MASS EFFECT™

RETRIBUTION

By Drew Karpyshyn

BALDUR'S GATE II: THRONE OF BHAAL

TEMPLE HILL

STAR WARS: DARTH BANE: PATH OF
   DESTRUCTION
STAR WARS: DARTH BANE: RULE OF TWO
STAR WARS: DARTH BANE: DYNASTY OF EVIL

MASS EFFECT: REVELATION
MASS EFFECT: ASCENSION
MASS EFFECT: RETRIBUTION

MASS EFFECT™
RETRIBUTION

DREW KARPYSHYN

BALLANTINE BOOKS • NEW YORK

Mass Effect: Retribution is a work of fiction. Names, characters, places, and incidents are the products of the author's imagination or are used fictitiously. Any resemblance to actual events, locales, or persons, living or dead, is entirely coincidental.

A Del Rey Mass Market Original

Copyright © 2010 EA International (Studio & Publishing) Ltd. Mass Effect, Mass Effect logo, BioWare and BioWare logo are trademarks of EA International (Studio & Publishing) Ltd. All Rights Reserved.

Published in the United States by Del Rey, an imprint of The Random House Publishing Group, a division of Random House, Inc., New York.

ISBN 978-0-345-52072-2

Printed in the United States of America

www.delreybooks.com
www.bioware.com

9 8 7 6 5 4 3 2

To my wife, Jennifer.
Thank you for always being there for me.
Because of you, I can follow my dreams . . .
and have someone to share them with.

ACKNOWLEDGMENTS

Once again I want to express my gratitude to the entire Mass Effect team at BioWare for all their hard work. Without your tireless effort and limitless dedication, Mass Effect would not exist.

I also want to thank all the fans who've shown such passion for what we've created. Without your support, none of this would be possible.

PROLOGUE

The Illusive Man sat in his chair, staring out the viewing window that formed the entire outer wall of his inner sanctum.

The unnamed space station he used as his base was orbiting a red giant-class M star. The semispherical edge of the burning sun filled the entire lower half of the viewing window, its brightness dominating but not completely obscuring the field of stars behind it.

The star was in the last stages of its six-billion-year life span. As the grand final act culminating its existence, it would collapse in upon itself, creating a black hole to swallow the entire system. The planets and moons it had spawned in its birth would be devoured in the inescapable gravitational pull of the dark, gaping maw left behind by its death.

The scene encapsulated everything the Illusive Man believed about the galaxy: it was beautiful, glorious and deadly. Life could spring up in the least likely of places in the most unimaginable of forms, only to be snuffed out in a blink of the cosmic eye.

He wasn't about to let that happen to humanity.

"Viewing window off," he said, and the wall

became opaque, leaving him alone in a large, dimly lit room.

· "Lights on," he said, and illumination spilled from the ceiling.

He spun his chair around so it was facing away from the viewing window, looking out over the circular holographic pad in the center of the room he used to receive incoming calls. When activated, it would project a three-dimensional representation of whomever he was speaking to, almost making it seem as if they were standing in the room with him.

They could also see him, of course, which was why the holo-pad was located so that it looked out over the chair by the viewing window. When the window was active, the Illusive Man would be framed by whatever astronomical wonder the station happened to be orbiting at the time: a bold and powerful visual to reinforce the image he had carefully fostered over the years.

He needed a drink. Not the synthetic, alien-produced swill that bartenders across the galaxy hawked to unsuspecting humans. He wanted something real; something pure.

"Bourbon," the Illusive Man said out loud. "Neat."

A few seconds later a door on the far end of the room slid open and one of his assistants—a tall, gorgeous brunette—appeared, an empty glass in one hand and a bottle in the other. Her heels clacked sharply as she crossed the room's marble floor, her long legs making short work of the distance between them despite her tight black skirt.

She didn't smile or speak as she handed him the

glass, her demeanor strictly professional. Then she held the bottle out for his approval.

Jim Beam Black, the label proclaimed, *Distilled to Perfection in Kentucky.*

"Three fingers," the Illusive Man told her by way of approval.

The assistant filled the glass to just past the halfway point, then waited expectantly.

As it always did, the first taste brought him back to the simpler time of his youth. In those days he had been an ordinary man, a typical citizen of Earth's upper class—wealthy, comfortable, naïve.

He savored the flavor, feeling a twinge of longing for those lost halcyon days: before he had founded Cerberus; before he had become the Illusive Man, the self-appointed protector of humanity; before the Alliance and their alien allies on the Citadel Council had branded him and his followers terrorists.

Before the Reapers.

Of all the enemies in the known galaxy and beyond, of all the dangers that might one day wipe humanity from existence, none could compare with the threat that lurked in the void of dark space at the galaxy's edge. Massive, sentient starships, the Reapers were ruthless machines completely devoid of compassion and emotion. For tens of thousands of years—perhaps longer—they had watched as alien and human civilizations evolved and advanced, waiting for the perfect moment to come in and wipe out all organic life in the galaxy.

Yet despite the apocalyptic threat they posed, most people knew nothing of the Reapers. The Council had sealed all official records of the Reaper attack on the Citadel space station, covering up the evidence and denying the truth to prevent widespread panic across the galaxy. And, of course, the Alliance, lapdogs of their new alien masters, had followed along without protest.

The lie ran so deep that even those who'd helped bury the truth had convinced themselves the Reapers were nothing but a myth. They continued on with their mundane existence, too weak and too stupid to acknowledge the horrific destiny awaiting them.

But the Illusive Man had devoted his life to facing unpleasant truths.

When the Alliance turned their back on the disappearing human colonies in the Terminus Systems, Cerberus had taken up their standard. They had even managed to recruit Commander Shepard—the Alliance's greatest hero—to aid them in investigating the mystery. And what Shepard discovered had shaken the Illusive Man to his core.

The Illusive Man dismissed his assistant with a slight nod; the woman spun expertly on her heel and left him alone with his thoughts.

Taking another sip of his drink, the Illusive Man set it down on the arm of his chair. Then he reached into the inside breast pocket of his tailored jacket and removed a long, slim silver case.

With an unconscious grace gained from years of practice, he flipped open the top, slipped out a cigarette, and closed it again in one seemingly continuous motion. The case disappeared into his jacket once more, replaced in his hand by a heavy black lighter. A flick of the thumb and a quick puff on the cigarette and the lighter also vanished.

The Illusive Man took a long, slow drag, letting the nicotine fill his lungs. Tobacco had been part of Terran culture for centuries, the act of smoking a common ritual in nearly every developed nation on the globe. Small wonder, then, that this ubiquitous habit had followed humanity into space. Various strains of tobacco had become popular exports for a number of colonies, human and otherwise.

There were those who even had the audacity to claim that several of the salarian brands of genetically engineered leaf were superior to anything humanity had produced. The Illusive Man, however, preferred his tobacco like his whiskey—homegrown. This particular cigarette was made from crop cultivated in the vast fields sprawling across the landscape of the South American heartland, one of Earth's few remaining agriculturally viable regions.

The traditional health risks associated with smoking were no longer a concern in the twenty-second century; advances in the fields of chemistry and medical science had eradicated diseases like emphysema and cancer. Yet there were still those who harbored a deep, fundamental hatred of this simple act. Ancient legislation passed in the mid-twenty-first century banning tobacco was still in effect within the borders of several of Earth's nation-states. Many viewed cigarettes as morally abhorrent: a symbol of the callous and exploitive corporate indifference that caused millions of deaths in the pursuit of shareholder profit.

For the Illusive Man, however, smoking represented something else entirely. The taste curling across his tongue and down his throat, the tickle of smoke spreading through his lungs, and the warm rush of nicotine spreading through his system brought both the comfort of familiar routine and the satisfaction of physical craving: two essential elements of the human condition. Smoking was a ritual to be celebrated . . . especially now that humanity's continued existence was at risk.

Smoke 'em if you got 'em, he thought, conjuring up an old line from a long-forgotten source. *Because none of us is going to see tomorrow.*

The Illusive Man took a few more puffs on his cigarette before stubbing it out in the ashtray built into the arm of the chair, then took another sip of his drink.

As grim as things might seem, he wasn't about to give in to melancholy despair. He was a man who tackled problems head-on, and this one was no different.

Commander Shepard had discovered that human colonists were being abducted by the Collectors, a reclusive alien species that served the will of the Reapers without question. Though trapped in dark space, the massive starships were somehow able to exert control over their hapless minions even across millions of light-years.

Acting on the orders of their machine masters, the Collectors had been gathering humans and taking them to their homeworld in the galactic core. There the abductees were repurposed: transformed, mutated, and finally rendered down into organic sludge as part of a horrific experiment to fuel the creation of a new Reaper.

Shepard—with Cerberus's help—had destroyed the Collector operations. But the Illusive Man knew the

Reapers wouldn't simply give up. Humanity needed to learn more about this relentless and remorseless foe in preparation for the Reapers' inevitable return. They had to study their strengths and weaknesses, expose and exploit their vulnerabilities.

Cerberus had salvaged key pieces of technology from the remains of the Collector operation. They were already beginning to set up a facility to undertake the first carefully controlled tests of the strange alien technology. Ultimately, however, there was only one way to gain the knowledge they sought: they would have to resume the Collector experiments on real human subjects.

The Illusive Man knew full well the abhorrence of his plan. But ethics and morality had to be cast aside for the survival of the species. Instead of millions being abducted, a few carefully chosen subjects would be chosen. A handful of victims had to suffer to protect and preserve the entire human race.

The plan to replicate the Collector experiments would progress in secret, without Shepard's knowledge or involvement. The alliance between Cerberus and humanity's most famous hero had been uneasy at best; neither side had fully trusted the other. It was possible they might work together again in the future, but for now the Illusive Man was only willing to rely on his own top agents.

A soft overhead chime indicated an incoming message from one of those operatives.

"Viewing window on," he said, sitting up straight in his seat and focusing his attention on the holopad.

The lights dimmed automatically as the wall

behind him became transparent. The dying sun to his back cast an orange-red glow over the room.

"Accept," the Illusive Man muttered, and the image of Kai Leng materialized above the holo-pad.

Like most of humanity, he was a child of a truly global culture. His Chinese heritage was clearly predominant in his dark hair and eyes, but around the jaw and nose were subtle clues pointing to some Slavic or Russian ancestry as well.

"We found him," Kai Leng reported.

The Illusive Man had no need to ask who he was talking about. A top Cerberus assassin, Kai Leng had for nearly three years been on a mission to track down a single target.

"Where?" the Illusive Man wanted to know.

"Omega."

The corded muscles of Kai Leng's neck momentarily tightened with revulsion as he spoke the name—a completely involuntary, but understandable, reaction. The space station represented everything Cerberus despised about alien culture: it was lawless, savage, and brutal. The reflex caused Kai Leng to turn his head, offering a glimpse of the tattoo on the back of his neck: a snake swallowing its tail.

The ouroboros was often used to symbolize eternity, but the Illusive Man knew it had a darker meaning as well: annihilation. Which was, in its own way, also eternal.

Cerberus had discovered Kai Leng a decade ago, liberating him from an Alliance prison camp. The Illusive Man had looked carefully into his past before recruiting him: a marine with N7 special forces training, he had been arrested after killing a krogan in a bar fight on the Citadel while on temporary leave.

The Alliance had come down hard on the former lieutenant, making an example of him. He was stripped of his rank and sentenced to twenty years in military prison. Kai Leng's long list of documented confrontational and even violent behavior toward aliens had no doubt contributed to the harshness of his sentence. For the Illusive Man, however, his anti-alien leanings were proof of character. That, combined with the fact that he had managed to kill a krogan while armed with nothing more than a standard-issue service blade, had made him a perfect recruit.

In the decade since Cerberus had arranged his escape, Kai Leng had become one of the organization's top wet-work operatives. But he was more than just a ruthless killer. He understood the need to be discreet; he knew how to plan and implement complex and delicate operations.

Now that he had found his target, the Illusive Man's first impulse was to give the exterminate order. But then an idea came to him. He still needed subjects for the upcoming experiments; why not kill two birds with one stone?

"Bring him in," he said. "Alive. Be sure to cover your tracks."

"I always do," Kai Leng replied.

Satisfied, the Illusive Man muttered, "Off," and the holographic image of the assassin flickered once, then disappeared.

He leaned back in his chair, casually swirling the

contents of the glass in his hand before downing the last of his drink in a long, satisfying gulp.

It's been a long time coming, Grayson, he thought, his mood much more cheerful than it had been only minutes ago. *But I'll make sure the wait was worth it.*

ONE

Paul Grayson knew the Illusive Man was still looking for him. It had been almost three years since he had betrayed Cerberus for the sake of his daughter, but even if *thirty* years had passed he knew they wouldn't give up the hunt.

He had changed his name, of course: Paul Grayson was gone; he went by Paul Johnson now. But creating a new identity for himself was only the first line of defense; it wouldn't hold up should any of the Illusive Man's agents come across his credentials. And his agents were everywhere.

Since its inception, Cerberus had seeded operatives throughout nearly every branch of the Alliance government. There was almost no place in Council space he could run where they wouldn't eventually track him down. So he had fled to Omega.

The Illusive Man had never managed to secure a foothold on the enormous space station that served as the de facto capital of the Terminus Systems. Cerberus was well known for its radical pro-human agenda, making its agents extremely unpopular among the various alien warlords, gang leaders, and despots who held sway on Omega. Even if they suspected that Grayson was hiding here, it wouldn't be easy for them to get to him.

It was something of an irony to Grayson that the skills he had learned while working for Cerberus—espionage and assassination—were proving so useful in carving out a new life for himself as a mercenary on Omega. He had been trained to kill aliens; now he was working for one.

"We're wasting time," Sanak grumbled, setting his sniper rifle to the side. He tugged at his combat suit as he shifted to find a more comfortable position behind the stacked crates that were concealing Grayson and him from view.

Grayson kept his own weapon trained on the ship on the far side of the loading bay. He was acutely aware of how careful his batarian partner was to not make any physical contact with him as he rummaged around.

"We wait for Liselle's report," he said flatly.

The batarian had turned his head to glare with all four eyes at the man crouched beside him. He blinked the uppermost pair, but the lower set remained still as stone.

"You always want to wait, human," Sanak snarled. "It's a sign of weakness."

"It's a sign of intelligence," Grayson snapped back. "That's why I'm in charge."

Sanak knew only one way to deal with problems: charge into them headfirst. It made working with him difficult at times. His general dislike of humans—and Grayson's deeply ingrained mistrust of batarians—didn't help matters.

The two species had a checkered history. Humanity

had expanded quickly after bursting onto the galactic scene, pushing the batarians out of the Skyllian Verge. The batarians had retaliated with violence, triggering a war between the two cultures—a war the batarians had lost. Now they were outcasts and pariahs in the civilized worlds of Council space—hardly ever seen, regarded with suspicion and mistrust.

On the streets of Omega, however, they seemed to be on every other corner. Since leaving Cerberus, Grayson had worked hard to overcome the xenophobia that had been drilled into him by the Illusive Man. But old habits died hard, and he was in no hurry to embrace the "four-eyed menace."

Fortunately, he and Sanak didn't have to like each other to work together. Aria had made that clear to both of them on several occasions.

"Seven targets in total," Liselle's soft voice chimed in his earpiece. "All members in position and awaiting orders."

Grayson felt the familiar rush of adrenaline coursing through his body in anticipation of the kill. Beside him he sensed Sanak training his weapon onto the ship, mirroring Grayson's pose.

"Go," Grayson whispered, the single word triggering a barrage of gunfire from the far side of the warehouse as Liselle and her team went into action.

A second later four turians stumbled into view from around the far side of the vessel. Their backs were to Grayson and Sanak, their attention and their weapons focused on Liselle's ambush.

Grayson released the air in his lungs in a long, slow breath as he squeezed the trigger. One of the turians dropped, the kinetic barriers of his combat suit too drained by Liselle's opening salvo to stop the sniper round that took him in the back of his bony skull.

An instant later two more went down, courtesy of a pair of perfectly placed shots from Sanak.

I may not like the bastard, Grayson thought as he took aim at the final adversary, *but he gets the job done.*

The last turian had just enough time to take two steps toward the cover of a nearby crate before Grayson took him between the shoulder blades.

There were several seconds of absolute silence before Grayson spoke into his mouthpiece. "Four targets neutralized on our side."

"Three more over here," Liselle responded. "That's all of them."

"Let's move," Grayson said to Sanak, leaping out from behind the cover of the crate and racing toward the fallen aliens.

The turians were members of the Talon gang, and the warehouse was a building deep inside Talon territory. Given the time of night and the remote location, it was unlikely anyone had heard the shots. But there was always a chance, and the longer they stayed the more likely they'd have to deal with reinforcements.

By the time he and Sanak reached the bodies, Liselle and the two batarians that made up the rest of her team were already rifling through their victims' clothes.

"Five kilos so far," the blue-skinned asari informed Grayson, holding up several plastic bags tightly packed with a fine, rosy powder. "Ninety, maybe ninety-five percent pure."

From personal experience, Grayson knew it took

only a small pinch of refined red sand to get a human high. Five kilos was enough to keep an entire apartment complex floating for the better part of a year. A stash this size could easily fetch six figures back in Council space. Which was precisely why Aria had ordered this hit.

There were no actual laws on Omega, no police force. Order was maintained solely by the gangs that ran the space station. But though there were no laws, there were rules. Rule number one: don't cross Aria T'Loak.

"Two more kilos on this one," Sanak said, pulling another tightly wrapped brick from inside the vest of the corpse he was searching.

"This one got caught in the cross fire," one of the other batarians said, holding up a bag so Grayson could see the grains of sand streaming out of the tiny hole in the side.

"Patch it up!" Grayson snapped angrily, taking a quick step back.

Red sand had no effect on batarians or asari, but one good whiff and he'd be dusted for the rest of the night.

"Aria wants it all," he reminded them. "The whole shipment. She's sending a message."

Known as the Pirate Queen, Aria had been the de facto ruler of Omega for over two centuries. Every other gang paid tribute to her in some form or another for the privilege of doing business on the station. Those that tried to cut Aria out—say by refusing to give her a piece of their red sand trafficking business— suffered the consequences.

"That's it," Liselle declared, standing up as she finished her examination of the last body.

Even though his mind was focused on the mission, Grayson couldn't help but be struck once again by the ethereal beauty of the woman before him. The asari as a whole were gorgeous by human standards: the mono-gendered species closely resembled human females, though their pigmentation was typically blue. Instead of hair they had sculpted, flowing folds of skin covering their scalp, but that did little to take away from their sexual appeal.

Liselle was considered extremely attractive, even among her own kind, and her form-fitted combat suit accentuated every curve. The part of Grayson's mind that still harbored the Cerberus-bred mistrust of aliens couldn't help but wonder if it was merely her physical appearance that was so stunning, or if it was something more.

In addition to being a species of biotics, the asari were known to have subtle yet powerful empathic— almost telepathic—abilities. Some believed they used these talents to influence the perceptions of others, making themselves appear more attractive than they actually were. If that was in fact the case, then Liselle was exceptionally skilled at the art.

"Secure the sand and move out," Grayson ordered, snapping his mind back to the task at hand. "Stay tight, stay alert. Remember—we're still in enemy territory."

Following his instructions, Liselle, Sanak, and the other batarians stuffed the packets into their gear before falling in behind him.

With Grayson in the lead and Sanak taking up the

rear, the small troop filed out of the warehouse and onto the district's shadowed streets. Moving quickly, they made their way down the twisting labyrinth of alleys and back lanes, eager to reach friendly—or at least neutral—territory.

It was late, well into the middle of the space station's night cycle. There were only a handful of people out on the streets. Most would be civilians, ordinary men and women from various species who—for whatever reason—lived or worked in the Talon-controlled neighborhood. These were easy to spot: seeing the heavily armed squad, they would turn away or slip into the blackness of a doorway, eager to avoid confrontation.

Grayson noted and dismissed these people with a single glance. He was on the lookout for Talon patrols. Any response to the attack on the warehouse would be random and disorganized; the Talons couldn't have expected Aria to strike at them here, in the heart of their own turf. But the turian gang was one of the few that regularly sent armed cadres out to walk the streets of their territory, as a way to remind people who was in charge. Armed and outfitted as his people were, Grayson knew that if they came across one of these patrols, the turians would immediately open fire on principle alone.

In the end, they were lucky. They crossed over from Talon territory into one of the central districts of Omega without incident. Just to be safe, Grayson kept them in formation for several more blocks, wary of signs of pursuit.

It was only when Liselle put a hand on his shoulder

and said, "I think we're clear," that he let his guard down.

"Aria's waiting for us at Afterlife," Sanak pointedly reminded him.

Grayson knew full well where their boss was. And that was the problem—everyone knew.

Afterlife was the social epicenter of Omega, a club where the wealthy and powerful mingled with the station's common folk, all in the pursuit of pure hedonistic satisfaction. Patrons came in search of music, sex, drugs, and even violence, and few left without finding at least some of what they sought.

Aria T'Loak was a fixture at the club, presiding over the pulsating chaos of the crowd from her private booth nearly every night. Her presence was part of what made the club what it was: Afterlife epitomized Omega, as did Aria herself.

"We're not strolling into the club loaded down with twenty pounds of red sand," Grayson replied. "We need to stash it someplace safe."

It wasn't likely the Talons would be able to mount a retaliatory strike so quickly; even if they did, he doubted they'd have the balls to take a run at Aria in her own club. But the Talons weren't the only ones he was worried about.

Security kept a tight rein inside the club, but shootings, stabbings, and random acts of violence were common in the streets and alleys surrounding it. Junkies desperate to score or street thugs too stupid to consider the long-term consequences wouldn't hesitate to go after Grayson's crew if they thought the payoff was big enough. It was a small risk, to be sure, but Grayson was all about minimizing risk at every opportunity.

"We hide the sand at my place," he declared. "Then we report to Aria and arrange a pickup for to-morrow."

Sanak's lip curled in disapproval, but he didn't say anything. Liselle, on the other hand, nodded her agreement.

"Lead the way, Paul," she cooed. "The sooner we drop this off, the sooner we can hit the dance floor."

It took them about fifteen minutes to reach Grayson's apartment. Several times he checked to make sure they weren't being followed; each time he did so, he couldn't help but notice Sanak rolling all four of his eyes.

That's why Aria put me in charge, he thought. *I worry about the details.*

It was just one of the many valuable lessons he had picked up from the Illusive Man.

His apartment was located in one of Omega's safest, and most expensive, districts. The guards at the district gate—a pair of heavily armed turians—recognized him and stepped aside so he and his squad could enter.

Reaching his building, he punched in the access code at the main door, instinctively shielding the key-pad from Sanak and the other batarians as he did so. The position of his body gave Liselle a clear view, but he'd already given the asari his building code several months ago.

The door slid open, revealing a small hallway lead-ing to a set of stairs and a single elevator.

"Third floor," Grayson said. "Take the stairs. The elevator's a little slow."

He led the way, with Liselle, Sanak, and the others following behind single file. At the top of the steps was another hall, with a single door on either side. There were only two apartments on each of the building's five floors; that was one of the things Grayson liked best about this building—only a handful of neighbors, and they all respected one another's privacy.

He went up to the door and placed his hand on the pad in the center. He felt a faint warmth as the biometric scan read his palm; then there was a soft click and the door slid open.

The well-furnished apartment beyond wasn't large, but Grayson didn't need a lot of room. A small entryway where visitors could take off their boots and coats led into a sitting room with a single couch and a vid screen. A small window looked out over the street below. Beyond the sitting room was a half-wall separating it from the functionally simple kitchen. Through the kitchen was another small hallway leading to the bathroom and then to the bedroom in the rear. The bathroom was small, but the bedroom was large enough not only for Grayson's bed, but also for the chair, desk, and terminal he used whenever he wanted to patch into the extranet.

"Just put the bags inside the front door," Grayson instructed, eager to keep the batarians from traipsing through his home. "I'll figure out someplace to hide them."

"What's the matter, human?" Sanak growled. "Don't you trust us?"

Grayson didn't bother to answer.

"Aria's waiting for our report," he said. "Why don't you and your friends go fill her in."

Liselle waited until the batarians were gone, then came over and draped her arms around his neck, pressing herself close against him. He could feel the heat emanating off her, and the faint perfume wafting up from her neck made his head spin.

"You're not coming to the club?" she whispered in his ear, disappointed.

Grayson could imagine the sultry pout playing across her lips, and he felt a flush rising up his neck and into his cheeks. Liselle always made him feel like a cradle robber, despite the fact she was at least a full century older than him.

It's different with asari, the churlish part of his mind admonished. *They mature slowly. She's still a babe in the woods, and you're a weathered geezer pushing middle age. She's probably got more in common with your daughter than with you.*

"I'll be there," Grayson promised, giving her a quick kiss even as he unraveled her arms from his neck and gently pushed her away. "I just have to take care of a few things first."

She turned away from him, letting her fingers trail along the length of his arm as she did so.

"Don't take too long," she called out over her shoulder as she headed for the door. "You might find me dancing with a krogan if I get bored."

When the door closed, he took a long, slow breath to clear his head. The lingering scent of perfume filled his nostrils, but without Liselle pressed up against him it didn't have the same overpowering effect.

Back to business, lover-boy.

He had to find somewhere to hide the red sand. It wasn't likely anyone would break into his apartment, but there was no sense leaving it out in plain sight.

First, however, he had to make a call.

TWO

Kahlee Sanders knocked lightly at the door of Nick's room.

"Come in," he called from the other side, his adolescent voice cracking on the second word.

She passed her hand over the access panel and the door whooshed open to reveal Nick and Yando, one of the newest students at the Grissom Academy, sitting side by side at the desk in the corner of the room.

"It's past curfew," Kahlee said. "Yando should have been in his own room thirty minutes ago."

"We're studying," Nick said, pointing at the haptic interface screens projecting up from the terminal on his desk.

Kahlee glanced at the assignment floating before her, then at the two boys. Nick stared back at her, his expression one of total innocence.

Nick had just turned fifteen. Always small for his age, he looked at least a year or two younger. His shoulder-length black hair and the wispy, curling bangs that fell down across his forehead did little to offset the impression of youth. But she knew he was mature beyond his years; if any of the students could look her straight in the eye and lie to her without giving anything away, it was Nick.

Yando, however, was another story. Eleven years old, he had had his amplifiers surgically implanted only a few months ago. Everything here was still new to him, strange. The instructors of the Ascension Project still filled him with a sense of awe, towering figures of authority looming over this unfamiliar world. Kahlee wasn't above using that to get to the truth.

"Yando," she said, keeping her voice low but firm, "what were you really doing?"

The young boy looked from Kahlee to Nick and then back to Kahlee, his eyes wide and white against his dark face.

"We were playing Conquest," Nick admitted with an exasperated sigh, letting his young companion off the hook. "But only for, like, ten minutes. Before that we studied for two hours at least!"

"You know the rules, Nick," she replied. "No extranet after curfew."

"It was just ten minutes!"

"I can check the logs," she reminded him. "See if you're telling the truth."

"I am!" he snapped back defiantly, before adding in a lower voice, "Well, maybe more like twenty minutes."

"Am I in trouble?" Yando asked, his lower lip trembling slightly.

Kahlee shook her head. "No. You're not in trouble. But it's time to get into bed, okay?"

The younger boy nodded, and she took him by the hand and led him to the door. Then she turned to Nick.

"We'll talk about this when I come back to take your readings."

"Yeah, right," he said, his voice dripping with teenage sarcasm. "Hate to go one whole week without someone jabbing a needle in my neck."

Kahlee led Yando to his room and tucked him in, but her mind was on Nick the entire time.

She wasn't sure if she should punish him or not. In his first two years at the Grissom Academy, Nick had been a holy terror. Always ahead of most of his classmates in the biotic Ascension Project, he had been arrogant, selfish, and prone to bullying the other children. In the last year, however, something had changed. Nick had gone from a problem child to a model student, the perfect example of everything the Ascension Project was trying to achieve.

Among humans, biotics—the ability of some individuals to use their mind to affect the physical world through small bursts of dark energy—was a commonly known, but still misunderstood, phenomenon.

Many erroneously believed that biotics were mutants blessed with superhuman telekinetic powers. Urban legends told of out-of-control biotics upending vehicles with a mere thought, or using their abilities to cause earthquakes while unleashing rampages of destruction that decimated entire city blocks.

The truth was much less terrifying. For one thing, contrary to what popular action vids portrayed, generating biotic fields took time and focus; it wasn't something that happened instantly. And without the surgically implanted amplifiers wired into their brains and nervous systems, most biotics could barely tip over a cup of coffee.

With the amplifiers and years of intense training, talented individuals could learn to generate dark energy fields strong enough to lift a full-grown man from the floor and toss him roughly against a nearby wall, but doing so required intense amounts of physical and mental energy. Two or three such displays were all that typical biotics could manage before total exhaustion would set in, leaving them as helpless and vulnerable as any other man or woman.

Making the general public aware of these limitations was one way the Ascension Project tried to bridge the gap between rumor and fact. The hope was that understanding would lead to acceptance, allowing biotics to integrate into normal human society without suffering the irrational mistrust and persecution they currently faced. Indeed, outside of the military, most human biotics preferred to keep their talents hidden whenever possible.

Kahlee didn't want children like Nick to grow up ashamed of their gift. But there was always the fear the pendulum could shift too far the other way, leading to an arrogant sense of entitlement or superiority among biotics. They could come to look down on others as inferior, making it even more difficult for nonbiotics to welcome them into society.

When Nick first came to the program, Kahlee had feared this was the direction he was heading. But the Ascension Project focused on more than just maximizing biotic potential; the curriculum also concentrated on building moral character, and in Nick's case it seemed to have made a difference.

As he'd matured, the bully had transformed into a

protector of the other students. He'd gone from sullen and selfish to helpful and cooperative. Now he regularly volunteered to tutor other students at the Grissom Academy—even the nonbiotics who weren't part of the Ascension Program.

In light of all the progress he'd made, Kahlee decided she wasn't going to come down too hard on him for his latest minor transgression.

When she got back to his room Nick was lying facedown on his bed, the nape of his neck exposed in preparation for the familiar procedure he was about to endure.

"I never meant for Yando to get in trouble," he mumbled into his pillow as he heard Kahlee come in.

She sat down on the bed beside him, then reached over and carefully pinched the nape of his neck between her thumb and forefinger, wincing at the inevitable—but still slightly painful—static spark as she made contact with his skin. The Ascension Project had tried to find a way to regulate the excess electrical charge that built up naturally in a biotic's body, but so far had experienced little success in coming up with a practical solution. For now, it was still a minor inconvenience the students and teachers simply learned to live with.

"Yando's still recovering from his surgery," Kahlee explained as she inserted a long, slim needle between the young man's vertebrae and into the tiny subcutaneous transmitter. "He needs his sleep."

The small ball on the top of the needle blinked green, indicating the data was successfully uploaded.

"He doesn't like being alone in his room," Nick

answered, muscles tense and teeth gritted against his discomfort. "I think he misses his mom."

He let out a long sigh when Kahlee extracted the needle, and his body relaxed.

"I thought maybe if we played some Conquest he wouldn't be so scared."

Kahlee smiled to herself and gently rubbed Nick's shoulder.

"You're a good kid."

Still facedown, he didn't answer, but she could see his ears turning red with embarrassment. He shifted slightly, and she realized he was trying to get more comfortable while being careful not to roll over, desperate to hide his body's involuntary reaction to her touch.

He's not a little kid anymore, she reminded herself, quickly pulling her hand away as what was happening to Nick dawned on her. *He's a teenager practically drowning in hormones.*

Kahlee was aware enough to know that several of the older students had developed crushes on her. It was understandable: she offered them comfort and compassion, and though she dressed conservatively while at the Academy, with her shoulder-length blond hair and trim figure she was still an undeniably attractive woman.

"I better go," she said, standing up quickly.

Uncontrollable erections were perfectly normal for someone Nick's age, but the last thing she wanted to do was make an awkward situation worse by drawing attention to what was happening. Better to just make a quick exit.

"Yeah, okay," Nick answered, his voice noticeably strained.

She flicked off the light and shut the door behind her, giving him some necessary privacy.

Once she got back to her own private quarters, she downloaded Nick's data into her private terminal, where it would automatically be relayed to the central database inside the Ascension Project's main laboratory.

The numbers were encouraging. Initial testing had indicated there was an upper limit to what each individual biotic could achieve. However, recent results from students like Nick seemed to imply that with hard work these so-called upper limits were hardly set in stone.

As she charted the latest results from her other students, she couldn't help but wonder what would have happened with Gillian Grayson if she had stayed in the program.

Although she was autistic, Gillian's potential had dwarfed the other children's in the Ascension Project. Kahlee suspected her remarkable talent and her autism were somehow linked, though it was also possible her abilities were the result of the drugs her father and Cerberus had been secretly pumping into her system.

In the end, Grayson had chosen his daughter over his loyalty to Cerberus, and with his help Kahlee had managed to get Gillian onto the crew of a quarian deep-space exploration vessel . . . one of the few safe places in the galaxy beyond the Illusive Man's reach.

Kahlee understood how hard it had been for Grayson to send his daughter away; it had been hard

for *her* to. But Gillian wasn't alone: Hendel Mitra—
the former security chief of the Grissom Academy—
was with her, and he cared for her as much as her
own father did.

Kahlee's train of thought was derailed by the soft
beeping of an incoming call over the extranet. The
point of origin was blocked, but she had a pretty
good idea of who was on the other end of the line.

She tapped the bottom right corner of the hovering
interface screen to accept the call, activating the video
feed on a separate screen. Staring back at her was
Grayson himself, as if Kahlee's thoughts about his
daughter had somehow conjured him up.

"Kahlee," he said, his face brightening as he spoke
her name.

For the past three years, Grayson had called her
every two or three weeks. Though he would never
openly admit it, she knew he was checking up on her.
She suspected that after Gillian was gone, he'd struck
some kind of bargain with the Illusive Man to guar-
antee her safety . . . though what that bargain was, or
what it had cost him, she'd never been able to find
out.

From the image on her screen, it looked as if he was
calling from a computer station set up inside a small
bedroom. She couldn't make out any other significant
details, however; Grayson was always careful to give
her no clue as to where he was calling from. So she
studied his physical appearance instead.

He seemed to be wearing some type of body
armor or combat suit, though it was hard to be sure
with only his head and shoulders visible. She was re-

lieved to see that his pupils and teeth were white, with no trace of the rosy pink hue that would indicate he had started using red sand again. Yet his face looked lean and haggard, as if he was under a great deal of stress.

"You look good, Grayson" she said, letting a smile slip across her lips to sell the white lie.

"I'm keeping busy," he responded, as vague and evasive as ever. "How have you been? Everything going well on the Ascension Project? Nothing unusual?"

"Unusual? You mean other than teaching children how to move objects with their mind?"

Grayson forced a polite laugh. Kahlee could see he was on edge.

"Is something wrong?"

"No," he answered quickly, shaking his head. "Everything's fine. Just got back from a job. Always leaves me feeling a little off."

"What kind of job?"

"The kind that pays my bills."

There was an awkward moment of silence as Kahlee debated whether to keep pushing for more information. In the end, she decided to let it go.

"I was thinking of Gillian when you called."

A wave of conflicting emotions flickered across Grayson's face at the mention of his daughter: longing, regret, and happiness ran in rapid succession across his features.

"I'm always thinking of her," he said softly. "Have you heard anything? From the quarians? Or Hendel?"

"I'm sorry. No."

After a pause, Grayson gruffly insisted, "It's better this way."

Kahlee couldn't help but feel like he was trying to convince himself, not her.

"You're welcome to come visit the Academy," she reminded him. "I've put you on my precleared-visitors list."

Grayson's association with Cerberus had never become known to anyone at the Academy other than Hendel and Kahlee, and she knew those days were behind him. As far as the rest of the staff knew, he was just the father of a former student . . . and a major donor to the program.

"I know how much you miss Gillian," she pressed. "Maybe coming here and meeting some of the other students and seeing the advances we've made would make things easier somehow."

"It's too dangerous," Grayson replied, refusing to even consider her offer. "For me and for you."

"I wish you'd let me help you," she said. "You don't have to do this alone, you know."

"I wish that were true. Goodbye, Kahlee. It was good seeing you."

And with that, the call abruptly ended.

Kahlee flicked off her screen and tried to turn her attention back to the files she'd been studying, knowing it was a lost cause.

Grayson wasn't exactly a friend. He had a dark history, and she was certain he'd done things that would horrify her. But they had a strong connection through their feelings for Gillian, and through the traumatic experiences they'd shared while on the run from Cerberus.

She knew he was trying to turn his life around; she truly believed that in his own way he was seeking redemption. Unfortunately, there was nothing she could do other than hope he someday found it.

THREE

Grayson sat for several minutes in front of the terminal after disconnecting his call to Kahlee, his mind filled with thoughts of his daughter.

She was in a better place now, and that gave him some comfort. But he couldn't help remembering all the terrible things that Cerberus had done to her. All the things he'd helped them do to her.

The familiar guilt washed over him, followed quickly by the inevitable self-contempt. There was nothing he could do to change the past; feeling bad about it was a waste of time. He considered himself a practical man, and he needed to stay focused in the here and now if he wanted to stay alive.

Unfortunately, rational arguments held little sway over matters of the heart, and—as he so often did after speaking with Kahlee—he felt hot tears streaming down his cheeks.

He had sworn he'd become a better person for Gillian's sake. And while it was true he'd turned his back on Cerberus, was what he was doing now really so different? He was a paid mercenary for a ruthless crime lord on the most dangerous, deadly space station in the galaxy. Did killing someone for credits become less amoral if the target had probably done something to deserve it?

In some part of his mind, the answer must have been yes. The nightmares that had plagued him during his time under the Illusive Man were gone; on some level he must have been more accepting of his new position. On the other hand, there were times when he felt fractured, as if he were two people. He knew the kind of man he wanted to be, but part of him—the little voice in the back of his head—wouldn't let him forget what he once was.

You can't change what you are, the little voice chimed in, as if on cue. *You're a killer. A violent man. And one day you'll die a bloody, violent death and the galaxy will be a better place because you're gone.*

The acceptance of his own incorrigible nature was strangely reassuring. It confirmed his decision to let Gillian go with Hendel and the quarians; better to put her as far away from her monster of a father as possible. It made it easier for him to distance himself from his past; made it easier to do what had to be done to survive in the present.

He wiped away the tears and got up from his chair. Liselle was waiting for him at Afterlife, but he wasn't quite ready to face the club scene yet. And he still had to hide the packets of red sand lying just inside the door of his apartment.

Maybe a quick dusting is what you need to pick up your spirits.

Grayson did his best to ignore the voice. He'd been clean for three years now. His body no longer craved the chemical-induced euphoria of the red sand.

But it was never really about the physical cravings,

was it? Dusting takes away the pain. Makes things bearable.

He'd cleaned himself up for Gillian's sake. She didn't deserve a junkie for a father.

Gillian's gone now. So who are you staying clean for? Liselle? Aria? They won't care if you dust up, just as long as you don't let it get in the way of a job.

During his last nine years with Cerberus, Grayson had been using regularly. Over that time, he'd never once let his addiction interfere with an assignment. But things were different now. He wasn't an undercover operative using his daughter to infiltrate an exclusive biotic training program. He was a man on the run; he had to stay sharp. Any given second of any given day could be his last.

Cerberus will find you. It's inevitable. So why not enjoy life until then. Ten kilos of red sand. Just one little hit. No one's going to miss it. No one will even know.

Grayson pushed the chair away from the extranet terminal and stood up slowly. He made his way from the bedroom down the hall, through the kitchen and sitting room, and over to the packets of red sand still piled just inside the door. He picked up all five bags, cradling them awkwardly in his arms, then took them back into the bedroom. Kneeling down, he slid them under the bed one by one. It wasn't much of a hiding place, but it was better than leaving them out in the open.

When he was done, he stood up and went into the bathroom. Looking at himself in the mirror, he noticed a small patch of pink residue on the front of his combat vest. He remembered that one of the bags had been punctured in the attack.

Damn batarians couldn't even seal it properly.

Brushing it away, he felt the fine granules rubbing coarsely against his palm. Most of them fell into the sink, but some adhered to his skin.

He held his palm up to his face, close enough so that he could make out each tiny, individual grain of sand clinging to his flesh. He stared at them for a long second, then shook his head and slipped his hands into the sink. The action triggered the faucet's motion sensor, and a stream of warm water washed the temptation down the drain.

Five minutes later he was changed into his civilian clothes and headed out the door. Walking at a smooth, easy pace, he reached the club in nearly twenty minutes.

As always, there was a throng of people outside waiting to get in. Human, asari, turian, krogan, batarian, volus, elcor: Afterlife catered to individuals from every species. But Aria had strict rules about crowd control, and those outside clamoring to get in would have to wait for some of the revelers inside to leave—or be carried out—before the guards at the door would grant them access.

The line stretched the entire length of the massive building, then disappeared around the corner at the end of the block. It would be hours before those at the tail end found their way inside. Fortunately for Grayson, friends of Aria didn't have to wait in line.

The krogan bouncer at the entrance recognized him, and let him in with a nod. Grayson passed through the short hall that led from the entrance into the ground-floor foyer, where a pair of scantily clad asari stood preening behind the coat check counter.

The asari weren't alone in the room, however. Two large, heavily armed and armored krogan flanked the sealed double doors leading to the hedonistic pleasures on the other side.

Outside, the music from the club was so muted and faint it could barely be heard above the noises of the street. Here, however, only a single insulated wall separated patrons from the waves of sound. Grayson could feel the beat from inside the club thrumming in his teeth—low, heavy, and fast.

"Anything to check?" one of the krogan growled, speaking loud enough to make sure he could be heard over the music.

Grayson shook his head. Many of the club-goers preferred to leave their valuables with the asari behind the counter, especially if they intended to end the evening too drunk or stoned to keep track of their belongings. Grayson, however, had no such intention.

The krogan stepped aside as the asari pushed open the doors. Taking a deep breath, Grayson walked inside.

The club consisted of four levels, each one made up of a large outer ring surrounding a square dance floor suspended by wires and walkways in the center. Each of the various levels appealed to its own particular crowd, with its own dance floor, unique musical style, and custom drinks and chemical recreations.

The common theme, as befitted the club's name, was the afterlife. The commingling of myths and legends from across the galaxy, including humanity, were represented in the club. On each level individuals could seek out the pleasures—or hedonistic debauchery—associated with Paradise, Heaven, Hell, the Halls of Athame, the Hollows, or any of a thousand other names for the promised realm allegedly waiting beyond mortal existence.

Grayson never gave much thought to what waited for him after death, but it was impossible to deny the primal appeal of the club. He had been here too many times to count, yet he still felt it each time he walked across the floor. There was something surreal and otherworldly about stepping inside Afterlife. The music, the lights, and the crowd created a palpable energy that seemed to free you from yourself, unleashing inhibitions and wild, dangerous desires . . . most of which could be satisfied on the lower levels of the club.

Adding to the exhilaration was the common knowledge that most of the patrons inside Afterlife were armed. Violence could—and often did—erupt without warning. Security forces were on hand to clamp down on riots and to prevent widespread chaos, but individuals were expected to look out for themselves. As a result, it was rare that a month went by without at least one death inside the club.

Grayson knew how to look after himself should trouble arise, but he couldn't deny that the savage undercurrent in the club enhanced the mood.

The entrance itself was on the third level. A stifling heat rose up from the bodies gyrating on the dance floors below. Well over a hundred patrons occupied this level, but the club was large enough to accommodate the numbers without making it feel overly crowded.

The strobing lights made it difficult to pick any one individual out from the crowd, but Grayson still made a quick search for Liselle as he crossed the floor. By the time he reached the spiraling ramp leading up to the VIP level above, he still hadn't seen her. He wasn't worried, however. Eventually she'd find him.

Climbing the ramp, he could feel the insistence of Afterlife fading slightly. On the topmost level of the club the music was less intense, the lights more subdued. It was less crowded, though Grayson still estimated the number of patrons at close to fifty.

Sitting behind the table of a large private booth on an elevated platform near the back was Aria T'Loak herself. From this vantage point Omega's infamous Pirate Queen could look out across the entire club, taking it all in like a god looking down from above.

Like all asari, she was beautiful by human standards. Unlike Liselle, however, Aria's complexion was more violet than blue. Grayson had often wondered if this had something to do with her age. He didn't know how old she was exactly—he doubted anyone did—but he wouldn't have been surprised to learn she was over a thousand years old. Despite this, she retained the youthful appearance and raw sexuality that was a hallmark of her species.

A familiar entourage surrounded her: a pair of asari handmaidens, a krogan bodyguard, and several batarians, including Sanak. However, the three turians standing at the table opposite Aria caught Grayson by surprise.

He had known the Talons would come to see her about the attack eventually; he just hadn't expected them to arrive so soon. He hadn't noticed an inordinately high percentage of turians in the crowd gathered outside the club, but if these three were in here to parley with Aria, it was a safe bet a dozen more were lurking in the streets and alleys outside.

His decision not to bring the red sand directly to the club was looking a lot less paranoid. He resisted the urge to say "I told you so" as he climbed the platform and took a spot beside Sanak next to the booth, close enough so his translator could pick up the conversation between Aria and her rivals.

Nobody paid any real attention to him; he was known to Aria and her associates, and the turians were focused only on her. There were private rooms on the VIP level, but Aria preferred to conduct most of her business in the booth, where others could see . . . especially when she was asserting her dominance over a potential challenger to her throne.

"I'm not denying what happened," Aria answered calmly in reply to part of the conversation Grayson had just missed.

The turians waited for her to continue, but she was content to let her words hang in the air as she took a sip from the tall glass elegantly cradled in her left hand.

Eventually overcome by the pressing silence, one of the turians—probably the leader—took up the dialogue.

"We're not looking to start a war—"

"Good," Aria cut him off. "Because you'd lose."

Momentarily thrown by the interruption, the turian was forced to start again.

"We're not looking to start a war. We came to parley in good faith. We want to come to an agreement."

"We already had an agreement," Aria reminded him. "Two percent off the top. Then you started moving product without giving me my cut."

"That was a mistake," one of the other turians admitted. "We came to apologize. You'll get your cut from now on."

"No apology necessary," Aria said, flashing a dangerous smile. "But you violated the terms of the contract. Now we need to renegotiate."

The turians exchanged a few quick glances, and Grayson could see them weighing their next words carefully. The Talons were an up-and-coming gang on Omega, but they weren't on par with the Blue Suns or Bloodpack yet. And they had no illusions about where they stood in the grand scheme. If Aria truly wanted to, she could wipe them out.

"A reasonable request, given what happened," the first turian conceded. "We'll increase your cut to three percent."

"Five," Aria stated, her voice making it clear the number wasn't open for negotiation.

"Nobody pays five percent!" the third turian objected, taking an angry step forward as his hand dropped to the pistol clipped to his hip.

In a flash the krogan was beside him, his mammoth eight-foot frame looming over the smaller man. Slowly, the turian's hand fell away from his weapon. Everybody else remained frozen until Aria gave a slight nod. The turian took a careful step back. A second later the krogan grunted, then did the same.

"You crossed me," Aria said coolly. "There are consequences."

"Five percent," the leader agreed.

He hesitated before continuing, choosing his words carefully to avoid further provocation.

"There is still the matter of the attack itself. Several of our people were killed. A large sum of product was stolen."

"Consider it the cost of doing business," Aria said, calmly taking another sip of her drink.

The turians collectively bristled. Grayson knew they weren't stupid enough to attack Aria here in the club; in addition to the highly visible bodyguards and biotics surrounding her, there were dozens of less obvious security personnel scattered around the VIP level. They'd be dead before they even got a shot off.

He did expect them to turn and storm out, however. Their friends had been gunned down, and the value of the sand was far more than what they had cheated Aria out of. She was adding insult to injury, making a point about who was in charge. She had backed them into a corner, and there was a chance they'd retaliate out of sheer desperation. The Talons couldn't win a war against Aria, but they could make it hurt before she broke them.

But Aria had a knack for knowing exactly how far she could push her rivals before they pushed back. For hundreds of years, she'd played various factions off against one another while keeping them under her thumb; no one was better at ensuring that the anarchy of Omega never got out of control.

In the end the turian leader nodded, accepting her terms.

"I'll inform our people," he said.

"I knew you'd see reason," she replied, dismissing them with a wave of her hand.

The turians turned and left without another word, the eyes of Aria's krogan bodyguard following them until they descended the ramp to the level below and disappeared from view.

"It didn't take them long to figure out what happened," Grayson commented once they were gone.

"The Talons are smart," Aria replied. "They're growing fast. A little too fast. They needed to be knocked down a notch."

"Glad we could do our part," Sanak chimed in.

You four-eyed ass-kisser, Grayson couldn't help but think.

"Sanak informs me the sand is secured at your place," Aria continued. "I'll send a crew over to pick it up in the morning."

Grayson nodded.

"I won't send them too early," Aria added with a sly smile. "I'd hate for you and Liselle to have to cut your evening short. You've earned the right to celebrate. Everything at the club is on me tonight."

"Thanks," he said, taking the compliment in stride.

Aria was hard on those who failed her, but she was generous with those who came through.

"Liselle mentioned she'd be on level two," Aria added, giving Grayson his cue to leave. He was smart enough to take the hint.

He went and got himself a drink at the VIP bar before making his way down to the second floor. He took his time, letting the atmosphere of Afterlife wash over him. In the end, it took him nearly twenty minutes to find Liselle. As he'd expected, she was on the dance floor, surrounded by a crowd of fawning young men and women.

Grayson had come to terms with Liselle's penchant for humans: she liked them, and they liked her. He knew the asari preferred to partner with those outside their own species; their unique biology allowed them to take genetic traits from alien partners and incorporate them into the DNA of their offspring. But Liselle was still young; it would be decades—or maybe even centuries—before she passed from the maiden stage of the asari life cycle into the childbearing years of matronhood. Whether she would still be attracted to humans, or if this was just an experimental phase of her youth, he couldn't say. And in the end, it didn't matter. All Grayson knew was that she was interested in him right now, and he planned to enjoy the relationship as long as it lasted.

He pushed his way through the others on the dance floor, drawing irritated looks that quickly changed to envy when Liselle saw him and draped her arms around his neck to pull him in close.

"Aria seemed pleased with your work tonight," she shouted, leaning in close to his ear to make her words heard above the music.

They were pressed tight against each other, Liselle's body gyrating to the music while Grayson did his awkward best to try and match the rapidly pulsating rhythm.

"I couldn't have done it without you," he reminded her.

As he leaned in close to her ear, the familiar alluring scent of her perfume rose up and engulfed him. For some reason, however, it didn't rouse the normal lust-filled urges.

Liselle was quick to notice his lack of reaction.

Grabbing him by the wrist, she quickly dragged him across the dance floor and into a corner where the music was only a dull roar.

"What's wrong?" she asked.

From her expression it was clear she was concerned, rather than upset. As it always did, her concern made Grayson feel guilty and somewhat ashamed.

He preferred to see their relationship as primarily physical. For the most part, Liselle seemed to have a similar perspective. To think it was anything more was ridiculous; even if they stayed together for the rest of Grayson's life, she would live on for hundreds and hundreds of years after he was gone. Her developing any serious emotional attachment to him wouldn't just be unlikely . . . it would be tragic.

"I'm fine," he said with a shrug.

"Maybe we should go somewhere quiet."

Normally he would have jumped at her suggestion. Tonight, however, it felt wrong for some reason. Like he would be taking advantage of her somehow.

"I think I'm just tired," he said apologetically, looking for a way to let her down easy. "Maybe I should go home and get some rest."

"You were talking to her again, weren't you?" Liselle said with a wan smile. "Your mystery woman. You always get like this after you talk to her."

Grayson had never told Liselle anything about his past. She didn't know about Kahlee, or Gillian, or his time with Cerberus. But there had been occasions when he'd mentioned the need to make a private call, and obviously Liselle had pieced some things together.

She's a lot more perceptive than you give her credit for.

Again, it was clear Liselle wasn't angry. She seemed a little disappointed, but she also seemed to understand and accept his reaction. Which only made Grayson feel even worse.

"I'm sorry," he mumbled, not sure what else he could say.

Liselle leaned in and gave him a quick kiss.

"If you change your mind tonight, give me a call."

And with that she was gone, disappearing back into the crowd of dancers, where she was quickly consumed by a wave of eager admirers.

No longer in the mood for the club, Grayson returned to the entrance on level three. One of the asari at the check counter winked at him. He nodded politely in response, then headed back out into the street, still wondering if turning Liselle down had been self-sacrificing or simply selfish.

FOUR

Kai Leng waited patiently in the line of patrons waiting to enter Afterlife. Though it was unlikely he'd run into anyone who'd recognize him on Omega—even Grayson had never met him—he'd still taken steps to hide his identity. He'd dyed his black hair blond and darkened the pigmentation of his skin. The signature ouroboros tattoo on the back of his neck—a snake devouring its tail—was covered with a temporary design of a Celtic knot.

Based on the length of the line, it would be several more hours before he reached the door and was allowed to enter Afterlife, and that was fine by him. He was here to wait, watching patiently for Grayson to reemerge.

Since tracking the former Cerberus member down on Omega nearly two weeks ago, Kai Leng had studied his routine from afar. He was learning Grayson's patterns, familiarizing himself with his routine.

He had been surprised to discover that Grayson was working for Aria T'Loak; he had risen quickly through the ranks until he'd become a valuable minion of Omega's most powerful crime lord. That complicated the extraction. Cerberus couldn't just grab him from a public place and make a break for one of the spaceports. Aria's influence spread too far on the station; someone would report the abduction. They'd end up having to fight their way through the Pirate Queen's people to try and escape, and Kai Leng didn't like those odds.

Secrecy was the key. Capture Grayson alone, where nobody would notice him missing. Get him off the station before anyone even knew he was gone. And make sure nobody could trace it back to Cerberus.

This had proved to be much harder than it sounded. Grayson was careful; he rarely went out in public unless he was on a mission for Aria. The club, a busy grocery store, and the apartment of his asari whore were the only places he ever seemed to visit.

Taking him at his own apartment was the preferred option, of course, but he lived in a secure district. Any attack on Grayson would have to involve some plan to first get past the guards protecting his neighborhood.

It would have been so much easier if the Illusive Man had simply wanted Grayson dead. Kai Leng could have completed that job within hours of locating him: a slow-acting poison slipped into his drink at the club; a sniper shot between the eyes from a hidden vantage point as Grayson walked down the street. But extraction was always more difficult than simple assassination.

Kai Leng wasn't acting alone, of course. He had six of his own people—loyal Cerberus operatives—on standby in an apartment in a neighboring, human-controlled district, just waiting for him to give the signal. With a little luck, it could happen in the next few hours.

Everything had been in place a few days ago, when Grayson had suddenly dropped off the radar. At first Kai Leng feared he'd been made, but some careful inquiries revealed that Grayson had gone on a special mission for Aria. He hadn't been able to learn all the details, but he'd gathered enough secondhand information to know it had something to do with drugs and one of the rival gangs.

Kai Leng had staked out the club, knowing Grayson's eventual return to his alien master was inevitable. For three nights he had waited for a glimpse of his target in vain. But tonight his perseverance had been rewarded.

Grayson had entered the club less than an hour ago. If he went home alone tonight, instead of accompanied by the young asari he was sleeping with, they'd strike. If he wasn't alone, they'd wait for another chance. Kai Leng was nothing if not patient.

Still, he was eager to get off the station. There were too many aliens on Omega, and too few of his own kind. He was an outsider here, subject to the whims of strange beings with cultures and values he had no interest in adapting to. The high crime rate, brutal dictatorship of the gangs, and relative powerlessness of humanity were a grim example of the Illusive Man's vision of an alien-dominated future. Kai Leng was convinced that anyone who had doubts about Cerberus had only to visit Omega to truly grasp the fundamental necessity of a pro-human organization willing to do whatever was necessary to defend the species.

The VIP door to the club opened and everyone in line craned their necks eagerly to see who was coming out. They hoped to see a large group: six, seven, or eight individuals leaving the club meant the same number waiting in line would be allowed in to take their place. On seeing only a single human exiting, a palpable murmur of disappointment rippled through the crowd.

Kai Leng felt the opposite emotion as he watched Grayson emerge and wander off in the direction of his apartment alone.

Several patrons near the back of the line gave up in disgust, stepping out of the queue in search of other entertainment. Kai Leng blended in with this crowd to avoid drawing attention, heading off in the opposite direction Grayson went. He continued around a corner until he was safely out of sight; he didn't want to risk Grayson noticing him if he happened to glance back for any reason.

Reaching up, he activated the two-way transmitter looped over his ear with a light touch.

"Target has left the club alone," he whispered, knowing the receivers worn by the rest of his team would automatically amplify his words so they could be heard clearly. "The plan is go."

Grayson made his way back to his apartment, his pace quickening with every step. He didn't feel right. Tense. Restless. Frustrated.

Leaving the club had been the right decision; the scene at Afterlife held no appeal for him tonight. But he still felt bad about brushing Liselle off.

She's right about Kahlee, you know. You always get moody after you talk to her.

He nodded to the guards at the district's gate as he passed, but didn't bother to speak as he blew by, his mind too caught up in his own thoughts.

Kahlee was a link to his old life; speaking to her was a way to keep the connection with his daughter alive. Their conversations were a reminder of what he'd once had . . . and what he had lost.

Those days are gone. Quit torturing yourself.

He reached his building, punched in the code, then quickly ran up the stairs. By the time he reached the door of his apartment he was breathing heavily. But while his physical exertion had raised his heart rate, it had done nothing to quell his inner turmoil.

Inside the apartment he locked the door, pulled the shade down in the sitting room, then stripped off his boots, shirt, and slacks. A few beads of perspiration had broken out on his skin; standing in his underwear in the middle of the room, he shivered in the cool air wafting down from the climate-control vents in the ceiling.

Part of him wanted to call Kahlee again.

Great idea. What are you going to say? You think she cares about your emotional bullshit?

She was probably asleep by now. There was no point in waking her up. And calling her might not make him feel any better; it might actually make things worse.

You're so messed up you don't even know what you want. Pathetic.

He began to pace back and forth in front of the couch, trying to burn off the restless energy.

Just leftover adrenaline from the job. You need to relax.

This feeling wasn't completely new to him. On edge. Wired. During his days with Cerberus, he'd felt this way most of the time. It wasn't hard to guess the cause: psychological stress.

Working for Aria was a little too close to what he used to do for the Illusive Man. He was falling back into old patterns.

What are you going to do? Tell Aria you quit? You really think she'll just let you walk away?

Leaving Omega wasn't a realistic option. He'd just have to find ways to cope. Like he did while working for Cerberus.

One quick hit of red sand and it's all good.

He couldn't deny the truth—he was an addict. He'd never last the entire night. Not with the drugs right here in the apartment. But there was a solution: replace one addiction with another.

Making his way into the bedroom, he activated the extranet terminal and tapped the screen to send out a quick call. Liselle answered on the second ring.

"I knew you'd call back."

Her voice was distorted slightly, the two-way transmitter in the bracelet she wore on her wrist struggling to filter her words out from the background noise of the club's dance floor.

"I'm sorry I was acting so weird," he said. "I just felt a little . . . off."

"Feeling better now?" she asked, her voice dripping with insinuation. "Want me to come over?"

"As fast as you can" was his earnest reply.

"I'll be there in twenty minutes."

The call disconnected, and Grayson pushed himself back from the terminal. Twenty minutes. He could last twenty minutes.

Kai Leng and his team—four men and two women—stopped at the gate leading into the district where Grayson lived. The turian guards studied them with something between boredom and contempt, not even bothering to raise their weapons.

It would have been an easy matter to take them out, but unfortunately, eliminating the guards wasn't an option. They were part of Omega First Security, an independent company hired by wealthy residents to provide protection in a handful of neighborhoods on the station. Each guard post had to check in with the main dispatch every twenty minutes; failure to do so would trigger an emergency response of two dozen reinforcements descending on the district.

"Name," one of the guards demanded.

"Manning," Kai Leng replied. "Here to see Paul Johnson."

The turian glanced down at the screen on his omni-tool. "He didn't put you on the list. I'll have to call him to get clearance."

"Wait," Kai Leng said quickly. "Don't call him. This is supposed to be a surprise. It's his birthday next week."

The turian hesitated, then gave the seven humans standing before him a closer look.

Kai Leng had dressed his people to fit their cover story. Nobody wore body armor; instead they were attired in colorful clothing befitting current Omega fashion. Instead of a weapon, each member of the team carried a gift wrapped in brightly colored paper.

They were armed, however; each team member had a small tranquilizer pistol carefully hidden somewhere on his or her person. Stunners were smaller and would have been easier to hide, but the tranqs had better range and weren't limited to two or three shots before needing to be recharged.

"This is a breach of protocol," the other turian said, though his tone wasn't one of flat refusal. "We could get fired."

"We're not looking to get you in any trouble," Kai Leng replied, holding up a pair of hundred-credit chips. "Just do us a favor and pretend we were never here."

Omega Security paid its people well, but that didn't mean they were immune to bribes under the right circumstances. The group before them looked harmless, and the offer was just enough to tempt them, but not so much it would arouse suspicion.

"Let me look in those gifts first," the turian said, snatching the chips from the human's outstretched hand.

Kai Leng had briefly considered having his team hide their weapons inside the gift boxes. Fortunately, his understanding of alien nature had made him reconsider. He knew the turian guards wouldn't be able to resist asserting their authority over a group of wealthy humans.

For the next few minutes, the turians pawed through the gift boxes. They tore off the wrappers and rummaged around inside, thoroughly—and roughly—inspecting the contents. Their search revealed several bottles of expensive wine, a watch, a pair of cuff links, and a box of premium cigars. When they were finished, the gift boxes had been reduced to shreds of brightly colored paper and a pile of crumpled cardboard strewn about the feet of the guards.

"Clean up this mess and you can go," the second turian said.

Kai Leng bit his lip and nodded to his crew. One further humiliation: picking up garbage off the street while the guards literally looked down on them. To their credit, his people took the insult without comment, knowing the mission was more important than their burning desire to punish the turians for their alien arrogance.

Just as they were leaving, one of the turians warned, "Mr. Johnson might not be that happy to see you. His asari friend came through here about ten minutes before you showed up."

"She's probably giving him her gift right now," the other added with a crude chuckle.

Kai Leng swore silently. Seeing that Grayson had left the club alone, he'd dropped surveillance and gone to meet up with his team. He hadn't considered the possibility that the asari might join him at the apartment later.

Keeping his anger in check, he smiled and said, "We'll be sure to knock."

He led his team past the checkpoint and around the corner leading to Grayson's building. As soon as they were out of sight of the guards he held up a hand, ordering everyone to stop.

He never would have given the go-ahead for the mission if he knew the asari would be there, but it was too late to abort. The guards were sure to ask Grayson about his surprise party in the next few days. He was smart enough to put the pieces together; he'd know Cerberus had found him. He'd either disappear or get a special security detail from Aria to shadow him. Tonight was their only chance.

"You heard the guard," he told his team. "Grayson isn't alone. The asari is with him. We have to take him alive," he reminded them, stressing the mission's primary directive. "However, the alien whore is expendable. If you get a chance, kill her."

He could see from the others' faces that they all understood this was easier said than done. They expected Grayson to have at least one weapon somewhere in his apartment; the asari could be similarly armed. Even if she wasn't, she was a biotic. Wearing nothing but party clothes and armed only with tranquilizer pistols, they were at a significant disadvantage.

"Stick to the original plan," he reassured them. "Strike fast; catch them unprepared. If we're lucky, it will be over before they even know what's happening."

Grayson was panting like a dog. He lay atop the covers of his bed, staring at the ceiling, trying to catch his breath. Liselle was pressed up against him, their naked bodies still intertwined.

"I'm glad you changed your mind," she murmured in his ear, running her fingers lightly down the center of his bare chest.

Still recovering from their session, he barely managed to croak out, "Me too."

Sex with Liselle went beyond mere physical pleasure. Like all asari, she established a profound and powerful mental connection with her partner during climax; for a brief instant two minds became one. Their identities crashed together, splintered, reformed, then tore apart with an overwhelming intensity that left Grayson literally gasping for air.

How are you ever going to go back to humans?

"I need a drink," he said, gently unraveling himself from Liselle's long, slender limbs.

He staggered down the hall into the kitchen. He pulled a bottled water from the fridge and drank it all in a single series of long, desperate gulps. He felt light-headed, but the restlessness and anxiety were gone, washed away by Liselle's incredible skills in the bedroom.

Just as he was about to call out to Lisclle to see if she wanted anything, the door to his apartment slid open.

His head snapped around in response to the sound, revealing a small group of people in the hall just outside his door. One was crouched at the edge of the door frame, where she had just finished overriding the security codes. The others were standing in a tight knot, making it hard to accurately gauge their numbers. But two things stood out to Grayson immediately: they all appeared to be human, and they were all armed.

His instincts kicked in and he dropped to the floor, the half-wall shielding him from a round fired by one of the intruders.

Professional. He got that shot off fast.

"Ambush!" he called out to Liselle. "Bedside

table!" he added, giving her the location of his weapon.

Told you Cerberus would find you.

He knew there was no way he could win this battle. Naked, unarmed, outnumbered—the odds were impossible. But he didn't care about survival. All he cared about was getting back to the extranet terminal in the bedroom long enough to send a warning out to Kahlee.

Assuming they haven't already gotten to her.

Knowing it was a huge risk, he popped his head up over the wall to sneak a peek at the enemy. Three of them fired as soon as his head came into view, but he was able to duck back down and avoid the shots.

Fortunately, they had no way of knowing he was unarmed. Instead of charging in to finish him off, they were still lurking in the hall, taking cover by the edges of the doorway to guard against any return fire.

Grayson made a break for the hall leading to the bedroom, crouching low to the ground. Behind him he heard heavy footsteps as several of the assassins burst into the apartment.

There was a series of sharp *twang*s as enemy bullets peppered the wall just above him. He heard the hiss as one whizzed past his ear. And then he was around the corner and out of the line of fire.

Odd. Bullets don't twang.

The stray thought was pushed from his head by the sight of Liselle rushing from the bedroom and down the hall toward him. She was still naked, her right arm extended, her hand clasped firmly around the butt of Grayson's pistol.

They were both moving fast, and in the split second

it took them to realize what was happening it was too late. They plowed into each other, the collision knocking them both to the ground.

Grayson sprang back to his feet, yanking on Liselle's left arm in a desperate attempt to pull her up. He was already heading toward the bedroom door again, moving backward as he half-dragged the asari with him. Amazingly, she'd managed to hold on to the pistol despite being bowled over and having her arm nearly wrenched from its socket.

A Cerberus agent skidded around the corner from the kitchen, bearing down on them. Grayson's grip instinctively tightened on Liselle's arm as he braced himself to receive a slug in the chest. From her half-prone position, Liselle waved the hand holding the gun vaguely in their enemy's direction as he took aim, the physical action triggering the synapses in her brain to unleash a quick burst of dark side energy.

The asari didn't have enough time to gather her power for a truly devastating attack. The biotic push didn't do any real harm, but it knocked their opponent off balance, sending his shot harmlessly into the ceiling as he staggered back around the corner and out of sight.

They were less than a meter away from the bedroom when the attacker ducked around the corner a second time, already firing. From point-blank range he unloaded a single shot, catching Liselle in the chest. She gasped and, with Grayson still dragging her down the hall, threw up her free hand to return fire.

The high-powered pistol unleashed a wild spray of bullets, the automated targeting computer compensating as best it could for Liselle's erratic aim. At least one round found its mark—a burst of red splashed across the wall and the Cerberus agent slumped to the ground.

Grayson kept his legs churning as Liselle's body went limp, the pistol sliding from her nerveless fingers as they crossed the bedroom's threshold. Releasing his grip on his lover, Grayson punched the panel on the wall and the door slammed shut, buying him a few moments of precious time.

He hoisted Liselle up and tossed her on the bed, frantically searching her naked body for the wound. He expected to see a hole torn through her sternum; instead he found only a small pinprick perfectly centered between her breasts.

The pieces finally fell into place when he realized that Liselle, though unresponsive, was still breathing.

The almost invisible wound. The strange twang *of their ammo. They're using tranquilizer rounds. They want to take you alive.*

He didn't know if that was better or worse. In either case, the realization did little to change the equation. He still had to warn Kahlee.

He could hear the intruders in the hall, just outside the bedroom door. It had no lock, but they were still being cautious—they knew their target wasn't using tranq rounds. But he didn't have long.

Leaving Liselle's unconscious body on the bed, he raced over to the extranet terminal on the far side of the room. Tapping frantically at the haptic interface screens, he logged on to the extranet and sent Kahlee the files he'd assembled over the past two years.

The second the message was away he activated the

purge, deleting every file on his system, including all records of his incoming and outgoing messages.

An instant later the door slid open. Grayson turned and charged his attackers.

He had taken but one step when he felt the sting of two tranq rounds in his chest. By the third step he was already out.

Kai Leng stood motionless for several seconds after Grayson's body slumped to the floor, the tranq pistol still pointed at the target in case he needed to fire another round. When it became clear that his adversary was unconscious, he lowered the weapon and began barking out orders.

"He was sending a message. Check the terminal—see if he was calling for backup."

Shella, their tech expert, ran over to inspect the computer in the corner.

"The rest of you search the room. Grab any weapons you can find. We'll need something more than these pop guns to take out those turians at the guard post."

"What about her?" Shella asked, nodding in the direction of the unconscious asari on the bed even as her fingers tapped away at the terminal's interface.

"Leave her to me."

He went back out into the hall. Darrin's body lay on the floor in a dark pool of his own blood. Jens was still crouched over him, injecting him with medi-gel, checking his vitals and hoping for a miracle. One glance at the body was enough for Kai Leng to know the medic was wasting his time.

Making his way into the kitchen, he began a quick

but thorough search; opening cupboards and pulling out drawers, he found a very large, very sharp carving knife. Picking it up, he hefted the weight. Satisfied, he went back into the bedroom.

"The terminal's clean," Shella informed him as he came in. "Must have wiped it before we came in."

Kai Leng frowned. He had no idea what kind of info had been on Grayson's system, but it had been important enough for him to spend time getting rid of it even while his apartment was under attack.

"Found this under the bed," one of the others chimed in, holding up a cellophane-wrapped package about the size of a brick. "Four more here, too. Looks like red sand."

They'd finally caught a break. He knew Aria was involved in a drug war with a rival gang; with any luck, she'd think they were behind Grayson's disappearance.

"Take the sand with us. Any weapons?"

"Just the one they used to shoot Darrin."

"How bad is he . . . ?" Shella asked, her voice trailing off.

Kai Leng simply shook his head as he crossed the room toward the bed. A shadow passed over Shella's face, but she didn't show any other emotion.

Standing over the naked asari's body, he drew the knife quickly across her throat. The cut was clean and deep. A river of blood ran down her neck and soaked into the sheets, the same dark color as the human blood pooling in the hall.

"Two of you grab Grayson, two more grab Darrin," he said, reaching around to slide the knife into the back of his pants, then untucking his shirt to hide the protruding handle. "Let's go."

The attack and search had taken less than ten minutes in total. Kai Leng was impressed with his team's efficiency, though in this case it wasn't really necessary.

Residents of the other apartments inside the building had probably heard the sounds of gunfire. But none of them were likely to get involved; people on Omega tended to mind their own business. Even if someone did want to report the incident, there was no one to contact. Omega had no police force, and the guards at the entrance gate a few blocks away wouldn't leave their post; they were paid to keep unauthorized people out of the district, not maintain order inside. News of the battle would reach Aria's ears eventually, probably even before morning. He hoped to be long gone by then.

Only one problem remained: getting Grayson's unconscious form, Darrin's still warm body, and eight kilos of red sand past the Omega First Security guards at the district gate.

He led the team through the winding streets, back the way they had come. They were fortunate enough not to run into anyone else. As they reached the last corner before the guard station, Kai Leng brought his crew to a halt. He extended his hand and Shella slipped Grayson's pistol into his palm. He registered with some disgust the fact that it was a turian-designed Elanus model before tucking it away under his shirt beside the knife. He could feel the two handles—blade and gun—pressing against the small of his back.

"Wait here, but be ready to move."

Taking a moment to focus his mind and body, he rounded the corner alone, moving with an easy but determined pace.

The turians noticed him as he drew near, but they didn't draw their weapons or seem alarmed in any way.

"What's the matter?" one of them taunted. "Get kicked out of the party?"

"Forgot something," he muttered, still moving toward them.

He was ten meters away—easily close enough to deliver an accurate kill shot. But the guards were wearing combat suits; their kinetic barriers would easily deflect a round from this far. He had to get up close and personal for either of his weapons to be effective.

"If you leave the district, it'll cost you to get back in," the other warned.

He didn't bother to answer. Five meters. Just a few more steps and it would all be over. He was close enough to read the expressions on their avian features; he recognized the exact moment they realized he was a threat.

Had either of them taken a few quick steps back while he reached for his weapon, he wouldn't have stood a chance. Fortunately, they both held their ground.

Moving with blinding speed, Kai Leng lunged toward them, his left hand reaching back to grasp the knife in his belt as he closed the gap. He whipped the blade out and drove the tip into the throat of the nearest guard. Twisting his wrist as it penetrated the leathery skin, he severed both the trachea and the turian equivalent of the carotid artery.

The second turian had his gun drawn, but as he extended his arm to shoot, Kai Leng slapped it down with his free hand, causing the weapon to discharge into the floor at their feet. He let go of the knife and went for his own pistol. In a blur of motion he yanked the gun from his belt, brought his hand back in front of his body, jammed the nozzle against the turian's temple, and squeezed the trigger.

There was a wet pop as the back of the turian's head exploded, spewing bits of skull and gray matter out the opposite side. Kai Leng was staring into his enemy's eyes at the moment of death; he saw the pupils dilate as the synapses from what was left of the brain ceased firing and the turian slumped to the floor.

Kai Leng turned his attention back to the first guard. He was down but still twitching, his hands feebly pawing at the knife jutting out from his larynx. Kai Leng stepped forward and finished him off in the same way as he had his partner: one close-range shot through the head.

Looking back, he saw his team was already moving, doing their best to run while carrying Grayson and Darrin. He didn't see anyone else; if there had been any witnesses, they were smart enough to make themselves scarce.

Moving at a quick jog and switching off the burden of the bodies every few blocks, the six of them made it to the spaceport in under ten minutes. Five minutes after that, they were aboard the ship and safely off the station.

Only then did Kai Leng allow a satisfied smile to cross his face.

"Call the Illusive Man," he said to Shella. "Tell him Grayson's coming home."

FIVE

Kahlee tossed and turned all night, constantly glancing over at the glowing clock by the bed. Each time she was surprised to see that only a few minutes had passed since she'd last checked; it seemed as if morning would never come.

She never slept well after one of Grayson's calls. She couldn't help but think about where he was, and what he was doing. And thinking of Grayson inevitably made her think of Gillian and Hendel.

She cared about each and every one of the students she'd treated, but Gillian had always held a special place in her heart. She knew Hendel was watching over the girl, but it didn't make her miss Gillian—or Hendel—any less.

The stoic security chief had been one of her closest friends on the station . . . one of the few close friends she'd had in her life. Despite her outgoing personality, she tended to keep others at a distance, a trait she'd probably inherited from her misanthropic father.

It was strange to think how much influence Jon Grissom had had over her life. She'd taken great pains to conceal the fact that the man the Academy was named after was in fact her biological father.

After her parents' divorce he'd vanished from her life, so she'd taken her mother's name. As she grew older, she tried her best to keep her relationship to one of Earth's most honored—and misunderstood—heroes secret.

Despite these efforts, her father had been thrust back into her life some twenty-odd years ago, when she had been on the run after being framed for the massacre of her fellow scientists at the Sion research facility. He'd hidden her at his home on Elysium, then later helped her and David Anderson—an Alliance soldier and the only other person who had believed Kahlee was innocent—escape off world.

Nearly two decades later Anderson had helped Commander Shepard expose Saren, the rogue turian Spectre, as a traitor to the Council. Kahlee had become a leading researcher in the field of biotics and the head of the Ascension Project. Her father, on the other hand, had stayed on Elysium. He had lived a lonely, isolated existence, refusing all interviews and doing his best to hide from a legendary reputation he never learned to bear.

She'd kept in regular, if infrequent, contact with her father up until the day he died. He had passed away from natural causes six months ago, at seventy-five: shockingly young by modern standards. But then her father had always been a relic from a bygone era.

There were hundreds of dignitaries at the funeral, all coming to pay their respects to a man they idolized, but never really knew. Kahlee had attended not as Grissom's daughter, but rather as a member of the Academy faculty: obviously she valued her privacy as much as he had.

The death of her mother when she was a teenager had shattered her world. Grissom's passing had had a much smaller impact. She never did feel close to her father: the two or three clandestine visits each year to his estate on Elysium had always resulted in uncomfortable conversations filled with long stretches of bitter silence. And yet, now that the surly old bastard was gone, she actually missed him. She still felt a small lump in her throat whenever she passed the memorial plaque in the mess hall that bore his name and likeness.

In an effort to turn her churning thoughts away from the people from her past, she tried to think of a way to smooth things over with Nick. She didn't want him to feel ashamed or embarrassed about what had happened, but talking to him directly might only make things worse.

If Hendel had still been here, she'd have asked him to handle it. But he was gone. Just like her father. And Grayson. And Anderson.

Why do all the men in my life tend to disappear?

That wasn't a question she wanted to mull over in the middle of a long, sleepless night. Fortunately, at that moment her terminal chimed to indicate an incoming message, giving her an excuse to jump out of bed and check it out.

She couldn't help but feel a twinge of apprehension as she flicked on the screen. At night the terminal was set to receive messages silently and store them until morning; it alerted her only when something tagged as *Urgent* came in. Seeing it was from Grayson made her even more anxious.

Unlike his call earlier in the day, this wasn't a live

feed. She could see from the formatting that it was a prerecorded message and an encrypted data file. Her throat was too dry to swallow as she tapped the screen and watched it play.

The instant Grayson's image appeared she knew the message had been recorded months or even years ago. His face wasn't as lean; the bags under his eyes weren't as pronounced.

"If you're watching this, that means Cerberus has found me."

He spoke the words with cool, almost clinical detachment, but that didn't keep Kahlee's heart from jumping into her throat.

"I don't know if they'll come for you, too. They might not; the Illusive Man is practical enough that he might decide you are inconsequential to his plans. But he can also be vindictive and petty. It's a chance you can't afford to take."

She tried to focus on what Grayson was saying, but her mind was having trouble processing the words. She couldn't disconnect the recording from the man behind it. Was Grayson dead? Had they taken him prisoner?

"There's a file attached to this message," the recording continued in the same calm voice. "Everything I know about Cerberus is in there."

Grayson's monotone delivery was a sharp contrast to the chaos crashing down on Kahlee. Her head was spinning, her stomach churning. The whole thing seemed surreal, a nightmare from which she couldn't wake up.

"The Illusive Man is smart. He's careful. He only

tells his operatives what they need to know. But I know far more than he suspects.

"Over the last several years working for Cerberus, I was gathering intel. Maybe some part of me knew even back then that I would turn on the Illusive Man. Or that he'd turn on me. Maybe I was just smart enough to want an insurance policy.

"Names of agents inside the Alliance. Locations of key facilities and safe houses. Shell companies owned by the Illusive Man. Whatever information I could gather, no matter how small, is there.

"Some of the information might be out of date—locations move; new operatives are brought in. But in the right hands what I know could do real damage to Cerberus."

A spark of hope flickered inside Kahlee. If Grayson was still alive, she might be able to use the files he'd sent her to figure out where Cerberus had taken him.

"Don't try to rescue me," the message continued, as if the recording could read her thoughts. "If you're seeing this, then I'm as good as dead."

Kahlee shook her head in an instinctive, unconscious refusal.

"You have to protect yourself. Get this information to someone in authority. Someone with the power to go after Cerberus. You have to destroy the Illusive Man; it's the only way you'll ever be safe."

The message went silent for several seconds, and Grayson's brow furrowed on the screen. Then he barked out a grim laugh.

"I don't know who you can go to," he admitted. "I wish I did. Cerberus has people at nearly every level inside the Alliance. Anyone in a position of power could be working for the Illusive Man.

"But you're smart. I know you'll figure something out. Just be careful who you trust."

The message ended abruptly, catching Kahlee off guard. There were no last words; no sentimental goodbyes. Grayson had told her what she needed to know, then simply ended the recording.

For several minutes she just sat in her chair, staring at the frozen image of Grayson's face on the last frame of the recording as she tried to absorb the horrific news.

Once she felt more in control, she muttered, "Replay," and watched the recording a second time to make sure she hadn't missed anything important during her first emotional viewing.

When it was done, she loaded an optical scan disk into her terminal and copied the information from the attached file. Then she got up, went to her closet, and began to pack. She wasn't panicking, but there was a definite sense of urgency in everything she did.

Despite the emotional shock, she was already thinking about a plan of action. She couldn't stay at the Academy; it might put the children and other staff at risk.

There were a number of people she could go to. She was recognized as one of humanity's most brilliant scientists; over her career she'd come in contact with any number of politicians and military liaisons who would listen to—and believe—her story.

But could she trust any of them? These weren't friends; they were acquaintances at best. Any one of them could be working for Cerberus.

If her father had still been alive she would have gone to him. If Hendel had still been here she would have asked him for help. But they were gone, just like Grayson.

There was only one person she could turn to. Someone she hadn't seen since her father's funeral, and only a handful of times in the decade before that. But Kahlee trusted him absolutely. And she knew she had to get Grayson's information to him as soon as possible.

Aria T'Loak stood motionless beside the bed, staring down at Liselle's naked, blood-soaked body. Two salarian technicians crawled around on the bedroom carpet, collecting samples of blood, hair, and fibers. Another was processing the room's extranet terminal while four more scoured the rest of the apartment, looking for any shred of evidence that might help reveal what had happened.

The signs of a struggle were obvious, though how many had been involved in the battle—and who they were—was impossible to tell. All they knew for sure was that the man known to them as Paul Johnson was gone, and so were the drugs.

That wasn't his real name, of course. As the enterprising human had worked his way up the ranks of her organization, Aria had had him checked out. It hadn't taken long to discover that Paul Johnson was an assumed name, but that hadn't alarmed her. He was hardly the only person in her organization using a forged identity.

A few months of careful surveillance assured her that he wasn't working for a rival gang or some law enforcement agency looking to move in on Omega, but she never had figured out who he really was. She'd had her people take biometric samples: fingerprints left on glasses at the club; retinal, facial, and morphology scans from the station's various security cameras; skin, hair, and even blood samples gathered by Liselle while Paul lay sleeping beside her. None of it came back as a match to any known database.

Aria didn't like uncertainty. Her first instinct had been to have Paul eliminated, just to be safe. She'd even ordered Liselle to do it. But the younger asari had pleaded for Paul's life. He had skills Aria could use, she'd insisted; he was valuable to the organization. Whatever his past was, he had left it behind when he'd come to Omega. He was loyal to Aria now, Liselle swore . . . as loyal as anyone who worked on Omega could be, at least.

In the end, Aria had let herself be persuaded. And now Liselle was dead.

Over the centuries, Omega's Pirate Queen had seen thousands, if not millions, of bodies: both those of her enemies and her allies. She'd stood over more asari corpses than she could remember, many of them slain by her own hand. But it was rare she had to face the death of one of her own offspring.

At her mother's insistence, Liselle had kept their relationship hidden. Aria didn't want her enemies to use the knowledge against her, and she didn't want Liselle to go through life with a target on her back. Yet in the end, it hadn't mattered.

Despite the seething rage she felt over the death of her daughter, Aria wasn't about to jump to any conclusions. There were too many possibilities in play.

This could have been a retaliatory attack by the Talons, though that didn't seem likely. Why come to make peace with her, only to start the war up again? They were smarter than that.

Plus, the Talons had no reason to take Paul with them. If they were responsible, his body should have been lying beside Liselle's. In fact, she couldn't think of anyone who would want to take Paul prisoner . . . which meant there was a good chance he was in on it.

She turned and strode quickly from the bedroom, her face an emotionless stone mask as she left her daughter's body behind.

Sanak was somewhere in the hall outside trying to find out if the neighbors had seen or heard anything useful. She'd sent a pair of krogans to accompany him—a not too subtle message that when Sanak asked a question, he expected a very thorough answer.

Unfortunately, there wasn't much chance of his learning anything new. Omega First Security had already offered a five-thousand-credit reward for any information that could lead to the apprehension—or elimination—of those responsible for killing their district guards. So far they had no significant leads. Aria's reputation was known to everyone on Omega, but if five thousand credits couldn't make someone come forward, neither could the legendary wrath of the Pirate Queen.

She crossed the kitchen and entered the living room just in time to see Sanak returning. From the batarian's expression she could tell his report wouldn't please her.

"We spoke to everyone in the building," he said,

tilting his head to the left in an unconscious gesture of respect peculiar to his species. "A few shots fired; a group of six or seven seen running from the apartment. All of them human. Nothing new."

Aria could have lashed out at him for his failure, but there was no point. She would use violence and intimidation to get what she wanted; they were valuable tools in negotiation and in motivating those working for her. But she knew Sanak was doing everything he could.

Although not her most intelligent employee, he was loyal and relentless in the pursuit of her goals. Getting angry at him served no purpose. She didn't berate her underlings without cause; it only led to resentment and eventual betrayal.

"So we still don't even know if Johnson is a victim or a traitor," she mused.

"My money's on traitor," Sanak offered. "You can't trust humans."

Rather than respond, Aria fixed him with a penetrating stare.

"Look at the evidence," he continued quickly, realizing she needed more than just his personal hatred of a species to be convinced. "Liselle's throat was slashed; she trusted her killer to let him get in close. And what about the drugs? I wanted to take them to you at the club. Johnson insisted we leave them here with him. Seemed kind of strange."

"Bringing the sand to the club would have been a foolish risk."

"It wasn't what he said," the batarian insisted. "It was how he said it. Seeing all that sand affected him.

He kept staring at it. His lip was twitching. He used to dust up. It was obvious.

"And he left the club alone," Sanak added. "I saw Liselle there by herself."

"Obviously you think that's relevant," she noted, impressed by how much thought he'd given this. "You have a theory?"

Sanak blinked his uppermost eyes, collecting his thoughts before he spoke.

"Johnson couldn't resist the sand. Felt that old craving deep inside. So he called some old friends on the station. Invited them over for a party. Liselle showed up to surprise him. He knew he was caught. Had his friends hide in the bedroom. Invited her inside. Cut her throat. Grabbed the drugs and took off with his friends."

Aria considered the explanation briefly before discarding it. "It doesn't make sense. Why was Liselle naked?"

"Humans are sick, twisted animals. Probably raped her before they killed her. Or maybe after."

"You said the neighbors heard gunfire," Aria countered quickly, eager to push away the mental images of her daughter being violated. "Explain that."

The batarian blinked all four eyes this time, struggling to come up with a plausible answer. Before he could, one of the salarians emerged from the bedroom hall.

"Extranet terminal. Wiped clean," he reported in the staccato manner of his kind.

Sanak pounced on the new information. "Bastard was covering his tracks. He had to be in on it."

"Get a trace from the network. I want copies of

every message going in or out of this apartment for the past month."

The salarian shook his head vigorously from side to side. "Human was smart. Scramblers. Encryption. Impossible to rebuild messages."

"We have nothing?" Aria exclaimed, her anger and frustration seeping into her tone for the first time.

"N-no m-messages," the suddenly anxious technician stammered. "Identify callers, maybe. Find where messages sent. Best we can hope for."

"Do it," Aria snapped. "Find out who he's been talking to. Understood?"

The salarian swallowed with an audible gulp. Unable to speak, he gave a quick nod.

"Clean up this mess," Aria added as she turned to go. "And for the sake of the Goddess, somebody cover up Liselle."

SIX

Consciousness came back grudgingly to Grayson. For a long while he floated in the half-world between wakefulness and sleep, until physical sensations began to intrude on the drug-induced blackness.

His mouth was dry. He tried to swallow, resulting in a painful, hacking cough as his parched throat nearly choked on his bloated tongue. His eyes fluttered open, then snapped shut as a searing light burned his pupils.

Even with his eyes closed, he could still see the brightness pressing insistently down on him. He tried to roll over to shield himself against it, only to find he was immobilized.

A jolt of adrenaline washed away the last remnants of the tranquilizer, and awareness came crashing in on him. He was naked and lying on his back atop a cold, hard surface. His arms were held down at his sides by thick straps on the wrists and elbows. His legs were similarly restrained at the knees and ankles. Three more straps—across his thighs, waist, and chest—completed his bondage.

He opened his eyes again, squinting to block out

most of the light. He tried to turn his head from side to side to get a sense of his surroundings, but it, too, was anchored in place. A strap under his chin kept his jaw clamped tightly shut; he couldn't even open his mouth to cry out for help. Not that he expected any help to come.

There's no escape this time. Cerberus will do whatever they want to you.

A wave of panic swept over him, and he struggled madly against his bonds, straining and twisting in a futile effort to gain even an inch of play in the straps.

"You'll only injure yourself," a voice said, speaking from close by his side.

The brightness dimmed substantially and Grayson opened his eyes fully to see the Illusive Man leaning over him. He was dressed in his typical attire: an expensive black jacket over a white designer shirt unbuttoned at the collar.

"Liselle?" Grayson tried to ask, but with his jaw restrained all that came out was an unintelligible grunt.

"You'll have answers soon enough," the Illusive Man assured him as he leaned back, though it wasn't clear whether he'd actually understood his victim.

With the Illusive Man no longer dominating his field of vision, Grayson could see a large lamp hanging down from the ceiling directly above him, like the kind found in an operating theater. It was off now, but it explained the unbearable brightness from before.

They weren't alone. He could hear the sounds of

other people moving about the room, along with the low electrical hum of machinery.

He cast his eyes from side to side, trying to take in as much as he could before they turned the light on again. At the edges of his peripheral vision he could make out just enough detail to realize he was in some kind of hospital or lab. A man in a long white coat passed by on his right, heading toward a bank of monitors.

The Illusive Man was standing just to his left, blocking out most of his view in that direction. But he did manage to catch a glimpse of what appeared to be several strange and terrifying pieces of medical equipment over his shoulder. And then the blinding light came on again, forcing him to once more close his eyes.

"It's been a long time," the Illusive Man said.

With his eyes closed, Grayson had no choice but to focus on his enemy's voice. The tone was calm, almost nonchalant. But Grayson knew the Illusive Man well enough not to be fooled.

"You're probably wondering what happened to the asari," the Illusive Man continued. "She's dead, of course. Quick and painless, if that makes any difference."

It doesn't, you sick son of a bitch!

Grayson concentrated on his breathing, struggling to keep it slow and even. Whatever was going to happen to him, he didn't want to give the Illusive Man the satisfaction of showing his fear, grief, or impotent rage.

"You might be worried about Kahlee Sanders, too," the Illusive Man added after a lengthy pause.

The bastard's watching you. Toying with you. Just stay still. Don't move. Don't give him anything to work with.

He could hear the others in the room—doctors or scientists, most likely. He heard footsteps, the flick of switches, and soft beeps emanating from computer consoles. Occasionally he would pick up a snatch of a low, whispered conversation, but the voices were too soft for him to make anything out.

"We haven't done anything to Kahlee," the Illusive Man finally admitted, once he realized Grayson wasn't going to entertain him with a reaction. "And we won't. She's irrelevant to our plans, and I won't kill a fellow human being without a good reason."

You're a real prince.

"That's why we brought you here. Why I wanted you kept alive. It wasn't so we could torture you. It wasn't to satisfy my lust for vengeance . . . though I don't deny I have those feelings. I'm only human, after all."

The Illusive Man laughed, and his hand patted Grayson on the shoulder like a father bestowing a lesson on his son.

"Humanity needs a hero—probably a martyr in the end. Not the kind of thing people are eager to volunteer for. But this is something that has to be done."

The overhead light dimmed again, and Grayson opened his eyes to see one of the scientists looming over him. Her face was utterly neutral; she showed neither pleasure nor remorse as she leaned in and affixed a pair of electrodes to Grayson's temples.

She stepped back and the Illusive Man leaned forward once more. His face was hovering mere inches above Grayson's own.

"The survival of our race depends on this. And I chose you for this . . . honor."

The hint of a smile, cruel and knowing, crept across the Illusive Man's features. Grayson peeled back his lips and tried to spit through his teeth into his tormentor's face. But his mouth was too dry, and all that came out was a hiss of air.

The Illusive Man leaned back and the overhead light snapped on again, forcing Grayson to shut his eyes once more.

Stop playing his games. If the light goes off again, keep your damn eyes closed.

He heard the sharp click of a metal case snapping shut, then the unmistakable flick of a lighter followed by a long inhalation of breath as the Illusive Man lit a cigarette.

"I know you hate me, Grayson," the Illusive Man continued, somehow managing to sound hurt. "But I don't hate you. That's why I'm going to explain what we're doing. At least you'll be able to appreciate your contribution to the salvation of our species.

"Have you ever heard of the Reapers?"

The question hung in the air. Cigarette smoke curled into Grayson's nostrils and crept down his throat, causing him to cough once.

The overhead light went off, but Grayson didn't fall for the bait this time. He braced himself, expecting to feel a hard slap across the face for his defiance, or maybe the tip of the Illusive Man's cigarette burning into his flesh.

When no punishment came, Grayson realized his enemy had no need of such crude methods. The Illusive Man had absolute power over him, and they both knew it. Petty tortures would only trivialize the situation, lowering the Illusive Man from the position of omnipotent god to pathetic despot.

"No, of course you haven't heard of them," the Illusive Man continued. "Knowledge of the Reapers has been buried for fear of causing a panic. But I know you're familiar with the Collectors, at least by reputation."

Grayson had never actually seen a Collector, but he'd heard plenty of stories. A reclusive race of insectlike humanoids, they were said to come from a world somewhere beyond the Terminus Systems' Omega 4 relay. Spoken of with fear and even reverence by the residents of the Omega space station, the tales told of the Collectors offering extravagant payments in exchange for very specific, and often bizarre, requests.

Their demands always involved the trafficking of live victims, but they were more than just common slavers. They wanted only individuals that matched very precise characteristics: a salarian clan mother with different-colored eyes, or a pureblood asari matron between the ages of two and three hundred.

The residents of Omega had regarded the prospect of striking a deal with the Collectors as akin to winning the lottery: a rare occurrence that would result in untold riches for anyone fortunate enough to cash in. Few of them ever bothered to imagine what it was like for the victims taken away.

Most believed the Collectors used them as subjects for genetic experimentation. But nobody really knew for sure; any non-Collector vessel passing through the Omega 4 relay vanished forever.

A few years ago, or so the rumors claimed, the Collectors had taken a particular interest in humans. Grayson himself had nearly been sold to them after being betrayed by Pel, his ex-partner. Fortunately, he'd managed to escape before the Collectors arrived, eliminating Pel in the process.

This time you won't be so lucky. The Illusive Man's made a deal with the Collectors. They're giving him some kind of advanced technology in exchange for you.

On the surface it seemed a logical conclusion, but Grayson quickly realized it didn't make sense. The Illusive Man would never agree to give a mysterious alien species human test subjects so they could learn the vulnerabilities of the entire race. It violated everything Cerberus stood for and believed in.

"The Collectors were agents of the Reapers," the Illusive Man explained. "A slave species under the total control of their masters. Everything they did, every strange request they made, was to satisfy the orders of the Reapers.

"They are the true enemy. A race of synthetic organisms—machines—that want to destroy or subjugate all organic life. And now they're targeting humans."

He paused as if he expected some kind of reaction

from Grayson. It was almost as if he'd forgotten this was a one-sided conversation with a bound and silenced listener.

"We need to study the Reapers. Learn more about their strengths and weaknesses so we can strike back at them. You're going to give us that opportunity."

"We're ready to begin."

The female voice emanated from somewhere off to Grayson's right. With his eyes still closed he had no way to be sure, but he assumed it was the woman he had seen earlier.

There was a high-pitched whine of a powerful machine revving up, and a few seconds later Grayson's world exploded as his body was racked with a powerful electrical current. His muscles went into spasm, causing his back to arch and his limbs to strain against his bonds with such force the straps bit into his skin and drew blood.

The current cut off suddenly and Grayson went limp. Every nerve in his body was still on fire; it felt like his skin was peeling away to reveal the muscle and tendons beneath. But despite the agonizing pain his body remained absolutely still; he wasn't even able to scream—completely paralyzed, yet fully conscious and aware.

"We have to replicate the procedures of the Collectors as closely as possible," the Illusive Man explained. "I'm afraid this is going to be . . . unpleasant."

He felt thumbs on his eyelids, lifting them open. With Grayson unable to control his muscles, they stayed that way, staring up into the excruciating brightness of the operating lamp. The silhouette of the female scientist momentarily blocked it out as she leaned over him to remove the strap from his chin. She opened his jaw and forced a long, flexible tube deep down his throat before stepping away, leaving him to be blinded by the light again.

"The Collectors implanted their victims with cybernetic Reaper technology. This allows the Reapers to communicate with and eventually dominate the organic host, even from across the galaxy."

The tube in Grayson's throat began to pulse as some type of viscous fluid was siphoned down into his stomach.

"Their technology is incredible," the Illusive Man continued. "Are you familiar with quantum entanglement? No, probably not. It's a complex field of study.

"Basically, there are particles in the universe that share certain complementary properties. If one has a positive charge, the other has a negative charge. Reverse the charge on one particle, and the other also reverses instantly, even if the particles are thousands of light-years apart.

"Humanity explored the phenomenon throughout the twenty-first century, but the cost of identifying and creating the particles was astronomical. In the end, the field was abandoned as impractical.

"But the Reaper technology we recovered from the Collectors is far more advanced. They've combined entangled particles with self-replicating nanotechnology, allowing them to infect, transform, and dominate organic hosts even while they're trapped in dark space."

Someone peeled the electrodes back from Grayson's skull; he felt them pulling at the skin as they were removed. Then he felt the sharp prick of a heavy-bore needle against each temple. There was an unbearable pressure as the needles burrowed into the soft tissue, penetrated beneath the skull, and finally buried themselves deep inside his brain.

"You're being implanted with self-replicating nanides. Their numbers will increase exponentially as they graft themselves onto your neurons and synapses. Eventually they will spread throughout your body, transforming you into a tool of the Reapers. You will be repurposed into a synthetic-organic hybrid unlike anything any of the Council races could possibly create.

"We need to study this transformation. Learn from it so we can defend ourselves against this alien technology. It's the only way we can hope to stand against the Reapers."

Grayson heard the words, but he could no longer understand them. His mind was being ripped apart. He could feel the nanides spreading through his head: alien tendrils wrapping themselves around his very thoughts and identity, strangling them out of existence until everything went black.

"He's catatonic," Dr. Nuri barked out. "Stop the procedure!"

The Illusive Man sat impassively as the scientists scurried to shut the equipment down. He waited silently as Dr. Nuri checked the screens monitoring Grayson's vitals.

"It's okay," she assured him after a few tense minutes. "No permanent damage."

"What happened?"

"It was too much for him to handle. It overwhelmed his system; he shut down."

"You pushed him too far."

"We knew the initial implantation would be traumatic," she reminded her boss.

"I told you to be conservative with your estimates," he reminded her. "We can't afford any mistakes. The Reaper technology is too powerful."

"We have no baselines," she answered defensively. "No data to extrapolate from. It's all theoretical. Nobody's ever tried anything even remotely close to this kind of procedure before!"

"That's why we must err on the side of caution."

Chastised, Dr. Nuri replied, "Of course. I'm sorry. It won't happen again."

"You said there was no permanent damage?" the Illusive Man asked, satisfied he'd made his point.

"He should rest for a few days. After that we can continue."

The Illusive Man nodded.

"Seal the room, but keep him hooked up to the monitors. I want him under observation at all times."

He stood up to leave.

"We've reached phase two of this project," he reminded the doctor. "The subject isn't human anymore. He's something alien now. Something dangerous.

"If you see anything unusual or unexpected—

if you have any doubt or uncertainty at all—
exterminate him immediately. I'd rather see the entire
project fail than risk having this thing we've created
break free. Do I make myself clear?"

Kai Leng stepped out from the shadows where he
had been silently observing the experiment.

"I understand," he assured the Illusive Man.
"Grayson will never leave this facility alive."

SEVEN

Admiral David Anderson was, above all else, a soldier. He understood the true meaning of words like honor, duty, and sacrifice. For twenty-five years he had served the Alliance without question or regret, giving up the chance for love and a family in order to protect humanity as it struggled to find its place in the galactic community. He'd served multiple tours of duty on godforsaken worlds. Fought in more battles than he could remember. Put his life on the line countless times without any hesitation.

Whatever his mission, whatever his assignment, he'd followed orders to the best of his ability and without complaint. But if he had to spend one more meal in the diplomats' lounge listening to the elcor ambassador drone on about his volus counterpart, he was going to go snap.

"With true sincerity," Calyn said in the ponderous style of his species as he sidled up to Anderson's table, "it is good to see you here."

The elcor were a large, heavyset species from the high-gravity world of Dekunna. Standing nearly eight feet at the shoulder, they used their long forelimbs to help their short back legs support their massive girth, giving them the appearance of gray-skinned gorillas walking about on all fours. They had no neck; Calyn's large, flat head seemed to be pushed back into his shoulders.

Though he was still technically an admiral in the military, Anderson hadn't seen active duty in several years. With the restructuring of the Citadel Council, he'd become one of humanity's key political representatives— a "reward" for all his years of dedicated service.

Over the past few months Anderson and Calyn had both been involved in a series of ongoing trade negotiations between the Alliance, elcor, volus, and turians. Anderson was little more than a figurehead at the talks; the Alliance had plenty of real politicians to handle the delicate negotiations. But that hadn't stopped Calyn from striking up a conversation whenever they met outside the conference room.

Every day, when Anderson would leave his Presidium office and come to the lounge for lunch, the elcor ambassador would invariably show up and plot a slow but relentless course over to his table to join him. Upon arrival, he would immediately begin grumbling about the volus ambassador.

"Without exaggeration," the elcor said, jumping right into it as he settled in across the table from Anderson, "Din Korlak is the rudest individual I have ever dealt with."

"I know," Anderson said through gritted teeth as he shoveled a forkful of food into his mouth. "You've told me. Many times."

As a result of evolving in such a high-gravity environment, the elcor moved—and spoke—with a painful deliberateness that Anderson found maddening.

Listening to Calyn vent his frustrations was like hearing a recording played back at one-quarter speed.

His frustration was compounded by the fact that the elcor had no concept of how to use inflection or tone in their speech. Among their own kind they relied on subtle body gestures and subvocal sounds below the threshold of human hearing to convey meaning and subtext. Unfortunately, these nuances weren't relayed through the universal translators that allowed the various species of the Citadel to communicate with each other. As a result, anything the elcor said invariably came across as a flat monotone devoid of any and all feeling.

To make matters worse, their faces were almost featureless. Their small, wide-set eyes and the vertical skin flaps where their mouths should have been revealed no discernible emotion, making it nearly impossible to read their mood.

"Genuine apologies," Calyn droned in reply to Anderson's objection. "It is not my intention to irritate you."

Anderson bit his lip and considered his next words carefully. Even without any contextual clues, it was clear he'd offended his dining companion. And even though he couldn't understand all the complexities of the negotiations, he knew enough to realize that they needed the elcor on their side.

The volus and the turians had a long history of cooperation; centuries ago Din Korlak's people had petitioned for military protection from the turians in exchange for preferential economic status. If the Alliance was going to make any headway in the negotiations, they needed the full support of Calyn's people.

"It's not you," Anderson lied. "The negotiations are just wearing me down."

"Understandable," the elcor replied. "Our jobs can be very stressful."

That's the understatement of the century, Anderson thought.

He was a man of action, not words. He liked to have a plan and implement it. But in the world of politics nothing was ever that simple. Among the ambassadors and Council members he was out of his element, drowning in a sea of bureaucratic red tape.

Calyn had accepted Anderson's apology, but it was impossible to tell if he was still feeling slighted. In an effort to smooth things over, the admiral decided to offer his own feelings on the volus ambassador.

"I probably shouldn't say this," he said, "but I share your opinion of Din Korlak. He's an arrogant, self-entitled whiner."

"With humorous intent," the elcor replied, "just be glad you do not share an office with him."

It was a classic military ploy: strengthen an alliance by focusing on a common enemy. Anderson was relieved to see that at least some of what he'd learned as a soldier could be applied to his new role.

"Next time that little butterball interrupts one of us at the talks," he told Calyn with a grin, "I should smack him hard enough to send him rolling out into the hall."

"Shock and horror," the elcor responded, his monotone words explicitly stating the emotional state completely absent from his appearance and demeanor. "Violence is not the answer."

"I wasn't serious," Anderson explained quickly. "It was a joke."

He'd managed to go twenty-five years as a soldier without stepping on a mine, but as a politician he couldn't even manage one meal without blowing himself up.

"Humans have a disturbing sense of humor," the elcor replied.

They continued the rest of the meal in silence.

By the time Anderson got back to his office after lunch, he was seriously thinking about retirement. He was only forty-nine; thanks to advances in science and medicine he had at least another twenty years before age began to take any significant physical toll. Mentally, however, he was exhausted.

It wasn't hard to explain. As a soldier he had always understood the value in what he did. As a politician, he was always frustrated by his inability to get anything done. In fact, the only time he ever felt like he made any difference whatsoever was when something went wrong . . . like with Calyn.

"How was your lunch, Admiral?" Cerise, the receptionist at the human embassy, asked as he entered the building.

"Should have stayed in the office," he grumbled.

"Be glad you didn't," she corrected him. "Din Korlak and Orinia came by looking for you."

Anderson wasn't sorry he'd missed the volus ambassador, but he wouldn't have minded speaking with Orinia. Anderson's turian counterpart during the ongoing trade negotiations was a former general. And even though they had seen action on opposite sides during the First Contact war, they shared a common set of military values: discipline, honor, duty, and a barely hidden contempt for the political bullshit they now endured on a daily basis.

"Do you know what they wanted?"

"I think Din wanted to file a formal complaint about something one of your aides said during the last session of negotiations."

"You think?"

"When they found out you weren't here, Orinia managed to talk him out of it."

Anderson nodded, certain he'd still get an earful from Din about it at the next round of negotiations.

"That reminds me," he said, trying to appear nonchalant. "Might be a good idea to extend a formal invitation to the elcor delegation to join us here at the embassy after today's talks."

"Why?" Cerise asked, suddenly suspicious. "What did you do?"

She's a sharp one. Can't sneak anything past her.

"I think I offended Calyn with a joke."

"I didn't know the elcor had a sense of humor."

"Apparently they don't."

"Don't worry," the young woman assured him. "I'll take care of it."

Grateful, Anderson took the elevator to his office. He had thirty minutes before the scheduled meeting with his advisers to prepare for the afternoon's talks. He planned to spend the entire time alone, just savoring some much-needed peace and quiet.

When he saw the blinking light on his extranet terminal indicating a message waiting for him, he nearly picked it up and threw it out the window. He thought briefly about ignoring it; he had a list of ten people he could imagine it being from, and he didn't want to hear from any of them. But in the end his soldier's training wouldn't let him be derelict in his duty. He logged on to the terminal, hanging his head in resignation.

"David: I need to see you right away."

His head snapped back up in surprise as he recognized the voice of Kahlee Sanders.

"It's important. An emergency."

He hadn't spoken to her since Grissom's funeral. Even then, they had exchanged only a few pleasantries, carefully avoiding any mention of their time together on the run twenty years ago.

"I'm on the Citadel. I can't say where. Please—contact me as soon as you get this."

Before the message had even ended he was sending a reply. Kahlee wasn't the type to overreact or blow things out of proportion; if she claimed it was an emergency, it had to be something very serious.

She answered immediately, her face appearing on the view screen.

"David? Thank God."

He was relieved to see she wasn't hurt, though it was easy to tell from her expression that she was upset.

"I just got back to the office," he said by way of apology for keeping her waiting.

"Is this a secure line?"

Anderson shook his head. "Not really. Standard diplomatic protocols. Easy to hack."

"We need to meet in person."

There was a long pause, and Anderson realized she

didn't want to openly suggest a location in case someone else was listening in.

"Remember where we said goodbye after Saren
filed his mission report from Camala?"

"Good idea. I can be there in twenty minutes."

"Give me thirty," he replied. "I need to make sure
I'm not followed."

She nodded.

"David? Thank you. I didn't know where else to
turn."

"It's going to be okay," he said, trying to reassure
her . . . though of what, he couldn't even begin to
guess.

The call disconnected. Anderson rose from his
chair, locked up his office, and headed back down-
stairs.

"I have to go, Cerise," he said to the receptionist
on his way out. Remembering the concern etched on
Kahlee's features, he added, "Don't expect me back
for a few days."

"What about the trade negotiations?" she asked,
taken aback by his sudden departure.

"Udina will have to take my place."

"This isn't going to make him happy," Cerise
warned.

"Nothing ever does."

Anderson took three monorails and two cabs,
transferring between four different levels of the
Citadel space station to make sure he wasn't followed. He didn't know what Kahlee was afraid of,
but the last thing he wanted to do was get careless
and lead whoever she was hiding from right to her.

Once he was confident nobody was tailing him, he made his way back up to the Presidium. In addition to the embassies for all the species residing in Council space, the Citadel's inner ring also housed a spectacular park. Grass, trees, flowers, birds, and insects from dozens of different worlds had been chosen and carefully reengineered to coexist in a verdant paradise where diplomats, ambassadors, and other functionaries could go to escape the stresses and pressures of government work.

In the center of the park was a shimmering lake. Twenty years ago he had met Kahlee there on the shore only minutes after learning his application to become the first human Spectre had been rejected because of a report filed by Saren Arterius.

Anderson didn't consider himself a vindictive man, but he couldn't help but feel a smug satisfaction knowing the turian who had derailed his candidacy had eventually been revealed as a traitor.

He made his way across the grass to the edge of the lake. He didn't see Kahlee. Knowing she was probably lurking nearby in an inconspicuous hiding place, he sat down, removed his shoes and socks, then dangled his feet off the bank. The temperature-controlled water was just cool enough to be refreshing.

A few minutes later Kahlee sat down beside him.

"Had to make sure you were alone," she explained.

"You told me not to tell anybody."

"I know. I'm sorry. I'm getting a little paranoid."

"It's not paranoia if someone's really out to get you."

In person she looked even more nervous than she

had over the vid screen. She sat with her knees pulled close up against her chest, her head low as she cast furtive glances from side to side.

"You're going to draw attention," he warned her. "Relax. Try to act casual."

She nodded and methodically removed her footwear, moving in tight beside him as she dipped her feet in the water. Anderson knew she was just getting close so they could speak in confidential whispers, but it still stirred up all his old feelings for her.

The one that got away. Only now she's come back.

He waited for her to speak, but after several minutes of silence he realized he would have to be the one to break the ice.

"Kahlee? Tell me why you're here."

He listened carefully as she told him about Gillian, Grayson, and Cerberus. He tried not to show any reaction, keeping his face and manner calm both for her sake and to avoid drawing the notice of the other park patrons. When she was finished, he took a deep breath and let it out in a long, easy sigh as he thought about everything she'd said.

"You said Grayson was part of Cerberus. Are you sure he's not still working for them?"

"He's not," she replied with absolute confidence. "He's been on the run for two years."

"And you're sure they're the ones who found him?"

"I'm sure."

"And now you're afraid they're coming after you?"

"Maybe. But that's not why I came to you. Grayson's a friend. He needs my help."

Anderson didn't say anything at first. He had more

experience dealing with Cerberus than Kahlee realized. For example, he knew that Cerberus had recently joined forces with Commander Shepard to
stop the Collector abductions in the human colonies
of the Terminus Systems. But he also knew that had
been a temporary alliance of convenience; the Illusive
Man was just using Shepard like he used everyone
else. And when Cerberus had no further use for someone, they tended to show up dead.

"You realize it might be too late for your friend,"
he said carefully.

"I know," she conceded, her voice a barely audible
whisper.

"But even if he's dead, I still want to take those bastards down," she added more loudly. "I owe him that
much."

"The Alliance has been trying to bring down Cerberus for thirty years," he reminded her. "So far we
haven't had much success."

"He sent me a file," she said, casting a quick glance
over her shoulder as if she expected to see the Illusive
Man standing right behind her. "Names of agents. Secret bases and meeting locations. Bank accounts and
corporate financial records. Everything you need."

"I want to help you, Kahlee. I really do. But it's not
that simple. Even if the information is good, we can't
act on it without tipping Cerberus off.

"They've got people in our government. Our military. Grayson may have given you a list of Cerberus
agents he knew of, but what about all the people
under the Illusive Man's thumb he doesn't know
about?

"The Illusive Man is smart. He's got a contingency

plan in place for something like this. We start arresting people, or gearing up for a raid on these locations, and he'll know about it almost before we do.

"If we're lucky we come up with a handful of low-level operatives. But we'll never get close to anybody important. And if Grayson is still alive, we might just spook them into killing him."

"You're telling me you can't do *anything*?" Her voice rose sharply at the end of the question, her anger and frustration spilling out.

"If you stay here on the Citadel, I can keep you safe," he assured her. "I'll handpick a team of four or five soldiers I trust to watch over you."

"It's not enough," she said, shaking her head in a stubborn defiance he remembered even after twenty years. "I'm not going to spend the rest of my life hiding from Cerberus. And I'm not going to give up on Grayson. There has to be a way to get to the Illusive Man."

"Maybe there is," Anderson exclaimed as a sudden flash of inspiration hit.

The ideal solution would be to call on Shepard for help, but that wasn't an option. The commander was off the grid, doing God knows what, God knows where. But there was another option.

He jumped to his feet and extended a hand to help Kahlee up.

"Do you have somewhere safe we can stay for a few hours?"

"I've got a place in the Wards," she replied, her eyes suddenly alight with eager expectation. "Why? What's your plan?"

"The Alliance can't help us. But I know someone else who can."

"We need to see Ambassador Orinia," Anderson told the turian receptionist. "It's urgent."

He recognized the young male behind the desk, though he couldn't remember his name. Fortunately, the turian recognized him as well.

"I'll tell her you're here, Admiral," he said, sending a message through his terminal.

It was well past supper time; most of the embassy offices were empty. But Anderson knew the turian ambassador would be working late.

"Go right in," the receptionist said, though he did give Kahlee what Anderson assumed was the turian equivalent of a suspicious glance.

Orinia's office was smaller than Anderson's—not surprising, given the fact he held a much higher position than her in the Citadel hierarchy. Like his own, it was functionally Spartan in décor. A desk and three chairs—one for the ambassador, two for guests— were the only pieces of furniture. Three flags hung on the walls. The largest was the emblem of the Turian Hierarchy. The second represented the colony where Orinia was born; its colors matched the markings on the hard carapace of her bony skull. The third was the flag of the legion she served in during her military career. A solitary, bedraggled plant stood out on the balcony, sorely neglected. If Anderson had to guess, he would have said someone had given it to her as a gift.

Orinia was already standing to greet them. Warned by her assistant's message, she showed no surprise at Kahlee's unexplained presence.

"I'm sorry you missed today's negotiations," she said, extending her hand. "Has Din Korlak become too much for you to handle?"

Anderson ignored the joke as he clasped the ambassador's hand. As always, the exchange was both awkward and clumsy. Orinia had readily adapted the familiar gesture of greeting in her dealings with humans, but she had yet to truly master the art of the handshake.

"This is Kahlee Sanders," he said by way of introduction.

"Welcome," the ambassador said, though she didn't extend her hand.

Anderson didn't know if Orinia had sensed his reaction to her handshake and decided not to repeat the effort, or if turian culture somehow viewed Kahlee as unworthy of the gesture.

You'd know all this if you were any good at your job.

"I'm guessing this isn't a social visit," the ambassador said, getting right to the point. "Sit down and tell me why you're here."

As they'd agreed on earlier, both he and Kahlee remained standing as a way to convey the urgency of this meeting. Taking her cue from them, Orinia did the same.

"I have a favor to ask," Anderson said. "One soldier to another."

"We're not soldiers anymore," the turian replied carefully. "We're diplomats."

"I hope that's not true. I can't go through official diplomatic channels for this. Nobody in the Alliance can know I'm here."

"This is highly unusual," she replied.

He could sense the suspicion and hesitation in her voice. But she hadn't given him a flat-out refusal.

"Are you familiar with Cerberus?"

"A pro-human terrorist group," she shot back sharply. "They want to wipe us out, along with every other species in the galaxy except your own.

"Cerberus is the main reason we opposed humanity's addition to the Council," she added, a hard edge to her voice.

"Don't define us by the actions of a criminal few," Anderson warned her. "You wouldn't want all turians to be held accountable for what Saren did."

"Why are you here?"

Her voice was curt; obviously, bringing up Saren was not the way to try and win her over.

The one time in your life you actually want to be diplomatic and you make a goddamned mess of it.

"We have information that can destroy Cerberus," Kahlee said, jumping into the conversation. "But we need your help."

The ambassador tilted her head to the side, fixing the humans with one piercing avian eye.

"I'm listening. . . ."

EIGHT

From the comfort of her private booth and flanked by her krogan bodyguards, Aria T'Loak watched Sanak make his way through the crowd at Afterlife.

She was a master at reading batarian body language, just as she could read nearly every sapient species in the known galaxy. Over the many centuries of her life she had learned to pick out the subtle cues that could tell her when someone was lying, or happy, or sad, or—as was often the case when one stood before the Pirate Queen—scared. Watching Sanak approach, she already knew that the news he was bringing her was not good.

For the past three days she'd had her people following up on Paul's disappearance. Inquiries with the typical Omega sources, ranging from simple chats to brutal interrogations, had turned up nothing. Nobody knew anything about the abduction, or even about the man himself. He was a loner; apart from Liselle he didn't spend time with anyone if it wasn't related to work.

Her last hope was his extranet terminal. It had been wiped clean, but her technical experts were attempting to salvage scraps of data from the optical drive. Another team was trying to track any messages sent or received through the terminal by scouring the data bursts transmitted through the relay buoys that linked Omega to the galactic communication network.

The cost of the investigation was astronomical, but Aria could easily afford it. And while part of her was doing this to avenge her murdered offspring, a more calculating part of her knew that sparing no expense to track down someone who might have betrayed her would send a powerful message to everyone else inside her organization.

Unfortunately, it looked as if all her efforts had been in vain.

"The technicians couldn't find anything," she guessed as Sanak reached her booth.

"They found plenty," he grimly replied.

Aria frowned. That was the problem with reading body language: it was imprecise. She knew Sanak was unhappy; she just didn't know why.

"What did you learn?"

"His real name is Paul Grayson. He used to work for Cerberus."

"Cerberus is making inroads on Omega?" she guessed.

The batarian shook his head, and Aria scowled in frustration.

"Just tell me what you know," she snapped.

Aria always liked to give the appearance that she was in complete control. By reputation, she was always two steps ahead of her rivals because she knew what they were going to say or do even before they did it. Nothing surprised her; nothing caught her off guard. It didn't look good for her to keep throwing out guesses that proved to be wrong; it weakened her image.

"Grayson used to work for Cerberus. Then he turned on them. It had something to do with his daughter and a woman named Kahlee Sanders.

"We couldn't locate his daughter. She vanished two years ago. But we found Sanders.

"The technicians said Grayson called her every few weeks. And he sent her a message the night he disappeared."

"Where is she?" Aria asked, suspecting she wouldn't like what she heard.

"She was working at a school for biotic human children. But she left the day after Grayson vanished. We tracked her to the Citadel; she's under the protection of Admiral David Anderson."

Aria's knowledge of politics and power extended far beyond the gangs of Omega. She recognized Anderson's name: he was an adviser to Councilor Donnel Udina, and one of the highest-ranking diplomatic officials in the Alliance.

The Pirate Queen ruled Omega with an iron fist. Her influence extended in various ways throughout the Terminus Systems. She even had agents operating in Council space. But the Citadel was another matter entirely.

In many ways the massive circular space station was a mirror image of Omega: it served as the economic, cultural, and political hub of Council space. And Aria was well aware that if the powers-that-be ever discovered she was taking an active role in events on the Citadel, there would be retribution.

Officially Omega was outside the Council's jurisdiction. But if they felt Aria had crossed a line—if they decided she posed a threat to the stability of Council space—they could always unleash a Spectre against her.

The Spectres weren't bound by the treaties and laws that shaped intergalactic policy. It wasn't inconceivable that one would come to Omega to try and assassinate Aria. The chances of such a mission actually succeeding were slim, but Aria hadn't survived over a thousand years by exposing herself to risk. She was careful and patient, and even the death of her daughter wouldn't change that.

"Don't do anything yet. But keep an eye on the situation," she ordered Sanak. "Let me know if anything changes. And keep trying to find out where Grayson went."

Grayson woke to find himself in a dimly lit cell. He was lying on a small cot in the corner. There were no blankets, but he didn't need any—despite still being naked, he wasn't cold. There was a toilet against one wall; against another was a built-in shelf stocked with enough military rations and bottled water to last several months. Apart from these few necessities, the room was completely empty. No sink. No shower. Not even a chair.

He had no idea how long he'd been unconscious. His limbs were heavy; his mind was groggy. As he sat up, a shooting pain laced its way from the top of his skull down through his teeth. Instinctively, he reached up to rub his head, then pulled his hand back in surprise when it touched bare scalp.

Must have shaved you while they had you strapped to that table, the familiar voice inside his head reasoned. *Probably so they could plant that Reaper technology inside your brain.*

The horror of what Cerberus had done to him in the lab was still fresh in his mind. He could remember the sensation of an invasive alien presence burrowing into his brain. For some reason, however, he no longer felt it.

Is it gone? Or just dormant?

He should have been afraid, terrified even. Instead, he just felt tired. Drained. Even thinking was a struggle; his thoughts were enveloped in a thick fog, and concentrating brought on more flashes of pain in his skull. But he needed to try and piece together what had happened.

Why had Cerberus put him in a cell? It was possible this was still part of the experiment. It was also possible something had gone wrong and the project had been aborted. In either case, he was still a prisoner of the Illusive Man.

His stomach growled, and he glanced over at the ration packs.

Careful. They could be drugged. Or poisoned. Or maybe they just need you to eat so whatever they implanted in your brain can start growing.

The last reason was enough to make him ignore his hunger, though he did open a bottle of water and take a long drink. He could go a long time without food, but he needed water to survive. And Grayson wasn't about to give up on life just yet.

He spent a few minutes examining the rest of the

cell, only to find there was nothing else of interest to discover. Then utter exhaustion set in and he had to lie down again. Before he knew it, he was in a deep sleep.

Grayson had no idea how long he'd been imprisoned in the tiny cell. He'd fallen asleep and woken up again five or six times, but that had little bearing on how many days had actually passed. He had no energy. No initiative. Just trying to stay awake required a monumental effort.

Nobody had come to see him. But he knew they were out there. Watching him. Studying him.

The bastards had planted probes inside him so they could monitor what was happening inside his head. He'd felt the tiny, hard lumps beneath the skin while running his fingers over the stubble growing back on his shaved scalp. Two on the top of his skull. Another pair centered at the top of his forehead. One behind each ear and a larger one at the base of his neck.

A while ago he'd tried to dig them out with his fingernails, clawing at the skin of his forehead until he drew blood. But he couldn't dig deep enough to dislodge the probes.

Or maybe you just don't want to. They're screwing with your brain, remember?

The rumbling of his stomach drowned out the rest of what the voice in his head was saying, hunger tearing at his gut like some kind of creature trying to rip its way to freedom.

Ignoring the risks, he grabbed one of the rations from the shelf and tore open the vacuum-sealed packaging. He wolfed it down, gorging himself on the bland, nutrient-rich paste. He was reaching for another when his stomach cramped up violently. He barely made it to the toilet in time to disgorge everything he'd just eaten.

Flushing the toilet, he wiped his chin in a half-hearted attempt to clean himself up without benefit of a sink or mirror. Opening one of the bottles of water, he rinsed and spit into the toilet until the foul taste of acidic vomit was gone.

The second meal he ate more slowly. This time his stomach managed to keep it down.

His best guess was that a week had passed. Maybe two. Probably not three. The passage of time was impossible to track in the cell. There was nothing to do but eat and sleep. But when he slept he had dreams—nightmares he could never quite recall on waking, but that left him shivering nonetheless.

He still had had no contact with anyone from Cerberus. But he couldn't really say he was alone anymore.

They were inside his head, speaking to him in whispers too faint to understand. These weren't like the critical, sarcastic voice he used to hear in his thoughts. That voice was gone. The others had silenced it forever.

He tried to ignore them, but it was impossible to block out their constant, insidious murmur. There was something simultaneously repulsive yet seductive about them. Their presence in his mind was both a violation and an invitation: the Reapers calling to him across the great void of space.

Somehow he knew that if he concentrated on them, he would be able to understand what they said. But he didn't want to understand. He was trying very hard *not* to understand because he knew understanding the voices was the beginning of the end.

With each passing hour Grayson could feel the whispers growing stronger. More insistent. Yet even though Cerberus had implanted him with this horrific alien technology, his will was still his own. For now, he was still able to resist them. And he intended to hold them at bay for as long as was humanly possible.

"I thought you said the transformation would only take a week," the Illusive Man said to Dr. Nuri.

They were staring down at Grayson through the one-way window in the ceiling of his cell. Kai Leng was lurking in the shadows over by the wall, standing so still he almost seemed to disappear in the darkness.

At the back of the room, the other members of Dr. Nuri's team were monitoring the readings on the hovering holographic screens projecting up from the individual computer stations. They were tracking and recording everything that happened inside the cell: Grayson's breathing, heart rate, and brain activity; changes in body and air temperature; even minute fluctuations in electrical, gravitational, magnetic, and dark energy readings emanating from the room.

"You told me to proceed with caution after we nearly lost him during the implantation," she reminded him.

"I just want to make sure nothing's gone wrong."

"The time line was only an estimate. Our research

strongly suggests indoctrination and repurposing varies greatly depending on the strength of the subject."

"He's resisting," the Illusive Man said appreciatively. "Fighting the Reapers."

"I'm amazed he's held out this long," Dr. Nuri admitted. "His focus and determination are far beyond anything I expected. I underestimated him in my initial calculations."

"People always underestimated him," the Illusive Man replied. "That's what made him such a good agent."

"We could try to artificially accelerate the process," Nuri offered. "But it would skew the results. And it might send his body into shock again."

"It's too much of a risk."

"Dust him up," Kai Leng suggested, stepping forward to join the conversation. "We still have the red sand we grabbed on Omega."

"It could work," Dr. Nuri said after a few moments of consideration. "Our testing shows narcotics have no impact on the Reaper biotechnology. And it could weaken his focus. Make him more susceptible to the indoctrination."

"Do it," the Illusive Man ordered.

Grayson didn't move when he heard the cell door open. He was lying on his side in the cot, facing the wall. He heard footsteps crossing the floor and he tried to tell how many people there were. It sounded like a lone individual, but even if there had been a dozen armed guards it wouldn't have made a difference; he knew this was probably his only chance to escape.

The footsteps stopped. He could sense someone standing beside the bed, looking down on him. He waited another half-second—just long enough to let them lean in to check on his motionless form. Then he sprang into action.

Whirling around, he kicked out with his feet, intending to send his target sprawling backward. His blow never connected.

Instead the person beside his bed—Chinese features, medium but muscular build—moved nimbly to the side and brought an elbow crashing down, dislocating Grayson's kneecap.

Under normal circumstances the agonizing injury would have ended the fight. But Grayson was driven by desperation and a primal survival instinct. Even as he screamed in pain, he curled his right thumb across a rigid palm, extended his fingers, and jabbed at his enemy's throat.

Yet again his attack was thwarted with ease. His adversary grabbed his wrist and twisted the arm up and back, yanking Grayson from the bed so that he landed hard on the floor, knocking the wind out of him. Momentarily stunned, he was unable to resist as the man plunged a needle into his arm and injected him with some unknown substance.

The man let go and Grayson tried to struggle to his feet. His attacker delivered a single punch to the liver, and Grayson collapsed back to the floor in a quivering ball.

The man calmly turned and walked away, never looking back. Helpless, Grayson could only watch him go. His eyes fixated on his assailant's ouroboros tattoo until the cell door slammed shut behind him.

A few seconds later he recognized a familiar warmth spreading through him. His face felt flushed and his skin began to tingle as the soft blanket of red sand wrapped itself around him.

Grayson had been a duster; he had always snorted the fine powder to get his high. But there were shooters, too. Red sand could be dissolved in a solution and injected directly into the bloodstream for those who wanted—or needed—a more powerful fix.

He curled up into a ball and closed his eyes, desperately trying to shut out what was happening. He'd been clean for two years. He'd put his body through the agonizing symptoms of withdrawal and battled against the powerful psychological urges of his addiction by clinging to the memory of his daughter. He had changed for Gillian's sake; staying clean was a symbol of the new man he'd become.

And now, with a single needle, everything he'd worked for was gone. He opened his mouth to scream at the unforgivable violation. Instead, he giggled softly as waves of euphoria washed over him.

He shivered with pleasure as the red sand coursed through his veins, the effects a hundred times more intense than anything he'd experienced while dusting. The first few minutes were a rush of pure ecstasy; yet already he was craving more. Every cell in his body savored the exhilaration of the concentrated drug even as he yearned for another hit.

Eyes glazed and a simpleton's grin plastered on his face, he managed to stand up. His dislocated kneecap sent signals of pain up to his brain, but the sand kept

him from caring. Still giggling, he collapsed back
onto the cot and closed his eyes in rapturous content-
ment.

Then, through the pink haze, he heard the whispers
once more. And this time, he could understand them
perfectly.

NINE

This wasn't the first time Kahlee had been taken in by an alien species while on the run from Cerberus. In contrast to her stay on the Quarian Flotilla, however, she didn't have to wear a full enviro-suit at all times inside the turian embassy.

At Anderson's request, Orinia had agreed to let Kahlee stay in the turian embassy for protection while they prepared to move against Cerberus. If Kahlee had known that would mean being shadowed by a pair of turian bodyguards day and night and not being allowed to leave the building for nearly two straight weeks, she might have objected.

Fortunately, she had plenty to keep her occupied. The files Grayson had sent on Cerberus were thorough, but far from complete and somewhat out of date. Understandably, Orinia had no intention of taking action until every piece of information that Grayson had provided was verified, updated, and cross-referenced against her own people's files.

Kahlee was initially surprised to discover that the turians were keeping tabs on Cerberus. In retrospect, however, it wasn't that shocking. Cerberus was intent on destroying, or at least dominating, every nonhuman species in the galaxy, making them a threat to the Turian Hierarchy. The turians weren't about to take that threat lightly.

The intel they had gathered on their enemy so far was impressive. It had taken a lot of convincing before Orinia had allowed Kahlee to look at the classified files; even though the First Contact war had happened thirty years ago, the ex-general still held a lingering mistrust of humans. Ultimately, however, the sheer overwhelming volume of information had forced the ambassador's hand.

Kahlee was one of the galaxy's foremost experts in complex data analysis. She'd used her skills to help Dr. Qian twenty years ago with his radical AI research. She'd used it to help the Ascension Project design and iterate new biotic implants to maximize the potential of the students at the Academy. Now she was using her talents to try and save Grayson.

With an organization as fluid and secretive as Cerberus, information was in a constant state of flux. Individual agents and cells were given virtually full autonomy to achieve their mission objectives, allowing them to operate across a broad spectrum of parameters. That made tracking their operations very difficult, with a high probability of error.

Grayson had even admitted in his own files that there had been numerous false leads and dead ends. There were only a few individuals inside the Alliance with whom he had worked personally; these were the ones he could confirm as agents of the Illusive Man. The other two dozen names on his list were only suspected Cerberus operatives; it was possible some of them were actually innocent.

He'd also provided the location of several key research labs, but had warned that Cerberus would periodically abandon certain facilities and relocate operations just to make it harder to shut them down. And the companies that helped finance the Illusive Man's illegal activities were all public corporations employing thousands of workers, most of whom had no idea that their efforts were helping to fund a terrorist organization.

The turians needed accurate information if they were going to go after Cerberus. They couldn't just start detaining and interrogating suspected operatives; in addition to the legal and political ramifications, it would alert Cerberus that something was coming, giving them time to relocate and evacuate.

Similarly, they couldn't just send soldiers to raid every suspected Cerberus location. If the information turned out to be inaccurate, they might end up attacking a civilian facility, which could be considered an act of war against the Alliance. Plus, Orinia had a limited amount of troops under her command for this mission; they had to choose their targets carefully. They were going to get only one chance to strike at the Illusive Man; wasting resources on abandoned locations could undermine all their efforts.

The only viable strategy was a blitz approach: simultaneously arrest all known Cerberus operatives on the Citadel while at the same time hitting key installations with military strike teams. By cross-referencing Grayson's files with the turian intel, and incorporating follow-up research of her own, Kahlee was creating a list of confirmed high-value targets.

It would have been easier if they had been able to

draw on Alliance resources for assistance, but that risked someone's reporting their activities back to the Illusive Man. Orinia had decided to keep this in-house: she and Anderson were the only nonturians who knew what was coming.

At least they had Citadel Security on their side. Technically C-Sec was a multispecies police force, but the top officials—and over half of the active force—were turian. Executor Pallin, the head of C-Sec, had served under General Oriana during his stint in the military, so he had readily agreed to create a special C-Sec turian-exclusive task force to aid in their efforts.

It all would have been so much easier if they could have simply arrested the Illusive Man himself. He was the mind, heart, and soul of Cerberus: eliminate him, and the organization would collapse into disorganized cells incapable of working together.

She had hoped that Grayson would reveal the Illusive Man's true identity, but in his file he had explained that was impossible. The Illusive Man wasn't living a double life, posing as a respected and powerful civilian as most suspected. He was the full-time head of Cerberus; he had no other identity. If he needed a public face for legitimate business, he'd call on representatives of the pro-human Terra Firma political party, or use clandestine agents in positions of authority to manipulate and influence events to get the results he wanted.

That was why it was so crucial to compile an accurate and effective list of targets. If the Illusive Man slipped through their fingers, it was inevitable that Cerberus would rise again. They had to either capture him, kill him, or deal Cerberus such a crushing blow that it would take decades for them to recover.

Kahlee understood all this; that was why she was willing to accept Orinia's careful and cautious approach. But she also knew that every day that passed made it less and less likely Grayson would still be alive.

It was possible he was already dead, but she wouldn't let herself believe that. The Illusive Man was cunning and cruel; he wouldn't simply execute someone who had betrayed him in the way Grayson had. He'd have some elaborate plan to exact his revenge.

As grim as this thought was, it gave her some small glimmer of hope to cling to as she analyzed all the disparate data in a desperate race to save him.

When Grayson woke up, he was horrified to discover he was a prisoner in his own body. He could see and hear everything around him, but it seemed surreal, almost as if he was watching a projection on a vid screen with the volume and brightness set way too high.

He rolled over in the cot, spun to put his feet on the floor, stood up, and began to pace restlessly about the cell—but none of these actions came from his own volition. His body refused to respond to his commands; he was powerless to control his own actions. He had become a meat puppet, an instrument of Reaper will.

He briefly registered the fact that his crippled knee had somehow repaired itself overnight. Then his eyes flickered downward, giving him a glimpse of his body, and his mind recoiled in disgust.

He was being transformed. Repurposed. The implants in his brain had spread throughout his body. The self-replicating Reaper nanotechnology had woven itself into his muscles, sinews, and nerves, transforming him into a monstrous hybrid of synthetic and organic life. His flesh had become stretched and semitranslucent. Beneath it he could see thin flexible tubes winding along the length of his limbs. Flickers of red and blue light pulsed along the tubes, the illumination bright enough to be visible through his opaque skin.

Even though he was no longer in control of his body, he could feel that the cybernetics had made him both faster and stronger. He was more aware of his surroundings; his senses were heightened to a supernatural level. The melding of man and machine had created a being that was physically superior to any evolutionary design.

But that wasn't the only change. He was also developing rudimentary biotic abilities beyond those temporarily granted by dosing up with red sand. He could sense his Reaper masters pushing and probing, eager to test the limits of his weak but ever-growing power.

The Reapers turned his body to face the shelf of provisions. Inside he felt a buildup of energy, like a static charge increased a thousandfold. His hand rose, palm extended toward the ration kits. There was a sudden jolt along the length of his arm, strong enough to send a flare of pain shooting up to Grayson's helpless consciousness.

The neat pile of carefully stacked rations was blown apart by the impact of a biotic push. Boxes shot up into the air, bouncing off the shelves and wall before clattering onto the floor.

It was hardly an impressive display. Grayson had seen his own daughter lift a thousand-kilogram piece of machinery and use it to crush a pair of Cerberus agents. The scattered ration packs weighed less than a kilogram each, and the impact hadn't even been powerful enough to burst the seals keeping the food inside fresh. But he knew his power would continue to grow, and he sensed the Reapers were pleased.

Grayson lowered his arm, and it took him a full second before the significance of the action struck him. *He* had lowered his arm; not the Reapers—him!

The biotic display must have temporarily weakened their control of his body. Recognizing that their domination of his will was not yet absolute was all the encouragement he needed to fight back.

The whispers in his head grew to an angry roar as Grayson struggled to regain control of his physical form. He shut them out, ignoring them as he focused all his energy on the simple act of taking a single step.

His left foot rose in response, moving forward half a foot before coming back down to the floor. Then his right foot followed suit, setting off a chain reaction in Grayson's body. He could literally feel each individual muscle tighten, then relax, as his mind reasserted its dominion over what was rightfully his.

As he came back to himself, his body began to tremble. His mouth felt dry, his skin itchy. He recognized the classic symptoms of withdrawal. The hit of red sand was wearing off, allowing him to regain his focus and concentration, his most valuable weapons against the aliens inside his head.

The Reapers were mounting a counterassault: pushing in on his thoughts, trying to twist and bend them to their control. But Grayson refused to surrender what he had fought so hard to regain. It was a battle to save his very identity, and he was winning!

He felt a rush of elation and adrenaline . . . and something else. He barely had time to realize what it was before the warmth of another dose of red sand swept over him.

His head began to swim in an ocean of narcotic bliss, and the Reapers seized the opportunity to wrest control of his body away from him.

Helpless, he could only watch from within as his body walked over to the cot and lay back down on the bed. Lying there in a dust storm fugue, he struggled to understand what had just happened. There was only one explanation that made any sense.

Cerberus was still watching him. Studying him. They knew he was resisting the Reapers; they had dosed him with concentrated red sand to weaken his resolve. Sometime during his previous high they must have surgically implanted a device to allow them to remotely administer doses of the drug to keep him in a perpetual state of intoxication.

It wouldn't have been hard; a small radio-controlled dispenser under the skin that released the sand directly into his bloodstream would do the trick. At a soluble mixture of near one hundred percent concentration, it would take only a few drops to send him flying each time. Eventually the supply in the dispenser would run out, but that didn't give him hope: he knew Cerberus would just refill it.

His eyes closed, shutting out the world. The Reapers needed him to rest; the transformation was still in progress. They needed him to sleep, and so he did.

The Illusive Man and Dr. Nuri had watched the entire episode through the one-way glass. The physical changes to Grayson's body were gruesome, but any guilt the Illusive Man had over what they had done was offset by the knowledge that the data they were collecting could prove invaluable at preventing or reversing the process in future victims. More important, they were learning the limits of what the Reapers were truly capable of.

At first the results seemed to mirror those collected from experiments on the so-called husks: human victims transformed into mindless automatons by the geth during Saren's campaign to seize control of the Citadel. But the Illusive Man knew the truth about that war: Saren and his geth army had all been servants under the control of a Reaper called Sovereign. And the technology to turn humans into husks hadn't come from the geth.

But Grayson's metamorphosis was something more subtle and complex. He was not becoming a mindless slave. He was becoming a vessel, an avatar of the Reapers—like Saren himself. And before his death at the hands of Commander Shepard, Saren had been very, very powerful.

"His strength is growing quickly," Illusive Man

noted to Dr. Nuri. "We won't be able to hold him prisoner for much longer."

"We're tracking his evolution carefully," the scientist assured him. "It will be at least a week before he poses any real threat of escape."

"You're certain of your data?"

"I'd stake my life on it."

"You already have," the Illusive Man reminded her. "And mine, too."

There was an awkward silence before he added, "I'll give you three more days to study him. That's all I'm willing to risk. Do I make myself clear?"

"Three days," Dr. Nuri promised with a nod. "After that we'll terminate the subject."

"Leave that to Kai Leng," the Illusive Man told her. "That's why he's here."

TEN

"Based on my analysis, we have to strike at the six locations highlighted on the first page of the report."

Kahlee had given plenty of presentations over the years, often to powerful and important people. But at her core she was a researcher, not a public speaker, and she couldn't quite ignore the cold, heavy knot in the pit of her stomach as she spoke.

"The names listed beneath each location are confirmed Cerberus operatives believed to have specific knowledge of the layout or defenses of the target in question."

This particular presentation wasn't made any easier by the fact that, apart from Anderson, everyone she was addressing was a turian military officer. They stared at her with the intensity of hawks tracking a mouse on the ground—eight pairs of cold, unblinking eyes.

"In order to use their intel without giving Cerberus advance warning, the strike teams will have to be en route before C-Sec arrests the operatives.

"Even if someone does send off a warning, these bases are in remote clusters that haven't been directly linked into the galactic comm network yet. It'll take time for any messages to get through to them."

"What kind of window will we have between the arrests and hard contact?" one of the turians asked.

His uniform sagged under the weight of all the medals pinned to his chest.

Upon entering the briefing room she'd been introduced to the assemblage, their names and ranks thrown at her in rapid-fire succession as they went around the table. She hadn't even made an attempt to try and remember them.

"Four hours," Anderson chimed in. "Plenty of time for C-Sec to interrogate the prisoners and transmit the info to you."

"Using the info, each strike team leader will have the authority to change the strategic plan for their target," Orinia added.

"This information is reliable?" another turian, this one female, asked.

A thin white scar ran along her jaw, its color making it stand out from the dark red facial tattoos that signified the colony of her birth. She was the only female turian other than Orinia in the room, meaning she stood out enough that Kahlee could actually recall her name: Dinara.

Kahlee could have gone into a lengthy explanation about statistical analysis, margins of error, and probability matrixes extrapolated from incomplete, estimated, and assumed data. However, doing so could have created doubt in the turians' minds.

"It's reliable," she assured them.

"Most of these targets are within the borders of Alliance territory," Medals, the first turian, objected.

"Just before Orinia gives the go to the strike teams, I'm going to authorize a joint-species military action inside Alliance space," Anderson explained. "Everything you do will be completely in accordance with existing Council laws and treaties."

"That's the kind of thing that could get you dismissed from your post," a third turian noted.

"Almost certainly," Anderson agreed.

"Two of the locations are inside the Terminus Systems," Dinara pointed out. "You can't grant us the authority to strike there."

"Those are the most important installations," Kahlee insisted. "The whole reason Cerberus has facilities outside Council jurisdiction is to allow them to engage in illegal or unethical research without fear of repercussions."

"Attacking a facility in the Terminus Systems means a Council review," Medals countered. "It could be grounds for a military discharge."

There were murmurs of agreement around the table, and Kahlee feared the turians were turning against them.

"That could happen," Anderson said, speaking loudly to be heard over the general grumbling. "But Cerberus doesn't play by the rules. Neither can we if we want to take them out.

"If that's a problem for any of you," he added sternly, "you can leave now."

There was a long moment of silence, but every turian remained seated at the table.

"The Terminus facilities are orbital space stations in uninhabited systems," Oriana said, picking up where Anderson had left off. "If the strike teams complete their mission, there won't be any witnesses to file a report against you."

"Understood," Medals replied with a curt nod. "No survivors."

"Except for any prisoners you find," Kahlee hastily added. "If Cerberus is holding someone against their will, they need to be rescued."

"This is a rescue mission?" Dinara asked, looking for clarification.

Anderson and Orinia exchanged glances before the turian ambassador answered the question.

"We can't confirm the presence of prisoners at any location. If you find any, help them if you can. But do not put the mission—or turian lives—at risk unnecessarily."

Kahlee bit her lip to keep from objecting. Anderson had warned her that getting the turians to cooperate wasn't going to be easy. They had to offer something the turians wanted: the elimination of Cerberus. If she pushed the prisoner angle, Orinia might pull her people out.

"What about the Illusive Man?" Medals wanted to know.

"Capturing him would be an ideal outcome," Orinia admitted. "But we have no pictures of what he looks like. All we have is a basic physical description. If you see anyone matching the profile, try to bring them back alive."

Kahlee wasn't sure what would happen next. She thought there might be a vote or some spirited debate regarding the mission. At the very least she expected others to voice their objections or raise concerns. True, the turians were a military culture, and they were used to accepting and acting on orders from their superiors; but this was an unusual situation, and technically Orinia was no longer part of the chain of command.

However, whatever window there had been to question the mission had apparently been closed.

"Strike teams leave in four hours," the ambassador declared as she rose from her seat.

Following her lead, the other turians stood and filed out, leaving Orinia alone with the two humans.

"I wish we could go with them," Kahlee muttered.

"Each commander has crafted his or her team into a finely tuned military instrument through thousands of hours of training," Orinia reminded her. "You'd only get in the way."

"They'll do their best to help Grayson if they find him," Anderson assured Kahlee, reading her thoughts.

"I know," she said, though secretly she had her doubts.

Kai Leng's muscles strained as he pulled his chin up over the bar one last time. Then he dropped to the floor and knocked out a final set of fifty push-ups.

When he was done he threw a towel over his shoulder, strode to the fitness room's gravity control, and dialed it back down from two hundred percent to one standard G.

He wiped the sweat from his bare torso and slung the towel back over his shoulder. He turned toward the locker room, then changed direction instantly when alarms began to wail.

Rushing over to the console by the wall, he punched in his security code to get a status update. The screen might as well have said: *ALL HELL IS BREAKING LOOSE.*

Three unidentified vessels were bearing down on the orbital space station. They were small enough to have slipped past the long-range sensors; that meant they didn't have the firepower to pierce the station's kinetic barriers and reinforced hull. Instead, they were coming in fast in an effort to get close enough to begin boarding procedures before the GARDIAN defenses could burn away their ablative armoring.

The database matched the energy signatures to turian light frigates, each capable of holding up to a dozen crew. The station had approximately forty hands, but the majority were scientists and support staff; only a handful had real military experience. It wasn't hard to do the math: the turians would win this battle.

Kai Leng raced to his locker, but didn't bother to grab his clothes. Instead, he grabbed his knife and pistol—a custom-modified Kassa Fabrications Razer. Gripping the Razer in his left hand and the twelve-inch blade in his right, he raced from the fitness center.

The station lurched as the first attack vessel's boarding ramp latched onto the exterior, nearly throwing Kai Leng to the floor. The ship shuddered twice more as the next two frigates made contact a few seconds later.

The invaders would use high-powered lasers to carve a seam in the station's hull, then apply concentrated explosives to blow open a hole so they could board. Given the turians' reputation for military efficiency, he figured they had less than a minute until the halls of the facility were crawling with enemy soldiers.

The station's main hangar housed several shuttles, but it was on the far side of the station. Going there was a fool's errand: if the turians were smart, they'd hit it first to cut off a primary evacuation route. Fortunately, there were several small escape pods located throughout the facility . . . though not nearly enough for all personnel to make it out alive.

Kai Leng had taken the time to memorize the location of every one of the pods; he knew the closest was easily in reach. But he couldn't leave yet—there was something too important he had to do.

The Illusive Man was asleep in his bed when the alarms rang out. Waking to the unexpected din, it took him a moment to orient himself. As soon as he had his bearings, he fired up the terminal at the desk in his private quarters.

He analyzed the information on the readout, evaluating their chances of victory. Seeing they were under assault by a trio of turian frigates, he immediately realized there was no hope in staying to fight. But if he was lucky—and quick—there might be enough time to terminate Grayson and still make it to one of the escape pods.

It had been over thirty years since he'd seen any active military service; he knew his skills were not what they once were. His best hope was to avoid enemy contact, but he wasn't about to go out unprepared. Moving quickly, he pulled a Liberator combat suit from his closet and slipped it on. From the drawer in his bedside table he grabbed a Harpy pistol before unlocking the door to his room and stepping out into the hall.

He was immediately assailed by a wall of sound: shrieking alarms, shouts of fear and panic, the pounding of booted feet as the station's crew ran up and down the hall. A scientist ran past him, his hands wrapped tightly around a Gorgon assault rifle, the heaviest armament on the station. The fact that someone had opened the armory was good; the fact that an untrained scientist was carrying one of its most powerful weapons was not.

The station was primarily a research facility; it wasn't properly equipped or staffed to defend against a direct assault. Orbiting an insignificant planet circling an irrelevant orange dwarf star in the Terminus Systems, they relied on the secrecy of their remote location to protect them.

The deck trembled beneath his feet and he heard the faint echo of a distant explosion, and he knew the turians had breached the hull. A few seconds later he reached a t-intersection in the hall. From the left-hand corridor, he heard screams and the sounds of gunfire. He turned in the opposite direction, realizing he'd have to take a longer route if he hoped to get to Grayson's cell while avoiding the turian patrols.

As he ran down the hall, his mind was already trying to piece together what had gone wrong. He liked to encourage the impression that Cerberus was all-knowing and all-powerful, but the truth was somewhat different. By galactic standards, they were a small organization, with limited people and finite resources.

Though the Illusive Man was a master of deploying those resources with maximum results, and had a knack for anticipating the actions of both his friends and allies, there were holes in his organization that left them vulnerable. Somehow the turians had found one. None of his agents on the Citadel had warned him of a potential attack, which meant the turians were acting alone. But how had they discovered the location of the base?

He saw Dr. Nuri coming toward him, flanked on either side by security personnel wearing heavy combat suits and armed with Gorgons.

"Come with me," he ordered. "To the lab."

Nuri shook her head. "We'll never make it. The turians overran the entire wing. We have to get to the escape pods."

Nuri was a valuable asset to Cerberus, but she had only the most basic level of combat training. Considering she wasn't even wearing body armor, he didn't see any point in forcing her to accompany them.

"Get to the escape pod," he told her. "Hold it until we get there."

To the guards he said, "You two stay with me."

There was no objection from the guards; they were trained soldiers, and knew better than to defy a direct order. Nuri responded with a nod before dashing off in the opposite direction.

Leading his small team, the Illusive Man was still trying to figure out how the turians had found them. He knew Grayson had information on Cerberus. The Illusive Man had assumed that Grayson didn't know about this facility, but it was possible he could have learned of it during the two years he was on the run. Still, even if Grayson was the source of the intel, how did it end up in the hands of the turians?

His musings were cut short as they rounded the next corner and came face-to-face with a six-member turian patrol standing less than five meters away. Both sides opened fire immediately, the turians dropping into crouches to present smaller targets while the Illusive Man and his guards retreated back around the corner for cover.

The brief initial exchange hadn't lasted long enough for the weapons to penetrate the kinetic barriers of either side. But the turians were better equipped and trained, and had them outnumbered two to one; further engagement was almost suicidal.

"Fall back," the Illusive Man shouted.

Keeping their weapons pointed at the corner should the turians emerge, the guards crab-walked backward in a shuffling retreat.

They'd gone roughly ten meters when two turians poked their heads around the corner and let loose a quick burst of gunfire. The Illusive Man pressed himself close against the wall, taking shelter behind one of the exposed steel ribs that ran vertically along the wall's surface every five meters to reinforce the station's hull. On the other side of the hall the guards did the same, the two of them cramming themselves tightly behind a single protruding girder.

The first two turians continued to lay down a wave of suppressing fire to keep their opponents pinned against the wall so they couldn't shoot back. At the same time the other four rounded the corner and took cover behind the beams in the same manner as their opponents.

The Illusive Man peeked out and squeezed off a few token shots with his pistol, but a barrage of return fire forced him to duck back into cover. The guards huddled together on the opposite side of the corridor had a similar idea, and they were better armed. Working in concert, they leaned out—one high, one low—and unleashed a storm of bullets.

One of the turians wasn't pressed tightly enough against the wall; his left side was partially exposed. By design, both guards aimed at this single target, their concentrated fire ripping through his kinetic barriers and shredding his combat suit in less than a second.

The turian screamed as the high-velocity rounds tore his arm and shoulder to pieces, nearly severing the limb. His compatriots returned fire as he slumped to the ground, blood gushing from his wounds. The Cerberus guards flattened themselves against the wall as rounds peppered their position, relying on the protruding edge of the vertical beam they were hiding behind to shield them from the assault.

With all the turian fire focused on the guards, the Illusive Man took the opportunity to lean out and let loose with his pistol, aiming at the injured turian lying on the floor before his kinetic barriers could recharge. The turian's body jumped and spasmed as the Harpy buried a half-dozen rounds into the helpless alien's torso, then went still. Before the turians could retaliate, the Illusive Man ducked back behind cover.

From the corner of his eye he caught a glimpse of something flying past his position. His gaze drawn by the movement, he turned his head to see a small, fist-sized black disk adhering itself to the wall beside the Cerberus guards.

The Illusive Man dropped to the floor and curled up into a ball, covering his head with his hands just as the grenade exploded. The concussive blast tossed the guards like rag dolls, bouncing them off the wall and sending them ricocheting out into the center of the hall. Any chance of their surviving was immediately snuffed out as their twisted bodies were riddled with turian bullets.

The Illusive Man knew his pistol didn't have the firepower to keep the turians at bay. But he was damned if he was going to let them take him alive. Rolling out from behind the covering beam, he grabbed for the nearest guard's assault rifle.

Wrapping his fingers around the weapon, he mentally braced to feel the impact of the enemy rounds as they overwhelmed his kinetic barriers. He came up on one knee and raised the weapon, but never fired.

The scene before him was a masterpiece of brutally efficient mayhem.

In addition to the turian shot by the guards, two more were already on the floor. One's throat had been slashed from behind, the cut so deep it nearly severed the head. The back of the other's head had been blown off, the result of someone's firing a pistol jammed against the back of his skull so the kinetic barriers couldn't protect him.

The remaining three were engaged in close-quarters fighting with Kai Leng. Despite not wearing a combat suit—he wasn't even wearing a shirt—Cerberus's top wet-work operative made short work of the heavily armored turians.

At melee range the heavy turian assault rifles proved to be a disadvantage; they were too slow and cumbersome to be brought to bear on a target as lithe and mobile as the human butcher attacking them. Kai Leng's weapons presented no such problems.

He stabbed his knife in an upward thrust toward the head of his nearest opponent. The sharply ascending angle brought it in beneath the turian's protective visor, impaling him through the underside of his chin. The blade penetrated up through tissue and bone and into the brain, resulting in instantaneous death.

The weapon was stuck fast in its victim, but Kai Leng had already released his grip on the hilt. One of the turians had thrown down his own ineffectual weapon and grabbed Kai Leng's wrist with both hands in an attempt to break his arm, or at least wrench the pistol from his grasp. But his combat suit made his movements clumsy and awkward, and the thick gloves prevented him from getting a proper grip.

Kai Leng slipped free and dropped to the ground, his leg sweeping out to knock the turian off his feet even as his partner fired a round from his assault rifle at the space where his human target had been standing upright an instant before.

Crouched low to the floor, Kai Leng shoved the nose of the pistol against the back of the still standing turian's knee. The joints of the combat suits were less protected to maintain flexibility; the thin mesh material did nothing to absorb the projectile when he squeezed the trigger. With a scream the turian fell to the floor, the assault rifle slipping from his grasp.

It had all taken less than a second. By the time the Illusive Man processed what was happening and dropped the Gorgon to reclaim his pistol, Kai Leng had grabbed the injured turian's helmet. One hand slipped beneath the chin, the other braced itself against the crown. The corded muscles of the tattooed human's bare chest flexed and he let out a grunt as he wrenched the turian's head at an impossible angle, breaking his neck and severing the spinal cord.

As the last turian was scrambling back to his feet, the Illusive Man shot him in the back. The first five rounds from the auto-repeating Harpy were deflected by the kinetic barriers. The next five were absorbed by the heavily padded layers of the combat suit. The final five pierced the flesh, damaging several vital internal organs.

The turian dropped to his knees, then slumped forward onto his face. Kai Leng added a final round to the back of the head from point-blank range for good measure before standing up.

"Is it clear the way you came?" the Illusive Man asked as he, too, stood up.

Kai Leng shook his head. "Our only hope is to get to the escape pod back in sector three."

The Illusive Man nodded. "Dr. Nuri's already there."

The two of them ran down the corridors of the doomed space station, knowing they could come across another turian patrol around any corner. The only reason they'd survived the last engagement was because Kai Leng had been able to sneak up on the turians from behind while they were focused on the Illusive Man and his guards. If they ran into another patrol, the ending would be much different.

Fortunately they didn't come across any enemy troops, though less than fifty meters from the escape pod they found grisly evidence that the turians had passed by earlier. Dr. Nuri's body was sprawled across the floor, her lifeless eyes staring up at the ceiling, a gaping shotgun wound in her chest.

Neither man made any comment as they stepped over her and continued on their way. A few seconds later they were in the escape pod. The vessel was capable of holding four passengers, but they weren't about to wait around and see if anyone else showed up.

Kai Leng sealed the door; the instant he was done the Illusive Man slammed his fist down on the button that jettisoned them to safety. As they shot clear of the station, the older man slumped across the padded seat, panting heavily in an effort to catch his breath.

It had been a long time since he'd seen any action; his body wasn't used to the intense physical exertions of combat. As he gasped for air, he was acutely aware that Kai Leng wasn't even breathing hard.

After a few minutes he had recovered enough to speak.

"You eliminated Grayson, I assume," he said.

Kai Leng shook his head. "There wasn't time. It was kill him or save you. I chose you."

The Illusive Man almost replied, "You made the wrong choice." Instead, he bit his tongue as he realized he could just as easily have asked Kai Leng the same question back on the station, while there was still a chance to do something about it.

The encounter with the turians had rattled him. He had thought he was going to die. Faced with a glimpse of his own mortality, he had decided not to ask Kai Leng about Grayson because he didn't want to know the answer. Not if it could cost him his life. He was a patriot, but deep down he wasn't ready to be a martyr.

He also had to accept the fact that this was all his own fault. There had been no need for him to come to the facility to oversee the experiments in person. He could have stayed on his secure station and received regular updates. But he'd wanted to watch Grayson suffer. He'd let his desire for vengeance override his common sense, and it had almost gotten him killed.

The truth wasn't pleasant, but the Illusive Man had made a career out of facing unpleasant truths. He wouldn't make the same mistake again. And he wasn't about to chastise one of his best agents for doing something he had tacitly approved of.

"That operation was too well planned to be a one-off mission," he informed Kai Leng. "Get on the secure channels. Find out who else was hit."

Damage control had to be his first priority. He

needed to evaluate the situation, take stock of his resources. After that, he could turn his attention back
to Grayson.

He couldn't be allowed to live. It wasn't about revenge anymore. They'd turned him into a monster, an
abomination. Grayson had become an avatar of the
Reapers, and now he was on the loose. Finding him
and destroying him was the only way to protect
humanity.

ELEVEN

Grayson woke when he heard the alarms. More precisely, when his cybernetically enhanced senses detected the distant sound of sirens echoing from somewhere outside his cell, the Reapers in control of his body caused him to sit up and open his eyes.

He was once again trapped inside himself. He could see and hear everything acutely, his senses relaying information along the network of synthetic synapses coursing through the gray matter of his brain. He could feel the temperature of the air, cool against his skin. The stench of his own flesh—unwashed in weeks—filled his nostrils. Even his sense of taste was heightened to preternatural levels: the spicy sauce from the rations he had devoured last night still lingered on his tongue.

But though he was fully aware of his surroundings, it was all somehow distant, as if it was filtered before being processed. This wasn't the pleasant fog of a red sand high, though he could feel that the effects from the last dose of drugs Cerberus had given him had yet to clear his system. This was something else. It was almost as if his consciousness had been removed from the equation, the inexplicable link between the physical and mental self severed.

The Reapers were growing stronger: it was the only explanation. The thought caused his heart to pound as adrenaline released itself into his system. The instinctive fight-or-flight response gave Grayson hope. His fear had triggered the reaction; if his emotional state could still exert any kind of influence over his body, then perhaps all was not lost.

He tried to reassert control, his battle against the enemy within temporarily making him ignore the distant sounds of battle coming from somewhere far away. As he pushed against the Reapers, he felt them push back. They were aware of him and his efforts, just as he was aware of them on a far deeper, more intimate level than before.

Horrified, Grayson tried to sever the link by flooding his mind with raw emotions: fear, hate, desperation. He hoped the primitive, animalistic thoughts would somehow disrupt or disgust the machines controlling him from beyond the edges of the galaxy, but it was immediately apparent that was not the case. He realized he was powerless; in this fight, he had no effective weapon to use against them.

The same could not be said of the Reapers. The sensation of a thousand red-hot needles piercing his skull made his mind scream in anguish, the suffering so brutally intense he instantly broke off his efforts to try and regain control of his body.

His enemy's victory was not absolute, however. In his torment, Grayson's physical shell had responded with a barely audible moan . . . further proof he was not yet entirely under their control. The memory of the searing pain was too fresh for him to try and resist them again, at least for now. Instead, he let his consciousness retreat, falling back into itself and leaving the machines unopposed for the time being.

Relegated to the role of observer, he was witness as the Reapers moved him over to the cell door until his ear was pressed up against it. He felt the alien technology focusing its energies on his ears, and amazingly his hearing became so acute he was able to discern sounds beyond the constant whooping of the alarms. He could pick out gunfire and even yelling coming from both near and far, punctuated with the occasional explosion or scream. The Reapers took it all in, desperate for information, using the auditory clues to try and construct a probable scenario of what was happening outside.

Grayson didn't know what was happening, either. He had a few theories, but he was afraid to consider them in detail. He didn't think the Reapers could actually read his thoughts—not yet—but he didn't want to chance it.

They held the position for several minutes, ignoring or not caring about the cramp forming in Grayson's neck and shoulders from the awkward angle necessary to keep his ear plastered tightly to the door. Eventually he felt the muscles seize and spasm, bitterly cursing the twisted irony that even though he couldn't control his body, he still suffered when it was harmed.

A few minutes later the gunfire tapered off, then ceased altogether. Soon after, he heard multiple footsteps as a small group approached the door. A second later they were fumbling with the electronic locking mechanism on the other side.

He thought the Reapers might brace for a desperate lunge for freedom the instant the door opened. The muscles in his legs trembled slightly as the option was considered, then quickly discarded. Instead, his body took several steps back so as to present less of a threat to whoever was about to come through.

Grayson was intently focused on everything his enemies did, on everything they had him do. Carefully studying his foe was his only hope of discovering any weakness they might have. The simple act of stepping away from the door told him the machines were rarely impulsive. They applied cold, unassailable logic to each situation, analyzing it for the most likely successful outcome. More often than not, he realized, they would choose to proceed with patience and caution.

The door slid open a few moments later to reveal three heavily armed turians. Discovering him inside the cell, they all took a step back and raised their weapons at Grayson's wild appearance.

His hair had grown back to cover his scalp, just as the scraggly, unkempt beard now covered his face. But he knew that wasn't what startled them. Completely naked as he was, the cybernetics weaving their way beneath his skin would be plainly visible; he suspected he barely looked human anymore.

"Who are you?" one of the turians demanded.

From the voice, it was obvious she was female. A long white scar ran across her chin, visible through the visor of her combat helmet along with the dark red markings painted on the bony carapace covering her face and skull.

"I'm a prisoner," the Reapers replied. "They tortured me. Experimented on me."

Grayson's voice rang hollow in his ears, like listening to a recording of himself.

"What's your name?" the turian demanded, keeping the gun leveled at his chest.

On some level Grayson was hoping she would shoot. She was obviously repulsed by the synthetic hybrid he'd become. Maybe she could sense the alien presence inside him. Maybe some finely honed self-preservation instinct would compel her to simply pull the trigger and end it.

The Reapers shook his head. "I . . . I don't know my name. They drugged me."

"Look at his eyes, Dinara," one of the other turians noted. "Totally dusted."

"Please help me," the Reapers begged.

No, don't! Grayson silently screamed.

At a signal from their scarred leader, the turians lowered their weapons. Grayson was deflated the ruse had worked, but the fact the Reapers didn't know his name verified his suspicion that his thoughts were still private . . . though for how much longer he couldn't say.

"Come with us," Dinara said.

The turians led him out of his cell, giving him his first glimpse of the facility where he'd been held prisoner. Beyond the door of the cell was a small hall; at the far end was a staircase leading up. At the top of the stairs was an observation room, made easily identifiable by the large, one-way mirrored window looking out over the cell below.

Beyond the observation room was what appeared to be a lab. A large console consisting of several computer stations filled the center of the room. The chairs were empty now, but Grayson had no trouble imagining his Cerberus tormentors sitting in the seats at the various terminals, monitoring the changes as his body was transformed into something hideous.

"See if you can find him something to wear in one of the sleeping cabins," Dinara ordered.

One of her followers disappeared out the door on the far side of the room, heading farther into the station in search of something for Grayson to wear. He returned a few minutes later clutching several pieces of clothing.

He handed them to Grayson, and the Reapers slowly made him get dressed. The pants were too large, as was the shirt. The boots were a size too small and pinched his feet. The Reapers didn't bother to complain.

Dinara reached up and placed a hand lightly on the side of her helmet, activating the built in receiver-transmitter.

"Status report," she demanded.

With his heightened sense, Grayson was clearly able to hear both sides of the conversation.

"Facility is secure," the voice on the other end replied. "Thirty-six enemy combatants confirmed dead. No prisoners."

"Shut down the alarms," the commander ordered, and a few seconds later the sirens abruptly stopped.

"We lost eleven of our own," the voice on the other end of her comm-link continued in a more somber tone. "Seven from second team, two each from first and third teams. Two escape pods are missing."

"Any sign of someone fitting the Illusive Man's description?"

"Negative. If he was here, we let him slip through our fingers."

"First and third teams stay here to hold the facility," she said. "Second team rendezvous back at my shuttle. We've got a liberated Cerberus prisoner for transport."

"Copy that."

She lowered her hand and the transmitter clicked off.

"Come with us," she said to Grayson. "We'll get you somewhere safe."

The three turians led him through the halls of what Grayson quickly realized was a space station. He didn't recognize it, though it had the distinctive utilitarian look of a Cerberus base.

He realized the Reapers were making his head and eyes turn and gawk constantly as they walked, trying to take in as much of their surroundings as possible. The machines were capturing data, storing it inside their infinite memory banks in case they ever needed it.

The turians didn't comment on his somewhat unusual behavior. Either they didn't know enough about humans to realize he was acting strangely, or they chalked it up to the effects of the red sand.

Grayson expected the turians to lead him to the docking bay. Instead, they rounded a corner to reveal a massive hole in the side of the station's hull. A chunk of metal two meters square lay on the floor, the edges scorched from where they had been partially sliced open by a powerful cutting beam, the metal itself twisted by the blast of the explosion that had finished the job.

The turian shuttle was visible through the hole, connected to the station by a fully enclosed platform extending directly into the shuttle's airlock. Three more turians—the surviving members of team 2—emerged from the airlock to greet them and salute the commander.

"Tell me what happened to the others," she ordered.

"Ledius, Erastian, and I split off from the others to cover more ground," one of them replied. "They engaged an armed enemy force. By the time we arrived, the battle was over and they were dead."

"All six of them?" their leader asked, her voice rising in disbelief.

"Most were killed at close quarters. It looks like they were ambushed from behind by three or maybe four assailants."

"Their bodies will be returned to Palaven," Dinara assured them, "and their spirits commended to that of the legion."

All six turians bowed their heads and shared a moment of silence. Then Dinara activated the transmitter in her helmet.

"We're ready to leave. Seal off this sector."

"Affirmative, Commander."

After a brief delay a warning siren let out three

long blasts, followed by the heavy thud of bulkheads slamming shut from either direction of the corridor to seal off the damaged area so that the entire station wouldn't decompress when the turian shuttle detached itself.

Satisfied, the turians boarded their ship. The Reapers had Grayson follow close behind. The shuttle wasn't large, but it had room for ten, not including chairs for the pilot and copilot. Five seats lined the wall on either side, facing each other.

Two of the turians went up front to fly the vessel. Three took seats on one wall, while Grayson and the commander took the other.

"We can't offer you anything to eat or drink," Dinara apologized as she helped Grayson into his seat. The chair was far from comfortable; it had been designed for turian morphology. "Our only supplies are turian; they could be poisonous for your species."

The Reapers nodded on Grayson's behalf.

"Take us back to the Citadel," the commander called out to the turians up front. "And send a message telling them we rescued a prisoner. Looks like he needs medical attention.

"Better transmit a retinal scan," she added. "He's too dusted to remember his name."

The engines fired up and the mass effect drive engaged. The pilot punched in coordinates, and then Grayson felt the familiar surge as the ship accelerated to faster than light speed, heading toward the nearest mass relay.

Until the shuttle dropped back to sublight speeds, they were completely isolated, undetectable by any scanners or tracking equipment and incapable of transmitting or receiving messages—the perfect time for the enemy within to strike.

Grayson could feel the Reapers gathering their power, and he fought to resist in any way he could. He had no great love for turians, but he didn't want to see any harm come to his liberators . . . especially if he was going to be the one to take the blame.

Everyone on board the shuttle was armed and armored except for him. It might be possible to eliminate two or even three of the turians, but the others would make short work of him. In the close confines of the shuttle, firing weapons was dangerous; they might resort to knives or simply bludgeon him to death with the butts of their assault rifles. It would be ugly, violent, and messy. He didn't want to go out like that.

The Reapers were too focused on the turians to lash out at Grayson with another debilitating bust of mental agony, but his efforts to stop whatever it was they were planning succeeded only in causing his face to twist into a grotesque mask.

Glancing over at him, the turian commander's eyes went wide with alarm.

"Are you all right? What's wrong?"

In response, Grayson's fist slammed into her face, shattering the visor of her combat helmet and caving in the hard carapace protecting her features, killing her instantly. Grayson's mind let loose a silent howl of agony as the bones of his hand shattered from the force of the blow.

Oblivious to his suffering, the Reapers unleashed a

powerful biotic wave at the three turians sitting across from them before they could react to the gruesome murder of their leader. The impact lifted them out of their seats and slammed them into the wall of the ship behind them, knocking the wind from their lungs and leaving them curled up on the floor gasping for breath.

Using Grayson's undamaged hand, the Reapers ripped the pistol from the belt of the commander's corpse, stood up, and delivered three kill shots execution style to the helpless turians on the ground.

Caught completely off guard by the unprovoked assault, the two turians up front were just now getting out of their seats to try and help their brethren. Grayson dropped the pistol and closed the distance between them, moving so quickly that everything around him became a blur.

His good hand wrapped itself around the wrist of the nearest turian and yanked him off his feet, tossing him to the back of the shuttle, where he landed with a heavy thud atop the bodies of the others.

This provided just enough time for the second turian to bring his assault rifle up. But as he squeezed the trigger Grayson slapped the nose of the weapon down. A stream of bullets deflected off the floor of the shuttle and ricocheted wildly around the reinforced walls of the cabin.

Several rounds ripped through Grayson's flesh: one through the shoulder of his damaged hand, another through the knee of the opposite leg, two through the thigh. There was a cry of pain as the stunned turian lying in the back of the shuttle was hit as well.

Grayson yanked the rifle from his opponent's grasp

with his one good hand, taking it away as easily as an enraged parent might snatch a toy from a petulant child. Then he swung the rifle like a club, slamming it into the side of the turian's helmet. There was a muffled grunt and the unconscious body went limp.

Ignoring the pain from the rounds in Grayson's knee and thigh, the Reapers spun him around and sent him leaping through the air to land on the turian at the rear of the vessel as he tried to get up, knocking him back to the floor. Then the Reapers had Grayson lift up one of the heavy boots and bring it smashing down on his back again and again and again, cracking vertebrae, severing the spine, and causing him to spew frothy indigo spittle across the floor as the internal injuries caused his dark blue blood to seep into his lungs.

When the turian beneath Grayson's boot had been reduced to a lifeless, pulpy mass, the Reapers stopped. Moving with purpose but without hurry, they piled all the bodies—including the still unconscious turian who had been bashed on the side of the head—into the airlock.

Had Grayson been in control of his body, he probably would have thrown up in reaction to the brutal assault. As it was, however, the Reapers kept him from having any physical reaction at all.

The most horrifying part was the cold, efficient way the savage attack had been planned and carried out. Grayson had sensed no anger or rage on the part of the Reapers as they had used him as an instrument of wanton slaughter. The massacre wasn't motivated by hate or even a sadistic desire to destroy organic life. The Reapers had analyzed the situation, determined a course of action, and followed it without any emotion whatsoever.

This, more than anything else, terrified their human host. It seemed to symbolize an inevitability about the Reapers, as if nothing could stop their relentless, passionless pursuit of their goal.

Once all the bodies were secured in the airlock, the Reapers had Grayson take a seat in the pilot's chair. Using his good hand, they punched in a series of commands that first disabled the vessel's transponder, then brought them out of FTL travel.

Grayson was an experienced pilot, but he had never been trained on a turian vessel. Alone, he probably could have fumbled through the process, but the Reapers moved with precision and certainty. They had an intimate knowledge of turian technology, and he could think of only one reasonable explanation.

The Reapers were gathering knowledge about him and his environment, recording everything they came into contact with. He didn't know how many of the aliens were in his head; sometimes it felt like a single entity, other times it felt like billions of individuals. In either case, however, it wasn't unreasonable to assume they shared whatever information they collected with others of their kind. Following this train of thought, if the Reapers had ever possessed a turian in the past for a long period of time, they could have learned virtually everything there was to know about that species. And now they were using Grayson to learn all they could about humanity.

The Reapers hit the eject button on the airlock, jettisoning the bodies into the cold vacuum of space.

Then they plotted a new course—too quickly for Grayson to catch the final destination—and made the jump to light speed again. Finally, despite his heroic struggle to oppose their will, the Reapers closed his eyes and made him fall asleep.

TWELVE

As she ran on the treadmill, Kahlee remained intently focused on her technique. She didn't believe in simply putting one foot in front of the other until she was out of breath and dripping with perspiration. There was an art to running; function followed form. She maintained an optimal stride length, kept her breathing under control, and focused on pumping her arms with each stride. Her pace never varied, and the kilometers—and minutes—rolled past.

The turian strike teams had left roughly twelve standard hours ago. Four hours after that, C-Sec had swooped in and arrested key Cerberus operatives for interrogation, including many high-ranking Alliance officials. As soon as the arrests were complete, Orinia had gone to oversee the interrogations. She had yet to return.

Anderson was gone as well, swallowed up by a maelstrom of meetings with representatives of the Alliance and the Turian Hierarchy in an effort to avert a political catastrophe. That left Kahlee alone in the turian embassy with nothing to do but wait for them to return. She didn't like to wait.

Patience had never been her strong suit. She was

used to tackling multiple tasks at once. Whenever she felt bored or restless, whenever she felt the world dragging itself too slowly for her liking, she would throw herself into her work and occupy her mind with difficult, complex problems.

In that vein, she had tried reviewing the Cerberus data one last time, but there really wasn't any point. Not with the turian strike teams already deployed. She had employed a number of other methods to distract herself—surfing the extranet, reviewing data collected from the children of the Ascension Project, even watching a romantic comedy vid—but nothing helped. Knowing the plan to destroy Cerberus had been set in motion made it virtually impossible to concentrate on anything else.

In the end she'd resorted to a crude but effective therapy to vent her frustration: physical exertion. The turians had been gracious enough to offer her access to the fitness facilities of their embassy, and for the last three hours she had engrossed herself in a punishing cardio workout while waiting for an update on the strike teams.

She noticed a small ache building in her left knee, and she reluctantly reduced the speed of the treadmill to a walking pace. As a classic type A personality, she had a habit of overdoing things. After suffering many painful repetitive-stress injuries in her youth, she'd finally learned to pay attention to the warning signs her body gave her.

With the slower tempo, however, her mind began to wander back to the very things she was struggling to avoid. Could the turians really bring down Cerberus? Was it possible they might actually capture the

Illusive Man? Would they ever find Grayson? And if they did, would he still be alive?

The questions gnawed at her, forcing her to pick up the pace again. But now that the ideas were firmly entrenched in her thoughts, even her run couldn't drive them back into her subconscious. After another twenty minutes she shut the treadmill down.

She'd promised to stay out of the way until the missions were over, but she'd reached a breaking point. It was time to march into the turian ambassador's office and demand answers!

Now that her mind had been made up, even taking the time to shower seemed like an unbearable delay. Wiping her neck and brow down with a towel, she marched over to the door, flung it open, and stepped right into Anderson and Orinia as they were coming in from the other side.

"Whoa, Kahlee," Anderson exclaimed. His hands instinctively reached up to wrap themselves around the biceps of her bare arms as he tried to catch her and absorb her momentum to keep them from crashing into each other.

His grip was firm, but not rough. Suddenly aware of the layer of perspiration covering her skin, Kahlee took a quick step back, breaking free of his grasp.

"We were just coming to find you," Orinia explained. "The strike teams have all reported back."

Unable to decipher the expression on the turian's unfamiliar features, she glanced over at Anderson to see if she could get a quick read on how things had turned out. She caught him rubbing his hands on his hips, trying to subtly wipe away the sweat that had transferred to his palms when he'd grabbed Kahlee's arms. She flushed with embarrassment, and hoped he would think her color was simply a result of her recent physical exertions.

"Udina was pissed," Anderson explained, and she could tell he was just as embarrassed as she was. "Says I created a political shit-storm that's going to take months to clean up."

He was avoiding the details of the mission, and she could tell by the expression on his face that things hadn't gone exactly as planned.

"Tell me what happened."

"All Cerberus bases were neutralized," Orinia informed her. "Unfortunately, turian casualties were almost twenty percent—nearly double what we anticipated. And we failed to apprehend the Illusive Man."

"What about Grayson?" Kahlee asked, fearing she already knew the answer.

"Dinara's team found him on a space station in the Terminus Systems," Orinia said.

"He was still alive," Anderson interjected quickly. "They sent us a retinal scan to confirm his identity."

She should have felt relief at hearing his news, but something about the way he said it gave her pause.

"Why a retinal scan? Why couldn't he just tell them who he was? Something went wrong, didn't it?"

"Dinara and her team took Grayson aboard their shuttle and transmitted a message they were returning to the Citadel. That was three hours ago. We haven't heard anything since."

"They'd need at least three mass relays to make it back to the Citadel," Kahlee offered, refusing to give up on Grayson. "That could take longer than three hours."

"Each time they pass through a relay they'd need to drop to sub-FTL travel," Orinia explained. "Standard turian military procedure would require them to transmit an updated ETA and flight plan each time. We've had no contact since the initial message."

"What do you think happened?" she asked, her mind struggling with the implications of what she was being told.

"We don't know," Anderson admitted. "It's possible they could simply be having comm issues."

Kahlee knew spaceships were designed with too many redundant backups for something like that to happen. Any mechanical failure that kept them from at least sending out a distress call would have to be catastrophic. If it was a technical issue, the chance of their still being alive was almost zero.

"There are other possibilities," Orinia reminded them. "The Terminus Systems are a haven for slavers and pirates."

"Would any of them be stupid enough to attack a turian military shuttle?" Kahlee wanted to know.

"Probably not," Anderson conceded. "We have to consider the option that their disappearance has something to do with Cerberus. Maybe some type of retaliation for the attacks."

"We found no indication they had the ships or resources to strike back so quickly," Kahlee objected. "Even if the Illusive Man is still out there."

"Unless they had an asset on the shuttle itself," Orinia said darkly.

It took Kahlee a second to realize what she meant, then she shook her head vehemently.

"No! That's not possible. Grayson isn't a traitor."

"It's a scenario we have to consider," Orinia insisted. "None of the other explanations make any sense."

"Grayson's the whole reason we got this information!" Kahlee protested. "Why would he help us bring down Cerberus if he was working for them?"

"Maybe he's trying to overthrow the Illusive Man," Orinia suggested. "Using the turians to do the dirty work for him would be a masterful ploy."

"I know Grayson," Kahlee vowed. "I trust him. He wouldn't do this."

She turned to Anderson, looking for support.

"You believe me, don't you?"

"Kahlee," he asked, his tone grave, "is Grayson a drug addict?"

The relevance of the question was completely lost on her. "Why?"

"The retinal scan Dinara sent to confirm his identity was discolored. Pink. Like he'd been mainlining red sand."

"Those bastards!" Kahlee hissed, her face twisting up with rage. "He was clean for two years. Two years!

"They must have drugged him while he was their prisoner to try and gain some kind of leverage over him. Sadistic sons of bitches!"

"How can you be sure that's what happened?" Anderson pressed. "Addicts aren't always the most loyal people. Maybe he was using again. All Cerberus would have to do was wait until he went into withdrawal and then offer him a fix in exchange for information."

"He's not like that anymore!" Kahlee shot back. "He turned his life around."

Anderson didn't say anything, but she could tell he had his doubts.

"There's no doubt in my mind," she assured him. "So why is this so hard for you to accept?"

"You're not always the best judge of character," he replied, choosing his words carefully. "It took a long time before you convinced yourself Dr. Qian's work was dangerous enough to report him to the Alliance."

"That was twenty years ago. I was young and naïve then," she explained.

"What about Jiro Toshiwa?"

Kahlee didn't realize Anderson knew about her former coworker at the Ascension Project, though it wasn't surprising the reports had crossed his desk. In addition to being Kahlee's lover, Jiro had also turned out to be a Cerberus mole inside the program.

"This is different," she muttered, fixing Anderson with a dark scowl. "Grayson isn't with Cerberus anymore. He turned against them for his daughter's sake. He would never start working for them again."

"Maybe not willingly," Orinia said. "But we found evidence of medical experiments at the facility where he was being held prisoner. The data is encrypted and very advanced, but we think Cerberus was investigating some form of mental domination or mind control."

"This is crazy!" Kahlee shouted. "Grayson is a victim, not the enemy!"

"Orinia's just worried about her people," Anderson said, trying to calm her down. "She doesn't want to lose any more soldiers, and we have too many questions without any answers."

"Then let me help find the answers," Kahlee said, jumping on the opportunity. "Send me to the Cerberus facility. Let me look at their test results, and I'll find out what they did to Grayson."

"We'll send our own experts to the station," Orinia said, dismissing her offer.

Kahlee bit her lip to keep from shooting back a reply that would do more harm than good. She wanted to say that she had twenty years' experience analyzing advanced scientific experiments in everything ranging from artificial intelligence to zoology. She wanted to remind Orinia that she was widely recognized as the most brilliant and accomplished complex statistical analyst in the Alliance. She wanted to mention that for the past decade she had been directly studying the effects of synthetic biotic implants on the human brain and nervous system. She wanted to point out that the odds of finding another individual in Council space with her combination of knowledge, experience, and talent was almost nil. And she wanted to scream that she could do more to help them in one hour than the entire team of turian so-called experts could achieve in a week.

But blowing up at the ambassador wouldn't help her cause. Instead, she tried to present a rational and reasonable argument.

"I have some experience in this field—."

"So do we," Orinia replied, cutting her off.

Kahlee took a deep breath to calm herself, then continued.

"The Cerberus scientists are human. They're going

to think like humans, use methodology and processes common to my culture, but likely very different from what your scientists are familiar with.

"Biology and society combine to create familiar, recognizable patterns in the minds of every individual within a particular species. The way the data is encrypted—even the way it's organized and categorized—will be more accessible to me than it will be to a turian, no matter how brilliant."

Orinia didn't answer right away, no doubt balancing the advantages of sending Kahlee to analyze the data against the risks of letting a human become an integral part of what was still technically a turian mission.

"If there's any hope of finding Dinara and her team alive, we have to move fast," Anderson pointed out, playing on the ambassador's sense of loyalty to her fellow soldiers. "Your people might figure this out eventually, but we'll see results a hell of a lot faster if Kahlee's there."

Orinia nodded, and Kahlee could almost forgive Anderson for doubting her about Grayson.

"My shuttle's leaving in an hour. How fast can you be ready to go?"

"Just tell me where to meet them, and I'll be there," Kahlee assured her.

"So will I," Anderson added.

"I thought you'd have to stay here to help smooth things over with the Alliance," Kahlee said, mildly surprised.

"Actually, I resigned my post," Anderson said. "Udina was threatening to launch some massive investigation into what he called my 'inappropriate diplomatic relations' with the turians.

"The Alliance brass was going to put me on administrative leave until it was all sorted out, so I told Udina to cram his investigation up his ass and I quit."

"David," Kahlee said, reaching up to put a hand on his shoulder. "I'm so sorry."

"Don't be," he said with a shrug. "I'm sick of being a politician. I used to be proud of what I did; I felt like I was making a real difference in the galaxy. Then I became a desk jockey and everything I tried to accomplish got buried in a mountain of political bullshit.

"Maybe this is my chance to do something that matters one last time before I pack it all in."

"I'll tell the shuttle commander to expect you both," Orinia said.

"Don't be late," she warned as they headed out the door. "We turians are nothing if not punctual."

THIRTEEN

The Illusive Man sat in the chair of his private office surrounded by darkness, staring out at the dying red sun that dominated the viewing window. He was letting his mind settle, his sense of confidence and control returning now that he was back in the familiar—and secure—surroundings. The turians may have hit Cerberus from all angles, but thankfully they had failed to strike at the true heart of the organization.

As cautious as the Illusive Man was with his operatives and operations, he was downright paranoid when it came to protecting this one location. Including Kai Leng, who was on board right now, only six Cerberus field operatives had ever set foot on this space station. Each time one of them visited he had the crew relocate the vessel to another system as soon as the guest departed.

The mobility preserved the secrecy, as did the harsh personnel screening practices used to recruit the onboard crew. The two dozen Cerberus agents who manned the unnamed space station that served as his inner sanctum were the most loyal and devoted of his followers. These were the fanatics, the zealots.

They were identified through a battery of psychological tests from among the Cerberus rank and file, and part of their training was a subtle yet effective program of propaganda that stoked the fires of their fervent belief in the cause and its leader. The individuals assigned to work here didn't just respect him; they revered him. Worshipped him. Each would have given his or her life without any question or hesitation if he commanded it.

There had been times when the Illusive Man had wondered if he was crossing a line. Was building himself up as a virtual god a necessary security measure, or merely a way to feed his own ego?

The events of the past twenty-four hours had irrefutably answered that question. The turians had dealt Cerberus a savage blow. Many of his key operatives inside the Alliance were now in turian custody. Some would refuse to talk, even when threatened with a capital sentence for treason against the Council. Others, however, would readily spill their guts to save their hides. A number of the undercover operatives not yet exposed would either turn themselves in to avoid the harshest penalties, or abandon their assumed identities and go on the run as the dominoes began to fall.

The vast financial network of companies and corporations that helped fund Cerberus—some knowingly, others unwittingly—was about to be exposed and dismantled. The Illusive Man would still have more personal wealth than he would ever need, but the cost of running an organization like Cerberus was astronomical, and until he rebuilt his financial support network it would be a considerable drain on his resources.

More troubling than the loss of his fortune and his inside sources in the Alliance, however, was the destruction of so many strategically vital operational facilities. The turians had captured two primary military training bases and four major research labs. From what he had been able to gather, few if any of the personnel had been taken alive, meaning that in addition to trillions of dollars of equipment, weapons, and resources, several of the most brilliant minds recruited to their cause had been lost as well.

However, despite the damage done, Cerberus still survived. The Illusive Man's network of followers was far larger than the Alliance could even imagine. There were other research bases and other training facilities located in systems both inside and outside of Council space. The network of scattered agent cells operating independently across the galaxy was still intact.

Through this unassailable space station known only to the most trusted few, the Illusive Man could still control and direct his followers while remaining hidden from both his enemies and his own people. Slowly he would regain what had been taken. He would gather resources and rebuild the political and economic shadow empire that had supported him. He would recruit new followers, and construct new facilities to replace those that had been destroyed. He had already put contingency plans in place to get new operatives assigned to key Alliance positions.

It would take time to recover completely, but humanity still needed Cerberus to protect and defend it. Despite what he had suffered, he wasn't about to turn his back on the people of Earth and its colonies.

But all that was for the future. In the present, he still had to deal with the problem of Grayson being at large. He knew Kai Leng was eager to go after the traitor, but he'd need help and support to hunt down and destroy the monster they had created.

Yet Cerberus couldn't do it alone. His organization was vulnerable right now. He had to be careful. His enemies wouldn't be satisfied with simply setting Cerberus back; they wouldn't rest until the Illusive Man was dead or in prison. They'd anticipate his efforts to rebuild, would be watching and waiting for him to reemerge, keeping a close eye on anyone who could possibly be sympathetic to his cause. Approaching potential allies right now was too dangerous; the solution lay elsewhere.

To bring Grayson down, he would have to look outside the human race, and even outside Council space. For the sake of humanity's future, he would have to swallow his pride and beg for help from those who represented everything Cerberus despised about alien cultures.

This all began on Omega. And if he wanted to end it, he would have to send Kai Leng back.

Kahlee and Anderson exited from the shuttle via the boarding ramp, falling into step behind the turian soldier who had been sent to greet them and take them to the lab. The half-dozen scientists Orinia had sent with them on the shuttle disembarked and followed close behind.

The docking bay of the Cerberus station was large enough to accommodate not only their own vessel, but also those of the turian assault teams that had originally secured the station. Yet even with all the ships, there was still plenty of room for the bodies.

The turians still hadn't finished cleaning up from the assault. A handful of their people were laid out respectfully in one corner of the bay, their arms folded across their breasts, their weapons lying beside them.

In stark contrast, the human casualties had been dumped haphazardly in the middle of the docking bay's cargo floor. They were being systematically stripped of anything of value by a team of turians. As they finished with each body, two of them would pick it up—one at the wrists, the other at the ankles—then carry it over and toss it onto the growing pile against the far wall.

Cerberus was the enemy, but Kahlee still felt a natural revulsion watching the aliens loot the bodies of her own kind. She glanced over at Anderson and noticed he was pointedly looking the other way.

"Thought they'd have more respect for the dead," she whispered, speaking softly so the turian guide a few steps in front of them wouldn't overhear.

"The turians show no quarter for an enemy," Anderson reminded her in a similarly low voice. "Look what they did to the krogan."

Kahlee nodded, remembering how the turians had released the genophage on the krogan homeworld— a biological weapon that effectively sterilized 99.9 percent of the population. Cerberus had brought this on themselves by openly declaring their intention to see humans eliminate or dominate every other species in the galaxy. As far as the turians were concerned, they were in a war for their very survival.

And it wasn't like they were going to jettison the

bodies into space; all the dead would be sent back to the Alliance for identification. That was what bothered Kahlee the most—she couldn't help thinking about those who would be tasked with notifying the families of the dead. Breaking the news to a parent or spouse was hard enough; it would be even more difficult having to tell the bereaved that the person they loved had been a traitor to the Alliance.

Fortunately their guide was setting a brisk pace, and they soon left the horrors of the docking bay behind. He wove his way down the corridors and halls of the Cerberus space station. The signs of battle— bloodstains on the walls and floor, scorch marks and scoring from the ammo—were still clearly visible.

Passing by an open door, Kahlee caught sight of something out of the corner of her eye.

"Wait," she called. "Hold on a second. What's that room back there?"

Their guide stopped and turned around slowly. It was clear he didn't like taking orders from a human. But Orinia had promised Anderson the turians on the station would cooperate with them, and he wasn't about to disobey his superior.

"It's some kind of operating theater," he answered.

"I want to see it."

The guide nodded, and Kahlee and Anderson went into the room. The turian scientists followed them, their own curiosity piqued as well.

The room was stark and utilitarian. A bright lamp hung down from the ceiling in the center. Beneath it was a gurney fitted with leather restraints. The straps and the gurney were stained with dried blood, as was the floor around it.

"They didn't use an anesthetic," Kahlee muttered, feeling sick to her stomach.

Medical equipment on wheels had been pushed up against the far wall. Some of it Kahlee recognized from her work with the Ascension program: an EEG monitor; an endoscope; a cranial drill. Other, more sinister-looking machines she could only guess the purpose of.

She gave each piece a quick examination, trying to get a feel for what it might have been used for. At the same time she struggled not to picture Grayson screaming as he was subjected to the bizarre medical tortures.

Once she was done, she and the rest of the group went back out into the hall, where the guide was waiting.

"I need to see where Grayson was being held," she said.

"We have to go through the lab," he told her. "Follow me."

They continued through the station until they reached what was obviously the station's primary research lab. There was a large bank of computer terminals in the center of the room. Several of the terminals had turians sitting at them, doing their best to hack through the layers of security on the system.

The process of analyzing what Cerberus had been up to was threefold. First the encrypted data had to be carefully extracted from the databases. Then it had to be decrypted. Finally, it would be analyzed by Kahlee and the other scientists.

One of the techs was walking around the room

from terminal to terminal, coordinating the work of the data extraction team.

"You must be Dr. Sanders," he said, extending his hand. "My name is Sato Davaria."

Kahlee shook his hand, as did Anderson.

"Admiral David Anderson," he said by way of introduction.

"An honor to meet you, sir," the turian replied with genuine sincerity.

The turians were a military society; it wasn't surprising that someone with as distinguished a service career as Anderson would be known by reputation.

"I need to see where Grayson was held," Kahlee said.

Sato looked over at their guide, who nodded to indicate he should comply with her request.

"This way," he said, taking them through a small door at the rear of the lab. The other scientists promptly fell in line behind them; at some point they had obviously decided to defer to Kahlee, at least for now.

The door led into an observation room. There was a large window in the far wall—probably one-way glass—overlooking a sparsely furnished prison cell below. The only other exit from the observation room was a small spiraling staircase leading down.

Sato led them down the stairs and into a small hall that terminated at the door to the cell. Kahlee pushed it open and stepped inside.

An unpleasant smell lingered in the stale air—a mixture of sweat, urine, and excrement. There was a small cot in one corner and a toilet in another. A shelf of bottled water and rations had been built into one of the walls. Several of the ration kits were scattered about the floor.

"No sink. No mirror. No shower," Kahlee noted. "They were treating him like an animal. Trying to de-humanize him."

"He was naked when he was discovered," Sato confirmed.

"Let's go back upstairs," Kahlee said. "I want to see what you've pulled from the data banks so far."

"We're making progress," Sato explained as they climbed the stairs, "but it's slow going.

"So far it looks like there was only one test subject in the whole facility. We've decrypted what could be preliminary results from the experiment. But our job is just to pull it out. You're the ones who have to de-termine what it all means."

When they reached the lab again, Sato took a seat at one of the open terminals. He started flipping through screens until he found the files he was look-ing for. Reaching out, he tapped the haptic interface, causing the data to balloon up so that all the hovering screens were suddenly filled with an assortment of charts, graphs, and raw numerical data.

He got up from the chair so Kahlee could sit down, then stood over her shoulder as she began to flip through the data. Anderson came over to stand by her other shoulder, showing his support.

"See this chart here," she said, touching one of the screens so that it expanded and moved to the fore-front of the display. "This is the kind of thing we track on kids recently fitted with biotic amplifiers."

"What does that mean?" Anderson asked.

"It confirms the theory that Cerberus implanted

Grayson with something. Possibly some kind of experimental cybernetics."

She continued to glance over the data, then stopped when she recognized something else, the cold chill of an old memory creeping down her spine.

"I've seen this before, too," she said softly. "Advanced AI research. The same kind of thing Dr. Qian was working on back at Sidon."

"Are you sure?" Anderson wanted to know.

"I'm sure."

"This must have something to do with the Reapers," Anderson said.

Unfamiliar with the name, Kahlee asked, "Who are the Reapers?"

Anderson hesitated, as if he was gathering his thoughts. Or maybe wondering how much he could say.

"They're a species of massive, hyperintelligent starships trapped in the void of dark space. They wiped out the Protheans fifty thousand years ago. Now they're looking for a way to return so they can wipe out all intelligent organic life again."

Kahlee blinked in surprise. "I've never heard anything remotely like that before in my life."

"I know how crazy it sounds," Anderson admitted. "But it's true. When Saren led the geth army against the Citadel, they weren't following him. They were answering to the Reapers. Saren was just an agent under his control."

"Saren Arterius was a traitor," Sato interjected, his voice sharp and bitter. "Don't try to excuse his actions with some crazy story."

Kahlee knew Saren was a sore point for the turians.

Though he was once revered as a hero of his people, his betrayal had made him a source of shame for the species. But Anderson had no love for him, either. He had no reason to mention this unless he believed it.

"If this is true," she said, still trying to wrap her head around the idea, "then why haven't I ever heard of it before? It should have been all over the vids."

"The Council suppressed the story. They said there was no real evidence, and they didn't want to cause mass panic. But I worked with Commander Shepard. I saw the uncensored reports. The Reapers are real."

"It's still a hell of a leap to trace this all back to Qian," Kahlee noted.

"You told me Qian had become obsessed with some kind of ancient, hyperadvanced AI technology. I think he found something connected to the Reapers. Saren must have gotten his hands on it during our mission to Camala."

"Okay. But I still don't see the connection with Cerberus."

"A few months ago, Cerberus learned the Collectors were abducting humans from remote colonies in the Terminus Systems so they could conduct horrific experiments on them.

"Cerberus stopped the Collectors, and they discovered they were working for the Reapers . . . just like Saren!"

"How do you know all this?" Sato demanded.

"I've seen the mission reports," Anderson assured them. "I've talked to people who were there. I'm not making this up.

"Cerberus must have recovered some of the Reaper technology from the Collectors. That's what they were doing here—experimenting on Grayson the same way the Collectors were experimenting on the colonists!"

"This is ridiculous!" the tech declared, and the general murmur from the turian scientists in the room seemed to support him.

"Look at the files," Anderson insisted. "You'll see I'm right."

Everyone turned to Kahlee, waiting for her opinion on the matter. She wasn't going to condemn Anderson's theory, but she wasn't ready to support it yet. Not without further evidence either way.

"The files will tell us the truth," she reminded them. "But whatever Cerberus was up to here, we need to figure it out."

FOURTEEN

Kai Leng wasn't worried about being recognized as he made his way through the twisting thoroughfares of Omega. The last time he had been here his appearance had been carefully altered. This time, as per the Illusive Man's instructions, he wasn't wearing a disguise.

Still, he was wary. Though he appeared calm on the surface, his senses had entered a state of hyperawareness. It was always a good idea to be on the lookout for trouble when visiting Omega. The lawless station was overrun with mercenaries and criminals; every encounter had the potential to suddenly erupt into violence.

Kai Leng glared at a pair of batarians approaching him, his eyes burning into them, sizing them up as potential threats. The four-eyed freaks noticed him staring. He could see a moment of indecision in their eyes: was this a threat worth confronting, or one they should just walk away from? In the end they made the right choice and crossed over to the other side of the street.

When the Illusive Man had first told him of his latest assignment, Kai Leng had expressed his skepticism.

"I don't think Aria T'Loak is a fan of Cerberus."

"She's a businesswoman," the Illusive Man had assured him. "At the very least she'll listen to our offer."

"And if she refuses?"

"We're not looking for a fight," the Illusive Man had reminded him. "We're trying to form a partnership.

"I need someone I can trust for this mission," he'd continued. "Just say and do everything exactly like I told you and it will all work out."

Kai Leng rounded the corner and came in sight of Afterlife. As was typical, the line to get in stretched down the block before disappearing around the corner. He had no intention of waiting in the queue, however.

Marching up to the krogan bouncer at the entrance, he declared, "I need to see Aria T'Loak."

"Name?" the krogan asked, ready to relay it to someone inside for confirmation that he was expected.

"I'm not on the list," Kai Leng admitted.

"Then you don't get in."

A pair of thousand-credit chips suddenly appeared in the assassin's hand. He reached over and pressed them into the krogan's massive palm.

"You can't bribe your way into Afterlife," the krogan declared with a deep laugh, extending his hand to return the credits to Kai Leng.

"Tell her I have information about a man named Paul Grayson," Kai Leng insisted, refusing to take the money back. "She might know him as Paul Johnson," he added.

The krogan's eyes narrowed to thin slits, but he did reach up to activate the transmitter built into the collar of his suit.

"Relay a message to Aria," he said to someone inside the club. "Some human here to see her about Paul Grayson. Or maybe it's Paul Johnson. He's not on the list."

There was about thirty seconds of silence as they waited for a response. Then the krogan's eyes went wide as he heard the orders coming from the other end.

"Yeah. Right. I'll send him right in."

He turned back to the waiting human. "Aria's sending someone to meet you. Head inside to the claim check."

Once again he offered the credits back to Kai Leng.

"Keep them," he told the bouncer, following the Illusive Man's orders to try and make a favorable impression.

The krogan shook his massive head. "Aria says you're to be comped for everything tonight. Including door fees."

Kai Leng took the credits back and slipped them into his pocket, then made his way down a short hall to the claim check. In addition to the two armed krogan and the pair of whorish asari behind the counter whom he'd seen here on a previous visit, a batarian was waiting at the checkpoint to greet him.

"Put all weapons on the counter," he insisted.

"I thought patrons were allowed to be armed inside the club," Kai Leng protested.

"Not if you want a personal meeting with Aria," the batarian replied.

Kai Leng hesitated, reluctant to leave himself vulnerable while walking into a veritable lion's den.

"You could always put your name on the list and come back after we run some background checks on you," the batarian mocked. "Should only take a week or two."

Kai Leng placed his pistol and knife on the counter. One of the asari took his weapons away and disappeared into the back. The other handed him a claim ticket and flashed him a lurid wink. Kai Leng ignored her.

"Stand still for the body scan," one of the krogan grumbled.

Once he was cleared, the batarian led him into the club. He pushed his way through the crowd, parting the way before them. Kai Leng was glad he didn't have to squeeze through the stinking, sweating bodies of the alien patrons himself.

The club was much as Kai Leng remembered: a den of disgusting filth, with drunk and stoned individuals from every species gyrating against each other on overcrowded dance floors to the relentless beat of uninspired techno music.

They climbed the staircase to the upper level, where the music's volume was at least bearable and the crowds were somewhat tolerable. The batarian led him across the club to where Aria T'Loak was sitting at a table in an elevated booth.

An asari handmaiden was seated on either side of her. Standing close by was the largest krogan Kai

Leng had ever seen. Well over eight feet tall, he had to weigh at least five hundred pounds.

In addition to the weapons Aria's menagerie carried, Kai Leng knew the three asari were all powerful biotics. It was possible the krogan was, as well; biotics were rare among the reptilian species, but not unheard of. Even if he wasn't, however, he was clearly capable of physically overpowering anyone else in the club.

The batarian led him up the small staircase into the private booth, then stepped off to the side. Aria didn't ask him to sit; even if she had, Kai Leng would have declined. Perhaps she knew that, which was why she hadn't made the offer.

Kai Leng suddenly understood why the Illusive Man had insisted on planning out everything he was going to do and say in such detail. They hadn't even made their introductions, and the negotiations had already begun.

"You have information on Grayson?" Aria said, breaking the silence.

"You want to find him," Kai Leng replied, following the script he'd memorized. "So do we. I think we can help each other."

Kai Leng noticed that the batarian and the krogan had subtly shifted their positions to stand behind him. Aria's people now had him surrounded.

"I don't get involved with people I don't know," the Pirate Queen informed him. "So let's start with you telling me your name."

"You know I wouldn't give you my real name," Kai Leng replied. "I can make something up if you want, but it seems like a waste of time."

"Are you willing to tell me who you're working for, at least?"

As instructed, he answered truthfully. "I work for Cerberus. Grayson used to be one of our people."

Every alien in the booth tensed, except for Aria herself.

"Why is Cerberus in my club?" she demanded coolly.

"My boss wants to make you an offer," Kai Leng replied.

"Why would I help an organization sworn to eliminate me and my kind?" Aria asked. "Maybe I should just kill you right here instead."

"I'd take at least three of your people with me," Kai Leng warned, forgetting his promise to stay on script. "Maybe even you, if I get lucky."

Behind him the batarian laughed. "You're not even armed. What are you going to do?"

Aria tilted her head to the side, a contemplative smile crossing her lips.

"Don't be a fool, Sanak," she said. "It's obvious our friend doesn't need a weapon to kill."

"This can end in violence," Kai Leng noted, his voice as calm as if he were discussing the weather. "Or it can end with you making a very tidy profit."

"You have my attention," Aria admitted.

Aria had studied the human as he'd crossed the floor of the club and approached her booth. The lean, tattooed man was obviously a highly skilled assassin. He showed neither fear nor bravado, moving through the crowd with the easy grace of a predator on the prowl.

Yet she was still able to pick up the revulsion in his body language. He was disgusted by the other patrons; they were lesser life-forms in his eyes. If pressed, he wouldn't hesitate to kill any one of them, and she was certain he would feel no remorse over his actions.

"The Illusive Man wants to speak to you himself," the assassin told her. "Somewhere more private."

"I prefer to do my business in the club," she informed him. "He can come meet me here if he wants to negotiate."

"He's not foolish enough to set foot on Omega. You can contact him through a secure comm channel. He's waiting for your call, if you're interested."

Aria had to admit she was intrigued. She was eager to find out more about the man she'd known as Paul Johnson and his possible role in Liselle's death. Plus, Cerberus's anti-alien bias was well known; she was curious to know why they had come to her so openly. And the chance to speak to the Illusive Man was an opportunity she wasn't about to pass up; it was amazing how much one could learn about an adversary through a single conversation.

"Come with me," she said by way of agreement.

Her handmaidens slid out from behind the table, allowing Aria to do the same. She led the human through the club to the private rooms in the back. Most of these could be rented out on an hourly, daily, or even weekly basis by patrons of the club. But there was one chamber Aria always kept reserved for herself and those rare occasions when she wanted to conduct business away from the eyes of Omega's curious public.

They entered the room and Aria took a seat at the comm terminal. The human stood off to one side while her own people took up positions scattered about the room.

"Do you have holographic relay technology?" the human asked.

Aria didn't rise to the obvious bait, but from off in the corner Sanak snorted, "We're not savages."

"Give me the comm channel," Aria said, ignoring the batarian as she activated the holo projector.

The human complied, and a few seconds later the image of a well-dressed older human with silver hair and bright blue eyes materialized in the center of the room. He was seated in a chair on what was obviously a space station. A swirling but unidentifiable nebula could be seen through an observation window behind him. In his right hand he held a lit cigarette.

"Aria T'Loak," he said with a slight nod. "I'm the Illusive Man."

"I'm disappointed you lacked the courage to meet me in person," she said, gently needling him in the hopes of goading some type of reaction.

"Are we here to play games, or talk business?" he asked, his demeanor unchanged.

Aria didn't reply right away. She wanted to make him sweat.

The three-dimensional holographic image was life-like enough for her to easily make out the subtle clues and body language projected by the man on the other end of the call. She studied him during the long silence as he took a slow drag on his cigarette, analyzing the unconscious mannerisms and expressions of his every movement.

To her disappointment, she quickly realized she wasn't picking up anything useful. His actions were a confusing mélange of false signals and intentional misinformation carefully orchestrated to hide his true feelings.

"I was told you wanted to speak to me," she finally said, opening the negotiations.

"Grayson betrayed our organization," the Illusive Man told her, putting his offer on the table. "We've been hunting him for over two years. Now I'm willing to pay you to kill him."

"Somebody went after Grayson while he was working for me," Aria said. "They killed one of my people. I think it was Cerberus."

"Nobody came after Grayson," the man corrected her. "He fled because his cover was blown, then staged the scene to make it look like he was abducted in order to buy time for his escape."

"His cover? Are you claiming he was spying on me?"

"Grayson infiltrated your organization. Climbed the ranks. Made himself invaluable. But the whole time he was working for you, he was gathering intel for his new employers."

Aria focused all her attention on the man as he spoke, carefully noting the inflection of his voice, his posture as he sat in his chair, his facial expressions and the involuntary movements of his eyes. But she was still unable to get any kind of read on him.

Only a handful of individuals in the galaxy could successfully lie to Arai T'Loak; with some dismay she realized the Illusive Man was one of them. But the fact that he *could* lie to her didn't necessarily mean he *was* lying to her.

She considered what he had told her so far. Grayson had worked for Cerberus, then betrayed them. Now they wanted revenge. That much she could believe; why else would the Illusive Man have sent his representative to Omega to bargain with her?

Given that he'd betrayed his previous employer, it wasn't hard to believe he had done the same thing to her. However, there were still too many pieces missing for her to accept the story without further investigation.

"Who was Grayson working for?" she wanted to know.

"A turian loyalist group. They're bitter over humanity's growing influence on the Council. The want to expand turian interests. They're planning to make inroads into the Terminus Systems."

The scenario was plausible enough. Though they were technically allies, everyone knew there was still lingering resentment between turians and humanity. If a group of nationalists did want to spread turian interests, the Terminus Systems would be the logical place to begin. And anyone who wanted to make inroads in the Terminus Systems would have to deal with Aria sooner or later.

Maybe Liselle had discovered Grayson's secret. He could have killed her to keep her quiet. But Grayson was smart enough to know he couldn't get away with her murder. Everyone knew they were sleeping together; if she turned up dead—or even disappeared— he would have been the prime suspect. So he fled

Omega, leaving behind a staged abduction scene to throw Aria and her people off his track.

The more she thought about it, the more plausible it all seemed.

"One thing I don't get," Sanak said, stepping forward as he barged his way into the conversation in his typical heavy-handed style. "Why would Grayson work for a pro-human group like Cerberus, then suddenly switch his alliance to a bunch of turian nationalists?"

The holographic image in the Illusive Man's chamber showed Aria T'Loak seated in what appeared to be a well-furnished suite. The projected image was centered on her, but at the edges it was possible to make out several aliens who were also in the room. Kai Leng wasn't visible, but the Illusive Man assumed he was there as well.

When the batarian stepped forward and interposed himself into the picture to ask his question, the Illusive Man didn't offer an explanation right away. He was building an elaborate lie, and if he wanted Aria to fall for it he had to let her do some of the work herself.

"Don't be dull," the asari said to her lieutenant, as if on cue. "Grayson's a mercenary. He has no loyalty to any cause. He works for the highest bidder."

The Illusive Man was well aware of an interesting phenomenon. The smarter someone was, the easier it was to make them believe a complex lie. The simple-minded focused on the holes in the story; they needed an explanation for every loose end. The intelligent filled in the holes themselves, using logic, reason, and creative thinking to weave the threads together into a perfect tapestry of deception.

However, it was also important to weave in bits of the truth to reinforce and support the layers of the story that were false. He knew Aria would have investigated Grayson's disappearance. If she had managed to track any of his communications, it was inevitable she would have come across one name popping up time and time again.

"Grayson doesn't work alone," the Illusive Man declared. "He has a partner. A woman named Kahlee Sanders."

He was hoping the name would elicit some type of reaction from Aria, but her expression remained unchanged. Grudgingly, he had to admit she was almost as good at concealing her true emotions as he was.

"Sanders is the key to finding Grayson," he continued. "She doesn't know the truth about him; she thinks he left Cerberus because he realized the error of his ways. She also thinks the turians they're working with serve the Council.

"She's nothing but a pawn in his games. He's using her. But we can use her, too.

"Sanders is the only person Grayson cares about other than himself," the Illusive Man explained, weaving in more bits of truth into his extravagant lie. "He will try to contact her sooner or later. Force her to send a reply asking for his help, and he'll come."

The Illusive Man paused, knowing a monologue was the least effective way to sell a fabrication. It was always more effective if there was some kind of give-and-take. He needed Aria or her people to engage in order to be truly persuasive.

Fortunately the batarian at her side was happy to oblige.

"Sanders is untouchable," he objected, confirming the Illusive Man's suspicions that Aria already knew about her. "She's hiding out at one of the embassies on the Citadel."

Kai Leng had filed extensive reports on Aria and her people during his preparations to grab Grayson. Based on the batarian's appearance and demeanor, the Illusive Man concluded he had to be Sanak, one of the Pirate Queen's longest-serving lieutenants.

"Sanders isn't at the embassy anymore," the Illusive Man explained. "The turians took her to a secret research station. Heavily protected, but a well-armed force with the element of surprise would be able to overwhelm the defenders and take Sanders hostage."

"Your information on this is solid?" Aria asked.

"My sources are always reliable," the Illusive Man assured her.

"So just go get her yourself," Sanak objected.

"The turian nationalists know we're their enemy. They try to keep tabs on all Cerberus movements. We'd never be able to pull off an operation like this without them knowing about it beforehand.

"But," he added, nodding in Aria's direction, "they will never see you coming."

"How much is this worth to you?" Aria wanted to know.

"Four million credits," the Illusive Man stated. "One million up front. The other three when Grayson's death is confirmed."

"Grayson's worth four million?" the batarian exclaimed in disbelief.

"What he knows about Cerberus is," Aria replied. "He has secrets they want to keep buried. Maybe I should try to take him alive."

The Illusive Man was impressed. Even though his offer was ridiculously high, he'd expected the Pirate Queen to haggle over the amount simply on principle. But she was smart enough to realize the key to the deal wasn't the amount of credits on the table, but rather Grayson himself.

"You might be able to sell his information, but you'll never find a buyer who can even come close to matching our offer," he told her. "He's worth more to both of us dead than alive."

Aria thought about it before nodding her assent.

"I accept your offer. Your representative can stay here as my guest until the deal is done."

"No," the Illusive Man replied, flatly declining her offer. "Cerberus will contact you with Sanders's location only after he is safely off Omega."

"Are you trying to offend me?" Aria asked. "Everyone knows my word is my bond."

"Nothing changes hands until we report back," the Illusive Man insisted. "When we contact you about Sanders, you can provide instructions to transfer the credits into your account and we'll send the down payment."

She considered the offer for several minutes before nodding her agreement.

"We have a deal."

The holographic image suddenly vanished as Aria immediately disconnected the call, determined to get in the last word.

The Illusive Man let the hint of a satisfied smile

cross his lips as he spun in his chair to better enjoy the magnificent view while finishing his cigarette.

Kai Leng bit his tongue to keep from commenting on Aria's abrupt end to her call with the Illusive Man. He suspected she had done it to try and get a rise out of him, and he wasn't about to give her the satisfaction.

"One of our operatives will contact you through the extranet once I'm off the station," he said, reiterating the Illusive Man's terms. "She'll make arrangements to transfer the funds."

"Why are you so eager to leave?" she asked. "We should celebrate this partnership. At least stay and enjoy a drink in the club. On me."

"Our business is done. I'm ready to leave," Kai Leng insisted.

He had no desire to stay any longer in her presence than was absolutely necessary, and he wasn't worried about offending her with his honest answer. Aria had made the logical decision to accept the deal; she wasn't about to change her mind because of a little rudeness on his part. She was far too smart to let emotions get in the way of business.

The asari shrugged indifferently, confirming his theory.

"As you wish. Sanak, escort our anonymous guest out."

The batarian led him from the private room, through the club, and back to the entrance. Kai Leng was only too happy to retrieve his weapons and leave the pounding music of Afterlife behind for the crowded Omega streets.

He made his way down the street for several blocks in the direction of the nearest spaceport, keeping an eye out to see if he was being followed. Once he was satisfied Aria hadn't put a tail on him, he changed course.

Despite what he'd told Aria, the Illusive Man had given Kai Leng specific instructions to remain on Omega after the meeting.

"Keep an eye on Aria and her people," he'd said. "Make sure they keep their end of the bargain.

"If they don't," he'd added, "take matters into your own hands. Do whatever it takes. Grayson cannot be allowed to live."

FIFTEEN

When Grayson came to he was sitting slumped forward in the pilot's seat of the turian shuttle, his chin resting on his chest.

He raised his head slowly, the muscles in his neck stiff and sore. His mouth was dry, he had a pounding headache, and he was sweating profusely: the familiar first stages of red sand withdrawal. With Cerberus no longer refilling the dispenser pumping the drugs into his system, his body was on its way to becoming clean again.

Lifting himself carefully from the seat, he reached his hands up to the ceiling to try and stretch out his aching back. Only then did he recall the injuries he'd sustained during the attack: the broken hand; the rounds in his shoulder and legs . . . injuries that had miraculously healed themselves while he had slept.

It took a few seconds before the full implications struck him. The Reapers had repaired his body while he was unconscious, but now he was the one standing and stretching! He was in control again!

The Reapers were still there. He could feel them deep inside his mind, slumbering like some great beast. The outburst of biotic and physical energy had forced them to withdraw into the dark recesses of his subconscious to rest and recharge.

This proved their power was not infinite, but he knew that when they attempted to seize control of him again they would come back stronger than ever. The cybernetics in his body were spreading . . . growing. Soon the Reapers would dominate him absolutely; he wouldn't have many more windows of opportunity left.

Sudden spasms in his stomach and bowels caused him to double over: another side effect of the red sand withdrawal. Moving quickly but carefully, he made his way to the head at the back of the shuttle. Turian and human physiology was similar enough for him to use the toilet, something he was grateful for as his body tried to purge itself through both ends.

It was nearly ten minutes before his stomach settled enough for him to feel safe leaving the bathroom. Even though the Reapers were dormant, he could sense their instinctive revulsion at the graphic display of organic weakness. Grayson didn't enjoy it, either, but his withdrawal gave him hope. Without the red sand clouding his thoughts, he'd have a better chance of holding the Reapers at bay when they tried to seize control of him once more.

He didn't know what the Reapers wanted. Their persistent presence in his mind gave him no insight into their ultimate goal. But whatever it was, he was determined to stop it.

Suicide was the quickest solution, of course. End his life now, and the threat would be eliminated. The easiest way would be to end it with a single shot to the head, but the Reapers had jettisoned the turians' weapons along with their bodies. He wondered if this was just coincidence, or if they had done this in anticipation of his reaction.

There were other options available to him, though. He got up and made his way over to the emergency kit in the back of the shuttle.

Something is wrong.

The Reapers sensed the changes in the brain waves of their host through the synthetic network monitoring his mental activity. They recognized the pattern flashing through his synapses: hopelessness; self-destruction. They had lost a vessel once before like this. This time they were prepared.

Grayson opened the metal emergency kit and examined the contents. There was medi-gel; a massive overdose could put him into a coma from which he might never wake. But would that even stop the Reapers? Or would they simply animate his flesh and send him stumbling around like some kind of zombie?

Dismissing the drugs, Grayson let his eyes fall on the next available option: the emergency kit's long, jagged utility knife. But it couldn't be a simple slit on the wrist; the incredible healing properties of his own flesh would betray him. He would have to slash his throat, making a cut so deep he bled out before the Reapers even realized what was happening.

The avatar cannot be allowed to harm itself.

The Reapers understood that Grayson had grown more resistant to their overt attempts to control him; his mind was adapting, developing new ways to protect itself from their domination. But there were other forms of control.

Tapping into his body's unconscious systems, the Reapers increased the levels of hormones being released into Grayson's system even as they subtly manipulated the electrical impulses in the brain to alter his emotional state.

Grayson's heart began to pound. He tried not to think about what he was going to do in case he lost his nerve. As he picked up the knife, his hands were shaking. He raised the trembling blade to his throat and closed his eyes.

A bizarre mix of emotions flooded through him. He'd expected to feel fear, and there was plenty of that. But he also felt an odd sense of hope and elation. He felt inexplicably energized. Defiant. Triumphant!

He tossed the blade back into the kit and opened his eyes. He refused to end it like this. Suicide was the coward's way out. He was better than that.

Marching back up to the pilot's chair, he sat down in the seat and took a look at the nav systems to get a sense of where he was. If he could figure out where the Reapers were heading, maybe he could figure out what they were up to.

To his surprise, he was deep inside Council space, orbiting a mass relay only one jump away from the Citadel . . . and from Kahlee.

He knew she was on the great station that served as the heart of the civilized galaxy. It was the only way to explain how the turians had found him. She must have passed the Cerberus files he'd sent her on to someone she trusted; that person had recruited the turians to help them.

He quickly plotted a new course for the shuttle— one that would take it in the opposite direction. Away from the Citadel. Away from Kahlee. He didn't have a destination in mind. Instead, he planned to send the shuttle out into the most remote, sparsely populated region of the galaxy. With any luck it would be a one-way journey; he would run out of fuel and be trapped floating on the edges of space, never to return.

It was another form of suicide, but now he was driven by the urgent need to put as much distance between himself and Kahlee as he could. He had to protect her.

As a further precaution, he decided to send her a message. He didn't activate the shuttle's video feature; he didn't want her to see what kind of monster he'd become. Instead, he'd send an audio file to her extranet account.

He had to warn her to stay away from him, no matter what. He had to tell her not to look for him; not to try and help him.

He has feelings for her.

The Reapers made another slight alteration to Grayson's thought pattern. Instead of his rational, conscious mind doing what was morally right, he momentarily succumbed to his primal, subconscious yearnings and desires.

"Kahlee, this is Grayson. Listen closely—I need to see you. Right away. Send me a reply as soon as you get this."

Grayson ended the recording and sent the message off, completely unaware of what the Reapers had done.

"Listen up!" Sanak shouted at the crew assembled in the cargo hold of the frigate. "ETA is five minutes. Expect resistance to be armed and organized."

Cerberus estimated they'd have about twenty soldiers to contend with. Just to be safe, Aria had sent forty of her best people on the mission—a mix of batarian, krogan, and asari mercenaries.

"Turians don't believe in surrender," Sanak warned them. "So expect this to get messy."

There was some knowing laughter from his team; they were eagerly looking forward to the carnage. Between the element of surprise and their superior numbers, they wouldn't have any trouble winning the battle. That wasn't what Sanak was worried about.

"Remember the primary goal—capture the human alive! Is that clear? Capture the human alive!"

A chorus of assent rumbled back to him, but he wasn't satisfied yet. He knew how easily things could get out of hand, particularly when krogan were involved.

"This isn't a suggestion. It's not even me giving you an order. This comes down from Aria herself. The human ends up dead, and so do we."

He could see from the expressions on their faces that the importance of what he was saying was sinking in. Just to be safe, however, he repeated it one last time.

"Capture the human alive!"

The bunk in the room Anderson had chosen for his quarters was comfortable enough, but he wasn't able to sleep.

It wasn't just the strangeness of the situation, though being on a Cerberus station manned by turians was more than enough to shake him. And there was something disconcerting about claiming the sleeping cabin of someone whose corpse was likely piled against the wall in the station's docking bay.

The issue keeping him awake was much more personal, however. He was worried about Kahlee.

She was obsessed with scouring the research files, trying to fully grasp everything that Cerberus had done to Grayson. The turian scientists and techs were doing their best to help her, working in alternating ten-hour shifts. But Kahlee hadn't taken more than a handful of ten- and twenty-minute breaks since their arrival. She was pushing herself too hard, and if she didn't take a break soon she was going to collapse from exhaustion.

Anderson had urged her to slow down, arguing that with each passing hour she was becoming less productive and more inclined to make a mistake. He pointed out that the turians could continue to pull files while she rested, giving her a completely fresh batch of data to analyze when she came back. As expected, she listened politely to his concerns, then brushed them aside with the reassurance that she knew her limits and a promise to stop whenever she reached them.

Knowing he had no chance of convincing her to take a break, Anderson had retired to try to get some much-needed shut-eye. Instead, he lay on his back, staring up at the ceiling in the dim light of the cabin.

It wouldn't have been so bad if he didn't feel so useless. His skills weren't suited to research and analysis; he was a soldier. He didn't like feeling helpless; he wished there was something he could do.

A second later he regretted that thought as alarms began to ring out through the station.

He sprang from the bunk and ran out into the hall, still in his undershirt and boxers. Several turians were emerging from the surrounding cabins, roused from their slumber by the emergency sirens.

With no clear idea of what was happening, Anderson raced down the halls until he reached the lab. Kahlee was there along with several armed turian soldiers, though the techs and scientists were gone.

"What happened to Sato and the others?" he asked, yelling to make his voice heard above the alarms.

"They went to grab their gear," one of the turian soldiers explained. "We're under attack!"

It wasn't surprising that the techs and scientists would have brought their combat gear with them: military service was mandatory for every turian. Given the nature of the mission, it was likely everyone on board except for Kahlee and Anderson was still in active service.

"What do we know?" Anderson asked, looking for a situation report.

"Single ship closing in. Medium-sized frigate. Not responding to hailing frequencies. Looks like they're going to try and board us."

The irony of the turians being on the other side of the equation this time was not lost on Anderson. He just hoped that this time the station's defenders would emerge victorious.

"You think it's Cerberus?" Kahlee asked.

Anderson shook his head. "I don't see how they

could have mounted a counterattack so soon. Not after the kind of damage we dealt them."

"Whoever it is, they'll be here any minute," the turian warned. "The captain wants us to rally here by the lab. Keep our forces together and face the enemy as a single unit."

"Understood," Anderson said. "Where do you want us to set up?"

The turian shook his head. "You stay in here with the door locked until the battle's over."

"We both have combat training," Kahlee protested. "We can help!"

"You don't have body armor or combat suits," the turian reminded her. "You don't know our tactics. You'll just get in the way."

"He's right," Anderson said, cutting Kahlee off before she could object further.

He didn't necessarily agree with the turian, but he knew that nothing was more disruptive to a fighting unit than individuals questioning orders.

"Can you at least spare some weapons just in case?" he asked.

The turian handed Anderson his assault rifle and pistol, then disappeared out the door. Anderson handed the pistol to Kahlee, hit the wall panel, and punched in the code to seal them inside.

He took a second to familiarize himself with the weapon: standard turian military issue. It was a good weapon, efficient and reliable . . . though if it got to the point where he had to use it, he suspected it would mean the battle had already been lost.

"Now what?" Kahlee asked him.

"Wait and hope that the next time someone comes through that door, they're on our side."

Except for the whooping of the alarms, everything was silent for the next few minutes. Then the sound of gunfire erupted from the hall, deafening even through the closed door. It continued without pause for several minutes, punctuated by the faint shouts of soldiers barking out orders and the periodic explosion of a grenade.

When it finally ended, it didn't taper off. Rather, it came to an abrupt and sudden halt. A few seconds later the alarms stopped, too—either shut off at the control room or disabled by someone hacking into the system remotely.

"Take cover," Anderson whispered.

He crouched behind one corner of the massive computer console in the middle of the room, resting his assault rifle on the edge and training it on the door. Kahlee took up a similar position with her pistol on the other side of the console.

They heard heavy footsteps in the hall beyond, then the unmistakable sound of someone hacking the door's access panel from the other side. When it slid open to reveal a krogan in heavy armor, both Anderson and Kahlee opened fire.

Instead of falling back, the beast charged their position. He managed to take three loping strides toward them before their combined fire penetrated his kinetic barriers. His momentum carried him two more steps forward, then they finally brought him down less than a meter away from the console.

Anderson vented the heat clip to keep his weapon

from overheating, waiting for the next attack. A pair of batarians, one on either side of the door frame, peeked around the corner and lay down suppressing fire, keeping the two humans pinned behind their cover long enough for an asari to step into the room and unleash a biotic wave.

The console rocked backward from the impact, and Anderson and Kahlee were spent sprawling toward the rear of the lab. Anderson managed to scramble back to one knee to take aim again. Out of the corner of his eye he saw Kahlee roll over onto her stomach and wrap both hands around the butt of the pistol so she could fire from a prone position.

Neither of them managed to get off a single shot before they were enveloped in a biotic stasis field launched by a second asari waiting in the wings. The powerful opposing gravitational and magnetic forces inside the stasis field held them completely immobilized for several seconds, allowing plenty of time for the batarians to rush in and disarm them.

One charged up to Anderson and slammed him in the face with the butt of his shotgun just as the stasis field dissipated, sending the admiral toppling backward to the floor, barely conscious. Beside him he heard Kahlee scream as the other batarian brought his foot slamming down on the pistol clasped in her hands, crushing her fingers beneath his heavy combat boot.

Anderson, his head spinning from the blow, tried to get up to fight. But before he could, the batarian landed on top of him, his knee driving into Anderson's chest and pinning him in place. Turning his head, Anderson saw Kahlee in a fetal position, writhing in pain, her mangled fingers clutched tight against her abdomen.

To his surprise, the attackers didn't kill them. Instead, they hauled them to their feet, forced their hands behind their backs, and slapped cuffs on their wrists.

"Sanak's waiting by the ship," one of the asari said.

Anderson could feel blood pouring down his face; the rifle butt had broken his nose and split his top lip. But he was more worried about Kahlee—her skin was pale and her eyes were glazed. The trauma of having all ten fingers simultaneously broken in multiple places had combined with her physical and mental exhaustion to send her into shock. Unfortunately, there was nothing he could to do help her.

Their captors dragged them out into the hall. Bodies were strewn along the entire length of the corridor; most were turians, but there were several batarians, a few krogan, and even the odd asari among the dead.

They were hustled through the station until they reached a large breach in the hull. A wide, fully enclosed gangway extended out from the breach, no doubt leading to the assault vessel the attackers had used to board the station.

Several enemy troops of various species were milling about the area, all following the shouted orders of a batarian who seemed to be in charge.

He was standing with his back to them, but turned as they approached. Seeing the prisoners, he blinked all four eyes in surprise.

"What are you doing with him?" he said, pointing his weapon in Anderson's direction.

"You said take the humans alive," one of the asari replied.

"I meant her, not him!" the batarian exclaimed.

"Are you sure that's what Aria wanted?" the asari asked, looking for clarification.

At least Anderson knew now who they were working for, though he had no idea why the legendary Pirate Queen of Omega had launched an attack on the station.

"Fine. Put them both on the ship."

Anderson decided to take a chance and speak up.

"She's going into shock," he said, nodding in Kahlee's direction.

His voice sounded strange to his own ears, distorted by the damage to his face.

"If Aria wants us alive, you better see to her injuries."

"Get them on board and give them each a shot of medi-gel," the batarian ordered. "Then load up those data banks from the lab and set the explosives. I want to be out of here before reinforcements arrive."

The batarians dragged them up the gangway and into the hold of what appeared to be some type of frigate. They were forced roughly down into two of the seats lining the wall. Anderson winced as his weight fell on the hands cuffed behind his back, causing a sharp pain to shoot through his shoulders. Kahlee cried out in agony, and he could only imagine what it felt like to have her broken fingers pinned between the seat and the weight of her body.

"You better get those cuffs off her," he said.

"You should worry about yourself," one of the asari suggested as she jabbed a long needle into his shoulder.

A few seconds later, everything went dark.

SIXTEEN

When Anderson came to, he was surprised to find himself lying on a large, comfortable couch in what appeared to be a well-furnished living room.

Shaking off the lingering effects of the medi-gel, he rolled over to put his feet on the floor and stood up. He realized he was naked, and then he noticed his undershirt and boxers folded and sitting on a chair nearby. They had obviously been laundered; there were no traces of the bloodstains from his broken nose. Next to his underclothes were pants, a shirt, socks, and even a pair of shoes.

Puzzled, he slowly got dressed as he took a quick survey of his surroundings. There was an archaic set of hinged double doors at one end of the room, open just a crack. Through it he could see a large, luxurious bed. At the other end of the room was a more contemporary sliding door, closed and—judging by the red light on the wall panel—locked.

Though they weren't his, the clothes fit him well enough. Doing his best to move silently, he approached the locked door and pressed the wall panel just to be sure. It beeped but didn't open. Despite the expensive surroundings, he was still a prisoner.

But where's Kahlee?

Moving quickly but quietly, he crossed to the double doors and gently pushed them open. To his relief, Kahlee was lying on a bed, under several covers. She appeared to be naked as well; someone had piled her clothes on a chair beside the bed. Unlike the unfamiliar garments Anderson wore, however, he recognized her outfit as the same one she had been wearing when they'd been taken prisoner.

She was snoring softly, her body still recovering from her recent lack of sleep and the medi-gel she'd been given on the frigate.

Coming closer, he was relieved to see her fingers had been splinted. It would probably be close to a week before the bones properly mended and she regained full use of them, but at least she had been tended to.

Curious, he made his way over to the bedroom's en suite to check his reflection in the mirror. Like Kahlee, his injuries had been tended to. His nose had been reset and his split lip was healed; apart from some minor bruising and swelling it was hard to tell anything had happened to him at all.

He considered waking Kahlee up, then decided to let her sleep. They couldn't do anything to escape their gilded cage at the moment, and she still needed to rest. He returned to the couch, where he lay down and closed his eyes, just for a moment.

"Hey, soldier," a voice whispered in his ear, "on your feet."

Anderson's eyes snapped open to discover Kahlee standing over him, dressed and fully awake.

"Must have dozed off," he mumbled, sitting up.

"You snore like an elcor with asthma," she told him.

"Not my fault," he objected. "Bastards broke my nose."

Kahlee held up her splinted digits. "I'd say you got off easy."

"How'd you manage to get dressed?" Anderson asked.

"It wasn't easy," she admitted. Coyly she added, "You could have helped me if you'd been awake."

The situation was too grim for Anderson to generate much of a smile, but he did his best.

"You look like you could use a drink," Kahlee said. "I know I could. I found a bar over in the corner, but I need someone else to pour."

Anderson got up and headed in the direction she pointed.

"Right there. Open the cupboard."

Doing as she said, he found an assortment of high-quality alcohol to suit a wide variety of species' palates, from krogan ryncol to asari elassa.

Not in the mood for anything too exotic, he poured two glasses from a bottle of brandy.

"On the rocks?" he asked.

"Neat," Kahlee replied.

Anderson brought the glasses over to the couch, where Kahlee sat waiting for him. She took one from him, cradling it awkwardly in her palms because of her splinted fingers.

"Any idea why we're here?" she asked after taking a sip.

"I figure Aria wants to meet with us," he said, still

standing. "Can't say how long we'll have to wait, though."

"Might as well get comfortable, then," Kahlee said, patting the cushion beside her.

Anderson took a seat beside her and kicked back his drink in one quick gulp.

"Is this related to Grayson?" Kahlee asked as he leaned over to set his glass on the nearby end table.

"Pretty big coincidence if it's not."

Kahlee continued to sip her drink. Anderson realized they were sitting much closer together than was necessary—there was plenty of room on the couch to spread out. But when he shifted his position he ended up moving closer to her, not farther away.

He knew there were things Kahlee might not like to talk about right now, but in the end he finally decided he had to ask.

"How much did you manage to find out at the lab?"

"You were right," she admitted. "Cerberus implanted Grayson with some kind of Reaper technology. Similar to cybernetics, but much more invasive. And far more advanced.

"Their results were still very preliminary, but they were *changing* him somehow. Turning him into . . . well, I don't even think they knew."

"Can it be stopped?" Anderson asked. "Reversed?"

"I don't know," Kahlee said softly.

"I'm sorry I got you involved in all this," she said after a few more sips of brandy. "You wouldn't be here if it wasn't for me."

"I've stayed in worse hotel rooms than this," Anderson replied, trying to make light of the situation.

"But at least they let you check out," she glumly replied.

Anderson reached an arm around Kahlee's shoulder and pulled her close. As he did so, she turned so she could snuggle into the crook of his arm, resting her head on his shoulder.

"We're going to get through this," he promised her. "Somehow. Someway. We *will* get through this."

He looked down into her eyes, and she tilted her head back so she could look up at him. Slowly, he tilted his head downward, bringing his lips to hers.

The room's sliding door opened with a sharp *whoosh,* causing them both to sit up suddenly.

"Christ!" Kahlee swore as the glass slipped from her grasp in her haste to disentangle herself, spilling what was left of her drink onto her lap.

From the door there came a chorus of crude laughter, emanating from the entourage that had just barged in on them: three asari, a krogan, and two batarians. As the door slid shut behind them, Anderson caught a glimpse of two more krogan standing guard out in the hall.

The batarians and krogan were all grinning; he guessed they were the source of the laughter. He recognized one of the batarians as Sanak, the leader of the attack on the station.

Two of the asari looked nearly identical, though whether they were actually twins or if he—as a human—was simply unable to discern the differences between them he couldn't say. The third asari, standing in the middle of the group, had to be none other than Aria T'Loak herself.

"Are we interrupting?" she asked, the corners of her mouth turning up in mild amusement.

Both Anderson and Kahlee got to their feet, but neither bothered to reply. Anderson could feel himself blushing with embarrassment, but Kahlee didn't seem to be suffering the same reaction. She glared at the intruders with nothing but hate in her eyes.

"You know who I am?" Aria asked.

"We know," Kahlee answered, her voice cold and hard. "What do you want?"

"I want Grayson, of course."

"Why?" Kahlee demanded.

"That's my business."

"We don't even know where Grayson is," Anderson objected, joining the conversation.

"No, but you can help me find him."

"What are you talking about?" Kahlee wanted to know.

"We hacked into your extranet account. There's a message from Grayson. He wants to see you. So you're going to send him a reply telling him to meet you here."

"What makes you think he'll come?" Kahlee asked.

"My sources tell me you and Grayson have a special relationship."

"Maybe not as special as we thought," Sanak chimed in with a snicker. "Or do you just stick your tongue down the throat of whoever you're with at the time?"

He was obviously hoping for some kind of reaction. Anderson was pleased to see that Kahlee was smart enough to stay silent and disappoint him.

"Your sources might be playing you," Anderson warned, his mind piecing things together. "That's what Cerberus does."

Aria didn't bother denying her relationship with the Illusive Man.

"Cerberus was right about where to find you," she said to Kahlee. "They were right about Grayson trying to contact you. Why shouldn't I believe them when they say he'll come if you reply to his message?"

"Why are you even working with a pro-human group?" Kahlee wanted to know.

"We share an interest in Grayson," Aria admitted. "He betrayed both our organizations."

"You're going to kill him!" Kahlee exclaimed.

"That's the plan," Sanak replied with a grin.

"You're crazy if you think I'll help you!"

"You'd really sacrifice your life—both your lives—to protect Grayson?"

Anderson jumped in before Kahlee had a chance to answer.

"How do we know you won't just kill us in the end anyway?"

"That's a chance you'll have to take," Aria said with a sly smile.

"I'll help you on one condition," Kahlee offered. "I'll try to bring Grayson in if you promise not to kill him."

"You don't get to make conditions," Aria pointed out.

"Grayson's smart. You need my cooperation if you want this to work."

"You'll cooperate eventually," Sanak said, and the other batarians laughed knowingly.

"I don't know what Cerberus told you," Kahlee continued, ignoring Sanak and speaking directly to Aria. "But I know they didn't tell you the whole story. Whatever deal they offered, you're getting the wrong end of it."

"Maybe so. But I doubt you can match their offer."

"You're right about that," Kahlee admitted, though Anderson could tell she wasn't backing down. "And I don't know what happened between you and Grayson.

"But all I'm asking is for you to let Grayson tell his side of the story before you make up your mind. You might be very surprised by what you find out."

"I'll think on what you said," Aria promised. "I suggest you do the same. I'll send someone for you in one hour to record your message for Grayson.

"Regardless of my decision, it would be in your best interest to cooperate," she added, her voice so cold it actually sent a shiver down Anderson's spine.

The Pirate Queen turned on her heel and left the room, her followers trailing along in her wake. The door to the hall slid shut and the familiar red *Locked* display lit up on the wall panel.

Once they were alone in the room, Kahlee turned to Anderson.

"Just so you know," she told him, "that was all a bluff. I'm not going to let them hurt you. When

Aria comes back, I'm going to do whatever she wants."

"Don't worry about me," Anderson assured her.

"The batarian was right," Kahlee said with a shake of her head. "In the end I'll do whatever they want. I might as well cooperate up front and save us both a lot of pain and suffering."

Anderson knew what kind of person she was. If she was alone, she would have resisted to the bitter end. The fact that he was with her—that he could suffer for her decision—forced her to compromise. But he also knew she wasn't the type to give up on someone. She was still holding out hope for Grayson.

"You're still hoping she'll agree not to kill him," he said. "You hope Aria will see what Cerberus did and then let you try to help him."

"I know it sounds crazy. But if you've got a better plan, I'm all ears."

"Why didn't you tell her everything?" Anderson wondered. "About how Cerberus implanted Grayson with Reaper technology?"

"Do you really think she'd believe me? I saw the research files and I barely believe it myself.

"Besides," she added. "I figured I better keep a couple of our cards hidden."

Anderson knew that Kahlee needed him to stay positive. But he couldn't shake the feeling this wouldn't end well.

"Even if she says she won't hurt him," he warned, "there's no way to know if she's telling the truth."

"I know. But it's better than nothing. At least I

planted the seed. Now I just have to wait and see if it grows."

There wasn't much else to say, so they simply sat down on the couch and waited in silence for Aria's people to return.

As promised, they arrived promptly one hour later to get Kahlee. Anderson had thought Aria might send Sanak; the batarian was obviously one of the alpha dogs in her pack. Instead, she sent the massive krogan and one of the asari twins.

"What did Aria say about Grayson?" Kahlee asked as they came in. "Is she going to take him alive?"

"She's still considering the offer," the asari replied. "Have you considered hers? Are you ready to cooperate?"

Kahlee nodded.

"Smart girl," the krogan growled as he led her out the door.

The half hour it took for them to return were the longest thirty minutes of Anderson's life. In his head he knew Kahlee was in the same amount of danger whether he was with her or not, but emotionally he felt like he could keep her safe just by staying near her.

When the door finally opened and Kahlee stepped through, she was alone. He jumped up from the couch and rushed over to her.

"What happened? Did they hurt you?"

Physically she seemed unharmed, but he could tell by her face that she was upset.

"I did what they wanted," she said quietly. "I sent Grayson a message."

"You had no choice," Anderson whispered, wrapping his arms around her in a reassuring hug. "You did the right thing."

"For us," she whispered. "But what about for him?"

SEVENTEEN

Grayson kept slipping in and out of consciousness as the shuttle drifted aimlessly through space. Every few hours he would suddenly become very tired and the world would slip away. When he awoke, he could never tell how long he had been out. He wasn't sure, but he suspected the Reapers were behind the black-outs.

Each time his senses returned he quickly checked the shuttle's navigational equipment to make sure the Reapers hadn't programmed a new destination into the ship while he was out. Each time he found the vessel's course unaltered.

It was almost as if they were waiting for something, harboring their strength until the moment was right. What that moment might be, however, he couldn't even begin to guess.

The sixth or seventh time he woke up, he saw a blinking light on the shuttle communications console, indicating an incoming message waiting to be heard. But that was impossible. He'd disabled all hailing frequencies; there was no way for someone to contact the shuttle directly. The only way there could be a

waiting message was if he had logged in to the comm
network . . . or someone had done it for him.

Suddenly the blackouts made sense—the Reapers
were temporarily putting him out so they could use
the communications equipment. He briefly wondered
why they didn't simply keep him unconscious. Based
on all the other times they had used him, he suspected
they needed him to be awake and alert to function
properly. By taking control of his body, they became
bound by the limitations of his physical form. If his
mind was pushed into an unconscious state, Grayson
suspected, his reactions would be slow and clumsy,
like a sleepwalker stumbling around in a stupor.

It could also be more taxing on the Reapers themselves. Taking control of his body while he slept could
have drained their reserves, which might explain why
recently he hadn't felt them try and reestablish their
dominance while he was awake.

If his speculations were true, then he'd learned
something new about the alien parasites feeding off
him. It might not amount to anything, but the more
he understood what was happening to him, the better
his chances of fighting it.

The message light was still blinking. His first instinct was to delete it unheard, perhaps thwarting the
Reapers' plans in the process.

*It could be important. A tool to use against the
enemy.*

As he was reaching up to delete it, a new thought
popped into his head. Knowledge was his only
weapon against the Reapers. If he listened to the message, it might reveal something useful. If he knew

what the Reapers were after, they might be easier to stop.

He hit the playback, and to his surprise Kahlee's face appeared on the comm panel's screen.

"Paul. I need your help. Meet me on Omega. I'm sending you the location. Please hurry. It's urgent."

There was something odd about the way she spoke. Her voice was flat, almost monotone. It didn't have its normal energy or spark. It made him suspicious.

Maybe she's scared. Or hurt.

He was being paranoid. There were any number of reasons she might not sound like her normal self. There was even the possibility that she hadn't changed at all, and that the physical changes the Reapers had wrought on his body were affecting his senses and perceptions.

Her message left him torn. He wanted to see Kahlee, and if she was in some kind of trouble he wanted to do everything possible to help her. But he couldn't risk exposing her to what he had become. He couldn't risk letting her come into contact with the Reapers.

She has nowhere else to turn. She's desperate. Don't abandon her.

He played the message again, focusing on the last four words: "Please hurry. It's urgent."

Kahlee wasn't prone to dramatics. If she said it was urgent, it had to be something serious. And there was a look of desperation in her eyes, as if he was her last hope. She needed him; he couldn't turn his back on her.

His mind made up, Grayson sent off a reply to the message.

"I'm on my way, Kahlee" was all he said.

Omega is dangerous. You'll need all your strength when you get there.

He plotted a course for Omega into the nav computer, then settled back in his chair and closed his eyes. He'd need to rest up so he'd be ready to face whatever might be waiting for him on the lawless space station.

"One at a time," Anderson said encouragingly. "Flex those fingers."

"You'd make a great nurse," Kahlee replied.

They were sitting side by side on the couch of the room they still had not been allowed to leave. They had turned so they could be face-to-face. Kahlee was holding her hands out in front of her, palms up. Anderson's hands were beneath, supporting her wrists. He had helped remove her finger splints so she could begin her physical therapy; when they were finished he would carefully help her put them back on .

They were sitting slightly closer than they needed to be, but not so close it could be considered intimate. Kahlee knew they were both wary of another sudden intrusion from Aria and her underlings; neither she nor David felt any need to endure that type of awkward embarrassment again.

She had noticed, however, that in the aftermath of any discussions of Grayson—like the one they had had with Aria yesterday—he always became a little more reserved and distant. She didn't think it was jealousy; not exactly. It was almost like he was waiting for her to work out her feelings for Paul before he let himself get too close.

"You're not concentrating," Anderson chided her, breaking her train of thought. "Focus."

Kahlee nodded, and turned her attention to her injured digits. One by one she curled them into her palm and extended them out again. The tendons felt stiff and brittle; she half-imagined she could hear them crackling as she went through the exercises.

They were only half finished when the door to the room slid open and Aria swept in. Her asari, krogan, and batarian escorts followed in her wake. Instinctively Kahlee snatched her hands out of Anderson's grasp, then cursed herself for caring so much what a bunch of criminals and thugs thought about her and her relationships.

"Grayson replied to your message," Aria informed her.

"I want to see it," Kahlee said, rising to her feet.

The asari shook her head. "There's nothing to see. He agreed to the meeting. You can see him then."

Kahlee felt like Aria was hiding something. She flashed back to some of what she had uncovered in the Cerberus research files: physical abnormalities; widespread mutations; repurposing of the host.

How bad is it? How far has his condition progressed?

"What happens now?" Anderson asked.

"I'll be alerted when he arrives on the station. At that time, my people will come to take Kahlee to the meeting."

"I want to go to," Anderson told her, getting up and moving over to stand beside Kahlee in a show of support.

"What you want is of no consequence," Aria reminded him.

"Where am I meeting him?" Kahlee asked.

"I wanted to keep this private. One of my warehouses near the loading docks."

Kahlee didn't like the sound of that. She would have preferred somewhere more public.

"Why not in Afterlife?"

"Too many people," Anderson answered grimly. "She thinks it's going to get violent."

"You promised you wouldn't hurt him!" Kahlee shouted, taking a half-step toward their captor.

In a flash her krogan bodyguard interposed himself between them. Anderson did the same, leaping in front of Kahlee. The two stared at each other, the krogan's massive reptilian form towering over Anderson. He didn't back down, however.

The krogan finally stepped aside when Aria reached up to put a hand on his shoulder, indicating she wasn't worried about the threat either of the humans posed. Satisfied, Anderson took a step back so he was once again standing beside Kahlee, rather than in front of her.

"I didn't promise you anything," Aria pointedly reminded her. "I said I would take what you told me about Cerberus into consideration.

"Grayson may already have killed one of my people," she added darkly. "I'm not going to take any chances with him."

"I want an assurance that Kahlee and I will be allowed to go free after this meeting," Anderson insisted.

"Everyone wants things they cannot get."

"Are you going to keep us here as prisoners forever?" Kahlee wanted to know. "Or are you just going to kill us when this is over?"

"I haven't decided your fate yet," Aria said with a smile. "But if you cooperate, your chances of leaving Omega will increase dramatically."

"How long until the meeting?" Kahlee finally said, realizing there was truth in Aria's last statement.

"I'll send an escort to accompany you in a few hours. I suggest you be ready when they arrive."

Kahlee and Anderson both remained standing until Aria and the others were gone and the door had closed behind them.

Neither of them spoke as they turned to look at each other. Kahlee wondered if the concern she saw in Anderson's face was reflected in her own.

He reached up and gently took her wrists, then drew her back down to a sitting position on the couch.

"You risk losing mobility if we don't finish the therapy," he told her.

With a nod, Kahlee resumed the exercises, eager to find something that could take her mind off the imminent meeting with Grayson . . . and the fear of what she might find waiting for her.

Aria still hadn't decided what she was going to do with her prisoners. She didn't want to kill them if she didn't have to; there was little long-term gain to be had from dead bodies. But she was also leery of letting them go. Anderson in particular looked like the type to carry a grudge, and she already had plenty of enemies. Ultimately, she knew, her decision would depend on the outcome of the meeting with Grayson.

He represented another decision she hadn't made yet. It was unlike her; she very rarely went ahead with a plan if she wasn't reasonably certain of the outcome. But she still didn't like the idea of getting into bed with Cerberus, no matter how lucrative the payoff might be.

"What's the plan for when Grayson arrives?" Sanak asked, causing her to turn her head in mild surprise.

She had never thought of the batarian as particularly perceptive; was it possible she had underestimated him? Or was it simply coincidence that had made him bring up the subject?

"We'll have plenty of people at the warehouse," she assured him. "More than enough to handle whatever happens."

"Why go to all this trouble? Why not just have someone take him out the second he sets foot on the station?"

"I haven't even decided for sure whether I want him dead or not," she cautioned.

"If you let him live you're throwing away three million credits!" Sanak protested. "And for what?"

"For what, indeed," she answered, causing him to shake his head in bewilderment.

She didn't bother trying to explain her thought process to him. The Cerberus offer was generous . . . a little too generous. What secrets did Grayson have that were so valuable to them? And was there any chance they could prove as valuable to her?

"It's a lot of money," Sanak muttered. "That's all

I'm saying. With those kind of credits on the table, no way I'd let him live."

Suddenly Aria knew what she was going to do, at least as far as Grayson was concerned. Sanak had many fine qualities. He was loyal, skilled, ruthless, and relentless in pursuit of his goals. But one thing he lacked was vision; he had a sense only of the now. The fact that he would take the Cerberus offer meant she should reject it.

"I want to try and take Grayson alive if possible," she declared. "But if he resists in any way, kill him."

Sanak's lip curled up in a snarl of disgust, but he had the common sense not to question her.

"I'm going to put Orgun in charge of the warehouse team," she added, deciding the bad blood between her lieutenant and Grayson only increased the chances of the meeting turning violent.

"What about me?"

"I'm putting you in charge of Kahlee. Make sure she's there to meet him."

EIGHTEEN

Grayson's fingers moved deftly over the controls of the turian vessel, bringing it in to dock with one of Omega's many landing ports. He was surprised by how easily he had picked up the feel of the alien vessel; it almost felt like he had piloted turian shuttles thousands of times before.

The meeting with Kahlee was at a warehouse in a district firmly under Aria T'Loak's thumb. Grayson didn't know if that was good or bad, however. Had Kahlee somehow become involved with Aria, or was it just random chance? The odds of any given location on Omega somehow being connected with the Pirate Queen were fairly high. She had direct control of at least a third of the station, and another third was held by various factions loyal to or affiliated with her organization in some way.

Aria is powerful. A threat. Avoid if possible.

Still, it didn't hurt to be cautious. He didn't know how Aria would react to his disappearance and Liselle's death. Rather than take a chance he chose to touch down at one of the rare Omega ports that didn't pay her tribute.

From there it was a long walk to the rendezvous,

but he covered the distance quickly. Though he wasn't running, Omega's landmarks rolled by quickly as he made his way through the labyrinthine streets. After several minutes he noted with surprise that, despite the brisk pace, he wasn't even breathing hard.

He would have made even better time if he wasn't constantly slowing down to study various structural and architectural features of the station. He had seen it all before, of course, but he almost felt like he was looking at it through fresh eyes: taking every detail and comparing it against some half-remembered blueprint he didn't actually ever remember seeing.

The cycle continues. Each civilization brings change, yet the works of our kind are eternal.

Omega was known for the haphazard, piecemeal way it had been constructed. Most believed that it had been carved from the heart of an ancient asteroid by the Protheans eons ago, but over the centuries any number of species had left their mark on it. Its discordant style gave it an almost random feel. And though it had never bothered him before, for some reason he now found the chaos offensive on a deep philosophical level.

But while the overall effect filled him with revulsion, each individual element he examined during his trek caused him to react with amusement. It reminded him of the ant farm he had as a child. The insects had worked with slavish dedication to build their network of tunnels, shaping and altering the tiny glass case that encompassed the entirety of their existence. He had observed them through the glass as they worked, industrious and relentless, completely oblivious of their own insignificance in the grand design of the universe.

He was nearing the warehouse district. Soon he would see Kahlee again. Just thinking of her caused his pulse, and his pace, to quicken. The walk felt effortless, as if he were being carried along by some invisible force. It felt different than when the Reapers had taken control of his body, however. Then he had been distanced from himself, a passive observer. Now he felt fully engaged in the process of putting one foot in front of the other to propel himself along. It just didn't seem to require any effort. It was almost as if someone was helping him.

A symbiotic relationship.

Grayson pulled up short, his calm, relaxed demeanor swallowed up by a dark cloud of suspicion. He tried to turn around and head back the way he came, but his legs suddenly felt heavy and awkward. He managed only ten steps before he was doubled over and gasping for breath. His own body was fighting him; resisting him.

The horrifying truth slowly dawned on him. The alien technology had become so deeply embedded into his body and mind that the Reapers were now an inextricable part of him. When he had been heading toward Kahlee they had been working in unison, parasite and host united in a common goal. Their insidious influence had burrowed so deep into the fiber of his being that he had not only been unable to resist their will, he had actively been helping them achieve their end.

"No," he shouted out, harsh and defiant. "I won't take you to her!"

He braced himself for the inevitable surge of pain as the aliens fought to bend him to their will. Instead, he felt nothing. The lack of opposition confused him. He knew they were still present; the wires and tubes protruding from his joints and crisscrossing beneath his flesh confirmed that beyond any doubt. But they had become invisible. He no longer processed them as *other*; they were part of him now, inseparable and indistinguishable from his own identity.

That's a good thing. Influence can work both ways.

A crazy idea began to form in his mind. If the Reaper technology was part of him now, maybe that meant he would be able to influence and control it the same way the Reapers had controlled his body earlier. Maybe he could draw on the cybernetic enhancements and his newfound biotic abilities whenever he wanted to. Maybe he could use them as tools to achieve his own goals.

You are superior to the pathetic beings of flesh that surround you.

The implications were staggering. Liberating. He had transcended the slow, laborious process of natural selection. He had broken free of the cycle of passing randomly mutated genes down from one generation to the next with the slim hope of gaining some minuscule natural advantage. He himself was changing, quickly and with purpose. He was evolving toward a perfect being.

Do not hide what you have become. Reveal your glory.

He had been afraid to see Kahlee because of what she might think of him. He looked strange. Different. But she was a scientist; she would understand and appreciate what was happening to him. She would see how he had been improved. Repurposed. She would admire him. Adore him.

Spinning on his heel, he set off once more toward the warehouse district, eagerly anticipating the meeting he had been defiantly refusing to go to only minutes before.

Kai Leng sat on the couch of the small room he had rented two nights before, staring intently at the image on his monitor as he absentmindedly spooned his dinner into his mouth. The monitor was linked to a surveillance camera pointed at the back wall of Afterlife.

His accommodations were less than a block away from the club; a run-down, ramshackle building converted into a pay-by-the-hour motel by an enterprising volus. It was primarily used by patrons of the club looking for a quick hookup who couldn't afford to rent one of Afterlife's private suites.

The room was poorly lit, and it reeked of what Kai Leng assumed was a mixture of alien sweat and vomit. But it was close enough to the club that he could maintain his vigil yet still have time to react if he saw anything.

The image on the monitor hadn't changed. He knew that what appeared to be a solid wall was, in fact, a well-disguised secret door leading to the private rooms in the back of the club. The wide-angle lens on the surveillance camera showed that the narrow alley was completely deserted; unlike the crowded doors out front, this hidden entrance was apparently known only to those who served in Aria's inner circle.

The Illusive Man had instructed him to keep an eye on Aria's people to verify they actually delivered on their promise to eliminate Grayson. With no other resources, it was impossible for Kai Leng to keep track of everyone in the organization. So he had initially decided to focus on Sanak, Aria's batarian lieutenant.

A less experienced agent might have tried to tail Aria herself. But the risk of being noticed was too great, and Kai Leng knew she wasn't going to put herself at risk by meeting Grayson face-to-face. Besides, she almost never left the club.

Sanak seemed the next logical choice, given what the Illusive Man had ascertained about his role in Aria's organization through a few discreet inquiries. The batarian was her attack dog, a blunt instrument. Whenever a situation called for violence or brute force, he would be her first choice.

Kai Leng's instincts had served him well. Three days ago Sanak had left the club through the VIP entrance out front. Kai Leng had tailed him as he gathered a squad of heavily armed mercenaries and boarded a ship. When the ship returned the next day, Sanak and the mercenaries weren't alone: Kahlee Sanders and Admiral David Anderson, one of the Alliance's most decorated soldiers, were with them.

It was immediately obvious the humans were prisoners and not guests. He could see the handcuffs on their unconscious bodies as they were carried by Aria's massive krogan bodyguard, one tossed over each shoulder.

Kai Leng had followed at a distance as Sanak's crew had taken the hostages back to Afterlife. They stuck to the unused back alleys to avoid drawing unnecessary attention. Upon reaching the club they had used the secret back entrance instead of going in the front, inadvertently revealing its existence to the inconspicuous shadow that had been following them the entire time.

So far everything was going according to the Illusive Man's plan—they had captured Sanders, and now they were using her as bait to lure Grayson in. Kai Leng estimated he had at least a day before the meeting would take place; wherever Grayson was, it would take time to contact him and set up the location. That gave him time to purchase the surveillance equipment, set up the camera on the back entrance, rent the repulsive room just down the street, and stock up on food and water in preparation for his vigil.

The wireless monitor was portable; when Kai Leng needed to use the bathroom, he brought it with him so he wouldn't miss anything. It was also set up to beep if the camera detected motion, allowing Kai Leng to grab a few sporadic hours of sleep as he waited. He never slept well or for very long, however. He didn't fully trust the merchant who'd sold him the equipment, and in the back of his mind he was worried it might simply short out while he was dozing.

He wasn't about to let that happen. Not when things seemed to be drawing to their conclusion.

Aria's people had brought Kahlee in through the back entrance; he had no doubt they would bring her out the same way when the meeting with Grayson drew near. All he had to do now was watch and wait.

* * *

Anderson knew the time was drawing near.

"Are you ready for this?" he asked Kahlee.

"Ready as I'll ever be."

"We'll be fine," he assured her. "Just stick to the plan."

They'd talked it over after Aria left them alone, and had agreed they had to stick together if they wanted to get out of this alive. Besides, there was no way in hell he was going to let them take Kahlee away to meet Grayson alone.

He took a deep breath to center himself, forcing his pounding heart to throttle itself back through sheer force of will.

A few minutes later the door whisked open and Sanak came marching in. Anderson hadn't been expecting him to be the one sent to retrieve Kahlee, but it didn't change anything. In fact, it might actually work in their favor.

A pair of krogan stepped into the room right behind him, weapons drawn in case the prisoners tried anything.

"Time to go," Sanak snapped. "Move."

Kahlee crossed her arms defiantly, careful not to bend her splinted fingers. Anderson did the same.

"We go together or I don't go," she said.

Sanak whipped out his pistol and stepped forward, jamming the barrel into Kahlee's forehead.

"He stays here. You come with me now, or you die."

"You won't kill me," she said, her voice calm and certain. "You need me for this meeting."

The batarian tilted his head to the right, an instinctive display of his contempt and frustration. Then he turned and pointed his gun at Anderson.

"We don't need him for the meeting," he warned her. "Come with me or I splatter his brains all over the floor."

"No you won't," Anderson declared. "Grayson's going to be suspicious. He's going to scout the location out; he won't reveal himself until he sees Kahlee. And if he senses something's wrong, he'll bolt.

"You need my cooperation to pull this off," Kahlee insisted. "Harm Anderson in any way, and you won't get it."

Anderson could see Sanak's mind churning. Aria would no doubt have emphasized the importance of getting Kahlee to the meeting; the batarian was trying to figure out a way to follow his orders without letting the prisoners dictate any terms.

"You have two options," Kahlee explained slowly. "One, David comes with me and we all go to meet Grayson. Two, you try to stop him from coming and the meeting doesn't happen."

"Then you get to explain to Aria how you blew this mission," Anderson added.

He suspected the lieutenant was good at following orders. He hoped he wasn't as good at improvising. Their gamble hinged on it.

Sanak let his pistol drop. He glared at them, then snapped it back into the clip on his thigh.

"If either of you try anything on the way, I'll kill you both," he warned.

NINETEEN

Kai Leng's monitor beeped its warning to indicate the camera had detected movement, but the alert wasn't necessary. He was already watching the screen intently as Sanders, Anderson, Sanak, and a pair of krogan guards emerged from Afterlife.

Grabbing his pistol and knife, he rushed out the door of the tiny rented room. He didn't bother to pack up the surveillance equipment. He didn't care if the next guest stumbled across it; he would have no further use for it after this meeting.

Ignoring the elevator, he took the stairs two at a time. He reached ground level and burst through the door out onto the street. Racing around the corner, he managed to catch his quarry just as they reached the intersection where the alley behind Afterlife joined up with the main thoroughfare.

To the casual eye they would have appeared to be nothing more than a group walking a little too closely together, but Kai Leng knew different. Sanak led the way, an assault rifle strapped to his back and a pistol on his hip. Anderson and Sanders followed, both unarmed. The two krogan brought up the rear, also carrying assault rifles. Unlike Sanak, however, the krogan had their weapons out, casually cradling them in their arms as they marched.

Keeping a safe distance behind, Kail Leng followed them as they wound their way through the business and residential sections of Omega's central district. Eventually the shops and homes gave way to warehouses as they reached a dimly lit industrial area.

They passed several nondescript two- and three-story buildings before disappearing inside the warehouse at the end of the block. Even through the gloom of the street, Kai Leng could see that the windows had been shuttered or painted over to hide whatever activities were going on inside.

He found a spot just inside the arch of a doorway in one of the nearby buildings that hid him from view, yet gave him a clean line of sight down both directions of the street. He settled in to wait for Grayson. An hour later, he arrived.

His appearance hadn't changed much from when Kai Leng had last seen him. The stubble on his head was a little longer; his beard a little more ragged; his synthetic upgrades slightly more noticeable. Despite the ill-fitting clothes covering up most of his exposed flesh, the tubes winding from his neck up into his skull were hard to miss. And it was possible to see the glowing, pulsating wires and circuits beneath the taut, almost translucent skin of his cheeks and hands.

The Illusive Man had warned him not to confront Grayson unless absolutely necessary. He was no longer the man Kai Leng had so easily beaten and then drugged in his prison cell; he had become something far more powerful. The plan was to let Aria's people do the dirty work; he was just here to report back in case something went wrong.

Even without the warning, Kai Leng would have sensed something different about him. Grayson moved with a fluid grace he hadn't possessed before. He had the sharp bearing of a predator now, a hunter on the prowl.

He passed less than five meters away from where Kai Leng was hiding. Though it was dark, the assassin instinctively pressed himself deeper into the shadows to avoid being noticed. Grayson passed by without seeing him and continued on to the warehouse at the end of the street.

He stopped a few meters before the door and paused, his head moving from side to side as if he was studying the building. He seemed suspicious, as if he sensed it was a trap.

Kai Leng held his breath, praying he would step inside.

Grayson made his way quickly down the dark row of buildings. Despite the low light, his augmented vision allowed him to see clearly. He noticed a lone figure lurking inside the doorway of a building as he passed, but dismissed him as irrelevant. He was here to meet Kahlee; nothing else mattered.

When he reached the entrance of the building bearing the address she had given him, however, Grayson hesitated, suddenly wary. Why had Kahlee chosen this remote location for their rendezvous? Why hadn't she wanted to meet him somewhere more public? Her message said she was in trouble; maybe she was too scared to show up anywhere else.

It could be a trap. Is Sanders loyal? Can she be trusted?

He shook his head, dispelling the ridiculous notion that Kahlee might betray him. She had risked so much to help him and Gillian escape Cerberus. She'd put her career and her life on the line for them, risking everything to help Grayson save his daughter.

Gillian.

Gillian was safe now; not even the Illusive Man could find her aboard the quarian deep-space exploration vessel. Memories of the daughter he hadn't seen in over two years came flooding back to him: the way she smiled; the ways she spoke. Gillian was special—she had an autistic condition that had made it difficult for her to communicate. Despite her incredible potential, she had lagged behind the other children of the Ascension Project.

Ascension Project.

The goal of the Ascension Project was to help biotic human children control and even master their latent abilities. Kahlee had made a special effort to help Gillian, giving her personal instruction above and beyond what the other students had received.

Biotic children.

He didn't know much about the other students. During Gillian's time in the program he had visited her only once or twice a year, as per the Illusive Man's orders. But he was certain Kahlee would have taken a personal interest in every student at the Grissom Academy. Knowing her, she would have memorized every—

Grayson forced his mind to a sudden, screeching halt as the truth dawned on him. The Reapers had grown stronger. The connection between them and him had deepened. His very thoughts had become exposed. They were sifting through his memories, picking through his knowledge piece by piece. And they suddenly seemed very interested in Kahlee and her role in the Ascension Project.

Terrified, he tried to turn and run. He had to get as far away from Kahlee as possible. In response, the will of his enemy came crashing down on him. He struggled to resist, but the Reapers would not be denied.

They forced him to march forward. Step by step he drew ever nearer to the door, until he was close enough to reach out his hand and tap the access panel.

Grayson fought against them, drawing on the mental tricks he had used to resist them in the past. But it was all in vain. The Reapers had grown far stronger than he'd realized. They'd been lying in wait, manipulating him instead of dominating him to hide their true power.

The door slid open and Grayson stepped into the dimly lit warehouse. He saw Kahlee standing in the middle of the room, her expression a mix of revulsion and pity when she saw his appearance.

"Oh, Grayson," she said, nearly breaking into tears.

But while his attention was focused completely on her, the Reapers were acutely aware of everything around them. Kahlee was not alone—at least a dozen armed individuals were scattered around the perimeter.

Adrenaline surged through him as his puppet-masters recognized they had been lured into a trap, and Grayson knew hell was about to be unleashed.

Aria's people were already in position when Anderson and Kahlee had arrived at the warehouse: a dozen on the floor, eight more perched on the catwalk running along the warehouse's rear wall. Shipping crates and forklifts had been strategically placed to provide cover for Aria's troops on the ground. The obstacles had also been arranged in a loose semicircle, effectively forming a corral in the center of the room.

It had been easy enough for Anderson to figure out the plan. When Grayson came far enough into the room, some of Aria's people would slip in behind him to block his retreat, leaving him surrounded on all sides. It was a good plan except for one thing: to lure Grayson into the right position, Kahlee herself would have to be inside the semicircle . . . and right in the line of fire if things turned violent.

He'd voiced his objections, only to have them fall on deaf ears. Orgun, the massive krogan in charge of the operation, had ordered Kahlee to take up her position and wait for Grayson. He'd confined Anderson to a dark corner in the rear of the building, and ordered Sanak to keep an eye on him. The batarian was standing a few steps off to the side, his assault rifle drawn and ready to dissuade Anderson from doing anything that might interfere with the meeting.

From their location, Anderson couldn't see Kahlee, though he had a line of sight to the warehouse's front door. He was staring right at it when Grayson came through.

Anderson was shocked by his appearance. Kahlee had mentioned he had been altered by the Reaper technology, but Anderson had never imagined anything like this. He could clearly no longer be called human; he had become some kind of nameless abomination.

His skin was stretched and discolored. Beneath it Anderson could see that the cybernetics had merged with his body, as if he was being devoured from the inside by machines.

It reminded him of the colonists who had been repurposed into husks on Eden Prime. There had been no way to reverse the effects of their transformation. He feared the same could be said of Grayson.

He heard Kahlee say his name, and then Orgun stepped into view behind Grayson, blocking his retreat.

"Surrender," the big krogan growled, raising his assault rifle so it was pointed directly at Grayson's back, "or we'll kill you where you stand."

Grayson responded by dropping into a crouch, spinning around, and charging the krogan, doubled over so low he almost seemed to be crawling on all fours. It happened in the blink of an eye; Orgun was moving so fast he seemed to be nothing but a blur.

Orgun fired a burst from his assault rifle, but the unexpected speed and uniqueness of Grayson's reaction caught him off guard. Trained to aim for the chest and upper torso, his shots sailed too high as Grayson scuttled toward him.

Some of his troops around the warehouse—the ones with quick reflexes—squeezed off a few quick shots of their own, but in their haste they aimed wildly and the rounds deflected harmlessly off the spot on the floor where Grayson had been standing an instant before.

He slammed into Orgun, a 160-pound man versus a nearly 500-pound krogan. Amazingly, it was Orgun who was sent flying by the impact, his assault rifle spinning free of his hands.

The warehouse erupted with the thunder of gunfire as Orgun's troops got over the initial shock of the unexpected attack. Grayson responded by throwing up a biotic barrier, the air around him shimmering with the sudden release of energy. The bullets were devoured by the powerful gravitational field, losing their momentum instantly and dropping harmlessly to the ground.

Anderson glanced over at Sanak from the corner of his eye. The batarian had been as surprised as anyone by Grayson's outburst; he was only just now recovering. His attention was focused entirely on the carnage before him, the prisoner beside him utterly forgotten.

As the batarian took his first running step toward the battle, Anderson delivered a back round-kick to the side of the head. It sent Sanak reeling, the assault rifle falling from his grasp to skitter across the floor as he pinwheeled his arms.

Anderson followed up his initial attack with a flying tackle, knocking them both to the ground. They wrestled briefly, trying to get possession of the gun clipped to Sanak's thigh.

They grappled at close quarters, grunting and cursing as they each fought to gain leverage. But Anderson was on top, giving him the advantage. He wrapped his hand around the butt end of the pistol, but the batarian managed to get him in an elbow lock, pinning his arm in place so he couldn't raise the weapon.

Anderson squeezed the trigger anyway. The round ripped a hole in the batarian's thigh, causing him to scream in pain and release his grip. Anderson quickly brought the pistol up and shoved the muzzle into the batarian's gut, then fired three more times.

All four of Sanak's eyes went wide in disbelief as his body went limp. Anderson rolled off him and stood up, still clasping the pistol. The batarian opened his mouth to speak, but all that came out was a wet gurgle. He coughed, and a dark trickle of blood seeped from between his lips.

Anderson fired one more time, aiming for the heart. Sanak shuddered once. Then his head lolled to the side, his eyes glazed and unfocused as his life ebbed away.

The entire encounter had taken less than thirty seconds, but in that time the shooting at the other end of the warehouse had stopped. Looking up, Anderson noticed several of Aria's troops—including Orgun— lying dead on the floor. Some were bent and twisted, limbs protruding at awkward angles in the unmistakable pose of those killed by powerful biotic attacks. Others appeared to have been beaten to death, their heads staved in as if someone had smashed them with a sledgehammer.

But he couldn't see Grayson anywhere in the carnage . . . or Kahlee.

Running toward the center of the room to get a better view, he realized he was the only one still alive inside the building. He had no idea what had happened to Kahlee, but a thousand scenarios were playing through his head, none of them reassuring.

Fearing the worst, he raced across the room and out the door, only to find her standing in the dimly lit street, alone and unharmed. She was staring off into the distance, her back to him.

"Are you okay?" he asked, panting slightly from his recent exertion as he ran up to her.

She turned in response to his voice.

"I'm all right," she assured him. "When the shooting started I just tried to stay low. Luckily nobody was aiming for me."

"What about Grayson?"

"He's gone," she said. "He broke through the circle of Aria's people and escaped out the door. They all ran off after him."

Anderson realized this was their chance. For the next little while it would be chaos as Aria's people tried to stop Grayson from escaping Omega. With everyone focused on him, they might be able to slip away unnoticed.

"Come on," he said to Kahlee. "We're getting off this station."

"How?" she asked.

"We just have to find someone with a ship who doesn't answer to Aria," he explained, knowing it wouldn't be nearly as easy as he'd made it sound.

A man he didn't recognize stepped out from the shadow of a nearby building.

"Maybe I can help with that," he said by way of introduction.

TWENTY

Kai Leng heard the sound of gunfire from inside the warehouse; the trap had been sprung. A few moments later, however, he realized Aria's people had failed as Grayson emerged from the building still alive. As before, Kai Leng pressed himself into the shadows rather than confront him. As loyal as he was to Cerberus, he wasn't suicidal.

Grayson broke into a run, and seconds later three armed krogan burst from the warehouse in pursuit. Despite their massive bulk they could run much faster than humans, their muscular legs powering them along. Grayson, however, was no longer human. The cybernetic enhancements of the Reapers gave him incredible speed, and he had already opened up a gap of at least thirty meters before the krogan even appeared on the scene.

They opened fire with their assault rifles as they chased after him, their accuracy compromised by the poor illumination of the street and their desperate efforts to keep up with their target. Grayson moved in an erratic, zigzagging pattern to make it even harder for them to line up a clear shot. But it was impossible to dodge the hail of gunfire completely, and a few stray rounds found their mark.

The impacts caused Grayson to stumble, momentarily knocking him off stride. In response he wheeled around and thrust his palm out toward his pursuers. The air seemed to ripple and distort with the power of his biotic push.

Kai Leng had no doubt that if the krogan had been closer the energy wave would have pulverized them, breaking bones and liquefying even their redundant internal organs. As it was, Grayson's flight had already left them so far behind that the force of the attack had dissipated considerably by the time it reached them. Instead of crushing them, it had only enough strength to knock them off their feet.

Before his enemies could pick themselves up, Grayson was off and running again. He was limping noticeably, but the awkward gait did little to slow him down.

Behind him reinforcements came pouring out of the building: half a dozen batarians and two more krogan. While the original pursuers picked themselves up, those newly arrived joined the chase. Like the others, they fired their assault rifles as they ran, but by this time Grayson was well beyond the effective range of their weapons.

As he raced past Kai Leng's hiding place, he passed under one of the few lights on the street, giving the assassin a brief but clear look at his wounds. Blood was streaming from several places in his right thigh. His left arm dangled awkwardly at his side; Kai Leng suspected a round had shattered his shoulder. His injuries were severe, but none appeared lethal—

miraculously, he didn't appear to have been hit in the torso or head.

And then Grayson was gone, fleeing down the street before vanishing around a corner. Kai Leng remained perfectly still as Aria's troops rumbled past several seconds later, knowing any movement might draw their attention to his hiding spot. He doubted they would bother to stop; they seemed intent on chasing Grayson down. But he wasn't taking any chances.

Several of them were shouting instructions into the transmitters of their helmets as they went by, no doubt calling in further reinforcements to help them bring Grayson to his knees. Kai Leng had a hunch they wouldn't be successful.

It was almost a certainty that Grayson was going to escape the station; the Illusive Man would not be pleased. But witnessing the failed ambush had still given Kai Leng hope. Grayson's wounds were proof that, as powerful as the Reapers were, they were not invulnerable. If any of Aria's people had managed a clean headshot, the threat might have been eliminated.

He was still concealed in his hiding place, wondering what to do next, when Kahlee Sanders stepped out onto the street. An idea began to form in Kai Leng's head.

Once Grayson left Omega, Cerberus would need to track him down again. The Illusive Man had told Aria T'Loak that Sanders was the key. That might no longer be the case, given her role in setting him up at the warehouse. But there was a chance she could still be used as bait to lure him out of hiding a second time.

As Kai Leng was contemplating his next move, David Anderson came out of the warehouse to join Sanders. He was armed with a pistol, though Kai Leng wasn't worried. If it came down to a physical confrontation, he was certain he was more than a match for Anderson and Sanders. But he wasn't sure that was the right way to proceed.

He stepped out of his hiding spot and began to move quickly but silently toward them. He stayed close to the edges of the buildings along the street, trying to make himself less conspicuous by sticking to the shadows. His efforts were helped by the fact that Sanders and Anderson were completely focused on each other.

"We just have to find someone with a ship who doesn't answer to Aria," he heard Anderson say once he was within earshot.

Acting on a sudden impulse, he stepped out into the open and declared, "Maybe I can help with that."

Kahlee took a quick step back, and Anderson raised his pistol.

"Who are you?" he demanded.

Kai Leng was close enough to easily disarm the admiral before he could fire a single shot. But he knew Cerberus would need Sanders's cooperation if they wanted to find Grayson. So instead of violence, he resorted to something even more radical: the truth.

"My name is Kai Leng. I have a ship docked at one of the ports outside Aria's sphere of influence."

"And you just happened to wander into this district?" Anderson said, making no effort to hide his skepticism. His pistol was still pointed directly at Kai Leng's chest.

"He's with Cerberus," Kahlee said, putting the pieces together. "The Illusive Man sent him to spy on Aria. He wanted to make sure she finished Grayson off."

"We have common goals," Kai Leng assured them, not bothering to deny her accusation. "We all want to get off the station, and we all want to find Grayson. We should work together."

"Or I could just shoot you where you stand," Anderson said, waving the pistol menacingly.

"You could try," Kai Leng answered. "But how will that help you escape Omega?"

"Not everyone here is in Aria's pocket," Kahlee replied. "We'll find someone willing to give us a ride."

"How long will that take? You don't have much time. Right now her focus is on stopping Grayson, but once he escapes—and he will—she'll turn her attention back to you."

"We'll take that chance," Anderson said, squeezing the trigger.

Kai Leng was already in motion, spinning out of the way. Before Anderson could bring the pistol to bear again, he seized the admiral's wrist, forcing it down and twisting it at a painful angle.

Anderson tried to fight back as the gun slipped from his suddenly nerveless fingers by bringing his knee up toward Kai Leng's groin. But he blocked the move by turning his hips so the blow only struck him in the meat of his thigh.

Kahlee jumped in to join the fray, driving her foot

into the center of Kai Leng's back. He absorbed the impact by tumbling forward in a somersault, still keeping his grip on Anderson's wrist. His momentum yanked Anderson off balance, dragging him down to the ground.

From his prone position, Kai Leng scissored his legs and swept Kahlee's feet out from under her, bringing her crashing down to the ground on top of the two men. He momentarily stunned Anderson with an elbow to the solar plexus, rolled free of the tangled mass of bodies, grabbed the pistol where it had fallen, and sprang to his feet.

He pointed the weapon at his two opponents, both of whom were still on the ground. He'd left them unharmed, though the blow he'd delivered to Anderson had him gasping for air.

He kept the pistol trained on them long enough to make it clear they would have been dead had he wished it, then slipped the weapon into the back of his belt.

"Cerberus is not your enemy," he told them. "We are defenders of the human race. We have no quarrel with you."

Kahlee cautiously got to her feet. Anderson was still having trouble catching his breath. She reached down and offered him a hand. He shook his head and waved her off, coughing and wheezing as he struggled up on his own.

"Don't pitch your propaganda to me," Kahlee spat, refusing to back down even after Kai Leng's display of physical superiority. "I know what you really are. I saw what you did to Grayson's daughter. I saw what you did to him."

"Sometimes individual sacrifices are necessary for the greater good."

"Bullshit," Anderson chimed in. "Justify your actions however you want. You're nothing but a bunch of terrorists."

"The Reapers are a threat unlike anything humanity has ever faced," Kai Leng reminded them. "You may think the Illusive Man went too far, but it was necessary to learn about our enemy. The survival of our species depends on it."

"You created a monster and set him loose on the galaxy!" Anderson shot back.

"That was as much your fault as ours. But blame gets us nowhere. We need to work together to bring Grayson back in."

"I'm not going to help you kill him," Kahlee declared. "So either shoot us, or leave us the hell alone."

"You saw what Grayson has become," Kai Leng pressed. "You can imagine what he's capable of. He has to be stopped."

"Clean up your own damn mess," Anderson answered, siding with his companion.

"We can help him," Kai Leng said, knowing there was still a way to get Kahlee to listen to him.

"We have the knowledge and resources to reverse the transformation," he lied. "But soon it will be too late. Everything Grayson is will be consumed by the Reapers."

Kahlee didn't say anything right away, causing Anderson to glance over at her.

"Is that true?" he asked her. "Can they reverse this?"

"Maybe," she said. "I don't know. But if there's even a chance to save him . . ."

She left the words hanging in the air.

"Even if it means working with Cerberus?" Anderson asked softly.

Kahlee nodded.

"Take us to your damn ship," Anderson grumbled.

"This way," Kai Leng said, pointing back down the street. "You'll understand if I prefer you didn't walk behind me."

Aria was at her usual spot in Afterlife when one of her asari underlings rushed in with news of the failed attempt to capture Grayson alive.

"Orgun and Sanak are both dead," she said. "Grayson is on the run, and Keedo is leading the pursuit."

The Pirate Queen kept her features calm, concealing her extreme displeasure.

"What about Sanders and Anderson?"

The attendant who had brought her the news shook her head. "I don't know. Keedo didn't say."

"Then why are you here?" Aria asked coolly.

"Keedo is requesting reinforcements. He says Grayson is . . . changed."

"Changed? In what way?"

"Cybernetic enhancements of some kind. He didn't go into details."

Aria silently cursed herself for trusting Cerberus. There was no doubt in her mind they knew about Grayson's upgrades; they might even have been responsible for them. Yet they had failed to warn her. If she had known, she might have sent more people to the meeting . . . and she might have reconsidered the idea of taking him alive.

But she was also angry at herself. Eager to avenge Liselle's death, she'd accepted Cerberus's proposal despite her misgivings. She had let her feelings for her daughter interfere with her judgment. She had let emotion get in the way of good business. She wouldn't make the same mistake again.

"Give Keedo whatever he needs," she answered. "And send an alert out to everyone we have: Grayson is to be shot on sight. Civilian casualties should be minimized if possible, but I won't hold anyone responsible for collateral damage."

The attendant nodded and rushed off to relay the orders.

Aria watched her go, sipping her drink while she thought about how she would have her revenge against Cerberus and the Illusive Man.

Grayson could do nothing but watch in fascinated horror as the Reapers sent him on a rampage through Omega. They had buried him so deep inside his own mind he had lost nearly all connection with his physical self. He could still see and hear, but he could no longer feel his own body. He knew in some academic way that he had been shot, but the pain was so distanced from his awareness that it had no meaning.

The escape from the warehouse had been only the beginning. As he raced down Omega's streets, it seemed as if everyone on the station was trying to kill him. Every time he rounded a corner he seemed to run into an armed patrol or a blockade. Aria was sending everything she had at him; Grayson wondered if it would be enough.

The Reapers had turned him into a devastating weapon, but their power wasn't infinite. The constant pressure kept them from replenishing the stored energy in his body; each time they drew on it they became fractionally weaker and more vulnerable. He was already seeing the effects of their exertions as each encounter became more difficult and more dangerous.

The first group to get in his way had been easily dispatched with a biotic singularity. With a mere flick of his wrist, the Reapers had caused a single point of near-infinite mass to be created right in the center of the four asari lying in wait for him around a corner. The gravitational field swallowed them up instantly, collapsing them into nothingness before they could summon their own biotic powers to strike back.

The next group of enemies—a mixed squad of humans and batarians—fell to a brutal physical onslaught. Grayson simply barreled into them before they had a chance to fire their weapons, his hands and feet becoming lethal weapons that bludgeoned, bashed, and tore his enemies to shreds. At the end of the encounter, the Reapers paused long enough to scoop up the weapons of his fallen foes, then sent Grayson racing off once more with an assault rifle in each hand.

The rifles allowed the Reapers to switch tactics. Instead of having to overwhelm enemies with biotics or melee combat, they were able to fight a running battle through the Omega streets. Unlike Aria's people, Grayson wasn't wearing a combat suit, so the

Reapers never went toe-to-toe with any of the patrols they came across. Instead, they would fire off a quick burst, then retreat, ducking around a corner into one of Omega's countless side streets or alleys. Using speed and maneuverability to offset the enemies' kinetic barriers and greater numbers, they would pick off the enemy squad one by one until the path was clear again.

The strategy would have been impossible under normal circumstances. Technological advances had helped reduce the kickback, but the sheer volume of rounds being discharged still required the use of both hands to stabilize the weapon. Even a krogan wasn't strong enough to use one in each hand effectively, but Grayson managed them as easily as if they were pistols.

Assault rifles also weren't known for accuracy. Even with the automated targeting systems built into the guns, the odds of repeatedly hitting a single target while on the move were low. But Grayson's synthetic enhancements gave the Reapers incredible accuracy, allowing them to focus both guns precisely on a single target. Kinetic barriers couldn't hold up under such a concentrated barrage, and as soon as the target became vulnerable the Reapers would finish the job with a perfectly placed head shot.

Aria's people fought back as best they could, but no organic foe could match the ruthless efficiency of a near-perfect killing machine. However, even aiming the weapons with laserlike precision was taxing his energy reserves. No matter how superior he was to his opponents, their numbers would eventually overwhelm him. He'd lost track of how many victims the

Reapers had claimed somewhere around twenty, but he knew Aria had plenty more fodder to throw at them.

Recognizing the futility of trying to defeat an entire army, the Reapers began to search for a way to escape the station. The layout of Omega was a confusing labyrinth of haphazard, unplanned construction. It was littered with dead ends and routes to nowhere. But in the two years he had worked for Aria, Grayson had become as familiar with the layout as anyone.

Now the Reapers were drawing on his knowledge, accessing it directly from his mind. There was nothing he could do to stop them; he'd been reduced to a reference library they could call on whenever they wanted.

Still battling swarms of Aria's soldiers, they plotted a course through the twisting, turning streets, heading for the closest of Omega's countless docking bays. None of the ports Aria controlled were heavily guarded—most people knew better than to steal a ship from Omega's Pirate Queen. This one was no different; only a handful of defenders were there to try to stop him. They quickly met the fate of so many of their comrades, though one managed to set off the alarms before she fell.

Grayson knew the blaring claxon meant that reinforcements would arrive in under two minutes, and even as the thought crossed his mind he realized the Reapers would now know it, too.

They had him race over to a small, single-pilot shuttle stationed in one of the bays. The boarding ramp was up, the hatch locked. The Reapers had Grayson reach out his hand and place it on the security panel. Blue sparks arced out from his fingers as he made contact. A sequence of codes flickered through Grayson's consciousness as the Reapers interfaced with the security system's programming, and a second later the hatch opened with a soft click.

The Reapers didn't even wait for the boarding ramp to descend. Dropping the assault rifles, they had Grayson grab hold of the underside of the hatch and haul himself up and in. Once inside, he resealed the hatch and took a seat in the pilot's chair.

A batarian squad arrived just as the engines were roaring to life. They opened fire on the shuttle, but their weapons were useless against the vessel's hull.

The ship rose up from the docking bay, passing smoothly through the shimmering, microns-thin energy barrier that kept the temperature-controlled atmosphere inside the docking bay from leaking out into the frozen vacuum of space.

Unlike the Citadel, Omega had no exterior defenses. There were no patrolling fleets, no GARDIAN turrets or mass accelerator cannons. No longer assailable by patrols and soldiers on the ground, the Reapers were about to complete their escape from Omega.

As the shuttle pulled away from the station, the Reapers once again began to pick through Grayson's mind and memories. He quickly realized they were digging for anything and everything he knew about the Ascension Project: names, locations, security procedures.

He didn't even try to fight them anymore; there was no point. The Reapers had broken his will to resist. His only solace was that even with full access to his thoughts, the Reapers would never be able to find Gillian. His daughter was safe . . . though the same could not be said of her former classmates.

The Reapers didn't immediately plot a course for the Grissom Academy. First, they opened the ship's comm channel and connected to the extranet. With access to trillions of terabytes of information from virtually anywhere in the galaxy, it didn't take them long to find what they were searching for.

Armed with the information they needed, the Reapers began to script lines of code. While with Cerberus, Grayson had been trained in basic computer hacking. He'd seen this type of thing before; it was clear the Reapers were compiling some kind of virus.

Driven by the AI intelligence of his masters, his fingers flew over the ship's digital interface. Grayson tried to follow what was happening, but the complexity and volume of the data was too much for his organic mind to process.

It took nearly fifteen minutes of effort for them to be satisfied with the program. Then they logged back on to the extranet and transmitted a message to the Grissom Academy. The Academy had firewalls and multiple levels of virus protection in place, but Grayson knew their security protocols would be no match for whatever malicious program the Reapers had created.

As the Reapers plotted a course for the Academy into the shuttle's nav systems, Grayson could sense they were almost spent. The desperate escape from Omega had pushed their avatar to its limits. They needed to recharge, but Grayson held out no hope he would have any opportunity to try and regain control of his body.

The shuttle accelerated to FTL speeds, heading for the nearest mass relay to begin the series of jumps that would take the Reapers to their destination. As it did so, they shut Grayson down, pushing him into a deep, dreamless sleep.

TWENTY-ONE

Kahlee and Anderson walked a few steps in front of Kai Leng as they made their way from the warehouse district back to one of the residential areas of Omega. He guided them by issuing directions when needed in a firm, businesslike voice.

"Left at the corner. Continue three blocks. Right here. Take another left."

They weren't running, but they were walking quickly, propelled by their mutual desire to get off the station as soon as possible. And as they wound their way through the crooked streets, Kahlee's mind was working in overdrive.

She was thinking about Grayson, and about Kai Leng's promise that Cerberus could save him. She wanted to believe him, but she knew that someone who worked for the Illusive Man wouldn't be above lying to coerce her cooperation.

Working solely from memory, she tried to reconstruct everything she had learned about the experiment on Grayson during her short time studying the lab reports. Much of it was theoretical and speculative; even the scientists in charge of the operation hadn't known exactly what to expect.

Try as she might, there was no way for Kahlee to confirm or deny Kai Leng's claim. She hadn't been given enough time with the data; Aria's people had attacked the facility before she'd had a chance to fully process everything.

She did manage to get a sense of the overall direction of their work, however. Their research had focused primarily on measurable and quantifiable data: physical changes and alterations to brain wave patterns. They hadn't bothered to do any kind of psychological testing; they hadn't bothered to try and figure out the purpose behind the horrific transformation. Why had the Reapers developed this technology? Why had the Collectors been abducting humans and repurposing them? What were the Reapers after? What did they really want?

Kahlee knew if she could figure out the answers to those questions, she'd be able to figure out where Grayson was going next. Whether she would actually share that information with Kai Leng remained to be seen.

Anderson could tell that Kahlee was deep in thought as she marched beside him. And he could guess what she was thinking about: she wasn't ready to give up on Grayson.

He wasn't ready to give up yet, either. The Cerberus operative had kicked his ass seven ways from Sunday, but he had no intention of simply following the orders of someone who answered to the Illusive Man.

Kai Leng was muscular, but he wasn't a big man. Anderson outweighed him by at least twenty pounds;

if they were in close quarters—like the pilot's cabin of a shuttle—he might be able to use that to his advantage. Whether it would be enough to offset Kai Leng's speed and superior training, however, remained to be seen.

"Right at this corner," Kai Leng told them.

They turned down a long, narrow alley. At the far end was a large door built into the bulkhead, separating the district they were in from the one on the other side. In front of it was a reinforced, waist-high barricade extending out from the bulkhead, across the alley, then back to the bulkhead again to form a small bunker. Behind the barrier were five armed turians.

At first glance they seemed to be almost bored, leaning casually against their protective wall or sitting on top of it, idly passing the time. On seeing the humans, however, they quickly took up defensive positions behind the barricade.

"Who are they?" Kahlee asked.

"Talons," Kai Leng answered. "They control the district beyond the barricade."

During his time as a diplomat, Anderson had received regular reports from Alliance intelligence from across the galaxy. The majority of these came from inside Council space, but some were focused on key locations in the Terminus Systems like Omega.

From these reports, Anderson knew that the Talons were the largest independent gang on Omega. Like most gangs, the Talons were into drug running, weapons smuggling, extortion, killing for hire, and slave trading. For a substantial fee, they also allowed ships and shuttles looking to avoid dealing with

Aria's organization to dock at Talon-controlled ports scattered around the station.

Their business model had proved profitable, and they'd slowly been extending their influence on the station by swallowing up smaller gangs. However, Anderson knew that much of the Talons' success had come from their willingness to maintain a mostly peaceful coexistence with the Pirate Queen, rather than opposing her directly.

"Aria might have sent our descriptions out to every gang on the station," Anderson warned. "If she's offering a reward, the Talons might just decide to turn us over to her to cash in."

"There's bad blood between Aria and the Talons right now," Kai Leng assured them. "Even if they knew she was after us, they wouldn't want to help."

The turian guards studied them as they approached. Two raised their weapons while a third climbed over the barricade and stepped forward to confront them. Anderson was surprised to see that in addition to his pistol he also had a short-range stunner clipped to his belt. He'd assumed the Talons were thugs determined to shoot first and ask questions later. Obviously, however, there were times when they preferred to disable an adversary instead of killing him.

In retrospect, it made sense. The clientele who hired out their docking bays weren't the most upstanding citizens; disputes over payments were inevitable, and shooting customers was bad for business. Blasting them with an electrical current strong enough to render them unconscious wasn't an ideal solution, but it beat the alternative.

"Halt," the turian ordered. "State your business."

"I rented bay 6358," Kai Leng stated.

"Step up to confirm identity," the guard replied.

Kai Leng came forward, holding out his palm so the turian could scan it with his omni-tool.

"Identity confirmed," the guard acknowledged. "Paid in advance until the end of the week."

"I'm leaving a little early," Kai Leng said.

"That's your business," the turian told him. "But we don't give refunds."

To emphasize his point, his hand hovered over the stunner on his belt.

"I'm not looking for one," Kai Leng assured him, and the guard relaxed and gave a nod to his companions.

Convinced the humans had a legitimate reason to be there and weren't looking for any trouble, the others lowered their weapons. The guard who'd greeted them climbed back over the barricade and hit a panel on the wall. The door behind them slid open, revealing nothing more dramatic than another long, narrow alleyway.

"You two first," Kai Leng said with a nod.

Anderson placed one hand on top of the barricade and vaulted over the top. He turned to look back at Kahlee. As his eyes fell on her splinted fingers, a hastily formed plan suddenly took shape.

"She's going to need some help," he said, tilting his head to indicate her injured hands.

He looked at Kai Leng, who, wary of some kind of trick, shook his head in response—just the reaction Anderson was hoping for.

"What about you?" Anderson said, turning to the guard with the stunner on his belt.

After a brief moment of hesitation, the guard stepped forward.

"Hurry up," he grumbled.

Kahlee approached the barricade and raised her knee high enough to set her right foot on top of the wall. With her other leg fully extended and her left foot still on the ground, she didn't have the leverage to propel herself over. Instead, she leaned forward awkwardly so Anderson and the turian guard could each grab hold of one arm, clasping her firmly by the wrist and elbows.

"On three," Anderson said. "One . . . two . . . three!"

Anderson felt Kahlee flexing her knee and shifting her weight with each count to try and help build enough momentum so they could haul her up and over. But as they pulled her toward them, Anderson twisted his hips and shoulders, throwing Kahlee off balance so she crashed into the turian guard as she came over the barricade. Anderson kept his grip on her arm throughout, letting her weight drag him down so that all three of them fell clumsily to the ground.

Kai Leng reacted almost instantly, springing over the wall without even touching it. The other turian guards responded to the situation just as Anderson had predicted, reaching for their weapons to defend themselves against what appeared to be an aggressive and hostile action.

With Kai Leng forced to engage the guards, Anderson had the few precious seconds he needed. He ripped the stunner from the fallen turian's belt, rolled onto his back, and fired at his target.

The stunner blast took Kai Leng right between the shoulder blades, causing him to drop to the ground unconscious. Two of the turians were already down, injured but not dead. The other two were still fumbling for their weapons, though whether they intended to use them on Kai Leng or Anderson wasn't clear.

"It's okay! It's okay!" Anderson shouted, tossing the stunner aside and raising his hands in a gesture of surrender.

The turians still standing rushed over and hauled him and Kahlee to their feet as their fallen captain angrily picked himself up. They slammed the humans back against the bulkhead, pinning them there by jamming their assault rifles into their chests.

Anderson didn't say anything as the nose of the weapon pressed painfully into his sternum. He knew he needed to let everyone calm down before speaking. He saw Kahlee wincing in pain, though he couldn't tell if it was from being roughly pinned against the wall or from banging her tender fingers during the scuffle.

The captain glared at the humans, then went over to check the two turians on the ground. They were both groaning in pain, but with the captain's help they managed to clamber to their feet, much to Anderson's relief. Convincing the guards to let them go would have been much harder if Kai Leng had actually killed anyone.

"I can explain all this," Anderson said, judging that emotions had cooled enough for him to make his case. "That guy on the ground was holding us prisoner."

"He paid for the docking bay," the captain snarled. "He's our customer. You're not."

"You're still going to get your money," Anderson reminded them. "Even if you let us go."

"Maybe we should hold on to you and wait for him to wake up," the captain countered. "He'll probably throw in a nice bonus for keeping you from escaping."

"He's with Cerberus," Kahlee said, jumping into the negotiations.

"Is this true?" the captain asked Anderson, stepping forward and leaning in until only a few inches separated their faces.

"It's true," Anderson declared, staring right into the turian's eyes.

The captain took a step back, but didn't speak right away. The guards cast quick glances in his direction, waiting to see what he would say. Anderson held his breath.

The anti-alien agenda of Cerberus was well known throughout the galaxy, even on Omega. It was only natural that most nonhumans would feel a similar bias against the Illusive Man and his agents. The only question was whether it would be enough to overcome the Talons' mercenary greed.

"You can go," the captain said at last. "Take his ship if you want."

In response, the guards lowered their weapons.

"What about him?" Kahlee asked, nodding in the direction of Kai Leng's still unconscious body.

"We'll think of something special," the captain

replied, and the other turians all squawked out evil laughs.

"Things will go worse for Cerberus if you let us take him," Kahlee insisted. "We're with an Alliance task force. We're trying to take the organization down. He has information we can use."

"You don't want to get mixed up in a war against the Illusive Man," Anderson added. "You already got paid. Just take the money and walk away."

The captain considered for a moment, then shrugged.

"Sure. Take him. Get the hell out of here. What do we care?"

Anderson didn't need to be told twice. He bent down and scooped up Kai Leng's unconscious body. With a grunt he tossed him over his shoulder in a fireman's carry.

"How far to the docking bay?" he asked.

"Not far. Take a right at the end of the alley. Bays are marked on the side. 6358's the one you want."

With Kahlee leading the way, they left the turians behind, Anderson struggling under the weight of his burden.

"I'm sorry I didn't warn you," he said once they were beyond earshot of the guards. "Are you hurt?"

"I'm fine," she assured him. "That was quick thinking back there."

"Why did you want to bring him along?" Anderson asked, indicating the unconscious man draped over his shoulder.

"Figured we'd hand him over to the Alliance for interrogation," she explained.

Her answer made Anderson feel better; he'd been

afraid Kahlee was still clinging to the notion that Kai Leng and Cerberus could somehow reverse Grayson's transformation.

Kahlee didn't say anything else, and Anderson decided it was more important to save his breath than continue the conversation. Five minutes later they reached the spaceport. Anderson was relieved to discover that bay 6358 was the second closest one to where they had come in.

"We better hurry," he warned Kahlee as they reached Kai Leng's shuttle. "I don't know how much longer he's going to be out."

It took her a few minutes to hack the security system so they could get inside. Anderson hauled Kai Leng into the vessel, then began searching for something to restrain him.

He found a standard emergency supply kit, complete with rations, bottled water, an electric lamp and heater, extra batteries, a small folding tent, fifty feet of nylon rope, and a military-style field knife.

Working quickly, he cut the rope into eight-foot lengths and used them to lash the still unconscious body of Kai Leng to the copilot's chair.

"Can you fly this thing?" Kahlee asked.

"Basic Alliance design," he assured her, firing up the engines.

After a routine safety check to confirm all the systems were working, he took the shuttle up and out of the docking bay, leaving Omega behind.

He hoped he'd never have to set foot on the god-forsaken station again.

TWENTY-TWO

They had just completed the first mass relay jump on their way back to the Citadel when Kahlee got up from her seat in the back of the shuttle and came up front to check on Anderson.

She glanced down at their prisoner; he was still strapped into the copilot seat, unconscious. With nowhere in the forward cabin for her to sit, she crouched down beside Anderson as he worked the controls.

"I realized I never thanked you for getting me off Omega," she said.

"I figured I was leaving, so I might as well take you with me," he joked.

Kahlee smiled, and reached to carefully place her injured hand on his arm.

"What happened in Aria's . . . ," she began.

Anderson shook his head. "Not with our friend listening."

Kahlee turned her head to look at Kai Leng. At first glance his eyes appeared to be closed, but as she studied him carefully, she realized his lids were open just a crack, allowing him to see what was going on.

"He's been awake for at least twenty minutes," Anderson said.

Realizing his ruse had failed, Kai Leng opened his eyes wide.

"Where are you taking me?" he asked.

"The Citadel," Anderson answered. "I've got some friends in the Alliance who are going to want to speak to you."

"That's a mistake," he warned them. "You should be going after Grayson. He's just going to keep getting stronger. He has to be stopped."

"You're probably right," Anderson agreed. "But unless you know where we can find him, we'll stick with the original plan."

"I don't know where he is," Kai Leng admitted. "I just assumed you did."

Kahlee sensed genuine surprise in his voice.

"Why would we know where he's headed?" she wondered aloud.

"The Illusive Man told me you were the key to finding Grayson," he told her. "He thinks you two have some sort of special connection."

"He's not the Grayson I knew," she said coldly. "Your people made sure of that."

"But you saw the files," Kai Leng continued. "You know what's happening to him. I thought you would be able to piece it all together to anticipate his next move."

"Don't listen to him," Anderson warned. "He's trying to get inside your head."

"No," Kahlee said softly, "he's right. I was thinking about this earlier. I feel like there's something I'm missing."

"You saw what he did to Aria's guards," Anderson reminded her. "Even if we knew where to find him, what could we do?"

"That's a coward's excuse," Kai Leng insisted.

Anderson didn't bother to reply.

Sensing that continuing the discussion would only make the tension worse, Kahlee retired to the rear of the shuttle again.

Taking a seat, she continued to mull over the problem. The thing she'd seen in the warehouse wasn't Grayson. It was his body—at least partially—but the Reapers were manipulating and controlling him.

If she could just figure out what the Reapers wanted, and how Grayson fit into their plans, she told herself, she could find the answer.

She thought back on the data from the experiments, trying to piece together everything she knew about the Reapers. They were interested in humans; that much was clear. They had even gone so far as to have the Collectors abduct humans so they could perform their own versions of the Cerberus experiments.

But if all they'd wanted was for Grayson to start abducting people, they'd have simply sent him out to the remote colonies in the Terminus Systems. The chances of finding him would have been almost zero.

She slammed her fist against the padded arm of her seat in frustration, sending sharp jolts of pain up through her splinted fingers. But she was too focused on trying to solve her problem to give it more than cursory notice.

Kai Leng had claimed she was the key. The Illusive Man felt there was some special connection between her and Grayson. Was he referring to Gillian? Was it possible the Reapers were going to go after Grayson's daughter because of her unique biotic abilities?

She felt like the solution was close, but she knew she wasn't quite there. The Cerberus data speculated that the Reapers would eventually be able to pull knowledge directly from Grayson's mind. But even if they found out about Gillian, there was no possible way they could find her. The best they could do would be to inspect her files from the Ascension Project—

The answer hit her with such force she almost cried out. Leaping to her feet, she raced into the forward cabin.

"Send a message to the Grissom Academy," she ordered, speaking so quickly her words nearly tripped over themselves. "Warn them Grayson is on his way."

To his credit, Anderson didn't argue or question her. Acting on her instructions, he dropped the ship out of FTL and sent out a signal to connect to the closest communications buoy.

"I've got a signal," he said a few seconds later, "but something's wrong. I can't connect to the Academy."

"Try emergency frequencies," Kahlee suggested.

"I'm trying them all," he said. "I'm getting no response. It's like they shut down all their comm systems."

"The Reapers," Kai Leng declared. "They found some way to block transmissions so nobody can warn them."

"How close are we to the Academy?" Kahlee wanted to know.

"Two relay jumps," Anderson informed her. "I can

have us there inside of three hours if I push the engines."

"Push them," Kahlee told him.

Grayson's shuttle decelerated from FTL speed only a few thousand kilometers from the Grissom Academy. At this range it wasn't necessary to use the comm buoy network to send a message; he was able to hail them directly.

Grayson knew Kahlee hadn't told anyone else at the Academy the truth about him. Convinced he had truly rejected Cerberus and was trying to turn his life around, she hadn't seen any purpose in poisoning his reputation. She'd also left him an open invitation to come visit her, though he'd never followed up on it.

The Reapers had discovered all this back on Omega while probing Grayson's mind for information about Kahlee. Now they were going to use what they had learned to gain access to the files of the Ascension Project.

"Grissom Academy, this is Paul Grayson. Do you copy?"

"Copy, Grayson," a voice came back over the intercom. "Long time no see."

Grayson didn't recognize the guard's voice, which meant the Reapers didn't either. But it wasn't unusual to have the guards remember him, even though two years had passed since Gillian had been part of the Ascension Project. While working for Cerberus, Grayson had played the role of a wealthy parent and frequent benefactor to the Academy, and Gillian had been one of the more unique students at the facility.

Any visit from her father was likely to stand out in the minds of the staff.

"I tried to let you know I was coming, but the message wouldn't go through," the Reapers lied.

"All our network connections are snafued," came the reply. "Haven't been able to link in for the last four hours. We're in a grade-two lockdown until the techs get it fixed."

The Reapers picked through Grayson's memories, reaching back to the days when Gillian was still attending the Academy. A grade-two lockdown was a relatively minor security precaution. Normally parents could visit their children at the Academy at any time, but in a grade-two lockdown they needed to get clearance from someone on staff.

"Kahlee Sanders told me to meet her here," the Reapers explained, spinning a story out of the bits and pieces they had drawn from their host. "She's supposed to arrive in the next hour or so. I'm guessing you didn't get the message."

"Affirmative. Like I said, nothing from the comm network for the last four hours."

"I know it's against protocol," the Reapers said, "but is there any chance you'd let me dock my shuttle and wait for her on board the station? I'd like to get out and stretch my legs. It's getting a little cramped in here."

There was a brief hesitation before the reply, probably the guard checking with one of his superiors. Grayson prayed they would deny the request.

"Sure thing," the guard's voice chimed a few seconds later, and Grayson knew the unsuspecting young man had just signed his own death warrant.

"Bring it around to bay three. But you'll have to wait in the security clearance area until Miss Sanders arrives."

"Roger that. Much appreciated."

Grayson's fingers flew effortlessly over the pilot's interface as the Reapers brought the shuttle around to align with one of the landing pads of the exterior docking bay. It touched down with only the faintest bump. Unlike the docks of Omega, here there was no mass effect field separating the Grissom Academy from space. Arrivals had to wait for one of the covered docking platforms to connect to the vessel's airlock in order to enter the station.

While waiting for the docking platform to get into position, the Reapers had Grayson rise from the pilot's seat and dig out the emergency kit stashed beneath his chair. He noticed that despite the fact that all his recent injuries were completely healed, he was moving much slower now. It had been several hours since the Reapers' frantic rush to escape Omega; obviously that hadn't been enough time to fully recover.

Inside the emergency kit was a knife with a long, heavy blade. The Reapers tucked this into the front of his belt before making their way toward the back of the vessel.

He could sense them picking through his mind for details about the security of the station. Technically, the Grissom Academy was a school, not a military base. But there were still enough security staff on-site—not to mention the biotic instructors of the Ascension Program—to pose a legitimate threat to the Reapers in their weakened and vulnerable state. Unable to simply overpower their enemies with irresistible biotic displays or incredible physical prowess and martial skill, they would need to rely on subterfuge and stealth to achieve their goals.

He couldn't say for sure whether the Reapers had selected this particular vessel during their escape from Omega in anticipation of this eventuality, though he knew it was possible. But by design or chance, they had ended up taking a standard passenger shuttle. Given their familiarity with the turian vessel they'd hijacked at the Cerberus lab, Grayson wondered if the Reapers simply had an affinity for that particular species.

In the back of the vessel was a sleeping cabin, with an assortment of clothes hanging in a small closet. The Reapers rummaged through the collection, looking for anything that could effectively cover Grayson's unnatural appearance and conceal the knife from the guards.

From the cut and style of the garments, it was clear the owner of the shuttle had been turian—unsurprising given the make of the ship itself. None of the pieces would fit Grayson in a way that could hide what he had become.

There was a soft chime from the overhead intercom, indicating the docking platform had connected with the shuttle's airlock.

Realizing the disguise had to last only long enough for them to get through the docking bay's security doors, the Reapers whisked the cover off the bed. As if it were a shawl, they draped the blanket over the back of Grayson's head, neck, and shoulders like a cape. Pulling the open sides at the front together and tucking the material beneath his chin left only his eyes and face exposed, peering out from a small opening in the formless tent of material.

As the Reapers passed through the shuttle's airlock and made their way slowly along the covered docking platform, Grayson speculated on what might happen to his new form if it was exposed to the unforgiving environment of space. Did the Reapers even need his organic systems to continue functioning anymore? He had seen ample evidence they were capable of repairing damaged organic tissue at an incredible rate, but at this point the cybernetics were so deeply ingrained in his body he felt as if he was more machine than man. As their avatar, could he somehow survive without oxygen in the freezing temperatures outside the docking platform?

He knew he was far from indestructible. But if his lungs and heart shut down while the synthetic network woven into the synapses of his brain remained undamaged, could the Reapers continue to animate his body? Or might there be a point where massive damage to the life-giving systems of the physical shell would cause them to finally abandon their host?

If the Reapers were aware of his speculations, they gave no sign. Perhaps they simply didn't care. They had absolute control of his physical form, and they had no intention of doing anything but plodding slowly along the ramp, swaddled in their bedspread cowl.

The docking ramp led him through another airlock and into a small hallway that sloped upward for several meters before turning around a corner and emerging inside the security screening area.

It was a large, open room. Behind him was a wall

with a window built halfway up, overlooking the docking bay. Before him was a reinforced glass wall. In the center of the wall was an open doorway equipped with a security scanner. All arrivals had to pass through the door in order to clear security.

Beyond that was another room with a small security booth built off to one side and another open doorway leading into the main section of the Academy. The security booth was on a raised platform, giving anyone inside a clear view of the docking bay through the glass wall and massive exterior window.

One of the guards—probably the young man he'd been talking to over the radio—had come down to meet him. He was standing on the other side of the glass wall, just beyond the security scanner. Grayson could see the head and shoulders of a second guard, this one a young woman, watching from the security booth.

The Reapers made a quick evaluation of their closest opponent. He seemed fit, and possessed the confident stance of someone who had received some basic training. At his side was a pistol, but instead of a combat suit he was wearing a Grissom Academy staff uniform: dark pants and a blue shirt emblazoned with the school's insignia.

Moving even more slowly than before, the Reapers approached the security scanner. They stopped a few steps before it, as if waiting for the guard's instructions before passing through.

"Uh . . . you okay, Mr. Grayson?" the guard asked from the other side of the scanner, taken aback by their guest's strange attire.

"Caught some kind of flu," the Reapers replied from beneath the blanket. "Can't stop shivering."

Obviously satisfied with the explanation, the guard noted, "That's an interesting shuttle you're flying. It's turian, right?"

Grayson's cover while working for Cerberus had been that of a high-ranking employee for Cord-Hislop Aerospace, a shuttle manufacturer that served as one of the Illusive Man's many front companies. Knowing this, the Reapers were able to come up with another plausible explanation.

"We're considering a merger with one of our turian competitors," they informed the guard. "Testing out their product before the deal becomes final."

The guard nodded, once again buying the story—a little too conveniently, Grayson thought. He wondered if the Reapers were somehow manipulating the young man, exerting a subliminal influence on his thoughts and emotions that made him more predisposed to believe their lies.

"I don't feel so good," the Reapers said, causing Grayson to sway unsteadily on his feet.

He stumbled forward and braced himself against the wall. Concerned, the guard took a step halfway through the security scanner to see if he was okay. The Reapers slowly toppled backward. The guard leapt forward and caught Grayson, supporting his weight with a grunt.

"Hey," he called out to his partner up in the security both. "I think he's really sick. Bring me the med-kit."

The young woman sprang into action, grabbing the med-kit and rushing down to help.

The Reapers kept the blanket clutched tightly around Grayson's body as the young man carefully lowered him to the floor. The woman ran up and crouched on the other side of him, setting the med-kit down beside her.

She turned her head to open it, and the knife now in Grayson's hand thrust up through the blanket, impaling the young man in the chest as he leaned forward to examine the patient more closely. He grunted in surprise, then let out a long, low gasp as the blade was withdrawn.

The young woman's head snapped around in surprise, and her eyes flew open in horror as she realized what had happened. The Reapers shoved the dying man aside and sat up, slashing out with the knife in an attempt to disembowel the female guard.

But the supernatural speed the Reapers had possessed on Omega was lacking, and she managed to scamper back out of range. The blade left a long gash in the belly of her uniform, but failed to make contact with the flesh beneath.

Scrambling to her feet, she ran toward the emergency alarm built into the wall right beside the security scanner. The Reapers brought Grayson to his feet, then snapped his arm forward. The knife flew from his grasp, end over end, before burying itself between the guard's shoulder blades.

She sagged to the floor, her hand desperately stretching out toward the alarm she would never reach before falling limp to the floor.

Ignoring the corpses of the two dead guards, the Reapers passed through the scanner and moved quickly up into the security booth. It took them less than two minutes to log in to the primary systems and disable the intercom and alarm systems across the entire station.

Next, they brought up a schematic of the Academy and committed it to memory. Returning to the security clearance area, they retrieved the knife sticking out of the dead girl's back as well as each guard's pistol.

Finally, they picked the blanket up from the floor and wrapped it around Grayson once more, reversing it to hide the bloodstains. On close inspection the large tear left by the knife was still visible, but Grayson suspected that anyone who got close enough to notice would already be as good as dead.

Moving with long, easy strides, the Reapers left the security clearance area behind, passing through the door into the main Academy as they headed for the wing of the Ascension Project.

TWENTY-THREE

"Grissom Academy, this is Admiral David Anderson of the Alliance. Do you copy?"

Anderson knew that the fact they were getting no response was a bad sign. They were close enough to the Grissom Academy to attempt to make contact through direct radio transmission, bypassing whatever technical glitch had isolated the school from the comm network. The silence on the other end meant something had gone wrong on the station itself.

"Try it again," Kahlee said, stubbornly refusing to accept the truth.

Knowing it was futile, Anderson closed the comm channel. They'd been trying to get a response for the past five minutes, ever since they had dropped out of FTL.

"There's no point," he said, hoping some hard truth might help to prepare Kahlee for whatever scene awaited them on the station. "We'll be there in two minutes anyway," he added to soften the blow.

"You won't be able to stop Grayson alone," Kai Leng warned them. "Untie me and let me help."

Neither Anderson nor Kahlee bothered to respond. The ship's sensors projected an image of the exterior docking bay onto the vid screen. Three of the bays were empty; the fourth was occupied by a small passenger shuttle.

"Turian," Anderson muttered, though everyone on board knew who the pilot had been.

He brought the shuttle in slowly. Without a signal coming in from the Academy, he had to land the shuttle freehand, relying on instrument readings and dozens of tiny manual adjustments to their course. A delicate operation at the best of times, it was made even more difficult by the fact that Kahlee was standing behind his chair, leaning over his shoulder and staring intently at the screen. She didn't say anything, but he could sense her urgency, as well as her frustration at how long it was taking. Despite all his care, when he finally touched down, the shuttle landed with a heavy thump.

They waited a few seconds to see if the docking ramps would connect to the shuttle's airlock, but sensors picked up no movement.

"Nobody manning the docks," Anderson muttered. "Going to need an enviro-suit."

"There's one in the back," Kai Leng offered. "A shotgun, too."

Kahlee glanced down at him in surprise.

"I want to stop Grayson as much as you do," he assured them. "Even if you leave me bound to this chair, I'll do whatever I can to help."

"Keep an eye on him" was all Anderson said as he got up from his seat and headed to the rear of the shuttle.

The enviro-suit was right where Kai Leng had promised. The resilient, insulated fabric easily stretched to fit over Anderson's clothes, and when he slipped the helmet over his head and flicked it on, it formed an airtight seal with the rest of the suit.

He touched the side of the helmet to activate the transmitter. "Kahlee, do you copy?"

"Copy," she replied from up in the cockpit. "Maintain radio contact at all times."

"Roger that."

He picked up the shotgun, the weight of the Sokolov noticeably heavier than the old Hahne-Kedar model he'd used during his tours in the First Contact war. Then he made his way over to the shuttle's airlock and stepped inside, closing the interior door behind him. There was a loud rush as the atmosphere whooshed out. Even through the insulation of his suit he felt the temperature drop, though it wasn't enough to make him uncomfortable.

He opened the airlock's exterior hatch and stepped down carefully onto the floor of the docking bay. The enviro-suit had magnetized boots for space walks, but they weren't necessary here—the artificial gravity generated by the station's mass effect fields was still active.

Scanning the dock for targets, he made his way over to the nearest airlock leading into the station. Fortunately it wasn't locked, and within a minute he was inside a small hall filled with heated, breathable air.

"I'm inside," he said to Kahlee, lifting the visor of his helmet.

He proceeded up the gently sloping passage, emerging in what served as the Academy's security clearance area for all passenger arrivals. The two bodies lying on the floor only confirmed what they had all suspected.

"We've got casualties," Anderson said softly, knowing the transmitter would amplify his voice enough for Kahlee to hear every word clearly. "Two. Look like security guards."

Keeping his shotgun at the ready, he crept toward the security booth, crouching low to the ground. He pressed up close to the wall beside the open door, then poked his head around the corner for a quick peek.

"Area is clear," he reported, some of the adrenaline-fueled tension fading from his muscles.

Making his way over to the control panel, he found the manual overrides and activated one of the docking ramps. Through the glass wall he watched as it slid into position, clicking tight on the shuttle's airlock.

"Docking ramp is in place," he told Kahlee. "Might as well come aboard."

"What about Kai Leng?" Kahlee asked. "You think it's safe to just leave him?"

"Don't see any other choice," Anderson replied. "Just in case, bring that knife from the first-aid kit with you."

"Copy that. I'm on my way."

Anderson debated stripping off the enviro-suit, then decided not to bother. He was already sweating under the airtight fabric, but the suit was equipped with standard kinetic barrier technology. If he ended up getting into a firefight, he'd need the protection.

He hustled down the steps from the guard station back to where Kahlee would emerge in the security clearance room. She probably knew the murdered guards; he wanted to be there for support when she came across the bodies.

He arrived just a few seconds before Kahlee. He didn't say anything as her eyes came to rest on the fallen guards, letting her mourn their deaths in silence.

She walked slowly over to the first body—a young man stabbed through the chest—and got down on one knee. Despite his glassy, unblinking eyes she pressed her fingers against his throat to check for a pulse. Finding nothing, she reached up and gently closed his eyes, then let her head drop.

Getting to her feet, she made a similar examination of the second body before coming over to stand by Anderson.

"Erin and Jorgen," she told him. "Good kids."

"Grayson did this to them," Anderson said, knowing it was something she didn't want to hear. "If we don't stop him, others will die."

Kahlee nodded her head in agreement.

"You don't have to worry about me," she assured him. "If we have to take him out, I won't hesitate."

Anderson didn't like the sound of that "if," but he knew it was the best he'd get from her. She still couldn't bring herself to admit Grayson was beyond salvation.

"The bodies are still warm," she noted. "And the blood is just starting to congeal. My guess is that Grayson came through here less than ten minutes ago."

"Do we set off the alarms?" Anderson asked.

Kahlee shook her head. "It's night—most of the

students and staff will be in their rooms. That's probably the safest place for them. We set off the alarm and they'll all come pouring out into the hall to see what's going on."

"What about security personnel?"

"We should be able to alert them from the guard station," Kahlee said.

They quickly made their way into the small control room overlooking the dock. Kahlee flipped a few switches, then slammed her hand down on the console in frustration.

"The whole system's fried."

"Any other security stations close by?"

She shook her head. "They're spread out everywhere. It'd take forever to gather them all."

"Do you have any idea where Grayson is going?" Anderson asked.

Kahlee thought about it for a moment before answering.

"If the Reapers are just looking for information, he'll head to the data archives. If they're after more victims, he'll head for the dorms. Either way he's heading for the Ascension wing.

"Come on," she added, turning to rush off.

Anderson grabbed her forearm, stopping her in her tracks.

"Grayson took the guards' pistols. We know he's armed. You can't go after him without a weapon."

"I have a knife," she reminded him, showing him where she'd slid it into her boot.

"You need a gun."

"This is a school, not a military base," she explained. "The only guns on-site are carried by the guards.

"Besides," she added, holding up her splinted fingers. "I couldn't fire one anyway."

"Where's the nearest guard station?" Anderson asked.

"Down the hall and to the right," she replied. "But the Ascension wing is in the opposite direction."

"Then we split up," Anderson declared, falling into the familiar role of an officer barking out orders.

"You go alert the guards. Get them to help you search the dorms. If you don't run into Grayson, round up all the kids and take them somewhere safe," he added, knowing Kahlee's primary concern would be for the safety of the children.

To his relief, she nodded in agreement.

"Take a left when you go out into the main hall," she told him. "If you just keep following it you'll end up at the main entrance to the Ascension wing.

"When you get there, look for the map painted on the wall. The data archive is off the main research lab. Look for the large room near the center of the map marked *Restricted Area*."

There was an awkward moment of silence. Anderson didn't know whether he should kiss her, hug her, or simply say "Good luck." Kahlee resolved the issue by leaning forward and giving him a quick peck on the lips, then turning and dashing out the door and down the hall.

Grasping the shotgun firmly in his hands, Anderson lowered the visor of his helmet and set off at a run in the other direction.

*   *   *

Back on the ship, Kai Leng was working to free himself from his bonds. His wrists and forearms were tied to the arms of the copilot seat; his ankles and calves were lashed firmly to the supports underneath. He wasn't completely immobilized, however.

By straining against his bonds he was able to gain just enough play in the rope to allow him to wiggle from side to side in the seat. Each time he did so the rope pulled taut, digging painfully into his flesh . . . but it also rubbed against the rough metal on the underside of the padded armrests of the chair.

He started slowly, rocking himself and twisting his torso, applying as much tension to the rope as possible, testing the limits of his movement. Then he began to pick up speed, side to side and back and forth, increasing the friction. In less than a minute the ropes had scraped his skin raw. After another they began to draw blood.

The blood mingled with the sweat of his exertion, making a warm, sticky mess that quickly covered his arms and dripped onto the seat and the floor around it. Kai Leng was oblivious, however; all his attention was focused on working the rope against the metal fittings of the chair, fraying it one woven nylon strand at a time.

It took nearly five minutes, but in the end the wear and tear caused one of the loops securing his left arm to snap. The others quickly went slack as he wriggled his arm, until they were loose enough for him to slide his crimson-soaked limb loose.

He attacked the knots holding his right arm in place, the fingers of his left hand slick with blood and sweat. It was frustrating work, but after another

minute he managed to free his dominant hand. Then
he set to work on the ropes around his legs and ankles.

The angle was awkward; he had to lean forward
and down to reach under his seat. Unable to see what
he was doing, he had to stop every twenty or thirty
seconds to keep the blood rushing to his head from
causing him to black out. In the end it took him
longer to free his legs than it had his arms, but ultimately he was free.

Breathing heavily from the exertion, he stood up
slowly. His legs had fallen asleep from being held in
the same position for so long. Gritting his teeth and
clutching the bloody copilot's chair for support, he
gingerly walked it off, doing everything he could to
get the blood circulating again.

When the pins and needles finally faded, Kai Leng
headed for the first-aid kit in the back of the shuttle.
He wiped away the blood with a sanitized towel, then
smeared a layer of soothing medi-gel on the gashed
and torn flesh of his burning forearms.

Then he paused to consider his next course of action. One option was to simply close the airlock and
fly away, leaving Anderson and Sanders to try and
deal with Grayson. This seemed to be the most sensi-
ble thing to do; he had no weapon and it was likely
everyone on the station would be as much against
him as they were against Grayson.

But he knew that would displease the Illusive Man.
There was a good chance Grayson would escape.
Once he left the Academy, he would be virtually impossible to find . . . especially if he killed Sanders before fleeing.

The more Kai Leng thought about it, the more he realized this might be the last chance Cerberus would have to stop the Reapers. And even if it meant confronting Grayson unarmed, he couldn't let the opportunity slip from his fingers.

With his mind made up, he didn't waste any more time. Moving quickly, he passed through the docking ramp and airlocks and into what was obviously a security clearance room.

Two bodies lay on the floor: one male, one female. A quick inspection revealed they had been killed with a knife. The fact that Grayson hadn't simply crushed them with some type of biotic power gave Kai Leng hope; it could mean his enemy was exhausted and possibly even vulnerable.

He felt the familiar spark of excitement flickering deep inside him. At heart he was a killer, a predator. He lived for the chase. And the hunt was about to begin.

TWENTY-FOUR

The Reapers were being cautious. Methodical. There was no need to hurry, so they didn't.

Eager to avoid unnecessary confrontations, they set Grayson off on a winding, circuitous route through the halls of the Academy, using the schematics they had downloaded from the guard station. It was night on the station, so they chose a route that passed by empty offices rather than dorm rooms where students would be sleeping.

With the blanket still wrapped tightly around his body, Grayson was nothing more than a passenger along for the ride. He was grateful their route kept them from running into anyone else, however. He didn't want to imagine what would happen if one of the students happened to stumble across them.

Eventually they reached the door of the Ascension Project's primary research laboratory. The door was closed, but the Reapers knew that the data archives for the entire project were stored in the room beyond.

They had Grayson lean forward and press his ear against the portal. Through the door and the blanket, his hypersensitive hearing picked up voices coming from the other side. Scientists working late, most likely.

They let the bloodstained blanket fall to the floor, then hit the panel to open the door. It slid back to reveal what was quite clearly a research lab. A bank of computer stations lined one wall. The opposite wall contained shelves of biological samples taken from the students to monitor their health and progress. In the back corner were various pieces of expensive equipment used to analyze the samples, as well as the electronic data collected weekly from the implants of every child in the program.

Two men and a woman occupied the room. One of the men was seated at a computer station, his chair turned away from the screens as he conversed with the other man and the woman. She was smiling knowingly, as if she'd just made a joke; the two men were laughing out loud.

All three turned in Grayson's direction as he came in. Their expressions transformed from laughter to fear, though it was impossible to say whether the cause was Grayson's mutated appearance or the twin pistols he carried.

The Reapers fired three shots in rapid succession. Each bullet was perfectly placed in the exact center of the forehead, causing instantaneous death. The three researchers fell to the floor, their lives forfeit simply because they had chosen this particular night to put in a few hours of overtime.

Standing perfectly still, the Reapers listened for the sound of any response to the three pistol shots that had echoed in the room. There were no cries of alarm from down the hall; there were no sounds of running

footsteps. Satisfied that the obstacles had been eliminated without alerting anyone else on the station, the
Reapers turned and casually hit the panel to close the
door.

In the back of the lab was another door; beyond it
were the data archives. The archives consisted of an
OSD library and server array that contained every
reading and every result from every test on every student who had ever participated in the Ascension Project.

Not surprisingly, the door to the data archives was
locked. Access to the information was restricted to
only a handful of senior staff on the project, and required a keycard, access code, and biological identification confirmed via voice and retinal scans. It took
the Reapers less than two minutes to hack the door
open.

Once inside, the Reapers began to access the data
using the lone terminal in the room. As the information flickered on the screen, Grayson scanned it,
processed it, and transmitted it instantaneously back
to his Reaper overlords in dark space.

The sensation was unlike anything Grayson had
ever experienced. It was exhilarating. Intoxicating.
Euphoric. Even a red sand high couldn't compare
with the rush of being a conduit for pure data transmission.

But it was also taxing. Draining. Exhausting.
Transmitting trillions of terabytes of data required a
tremendous output of energy, and the Reapers knew
their avatar was already weak. So they went slowly,
taking their time, careful not to destroy their precious
vessel.

* * *

"We've got an emergency," Kahlee said as she burst into the guard station closest to the security clearance room, slightly out of breath from running the entire way.

"Three of you come with me. The other two go alert the other guard stations and put the whole Academy on stage-four lockdown."

Hendel Mitra, the former security chief at the Grissom Academy, had been a close personal friend of Kahlee's. His successor, Captain Ellen Jimenez, was a capable replacement, but Kahlee and she had never formed the same close, personal bond. Fortunately, she still respected Kahlee enough not to question her when she burst into the guard station and started barking out orders to the staff.

"Jackson and M'gabi," the new security chief said, nodding at two of her people, "go warn the others. Seal off this wing—nobody gets in or out."

Turning to Kahlee she said, "Lead the way."

The fact that Jimenez had been on duty was pure coincidence. Racing down the hall toward the Ascension wing, Kahlee couldn't help but wonder if the other security personnel would have been as quick to listen to her if they hadn't seen their supervisor so easily falling into step.

We're going to need a few more lucky breaks if we want to get out of this alive, Kahlee thought.

"What's going on?" Jimenez asked as she ran beside her.

Not wanting to go into the whole story, Kahlee decided to stick to the details that mattered. "Someone infiltrated the station. We have to evacuate the Ascension Project dorms. Get the children somewhere safe."

"The cafeteria," Jimenez suggested. "Get everyone inside, and reinforce the room with as many security personnel as we can spare."

"Good idea," Kahlee replied.

When they reached the dorms, they had to split up. There were three separate student halls, plus a fourth for the faculty. Jimenez dispatched her people with the calm, cool efficiency of a true leader.

"Giller, take the far hall. Malkin, the one next to it."

"Don't let anyone out of your sight," Kahlee warned them. "Not even the staff. We've already had two casualties."

She didn't offer the names, uncertain what effect it might have. To the credit of Jimenez and her staff, they didn't ask.

"Rendezvous back at the cafeteria," Jimenez called after the others as they ran off. "The same goes for you," she said, turning to Kahlee. "Are you armed?"

"Got a knife in my boot."

Jimenez glanced down at the splints on her fingers.

"Can you fire a pistol with those things?" she asked.

"I doubt it," Kahlee replied.

Jimenez unclipped the gun from her side and offered it to Kahlee anyway.

"Just in case," she said before rushing off to start rousing the children from their beds.

Kahlee awkwardly tucked the pistol into her belt, then hurried over to the closest room. She opened the door and flicked on the light to find Nick asleep in his bed. The teenager rolled over and looked at her with the confusion of someone still half asleep.

"Get up, Nick," she said. "Right now. Hurry."

"What's going on?" he mumbled.

"Please, Nick. Just get up and meet me in the hall right away."

Not waiting for a response, she went to the next door and repeated the process.

Within five minutes she had all sixteen students following her to the cafeteria.

"Miss Sanders," Nick said, falling into step beside her. "What's going on?"

He'd pulled on a pair of pants and a shirt after she'd woken him up, but his dark hair was still a tangled, uncombed mess.

"Not in front of the children," she replied, knowing he'd be less likely to argue if he felt like she was treating him like an adult.

"Gotcha," he replied, his chest puffing out just a little.

Even in these dire circumstances, Kahlee couldn't help but let a quick smile slip at his reaction.

They were the third group to arrive in the cafeteria. Jimenez showed up with the fourth a few seconds later.

Everyone was milling about, confused and a little alarmed. Being roused from slumber by armed guards—even guards meant to protect you—was more than a little frightening.

"What do we tell them?" Jimenez wanted to know.

"Listen up!" Kahlee called out, projecting her voice so everyone could hear. "Nobody is allowed to leave

this room without permission from me or Captain
Jimenez."

She paused, and there was an instant onslaught of
questions, mostly from the other members of the
staff. "What's going on?" . . . "How long do we have
to stay here?" . . . "Are we in danger?"

Kahlee wasn't about to tell them the whole story. It
would take too long, and they probably wouldn't believe her anyway. And if they did believe her, it might
cause panic.

"It's possible we have an abduction scenario in
progress," she continued, shouting to be heard above
everyone else. "We haven't confirmed that yet, but
we're not taking any chances."

The threat of a student being kidnapped was something everyone in the room could easily accept and
understand. Every child at the Grissom Academy was
special in some way. In addition to the biotics of the
Ascension Project, the school had a high proportion
of academic geniuses and artistic prodigies, as well as
a large number of children with parents rich and in-
fluential enough to get their offspring onto the enroll-
ment list of the best school in Alliance space.

"We have security forces clearing this wing, but
until they're done you all have to stay here where it's
safe," Kahlee continued. "You might be here all
night, so try to get comfortable."

As she spoke, Jimenez glanced over at her with a
curious look. The security captain wasn't buying the
story, not completely. She knew her people weren't
scouring the halls looking for an unauthorized intruder.

Kahlee considered pulling her aside and asking for her help in tracking down Grayson. But more armed guards in the cafeteria meant a better chance of keeping the children safe. And she was still clinging to the hope there might be some way to end this without further bloodshed. She was convinced some part of Grayson was still alive inside him; if she could get through to him, she could get him to surrender so they could try to help him. If Jimenez joined the hunt for Grayson, however, it would almost certainly end with either Jimenez's death or his.

"I have to go," Kahlee told her. "Make sure nobody leaves until I give you the all-clear."

It was obvious Jimenez wanted to say something, but she just bit her lip and nodded in acknowledgment.

"I better go with you," a voice behind her said, the manly timbre cracking on the last word.

Kahlee turned to find Nick standing there.

"I'm the strongest biotic at the school," he reminded her. "I can help you stop these kidnappers."

"I need you to stay here with Captain Jimenez," Kahlee told him. "Keeping the children safe is the most important thing."

"I'm not stupid," Nick told her. "You're just saying that so I won't feel bad you're leaving me behind."

"She's leaving me behind, too," Jimenez reminded him.

"Whatever," Nick replied, turning away from them and trudging off to disappear into the crowd.

"He has a point," Jimenez noted once he was gone.

"Whatever's going on, you shouldn't be heading out there without backup."

"I'll manage," Kahlee assured her, slipping out the cafeteria door to avoid further argument.

A second later she heard Jimenez barking out orders.

"Come on, everyone. Don't all crowd around the doors. Find somewhere to sit and we'll bring drinks around to the tables."

Satisfied the cafeteria was in good hands, Kahlee set off at a brisk jog, heading in the direction of the data archives.

The station was on an Earth-standard day/night cycle, meaning the offices that Anderson passed were all dark. The overhead illumination in the halls had been dimmed to conserve energy while most of the people on board were sleeping.

On reaching the entrance to the Ascension wing, he'd studied the map long enough to commit it to memory. Then he began to make a slow, cautious trek toward the data archives.

Time was of the essence, but he knew carelessness and impatience had killed more soldiers than any other enemy. Even though his enviro-suit was equipped with kinetic barriers, he had no intention of walking into an ambush. He hugged the walls as he went, hiding in the shadows. He poked his head around every corner, warily scanning the halls for signs of the man he was hunting.

At one point he heard the sound of distant gunfire—three quick shots from a pistol—and he froze. It was impossible to tell exactly, but the sound seemed to have come from the direction he was heading. There were no further shots, so Anderson continued his methodical progress. Whatever encounter had triggered the shots was obviously over; there was no sense recklessly charging in now and possibly getting himself killed.

After several minutes he finally reached the hall leading to the main research lab where the data archives were stored. As he peeked around the corner, he saw something lying on the floor right in front of the lab's sealed door.

He ducked back quickly on instinct, then paused while his mind processed the memory of the image. It looked like a bundle of clothes, or maybe a blanket. He couldn't imagine how it had come to be there, but it didn't seem to pose any threat.

Creeping into the hall, he approached the lab's door with his shotgun at the ready. As he drew nearer he was able to confirm it was a blanket on the floor; he could see that it was stained with blood. An image of a child getting up in the night to wander the halls and stumbling across Grayson forced its way into his consciousness, and he struggled to push it aside.

He hit the panel on the wall and the door slid open with a soft *whoosh*. Anderson wheeled into the doorway, ready to fire. But what he saw in the lab didn't prompt him to pull the trigger. Three bodies lay on the floor, each shot once between the eyes—a clear explanation for the pistol fire he'd heard earlier.

The adrenaline was pumping through his system; his senses were hyperalert, and he could hear the sound of his own breath inside his helmet. Grayson had to be close. If he wasn't in the lab, there was only one other place he could be.

With the shotgun pressed tight against his shoulder, Anderson carefully approached the door at the back of the lab. It was closed, but the green light glowing on the nearby wall panel indicated it was unlocked. He pressed himself against the wall just beside the door, took a deep breath to steel himself, then hit the panel.

Grayson was standing inside the room only a few meters away from Anderson, intently focused on the display screens of the room's lone terminal. He was so absorbed in whatever he was looking at that he didn't even seem to notice the man now standing in the doorway with a shotgun aimed directly at him.

Up close, Anderson was shocked to see how invasive the Reaper cybernetics had become. Even through his visor it was clear the thing before him could no longer be considered a fellow human being. Despite this, Kahlee probably would have given him a chance to surrender. Anderson felt no such compulsion.

All this flashed through his head in the fraction of a second that it took for him to squeeze the trigger. He aimed at his target's center of mass to inflict maximum damage. At point-blank range the projectiles mushrooming out from the shotgun's barrel maintained a tight dispersal pattern; the blast took Grayson square in the side of his torso. The impact spun him around and sent him sprawling face-first onto the floor.

Without a combat suit or kinetic barriers to protect him, the damage to Grayson's internal organs was almost sure to be instantly lethal, but Anderson wasn't taking any chances. He stepped forward as he prepared to fire again, only to be suddenly lifted off his feet and tossed back through the open door to crash against the computer terminals in the lab. He fell in a crumpled heap to the floor, stunned but not seriously injured.

It took him a second to recover from the biotic attack, enough time for Grayson to rise to his feet. His right side had been reduced to hamburger; blood was oozing from a hundred tiny holes in his torn flesh. But somehow he was still going.

From his prone position Anderson fired again, taking aim at his enemy's head. Grayson dodged out of the way by throwing himself awkwardly to the floor. Then he scrambled back to his feet, yanking a pair of pistols from his belt.

He was still quick, but he didn't have the unfathomable speed Anderson had witnessed during the ambush at the warehouse on Omega. In the time it took him to get up and draw his weapons, Anderson was able to roll into cover behind the edge of the lab's massive computer console.

Grayson fired the pistols several times, keeping Anderson pinned down. And then Anderson was rocked again by another biotic attack. This time instead of a simple push to send him reeling, his enemy created a series of microscopic, rapidly shifting mass effect fields that completely surrounded him. They flickered in and out of existence, subtly warping the very fabric of the space-time continuum. The powerful push and pull of the opposing forces tore at his flesh, causing him to scream in pain.

It felt like he was being ripped apart at the sub-atomic level. Anderson knew if he didn't get out of the shifting fields, they'd cause all the cells in his body to hemorrhage and rupture.

Ignoring the pain, he popped up from behind cover and fired off several rounds with the shotgun. Grayson fired back with the pistols as he dove for cover. The kinetic barriers in Anderson's enviro-suit shielded him from the opposing fire, allowing him to fall back into the hall.

He backpedaled quickly, putting some space between himself and the door, then dropped to one knee and took aim at the opening, waiting for the enemy to emerge once more.

Grayson could feel his heart fluttering erratically. His lungs were drowning in blood from his wounds. He knew the only things keeping him alive were the cybernetic implants and the irresistible will of the Reapers.

He thought the wounds might cause their hold on him to slip, but if anything they were holding on even tighter. Try as he might, he could find no purchase in his efforts to wrest back control of his body. It was like grasping at thin air; there was nothing left for him to seize onto.

The Reapers knew their enemy was lurking just outside the door. Another well-placed hit from the shotgun and even the synthetic elements of their avatar might begin to fail. So rather than step out into the hall, they waited, gathering their strength for one last attack.

TWENTY-FIVE

Nick couldn't get comfortable in his seat. He kept casting glances over at the cafeteria door, where Captain Jimenez stood watch.

He'd seen the gun in Miss Sanders's belt, but her fingers were all bandaged up. There was no way she'd be able to use it. What was she going to do if she ran into the kidnappers? She wasn't even biotic.

Focusing on the glass on the table in front of him, Nick briefly gathered his strength, then caused the glass to slide across the surface toward him. He caught it with his hand just as it was about to topple off the table's edge.

I could yank the guns right out of the kidnapper's hands. Send them flying back to smash against the wall. But they want me to sit here like I'm some kind of kid!

He glanced over at Yando, who was sitting beside him. The younger boy was staring at him with wide eyes.

"You're not supposed to do that," he whispered.

Nick knew he was referring to the trick with the glass. The instructors would have called it a "gratuitous display" of biotic ability, something that was frowned on in the Ascension Project. They didn't want kids to push themselves too far by experimenting on their own. But for Nick, moving a glass was easy. He'd been using biotics for years. He knew what he was capable of, even if nobody else believed in him.

"Hey, Yando," he said, getting a sudden flash of inspiration. "I need your help."

"With what?" The younger boy was suspicious. He was always worried about getting in trouble, but in the end Nick knew Yando would do whatever he told him to.

"I need you to go up to Captain Jimenez and tell her you've gotta use the bathroom."

"The bathroom's right over there," Yando said, pointing to the rear of the cafeteria.

"I know. Just tell her you gotta go, but you're scared. Tell her she has to come with you."

"She's a girl! She can't come into the boys' washroom!"

Nick gave an exasperated sigh.

"She's a security guard. She can go wherever she wants. Let me finish."

"Sorry," Yando muttered.

"Go inside the bathroom and count to ten. Then start crying and screaming like you're freaking out."

"What? No way! Everyone will make fun of me for being a baby!"

"I won't let them," Nick assured him. "You know I've got your back."

It was true; Nick had been watching out for Yando ever since he got here. But the younger boy still wasn't entirely convinced.

"Come on, buddy. I need you to do this. It's important."

"Why? What are you going to do?"

"I can't tell you," Nick said. "That way, if I get caught you won't get in trouble."

Yando thought about it, shaking his head slowly back and forth. But when he spoke, he didn't say no.

"Okay. I'll go tell her."

"Attaboy," Nick told him. "I knew I could count on you."

Nick turned in his seat to watch the action as Yando got up and crossed the cafeteria to speak with Captain Jimenez.

He was too far away to hear them talking, but he could see Yando shifting uncomfortably from foot to foot, just like he had to pee and was fighting to hold it in.

For a minute he thought Captain Jimenez was going to refuse or maybe send him with someone else. Then she took a quick glance around and took Yando's hand, leading him off to the restroom.

Careful not to move too quickly, Nick got up and made his way over to the door. Nobody paid him any attention. The younger kids were half asleep in their seats. The older ones were sitting in tight little groups, excitedly discussing the evening's strange events. The instructors and security guards were distributing food and drinks to the kids and trying to act like they knew what was going on.

He stood off to one side, trying to appear inconspicuous. And then he heard a high-pitched wailing coming from the rear of the cafeteria as Yando delivered on his promise.

As everyone turned to see what was happening, Nick opened the cafeteria door and slipped out into the hall, quietly closing the door behind him. He knew Yando wouldn't rat him out, and with so many kids to worry about he didn't think anyone would even notice he was gone.

Impressed with himself for carrying out such a brilliant plan, he realized there was one fatal flaw: now that he was free to go after Kahlee, he had no idea where she'd gone.

He hesitated, trying to figure out what to do next. Going back to the cafeteria wasn't an option, not after he'd worked so hard to get out. So he headed down the hall back toward the dorms, hoping he'd figure something out or simply get lucky and stumble across either Miss Sanders or the kidnappers.

Kai Leng had never been to the Grissom Academy. Fortunately, the school was designed to accommodate unaccompanied visits from parents of the students. The walls were marked with maps showing the general layout to help visitors unfamiliar with the station find their way around.

It was easy enough to guess that Grayson had gone to the Ascension wing, given the history of his daughter. Using the maps, Kai Leng was able to find his way there without any real difficulties.

The halls were completely deserted; not even a security patrol crossed his path. Kai Leng considered that a stroke of bad luck—if he had run into some guards he would have been able to arm himself with some kind of weapon. As it was, he had nothing to go on at the moment but his training.

When he reached the Grissom Academy's entrance, he briefly studied the map on the wall. There was no way to be certain, but his instincts told him Grayson would be heading for the large area marked *Restricted Area*.

He wound his way through the halls, but before he reached his destination he heard a young man's voice coming from behind him.

"Don't move unless you want to find yourself thrown through a wall."

Kai Leng stopped and turned to face the unexpected threat. A young teenager with dark, messy hair was standing in the hall.

"I'm a biotic," the kid warned. "I can bounce you around like a basketball!"

His words were defiant, but it was clear to see he was terrified.

Kai Leng had no doubt he could close the distance between them before his opponent could gather himself and unleash a biotic power. But violence wasn't always the best solution.

"You're one of Kahlee's students," he said.

"You know Miss Sanders?" the boy replied, a look of uncertainty coming over his face.

"I came here with her. We're working together."

The kid let out a deep breath and relaxed. "Sorry. I thought you were one of the kidnappers."

Kai Leng wasn't exactly sure what he was talking about, but it was easy enough to play along.

"If I was a kidnapper, wouldn't I have some kind of weapon on me?"

The kid shrugged. "Maybe you don't need one. You look like sort of a badass."

"This badass is on your side," he assured the young man. "I need to find Kahlee. Do you know where she went?"

The kid shook his head. "She had security take us all into the cafeteria, then she ran off. But I snuck out to help. I'm the strongest biotic in the school."

"I don't doubt it," Kai Leng said with a nod. "What's your name?"

"Nick. Nick Donahue."

"My name is Steve. Maybe you can help me."

"Sure," Nick eagerly agreed. "What do you need?"

"The maps on the wall have a section marked off as a restricted area. You know what's there?"

"If I tell you," the kid replied, "you have to take me with you."

"Deal," Kai Leng answered, knowing it couldn't hurt to have a powerful biotic around—even one as young as Nick—if he ran into Grayson. Plus, he could always use him as a hostage if he got into a tight situation.

"That's the lab and data archives," Nick explained. "You figure that's where Miss Sanders went?"

"There's a good chance. Care to show me the way?"

"Sure thing. Follow me."

Kahlee rounded the corner and stopped when she saw Anderson crouched in the middle of the hall. He was facing away from her, his shotgun pointed at the door of the lab.

She was about to call out to him when Grayson suddenly came barreling through the door. Anderson fired with the shotgun, but the bullets were repelled by a shimmering biotic barrier. Grayson thrust his fist out and a rippling biotic wave rolled down the hall.

Her brain had just enough time to register Anderson hurtling backward in her direction as if he had been fired from a cannon before the wave struck her, too. Fortunately, she was far enough away to be spared the brunt of the concussive impact; much of the energy had dissipated, and she was only knocked off her feet. But Anderson had been much closer to Grayson when the power was unleashed, and had been hurtled a good twenty meters before landing in a crumpled heap beside her.

Kahlee grunted in pain as she had to use her fingers to struggle back up. At her feet, Anderson didn't move or make a sound. Before she could check on him, however, Grayson was standing in front of her, pointing a pair of pistols in her face.

Grayson knew the Reapers were going to kill Kahlee, and there was nothing he could do about it. They had locked him inside his own body, helpless to affect the physical world.

In desperation, he tried one last time to exert his influence over the alien machines controlling him, in what he realized might quite possibly be the final act of free will before they devoured him completely. But instead of struggling for physical control, he threw all his energy into projecting a single thought: *Kahlee is too useful to kill.*

He didn't know if his gambit worked, but he suddenly felt the Reapers pawing through his mind, digging up everything he knew about Kahlee Sanders.

Not even knowing if it was possible, he tried to direct and influence their search.

She knows more about the Ascension Project than anyone else. She's studied the children for years. She's analyzed the data from every conceivable angle. She's one of the most brilliant scientific minds in the galaxy. She's worth far more alive than dead.

Instead of squeezing the trigger, the Reapers tucked one pistol into Grayson's belt. With their free hand they grabbed Kahlee by the forearm in a viselike grip, causing her to gasp in pain.

"Come with me," they said, dragging her away.

Kahlee didn't argue as Grayson seized her by the arm and led her off down the hall. He seemed to have forgotten all about Anderson, as if he had suddenly become entirely focused on her and her alone.

She had no way to know if Anderson was still alive as they left his motionless body behind and marched back up the hall, but she wasn't about to draw attention to the possibility that he might be.

Once they had rounded the corner and Anderson was out of sight, she dared to speak.

"Grayson, please—I know what's happening to you. I want to help you."

"Grayson is gone," the man pulling her along replied.

They were moving so fast he was practically carrying her, her feet scuffling along the floor in a desperate attempt to keep up and take pressure off her arm.

"Slow down! You're hurting me."

To her surprise, they did slow down. Just a fraction, but enough so that she was able to keep pace. In her mind, there was only one possible explanation: somewhere, deep inside the abomination manhandling her down the Grissom Academy halls, a tiny part of Grayson still lived.

TWENTY-SIX

David Anderson's return to consciousness was not pleasant.

It began with a sharp, stabbing pain in his left side that flared up intensely with every breath. His mind wasn't thinking clearly yet; it couldn't quite remember where he was or how he'd got here. But his soldier's training allowed him to focus on the pain and try to make a self-diagnosis.

Broken ribs. Collapsed lung.

Neither condition was fatal, but either would definitely slow him down. He rolled gingerly onto his back and tried to assess the extent of the damage by reaching up to feel around with his right hand. The simple motion nearly caused him to black out.

Fractured collarbone. Possible dislocated shoulder.

He felt like he'd been hit by a high-speed monorail.

Or one hell of a biotic push.

Everything came back to him in a flash. He didn't know how long he'd been out or why Grayson hadn't finished him off, but he was still alive. And that counted for something.

Come on, soldier. On your feet.

Trying not to twist, which would aggravate his

ribs, and careful not to jar his arm, which would set off his collarbone, he tried to get to his feet . . . only to fall back hard to the floor as the torn ligaments in his left ankle collapsed under his weight.

As he hit the ground, he was swallowed up in waves of pain so intense they made him vomit inside his helmet. The reflexive spasm of his stomach caused his broken ribs to scream out, which started a coughing fit that squeezed his collapsed lung even tighter, making it feel like he was being strangled by someone inside his chest.

Knowing that the only way to stop the chain of injuries from setting each other off like toppling dominoes was to lie still, Anderson somehow forced his body to quit writhing despite the throbbing pain in his ankle, chest, and shoulder.

He opened his lips and took several slow, shallow breaths, ignoring the foul taste of his last meal that coated his mouth. As bad as the taste was, however, the stench inside his helmet was worse.

When the excruciating pain finally subsided to a dull agony, he very slowly took his one good arm and unbuckled his helmet, letting it fall to the floor beside him. Fighting the urge to take deep, greedy gasps of the clean air, he very carefully maneuvered himself up into a sitting position.

Using the nearby wall for support, he managed to stand up, keeping all his weight on his right leg. He spotted his shotgun on the floor a few meters away.

The enviro-suit was releasing a steady trickle of medi-gel into his system. It was regulated to keep the doses small; too much of the wonder drug and he'd slip into unconsciousness. The limited doses weren't enough to heal his injuries, but did make it easier for him to cope with the pain.

With slow, careful steps, he made his way over to pick up the shotgun, wincing each time he put weight on his injured foot. He was able to hold it with his injured arm. The weight of the weapon pulling down in his grasp caused jolts of pain to shoot through his broken collarbone, but he had no other way to carry it. Not when he needed his good hand to help support his weight against the wall.

Gritting his teeth, he hobbled down the hall in the direction of the landing port, hoping to catch up to Grayson before he escaped. The collapsed lung limited him to short, shallow breaths, making his creeping pace as exhausting as an all-out sprint.

It wasn't long before the painkillers coursing through his body were going into overdrive, staving off shock and giving him a nice little buzz as well.

Stay focused, soldier. No R and R until the mission is done.

Kahlee was trying to think of a way to reach Grayson. When she'd tried to appeal to him directly, the Reapers had shut him down. But when she'd asked the Reapers to go slower, Grayson had been able to exert some kind of subtle influence over them. It almost seemed as if making the Reapers focus on something external loosened their hold on Grayson, allowing him some limited type of freedom.

"Why are you here?" Kahlee asked. "What do you want from us?"

She wasn't sure if the Reapers would even reply. All she was hoping for was that she might be able to engage the Reapers enough to give Grayson a fighting chance. A fighting chance to do what, however, she couldn't say.

"We seek salvation," Grayson said, much to her surprise. "Ours and yours."

"Salvation? Is that what the Collectors were doing? Saving those human colonists? Is that what you did to Grayson?"

"He has been repurposed. He has evolved into something greater than a random assortment of cells and organic refuse."

"That randomness is what made him unique," Kahlee countered. "It made him special."

She noticed that their pace had become more measured and deliberate. If Grayson was still inside there, if he had any influence at all, he was using it to slow the Reapers down. He was trying to buy her time to escape. The best thing she could do was try to keep them talking.

"Why can't you just leave us alone? Why can't you just let us live our lives in peace?"

"We are the keepers of the cycle. The creators and the destroyers. Your existence is a flicker, a spark. We can extinguish it—or we can preserve it. Submit to us and we can make you immortal."

"I don't want to be immortal," she said. "I just want to be me."

They were barely moving at all now. Grayson had managed to bring their hurried escape from the Academy down to a crawl.

"Organic life lives, dies, and is forgotten. You cannot fully comprehend anything beyond this. Yet there is a realm of existence beyond your understanding."

There was something odd about the things Grayson was saying. She knew he was speaking on behalf of the Reapers, but it seemed like he—or they—actually wanted her to understand their position. It was like they were trying to persuade her to agree with them, but they didn't know how to frame their arguments in a way she could relate to. Or maybe there simply was no way for organic beings to relate to hyperintelligent machines.

"We are the pinnacle of evolution," they continued. "Yet we see potential in your species. You can be elevated. The weakness of organic flesh can be cast aside. You can transcend yourselves."

The words didn't really make any kind of compelling argument, but she felt as if there was some deeper meaning to them.

"Your understanding is limited by genetics. You cannot see beyond the brief instant of your own existence. Yet our knowledge is infinite, as are we."

The more Grayson spoke, the more his words seemed to make sense on a deep, almost subconscious level.

"The laws of this universe are inviolate. Immutable. Your resistance will only lead to your extinction. What are—what we do—is inevitable."

Kahlee was so far under the Reapers's spell, she wasn't even aware she was nodding along in agreement.

Kai Leng heard the voices coming from down the hall. They were faint, still too distant to decipher what was being said, but he recognized the tone of Grayson's voice.

He reached out and put a hand on Nick's shoulder, signaling him to stop. The boy hadn't noticed the voices, and he turned and looked back up at Kai Leng with an inquiring stare. To his credit, he knew enough to keep quiet.

The assassin continued to listen, focusing on the distant voices until he was certain they were drawing closer. Then he pointed in the direction of a nearby dark office with an open door. The two went inside, and Kai Leng promptly closed the door and flicked on the light.

In a careful whisper he said, "I heard something down the hall. The kidnappers are coming this way."

"What are we going to do?" Nick asked, his adolescent voice cracking with a mixture of fear and excitement.

"I think they're heading back to the docking bays. They're going to go right past us."

Nick nodded to show he was following along so far.

"I don't have a weapon, but you do," Kai Leng continued. "If we wait here for them to pass by, will that let you build up enough energy to hit them with a blast powerful enough to take them out?"

"You mean kill them?" Nick asked in wonder.

"These are dangerous men," Kai Leng warned him. "If we don't kill them, they'll kill us."

"I've . . . I've never killed anybody before."

Kai Leng nodded sympathetically. "That's okay. I understand. It's a lot to ask from someone your age. Maybe we should just hide and let them go by."

"No," Nick answered hastily. "I don't want to hide. I can do this."

"Are you sure you're up to it? It's not going to be easy."

"I can do it," Nick swore.

"Good. Here's the plan. We wait in here with the door closed and the lights off until they pass by. Then I hit the panel and you jump out into the hall and hit them with everything you've got before they can turn around."

"Isn't that like stabbing them in the back or something?"

"This isn't a game, Nick. There's no such thing as playing fair."

"Yeah. Okay. Right."

"I'm going to turn out the light now. You ready for this?"

Nick nodded, and Kai Leng cast the room into darkness. At first it seemed there was no light at all, but after a few seconds their eyes began to pick up on the subtle illuminations from various sources around the room: the blinking message light on the office's extranet terminal; illuminated power buttons on the computer console and video display screen; the ghostly green glow of the wall panel that indicated the door was unlocked. It wasn't much, but it gave them just enough light to make out their own silhouettes in the gloom.

Kai Leng pressed his ear to the door and listened carefully. He could hear Grayson speaking; occasionally Kahlee's voice would interject. He wouldn't tell Nick about Kahlee—it might make him reluctant to launch his attack, and Kai Leng was more than willing to sacrifice her if it meant they had a chance to eliminate Grayson.

He looked over at Nick, and was surprised to see a tiny spark run the length of the young man's neck. As he watched the teenager gather his power, the sparks became more plentiful as his body began to discharge the dark energy in tiny bursts.

It took them a long time to finally reach the door; they were moving far slower than Kai Leng would have imagined. Once they were past, he waited a few more seconds to let them get a few meters down the hall, then he hit the panel and jumped back out of the way.

Nick sprang into action, rushing out into the hall with a shrill scream of youthful rage.

The buildup of stored biotic charge was causing Nick actual physical discomfort. His teeth felt like they were chewing on tinfoil, his eyes itched, and he could hear a high-pitched hum in his ears. But it was worth it if it meant he had a chance to help stop the kidnappers and impress Miss Sanders.

When the door to the office opened, he charged through, unleashing all his pent-up energy against his enemies. Too late he realized that Kahlee was one of the two people he was about to crush with the most powerful biotic display of his young life.

The barely contained power was already pouring out of him in an uncontrollable flood, and he didn't have the mental discipline or control to simply shut it off. The best he could manage was to try to refocus it. Instead of a concentrated beam of deadly force, he pushed out with his mind, distorting it into a swooping wave so the impact would be dispersed across a much wider area.

His yell had caused both Kahlee and the man beside her to turn in his direction. He saw their faces clearly, their eyes going wide in surprise as they were lifted from their feet and thrown sideways against opposite walls before falling hard to the floor.

"Hit them again!" the tattooed man who called himself Steve shouted from inside the office door. "Finish them!"

Confused and overwhelmed, Nick could only stand there, staring in horror at the bizarre-looking half-man/half-machine rising to its feet and turning toward him.

Nick's scream had given Kahlee just enough time to realize what was happening and brace herself for the impact. Nevertheless, the biotic wave hit her so hard, the pistol in her belt was jarred loose and sent skittering across the floor.

Fortunately, she hit the wall with her shoulder rather than her head, and she managed to keep her senses about her. She didn't know how Nick had found them; she knew only that by attacking Grayson he had marked himself as a threat in the Reapers's eyes.

Reacting rather than thinking, she got off the floor and threw herself across the hall toward Grayson, slamming into him as he raised his pistol and fired at his young assailant. She was able to knock him off balance, but as the pair tumbled to the ground, she heard the explosion of the gun and the sharp grunt of surprise from Nick.

Grayson sprang to his feet and grasped the back of her belt with his free hand. He hauled her up by the belt, holding her suspended horizontally like a sack of flour before heaving her aside.

The throw sent her helicoptering through the air, her arms and legs flailing wildly. Caught off guard by the sudden move, she didn't have time to brace herself for impact this time, and slammed face-first into the floor.

The blow left her seeing stars. Dazed and stunned, she couldn't even roll over to see what was happening behind her.

From inside the office Kai Leng saw Nick get shot, the bullet catching him in the stomach. As the young man gasped in pain and fell to his knees, Kai Leng was already in motion.

He'd seen the pistol fall from Kahlee's belt; he knew he had to get to it if he had any hope of surviving the confrontation. Grayson tossed Sanders aside, his distraction buying Kai Leng a few precious fractions of a second. He slid across the floor and wrapped his hand around the pistol, rolling over onto his back so he could fire at Grayson.

But the Reapers were too quick. In the time it had taken him to secure the weapon, they'd crossed the hall to where he was lying on the floor. Grayson's foot kicked the gun from his hand, striking with such force it shattered Kai Leng's wrist.

The assassin knew it was over. He stared up at the monster looming over him, prepared to meet his end. He flinched at the thunderous echo of a shotgun, his mind taking a second to realize he had not been shot.

Grayson staggered away from him, revealing the source of the blast. Anderson stood halfway down the hall, the stock of his weapon wedged firmly into his stomach as he held it with one hand. His right arm hung limp and useless at his side.

He fired a second time, and Grayson's body shuddered and collapsed to the floor.

As Grayson lay on his back, staring up at the ceiling and gasping for air, he felt the Reapers abandoning his body. Their vessel broken, they directed their consciousness back into the void of dark space, leaving Grayson alone as the last sparks of life flickered away.

Finally free of their control, he turned his head as the world began to grow dim. He saw Kahlee gamely hauling herself back to her feet, and he smiled.

His head lolled back to its original position, leaving him staring up at the ceiling once again. The head and shoulders of a dark-haired man of Asian descent appeared in his field of view; it took Grayson a moment to recognize him as the one who had attacked him in the Cerberus holding cell.

Life seemed to slow down, and he heard the familiar *pop-pop* of a pistol, the standard double-tap taught to all Cerberus assassins. As the pair of bullets entered his skull, everything went dark for the last time.

TWENTY-SEVEN

To aim the shotgun, Anderson had to brace the butt against his stomach. When he fired, he had to hold his breath and keep his abs tight to try and absorb the kickback so he wouldn't pass out from the pain. Despite these precautions, it took him a few moments to recover each time he pulled the trigger.

He managed to score a hit on Grayson with his first attempt; fortunately, with shotguns it wasn't necessary to be particularly accurate at short range. Grayson was staggered by the first shot, but didn't go down. Between this blast and the one Anderson had delivered when he caught him in the data archives, however, he had sustained such grievous injuries that it was all the Reapers could do to keep him on his feet.

That gave Anderson time to gather himself and fire again, finally dropping Grayson to the floor. In the time it took Anderson to recover from the kickback of the second blast, Kai Leng had scooped up a pistol from the ground and finished Grayson off with two point-blank shots to the head.

Before the assassin could turn his attention toward

another target, Anderson said, "Drop the gun and don't move!"

He didn't shout or yell; despite his being dosed with medi-gel, his collapsed lung and broken ribs were too painful for him to take a deep breath. But he knew that Kai Leng had heard him clearly.

The assassin stood frozen, his weapon still pointed at Grayson's corpse on the floor. Anderson knew what was running through his mind. Could he bring his pistol up and get off a shot before Anderson could squeeze the shotgun's trigger? He was quick, but was he quick enough?

"Don't do it," Anderson warned. "I've got you dead in my sights. At this range even *I* can't miss."

To his relief, Kai Leng let the gun slip from his hands.

Anderson had seen the unconscious teenager lying on the floor bleeding from his gut when he'd arrived on the scene, and in his peripheral vision he could see Kahlee trying to shake off the cobwebs and regain her senses after being thrown by the Reapers. But he couldn't offer help to either one. Not yet. Kai Leng was too dangerous to take any chances with; until he was neutralized Anderson had to push everything else aside and focus on this true threat.

"I want you to take it slow and easy," Anderson told him. "Gently—very gently—use your foot to slide that pistol over to me."

He kept his trigger finger ready as Kai Leng complied, ready to fire at any sudden movement; God help the man if Anderson sneezed. The gun skittered across the floor and stopped a few inches from Anderson's feet.

"Now put your hands behind your head, turn around to face the wall, and get down on your knees."

The assassin complied, and Anderson finally felt like he had the situation under control. From that position even Kai Leng wouldn't be able to react fast enough to avoid a shotgun at point-blank range.

"What do we do now?" the assassin asked.

"All this gunfire is sure to attract someone's attention. I figure the security patrols will be showing up in a couple of minutes. We'll just wait for them to arrive."

He glanced over at Kahlee and saw she was on her feet, bracing herself against the wall and trying to get her bearings. She glanced down at Grayson's body lying just across from her, and then her eyes fell on the boy farther up the hall.

"Nick!" she shouted, racing over to him and crouching down to inspect his wounds.

Anderson kept his shotgun trained on Kai Leng, wary in case he used the distraction to try to escape. He didn't move, but he did speak.

"I could have killed you, you know," Kai Leng said, keeping his eyes fixed firmly on the wall. "But I didn't. I have no reason to harm you."

"David," Kahlee said, looking up from the body of the unconscious boy. "He's losing too much blood. I need a med-kit."

"All I wanted was to stop Grayson," Kai Leng continued on as if he hadn't heard her. "My job is done. Just let me go."

"You're not going anywhere," Anderson snapped

at him. "This is all your fault. Grayson. This kid. Their blood is on your hands!"

"David!" Kahlee barked out. "I can still save him. But I need that med-kit!"

"Go," Anderson told her, not taking his eyes off Kai Leng. "I don't know where they are. Grab one and bring it back."

"We need to keep pressure on the wound," Kahlee protested. "He'll bleed out before I get back."

"I can't take my eyes off this guy," Anderson told her with a shake of his head. "We'll just have to wait for security to show up. Shouldn't be long now."

"There isn't time," Kahlee insisted.

"You," Anderson said to Kai Leng, coming to a decision. "On your feet. Nice and slow. Come over and put pressure on this kid's wound. Hold it until Kahlee gets back."

"No," Kai Leng replied without moving, his voice completely devoid of emotion.

"No?" Anderson repeated incredulously.

"You have a choice," the assassin calmly told him. "You stanch the flow of blood while Kahlee retrieves the med-kit, and I disappear. Or you keep that gun pointed at me until security shows up and we all watch as the boy dies."

"You son of a bitch!" Kahlee screamed. "He's just a boy!"

"It's Anderson's choice," Kai Leng told them. "All he has to do is let me go."

Kai Leng was still facing the wall. Anderson took the opportunity to set the shotgun down and gingerly pick up the pistol. Moving carefully, never taking his eyes off Kai Leng, he made his way over to where

Kahlee was sitting beside Nick. She had her injured hands stuffed up inside the wound in the boy's stomach, her arms trembling from exertion as she pressed with all her might.

"I've only got one hand," Anderson warned her.

"You've got more good fingers than I do," Kahlee reminded him. "Reach inside and press as hard as you can."

"I assume this means I'm free to go," Kai Leng said confidently.

He was still facing the wall, but he became bold enough to get to his feet. Anderson took careful aim with the pistol and fired. The bullet lodged itself in the thick muscles at the back of the assassin's right thigh, causing him to cry out and drop back down to the floor.

Writhing on the ground, he reached his hands down to awkwardly try to clutch at the wound. Anderson fired the trigger again, this time catching him in the calf of his other leg.

Kai Leng roared in pain and anger, then rolled onto his stomach and looked up at Anderson with death in his eyes.

"Security's on its way," Anderson noted. "If you want to get out of here you better hurry."

Kai Leng flashed him a hateful grin, then turned and started crawling on his belly in the opposite direction in a desperate attempt to escape before reinforcements arrived.

Finally able to turn his full attention to Kahlee and her patient, Anderson let the pistol fall to the floor.

"Show me what to do," he said.

"Reach into the wound and follow along my fingers," Kahlee told him.

Anderson followed her instructions, carefully pressing his hand up and into the warm, sticky hole in Nick's abdomen.

"Feel that tube my fingers are pressing against?"

"Yeah. I think so."

"When I pull my hands out, you press down on it as hard as you can. Whatever you do, don't let go."

"Got it."

"On three. Ready? One . . . two . . . three!"

Kahlee slipped her hands out of the way, and blood began to seep from the wound as Anderson fumbled to get his own hand in position to clamp down on the bleeding.

"He's still bleeding!" Anderson said, his voice frantic.

"Press harder!" Kahlee shouted. "As hard as you can!"

Anderson leaned the entire weight of his body into it, and the oozing blood slowed to one thin trickle.

"Good," Kahlee said, standing up and patting him on the shoulder. "Can you hold it?"

"For a bit," he answered. "But hurry."

She didn't need to be told twice. He heard her footsteps disappearing down the hall, and then he was alone with Grayson's corpse and the dying boy.

Nick's breathing had become rapid and shallow. His skin was so pale it looked like he'd been rolled in chalk, and beads of sweat covered his forehead.

"Don't die on her, kid," he whispered. "She's lost too much today already."

Kahlee was back inside of two minutes.

"How is he?" she asked as she set the med-kit on the floor beside him.

"Still with us," Anderson replied.

She pulled out a hypodermic, grasping it clumsily in her palm because of her injured fingers, and injected it right through Nick's pants and into his thigh.

Unlike the small amounts of medi-gel Anderson had been receiving from his suit, a concentrated dose could have immediate, almost miraculous, effects. The clotting agents would stop the bleeding and the biologocial nanides would begin to repair damaged tissue and cells. At the same time, the powerful sedative properties would send the patient into a state of virtual hibernation, the medically induced coma maintaining vital systems and preserving internal organs. Surgery would still be required for serious wounds, but except in the most extreme cases medi-gel could stabilize patients long enough to get them proper medical attention.

Within seconds Nick's color returned and his breathing became slow and regular.

Kahlee leaned in and scanned his vitals with the omni-tool from the med-kit, clasping it awkwardly with both hands.

"It's working," she said. "You can let go."

Anderson carefully slid his hand from the wound and rolled gingerly out of the way, giving Kahlee room to work.

From the med-kit she retrieved bandages and a thick tube of ointment. Unlike the liquid medi-gel she'd injected into Nick, this batch had been processed into a thick, gooey salve. She struggled to open the cap, her splinted fingers unable to find any purchase.

"Hold the tube," Anderson said, reaching over with his one good hand to grasp the cap.

He twisted and the cap came loose. Kahlee spread the salve directly on and into the wound, then covered everything with a bandage. Using the omni-tool, she scanned him one final time, just to make sure nothing had been missed.

"I think he's going to be okay," she announced, wiping the back of her hand across her sweat-drenched brow.

"We make a good team," Anderson remarked. "Maybe we should open a med-clinic."

"You are looking for a job," she reminded him. "It's either that or—"

Anderson held up his hand, cutting her off mid-sentence. "Hear that?"

She tilted her head to the side. "Footsteps!"

Kahlee scrambled to her feet and began to yell at the top of her voice. "Over here! By the admin offices!"

Soon four security guards—two men and two women—came around the corner.

"We heard gunfire, so I figured we better send some reinforcements," the woman in charge said. "I left the others to keep an eye on the children."

She glanced down at the bloody carnage and Grayson's mutated corpse, and her face became grim. When she saw Nick, her expression changed to one of shock.

"I'm sorry," she blurted out to Kahlee. "I don't

know how he got out of the cafeteria. I didn't even notice he was gone!"

Kahlee shook her head. "It's not your fault, Captain. And he's going to be okay . . . though we should still get him to the hospital."

The security chief nodded at one of the men in her detail, and he carefully picked Nick up off the floor.

"Hate to be the one to interrupt," Anderson chimed in from where he was still sitting on the floor. "But maybe the rest of you should go after Kai Leng."

"Right," Kahlee agreed. "Asian male. Tattoo on the back of his neck. Not armed, but still dangerous."

"Wounded in both legs," Anderson added, pointing at the trail of blood drops leading off down the hall. "Shouldn't be hard to find."

While the guard carrying Nick set off at an easy pace so he wouldn't unnecessarily jar the young man, the other guards sprinted off at a full run, leaving Kahlee and Anderson alone.

Kahlee crouched down beside him. "You look like you're in pretty rough shape," she said, holding up the omni-tool. "Better let me check you out, too."

"In a minute," Anderson told her. "After you say your goodbye."

She glanced over at Grayson, then let her eyes fall to the floor. She got up, went slowly over to the body, and knelt down beside it.

Anderson turned away, giving her some privacy. He could hear her whispering, but he made no effort to listen in on what she was saying. When he heard the faint sound of Kahlee's sobs, he couldn't help but glance back to see if she was okay.

She was clasping Grayson's hand in her lap, a few tears trickling down her cheeks. She brought his hand up to her lips and gave it a single soft kiss before letting it slide gently back to the floor. Then she wiped her eyes, took a deep breath, and got back on her feet.

Anderson didn't comment as she sat down beside him. He wondered what she had whispered, but he had no right to ask. The moment hadn't been his; it was between her and Grayson.

"Let's see if we can get you patched up," Kahlee said, holding up the omni-tool and giving him a tired smile.

TWENTY-EIGHT

A number of things flashed through Kai Leng's mind after Anderson rendered both of his legs effectively useless.

He knew right away the wounds weren't life-threatening. Both shots had struck muscle; no major arteries had been hit. His legs were bleeding, but not profusely—it would take at least twenty minutes before he lost enough blood to put his life in danger.

Knowing he wasn't going to die, Kai Leng's first instinct was to get even. As he crawled along the floor, he glanced back and saw Anderson and Kahlee focusing on the injured boy. Kai Leng figured he had a better than even chance at getting to Grayson's body—and the pistol beside it—before they noticed him.

But once he had the pistol, what could he do with it? Anderson had chosen not to execute Kai Leng; he had too much of the noble hero in him to kill a helpless opponent. But if Kai Leng got his hands on a weapon and started shooting, he was pretty sure Anderson wouldn't hesitate to finish him off.

Normally Kai Leng would have taken his chances anyway. But Anderson was wearing an enviro-suit equipped with kinetic barriers. He'd survive the first few shots, giving him a chance to grab either the pistol or shotgun and start firing back. Given Kai Leng's current state, it didn't seem like a battle he could win.

He could use the pistol to kill Sanders, but that wouldn't accomplish anything except pushing Anderson into enough of a rage to kill him. He could use the pistol to threaten Sanders, putting them all into a hostage situation, but that would only give the security guards more time to arrive. Against such overwhelming odds, there could be only one realistic outcome.

Kai Leng realized he wasn't ready to die just yet, so he decided to ignore the pistol and focus on escape. He continued to crawl on his belly until he disappeared around the corner, moving at a snail's pace. It wasn't the pain that slowed him down; mentally, he was strong enough to ignore it. But Anderson was a crafty old bastard—he'd placed his shots carefully, knowing the damage to the muscle tissue would make it impossible for Kai Leng's legs to bear any weight at all.

The smooth floor of the Academy's halls offered little purchase for his hands and fingers; escape would be impossible if he had to drag himself along like a slug. But the Academy was a space station—gravitational fields inside the halls were maintained by the facility's mass effect field generators. In the event of an emergency, it was possible the artificial gravity could fail.

On his way in, Kai Leng had noticed a series of metal rungs running the entire length of the ceiling. Their purpose was to allow people to move around should the environment suddenly become weightless. He'd also noticed a small maintenance ladder built into the wall farther up the hall to provide access to an overhead electrical duct. If he remembered correctly, the ladder was on the same side of the corridor as the rungs in the ceiling.

The ladder was less than fifty meters away. Moving as fast as he could, it still took Kai Leng well over a minute to reach it. Then he grabbed the first step and hauled himself up the ladder one rung at a time, his injured legs dragging behind him.

When he reached the ceiling, he wrapped his left arm around the ladder's topmost rung and reached out to grasp the handhold in the ceiling with his right hand. But he couldn't quite reach; his fingertips just brushed against the rough, rounded metal.

Refusing to be defeated when possible salvation was only inches away, he lunged toward the handhold, simultaneously pushing off from the ladder with his other arm. His fingers locked around the rung, leaving him dangling by one hand from the ceiling.

He rocked his body back and forth several times to build momentum, then pulled himself up as he swung forward so that he was able to grab the next hold with his left hand. At the same time he let go of the rung in his right and swung his arm forward to grab the next hold in the line. Keeping the rhythm going, he was able to go from rung to rung, his legs dangling below him as he propelled himself along like one of his simian ancestors swinging through the branches of Earth's long-forgotten jungles.

It didn't take long for his arms and shoulders to

start aching from the strain of supporting the entire weight of his body, but as with the pain from the bullet wounds he simply blocked the sensation out. By the time he reached the security clearance room outside the docking bay, his arms were trembling with fatigue, and his grip finally faltered.

As his fingers slid off the rung, he barely had time to brace himself before his body fell back down to the floor with a heavy thud. The impact sent a fresh wave of pain through his wounded legs. He saw stars, and for several seconds he had to fight to keep from blacking out.

It took him close to a minute before he had recovered enough to press on. His heart was pounding and he was gasping for air, but salvation was in sight. There was no way he could get back up to the rungs in the ceiling; even if he could, his exhausted shoulders and arms would probably refuse to support his weight. With no other options available, he once again began to crawl toward the passage that would take him to the docking ramp.

He passed by the bodies of the two dead guards, inching his way along. He was halfway up the docking ramp—less than ten meters from the shuttle's airlock—when he heard voices coming from the hall behind him.

"Got another spot of blood here!" someone shouted. "Looks like he's headed out to the shuttles!"

Kai Leng redoubled his efforts, crawling across the hard metal floor of the docking ramp as fast as he could. Behind him he heard the heavy clunk of boots coming for him.

He reached the shuttle's airlock just as the first two security guards stepped onto the docking ramp.

"Freeze!" one of them shouted.

Ignoring the order, Kai Leng rolled through the airlock's door and lunged up to slam his palm against the button halfway up the wall.

Kai Leng wrapped himself into a ball, covering his head with his hands as the guards opened fire. A few stray rounds snuck into the airlock and ricocheted around before the heavy panel slammed shut, but none made contact with their target.

Kai Leng knew he didn't have much time. The guards' guns wouldn't be able to penetrate the hull, and the airlock door was locked. But they could still try to hack it open and get on board before he could take off.

He crawled through the shuttle and up to the forward cabin. Hauling himself into the chair, he punched the controls and fired up the engines.

Fortunately, the Academy had been designed with an exterior docking bay—far less expensive to maintain than a fully enclosed landing port. That meant there were no doors or ceiling that could be closed to prevent his escape.

A few seconds later the vessel lifted off and pulled away from the station. Kai Leng punched in a course for the nearest mass relay, but he knew he was already free and clear, so he didn't accelerate to FTL speed yet.

Instead, he slid down from the chair and crawled back to the rear of the cabin, where the first-aid kit was still lying on the floor. Anderson had raided it for the rope to tie him up, but there were still basic medical supplies.

He found a tube of medi-gel and smeared it onto his wounds to dull the pain and prevent infection, careful not to overdose and black out. Then he crawled back to the front, hauled himself up into the pilot's seat, and opened a comm channel.

The display flickered, and then the face of the Illusive Man came into focus.

"Is it over?" he asked.

"Grayson is dead," Kai Leng assured him. "But I couldn't recover the body."

"It's still on Omega?" the Illusive Man wanted to know.

"No. The Grissom Academy."

The Illusive Man's face showed no reaction to the unexpected news.

"What about Sanders and Anderson?"

"Also at the Academy. Both still alive."

"I think you'd better come deliver your mission report in person," he said.

Just as Kai Leng was wondering if he would leave that meeting alive, the Illusive Man said, "I knew I could count on you to complete this mission.

"You're a valuable asset to the organization," he added, almost as if he had read Kai Leng's thoughts. "Cerberus is lucky to have you."

"It's my honor to serve the cause," Kai Leng replied.

"The station has been moved," the Illusive Man told him. "I'm sending the coordinates."

The comm channel beeped to confirm the receipt of

the incoming data. Then the view screen went dark as the Illusive Man killed the connection.

Kai Leng leaned back in his chair and let out a long breath he hadn't even realized he'd been holding.

He had the autopilot plot a course for the station and fired up the drive core, sending the ship into FTL. Glancing at the flight plan, he saw he had close to an hour before he'd have to manually coordinate the first mass relay jump of the trip.

"Lights off," he said, closing his eyes as the shuttle's illumination dimmed. "Wake in forty minutes."

For the first time since this whole thing had begun, his body was able to truly relax, slipping easily into a deep and dreamless sleep.

Three days had passed since Kai Leng had escaped the station. Anderson's injuries had been tended to; his ribs were still a little tender and it would be another week or so before the ligaments in his knee were completely mended. Still, he was well enough to return to the Citadel. But first he needed to speak to Kahlee.

He found her where he'd expected: sitting beside Nick's hospital bed to keep him company as he recovered from his wounds. Over the past three days her time had been split between this room, Anderson's room, and twice-daily physio sessions to help her regain full use of her fingers.

"How you doing, champ?" Anderson asked as he entered the room.

"Fine" was all Nick said.

He didn't talk much when Anderson was in the

room. That was to be expected. It was obvious he had a crush on Kahlee. When it was just the two of them, all her attention was focused on the boy.

"You're looking well," Kahlee said, flashing Anderson a warm smile.

From the corner of his eye he caught a momentary scowl cross Nick's face, and he had to fight to keep from laughing at the young man's reaction.

Get over it, kid, he thought. *Go find someone your own age.*

"How are the digits?" Anderson asked.

"Good as new," Kahlee said, holding her fingers up and twiddling them in the air. "I can start taking piano lessons tomorrow, if I want."

"I've got another proposal you might want to consider."

She raised a curious eyebrow. "What are you talking about?"

"Can we talk in private?"

"Back in a minute, Nick," Kahlee said, patting the young man's hand as she got up.

"Whatever," he grumbled, though she didn't seem to notice his suddenly surly attitude.

Anderson led her out into the hall, then into a nearby patient room that was currently empty.

"Shut the door," he said once Kahlee was inside.

"Sounds serious," she said, complying.

"I checked with some old friends inside Alliance Intel," he told her. "No sign of Kai Leng or Cerberus."

"Like cockroaches when the lights come on," Kahlee noted. "You think they'll come after us?"

"I doubt it. There's nothing for them to gain. Besides, we're too high-profile. Cockroaches like to stay in the dark corners."

"So what are your plans now?" she asked.

"I'm heading back to the Citadel in a few hours," he told her. "I need to take Grayson's body with me."

"Do you think this will finally convince the Council the Reapers are real?"

"You saw the research. You tell me."

"Doubtful," she admitted. "The technology inside him may have been based on Reaper designs, but it's got Cerberus's fingerprints all over it. And there's no way to know who or what was controlling him. Not anymore. They'll probably just put all the blame on the Illusive Man."

"I may not be able to get the Council to listen to me, but there are people I can turn to . . . both in and outside the Alliance. We can't ignore this anymore; something has to be done to try and stop the Reapers."

"You want my permission to study him," she said softly as the realization of what he was asking dawned on her. "You want to conduct autopsies. Take him apart and see what you can learn about their technology."

"This isn't the same as what Cerberus was doing," he insisted. "I don't condone what they did to him in any way. But they were right about one thing: the Reapers are coming, and we have to find a way to fight them.

"I promise he'll be treated with respect and dignity," he assured her. "But there are things we have to know."

"I understand," she said softly.

"There's more," Anderson continued. "I want you to come with me. You're the most brilliant scientist in Alliance space. If we have any hope of figuring this out, we need you."

He paused to give weight to his words before continuing. "*I* need you."

"You're asking me to leave the Ascension Project?"

"I know you love these kids. And you're doing good work here. But nothing is more important than this."

She mulled it over in silence for a few moments, then nodded her acceptance.

"It's what Grayson would have wanted."

"It has to be what you want, too," Anderson insisted. "Don't do this out of guilt."

"It's not guilt," she said. "I spoke to them through Grayson. The Reapers, I mean. They kept talking about a cycle. They said our extinction was inevitable. I'm not going to sit on the sidelines and let that happen."

"I'm glad," he said, reaching out to take her wrist, then pulling her close. "I didn't want to lose you again."

He held her head in his hands, then leaned in and gave her a long, deep kiss on the lips.

"Better not let Nick catch you doing that," Kahlee said with a soft laugh when he was done. "He'll bounce you off every wall in the station."

EPILOGUE

The Illusive Man sat in his chair, staring out the window at the brilliant blue sun the station was orbiting. It was a suitably stunning, and perfectly nondescript, background for the call he was expecting.

Occasionally he would take a sip from the whiskey rocks in his right hand, or pull a long, slow drag on the cigarette in his left. He was thinking about everything Kai Leng had told him, and what the implications were both for humanity and for Cerberus.

He knew enough about Admiral David Anderson to know he wasn't going to ignore this. Finally someone other than Cerberus was going to start doing something about the Reapers. That didn't mean the Illusive Man was simply going to step aside, however.

Working with Anderson probably wasn't an option. Not in the immediate future, anyway, though he wasn't willing to rule it out entirely. But for the time being he needed to make sure his own work continued, even as he tried to rebuild his fallen empire.

And that meant smoothing things over with Aria T'Loak. He couldn't afford a war with her, and she had something he needed.

He had just finished his cigarette and started another when he heard the soft *beep* indicating an incoming message. He spun his chair to face the holopad.

"Accept call," he said.

A flickering, three-dimensional image of Omega's Pirate Queen materialized in the center of the room. She was alone, seated in the same room she had called him from the last time they had spoken.

"I'm not very happy with Cerberus right now," she declared, skipping the formalities and getting right down to business. "You didn't warn me what Grayson had become."

"It wouldn't have been a problem if you hadn't tried to take him alive," the Illusive Man countered. "You're the one who reneged on the deal."

"I've heard Cerberus has suffered some rather serious setbacks of late," she said, changing topics in a blatant effort to rattle him.

"The stories of our demise are greatly exaggerated," he assured her, borrowing a quote from one of his favorite literary figures.

"I lost a lot of good people because of you," Aria told him. "I don't forget something like that."

"A war doesn't help either one of us," he countered. "I thought you were smart enough to know that."

"Is that why you called me? To sue for peace?"

"I have a business deal."

She laughed.

"What makes you think I'll say yes after the way the last one turned out?"

"This one won't cost you anything. No risk. Only reward. It's a deal you can't pass up."

"I'm listening."

"I want the research files from the station where you attacked the turians."

"That was your lab originally, wasn't it? You used me to get revenge on them."

"I think we used each other. What about those files?"

"Why should I turn them over to you? Maybe I'll just keep them for myself."

"So keep the originals for yourself. Just send me a copy."

"Were these experiments really what I think they were?" she asked.

"I don't know what you think they were," the Illusive Man replied evasively.

"What's your offer?"

"Send me the files and I'll give you three million. One up front, two on final delivery."

"Three million, and I can keep the originals?"

"All I want is the data," he assured her. "But I'll know if you hold anything back. If you want to get paid, you send everything."

"You really believe in this, don't you," she said. "The Reapers. Galactic extinction. You don't think it's some crazy story."

"Let's just say I'm not willing to take that chance."

"I'll send you the files," Aria agreed. "You'll have them by tomorrow."

"I'll put the down payment into your account tonight. Same as last time?"

"The same," she said with a coy smile. "Unlike you, I don't care if people know what I'm up to."

Before he could reply, she disconnected the call. He

laughed in spite of himself, amused at how important to her it was to get the last word.

He spun his chair to face the viewing port and pulled out a cigarette. He'd half-finished it when one of his assistants arrived to slip a glass into his hand before quickly removing herself from the room.

As he sipped his drink and smoked his cigarette, the Illusive Man's gaze shifted from the glowing blue star to the cold black curtain behind it. One thought kept running through his head, over and over.

The Reapers are out there somewhere. And they're coming.

By Kathryn Casey

Non-Fiction
DELIVER US
DEADLY LITTLE SECRETS
SHATTERED
EVIL BESIDE HER
A DESCENT INTO HELL
DIE, MY LOVE
SHE WANTED IT ALL
A WARRANT TO KILL

Fiction
SINGULARITY
BLOOD LINES
THE KILLING STORM

KATHRYN CASEY

DELIVER US

THREE DECADES OF MURDER AND REDEMPTION IN THE INFAMOUS I–45/TEXAS KILLING FIELDS

HARPER

An Imprint of HarperCollinsPublishers

DELIVER US is a journalistic account of the murders of young women around the I–45 corridor that runs south from Houston into Galveston between 1970 and 2000. The events recounted in this book are true. The personalities, events, actions, and conversations in this book have been constructed using court documents, including trial transcripts, extensive interviews, letters, personal papers, research, and press accounts. Quoted testimony has been taken from court transcripts and other sworn statements.

HARPER

An Imprint of HarperCollins*Publishers*
195 Broadway
New York, New York 10007

Copyright © 2015 by Kathryn Casey
Map by forensic artist Suzanne Lowe Birdwell (www.dovelyart.com)
ISBN 978-0-06-230049-2

First Harper mass market printing: February 2015

HarperCollins ® and Harper ® are registered trademarks of Harper-Collins Publishers.

Printed in the United States of America

Visit Harper paperbacks on the World Wide Web at
www.harpercollins.com

10 9 8 7 6 5 4 3 2 1

*This book is dedicated
to all the lost boys and girls.*

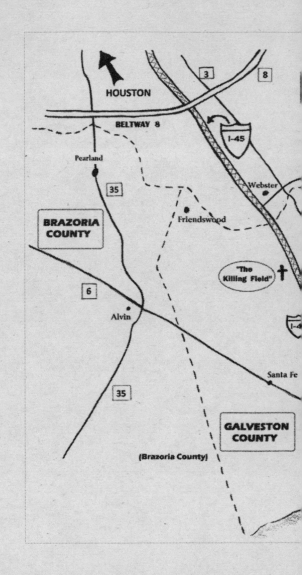

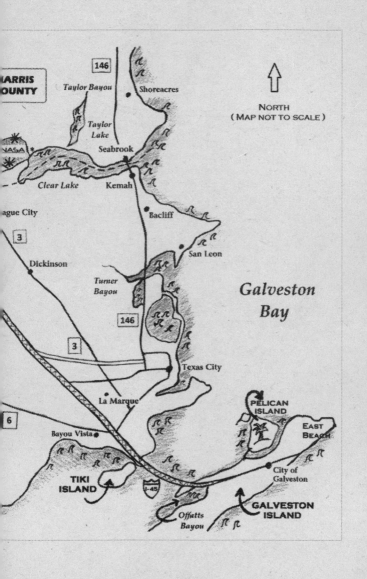

Contents

DELIVER US

Prologue

It's only natural to want to believe we are in control, that when we wake each morning, *we* decide what we do, that our lives don't rest in the hands of others or, even worse, of that unseen yet eternal influence commonly referred to as destiny. We humans crave the ability to plan. We set goals, bargaining off today in exchange for where we want to be tomorrow, even what we hope to be doing a decade in the future. Much of the time, that's a wise decision, one that brings prosperity and happiness. Yet doing so is a risk, for fate is always a factor, and fate can be capricious.

In 2006, a few months after my mother died, I was preoccupied and missed my freeway exit. Instead, I took another. A mile down the road at a traffic light, a young man texting behind the wheel plowed into the rear end of my small SUV. The result: a back problem that's plagued me ever since that day. How many times when I push myself out of bed in the morning have I lamented missing that exit, wondered if the pain I endure could have been avoided by simply paying more attention and getting off the interstate sooner. A fleeting moment, I was distracted, and chance claimed control.

Yet, I've been lucky. I have few complaints.

Thirty years writing true crime, first for magazines, then books, and I understand what can happen when chaos truly takes over. Others may debate if evil exists in this world; I've looked it in the eye. In courtrooms, in prison interviews, killers describe how lives were taken. Sometimes there's sadness, the belated realization that wrong has been done, yet more often, years later, there's no empathy for the victim. Instead, even when a murder is admitted, I've witnessed an indignant righteousness, an entitled anger, a scowl as a killer describes a victim, one that implies the dead bear the blame. The victim was flawed, she caused the events that led to her death, or she was simply too accessible, not careful enough, and that led to her murder.

Since 1985, I've often written about sensational Texas murders. But my journey didn't begin on the Gulf Coast. In the fifties and sixties, I lived in Milwaukee, Wisconsin. My father was a factory foreman, my mother a school secretary who loved to read. I have three brothers, and we lived in a small house on an abbreviated street where maples and elms shaded the homes in summers, and in winters we shoveled snow into banks that we recycled into stiff, twig-limbed snowmen with clichéd carrot noses and button eyes.

My parents cautioned me when I was very young that there were dangers hidden in the shadows. I heard tales about the ubiquitous boogeymen, the frightening Rumpelstiltskin-like figures that waited for imprudent children, especially little girls who strayed from the safety of their homes. The outcome was always described in obscure manners, perhaps nothing more than the raising of eyebrows or tight-lipped frowns that implied unlucky children suffered tragic ends. Yet the message was clear: There were forces to be wary of, people to fear.

Sometime in the sixties, a segment aired on the local news reporting that a girl had disappeared from a nearby park. Then a teenager, I'd walked a dirt path that led from my home to the community swimming pool for years, a trail that bordered the verdant banks of the meandering Menomonee River. I'd grown up playing on the riverbank, among the trees. It was where I smoked my first and last cigarette while reclining on a sturdy yet graceful branch of a massive oak.

When my parents handed me a newspaper account of the kidnapping to read, I was ordered to stay out of the park. From that day forward, I was to walk not on the trail but across the street, on a sidewalk that ran in front of the homes facing the parkway. I argued against it, but they were steadfast. A young girl had mysteriously vanished, a warning that wasn't to be ignored. All girls were in danger. But it was the sixties, a time when the hubris of youth made news across the country, a stormy era when danger seemed in the very air as neighborhood boys headed off to war. Vietnam dominated the evening news. Flags burned and life felt electric. With so much to consider, the disappearance of one girl carried little impact. I was coming of age, and the world was opening up for me. I felt strong and invulnerable.

So I ignored my parents' entreaties and continued walking the footpath until the day the lost girl was found. I honestly can't recall where her body was or how long she'd been missing. Yet I'll never forget the fear in my mother's eyes as she repeated her warning to be vigilant because there were wicked people in the world.

I can't say that I never entered the park again or walked leisurely yet defiantly along the peaceful pathway, where I tore off the tips of evergreen branches. I rubbed the weblike needles between my fingers, releasing a near-intoxicating fragrance of pine. But there were times, when a car slowed or I sensed movement in the dense shadows of the trees, that I darted across the street to the perceived safety of the sidewalk, within shouting distance of front doors. Was I safer there? I don't know.

In truth, Milwaukee even then was a fairly big city, home to many young girls, the vast majority of whom grew up playing safely in their front yards, skipping to their friends' homes, walking to and from school. The movement in the bushes? Undoubtedly a soft breeze. For the most part, we were safe. Yet a girl had been murdered.

It was disquieting.

Then something happened in July 1966, an event that

made an even bigger impression. Again the news came in headlines, this time describing a scene of horrific carnage. In a Chicago flat a little more than an hour from my home, Richard Speck had raped, tortured, and murdered eight student nurses. How was such evil possible?

It would be another decade, the late seventies, before I first heard the term *serial killer*. It was in conjunction with the unfathomable darkness that was Ted Bundy. Like many across the globe, I read and watched legions of news accounts on the handsome, charismatic young man with the piercing eyes, mesmerized by the former law student who'd left a trail of blood extending from Washington State to a sorority house in Florida.

Just before his execution, Bundy admitted committing thirty murders, but authorities speculated that he'd killed many more. His name became synonymous with wanton slaughter, and he forever changed the image of the dangerous stranger. No longer could we tell ourselves that we would recognize the face of evil. Now it could be lurking behind the eager smile of a neighborhood boy or the pleading face of a handsome stranger asking for help in a parking lot. For the first time, America wondered what lingered in the hearts of the solitary figures jogging our streets, the drivers of the big rigs that passed us on the interstates, the good Samaritans who stopped to help us change flat tires along the sides of deserted roads. Good deeds were not to be taken at face value. Bundy tricked his victims, and they paid with their lives.

In 1981, my husband and I settled in Houston. I can't remember the first time I encountered an article in the *Houston Chronicle* that detailed a strange phenomenon along Interstate 45, beginning south of the city and extending onto Galveston Island. It was most likely around the time fourteen-year-old Sondra Ramber ambled out her front door in Santa Fe, a small, mostly rural community not far from the interstate corridor. In October 1983, Sondra was last seen walking to a store. When her father returned home that evening, the house was unlocked and empty. He reported her missing the following morning. Who took her? Why? Did she simply walk away? If so, she left with biscuits baking in the oven and without her coat and purse.

Frightening? Yes. It would have been more so had I known that over the previous decade nearly a dozen other girls had disappeared in and around that same slice of the metropolitan area. Some bodies were eventually found. Others were never recovered.

The first reference I read to the plot of land dubbed *The Texas Killing Field* was around September 1991. A body had been discovered in an oil field off Calder Drive, not far from I-45. Janet Doe was the fourth victim found in that same location over a period of seven years. It was then that the *Houston Chronicle* ran a full-page article documenting the history of unsolved murders of young women along the southern I-45 corridor, two decades of murder: sixteen young women, sixteen grieving families.

It seemed that there was no end to the horror.

Five years later, in March 1996, thirteen-year-old Krystal Jean Baker, by family legend a great-niece of screen-icon Marilyn Monroe, walked a few blocks from her grandmother's house and called her mother from a tire-store phone. Moments later, fuming over not getting her way, Krystal huffed off toward a friend's house. Her bloodied, bruised, strangled body was discovered in a neighboring county under a freeway overpass.

The next murder sent waves of anger throughout all of Houston, when in April 1997, Laura Kate Smither, a bubbly twelve-year-old ballerina with curly brown hair and playful eyes, went for a jog on the rural roads surrounding her home. Laura was only supposed to be gone for twenty minutes, but seventeen days later her corpse was recovered from a retention pond. Thousands of volunteers had scoured the fields surrounding her home, and law enforcement, including the FBI, searched for clues, all to no avail.

That hot Texas summer, the tally grew when, four months later, Jessica Cain, a young actress and soon-to-be college freshman, disappeared within a few miles of her home. Her pickup was found on I-45's shoulder, heading south. Did someone force her off the road? Jessica left her purse inside the truck, as if only planning to step away for a moment, but she never returned.

Houston-area newspapers published the first illustrations of the terror, charts depicting the abductions and murders, in the late nineties under headlines that read variously MYSTERIES ALONG I-45, and UNSOLVED. With her disappearance, Jessica Cain joined so many others whose faces stared out from grainy newspaper photos, a black-and-white gallery of smiling girls and young women, school pictures, snapshots, family photos, the last images of the dead. Below each ran a name, dates, and brief descriptions of their disappearances. At times, the heartbreaking list changed when crimes were solved. Serial killer Anthony Allen Shore, for instance, was arrested in 2004 and the photos of three of his alleged victims, Dana Sanchez, sixteen, Maria Carmen del Estrada, twenty-one, and Diana Rebollar, nine, were deleted from the list.

Sadly, more often than the deletions came additions, new photos appearing as more girls and young women died along I-45 at the hands of unknown killers. Through it all, grief spread from family to family. Unimaginable pain. Unforgettable horror. No closure. Rarely justice.

I don't know when I first realized that I would write about these tragedies just down the highway from my Houston home. Perhaps I always knew. As I went from reporting on sensational murders in magazines to books, I cut out and kept articles on the I-45 murders. The young girls in the newspaper pictures troubled me, seemed to ask for help, wanting their stories to be told. Whenever I saw their faces, I considered how quickly and unexpectedly life turns. I knew it could have been my photo or that of someone I loved, and I wondered how so many cases remained unresolved. I had to do something because the victims were real, they mattered, and they deserved not to be forgotten.

One version of the chart documenting the unsolved I-45 cases.
(Courtesy of the Galveston County Daily News*)*

As I began writing this book, my goal was simple: to tell not all but some of the victims' stories along with those of the people who toiled to bring their killers to justice. I hoped to share the trials of the families, those who never overcame their grief and others who used it to build a better world. For even in the deepest despair, there were those who found inspiration and redemption.

At the same time, I wanted to give a voice to those suspected of the crimes, for they, too, had important stories to tell.

In many ways, recounting these murders transported me on a journey through my own life, back to the seventies, when I was young, through the eighties and nineties. The world changed drastically throughout those years. Wars began and ended. Science made great strides. Presidents came and went. Our cities and our towns were redesigned, along with our styles and our habits.

What remained the same was that despite our best intentions, despite all we wish for our world, for our families, in 2014 we have little better grasp of the true nature of evil than we had when the first victim discussed in this book died in 1971. We were no more adept at recognizing its face. And we still didn't know how to stop it.

This book is divided into three sections organized by decades: the seventies, eighties, and nineties. For the most part, the first two, the seventies and eighties, are organized chronologically. In contrast, the nineties unfold in two distinct parts. The first set of chapters explores the 1996 murder of Krystal Jean Baker, the investigation into her death, and the trial of her killer. The final chapters examine one of the Gulf Coast's most infamous cases, the 1997 abduction and killing of little Laura Kate Smither.

What binds these cases? They all center on a fifty-mile section of Interstate 45, running south of Houston, the nation's fourth largest city, onto Galveston Island.

The dead as well share a common bond—all were young women, the majority teenagers, and victims of chance. If they'd taken another road, refused to accept an offer of a ride, or called in sick to work on the days they died, they would likely still be alive. Most if not all would have gone on with their lives, unaware that one choice could have brought them face-to-face with stark terror. By now, they could be mothers with children, some even with grandchildren. Instead, their faces and their stories haunt the Texas Gulf Coast.

Deliver Us is an account of the slaughter, the brutal murders of young women around the corridor that runs south of Houston into Galveston, an area loosely dubbed by the press as the I-45/Texas Killing Fields. Three decades of loss and redemption along a busy highway, in our midst, where more than a hundred thousand commuters drive each workday.

"Deliver us from evil," believers plead in an ancient prayer. Deliver us from the evil among us, the hunters, the killers concealed in the shadows. For they exist.

THE 1970s

- Colette Wilson: 13, taken from beside the road on June 17, 1971, while waiting for her mother after a school band competition.

- Brenda Jones: 14, disappeared after a hospital visit with her aunt, on July 11, 1971.

- Sharon Shaw: 14, vanished with her best friend, Renee Johnson, on August 4, 1971.

- Rhonda "Renee" Johnson: 14. Shaw and Johnson were last seen by a friend on Galveston's Seawall Boulevard.

- Gloria Ann Gonzales: 19, a grocery-store bookkeeper, left on a vacation in October 1971. She was never seen again.

- Maria Johnson: 15, got into a white van on November 15, 1971, with Debbie Ackerman

- Debbie Ackerman: 15, hitchhiked, with her best friend, Maria Johnson.

- Kimberly Rae Pitchford: 16, walked out of a driver's education class on January 3, 1973, and never called her parents for a ride home.

- Brooks Bracewell: 12, allegedly skipped school on September 6, 1974, with her friend Georgia Geer.

- Georgia Geer: 14. Last reported sighting was at a convenience store with her friend Brooks Bracewell.

- Suzanne Bowers: 12, left her grandparents' Galveston house on May 21, 1977, intending to walk home and get a swimsuit. She never arrived.

Chapter I

A Serial Killer on the Island

Galveston, Texas
1971

Man is drawn to water. It is part of us. It comprises more than half of our bodies, and we require a supply each day to live. Scientists say the sea is where our species began. Perhaps that's true, for certainly it calls to us. Rarely do we feel as invigorated, as cleansed as when we stand on a beach, the sun warming our skin, watching light dance on waves, as we breathe salted breezes

Maria Johnson, like so many of the girls, worshipped the sun and the beach.

and absorb the rhythm of the surf. The tides come and go, the water climbs and recedes, and we stare entranced, engaged in a primitive ritual. Even if we never venture into the white-foam waves, for most of us simply being near a vast expanse of water has the power to clear our minds and relax our bodies. At the end of the day, as the sun sets, we leave refreshed.

In hindsight, water would play a part in many of the I-45 cases, if not in the girls' lives, in the aftermaths of their murders. Nearly all the bodies were found in or near water. Yet it was obviously not for its healing qualities. Why? "Water washes away evidence. It makes it harder to solve the crimes," an aging investigator told me. "They know that."

"They?" I asked.

"The killers." After a long pause, he concluded, "They know."

Despite its name, Interstate 45 is an intrastate highway, linking the Lone Star State's two largest, and two of the nation's biggest cities. From I-45's northern point, Dallas, it slices through the countryside, traveling two hundred miles south to Houston, an immense, sprawling metropolis fueled by the oil industry and the businesses that feed off it. But 45 doesn't end in the mirrored and granite skyscrapers at H-town's bustling center.

Instead, the interstate continues its arrow path. South of Houston, I-45 becomes the Gulf Freeway. It skirts the University of Houston's split-obelisk-guarded campus, then continues on, surrounded by commercial and retail businesses, clusters of stores, car dealerships, businesses, and shopping malls, typical metropolitan spread. Half an hour from the city, the economic forces switch from what's found within the earth to the skies above it, as the Clear Lake exit leads to the Johnson Space Center, NASA's mission control, where engineers and scientists monitored the men who walked upon the moon and shuttle traffic to the space station.

Past Clear Lake, the landscape is wooded but not particularly interesting, flat coastal plain. Flash back to the seventies, when the killing began, and much of this southern I-45 corridor remained undeveloped land dotted by small towns. During the three decades the murders in this book took place, the population mushroomed, as Houston grew from the sixth to the fourth largest city in the nation. In its shadow, the population of Galveston County, including the majority of the I-45 towns, expanded from less than 170,000 to more than 217,000.

Jobs brought many of those who settled here. Residents commuted to work by joining the flow of traffic on I-45 north into downtown Houston, west to the I-10 energy corridor, or east to the pipe jungles of chemical plants and refineries that proliferate along Galveston Bay's winding coastline, immense facilities operated by goliaths Exxon, British Petroleum, Dow Chemical and others. From towering steel stacks, torchlike flares burn off excess hydrocarbons. At night, the flames and refinery lights shimmer against the darkness.

Their names give the towns and small cities separate identities: Alvin, Santa Fe, Hitchcock, Friendswood, La Marque, Kemah, Bacliff, Dickinson, La Porte, San Leon, League City, Texas City, Seabrook, and Webster. Yet as the region developed, many absorbed any vacant land between them, until it became common to leave one burg and enter another without notice.

The official boundaries, however, have importance, including a substantial effect on law enforcement. The towns and cities where the killings took place fall into three counties: to the north, toward Houston, Harris County; to the south Galveston County; and to the west Brazoria County. Each employed a separate sheriff's department, and each municipality its own police department. The result: The investigations, as the murders unfolded, fell under the jurisdiction of eleven different law-enforcement agencies.

What is consistent? Water.

Fingerlike bayous weave through cities and towns, neighborhoods, alongside roads and past oil-collection tanks housed on vast empty acres. These usually shallow waterways flood during downpours, eventually washing discarded rubble into Galveston Bay. At times the debris isn't only fast-food containers or empty beer cans, however, but something far more sinister: human bodies, used and discarded.

In Galveston, I-45 comes to an abrupt end.

A barrier island, 28.9 miles long and 3.2 miles at its widest point, Galveston lies 50 miles southeast of Houston. Attached to the mainland by a mile-and-a-half causeway, the city has an aura all its own, a presence, the feel of a notorious past, a seedy sophistication—think New Orleans or Venice—places haunted by history.

On September 8, 1900, Galveston ranked among Texas' five largest metropolises, a wealthy, thriving commercial center with a busy harbor and a bright future. Then came the hurricane. Standing on the beach staring out into the Gulf of Mexico's pewter surf, it's easy to visualize what it must have been like on that awful day. Decades before television and storm-tracking radar, when horse-drawn carriages provided the primary means of transportation, a blue sky with scattered clouds darkened by midmorning into what at first appeared to be merely a particularly tumultuous tropical storm. But the waves swelled, and the water rose. By the time the island's residents realized a massive hurricane approached, they had no opportunity to flee. The Great Storm, as it's still called, remains the deadliest natural disaster in U.S. history, killing at least six thousand and perhaps as many as twelve thousand. At St. Mary's Orphans' Asylum alone, ten nuns and ninety children perished.

In the decades that followed, Galvestonians built a seawall, a ten-mile, seventeen-foot-high buttress designed to hold back Gulf waters. Based on lessons learned, they trucked in earth and raised the land and more often built homes on stilts. Some of the grand Victorian mansions survived, yet the island was forever changed. Houston dug its own port and flourished, dominating southeast Texas, and Galveston became a beloved appendage, a playground. Prohibition brought bootleggers and The Balinese Room, a casino that attracted A-list celebrities: Frank Sinatra, Bob

Hope, the Marx Brothers, and Texas billionaire Howard Hughes.

This brush with celebrity ended quickly. The Texas Rangers moved in, staking the nightclub out to prevent gambling. The glitter moved to Las Vegas, then to Atlantic City, and from that point on, Galveston's light faded. As time passed, the island drew mainly tourists, college students celebrating spring break, summer-vacationing families, and wealthy Texans who wanted second homes with a beach view.

By 1970, except for the summer months, when tourists elbowed onto the beaches and the population could top 250,000, the island was a sleepy place with approximately 61,000 full-time residents. Along with tourism, the main employers were American National Insurance, founded by the Moodys, one of the island's wealthiest families, and UTMB, the University of Texas Medical Branch, with its teaching hospital and research center.

Off and on, more hurricanes battered Galveston, some dealing devastating blows. Always there was the threat of the next big storm. Perhaps that's part of the city's appeal, the expectation of impermanence, the knowledge that any summer could bring a direct hit from a category five, and much of the island—like the mythical Atlantis—might disappear under the sea.

The killing began in 1971, at a time when the United States experienced a transformation.

Danger and turbulence seemed to permeate the country. In the prior decade, assassination had become not history but reality as a president, his brother, and the nation's most prominent civil rights leader all fell. Despite President Richard Nixon's pledge to end the bloodshed, the Vietnam War still raged, and the draft forced neighborhood boys to risk their lives a world away. Meanwhile, at home, discord invaded living rooms, spawning what became known as the generation gap. "Don't trust anyone over thirty!" the young were advised. "Turn on! Tune in! Drop out!" Drugs invaded popular culture, and intimacy moved out of marital bed-

rooms, reemerging as a call to casual sex. America's disil-
lusioned youth worshipped freedom, the call of the open
road, and the pull of sunshine and water. Teenage girls grew
up playing with Barbie dolls, and beauty became redefined
as slender, spirited and independent, the tanned and lithe
California Girls celebrated by the Beach Boys.

Athletic and tan, Maria Johnson
didn't understand the dangers.

This milieu surrounded
Maria Andrews Johnson,
the pretty, chestnut-haired
fifteen-year-old pictured
here and in the bikini
under this chapter's heading. As it would for so
many, the world changed
around Maria, appearing
to offer a limitless future,
one without the bonds that
tethered women to family
and home. Yet for Maria
and the other young vic-
tims in this book, such
freedom was an illusion,
one that would end all too
quickly in horrific deaths.

Maria Johnson was one
of eleven girls, ages twelve
to nineteen, murdered
south of Houston along I-45 during the 1970s. When the
I-45 Unsolved Mysteries charts first appeared decades later,
their pictures formed the first two lines of black-and-whites.
Many who investigated these vicious crimes believed that
during those years a monster roamed Galveston Island and
the surrounding area, a serial killer hunting for prey.

Some of the dead put themselves in peril by buying into
the belief that they could be footloose and free, uncon-
fined, without worry. Although they weren't to blame, their
choices put them in jeopardy. Others were less adventurous,

teenagers who did as they were told and never strayed from their parents' example. Yet they, too, died. For all, chance intersected their lives with danger; they could never have anticipated the terrors that awaited.

"Cruising the seawall really was our life," said a woman who grew up on the island and came of age in the early seventies. Her Galveston was one where teenagers in their parents' cars or their first hot rods revved their engines on Seawall Boulevard, surrounded by hotels, condominiums, restaurants and shops, bedrooms for rent with Gulf views. Tourists pedaled surreys topped by awnings on the sidewalk bordering the seawall, while vacationers and locals in swimsuits played volleyball on the sand or perched on gray boulders along the shoreline. Palm trees lined streets, and breezes filled with the invigorating scent of salt water. Summers, the sun beat down resolutely on its worshippers scattered across the beaches. Tropical-afternoon storms cleared the air, and at night the coastline disappeared into darkness that never muffled the cadence of the waves.

The first incident may have been on Galveston's East Beach.
(Courtesy of Kathryn Casey)

"The island felt safe. It was this quiet place when the tourists weren't around. And during the summers, it was a never-ending party," she said. "There were different beaches for different groups, the party kids and the banditos, the druggies, the families who brought their kids. But everyone got along, and no one worried . . . not until the killing started."

An unusual event occurred at 4:45 in the afternoon on April 27, 1971.

On that day, a sixteen-year-old girl sunbathed on East Beach, on the island's far eastern tip. It was a Tuesday during the school year, before the crush of summer, and the shoreline was deserted. Later, the teenager would tell police that a white man approached her and forced her into his car, then drove her to the south jetty, a secluded area near the red and green beacons that mark the narrow entrance from the Gulf into Galveston Bay. The girl, unnamed in news accounts, was beaten but somehow managed to escape. When a small article ran about the assault in the *Galveston County Daily News,* it's probable that few on the island paid much attention. After all, what was one such incident? Locals undoubtedly assumed it was someone who'd had too much to drink, a tourist from the mainland. What were the odds that it would happen again? How could anyone have predicted that it would later appear that the crime was an omen of so much more to come?

COLETTE WILSON

In the blink of an eye,
Colette Wilson vanished.

On Thursday June 17, 1971, at 12:30 P.M., thirteen-year-old Colette Anise Wilson stood in Alvin, Texas, at the intersection of Highway Six and County Road 99, northwest of Galveston on the mainland. The eighth-grader wore a Mickey Mouse T-shirt and purple shorts.

Her hair long and dark, she carried a black clarinet case and a file of sheet music. Surrounded by cattle pastures bordered by trees, the intersection was a lonely place, the crossing of two sparsely traveled country roads. Yet there was no reason for the girl to be wary. The woods stretched out around her, but the location was familiar, only two and a half miles from her home.

In that day's headlines, President Richard Nixon asked Congress for $371 million to fight America's growing dependence on drugs, and sources unmasked military analyst Daniel Ellsberg as the informant of the leaked Pentagon Papers, a trove of top secret government documents that theorized the U.S. couldn't win the Vietnam War.

On that country road, such concerns must have seemed inconsequential to the teenager. It's far more likely that music drifted through Colette's mind, snatches of selections she'd played with her classmates. She'd just left a multischool band camp, and her instructor dropped her off, then quickly drove away with a car full of other students to deliver. "This was a different time," said Colette's mom, Claire Wilson. "People wouldn't do that today, but back in the seventies, it seemed safe."

At the Wilson house, Claire tended to her other nine children. It was summer, and the house hummed with young voices as she called out asking which of the children would like to drive with her the short distance to pick up Colette, the second oldest. Two of the boys responded, and one of the youngest children, a daughter named Alice. Minutes later, Claire pulled out of the driveway.

Meanwhile Colette presumably stood alone at the corner, expecting her mother to arrive at any moment. A sweet, happy girl, she was unusually eager to get home. There were big doings at the Wilson house. The entire family was preparing for a wedding. Their neighbor was getting married the following day. Close friends of Claire and her husband, Tom, a dentist, the bride and groom were honoring the Wilsons by holding the ceremony on their anniversary. At home,

Colette had a half-sewn dress that needed to be finished, one she wanted to wear to the wedding.

The Wilsons

When this Christmas photo was taken in 1969, the Wilsons had nine children (Colette is in the back row, second from the right).

With so many children, the Wilson household could be a bit hectic. That meant things didn't always happen on schedule. If her mother was late, Colette had standing instructions to walk to her best friend's house, hidden in the trees just a short distance down the road from the intersection. Did Colette follow those orders that day, or did she wait on the corner? Perhaps she stood in the hot Texas sun for a minute or more, shading her iridescent blue eyes as she looked off to the distance, to where the intense heat radiated off the pavement, melting into a shimmering mirage pool.

Six minutes. Just six quick minutes elapsed between the time Colette exited her instructor's car and Claire Wilson arrived at the designated corner, where she expected to see Colette patiently waiting. But when Claire drove up, Colette wasn't there. Someone else was, someone pulled off the road in an old car. Claire sat for a few moments, looking at the car. A man was behind the wheel. Wondering why he was parked along the road, Claire surmised that the car must have broken down. With little hesitation, she drove off toward Colette's friend's house to collect her daughter.

Colette, however, wasn't at the friend's house. The friend hadn't seen her. On the drive home, anxiety overcame Claire. Where was her daughter? This time when Claire passed the intersection, it was empty. No Colette. And the stranger in the car—the one she'd assumed had mechanical problems? He was gone.

At the house, Claire called Tom at his dental office. "Something's wrong," she said. "Colette's missing."

Authorities were called. Years later, Claire would try to explain how the disappearance of a thirteen-year-old initially caused little official concern. "There weren't any Amber Alerts. The police weren't worried. They said she was probably taking drugs or something, that she'd run away. We knew Colette. We knew that wasn't true. But they wouldn't listen to us."

Frustrated, it was the Wilsons who investigated that afternoon.

One after another, Claire contacted Colette's friends, but no one had seen her. None of her daughter's friends or their families knew where Colette could have gone. Meanwhile, Tom and the older children combed the site where Colette was dropped off. They searched the surrounding woods, hoping to find someone or something that would lead them to Colette. As word spread, their neighbors helped, organizing search parties, doing the things authorities weren't, looking frantically for any sign of Colette. Frustration welled, especially when someone found an unemployment check stub near the site and gave it to the police. To the Wilsons' amazement, the officer threw it away. "Our neighbors were wonderful, and I'll be forever grateful for all they did. But the police didn't take any of it seriously," said Claire. "If it weren't for our neighbors, no one would have been looking for Colette."

Meanwhile, Claire thought back to the car on the side of the road. Could that have been a stranger taking away her daughter?

Finally, on Saturday, two days after the disappearance, police admitted that it appeared Colette Wilson had been kidnapped. It was only then that they issued a statewide alert and brought in helicopters. But it was too late. Whoever had taken Colette had an insurmountable lead. Even when authorities admitted they had a missing teenager, it seemed to Claire that local officers did little but congregate at the intersection where Colette was last seen and talk to reporters. "I don't think they knew what to do," she said.

Not dissuaded by the lack of effort on the part of police, the neighbors continued their searches, extending their efforts westward, into Brazoria County. Despite their hard work, they uncovered no solid clues. Frantic to find his daughter, Tom Wilson raised $10,000 for a reward. Eager to do everything possible, still thinking about the lone car that day on the road, Claire agreed to be hypnotized. Sadly, nothing developed from the experiment; she recalled no description or license-plate number to help with the search.

Before long, Texas Rangers and state troopers joined the efforts, but again to no avail. Disheartened, when Tom heard that his daughter might have been seen in Louisiana, he didn't rely on authorities but went himself, following what turned out to be one of many false leads. As the investigation faltered, Claire and Tom hired a private investigator, but he, too, failed to uncover any solid evidence.

As time passed without word of Colette, the Wilsons, a deeply religious family, adopted a ritual, every evening kneeling around their missing daughter's bed and praying for her return. Where was Colette? How could she simply disappear? "We prayed that the Archangel Michael would lead us in our battle," said Claire. "We prayed that God would bring our daughter home."

Less than a month after Colette Wilson's disappearance, on Monday, July 12, 1971, a crew on scaffolding painted the Pelican Island Bridge, a steel-and-cement structure extending north from Fifty-first Street, not far from the Galveston Harbor Channel, an industrial zone near the shipyards. They worked and talked, as the water around them glistened, sunlight dazzling on the surf. Around ten that morning, one worker noticed something floating in the distance. Before long, they were all staring at it, calling out ideas, guessing what it might be. A slight chop in the water lapped against the bridge as they worked, an echoing *thunk, thunk, thunk*. Slowly, the object floated closer, growing in size. It was then that they realized they were staring at a dead body.

The call came into the Galveston Police Department at 10:30 A.M., a report of what appeared to be a woman's corpse in the water. When officers arrived, they pulled a lifeless figure from the bay, a young, light-skinned African-American woman. She was nude, her wrists and ankles bound with long, plastic laces. With no identification to tell them otherwise, police estimated that the dead girl appeared to be approximately twenty.

At the scene, however, an officer arrived who recognized the girl. Brenda Jones was only fourteen years old. Entering eighth grade in the fall, Brenda attended the island's Holy Rosary School, the first African-American Catholic school in the state. She was a good student, and she was responsible, so when Brenda didn't arrive home on time the previous afternoon, her family quickly grew worried. "I called and reported Brenda missing that same evening," said Phyllis Southern, one of Brenda's three sisters, describing how everyone in her family impatiently awaited news, wondering where Brenda had gone.

Outspoken and always ready with a wide smile, Brenda loved children and planned to one day be a teacher. The

baby of the family, she tended to be a bit of a tomboy, whipping the neighborhood boys at marbles. Around the house she was a joyous presence, practicing her clarinet for the school band and singing her favorite Rhythm and Blues songs. Her mom, Evelyn, was a widow, and just the year before moved the family into the Cedar Terrace Projects, housing for economically strapped families on the island. "We'd led pretty sheltered lives," said Phyllis. "Mom didn't want to move us there, but she couldn't afford anything else."

Brenda Jones had a personality that could light a room. *(Courtesy of her family)*

Hoping to uncover clues to what led to Brenda's disappearance, her family reconstructed what they could about the afternoon she vanished. It began like any other Sunday. They attended mass at Holy Rosary, then Brenda stayed to teach Sunday school. They gathered and ate dinner, and Brenda told her mother that she wanted to go to the University of Texas Medical Branch's John Sealy Hospital to visit an aunt who'd fallen and broken a leg. Evelyn agreed and gave Brenda bus fare. Brenda kissed her family good-bye and left. "We didn't have a car. Our mom couldn't afford one," said Phyllis. "Brenda took the bus to the hospital. She saw my aunt, and left. Later, the bus driver told us Brenda

got on the bus at the hospital and got off at the stop just a
few blocks from the house, on the corner of Avenue I (later
renamed Sealy Avenue) and Thirty-first Street."

Phyllis Southern and Pearl Smith, two of Brenda Jones's sisters,
holding her school photo. *(Courtesy of Kathryn Casey)*

Brenda was in a hurry to get home. Phyllis had just given
birth to a son four days earlier, and the infant had entranced
his young aunt. "Brenda wanted to come home to hold him,"
said Phyllis. "She loved babies."

On the corner where she disembarked from the bus stood
the school Brenda was scheduled to attend in the fall, Central Middle School. The bus driver saw her walking toward
home as he drove off.

So close to the safety of her front door, but Brenda never
arrived.

Police wouldn't take a missing person report on the phone
from Phyllis that night, saying it was too soon. If Brenda
didn't return home the following day, the officer suggested
the family could come to the station to file paperwork. That
never happened. Instead, early that Monday afternoon, an

officer knocked on their front door. Once inside, he asked
to see a photo of Brenda. One glance, and he asked Evelyn
to accompany him to the morgue. A body had been found
floating in the water. There on a slab, Evelyn identified her
youngest child. When she'd disappeared, Brenda had worn
a satiny white blouse, a blue skirt, and Roman-type sandals
that laced up to her knees. When found, her body was nude.
Her sandals' long laces had been torn off the soles and used
to bind her wrists and ankles.

"Our mother was shattered," said Phyllis. "She couldn't
believe anyone would do that to her baby." When police
asked if anyone was angry with Brenda, if anyone in the
family knew anyone with a reason to kill Brenda, no one had
a name to give them. "Everyone loved Brenda. Why would
anyone want to hurt her?"

The following day, at the Galveston County Morgue, a
medical examiner conducted an autopsy, looking for any
visible signs of trauma. Quickly, he noticed something
jammed inside the teenager's mouth. Carefully, he pulled at
thin fabric, removing the item from between her teeth. Once
unfolded, he realized it was a pair of women's underwear. It
seemed such an odd thing for the killer to do. Was it to prevent Brenda from screaming? That couldn't have been the
case. From the condition of the tissue, the physician speculated that the panties had been forced in Brenda's mouth
after she was dead. Why then?

The medical examiner made notes, then continued the
autopsy. Based on a lack of bruising, scratches, and cuts,
he theorized that the most likely scenario was that Brenda's
corpse had been thrown into the water from a boat or pier.
As to time of death, a lack of rigor mortis led to the determination that she'd died at most a few hours before being
found. That suggested that someone had abducted the girl
the afternoon before and kept her alive all night, before killing her around sunrise.

How had Brenda died? The medical examiner documented bruising across Brenda's neck. Under cause of death, he wrote: manual strangulation.

In Alvin, Tom and Claire Wilson continued their search for Colette, following leads that quickly turned cold. On Galveston Island, Brenda Jones's family waited for police to find her killer. They saw little being done. "My mother and I went to the police station, we tried to get them to do something, to find out who did this," said Phyllis. "I had the feeling that they didn't care. Brenda was a black child from the projects. My impression was that they thought her murder wasn't worthy of any real investigation."

Two dead teenage girls in two months, and no answers.

What no one would speculate about until later was that the two cases could be connected. Was it a coincidence that both girls played musical instruments? No one knew. "Brenda was black, and Colette white," said a woman who knew Brenda. "Why would anyone think that the same person could be responsible?"

The Wix Ski School on Offatts Bayou. *(Courtesy of Johnnie Wix)*

"The police came asking questions, I remember that," said Johnnie Wix, her voice heavy with sadness.

In her nineties, Johnnie was a diminutive figure seated on a couch in her daughter's living room, a frail bump under a pile of blankets. I'd arrived unannounced and entered when she yelled at me to come inside. She thought I was a nurse, there to help her dress for the day. On her schedule, a doctor's appointment was inked in for the afternoon. When I identified myself as a writer and explained that I'd come to talk about the girls who died in Galveston in the 1970s, the old woman with her white hair in loose curls cast her eyes down at her gnarled hands on her lap and sighed. "I don't like to think about that. It is more than forty years ago now. I never forgot about the girls, but I got to the point, I didn't like to remember."

Back in those days, Johnnie and her deceased husband, Sam, a marine engineer who'd served in the navy during World War II, ran Galveston's Wix Ski School, on Offatts Bayou, just blocks off I-45. A favorite spot for birdwatching, the estuary between Galveston and West Bays was named after steamboat captain Horatio J. Offutt, who in 1847 bought the surrounding two hundred acres. Urban legends erroneously touted other theories for the source of its name, the most popular that it stemmed from the bayou's location as the first exit past the causeway onto the island. In that version, "off at the bayou" morphed into Offatts Bayou.

The ski school, located on a boat dock attached to the back of the Wixes' small frame house, was a hangout for teenagers who congregated to ski and buy dime cans of pop out of the old, red, soft-drink box Johnnie kept well stocked. Gas was nineteen cents a gallon, and Johnnie charged a dollar to pull a skier on a turn around the wide bayou. When the teens were short of money, she let them earn rides by helping with tasks around the school, cleaning the old boat Sam labored to keep running or working on the ski lines. Sometimes professional skiers from Sea-Arama Marine World, a theme park that had opened on the island in the midsixties, dropped in. "All those who came around, they were nice kids," Johnnie said. "I liked them. And people loved coming to the ski school. Rich people, just regular people. Lots of different kinds of people. It was our sport, and we loved it."

The first two girls the police questioned Johnnie and Sam Wix about were fourteen-year-old friends Sharon Shaw and Rhonda "Renee" Johnson. They disappeared on August 4, 1971. That afternoon, they'd dropped in at the Wix Ski School. Sam told police that Shaw and Johnson stayed only briefly, leaving when he told them that the ski boat wasn't going out because of choppy waters. The Wixes' neighbors later said that they saw the girls leave the ski school and walk east toward Sixty-first Street, a main thoroughfare that led to Seawall Boulevard and the beach.

The girls must have been disappointed that day. Shaw and Johnson worshipped the water, skied, and belonged to a local surfing club. They'd been looking forward to the afternoon at Wix. "They weren't regulars, but they'd show up sometimes. They came maybe once or twice before that day," Johnnie said, her face taut with a troubled frown. "They weren't local. They were rounders."

When I asked what she meant by that, Wix shook her head. "They were attractive girls, and street-smart."

Shaw and Johnson lived in Webster, a small town half an hour north of Galveston on the mainland, just off I-45. When they didn't return home, their parents began searching. One friend speculated that they might have run away. The girls had been talking about following friends to California, to ride the grand waves—so much bigger than Galveston's meager surf—in Malibu. "I don't think at first anyone thought it was anything but that those first two girls had taken off," said Johnnie.

A brief two months after the Webster girls disappeared, there was again little notice when a nineteen-year-old book-keeper working at a Houston Kroger store, Gloria Ann

Gonzales, was reported missing by her roommate in late October. Gonzales had last been seen at their apartment on Jacquelyn Street in Houston. Brenda Jones's body had been found quickly, but like Colette Wilson, and Shaw and Johnson, Gonzales appeared to have inexplicably vanished.

"If people were really worried, well, I didn't hear anything," said Johnnie Wix, her parchment-thin eyelids fluttering down, then resolutely closing, as if shutting out the memories. "Then we heard about Maria and Debbie. And then we all knew something really bad was happening."

Best friends Debbie Ackerman and Maria Andrews Johnson.

"Debbie was a good kid," said her sister-in-law, Denise. "She loved the water, surfed, and skied. All summer, she was tan, and the sun streaked her hair blond. She and Maria were best friends, together constantly. Debbie was the apple of her daddy's eye. The only girl. And no one in the family ever got over it."

Coming from very different backgrounds, Debbie and Maria weren't an obvious pairing. Debbie had two older brothers, Glenn and Wayne, and lived with her parents, German immigrants, in a small house on the island. Her dad, Joseph, was a janitor, and her mother, Deomeria, called Dee, worked as a supply clerk. They were a close family, and since she was the little sister, they all doted on Debbie. At Ball High School, Debbie was a popular fifteen-year-old, elected to student council, and friends who grew up with her remembered an outgoing girl with an athletic build. She danced on the school football field as a member of the Tornettes, the drill team, alongside the mascot, a menacing-looking yellow tornado.

While the Ackermans were well-known in Galveston and Debbie was BOI (born on the island), Maria, her long dark hair parted down the middle, had just moved to Galveston the previous year. Her father a gynecologist, her parents' marriage ended in a divorce that split her family. At fifteen, Maria moved often in the aftermath, ultimately following her stepfather's work to Galveston. One of Maria's great loves was collecting antique glass bottles that she displayed in her bedroom window.

What Debbie and Maria had in common was a love of the water. They wore bikinis on the beach, surfed with friends, and frequented the two surf shops on the island and Wix Ski School.

That summer, Debbie competed in surfing contests and won her first trophy. "They'd come in and hang out with the other kids," said Doug Pruns, the owner of Doug's Surf Shop. "They were nice girls. They were dating a couple of the guys who came to the shop."

On that fateful fall Saturday in 1971, there was a disagreement at the Ackerman house, when Debbie wanted to spend the weekend at Maria's rather than stay home to help her mother clean. The coming Monday was a school holiday. "Dee was angry about Debbie's leaving. She didn't like Debbie's hanging out with Maria," said Johnnie Wix. "She thought Maria had been around more and was too advanced for Debbie."

As teenagers often do, Debbie divided and conquered by asking her father, who gave his permission. Her parents argued, but Debbie left. After two days at Maria's, on Monday morning, Debbie called and talked to her father again, this time explaining that she wanted to spend the school holiday with Maria as well. Joseph gave his daughter permission but with strict orders to be home by 3:15 that afternoon. The date was November 15, 1971.

That afternoon would be an eventful one in U.S. history, one on which the U.S. government announced plans to concentrate bombing on Laos and Cambodia during the dry season, to cut off supplies to North Vietnam. Meanwhile at the Globe discount store in Galveston, bedspreads sold for $10.88 and women's bellbottoms for $2.97. Once Debbie had her father's consent, she and Maria took off for the day.

A couple of hours later, at approximately 11:15 that morning, two teenage girls working at the Baskin-Robbins ice-cream parlor at Galveston's Port Holiday Mall saw Debbie and Maria on the street and called them over. Debbie had her small suitcase with her from her sleepover at the Johnsons' house. Asked what they were doing, the girls gave the usual teenage reply: "Nothing."

When they parted, one of the girls in the shop looked out and saw Debbie and Maria hitchhiking. Moments later, a white man in a white van with a peace sticker on the back window pulled over. The driver lowered his window and talked to Maria, and both girls scrambled into the van on the passenger side. As the van pulled away, the girls in the ice-cream shop noticed curtains behind the van's back window, blocking the view inside.

The appointed time, 3:15, came and went, and Debbie failed to return home as she'd promised.

At about four, Dee Ackerman contacted Maria's mother, looking for Debbie. The calls continued into the evening, but the Johnsons insisted that they had nothing to tell her. They hadn't seen Maria either. In fact, the last time they'd seen the girls was that morning just after 9 A.M., when the Johnsons said good-bye and left for work. They had no idea where their daughter and her best friend could be.

The following morning, Tuesday, the girls were still missing, and their parents were growing increasingly apprehensive. Maria's father notified the Texas Rangers, and the Ackermans called their sons home from college to help search for their sister. That afternoon, the family canvassed Maria's and Debbie's usual haunts, including the beach, where they stopped passersby and asked if they'd been there the day before and if they'd seen the girls. No one had. The Ackermans went to the mall and the surf and ski shops, but returned home with nothing to help in their quest. Meanwhile, the police put out a BOLO, a be-on-the-lookout, for the two teenagers.

The road leading to Turner Bayou, a remote field with an oil-collection tank. *(Courtesy of Kathryn Casey)*

The call came in the following afternoon, Wednesday, November 17, two days after the girls' disappearances. While fishing, an elderly man happened upon a body in Turner Bayou, on the mainland, near Texas City, a short drive north on I-45 from Galveston.

Police quickly flooded the area, driving down country roads surrounded by cattle pastures, then through a gate onto a gravel-and-dirt one-lane road, onto vacant land where Humble Oil had a collection site. The corpse was partially submerged, near a small wooden bridge that extended across the narrow bayou. Ropes were used to reel it in. The dead girl had long, dark, reddish brown hair. She wore only a pink bra under a shirred maroon blouse, pierced earrings, and rings. From the waist down, she was nude. The first officers on the scene noted what appeared to be bullet wounds, especially one on the right side and center of the neck. Like Brenda Jones's corpse when pulled from the water at the Pelican Island Bridge, this dead girl's hands and ankles were bound.

That evening, Maria's frantic mother and stepfather were called to the Texas City police station. The girl's corpse had been taken to the morgue, but her jewelry was at the police station waiting to be inspected. As soon as they saw it, the Johnsons verified it was Maria's.

ISLE GIRL'S BODY FOUND, Texas's oldest newspaper, the *Galveston County Daily News,* reported the following morning. The coroner estimated that Maria's remains had been in the water for approximately thirty-six hours, suggesting that she was murdered sometime late Monday or early Tuesday morning, ten to eighteen hours after she and Debbie disappeared. Someone in the area of the Humble Oil field reported hearing gunshots that Monday evening. But the search wasn't over. By the time newspapers slapped down on front porches that drizzling, overcast morning, every available officer from Galveston County and Texas City was at the Turner Bayou Bridge searching for a second body.

"Once they had Maria, we all pretty much knew that this wasn't going to turn out well," said Denise. "We knew the likelihood was that Debbie was dead."

"I see something!" a Texas City fireman shouted, when he spotted skin protruding from the water 150 feet downstream from the small wooden bridge where Maria Johnson had been found. There in the tall grass around the bayou's marshy edge, all that was visible was the naked buttocks of a young girl facedown in the water. The corpse, again, was nude from the waist down. And like both of the previously recovered victims, Maria Johnson and Brenda Jones, the girl's wrists and ankles were bound, this time with long black cords that looked like shoestrings. The most recently discovered corpse wore only a bra and a dark purple Banlon-type shirt with a zipper up the front. Robbery obviously hadn't been a motive, as this body, too, wore jewelry. Officers noticed gunshot wounds to the upper back and the right of the spine.

That evening, Debbie's father and one of her brothers went to the morgue to identify the body. "When they got home, they pretty much collapsed," said Denise. "It was over, but it wasn't. The whole family wanted to know who'd done this."

The next day, the *Daily News* banner headline read BODY OF 2ND GIRL FOUND: LEADS SLIM, POLICE SAY. Along with photos of the girls, the newspaper ran one of the fields surrounding Turner Bayou, with a large oil-collection tank in the background and a group of cowboy-hatted men carrying Debbie Ackerman's body covered by a sheet on a stretcher. "That was the first time any of the murders got our attention," said a woman who went to school with the dead girls. "I don't remember being aware of the killings until then."

Word circulated that the last time Debbie and Maria were seen they were hitchhiking. After a hesitation, their schoolmate continued: "We told ourselves that Maria and Debbie were a little wild. We told ourselves we wouldn't do that, hitchhike, so it could never happen to us. But everybody was freaked out. No one wanted to be out at night. Our parents kept us home. We were all afraid."

The next day, the Galveston police chief told not only local press but reporters from big-city newspapers that converged on the island that he believed the motive for the girls' killings was sexual. Noting Brenda Jones's death, he added that Debbie and Maria weren't the first girls to die on Galveston that summer and be found with their hands and wrists tied. The medical examiner, too, granted interviews, detailing a theory that Debbie had been killed first, perhaps shot from above as she tried to shield Maria.

While news of the girls' murders rocked Galveston, investigators tried to nail down Debbie and Maria's activities on their final days. As reports came together, police drew up a timeline. What they discovered was that the day before they disappeared, Maria and Debbie had been seen at a shopping mall on the mainland near Texas City, the closest town to where their bodies were found. They were looking for a birthday gift for Debbie's boyfriend. That afternoon, they returned to Galveston in a taxi but forgot Debbie's purse in the backseat and ended up at a cab stand at eight that evening retrieving it. They slept at Maria's house. The last time they were seen was the following morning, entering the white van in front of the ice-cream parlor.

The investigation continued, but while the police attempted to find the killer or killers, the girls' families turned their attention to the pressing business at hand, burying the dead.

That same week, Maria's body was shipped to a family plot in Plainview, Texas. But Debbie had strong island roots. She'd been born in Galveston, and she'd be buried there. The church overflowed with mourners on the day the Ackermans memorialized their daughter. "People were standing everywhere. Kids, parents, teachers, neighbors, folks that knew the family," said a school friend. "There was a lot of sadness, and a lot of fear. Everyone felt on edge. We couldn't understand what was happening."

As bad as things seemed, they were about to get much worse.

At eight in the morning on the same day Debbie Ackerman was laid to rest, November 23, a man wielding a metal detector walked through a heavily wooded area near the Addicks Reservoir, west of Houston and just north of I-10. A bird sanctuary, the lake is man-made, a dammed-up area used for flood control, to help prevent low-lying downtown Houston from flooding during hurricanes and the Gulf Coast's sometimes torrential rains. Rather than buried treasure, what the man found was a decapitated, decomposing body.

In this era long before the advent of cell phones, the man drove to the nearest neighbor's. A call went out, and police responded, bringing troops to comb the area, in search of clues. One of the first discoveries was a skull a short distance away in the underbrush. Based on items found on the corpse—a white knit pullover and striped slacks, and a ring that read LOVE—it was quickly assumed that the decomposing body belonged to Gloria Ann Gonzales, the nineteen-year-old Kroger bookkeeper who'd been missing for nearly a month.

That same day, the remains were transported to the morgue for autopsy. On the stainless-steel table, the physician in charge noted that based on pressure-point marks, it appeared the remains laid facedown in the woods for an extended period of time. The decapitation, the ME speculated, hadn't been done by Gonzales's killer but animals that ravaged the corpse.

Yet there was an odd circumstance, a puzzling one. While the body remained covered with decomposing flesh, the skull was nearly skeletal. Why would the skull be nearly cleaned off and not the body? Could animals have devoured all the tissue off the skull? Perhaps, but he saw no signs of such animal activity. And if that was the cause, why hadn't they attacked the body as well?

When it came to the cause of death, the medical examiner focused on the skull. On its bony surface, he noted a series of fractures, including a flat one that appeared to have been administered by a powerful blow. Could Gloria have been bludgeoned to death?

Events tumbled one after another, fate twisting and turning. It would later seem that the murders were piling up so quickly that it was difficult to keep the evidence straight. Perhaps this was never more apparent than during the Gonzales autopsy, when suddenly the physician in charge faced a second perplexing find.

Gonzales's mandible remained with her body, and he inspected it carefully. Decades before DNA mapping in criminal cases, dental records played the most important role in identification. Along with the jawbone, the doctor examined teeth found on the scene. Some were still attached. The others, found near the body, he carefully inserted into the bone, to reconstruct the lower jaw to aid in matching it to Gonzales's dental X-rays. When he picked up a molar, however, he suddenly had a problem. The tooth didn't fit the jaw.

Perplexed, the medical examiner took another look, lined up the tooth a second time, tried to insert it, only to again pull the tooth away when it was apparent that it wasn't a match. With that, the physician paused and considered the possibilities. Eventually he came to the only possible conclusion, writing on the Gonzales autopsy: "It was evident that the molar came from another individual."

"Another individual." Another body?

Three days later, deputies returned to the site in the Addicks Reservoir where Gonzales's body had been found, this time with dogs and equipment to mount a wider inspection of the area. They were looking for a second dead body.

Among those walking through the tall grass, picking his way through the thick underbrush, was the Harris County Sheriff, C. V. Buster Kern, a square-faced, heavily jawed man with horn-rimmed glasses and graying hair. He was a political man, put in office by the voters, and it was a good public-relations move to be photographed aiding in the hunt for evidence. But that wasn't the only reason he'd shown up to help. "The cases of the missing girls ate away at him," said someone who knew Kern. "He wanted answers."

Ironically, the sheriff would be the one to find an important piece of the puzzle. Around 10:30 that morning, after fighting off bugs and wading through knee-high grass watching for venomous snakes, Kerns spotted a pile of bones on a bed of decaying leaves fifty yards from the flags that marked the spot where searchers had recovered Gonzales.

The horror of that day would stay with many of those in attendance in the reservoir throughout their lives. First the discovery of Gonzales's decomposing body, a skull, and now a human skeleton. As they compared notes, someone noticed a clue to the second victim's identity, a ring that spelled out the word PEACE on a fragile finger bone. Colette Wilson's parents had described just such a ring when they told police what their daughter wore on the day she disappeared.

No skull was found with the skeleton, but the medical examiner honed in on a mandible with some teeth, a way to find out if their suspicions were true. That afternoon, a call went out to the Wilson household, asking to have Colette's father report to the scene. As Tom Wilson drove to the reservoir to join the search party, his wife had mixed emotions. "We'd been praying and praying that Colette would be found," said Claire. "All we cared about was that we'd find her. We'd hoped to find her alive. Yet if she was dead, we wanted to bring her body home. The worst case was not knowing."

Once he'd joined the others at the Addicks Reservoir, the middle-aged dentist was shown the recovered peace ring. Immediately, he began crying, nodding that it had belonged to his daughter. Yet his obligations weren't finished. In addition to being Colette's father, Tom Wilson was her dentist, and the next thing he did must have been one of the most difficult tasks of his life. Wilson was handed the skeleton's jawbone for identification. "I recognize my work," he said later, after examining the jaw and teeth, some of which contained fillings, sad remnants of a young life. "It's Colette."

Remembering that day, Claire Wilson would attempt to

describe the emotions that overwhelmed the family. "It was terrible, and in another way, we were so grateful," she recalled. "Colette was dead, but we could bury her. We could bring her home. It was so awful, but at the same time, we were happy."

More than five months after Colette had disappeared, the Wilson family's search was over. It had ended in a nightmare.

"There's no doubt about it. That's my daughter," Wilson told reporters as he left the scene, his eyes welling with tears. "Colette was very happy, and God, she was beautiful. I guess we knew that it would probably end this way. We've been looking for Colette since she disappeared, and we won't stop now. We don't have any clues as to who did this, but he'll be found."

While no doubt remained, during his examination of the bones, the Harris County medical examiner found further evidence confirming that the skeleton belonged to Colette. The bones were consistent with coming from a young girl, thirteen to fifteen years of age. And this particular girl, he noted, had a congenital defect in her right hip. Colette's parents had already told police that their daughter had been born with a malformed hip and had spent the first two years of her life with her lower body in a cast.

The following morning, newspapers across Texas reported the findings, and something else, that there were now five unsolved murders of young girls since the beginning of the year in the area around I-45 extending south from Houston into Galveston: the only African-American victim, Brenda Jones; best friends Debbie Ackerman and Maria Johnson; the Kroger bookkeeper, Gloria Gonzales; and the dentist's daughter, Colette Wilson. AUTHORITIES SEEK LINK IN HOUSTON, ISLE GIRLS' DEATHS, Galveston's *Daily News* reported. The *Odessa American* ran the headline: UNSOLVED MURDERS MOUNT IN HOUSTON.

In the days that followed, the searches in the reservoir

continued. Colette Wilson's body had been found without a skull, and there remained the possibility of unearthing more evidence. What searchers weren't prepared for was the finding of a decomposing head on November 30, hidden in the brush twenty-five feet from where Gonzales's body had been located.

The ME now had a decomposing body, a decapitated head, one skeleton, and one skull.

From the beginning, the condition of the original skull, the one found with the body, must have bewildered the physician. Why was it devoid of nearly all tissue when the body was still covered in flesh? When he examined it, he determined that the skull did come from a young woman. Yet the features that identified race, including the thin nasal aperture and rounded shape of the forehead, suggested that the skull found near Gonzales's body was from a Caucasian. Gloria was Hispanic. He then tried to fit that skull to the mandible found with the skeleton, the one Tom Wilson had identified as belonging to his daughter. They fit.

Meanwhile, the decomposing head, still bearing flesh and curly dark hair anchored in a silver barrette, could have come from Gonzales. Its features were consistent with those of a Latin-American woman. The physician placed the head onto the mandible attached to the body and found he had a second match.

Once he had all the remains identified, the ME revisited the question of causes of death for the two girls. Based on the fractures in the skull, the one he now knew belonged to Colette Wilson, he was able to determine how the thirteen-year-old had died: "It is our opinion," he wrote, "that the decedent, Colette Anise Wilson, came to her death as a result of a fractured skull, blunt trauma—homicide."

He then turned his attention to Gonzales's cadaver. Here cause of death was less certain. Yet he had obvious suggestive evidence. When her body was recovered, it was found with a two-foot cotton cord attached to a four-inch piece of wood cinched around her neck. Based on the noose, the physician wrote: "it was probable that Gloria Gonzales was killed by strangulation with the cotton rope ligature."

The headlines were terrifying. Parents across the Houston area held their daughters close, refusing to let them leave the house except to go to school, and a sense of near hysteria invaded living rooms. Politicians called for action, and a meeting was quickly set for all the law-enforcement agencies involved in downtown Houston, at the Harris County Criminal Courthouse. By then, factions were developing, those who saw no connection between any of the killings and others like Kern who leaned toward believing otherwise, describing the killer responsible for Gloria Gonzales's and Colette Wilson's murders as "a homicidal maniac who may or may not be the same person or persons that killed the two Galveston girls [Debbie Ackerman and Maria Johnson]."

Hours after the meeting, which ended with the debate still raging over possible links between the killings, the Houston/Galveston cases were featured on the *CBS Evening News*. The realization that young women's bodies were piling up in Texas was beginning to draw national attention. A somber tone in his voice, Kern told Walter Cronkite that law enforcement had a suspect, one who'd told a woman, "He wanted the law to catch him because he was crazy."

That lead would turn out to be futile, the ravings of a man who'd confessed simply to gain attention. Days later, Kern released a composite drawing of another man he said could have been a homicidal "sex maniac." Kern never explained but later described that, too, as a false lead. Polygraphers were kept busy in Texas that fall, running examinations on suspects. One after another, investigations and lie-detector exams cleared each one.

The beginning of a new year is a time for reflection, and when the months before have been difficult, it's only natural to hope that the change will bring relief from pain, happiness, and in the case of 1971 Galveston, an end to the terror. It wasn't to be. Quickly, 1972 took up where 1971 had ended.

In January, the remains of two more girls were found, again near water, on the banks of an overflow ditch running off Taylor Bayou, east of I-45 and thirty miles north of Galveston near the affluent waterfront community of Shoreacres. This time the dead were quickly bestowed with names: Sharon Shaw and Rhonda Renee Johnson, the fourteen-year-olds who five months earlier friends believed had run away to surf in Malibu.

That meant that the number of young girls murdered in the Galveston/South I-45 area in the previous eight months stood at seven.

The dead girls' parents were frantic, begging for answers. They went before the press, pleading with anyone with information to come forward, hoping to find the man or men who'd murdered their daughters. They demanded law enforcement take action, but the small police agencies along the Gulf Coast had never experienced such carnage, and looking back, many would surmise that they simply didn't know what to do, how to proceed to solve the crimes.

"My sister's death crushed my family," said Renee Johnson's brother. "I don't think people understand how devastating it is for parents to lose a child this way. My father was never the same. It just tore everything apart."

That very year, the Behavioral Science Unit at the FBI would be formed, and profilers would begin studying such cases, yet it would be decades before the practice would move into mainstream law enforcement. For his part, Chief Deputy Sheriff Lloyd Frazier told the *Houston Chronicle* that he suspected the girls' deaths were linked. "I believe that a killer of young girls is lurking in the area," he said, but then admitted that suspicion was all he had. The investigations were stalled. By then, fifteen suspects had been given lie-detector tests, but no arrests had been made.

When questioned further about the cases, Frazier said, "Our problem in each case is that the bodies were found . . .

long after any footprints or tire tracks had disappeared . . .
We don't have anything concrete to link these cases except
that they were all young girls, but we don't have anything
that would lead us to believe they were separate cases. I believe we have one killer."

It wasn't that investigators didn't try. In the months that
followed, reports filtered off and on into newspapers of even
more suspects brought in for questioning, some of whom
confessed to the killings. Yet each led to disappointment
when none seemed to be genuine possibilities.

"At school, everyone was talking about it," said a woman
who was a girl on the island at the time. "We were calling
him the Purple Passion Killer, because there were rumors
that every girl who'd died had something purple on." In fact,
Maria Johnson and Debbie Ackerman had both been wearing maroon blouses and Colette Wilson purple shorts. "Our
parents wouldn't let us leave the house alone, and they'd stop
us at the door and make us change our clothes if we started
to walk out wearing anything purple. We were all afraid."

Off and on in the newspapers, authorities speculated that
they were nearing a break in the cases. In the first months
following the discovery of Shaw's and Johnson's skeletons,
there were serious suspects. In fact, at one point in March,
the Harris County sheriff announced that he had yet another
theory about who'd murdered all the girls. This time the
man was a former mental patient, one who'd tried to abduct
a woman after stalking her. She said the man mentioned the
killings, suggesting he could be responsible. That lead faded
away, and no arrest was ever made.

Another possibility was a young hippie with a VW bus
and California license plates pulled over on a traffic stop. He
raised suspicion by asking the officer about the girls' deaths.
Police searched the man's vehicle and discovered a rifle.
Again, however, a promising possibility ended in frustration
when police verified that the man had only recently arrived.
He'd come because he'd heard news of the murders on television and had driven all the way to Texas, intending to solve

the crimes and collect the thousands of dollars being offered as reward money.

The investigations continued, and off and on men who in a later day's vernacular would be called persons of interest cropped up only to later be ruled out. Perhaps the most viable suspect was a twenty-four-year-old Houston wrecker driver named Harry Lanham. He and a friend, a Vietnam vet named Anthony Knoppa, Jr., were arrested in April 1972 for the murder of Linda Fay Sutherlin in Pearland, a suburb just south of Houston. Her body had been found the previous November, around the time of the Ackerman and Johnson killings, lying in the weeds under a bridge along County Road 89.

In hindsight, Linda Faye's killing didn't bear a lot of resemblance to the other murders beyond that the twenty-one-year-old barmaid's body was found in a ditch. Unlike the others, Sutherlin was fully dressed, still wearing brown go-go boots and a short pink dress, even her sweater. A leg from her panty hose was tied around her hands, and the second leg had been cinched around her neck. She'd been beaten, and shotgun-pellet holes covered her shoulder. The break in the case came when witnesses remembered seeing Sutherlin in a convenience-store parking lot, her car apparently not working, talking to two men in a red tow truck. Police tied the truck to Lanham, who had a long history of violence. Once Lanham, a husky six-footer who weighed 240 pounds, was brought in for questioning, he fingered Knoppa for the killings. Knoppa returned the favor, claiming Lanham pulled the trigger, delivering the fatal injuries.

One of the most chilling admissions was in Knoppa's statement, when he said that after they picked up Sutherlin, they drove around with her in the wrecker for hours. "Harry and I both knew what was going to happen, but we didn't talk about it. We both knew that we were going to kill the girl."

That October, Lanham and Knoppa were convicted of murder with malice aforethought, Knoppa getting fifty years and Lanham twenty-five.

It was while he was in jail awaiting transport to prison in the fall of 1972 that Lanham made claims that he'd murdered the Galveston-area girls. Police from all the towns where killings had taken place descended on the jail to interview him. Whatever Lanham said during those interviews, no additional charges were ever filed.

Not reported in the press was that Lanham had another visitor while in jail, one who had a very personal interest in getting at the truth; Tom Wilson, the dentist who'd identified his own daughter's remains, had heard about Lanham's confession and made arrangements to talk to the man who claimed to have murdered Colette. That day, whatever the convicted killer said, Wilson didn't believe him. When he returned home, Tom told his wife that Lanham's confession didn't ring true. "Tom said that man wasn't the one who killed Colette," said Claire, a painful catch in her throat, the sadness still palpable. After a pause, she whispered, "He wasn't the one."

Speculation about Lanham's possible involvement in the killings would continue, but hope of interviewing him further and confirming or disposing of his claims faded months later, in December, when the convicted killer was shot and killed while wielding a knife during a botched jail escape.

So many unanswered questions; so many false leads.

The victims' families prayed for answers that never came, and their misfortunes seemed to multiply. Many found no peace, as they anguished over a lack of even modest closure, not knowing who'd murdered their daughters. In Galveston, the Ackermans could never forget what happened to Debbie, going to the media on the anniversaries of their daughter's death, pleading for help in finding her killer. Every year when November approached, Dee Ackerman walked resolutely into the Texas City police station demanding assurance that the police hadn't stopped looking for Debbie's murderer. Her heart remained broken, and many would say that it would never mend.

"We're still wanting to know who did it," Dee told reporters. "We're still grieving. The hurt is still there. No, no, never will I get over it. It will be in my mind forever."

Tears spilling from her eyes, Brenda Jones's mother, Evelyn, talked of her lost daughter often, considering how the future would have been different if Brenda hadn't died. "I wonder what she would have done, if she would have become a teacher," Evelyn said. The loss seemed to envelop her at times, a sadness that would never leave her. "I wonder if Brenda would have had children, and what she'd look like all grown."

In the Wilson household in Alvin, Colette's family, too, grieved.

"I believe what happened to our daughter killed my husband," said Claire Wilson, painfully considering all the killer had taken from her. Four years after their daughter's murder, Tom Wilson died at the young age of forty-two. He'd never stopped looking for Colette's killer, and he'd never been able to move past the grief. "By then we had two more children, but he never got over what happened to Colette. I have no doubt that grief over Colette's death caused the heart attack."

The one ray of hope, one promise of closure for any of the cases, centered on an arrest in June 1972, charges tied to the murders of the two Webster girls, Sharon Shaw and Rhonda "Renee" Johnson. So many cases unsolved, so many questions, but for Shaw and Johnson, perhaps, there would be answers. Yet later many wondered if such tattered justice yielded yet another tragic turn.

Chapter 2

All That Remains
The Murders of Sharon Shaw and
Rhonda "Renee" Johnson

Webster, Texas

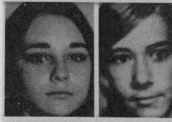

"It was a different time. We were young, and we felt like nothing could hurt us," said Glenda Willis. "Looking back, of course, it was foolish. I mean, we weren't afraid of anything. We never thought anyone was truly evil. I guess that wasn't a good thing, but we just didn't know."

I'd contacted Willis the week before, asking for an interview. She'd been close to Sharon Shaw and Rhonda "Renee" Johnson throughout the summer of 1971, the final months of their lives.

The Taylor Bayou Ditch, best friends Sharon Shaw and Rhonda "Renee" Johnson, and Renee's grave.
(Collage courtesy of Kathryn Casey)

Willis agreed, and we met at her home in League City, the largest of the communities bordering I-45, five minutes south of Webster, the murdered girls' hometown. In 1970, ten thousand resided in League City. On the day Willis and I met, nine times that made it their home. "This house is where we spent a lot of our time," said Willis, a raspy-voiced woman with startling red hair. As she talked, her right hand swept the living room. "This is where Renee and Sharon hung out. I'll always remember them here."

At that time, the rambling one-story on a quiet, suburban street was owned by Willis's parents. Her father was an accountant and a prominent local businessman. He and Glenda's mother had recently divorced. She took off with a friend for Europe, and Glenda's dad remarried. The result was that Willis, who was then just sixteen, was home alone. Once word spread that she had a house unrestricted by parental oversight, teenagers fast-tracked to her front door. Soon, to the chagrin of neighbors, the street filled with beat-up cars and VW buses with surfboard racks, rock and roll pounded from open windows, and packs of teens camped out in the backyard.

Around the time school ended that May, Willis met Shaw and Johnson at a mutual friend's apartment, and soon they, too, were regular visitors. Although at fourteen, two years younger than Willis, in many ways Shaw and Johnson seemed more advanced. "Up until that spring, I'd been in a Baptist boarding school in San Marcos. I moved back to League City, and a friend introduced me to Sharon and Renee, which is what we called Rhonda," Willis explains. "They started coming over. It was a wild time. Sharon and Renee would do anything. We were so naive, like hitchhiking on the freeway even though I had a car."

Forty years later, the dangers of thumbing a ride would be well-known, mothers and fathers warning their children that getting in a car with a stranger was a dangerous proposition. But in the early seventies, the counterculture scene portrayed sticking out a thumb and jumping into any car that stopped as a romanticized rite of passage. The open roads called, and teenagers with light wallets viewed it as an easy and cheap way to claim independence.

"I only did it once, and my dad was the one who saw me and picked me up. Then it became an argument about if I was going to hitchhike, I didn't need my car," said Glenda, whose absent-albeit-wealthy parents supplied her with not only an unsupervised home but a brand-new orange Cougar XR7 convertible and credit cards. "Renee and Sharon hitched all the time."

Glenda Willis walking along the banks of the Taylor Bayou ditch, looking for the spot where her friends' bodies were found.
(Courtesy of Kathryn Casey)

Perhaps their sense of security would have suffered a blow if they'd read the newspapers, but none of them did that summer. The girls had missed all the troubling news, including the accounts of the murder of Brenda Jones and Colette Wilson's disappearance earlier that summer. Like many teenagers, Shaw and Johnson felt invincible, and their worldviews centered firmly on their own wants and needs. "Our big deal was whether there was going to be sunshine, because we wanted to go to the beach," Willis said. "That's all we cared about. Having fun. Then, Sharon and Renee disappeared, and it all unraveled . . . Nothing was ever the same."

"I was the conservative one," said Willis.

Sharon Shaw, an outspoken, stunning young girl with a feisty temperament, long dark hair parted down the middle, and thick straight eyebrows, was something of a tomboy. All the girls were athletic, but especially Shaw, who lived for the beach. In the group of friends, her nickname was "Wild S." Highly competitive, she seemed older than her years and intent on having her way. "We didn't want to wear bikinis around Sharon and Renee, because they were so in shape. Really toned. There wasn't anything, any sport that Sharon couldn't do. Once she learned to water-ski, she outskied everyone. A couple of weeks, and she was doing jumps and flips like the Sea Arama performers."

Of the two girls, Renee, her dark blond hair swept over her forehead and trailing down her shoulders, was the more reserved. "But if Sharon did it, Renee was going to do it," said Willis.

In Webster, Shaw and Johnson were neighbors. And in the rural town surrounded by cattle and rice fields, the Johnson family was well situated. Renee's grandfather, Roy Johnson, was a councilman who later became mayor, and her father was a local businessman. "Renee was the one the boys were all crazy about. She was petite and a flirt. She was a magnet for boys, always laughing, never took anything seriously," said Willis. "She knew how to talk to boys."

Much of that summer was spent twenty-two miles south of Glenda Willis's house on the island. They hung out with friends, including two Galveston girls named Deb and Peachy. "That was how we started going. We went to their houses, then to the beach," said Glenda. If they didn't take her car, they rode bikes. But for Johnson and Shaw, no method of transportation held as much allure as sticking out a thumb to attract a ride. "They loved it. Sometimes I'd offer them a lift, and they'd turn it down, preferring to find someone to pick them up along the road," said Willis.

Galveston was a natural destination for their daily treks. They felt the pull of the water, the beaches, and the venues where teenagers congregated, a triangle made up of the Wix Ski School and the island's two surf shops, Jericho's and Doug's. Rather than splinter off, the teens circulated in groups, whiling away lazy afternoons on the beach, listening to music, slathering up with baby oil and perfecting their tans. When the hot Texas sun burned, they retreated to the water. While far from the spectacular surf in California or Hawaii, on days when Gulf waves built enough to give them a modest ride, they grabbed their boards and rode on a crest of white foam.

As evening approached, the friends habitually returned to Glenda's house. "Everybody would come here. And on Saturday nights, this house rocked," said Willis. "It was the seventies. Back then it was drugs, free love, the hippie era. We listened to Alice Cooper, Chicago, the Rolling Stones, the Beach Boys, and the Beatles. We all went to hear Rod Stewart in the old Coliseum in downtown Houston."

When Willie Nelson hosted an open-air concert in an Austin field, the friends packed Willis's car and went, claiming a patch of land to camp out. "There were probably a hundred kids from this area, thousands from all over Texas," she said. "It was a blast."

Rock and roll scored their lives that summer. Liberty Hall had recently opened in a shabby section of downtown Houston, and there the girls danced and sang along to ZZ Top. "You could smell the pot, and everyone was drinking." Although the legal age was twenty-one, that never presented a problem. Older guys in their twenties escorted the girls into bars and clubs where the rock and roll blared, including one on the island where they danced on the sand. "It was a dump, but it had music, so we didn't care."

Rather than drive back to Willis's house in the early hours of the morning, they often stayed on the beach, sleeping in tents, on the sand, or on the bed of a friend's pickup truck. "One weekend, there must have been a hundred kids camped on the beach," said Willis. "We were up partying most of the night."

Like many of their friends, Renee and Sharon sometimes smoked pot, one night getting so high they danced naked on the roof of the Willis house in the rain. A neighbor woman called the League City police, who responded but rather than immediately end the show, took their time and watched. "They let them dance for fifteen minutes before they made them get off the roof," Willis said, laughing at the memory. "Sharon and Renee weren't hippies or flower children. They were just themselves. They wore their bikini tops, blue jeans, and cutoffs, hip huggers, halter tops, and no bras. We were all young and free."

What seemed unimportant was the future. They never discussed what they wanted to accomplish when they became adults, what they hoped the world held in reserve for them. "Our big thing was to get out of school and get out on our own," said Willis. "We were living in the moment. All we cared about was where the party was the next day."

Then something changed. In mid-July, Sharon complained that her mother talked about shopping for school clothes. Sharon and Renee were scheduled to start high school. Neither of them wanted to go. "I don't know why they were upset about high school," said Willis. "And Sharon didn't want to go shopping with her mother. She didn't want to have to wear the clothes her mother picked out. Both the girls said they didn't want anything to do with high school."

As the days of summer ticked off, Shaw and Johnson became increasingly distraught. Before long, conversations on the beach and in Willis's living room dissected ways to leave the Houston area, how and when to run away, and where they could find a parent-free refuge. They talked longingly about the hippie movement and the throngs of teenagers descending on San Francisco's Haight-Ashbury district, the media-christened center of the hippie subculture. The site was so storied that it was held in special reverence. Four years earlier, The Mamas & the Papas hit single commanded those who went to arrive adorned with flowers in their hair.

Yet Shaw and Johnson, for all their pluck, were leery of going alone. After a chance meeting, it appeared that they wouldn't have to. "Sharon and Renee met these older guys," said Willis. "The guys talked about going to California, and Sharon and Renee started saying that they were going with them. They were dreading high school. Their plan was to be gone."

August 4, 1971, a Wednesday, Sharon Shaw and Renee Johnson woke up at the Johnson house. They were so close, they rarely spent a night apart. That morning, they grabbed breakfast and, since the sky was blue and the sun shining, cajoled a neighbor into providing a ride to Galveston for a morning on the beach. Their only instruction was to be sure to return to the Johnsons' home by one for lunch, when Renee's parents would call to make sure they'd followed orders.

A little more than half an hour later, the neighbor dropped Sharon and Renee off at the Wix Ski School, on Offatts Bayou. Despite the sunshine, the chop was substantial that morning. Sam Wix would later tell police that the two girls were there only briefly. Once he explained that the water was too rough for skiing, they left, swimsuits in hand, heading toward the beach.

In League City that morning, Glenda Willis slept in. When she awoke, she packed her car and drove to the island, picking up a couple of boys who were friends along the way. Then late that morning, she crossed paths with Shaw and

Johnson at their usual meeting place, Thirty-ninth and Seawall Boulevard, across the street from a Galveston landmark, Gaido's, a low-slung seafood restaurant with a giant,
blue-clawed crab sculpture perched menacingly on its roof.

The front occupied by Willis and the two boys, Sharon
and Renee scrambled into the convertible's backseat, and
the teens drove along the seawall. By then, Shaw and Johnson were contemplating how to get home. Glenda offered to
drive them but not until later, not before three. She and the
boys were meeting other friends on Stewart Beach. Shrug-
ging it off, Sharon and Renee explained that they needed to
be at the Johnsons' at one for the phone call. Rather than
wait for Glenda, they said they'd hitchhike home to Webster,
check in at the house, then find a ride back to Galveston.

"Okay. If you want a ride home later, I'll be around,"
Glenda said. She drove a few miles down Seawall Boulevard before dropping the girls at the sidewalk in front of the
Flagship Hotel, a boxy structure built over the water. Sharon
and Renee scurried from the car.

"I'll be heading back to the house about five thirty. I can
meet you here," Glenda called out as they rushed off. The
two girls waved, shouting that they'd see her then. With that,
Glenda drove away. "They looked really happy. They were
both laughing, walking along the seawall."

Moments passed, and Willis, recounting that day, said
nothing but closed her eyes as if reliving that painful instant
out of her past. Her voice broke with aching emotion, as she
whispered, "I never saw them again."

At five thirty, after her day on the beach, Glenda drove
back to the spot where she'd dropped Sharon and Renee.
Glenda assumed her friends would be waiting, that they'd
wave at her and run to the car, eager for a ride home, banter-
ing about the evening's plans. But that didn't happen. Sharon
and Renee weren't there.

Presuming that they'd arrive at any moment, Glenda
pulled the Cougar over in front of the hotel and parked. She
watched sunbathers on the shore and occasionally scanned

the seawall. Time passed, and Johnson and Shaw didn't come. "I had to be home by six. About then, my dad drove by each day to check on me," Glenda said with a shrug. "So I left. When Renee and Sharon didn't show up at my house that night, all of us didn't think anything of it because it wasn't unusual for them to stay overnight in Galveston. For all we knew, they were sleeping on the beach."

When the girls' parents called, Glenda covered for her friends, making up excuses, telling them that Renee and Sharon had just stepped out. When it went on for days, Glenda became worried. "I talked about it with the other kids, about how Sharon and Renee better get their asses home. You can only tell parents so many times that the girls are sleeping. The next thing I remember is Sharon's mother knocking on the door. She said they hadn't been home. I admitted I hadn't seen them, and that's when she filed a missing persons report."

Yet Glenda and the girls' other beach friends still weren't worried. They never considered that Shaw and Johnson could have been in danger, instead agreeing that the two girls had undoubtedly carried out their plan and run away, maybe to California. By then they could have been in San Francisco, or surfing in Malibu.

In the weeks that followed the girls' disappearances, police officers descended on the Willis home asking questions. When they stopped, Sharon's mother arrived, demanding answers. Presumably desperate and disconsolate about her daughter's disappearance, Sharon's mother, like so many of the other victims' parents and siblings, undoubtedly struggled with the uncertainty and the insurmountable fear. Where was her daughter?

As she remembered those grim times, Glenda spent long hours with Sharon's mother, traveling the streets of Galveston, pointing out places the girls hung out and helping Sharon's mother in her frantic search. "We drove from place to place, but no one had seen them. I didn't think anything of it. I knew they'd just taken off and that they'd be back at some point," said Willis. The weeks passed, and Sharon's mother stopped coming. Glenda continued searching on her own. "I wanted to find someone who'd had contact with them, to tell them to call their parents."

School started in September, and the freshman class arrived at Clear Creek High School. Sharon Shaw and Renee Johnson weren't among them. By then, Glenda's father had heard about the girls' disappearances. Not wanting her involved, he packed her up and moved her back to the Baptist boarding school in San Marcos, south of Austin.

At school, Glenda Willis didn't hear the news a month later, in November, when Debbie Ackerman and Maria Johnson disappeared, their decomposing bodies found days later in Turner Bayou, their wrists and ankles tied. If Willis had, perhaps she wouldn't have been as certain that Sharon and Renee had willingly absconded in search of freedom. The holidays came and went, and still Glenda refused to consider any possibility other than that Sharon and Renee had left voluntarily to enjoy life on the road.

Five months almost to the day after Sharon Shaw's and Renee Johnson's disappearances, on January 3, 1972, two teenage boys in small boats rowed down a drainage ditch attached to Taylor Bayou. Situated near State Highway 146 and the upscale community of Shoreacres, a coastal town across the bay from Galveston, Taylor Bayou resembled the site where Maria Johnson's and Debbie Ackerman's bodies had been found nearly two months earlier. The land surrounding the ditch was covered in brush and trees. It was a lonely patch of ground, one with few visitors.

On that afternoon, the boys saw what they at first thought could have been a volleyball bobbing in the water. Yet when they ventured closer, they realized it was something very different. Marking the spot with a broken oar plunged into the mud, they rushed home to bring one of their fathers to investigate. It was late, and the man suggested they wait until the next morning.

At first light, the tide rolled lazily in, while the two boys and the man in a boat searched the shoreline. When the man saw something glistening under the water near the broken oar, he reached deep into the muck and brought the object up. He put it in the boat, and they hurriedly rowed home. When police arrived, the boy's father directed them to the garage. There he unwrapped a blanket, revealing the object pulled from the Taylor Bayou ditch: a human skull.

At any time, such a grisly discovery would have required further investigation, but in the context of so many murdered girls, law enforcement moved in quickly. In the days that followed, divers explored the water for clues, while deputies searched the land surrounding the ditch where the skull had been found. Once the skull was in the hands of the medical examiner, he inspected its delicate features and determined that it came from a girl. After he measured her thin nasal aperture, he wrote on the autopsy report that the skull was from a Caucasian. Finally, he examined the skull's suture lines, areas that fuse as humans age. When he assessed the degree of ossification, rigidity caused by the growth of bone, he judged the age at between thirteen and seventeen.

Another dead teenage girl.

Even with such a small piece of a skeleton, there was hope that the dead could be identified. In a lucky twist, the skull included a jaw segment and five teeth, some with fillings and one with a crown. A list of missing girls in the Houston/ Galveston area was compiled, and investigators fanned out, beginning the grim task of notifying parents and tracking down dentists, bringing pictures and written descriptions of the skull's dental work to interviews.

At the same time, on the banks of the Taylor Bayou ditch, others congregated, and the search continued, in hopes of finding more of the girl's skeleton. That the ditch was a popular place to dump garbage made the task tedious. A substantial complication was that floods had come and gone during the previous year's back-to-back hurricanes, leaving behind a thick layer of silt. Heavy equipment and dogs were brought in, and mechanical sieves were employed to sift through the sludge. Slowly, more teeth were recovered and sent off to assist in identification. Then a handful of bones were found. Some turned out to be from animals, but a singular delicate left-arm bone was spied in the woods. Not long after, a human sacrum, the large triangular bone at the base of the spine, the one that forms the back of the pelvic cavity, was found under a pile of dead leaves.

On the surface, it all appeared to fit. The medical examiner pegged the sacrum, too, as being from a young female. Yet did all the bones come from the same girl? Although they had no way to conclusively tie the bits of recovered skeleton to the skull, the coroner tentatively linked the findings based on their proximity.

While the search of the recovery site continued, investigators compared dental records. Finally, nine days after the skull's discovery, its owner had a name: Rhonda "Renee" Johnson. The young, blond teenager with the flirty personality was dead. The day her skull was found would become Johnson's official death date on state records, but it was obvious to all who saw her sun-and-water-bleached bones that the teenager had died months earlier, probably not long after her disappearance.

Johnson's identification, of course, raised the question: Where was Sharon Shaw? The obvious answer was that there was a strong possibility that she'd met a similar fate.

The quest continued, this time searching the ditch and surrounding area not only for additional pieces of Johnson's skeleton but also for any signs of Sharon Shaw. "We were out there all day, day in and day out for what seemed like forever," said an officer who helped look for the bodies. "We had sieves, and we went through the mud looking for bones, anything we could find. We found some pieces of jewelry, things a young girl would wear. We fanned out, walking the bayou, poking into the high grass, watching out for nests of snakes."

Eventually, the hunt was abandoned. While it was presumed that Sharon Shaw was dead, blaming the hurricanes that flooded the Gulf Coast the previous September and the animals that roamed the area, including coyotes, authorities reasoned that the second teenager's bones were most likely scattered and would never be found.

That wasn't what fate intended, however, for on February 17, six weeks after the discovery of Johnson's skull, at just after 5 P.M., a twenty-year-old man walked the banks of the bayou. Why? Decades later that would be unclear. Perhaps he'd heard about the search and wanted to help. Or maybe he was simply a local taking a stroll along the bayou just as dusk fell. As he made his way along the bank, he noticed something hidden in high grass. Bending down to investigate, he identified the curious objects as a pile of human bones. The man marked the spot, then ran quickly up the banks. He drove to a chemical plant, one of the many under construction on the nearby coastline, and rushed in and asked to use a telephone.

Sharon Shaw's remains lay a mere half a mile from where Johnson's skull had been found.

Recovered along with nearly a full skeleton was a skull, like the first, detached from the body, but not necessarily by a killer. Instead, it was thought that both skulls might have become dislodged through decomposition. Five days later, the newly discovered jawbone and yet another set of dental records led a medical examiner to officially rule what everyone involved in the case already assumed—the pile of bones found on the edge of the Taylor Bayou ditch belonged to Sharon Shaw.

One coincidence—or was it—caught investigators' attention. The previous September, just a month after Shaw and Johnson vanished, a decomposing, headless, handless, footless torso wearing a shirt from one of Galveston's two surf shops, Jericho's, had been found in that same area along Taylor Bayou's shores. At the time, the torso was misidentified as belonging to a missing teenage boy, but years later he reappeared alive and well, explaining that he'd changed his name and served in the armed services.

In hindsight, pondering the discovery of the two girls' remains and the lack of Johnson's full skeleton, many wondered if that unidentified torso could have been hers. Yet based on the structure of the pelvis—one of the two bones along with the skull used to determine sex—the assistant medical examiner who conducted the autopsy of the torso in the fall of 1971 pegged the body not as female but that of a teenage boy, sandy-haired and standing about five-foot-seven.

Over the decades, many would come to wonder if the assistant medical examiner was wrong and that the Jericho Surf Shop T-shirt torso was Renee Johnson's body, found months before her skull and her friend Sharon Shaw's skeleton. That led to theories about why Johnson's body might have been beheaded, and why its hands and feet were removed. Did that shed any light on the murders?

To unravel the mystery, decades later the Harris County Medical Examiner's Office would attempt to locate the torso's remains to run DNA, to determine sex and answer the questions surrounding the unidentified body. In the end, the ME's office would issue a statement saying that no remains were found from which to obtain DNA. In the four decades since the torso's discovery, everything had been lost.

The identity of the Jericho Surf Shop torso remained like so much else about the cases, an unanswered question.

In the weeks following the discovery of Shaw's and Johnson's bones, investigators considered their deaths, comparing the evidence to the murders of the other dead teenage girls, especially the two Galveston girls whose bodies were found just two months earlier, Debbie Ackerman and Maria Johnson; Sharon and Renee, too, were best friends who'd disappeared together, apparently been murdered together, and their bodies dumped together into a water-filled ditch,

where the killer could count on the water and wildlife to
consume their flesh and destroy physical evidence. Keys
were found on the site, but police failed to determine who
they belonged to. And on a later search, some clothing discovered in among the trees matched the description of what
the Shaw and Johnson girls wore on the day they disappeared. The searchers also collected thick black string they
theorized might have been used to tie Shaw and Johnson,
reminiscent of the bindings found on not only Ackerman
and Johnson but Brenda Jones, whose body had been found
months earlier floating near the Pelican Island Bridge.

So little remained to glean information from, the medical
examiner ruled Johnson's and Shaw's causes of death as undetermined. On the cover of both girls' autopsies, he wrote:
"There was no evidence of trauma. However, in view of the
known circumstances of this case, it is our opinion that the
manner of death was homicidal."

That February, Glenda Willis was at home in League City
for a few days when police knocked on her front door. They
told her that Sharon's and Renee's remains had been discovered, and they wanted her to identify the jewelry found
near the scene. "I was the last one to see them alive, so they
wanted me to verify that I remembered what they'd found,"
she said. On the trip to the police station, she felt noncom-
mittal about even participating. "I didn't believe it was them.
I told the police that they were wasting their time. I kept
telling them that the girls weren't dead; they were in California."

At the Webster police station, however, she was shown
photos of the skeletons and jewelry found nearby, including ankle bracelets. One piece she knew instantly, a thick,
rustic-looking surfer's cross on a chain. "That's Renee's,"
she confirmed. Although she'd been told of their fate, Willis
remained unable to comprehend what she'd just learned, so
much so that she asked, "Where are the girls?"

"Your friends are dead," the officer said, his voice firm yet quiet. "Like I said, this was found near their skeletons."

"Even then, I didn't believe it," Glenda would admit years later. "It was a long time before I could accept that Sharon and Renee weren't ever coming back. From that point on, my parents went into serious protection mode and shipped me off."

Her friends' deaths had left Willis traumatized. She suffered nightmares and thought back often to that summer. "I had dreams where we were in my car, and Sharon and Renee wanted to hitchhike, and I'd tell them no," she recalled. "I'd tell them no, but they'd go anyway. Then I'd wake up, and they'd be dead."

The next painful event would leave Glenda Willis with still more to regret. "I wish I'd known about Mike Self," she said, accompanied by a sad shake of the head. "I would have told them that he didn't do it. He didn't murder Sharon and Renee."

Chapter 3

A Case of Russian Roulette
The Prosecution of Michael Lloyd Self

Webster, Texas

One of Michael Lloyd Self's mug shots. *(Courtesy of the Harris County Sheriff's Office)*

"If you put what happened to Mike Self in the context of the law and what we do today, you're never going to be able to reconcile it," said Dewey Meadows, the former prosecutor turned defense attorney who in 1972 was assigned by a judge to represent Michael Lloyd Self against charges that he'd murdered Sharon Shaw and Renee Johnson. We were in a windowed conference room inside the modern Houston high-rise where Meadows's firm was located, a building that didn't exist at the time the drama we gathered to discuss unfolded. "Back then, things were different. We defense attorneys used to carry guns to the courthouse, then sit in the coffee room, talk about the judges, and show the guns off, sometimes trading them. Things were wilder then, not so controlled. And the police got away with more."

In 1972, when Renee Johnson's and Sharon Shaw's bodies were found, Michael Lloyd Self worked at a gas station on Nassau Bay Road in Webster, close to the Johnson Space Center, then in full throttle with the burgeoning space program. A slender man with soft dark hair and a longish, slightly crooked jaw, Self had grown up in the area. Glenda Willis had crossed paths with him over the years. "My family knew his family," she said. "It was such a small town back then, everyone knew everyone around here. We always referred to him as Slow Mike. We joked about it. There was something not quite right with Mike Self."

Adopted as a young child, Self lost his father when he was only ten. His mother, a second-grade schoolteacher, became a single parent, and friends described Self as a shy momma's boy. He never did well in school, frequently on the verge of failing, and a doctor who examined him in fourth grade pegged the cause on what he called "minimal brain injury." From a young age, Mike Self talked haltingly and sometimes appeared to have difficulty comprehending. Family friends and his mother would say he was "vulnerable" and "easily led." They used words like *passive, nonaggressive*, and *insecure*.

Out of high school, Self signed on at the gas station back in the days when full-service attendants filled tanks and checked oil. But his true love was volunteering at Webster's fire department, housed next door to the police station. Those who knew him described Self as something of a law-enforcement hanger-on, making friends with the police chief and frequenting the station. Mike Self liked to banter about cases in the news although there weren't a lot of serious ones in the small town, at least not until Sharon Shaw and Renee Johnson turned up dead. At that point, what Self wanted to talk about were the two girls' murders.

In those first few months after Shaw's and Johnson's remains were found, there wasn't a lot to discuss. Like the investigations into the murders of the other five girls who'd perished in the area in the previous year, 1971—the dentist's daughter, Colette Wilson; the schoolgirl whose body was found floating near the Pelican Island Bridge, Brenda Jones; the grocery-store bookkeeper, Gloria Gonzales; and the two best friends whose bodies were found near the Turner Bayou Bridge, Debbie Ackerman and Maria Johnson—the inquiry into Shaw's and Johnson's deaths quickly stalled. After the discovery of their bones, months went by without a solid lead. Until attention turned to Mike Self.

Glenda Willis would be perplexed at the idea that Self would have even been considered: "Mike wasn't a part of that group. He didn't even know the girls. And he just wasn't the kind of guy who would have hurt anyone." Those are the things she'd later wish she'd been able to tell the police, but that opportunity wasn't there. "My mom told the police that I was away at school. She never told me they wanted to talk to me. I didn't find out until later."

How did the case against Self come together?

Decades later, the story those involved told was that Renee Johnson's grandfather, the Webster City councilman, pulled strings. The loss of his granddaughter was understandably devastating to the entire family, and Roy Johnson took it particularly hard. Infuriated that the murders remained unsolved, the politician and his political allies jettisoned much of the city's police force, including the chief.

At the time, Donald Ray Morris was a Texas Department of Public Safety trooper, a traffic officer assigned to the Webster area. On May 20, Morris hired on as Webster P.D.'s new chief. He brought with him his DPS partner, Tommy Lee Deal, as assistant chief. Their prime duties, of course, included solving—in all hopes quickly—the double murder case, thereby bringing Renee's family justice.

How did Mike Self become a target? Days after Morris took the job, the gas-station attendant attracted the new chief's attention.

In the beginning, Morris's interest in Self revolved around a completely different matter: whether Self had stolen gas from the fire chief's station wagon. It would later seem that brief investigation set the tone for their future encounters. "I leaned on Mike real hard about it," Morris later testified, describing the first time he interrogated Self. "He respected me as far as what I could do to him."

"Was Mike Self afraid of you?" a lawyer asked.

"That's a fair statement. Yes," he responded. At other times, Morris said much the same in even stronger terms, admitting that Mike Self was "scared to death of me."

When it came to the question of where the bad blood originated, some said that Morris resented Self because he was a friend of the former police chief, whom Morris made it clear he couldn't abide. Weeks before he was even questioned about the two murders, Self, who'd had psychiatric treatment after he'd been accused of being a Peeping Tom, told a Webster police officer that Morris had "threatened to get him."

It was around daybreak less than a month after Morris took over as Webster's police chief, when Tommy Deal and another officer were dispatched to the Texaco station where Self worked to talk to him about the girls' murders. Finishing up after working the night shift, Self agreed to report to the police station when he punched out. By seven thirty, he was in an interrogation room where Deal read Self his Miranda rights. Half an hour later, Don Morris arrived at the police station. At approximately nine thirty, Self allegedly confessed.

What happened would later be recounted in depositions by other officers who ventured in and out of the interrogation room that day. They heard Morris shout at Self, who cowered, handcuffed, in a chair. At one point, witnesses said Morris held a billy club in his hand, hitting his palm with it while he cursed at Self, demanding the confession. Mike Self would later contend that Morris rammed the stick into his abdomen and hit him across the back, telling him that he wouldn't get out of the interrogation room until he admitted killing the girls.

It would later appear that the tactics worked. One officer reported that he saw Mike Self looking to Morris to tell him what to write in the confession. The officer, who initially heard Self adamantly claim his innocence, described Self as terrified.

Looking back, Dewey Meadows believed Self could have been an innocent man. *(Courtesy of Kathryn Casey)*

That same June 1972 morning, Michael Lloyd Self was arrested by Webster police for Shaw's and Johnson's murders. Using a common tactic, a Harris County assistant DA charged the gas station attendant with murdering both girls, but proceeded toward trial only with the murder of Sharon Shaw. The plan was to try him on the Shaw case and hold the Renee Johnson murder in reserve. If they failed to get a conviction on the first murder, prosecutors had the option of trying Self on the second. Soon after, a judge contacted Dewey Meadows and appointed him to represent the defendant.

Once assigned to the case, Meadows, who'd just left a

slot as a Galveston County prosecutor, picked up his office phone and called the Webster Police Department, asking to talk to his client.

"He can't talk to you right now," someone told him. "He's being interrogated."

"Well, I'm his lawyer," Meadows said. "You need to stop talking to him right now. Tell Mr. Self that his lawyer told him not to talk until we've had the opportunity to consult, and I can be there with him."

That, however, didn't happen. Instead, Self was questioned for hours. By the time Meadows met with him, Self had signed a confession, describing in detail how he murdered the two girls. Yet when Meadows talked to Self, he insisted that he wasn't guilty, that he'd never even met the girls.

"I asked him, 'Why'd you sign that?'" said Meadows. "Mike told me he was afraid the police chief was going to kill him."

In that first meeting with his lawyer, Self rolled up his shirt to display a reddened area on his abdomen where he said Chief Morris had jabbed him with a nightstick. "Then Mike described how Morris pulled out a gun," said Meadows. "Mike demonstrated how Morris took bullets out of the chamber but said that he left one in. Morris spun the barrel and put it to Mike's head. What Mike said was that Morris played Russian roulette, pulling the trigger."

"I think that man's crazy," Self told Meadows. "I'm afraid of him."

The following morning, news articles announced Mike Self's arrest, reporting that he'd voluntarily confessed. It seemed an open-and-shut case. Chief Morris crowed to the media about his success, boasting that his hard work could pay off for other police departments in the area. In Morris's assessment, Self looked like a viable suspect in the other girls' killings.

Time passed and, eager to explore the possibility, Galveston County deputies and Texas Rangers dropped in at the jail and interviewed Self about their three unsolved murders of young girls: the girl found floating near the Pelican Island Bridge, Brenda Jones, and the two best friends from Galveston, Debbie Ackerman and Maria Johnson. The deputies and Rangers left, however, without connecting Self to any of the crimes. Harris County detectives showed up as well, asking Self about the murders of the Kroger bookkeeper Gloria Gonzales and the dentist's daughter Colette Wilson, whose remains were both found in the Addicks Reservoir, their turf. Yet they also never pursued any charges.

Despite Morris's contention that he'd caged a heinous double murderer, the case against Mike Self had problems. The first: Two days after his arrest, Self was given a polygraph. He failed. The examiner judged that the confession of the man under arrest was not truthful.

Adding to the muddle it quickly became apparent that much of what Mike Self had written in his confession didn't match the physical evidence.

The contradictions were glaring. In the confession, Self wrote that he threw the girls' bodies into not Taylor Bayou or the ditch where they were found but nearby Taylor Lake. Another inconsistency was that he said he picked up one girl at her house. That wasn't possible since it supposedly occurred hours after her parents were home and had reported her missing.

One of the most obvious examples of the discrepancies between the confession and the physical evidence, however, involved his description of how he murdered the girls. Self wrote that he beat the girls on the head with a Coke bottle, knocking them out. The problem was that neither Shaw's nor Johnson's skulls were fractured, which seemed unlikely if he'd pummeled them hard enough to render them unconscious. Finally, Self claimed he removed the girls' clothing from the scene, driving miles away before disposing of it. Yet Renee's and Sharon's clothes were found not far from their bodies.

Such inaccuracies were potential land mines in a trial. In response, Self was again interrogated by Webster police. Before they finished, the agency's prime suspect had signed confession number two. This time Self's account of the murders more closely resembled the case facts.

Meanwhile, Self's defense attorney, Dewey Meadows, felt exasperated. He'd never been notified by police that his client was again being interrogated. "The police questioned Mike even though I said they couldn't. He signed confessions, then told me and his mother that he didn't kill the girls." At their meetings, Meadows noticed how Mike Self appeared unable to defend himself, instead looking to his mother for guidance. The man seemed weak but not necessarily guilty. "But what about the confessions, Mike?" Meadows prodded.

"They told me what to put on the paper and told me to sign it. They said it would make me feel better," Self answered. "They said if I did, I'd be able to see my mother."

"Why did you sign it if you didn't do it?" Meadows asked.

"I was scared," Self answered yet again.

Later, it would be alleged that Mike Self led police to the site where the girls' bodies were found. In pictures snapped that day, Self could be seen gesturing, as if indicating where he'd dumped Renee's and Sharon's bodies in the Taylor Bayou ditch. Did he really know the details, or was someone instructing him to act out the scene for the camera? "I don't know," said Meadows. "But Mike said they told him what to do, and he did it."

There seemed little question that Morris and Deal enjoyed the publicity heaped upon them for being the first to make an arrest in any of the notorious cases. Even before Mike Self's trial began, the chief and his assistant granted interviews to detective magazines. Praise was abundant, as Deal was described as "an outstanding officer" with "a sterling record."

The title of one of the articles read TWO PASSENGERS TO ETERNITY, accompanied by suggestive photos of young girls on a beach. Another was called: "Sex Slayings of Two Pretty Teenage Surfers." "Within a few minutes of questioning and having been shown pictures of the girls, Self allegedly admitted that he knew both girls and had killed both of them," the latter article stated. In the depiction of events in the piece, Mike Self voluntarily waived all of his rights, signed a confession, and then led the investigators to the scene of the crimes.

If Self had any luck at all, it came not from Texas but Washington, D.C. Shortly before his trial, in a case entitled Furman v. Georgia, the United States Supreme Court ruled the death penalty unconstitutional due to the "arbitrary and capricious" manner in which it was applied. It was a ruling that would stand until 1976, when modifications were made to the laws. The result: When Mike Self walked into the courtroom on May 7, 1973, his life didn't hang in the balance, but his freedom did.

The first day of Self's trial, before the jurors were seated, attention focused on the all-important subject of Mike Self's confessions. "They were the ballgame," said Meadows. "Nothing else tied Mike to the murders. Not one piece of evidence."

A motion brought by Meadows contended that the confessions had been coerced. If successful, both would have been ruled inadmissible. The case rested on the outcome of the hearing, and each side argued hard. For the prosecution, Assistant Police Chief Tommy Deal testified that Self freely and voluntarily confessed. Meadows countered by putting Self on the stand, who repeated his account, that he'd signed the confessions only after being threatened, intimidated, and terrorized by the Webster police. Before the judge, Self recounted Chief Morris's alleged game of Russian roulette. Bolstering his friend's claims, Self's roommate took the stand and relayed his experiences with Morris, including that the police chief appeared out to get Self. The judge's decision, however, went against the defense. The confessions would be admissible at trial.

That week in the courtroom, the prosecutor presented jurors with copies of Mike Self's second confession, pictures of the girls' remains, and photos of the accused at the scene pointing to where the girls' bones had been found. He also put on the stand a witness who said that he thought he once saw Self talking to Renee and Sharon outside a convenience store.

The defense had only one witness, the defendant, who again told his version of how Webster police obtained his confession. On rebuttal, Chief Morris denied that any of it had ever happened, describing Self's confession as Deal had, voluntary. The jury took thirteen hours to deliberate and returned a guilty verdict—the sentence, life in prison.

It was what happened after the trial that would convince many that a nest of crooked cops might have condemned an innocent man to life behind bars.

Months after the trial, Don Morris resigned and returned to DPS to work as a trooper. His friend, Tommy Deal, left Webster a little more than a year later.

Then in September 1975, in the little town of Caddo Mills, northeast of Dallas, word spread that the State National Bank was being robbed. Men carrying guns and paper bags were demanding money out of a teller's drawer. The mayor was called, and he ran to the barber shop, knowing that the proprietor had a rifle. A group of townsfolk, alerted by police-band radios, descended on the bank in time to see two men escaping, one holding the teller, the daughter of the bank president, hostage. The robbers sped off, followed by a posse of twenty-five brave citizens. Outside town, the getaway car slammed to a stop, and the robbers pushed the hostage out the door. That gave the citizens in pursuit the break needed to move in. The robbers jumped from the car and ran, only to find they stared down the sights of a young boy's rifle.

The bank robbers corralled that day were former Webster police officers Tommy Deal and a friend, also a former

DPS officer. The man who was later labeled the ringleader of this band of thieves, which had been active in the area for more than two years, including the time that they were fingering Mike Self, was none other than former Webster Police Chief Donald Ray Morris. An article that ran when they were convicted in 1975 called them the three musketeers. Others described the scene in Caddo Mills on the day of the robbery as a comedy of errors on the part of the two hapless bank robbers.

When Self's appeal came up for review in 1979, Morris and Deal, the two men who'd secured his confession, were serving time in federal prisons. The argument at the appeal hearings, as it had been at the trial, centered on the validity of Mike Self's confession. By then, investigations into the circumstances had yielded valuable new witnesses. Depositions were submitted in which Webster police officers on the scene the morning Self was brought in for questioning recounted how the suspect insisted on his innocence until Morris put the fear of God in him. One officer described Morris as sounding "sadistic" that day. "He scared the daylights out of Mike Self," said another officer.

In the interrogation room, when Self said he was innocent, Morris called him a liar. One man heard the chief say, "Mike, you're not going to leave here until you tell me you killed those girls." What the officer would most remember was how frightened Mike Self appeared.

At the hearing, Morris disputed little of what was said, admitting that he'd come on strong with Self. "I told Mike before he ever confessed that I was going to arrest him for murder, you know, of the girls," Morris said.

Gerald Birnberg, Mike Self's attorney for his appeal, found the history of what had happened to his client abhorrent. "Mike had been basically convicted only on the basis of his confession, and it was bullied," he said. "There was no other evidence linking him to the crimes. Was Mike kind of an odd guy? Yes. He wasn't playing with a full deck. He was the perfect patsy."

Before long, articles appeared in Texas newspapers about the bizarre case of a man whose confession may have been forced by police officers who'd turned out to be bank robbers. When Mike Self explained to a *Houston Chronicle* reporter in 1989 why he'd signed the confessions, he said, "To keep Chief Morris from blowing my brains out . . . He said that if I didn't sign the confession, he'd shoot me and say I tried to escape."

Even after years in prison, Self said he didn't blame the jurors who'd ruled on his fate, insisting that they were just doing their job "based on what they heard."

By 1990, Mike Self had been in prison for seventeen years for a crime that few believed he'd committed. Even the prosecutor assigned to represent the state on the appeal doubted that justice had been served. That August, a U.S. magistrate agreed, ruling that the confessions should have been suppressed at the trial. "Dirty pool abounded in the Self case," he wrote. "Self was illegally arrested without a warrant and no independent evidence . . . was ever developed to establish probable cause." Based on that finding, a U.S. district judge threw out Self's conviction, stating that he should be released, unless the state filed for a retrial. If they chose to prosecute him again, however, the judge further ruled that the state would not have the use of the confessions.

For a while, it appeared that doors would finally open and Mike Self, by then middle-aged, might live outside prison walls. That wasn't destined to happen.

Instead, prosecutors challenged the ruling and continued to fight the appeal.

The final resolution came in 1992. While calling the case disturbing both in claims about the circumstances of how the confessions were obtained and the later convictions of Morris and Deal, the U.S. Fifth Circuit Court of Appeals ruled that the federal district court could not overturn the state court's ruling. The judges concluded that there was sufficient evidence supporting the state court's decision that

Self had been advised of his rights prior to signing the confessions and voluntarily waived his rights. The Fifth Circuit also noted that Mike Self had his opportunity to make his case that the confessions had been coerced at the trial, and the decision of the state court and the jurors had gone against him. That decision ended Mike Self's appeals.

Three years later in 1995, twenty-two years after his conviction, Self became eligible for parole. One day, Dewey Meadows saw his old client at one of the prisons. Meadows approached Self to talk to him. The attorney knew how parole boards worked and that Self had a good shot at being released, if he played ball. "You know, Mike," the attorney said. "You could get out of here. All you have to do is tell the board that you're sorry, that you regret your actions."

"But I didn't do it," Self said in his slow, deliberate speech. "I didn't kill those girls."

Years later, the Texas appeals courts would rule that a confession alone was not enough for conviction; collaborating evidence was required. That decision came too late for Mike Self, who died in 2000 of a heart attack in prison.

Looking back on the case even with the benefit of hindsight, Meadows wasn't sure how he would have represented Self differently. "That he signed those confessions was a big problem. The law then wasn't in our favor," said the attorney. "But then, I never thought the judge would let them in. And I didn't believe a jury would find him guilty when there wasn't any other evidence tying him to the two girls' murders."

"I didn't believe Mike Self was guilty," said Doug O'Brien, a former Harris County prosecutor who for a short time worked on the case. In hindsight, not only the circumstances surrounding the confessions bothered O'Brien but something else; while Self lived locked behind bars, more girls died around I-45 and on Galveston Island. "That was a big clue that we had the wrong man. Mike Self was in prison, and the murders continued."

Chapter 4

Lambs to the Slaughter
The Killing Continues

1973 through 1978

In fact throughout the seventies, while Mike Self's fate played out at the hands of Webster police and the court system, girls south of Houston continued to die at the hands of one or more killers. When he talked to his wife, Tom Wilson, the dentist who'd had to identify his own daughter's skeleton, described Colette's innocence and the evil that stalked Texas those years in graphic terms: "It was like sending a lamb to slaughter."

Suzanne Bowers, Kimberly Rae Pitchford, Brooks Bracewell, and Georgia Geer. *(Collage courtesy of Kathryn Casey)*

Michael Lloyd Self was arrested on June 10, 1972. While he sat in jail awaiting trial, on January 3, 1973, a strawberry blond sixteen-year-old with hazel eyes, a sophomore, arrived early at J. Frank Dobie High School in Houston's far southeast reaches for her first day back after the winter break. Kimberly Rae Pitchford enjoyed roller skating at a rink near the house, but not helping her mom clean. She was self-conscious about the new braces on her teeth, and coworkers at a fast-food restaurant where she worked part-time noticed that she covered her mouth to hide them when she smiled.

On that day after school, her learner's permit in hand, Kimberly left the school campus and reported to her first driver's education class. Her father was at work, and Kimberly's mom instructed her to call home when class ended, promising to pick her up.

Later, when police pieced together that day, it would seem that nothing unusual had happened. As she did every day, Kimberly took the bus to school. She attended all of her classes and ate lunch with her best friend. At 3:45, Kim reported to detention, punishment for showing up late to a class. At five she was at the driver's school. At six, wearing a new black coat she'd received as a Christmas gift, she walked out of driver's ed.

Then she vanished.

Although she showed signs of some typical teenage rebellion, Kimberly was a responsible young girl, the kind parents didn't worry too much about. When the phone didn't ring, Elmer and Carol Pitchford called their daughter's friends. When none could tell them where to find Kimberly, the Pitchfords called police. Later that same evening, they filed a missing person report.

The bad news came days later.

The next afternoon, two teenage boys walked by a wooden bridge on County Road 65, a rural lane twenty-two miles from the driving school, and noticed something black billowing against a fence. The following day, curious, they returned to investigate. Parking on the shoulder, they walked toward the object and discovered a black coat. That was odd, but not enough to cause any alarm. It was as they returned to the truck that their attention was drawn to something else, something in a nearby bayou. They cautiously approached. There'd been a recent rainstorm, and whatever it was appeared to be pinned against a bridge in the rushing current.

When they realized what they were looking at, they turned and ran.

The teenagers rushed home to tell one of their fathers, who returned with them to the scene. Once there, he saw what they'd described: a girl's body, facedown, partially underwater. Wondering if it could be some kind of doll, looking for a less horrific explanation, the man retrieved a long branch and poked it. It appeared real. Reluctant to touch anything else, they ran back to the car and drove to a nearby home, where they rang the doorbell and asked to use a phone to call police.

On the scene, police recorded that the dead girl wore a blue-and-red dress, a red bra, and a small gold cross on a chain around her neck. The clothing matched the description on a recent missing person report. By then, however, there was little question. A driver's license application retrieved from the coat pocket bore the name Kimberly Pitchford. At nine that evening, the police arrived at the Pitchfords' house. "They brought us the bad news," said Kimberly's father, Elmer.

The medical examiner assessed the cause of death as ligature strangulation.

Twenty months later, on September 6, 1974, law enforcement in the Houston and Galveston area again searched for two missing girls. That day the youngsters were from yet another I-45 town, Dickinson. Brooks Bracewell, twelve, and Georgia Geer, fourteen, didn't show up at McAdams Junior High School. Georgia's mother called to report the girls missing, telling police that she thought they'd skipped school. For a while, police assumed that this time they might just be dealing with runaways, especially after reports came in that the girls were seen at a motel on County Road 517 near Alvin playing football with a group of unidentified men. Afterward, another witness claimed to have noticed the girls hitchhiking, and yet others said the girls had stopped at a convenience store.

Many couldn't understand what was happening along the Gulf Coast. Some wondered about theories that one man, one lone man, could be responsible for so much death. Was that possible? The following year, the entire country talked about a new phenomenon. The term *serial killer* entered vocabularies and took over headlines with the arrest of a handsome former law student named Ted Bundy. It was in 1975 that he was incarcerated for the first time. Held in Utah on a charge of aggravated kidnapping and attempted criminal assault, Bundy was the prime suspect in a long list of unsolved homicides spanning the nation. In the years that followed, he escaped twice, only to finally be arrested in Florida in 1978.

"When we heard about Ted Bundy, we wondered if that was what was going on down here," said a woman who remembered the fear that permeated the southern Houston and Galveston areas during her teenage years. "We thought it must have been someone like Ted Bundy responsible. But we thought that since no one had died since the Pitchford girl, maybe it was over."

It wasn't.

On April 18, 1976, yet another devastating discovery turned into banner headlines. On that day, a roughneck working a Phillips Oil site stumbled upon the skulls of Brooks Bracewell and Georgia Geer. This time, prisoners were brought out to help with the search of marshes in Alvin, not far from where Colette Wilson had been abducted nearly five years earlier. Because of floods in the area the previous year, the search proved difficult and more than four thousand man-hours went into collecting bits of clothing, teeth, and pieces of jaw. At that time, none of the girls' other bones were found. Again, dental records identified the dead. Both Bracewell and Geer suffered blows to the head.

Still, Bracewell and Geer had been missing for nearly two years. During that time, no other girls disappeared. The towns along I-45 and the island held on to hope. Assuming the girls were murdered by the same killer, perhaps the man had moved on. Perhaps he'd died. Perhaps he was in prison or jail for another crime. Perhaps, but no one knew, not for sure.

Perhaps he was just lying low, letting the spotlight wander. Perhaps he waited and watched, hoping for another opportunity.

At 10:40 A.M. on May 21, 1977, twelve-year-old Suzanne "Suzie" Bowers left her grandparents' home two and a half blocks off the Galveston seawall. Her plan: to walk a mile home, change into a bathing suit, and grab her bike, then ride three miles east on Seawall Boulevard to meet friends at a popular hangout, Stewart Beach. It had rained earlier in the day, but the sun came out, transforming that Saturday into a good day to work on her tan. Suzie loved the water, worshipped it, swam, surfed, and skied. She'd asked her grandfather for a ride home, but he later said that he thought the exercise would be good for his granddaughter and sent her on her way. There didn't seem any reason to worry; Suzie had traversed that same route often, and there'd never been a problem.

Something of a tomboy, Suzie Bowers posed for this photo in sixth grade.

The second of four children, Suzie lived with her father and stepmother but stayed many weekends with her siblings at her grandparents' house on Avenue S1/2. The soon-to-be-eighth-grader had shoulder-length brown hair, green eyes, and, at just under five feet tall, weighed approximately ninety pounds. A spirited tomboy, Suzie favored baggy clothes to cover up the fact that she was developing into a teenager.

That afternoon on Stewart Beach, her schoolmate and good friend Sara Groves watched for Suzie. When Suzie didn't show up as she'd promised, Sara wasn't initially worried. Then when she got home later that afternoon, Suzie's grandmother called and said that Suzie had never arrived at her parents' house that morning. They couldn't find her. At first, Sara still wasn't too troubled. "But Suzie's grandmother kept calling. When she was still calling at six that evening, I figured something was really wrong," said Groves.

That same evening, Suzie Bowers's parents reported her missing to Galveston police.

Even with so much recent evidence suggesting that reports of missing teenagers could end very badly, officers at first wrote off the parents' fears, saying that Suzie had probably run away. Groves remembered telling them that Suzie wouldn't do that, that she wasn't that kind of a girl. And Bowers's stepmother told the *Galveston County Daily News* she didn't believe it either: "All the money Suzanne had saved for a choir trip is still here, as are all her clothes. Her friends are all accounted for. She didn't run away . . . We just don't know what happened. It's as if she was swallowed up in thin air. We have no clues. She's just gone."

Suzie Bowers would be the last of the 1970s killings of teenage girls tied to the I-45 mysteries. Nearly two years later, in March 1979, two boys on dirt bikes rode through a field on the mainland, not far from where Colette Wilson, the dentist's daughter, disappeared, and found Suzie's skeleton. What first caught their attention was a training bra and small bits of red, blue, green, and brown cloth.

In hindsight, four of the girls' killings would have ties to Alvin. Colette Wilson lived in the small town and was abducted not far from her home. Suzie Bowers's skeleton and Brooks Bracewell's and Georgia Geer's skulls were discovered in the Alvin area. Another tie was that Bowers's skull, like Wilson's, Bracewell's, and Geer's, showed evidence of trauma.

"A friend called me and said Suzie had been found," said Groves. "I asked if she was okay, and the girl said, 'What do you think?' I knew then she was dead."

"We've been praying for an answer, but we didn't want to hear this," Suzie's grandmother told reporters. "The only relief we can try to feel is that Suzanne is not suffering."

Sara Groves kept in touch with the grandmother over the years, visiting and talking on the phone. When Suzie's grandfather died, his wife told Groves that the last word on his lips was his dead granddaughter's name.

Later, when police circulated through the country taking alleged serial killer Henry Lee Lucas on trips asking about cases, he'd say he thought he remembered murdering little Suzanne Bowers. Yet many would eventually discount his story, as they did those of so many murders he claimed to have committed. Sara Groves would spend her life remembering what happened to her friend, urging police not to close the case. Her impression was that no one was investigating. "Once Lucas confessed, they wrote it off," she said. "It was like it was over, but it wasn't, because the dates, what Lucas said, didn't match what happened."

While Lucas was in prison, Groves wrote him, asking if he murdered her friend. The killer wrote back denying that he had, saying that he'd only claimed he'd murdered Bowers and others to get extra favors from authorities, perks like access to a television and cigarettes. "You ask me if I was guilty of killing your friend, the answer is no. I did give a false confession to the murder, but I was not guilty of it. I was given all the evidence about it," he wrote. ". . . I know that was wrong now, because I hurt a lot of people by making the false statements. I hope you will forgive me."

Over the decades, Groves mounted her own inquiry, including calling the man who leased the property where her twelve-year-old friend's bones were found. He said he'd seen two vehicles in the field about the time Suzie disappeared. One was a truck, but the other—like the last vehicle Debbie Ackerman and Maria Johnson were seen entering in front of the Galveston ice-cream shop on the November 1971 morning they disappeared—was a van.

Often, Sara called Suzie's grandmother and compared notes. "Grandma Bowers never stopped trying to figure out who murdered Suzie," said Groves. "Until the day she died, Suzie's grandmother left the room Suzie slept in the way it was on the day she disappeared. Her clothes and stamp collection were still there. Suzie's grandmother never got rid of anything."

Death was all around Groves during those years. In 1971, when Debbie Ackerman was murdered and her body thrown in Turner Bayou, Groves lived only a block away from the girl's family. Then Groves's good friend Suzie Bowers died, perhaps slain by the same man. Hearing a Bee Gees or Barry Manilow song brought memories flooding back. "Suzie and I were in choir, but neither one of us could carry a tune. We just murdered their songs. We called the local radio station all the time and requested 'Jive Talking,' then sang along at the top of our lungs. Suzie was so much fun."

When asked how her friend's death impacted her life, Groves didn't hesitate: "I never got over it. I've always watched my back."

The seventies ended, and so did the killings. Yet more discoveries remained. In April 1981, the remainder of Brooks Bracewell's and Georgia Geer's skeletons were discovered in a Brazoria County oil field south of Alvin.

In the end, the list of the eleven teenage girls murdered between 1971 and 1977 along south I-45 included: the dentist's daughter, Colette Wilson; the girl found floating near the Pelican Island Bridge, Brenda Jones; Sharon Shaw and Rhonda "Renee" Johnson, who were at first thought to have run away to California; the Kroger bookkeeper, Gloria Ann Gonzales; Galveston best friends Debbie Ackerman and

Maria Johnson; Kimberly Rae Pitchford, who disappeared after driver's ed; Brooks Bracewell and Georgia Geer, thought to have skipped school; and Suzie Bowers, who disappeared while walking home to grab a swimsuit for a day on the beach.

Four of the teenagers died while Michael Lloyd Self languished behind bars.

After Self's trial, no defendant ever again entered a courtroom to be tried for any of the killings. Based on Self's conviction, Sharon Shaw's and Renee Johnson's cases were considered solved and closed. The rest of the girls eventually became the first rows of black-and-white photos in newspapers under the heading MYSTERIES ALONG I-45.

The families grieved, and the girls were never forgotten.

Yet life did go on. Four decades after her daughter's murder, I interviewed Claire Wilson for this book.

From the beginning of our talk, I was struck by how many reasons Claire had to allow life to slip through her fingers. Her second child, Colette, was the first of the eleven 1970s/I-45 murder victims. Then just four years after Colette's murder, Claire's husband died of a heart attack attributed to his overwhelming grief. Sadly, the following year, Claire lost another child, this time in a car accident. So much tragedy. Yet that wasn't what Claire wanted to discuss.

While acknowledging the anguish brought on by Colette's horrific killing, Claire refused to dwell on what could have been, instead preferring to focus on the good in her life. In her eighties, she had ten surviving children, thirty grandchildren, and five great-grandchildren. "I am so blessed," she said. "I have a wonderful family. All the kids turned out to be good people. Did Colette's murder change us? It did. But we never allowed her death to take over our lives. We couldn't."

"If you could find him and talk to him, the man who did this, what would you say to him?" I asked. My assumption was that she would want to retaliate, if not by striking out

physically perhaps with her words, attempting to punish the
source of her loss and suffering.

"I'm not sure. I've never thought about that. I believe in
God, and a long time ago, I put this in his hands," she said.
For a moment, Claire Wilson was quiet. When she spoke
again, she said, "I guess I'd just ask why. Why did he do
this? Why Colette? But I guess I know the answer. Because
on that day, she was the one he saw on the side of the road."

A few nights later, I sat in a sushi restaurant with a retired
FBI profiler who'd worked many of the cases I was investigating. I told him about my research into the murders of the
eleven girls in the 1970s.

"One thing to look at is the timeline," he said. "When the
killings start and when they stop, and pair that up with
the suspects. An important clue is who was available to
do the killing."

Decades after the eleven girls' murders, a lone cop on
Galveston Island would pull together all the records he
could find and assess just that. He'd construct a chronology
of the events as they unfolded. His conclusion? That speculation at the time of the killings was most likely right and all
eleven murders—including the two Mike Self died in prison
for—could have been committed by one killer. The suspect
he'd focus on was one who moved into a house on the island
in 1970, a year before the first killing, and disappeared in
1978, a year after the final victim, Suzanne Bowers, died.

Chapter 5

The Cop and the Killer
Fred Paige's Quest

Galveston, Texas

Alfred "Fred" Paige, believes he knows the name of the Galveston killer. *(Courtesy of Kathryn Casey)*

Between 1970 and 2000, the various versions of the I-45 Mysteries charts would grow to include the photographs of approximately twenty young women. But it all began in the 1970s on Galveston Island with the murder of the first eleven girls. On the day I met with Alfred "Fred" Paige, it was clear that he was haunted by a belief, the certainty that he knew the face, the name, the man behind the brutal slayings of the island's teenage girls. His frustration was that nothing had been done about it.

In his natty Galveston P.D. uniform, Paige had just finished his shift, patrolling the island's streets. With a flat top
of graying brown hair, a wide smile, and an inquisitive gaze,
in November 2005 the veteran cop was a Galveston P.D. detective working property crimes. Eight years later, he was
back in a squad car. Paige didn't say if his belief that he'd unmasked the serial killer had affected his career, but he made
it clear that his was a lonely battle. "No one ever connected
the dots," he said. "When I started looking at this, it was fascinating how it all laid out. To me, it all seems pretty clear."

The fiftysomething Paige didn't sign on at Galveston P.D.
until two decades after the island's serial cases turned cold.
The freewheeling seventies were a distant memory when a
retired supervisor of Paige's forwarded a letter to him from
an elderly woman, an inquiry into the status of the investigations into the two Galveston best friends, Debbie Ackerman
and Maria Johnson. The woman had been a friend of Dee
Ackerman, Debbie's deceased mother, and she wanted to
talk to someone in authority about the killings. Days later,
the woman called Paige directly, inviting him to the nursing
home where she lived.

In her room, the old woman pulled out a scrapbook of
yellowed newspaper articles, the original clips from the
Galveston County Daily News and *Houston Chronicle* documenting the disappearances of Ackerman and Johnson and
the accounts of finding their bodies near the Turner Bayou
Bridge. "Please, look into this," the old woman begged
Paige, as if she'd carried the horror of what had happened to
her friend's daughter with her and never forgotten. "Please
try to find out who killed these girls."

That day began a journey, one that took Paige back to
a different time, when eleven young girls, six of them in
pairs, vanished and died. Over the coming year, the veteran
cop put a fresh set of eyes on the old cases and quickly focused on a shadowy figure he believed was the man who
once roamed the palm-lined streets, murdering Galveston's
daughters.

Carla Costello in her Texas City office, the files on the unsolved cases behind her. *(Courtesy of Kathryn Casey)*

In November of 2005, Paige had never even heard his main suspect's name. That happened a few months later, one afternoon the following January when the fast-talking cop drove across the causeway to the mainland and then north on I-45. Before long, he'd pulled into the parking lot of the Texas City Police Department. Paige was there to see Senior Officer Carla Costello.

The appointment with Costello was a logical place for Paige to start an investigation into Debbie Ackerman's and Maria Johnson's deaths. In the early nineties, twenty years after the first of the Galveston-area girls died, Costello was the one who entered all the 1970s victims into VICAP, the FBI's Violent Criminal Apprehension Program, a national database used to document and compare murders and sexual assaults, in hopes of identifying serial cases. "I'm a big believer in VICAP," said Costello. "We worked hard at that point to get everything organized."

During that process, Costello collected many of the records on the cases, and over the years she became the go-to person for anyone in law enforcement needing information, hence Paige's pilgrimage to her office.

With soft features and tired eyes, Costello had seen much misery over her more than three decades in law enforcement, including the pain of the parents of the murdered girls. Some continued to check on their daughters' cases, calling her or dropping in to ask if anything was being done decades after the killings.

Because of Costello's interest, it was a natural outcome that she became the record keeper, the one who organized the bulk of the cases into white, three-ring binders she kept on the lower shelf of a bookcase beside her desk. In a translucent white plastic file box nestled into a corner, she'd amassed everything from the case that most haunted her: the 1971 double murder of Debbie Ackerman and Maria Johnson, who'd been found in a Texas City oil field, their bodies partially submerged in Turner Bayou. One reason Costello never forgot the girls was that up until her death, Debbie's mom made annual visits to Costello's office. "I'd always hoped that someday I'd be able to tell Mrs. Ackerman that we'd arrested Debbie's killer," said Costello with a slight shrug. "One of the hardest days was the day I heard that Mrs. Ackerman died. I knew then that we'd never be able to give her justice."

That January day in 2006 when Paige walked into Carla Costello's office, he explained his encounter with the old woman in the nursing home and his promise to do what he could to find Debbie and Maria's killer. "Did you ever have anyone you liked for this?" Paige asked Costello. "Anyone you thought might have been behind the killings?"

There was one man, she said. Years earlier the guy, a convicted killer already incarcerated in a Texas prison, had written two letters: one to the Harris County District Attorney and the other to his counterpart in Galveston County. "He confessed," Costello explained to Paige. "But when we tried to follow up, he refused to talk to us. I've always wondered if maybe he's telling the truth, if he could be the killer."

With that, Costello pulled out a copy of one of the man's letters, written from prison and dated January 4, 1998, at a time when the inmate was five years into his seventy-year sentence. The correspondence, addressed to the Galveston district attorney, was disjointed and crudely crafted. In it, the convict contended that he'd murdered all eleven of the girls who'd died along I-45 in the 1970s: seven in Galveston County and four in southern Harris County. Why would he commit such monstrous crimes? In the letter, the man claimed that he'd been brainwashed into committing murder.

Although brief, the inmate's note offered details about two of the crimes: the homicides of the same girls the old woman mentioned to Paige, Debbie Ackerman and Maria Johnson.

In his letter, the self-described serial killer said he'd shot Ackerman and Johnson with a .357 Magnum pistol: Debbie in the neck or the head, and Maria in the neck or back. At the time, he said he stood above the teenagers on a small bridge. Their hands and feet were bound in front with a white nylon string. Knowledge of these facts, the man maintained, proved he was the killer. Yet he added that if he was ever brought into a courtroom he would plead not guilty, laying the blame on the "brainwashing program." In a postscript, the prison inmate said that the "powers that be" knew he had murdered the eleven girls and had done nothing.

The letter was signed: *Yours truly, Edward Harold Bell*

"Does this match the evidence?" Paige asked Costello.

"Pretty close," Costello said.

"Why hasn't this guy been charged with these murders?"

"This is all we have, and he could have gotten it out of the newspapers. We can't prove he did it." Costello said, "He won't talk to us. He could be the killer, or he could just be crazy."

That afternoon, Costello made copies of the letter, the autopsies, investigation records, and other records from the murders for Paige, who thanked her and left.

One of the things Costello told Paige, one of the reasons she entertained the possibility that Bell told the truth in his confessions, was that Bell lived on Galveston Island at the time of the serial killings. "He was part owner in a dive shop on S-Road," she said. That bit of info came to her through the Harris County DAs, who'd briefly investigated after they received their letter from Bell.

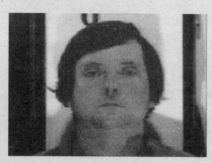

Ed Bell was always a good businessman.
(Mug shot courtesy of the Harris County Sheriff's Office)

As Costello had said, the Galveston DA, too, had tried to reopen the cases, asking to talk to Bell in prison. He'd refused the requests, and both agencies' investigations were tabled for lack of evidence. The laws had changed. Michael Lloyd Self had died in prison, perhaps an innocent man after being convicted on only a questionable confession. In the decades that followed, court decisions decreed that without corroborating evidence, a confession wasn't sufficient evidence of guilt. What if the confessor was delusional? It wasn't unusual for disturbed people to falsely claim they committed sensational crimes. Some did it simply to attract attention.

Despite such doubts, Paige was intrigued. Eleven murdered girls. Ed Bell claimed to have killed eleven girls. Was the man telling the truth?

Later in his office, Paige reviewed the copies of the old files. The only murders Bell discussed in any detail in his letter to the Galveston County DA were those of Debbie Ackerman and Maria Johnson, so Paige began there, listing the specifics. In his letter, Bell had written that:

1. Ackerman and Johnson were shot with a .357
   Magnum pistol
2. Ackerman in the neck, possibly the head
3. Johnson was shot with the gun pointed downward,
   possibly in the back of the head or the neck from
   above. "I was standing on a bridge at the time,"
   Bell claimed.
4. Their hands were tied in front; their feet were also
   bound.

From the evidence records in the case files, Paige pulled
together the corresponding details. According to the autopsies, the bullets used to kill Ackerman and Johnson were
.38 caliber. That was a type Paige knew could have been
fired from a .357 Magnum pistol. There were similarities
in the way the girls were dressed when found. Both were
naked from the waist down but wore their bras, shirts, and
jewelry.

The Turner Bayou Bridge, where Ackerman's and Johnson's bodies
were found. *(Courtesy of Fred Paige)*

As part of his investigation, Paige drove to the mainland, to the location where the teenagers' bodies had been found, through a gate and onto the oil field, then down a gravel and dirt road, one that led to Turner Bayou. Once there, he stood on the narrow wooden bridge, imagining what had transpired decades earlier. Paige took a picture, and reviewed what he'd read in the police reports.

In January 1971, the first body found in Turner Bayou was that of Maria Johnson. It was positioned, as Bell had said, close to the bridge. Also consistent with Bell's description, Maria had a bullet hole on the right side and center of her neck, as well as other gunshot wounds around the head. At the scene, Paige stood on the bridge and visualized how it might have taken place as Bell described in his letter, realizing that the killer could have stood above Johnson—perhaps on the rugged wooden slats of the bridge—when he fired his weapon. Also fitting Bell's letter, Johnson's ankles and hands were bound. Could the fishing cord used to tie Johnson's hands have been what Bell called a "white nylon string?"

Paige then considered Debbie Ackerman's killing. When found, her body lay in the water a hundred yards from her friend's remains. Matching Bell's assertions in the letter, Debbie's ankles and hands were tied, but this time by black cords resembling long shoelaces. Like her friend, she had been shot. One bullet tracked through Ackerman's back and out her chest, but the second was—again as Bell had written—in the neck or head region, more exactly on the left side below the chin.

After comparing the evidence to Bell's written description and assessing that he had a match, Paige called the Galveston DA's Office, and one of the prosecutors answered. "There's a letter," Paige said. "Dude, there's a letter!"

The prosecutor hadn't been at the District Attorney's Office when Bell's letter arrived and knew nothing about it. "I told him that I was all over it, and I'd let him know when I came up for air," Paige said. "So then I set about trying to figure out more about who this guy was and could he possibly be the guy who murdered all those girls."

As Paige investigated, a confusing picture emerged of Ed Bell, that of a young man who initially had a bright future but succumbed to dark urges that eventually dominated and destroyed his life.

Ed Bell was born in Houston. His father, Carl Clayton Bell, was an East Texas oil-field worker and his mother a housewife. He had one brother, Larry, who was two years older. They moved often, following Clayton's latest job, but by junior high had settled on a ranch in New Ulm, a small town a little more than an hour west of Houston, outside of Columbus. Young Ed Bell was an amiable young man who focused on his studies and concentrated on bettering his life. "It was a typical American family," said a relative. "The mom was a sweet woman, maybe a little dingy. The Bells had a house in the country, and as boys, Larry and Ed raised livestock."

During Ed Bell's impressionable childhood years, his family witnessed a shocking act of violence, when Bell's cousin reportedly killed his own father. Ed Bell would later contend that their uncle was torturing his wife at the time, forcing water down her throat, and his son shot him to make him stop.

Despite the chaos of his childhood, those who knew the young Ed Bell judged him like pretty much any small-town kid. To family and friends, he was simply "Butch." One of his former classmates at Columbus High School remembered Butch Bell as a close friend, a happy sort of boy. "He was an Eagle Scout, a really good kid. He had a lot of friends. And he was smart."

Other friends agreed, describing Bell as intelligent and gregarious. "The girls seemed to like him. He dated one girl after another in our class," remembered an old school friend. "Butch was just a really nice guy. I never saw him be violent, not in any way."

After his 1957 high-school graduation, Bell enrolled in one of the Lone Star State's premier universities, Texas A&M, the home of the Aggies, where he played his trombone in the marching band during football games. To pay his way, he worked in the dining hall and sold Christmas cards and fruit in the dorms. "He was a hard worker and a real entrepreneur," said a friend. "He was one of the most liked guys in the Aggie band."

At A&M, Ed Bell majored in physical education and minored in biology. His grades in high school had been exemplary, but in college turned average. While there, he learned to scuba dive, and over one summer he worked as the aquatic director at a boys' camp. It was in San Marcos that Bell met his future wife, Bonnie, who attended Baylor University in Waco. Those who knew her described Ed's young wife as a pretty woman who was into health food. They dated, marrying while he was still at A&M.

Were there early signs that Ed Bell was capable of violence? Later, no one would recall any. None of his friends would report seeing any evidence of a volatile temper. Rather, Bell was someone who tried hard to please, a bright, outgoing young man who quickly made friends.

Not dark and introverted, Bell had a buoyant personality and a jovial laugh. Larry's wife, Janice Bell, described her brother-in-law as a big-talking Texan. "Ed was very friendly, made friends with everyone. He could be very likable. I never liked him, but I can't say why. It just seemed that he was always tooting his own horn."

Many believed that Ed Bell would one day earn such bragging rights, by combining his hard work and goals to become a great success. "I think Ed was a big dreamer," said an old friend. "And that's not a bad thing."

Over the years, Bonnie and Ed Bell had three children. The first time he was picked up for exposing himself to young girls was in 1966 in the rural ranching community of Sudan, Texas, just west of Plainview. Bell was ordered into treatment, and would later characterize his stay at Big

Spring State Hospital, a two-hundred-bed psychiatric facility, as a waste of time.

By the late sixties, the family lived in Lubbock, where Bell had a job as a pharmaceutical rep calling on physicians. At the time, he also attended Texas Tech University, working on a master's degree. There, in April 1969, Ed Bell's dark side reemerged when he was arrested for again exposing himself. The repercussions were swift. In response, Bell was kicked out of Tech and a deal was brokered, one in which he escaped prison time by agreeing to inpatient treatment for what were labeled as his "perversions." In his instructions, the judge specified that Ed Bell be treated for nine months in a psychiatric facility, or until a consulting physician deemed Bell cured. About that time, Bell and his first wife divorced.

Ed Bell arrived in Galveston in April 1969 accompanied by his father, Carl Clayton Bell, at the suggestion of a psychiatrist who recommended the University of Texas Medical Branch's psychiatric program. Once there, the two men entered the austere hospital lobby. In the admissions area, Bell and his father answered questions. The reason he was there, Bell said, was because of his "sexual problem."

In response to the interviewer's questions, Bell's father maintained that his son had always seemed a "normal" young man, bright, with friends and healthy relationships with girls. "He seemed to date in a regular manner. Ed never showed any signs of perversions."

When asked about his son's early life, Ed's father responded that his wife had no difficulties during the pregnancy and that Ed suffered no childhood trauma or high fevers, no head injuries to explain his actions. Carl Bell also said that as a youngster, Ed displayed no signs of a propensity toward violence, such as cruelty to animals. He'd played well with other children and was bright, earning good grades.

When it came to Ed's problem, Carl maintained it began in his son's second year of marriage. While still in College

Station, Ed exposed himself at least twice to young girls. From that point on, such incidents escalated, until Ed had been picked up by police five or six times. The most recent offenses were that past April, for which he'd been ordered into psychiatric treatment.

What did the interviewer see in the thirty-year-old Ed Bell sitting across from him that day?

In many ways it wasn't different from what Ed's old friends in Columbus described. When documenting the admission, the interviewer characterized Ed Bell as friendly, a personable man. Yet he did note that the hospital's new patient seemed perhaps *overly* helpful, as if wanting desperately to be liked.

Why had Bell turned from model student and young husband to having what he described as "a sexual problem?" When asked, Bell labeled the root of "his perversion" as a combination of pressures at work and home. He took no responsibility for the incidents that led to his arrest, blaming his actions on others. "Is there anything else going on?" the interviewer asked, seeking information on any signs of mental illness. Was Ed experiencing hallucinations, auditory or visual?

Bell denied both.

On that day in April 1969, Ed Bell entered UTMB's psychiatric program, where he was put on Valium. At the hospital, the physicians eventually came to two diagnoses: a personality disorder and depression. Presumably, his treatment went well, because just three months later, in July, Bell essentially moved out of the hospital on overnight passes although he wouldn't be officially discharged until July 1970. While attending day sessions, he came and went as he pleased.

In Galveston, Bell began a new life. Not long after checking out of the hospital, thirty-one-year-old Ed married again, this time to a twenty-year-old named Debbie, a fellow patient he'd met in the hospital.

The newlyweds moved into a rented second-story apartment in a large waterfront house on Offatts Bayou. "Ed loved Galveston," said an old friend who visited him there. "He loved the water, scuba diving, the casual lifestyle. He seemed to flourish."

On the island, Bell met Doug Pruns, who ran Doug's Dive & Surf Shop in a strip center on Fifty-seventh and Avenue S, next door to a wrecker service. Bell proposed that they partner up. Somehow, he'd pulled together a stash of scuba equipment he wanted to rent through the shop. Pruns and Bell struck a deal. Decades later, when Fred Paige investigated Bell's past and heard about the surf-shop arrangement, it piqued his interest further.

Connecting Bell to the surf shop was an enticing bit of information. "What I learned was that Debbie Ackerman and Maria Johnson (the Galveston girls whose bodies were found near the Turner Bayou Bridge), along with many of the other victims, used to frequent the surf shop. They hung around there." Also interesting was that geographically everything fit. The waterfront apartment Bell and his new wife rented was walking distance to both Doug's Surf Shop, a hangout for the teens, and the Wix Ski Shop, the last place the two Webster girls, Rhonda Johnson and Sharon Shaw, were seen on the August 1971 day they disappeared. Ackerman and Johnson had been at Wix, just down the block from Bell's apartment, skiing the day before they vanished. "Everything is right there," said Paige. "And Ed Bell was right in the middle of it."

While Doug Pruns ran the surf shop day to day, Ed Bell made most of his money selling real estate in Terlingua Ranch in far-west Texas near Big Bend National Park, out of an office in downtown Houston. Later, in the midseventies, Bell expanded his interests, investing in tugboats used to service offshore oil rigs. "Ed always seemed to have a bunch of money, a roll in his pocket," said an old friend. "He talked big and moved around a lot."

There were other indications that Paige interpreted as

confirmation that he was on the right track. An old witness statement from the time of Debbie Ackerman and Maria Johnson's disappearance placed them at the Baskin-Robbins ice-cream shop in Galveston. The last time they were seen, the girls were getting into a white van with a peace-sign sticker on the back window. An unidentified white man was behind the wheel. What made this particularly important, in Paige's estimation, was that just a few months later, in February 1972, Bell was again picked up for exposing himself to yet another young girl. This time he was in Louisiana, and the arresting officer recorded the type of vehicle Bell drove that day: a 1971 white Ford van.

When Paige talked to Glenda Willis, Sharon Shaw and Renee Johnson's friend, he heard something else interesting. In the weeks before her friends disappeared, Shaw and Johnson hung out with two older men, in their twenties or thirties. "It was creepy," Willis said. "What were guys like that doing hanging out with high-school kids?" Just before they vanished, the girls began talking about running away with the men to California. One of them, Willis mentioned, drove a van.

Another source gave Paige more enticing information on ties between Ackerman, Johnson, and Ed Bell. One of Debbie Ackerman's good friends told the veteran cop that the group of friends they ran with that summer spent time at the same waterfront house where Bell lived. They knew the man who owned the property, and some took diving lessons from him.

Working through the evidence, Paige continued to connect the dots linking Bell and the girls as the veteran cop delved ever further into the past and his inquiry into the murders. Some of those Paige interviewed recalled that Bell and his young wife lived at one point in a red trailer that resembled a caboose. At first the trailer sat on land in the Bayou Shores RV Resort, not far from their waterfront apartment. Later, however, Bell moved the caboose onto a rural lot situated two hundred yards from Humble Camp Road.

What made that fact important was that Humble Camp was the road that led to the Turner Bayou Bridge, the site where Debbie Ackerman's and Maria Johnson's bodies were found.

Then there was the timing. The strange events on the island began not long after Ed Bell was released from UTMB's psychiatric program in July 1970.

When Paige expanded his investigation from his initial look at Johnson's and Ackerman's murders to those of the other girls, he again quickly found suspicious links with Bell.

What about Colette Wilson, the dentist's daughter? What caught Paige's attention was her location that final day of her life, attending a multischool band competition. That brought to Paige's mind Ed Bell's own years participating in bands at Columbus High School and A&M. Had Bell gone to the competition and seen Wilson that day? Did he follow her instructor to the corner where she let Colette out of the car?

Brenda Jones, the only African-American victim, also played an instrument. And she was at UTMB visiting her aunt on the July 1971 afternoon of her disappearance, not far from where Bell spent months as an inpatient in the psychiatric unit and where he routinely reported for outpatient therapy.

Was it a stretch to believe that Bell could have been the killer? Paige had ample evidence documenting that in 1971, when the killings began, Ed Bell actively pursued young girls in Galveston.

Two weeks after Colette Wilson's abduction in June 1971, for instance, an island teenager sunbathing in her backyard looked up to see a stranger masturbating as he watched her. The man the girl identified was Ed Bell. The following month, in August, the two Webster best friends, Renee Johnson and Sharon Shaw, disappeared, after last being seen at the Wix Ski School, just down the block from Bell's apartment. Was there any connection to Gloria Gonzales, the grocery-store bookkeeper whose body was found near Colette Wilson's skeleton? During his research, Paige discovered that Bell had business connections in Gonzales's neighborhood and near the Addicks Reservoir, where Wilson's and Gonzales's bodies were found. A month after Gonzales's disappearance, Debbie Ackerman and Maria Johnson were murdered. Both girls frequented the surf shop where Bell was a part-owner and were last seen entering a white van. Perhaps the one Bell owned?

Although 1971 ended, on Paige's list the killing continued.

What happened to Kimberly Pitchford, the sixteen-year-old who vanished after leaving her driving class in January 1973? Had she, perhaps, gotten into Bell's van? Paige had no way of knowing. The following year Bell was again in trouble in Galveston County, this time for exposing himself to two girls he happened upon on a road. That day he drove not the van, but a rented Volkswagen. Not long after, a former psychiatric patient accused Bell of rape but ultimately dropped the charges.

Then the final set of two: Brooks Bracewell and Georgia Geer. Like the others their bodies were found in or near water, this time in a marsh. When Paige ran a records search, he discovered that Bell owned land in the area.

The last of the girls to die, twelve-year-old Suzanne Bowers, vanished near her grandparents' Galveston house in 1977. Here Paige documented a tantalizing connection to his suspect. One of Ed Bell's tugboat captains lived just behind the grandparents' house. "The guy told me that Bell was at his house all the time," said Paige. "It wouldn't be a stretch to think he'd seen the girl."

Then all went quiet. Or at least it appeared to.

The following year, on August 24, 1978, Bell pulled up in front of a house in Pasadena, Texas, southeast of Houston. On the street Bell spied a group of children playing. He got out of a red-and-white GMC pickup nude from the waist down and began masturbating. The girls screamed, and a twenty-six-year-old vet recently home from the service, Larry Dickens, heard his mother, Dorothy, calling the police. His light brown hair swept over his forehead, his mustache trimmed, the former Marine shouted at Bell. Hoping to detain the man until police arrived, Dickens ran to Bell's truck and grabbed the keys out of the ignition.

Furious, Ed Bell retrieved a .22 pistol from inside his pickup. He shot Dickens four times in the chest. Somehow, Dickens managed to run toward the garage, wounded but trying to escape with his life.

Inside the house, Dickens's mother again called police, pleading for help, while outside her son staggered down the driveway before collapsing. Bell grabbed a high-powered rifle from his pickup and walked back up the driveway. As Dickens pleaded for his life, Bell straddled the ex-Marine and pulled the trigger.

Larry's teenage sister, Dawna, pulled up just in time to see Bell fire that fatal shot. "I don't think my mother ever got over losing Larry that way," said Dawna.

Twenty minutes later, after a car chase and gun battle, police had Bell secured in the back of a squad car. They drove him to the Dickens house, where Dawna and her mother identified him as the man who'd murdered Larry. Astonishingly, his lawyer posted bond, and Bell was out of jail in twenty-four hours.

Two months later, Ed Bell was back at UTMB in Galveston, where he admitted himself for another psychiatric evaluation, again for his self-described "sexual problem." After his testosterone levels were deemed high, doctors put him on depro provera, a drug used for chemical castration, one known to diminish male sex drives. What authorities didn't know was that at that same time, Ed Bell was liquidating his assets, including selling all but one of the boats he'd been running to supply oil platforms in the Gulf.

When the next hearing on his case came up, Ed Bell and his remaining boat were gone. He'd jumped his bond and was on the lam with more than $140,000 in his pocket.

In the years that followed, off and on, reports came in of sightings, like one in 1984 from a woman who identified Bell as the intruder who entered her house in Bryan, Texas, near A&M. She screamed when she saw the reflection of a man carrying a large hunting knife in her bathroom mirror. That afternoon, the woman grabbed a gun and chased the stranger from the house.

For fourteen years, Bell was on the run. Based on the brutality of the Dickens murder, in 1985 he was named Texas's most-wanted criminal, his picture displayed in post offices and government buildings across the state. Yet his trail went cold. In Houston, Dawna and her mother worried that Bell would one day come after them, to silence them as witnesses. "Even when I was thirty, I'd look over at the next car on the road and think that I saw him," said Dawna. "My mom did the same thing. We were terrified of him."

Then, on December 2, 1992, *America's Most Wanted* aired an episode including a dramatization of Larry Dickens's murder. A young Matthew McConaughey portrayed the victim, illustrating for the cameras how the courageous ex-Marine attempted to corner and detain Bell. "That was McConaughey's first acting role, playing my brother," said Dawna. "After the program aired, tips started coming in."

Those phone calls led authorities to Panama, where Bell lived under an alias, the name of a dead cousin. He'd married again and had begun a new life, running tourist boats and prospecting for gold on land he bought outside of Panama City. Although he fought extradition, Bell lost and was escorted back to the U.S. by FBI agents.

In June 1993, Bell was finally tried for Dickens's murder. On the stand at his trial, he described the dead ex-Marine as a religious fanatic. "Mr. Bell said he was just sitting there and that my brother attacked him for no reason," said Dawna, who testified at the trial. "His story was so far out there."

While Bell was on the stand, Dawna said he appeared focused on what was going on around him and showed no signs of any delusions or mental illness. "He knew what he was saying."

During his testimony, Bell claimed he shot Dickens in

self-defense and that the fatal shot had been an accident, that he'd tripped and the gun had gone off. According to the autopsy, the bullet traversed front to back through Dickens's forehead.

One day during the trial, Larry Bell, Ed's older brother, approached Dawna. "I'm so sorry," he said, appearing heart-broken. He cried, saying he regretted what Ed had done. "My brother wasn't always like this. He used to be a kind and gentle person. I don't know what happened to him. He just snapped."

The jury rejected Ed Bell's depiction of the events and handed down a seventy-year sentence. In July 1993, Bell disappeared inside the Texas prison system. Five years later, he wrote the letters to the two district attorneys in which he confessed to murdering the eleven teenagers.

After he reviewed Ed Bell's past, Fred Paige believed Bell's claims in his letter. "If you can give me a better suspect, I'd love to hear it," said Paige on the afternoon of our interview, his arms folded defiantly across his chest.

His file on the case in hand, Paige contended that he consulted with the Galveston District Attorney's Office and tried to convince a prosecutor to take his evidence along with Bell's confession letters to a grand jury. "They put me off and put me off. They'll never prosecute it," he said. "They won't because, in a nutshell, the bullets were lost, the clothing was lost, the evidence from these cases is gone. Plus most of the witnesses are gone."

At this point, Paige and I had been talking for a very long time, recounting an investigation into events that were nearly four decades old. For all Paige's hard work, Ed Bell's guilt was still just speculation. Paige had been unable to bring any closure to the cases or the victims' families. "Sure, Ed Bell is in prison for killing Larry Dickens, but Bell killed a lot of other people," Paige alleged, his disgust apparent. "The bottom line here is that Ed Bell will probably never be prosecuted for any of them."

Although Paige couldn't drum up the interest of a prosecutor, he did get the press interested. In May 2006, the first
article ran in the *Galveston County Police News,* a monthly
newspaper that serves the area's law-enforcement community. In it, Paige named Bell as a suspect in the murders and
asked for help from anyone who might have photos of the
white van Bell drove at the time of the Ackerman and Johnson murders. Perhaps he hoped to see that peace sign a witness noticed on the back window of the van the girls drove
away in. Other articles in the *Police News* followed, about
Michael Self's questionable conviction and the evidence
against Ed Bell.

Bell turned down interview requests from the *Police
News,* but five years later, *Houston Chronicle* reporter Lise
Olsen learned of Paige's suspicions. Olsen corresponded
with Bell in prison, and he wrote that he had murdered
eleven girls, five in 1971 and six more in the mid- to late
seventies.

The list Ed Bell scratched out wouldn't turn out to precisely match the one Fred Paige had drawn up. It wasn't
identical to the names that had run for so many years of
the murdered girls in the chart. Yet many of the cases were
accounted for in the handwriting of a man who claimed to
be a serial killer. For the 1971 murders, Bell left out Brenda
Jones, but included the other murders that made headlines
that year: the dentist's daughter, Colette Wilson, the two
Galveston girls whose bodies were found in Turner Bayou,
Debbie Ackerman and Maria Johnson, and Sharon Shaw
and Rhonda Renee Johnson from Webster, who Mike Self
was convicted of murdering.

Then there were the later murders, the final six. The next
on Bell's list he called simply Pitchford. That bit of information made it easy to peg Bell's sixth victim as Kimberly
Rae Pitchford, the sixteen-year-old who disappeared one afternoon in 1973 after leaving her driver's education class.
In his letter to Olsen, Bell talked of two more girls who'd

died together. The reporter thought this third pair of murder victims was most likely fourteen-year-old Georgia Geer and twelve-year-old Brooks Bracewell. In her article, Olsen recounted what Paige had discovered, that in 1974, at the time of the murders, Bell owned pastureland minutes away from the Dickinson convenience store where Geer and Bracewell were last seen.

In his letter to Olsen, Bell described a dark-haired girl. Was he referring to the Kroger bookkeeper, Gloria Ann Gonzales? It seemed likely, especially since Gonzales's corpse was discovered near the remains of one of Bell's other named victims, Colette Wilson.

In prison, Olsen interviewed Bell, and again he claimed the murders, calling the slain girls "the eleven who went to heaven." That became the headline of Olsen's *Houston Chronicle* article which ran on September 26, 2011. When Olsen asked officials why Bell hadn't been prosecuted, the reply was as Paige had suspected. Current Texas laws stipulated that a confession alone couldn't be used to convict. The courts required corroborating evidence. "I didn't believe we had sufficient evidence that we could proceed to a grand jury with, and without getting into specifics, that's the decision that had to be made, no matter the temptations to proceed otherwise . . . It wasn't for a lack of effort," former Galveston DA Kurt Sistrunk told Olsen.

The day I read Lise Olsen's article, I decided it was time to look into the girls' murders, starting with the oldest crimes, the killings on the island. Before long, I, too, was writing to Edward Harold "Butch" Bell, asking for an interview.

While he responded quickly, he refused to grant me an interview. I kept writing, hoping to convince him to sign the forms that would result in a prison interview. Each time I made my request, Ed Bell declined, instead issuing orders, telling me to do one thing or another and report back to him. Finally, a friend, a trained profiler, suggested I stop writing.

"He's pulling your chain," she said. "Serial killers are big on control. He's trying to control you from inside prison. Pull back for a while. See what happens."

I did, and I waited. Then months later, I wrote Bell again. This time, his answer was the one I wanted. As I prepared for the interview, I wondered if Fred Paige was right. Would I soon meet the Galveston serial killer? Was it Ed Bell? Or was this simply a red herring, an enticing dead end?

Chapter 6

The Eleven Who Went to Heaven
Edward Harold "Butch" Bell

Brazoria County, Texas

"If I cut your head off right now, they can't do anything about it," said Ed Bell with a satisfied smirk, his chin jutted out, defiant. "There's nothing anyone can do to me."

Late that morning, I'd traveled south of my Houston home to the Stringfellow Unit, a rambling old prison surrounded by double rows of chain fencing topped by curls of concertina wire in the flat, wooded terrain of Brazoria County. I was there to finally talk to Bell.

Ed Bell in 2012.
(Courtesy of the Texas Department of Criminal Justice)

The meeting was the culmination of more than a year during which I'd attempted to interview him. I'd written letters and made repeated requests. In response, I received letters from Bell packed with name after name, people out of his past he suggested I contact. He wanted me to do my research, but not on the killings, rather on what he called the Program, psychological and physical abuse he claimed to have been subjected to since shortly after his birth in 1939.

"I've been in the Program my whole life," he told me. In the prison visitors' room, we talked through a Plexiglas-and-wire-mesh divider. His hair chopped short, his nose and ears elongated by age, brown patches mottling his pale skin, at seventy-four Bell had cold muddy eyes and thin lips that seamlessly transitioned from amusement to disdain to anger. "I believe in free will. But I didn't have it, because of the Program. And I'm not responsible for any of the bad things I've done."

From outward appearances, it seemed that Bell suffered from some form of mental illness. Exactly what, I didn't know, although he repeatedly referred to having been placed in psychiatric hospitals, to people trying to push him into becoming "nuts," and he often brought up paranoid schizophrenia. Was that what psychiatrists had labeled him over the years? He certainly displayed signs of paranoia, insisting that newspapers were being altered to distort his take on reality. In his mind, he was the focus of a large, international conspiracy. He was so important that not only were television shows regularly doctored specifically to mislead him, but he claimed that the FBI had paid off hundreds of people for decades to keep his involvement in the Program secret.

"I have one question," he said. "Who's the president of the United States?"

His hearing nearly gone, he shouted and cupped his good ear to hear my response. "Barack Obama."

Bell frowned and shook his head. "I don't believe it. I'm pretty sure nothing I see on television is true. Those news programs are just set up to play with me."

This wasn't the Ed Bell of 1970s-era Galveston as described by his friends and family. That Bell had been gregarious, a big-talking businessman, and no one had said that they'd noticed any indication that his take on reality was distorted. Rather, he was the kind of guy who always had multiple jobs brewing, who habitually flashed a bank roll. "I was a college graduate. I never had a problem getting a job.

I made a lot of money," he confirmed, with a broad grin. "I knew how to bring it in. No question."

How did his current condition impact the believability of his claim that he was the 1970s Galveston serial killer?

"He may be mentally ill, that doesn't mean that what this man is saying isn't true. It's still possible that he's a serial killer," said Dr. Richard Coons, an Austin-based forensic psychiatrist known as one of the top experts in criminal behavior in the United States. "The problem in this type of situation is sorting out reality from delusion."

Certainly, there have been serial killers with recorded evidence of mental illness: Wisconsin's Ed Gein, who killed two women and tanned the hides of bodies he exhumed to make furniture, one of the inspirations for Hannibal Lecter in *Silence of the Lambs*; Albert Fish, the Brooklyn Vampire, who preyed on children; and Britain's Peter Sutcliffe, a prostitute killer known as the Yorkshire Ripper. So the combination of mentally ill and serial killer wouldn't be new.

Dr. Coons advised that to weed through the maze of Bell's distorted thoughts, solid evidence was needed to determine if Bell told the truth when he confessed to murdering the girls. The best route was through corroborating scientific findings, but that wasn't possible. Fred Paige said there wasn't any DNA available from any of the seventies-era murders. All the evidence had been lost or misplaced decades earlier. "We looked in 1993, when we had a task force on the murders," confirmed another of the investigators. "We couldn't find anything. No clothing. Nothing."

Unless an eyewitness came forward, without physical evidence, the only remaining way to determine if Ed Bell was the man who'd terrorized Galveston Island and the surrounding area was to determine whether or not Bell knew facts about the crimes that hadn't been made public in news reports, the things only the person responsible could know. If not? Perhaps his role was simply imagination, the fantasy in a disturbed mind.

Yet from the moment the interview began, Bell refused to

discuss anything other than what he called the Program. He claimed he was above the law. He argued that his position ensured that he literally could not be punished. It seemed incongruous considering the circumstances. Bell claimed the Program protected him from punishment for any crime. "It means I can't be arrested or charged with anything. I can't be detained. I'm above the law."

Clearly, however, that wasn't the case since he'd been an inmate in Texas prisons for two decades. The contradiction didn't appear to give the dough-faced man any concern. "You just have to understand the Program," he said. "Then it all makes sense."

It was in 1997, the year before he wrote his letters to the two district attorneys, that Ed Bell said he'd figured out that he wasn't responsible for what he referred to as "the bad things I've done." When asked if he meant killing Larry Dickens and the eleven girls, he nodded. Off and on his eye twitched when he talked about the murdered girls. "The twelve people I killed . . . Those bad things?" Why wasn't he guilty? Because, Bell said, he'd been an unwitting pawn, manipulated by a government-sponsored experiment.

Bell said he didn't know why he was chosen. But he contended that it might have had something to do with his grandfather, who he suspected personally knew President Franklin D. Roosevelt. The goal, Bell said, was to experiment with a good kid, subject him to abuse and manipulation, to toy with his physiology and determine if he could be made bad. The first step in Bell's definition of turning to the dark side included becoming gay. And the final step centered on belief in a higher being.

"They wanted me to become a homosexual, then homicidal. What comes after homicidal? Suicidal! Then crazy. Nuts. Paranoid schizophrenia. And finally they want to turn me into a Jesus freak," Bell insisted, his arms crossed resolutely across his chest. "Then they think I'll tell them what they want to know."

"Tell them what?" I asked.

"Why people do bad things," he said with an exaggerated frown.

As he talked of the Program, Bell's demeanor appeared increasingly agitated. In his tortured mind, he remained locked in the injustices and horrors of his childhood. "It was a brainwashing program," he said. "The Program has been so absurd and asinine; almost no one will believe it." Although he knew of no one else who'd been subjected to it, Bell contended that everyone around him was part of the charade. Who was behind the plot? Bell described those in charge as government agents, somehow affiliated with the FBI. The vast majority of the time he referred to them as simply *they*. Those in the know included not only the ones pulling the strings but also everyone around Bell. "I think almost anyone on Galveston Island can tell you about the Program," he said.

What did *they* want? Why were *they* doing this?

"To see if they could turn me," he snarled. "I was a good kid, an Eagle Scout. They wanted to see if they could turn me homicidal."

The treatment, Bell said, began when he was a toddler, and at each stage seemed to have been intertwined with sex. At three, he described taking his clothes off and playing show-and-tell with a little girl. The episode was interrupted by Bell's mother, who beat him with a stick. "She really let me have it. No food. Eight hours later, my father comes home. He beats the hell out of me. Again, no food. That's what started it. That caused me to do the bad things."

Bell contended that the beatings accompanied by not being fed forced his endocrine system into overdrive, pumping out hormones. "This was done intentionally. It just threw everything out of whack, all the hormones, including testosterone. It made me oversexed."

Looking back, he said he knew from early on that his sex drive was exceptional. As a teenager, he masturbated five or six times a day. At fifteen, he claimed, his father, an oilfield worker, hired a hit man to kill him. When I asked why, Bell didn't mince words. At the time, his family lived on a ranch: "I was doing things I wasn't supposed to do. Sex with animals."

Looking back, Bell said his one regret was that he hadn't turned the tables on his father by murdering him. "He wanted me dead? I should have killed him. I should have killed my daddy, shot him through the head and buried him in the woods."

Bell had spent the past two decades in prison, and his only news of his contacts on the outside came from family and friends. His older brother had told him that both his parents were dead. They would have been nearing one hundred if still alive, but Bell didn't buy it. He also didn't believe his uncle had died six decades earlier as he'd been told, arguing that the entire episode was a charade staged for his benefit. At the funeral, the dead body in the casket wasn't his uncle's, Bell insisted. "That was a wax figure. It was all part of the Program.

"Why? They wanted me to get ideas. At eight, I could pop a snake's head off at fifty paces. I was really a good shot. What were they trying to get me to do? To kill my father . . . to take me to trial and sentence me to a shot in the arm. Bingo, I'm dead."

His upbringing turbulent, Bell said that when the bad thoughts first came to him, he wondered if it was heredity. While in prison, he came to another conclusion. "My father and my grandfather were both crazy," Bell said, his voice rising. "I thought it was bad blood. Until I got in here. Then I figured out what they'd done to me, about the Program."

When he brought up the "bad things" he'd done, I pushed for details, trying to get him to talk about the girls. "You know the things I've done, the things you're here to talk to me about," he said, referring to the Galveston serial killings he knew I'd come to discuss. As we talked, he became increasingly disturbed. "It was all because of the Program. They pushed me and pushed me. And it kept building inside me. It built and built, until one day, it just blew. I exploded."

"And what happened?" I asked.

"The bad things that you're asking about. I am of the opinion that the Program itself caused me to do those things," he said.

To Bell's mind, this program aimed at testing his ability to turn away from evil had an effect the collective *they* should have predicted. "At six or seven years old, I had enough upstairs to know that if you torture someone, you can get them to do bad things," said Bell. "I don't think it's right that I'm in here. They should be in here . . .

"As a sex offender, because of my hormones, I don't think I was in charge of my free will . . . They tried to get me to kill people. I didn't want to do it. They wanted me to rub people out. They wanted me [to be like] Al Capone."

Why had he confessed to the killings? Bell said it was a way to expose the injustices he'd suffered. Once his fate was known, Bell argued that he would have to be released from prison. "I wrote the letters because I figured out the Program. When I figured out what had been done to me, the pressure came off of me. I realized this was done to me on purpose, so I would do bad things," he explained, absolving himself from any responsibility for the twelve murders he claimed to have committed. "And I wanted people to know about the Program."

Throughout his past, there were times when he said he fought off urges to do bad things. There were times he thought he was supposed to murder people. When he didn't, Bell believed those people rewarded him, giving him ranches, money, even a large office building. "If I come out of here, I'm going to have plenty of money," he contended. "I believe I own much of downtown Houston."

Yet here, too, much of what he said made little sense. For if he'd been rewarded for not killing those on his hit list, didn't there have to be a hit list? "Did *they* pick the girls out for you, the people running the Program?" I asked. "Did they tell you to kill the eleven girls?"

"I don't think they picked anyone out," Bell said, his

twisted mind mulling over the question. "I don't think they told me *what* bad things to do."

Edward "Butch" Bell in the prison visiting room, 2013.
(Courtesy of Kathryn Casey)

Over the years, Bell said, however, there were scenarios—or as he called them "setups"—the faceless entities behind his torture set in motion. When he met his first wife on a blind date, he speculated that there was an ulterior motive for introducing them. Off and on he appeared distracted and hummed, and I wondered if he was trying to block auditory hallucinations. He did that at this point in the interview, the hum getting louder and more determined. When he stopped, he said that although he hadn't done as they'd wanted, "I was supposed to rape her. So they could lock me up then."

There were others, including a woman with a young son in 1963 in Paducah, Texas, stranded with a flat tire along a deserted road. As Bell described that day, he was the kind stranger who pulled over and fixed her flat. Looking back he classified it as another of what he calls the many situations the powers that govern his life drew him into. "I wasn't supposed to help that poor lady with her tire. I was supposed to rape her and kill her kid," he insisted, his voice rising. While he fixed the tire, apparently fighting homicidal urges, Bell suspected strangers watched from the woods, monitoring his actions.

When it came to the day he jumped bond on the murder charge, Bell claimed that wasn't what happened. Instead, he insisted that when he was released on bail, those in charge knew he would run and wanted him on the lam. "They wanted to follow me. They wanted to see what I would do. They wanted me south of the Rio Grande River. They thought it would be easy to corrupt me down there," he insisted. In Central America, he adopted the name and identity of a dead cousin but still spotted so many people in bars and restaurants, on the street that he believed were FBI agents in disguise, that he said he made it a point to stop noticing.

In addition to his two wives in the U.S., Bell said he'd married twice more, once in Costa Rica and to a fourth woman in Panama. Yet he contended that none of the marriages, not even those in Texas, were real. Why? The women were in on the conspiracy, Bell suggested, and the marriages didn't abide by the letter of the law, which made them merely masquerades. "They wanted it that way," he said. "So that when I got railroaded into prison on these bogus charges, they could just walk away."

In prison, he said the torture continued. "I've been poisoned in here six thousand times," he railed. "They're trying to make me be a homosexual. I'm not going to do it." Why did they want him to be homosexual? Bell said it was so those in charge of his torture could put him in lockup whenever they wanted.

Now that he'd unmasked the Program, Bell said he was blameless for all he'd done. "My daddy was a total complete fruitcake. Nuts," he said, again referring to his treatment as a child, when he contends his family and a conspiracy of others abused him to turn him into a killer. The result? "I killed twelve people. And maybe a lot of others who committed suicide because of what happened."

What did he hope to accomplish? He speculated that exposing the Program mandated that he had to be released from prison. Once word spread that he wasn't at fault, that he was a victim not a predator, authorities had no alternative other than to set him free. "The people who did this to me belong in prison, not me. Let's expose them for what they are. Who belongs in prison, me or them? They do."

Once he was out? Ed Bell said he'd then answer all the questions about the girls he claimed to have murdered. "But not until I'm out on the street where I belong."

Would he hurt anyone again? No, Bell insisted. Now that he understood the Program and why he'd murdered the girls, he didn't feel drawn to violence. Besides, at seventy-four, he argued that he no longer had the sexual urges that drove him. "If Elizabeth Taylor was in her prime right here, I'd be afraid to even kiss her. Because that might be all I can do," he said, with a curt laugh. Once released from prison, he mused that maybe he'd settle in southern Spain. "I don't want to live in this country, not after what they've done to me."

Why did he kill the girls?

"It was an accumulation from when I was three years old. It built and built, and I exploded. I finally just exploded. It was an explosion. It wasn't the bad blood. It wasn't being oversexed. The buildup is what caused it."

When asked again why he killed those particular girls, he answered, "I can't tell you why they wanted me to do individual things. *They* wanted me corrupt. They wanted me Al Capone. Baby Face Nelson. Bonnie and Clyde. I was a good boy, and they did this to me."

"Did it bother you, Ed?" I asked.

"What?"

"What you did to those girls? Did it bother you?"

He looked at me, then stared down at his hands on the

counter in front of him. Whether he meant it or not, for a moment, he looked repentant. "Of course."

Ed Bell saw proof of the Program's existence all around him. He'd repeatedly confessed to murdering eleven teenage girls. Why hadn't he ever been prosecuted? It was all part of the conspiracy. "Because if I get in front of a judge, and I tell them that I was on a U.S. government program from birth, he'll have to let me out. So they don't want me in another courtroom."

A lull, then Bell went on, explaining his view of faith and eternity. "I don't believe in heaven or hell. I don't believe there's a God or Jesus or Mohammad or somebody. I don't believe it. Jesus Christ was a con artist . . . I don't think there's a god. That throws the whole religion thing into the street."

So there would be no day of reckoning, as Bell saw it, not on Earth or after he died. And why should there be? Even if hell existed, Bell maintained he'd done nothing to ensure that was the road his soul would travel. As the interview wore on, he became defiant. "If people tell you that I'm incompetent, they're the ones who are incompetent!"

At times, Bell displayed his gregarious-salesman side, laughing and telling jokes. "When I die, here's what I want you to do," he said at one point, his tone conspiratorial. "You'll get the word. I want you to tell them to bury me nude in the casket. I'm an old flasher, so I want to be nude. And I want to be facedown. That way, when all those people who don't like me walk by the casket, they can kiss my ass."

What happened on the day he shot Larry Dickens? "I think the whole thing was a setup that went bad," Bell said. "I was coming up from Galveston. The traffic snarled in front of me on I-45. They forced me off the road to go to Pasadena, Texas, for the setup."

As he talked, Bell's voice became increasingly agitated. "I'd been flashing people all over Houston for years. The police knew my license number, what I looked like. But they told everyone, my daddy, the others, they told them, 'You caused this . . . we ain't gonna touch him . . . We're not going to prosecute him. We're not going to mess with him. You did this. You fix it.' They channeled me into Pasadena." In Bell's account, he hadn't taken off his pants and masturbated in front of a group of children that day. He hadn't done anything wrong, nothing to explain why Dickens confronted him.

"This guy comes out of his house, he takes my keys. He's yelling and screaming at me . . . I pull a pistol out from behind the seat of my truck . . . I said, 'I want my keys.' He said no. I shot over his head. Boom! I said, 'I don't want to hurt you.' He throws his hands up in the air. This is not what you want to do with an atheist. I'm an atheist. He starts screaming that Jesus is going to save him. He believes in Jesus. He said he's going to kill this man in the name of Jesus. He comes at me. I emptied the gun. Blood starts coming out of his nose like you'd opened a faucet. Whew!

"He goes into the garage. I need my keys. I get the M-1 carbine out of the truck. He's sitting there . . . I said, 'Give me my goddamn keys!' I shoot from the hip."

The twelfth person Bell claims to have killed, Larry Dickens, lay dying. Yet Bell insisted he wasn't accountable. He admitted shooting Dickens with a pistol then a rifle, but he denied discharging the fatal shot through the head, despite Dawna Dickens's painful memories of seeing Bell shoot that final bullet. "Someone else did that," he said. "I don't remember shooting him through the head. I don't. Someone else did that."

So in Bell's world, he was innocent of the girls' murders because he was manipulated to kill them and Dickens's murder because some unseen person fired the fatal shot. An old man, who claimed not to believe in either heaven or hell, appeared determined to wipe away any responsibility for his sins, to clear his earthly record by blaming others.

Yet what little remorse Ed "Butch" Bell might have shown earlier was now gone, and his voice swelled in anger. "I have known since I was eight years old that there is no

God!" he shouted. "I don't think there's any way I could be farther from Jesus Christ . . . when you die, they take you apart. Take your brain out. Take your internal organs. You going anywhere but a hole in the ground?"

Our time together wore on, and I tried again to maneuver him into talking more about the girls' killings. When he balked, I offered to show him a printout of the I-45 unsolved murder chart with pictures of the victims, one I'd brought with me. Many of the girls were those he'd claimed to have murdered. "Would you look at it?" I asked, pulling it out of a file.

"No," he said, spitting out the word. He turned away, angry. "You don't have to show that to me . . . I think the bad things I've done in my life were because of the Program."

At that point, Ed Bell addressed the invisible others he claimed monitored us and recorded each of his words. "They're going to school on us," he said. "They want to know how I think. They keep looking for a weakness. But I don't have any. I'm King Kong!"

Later, one thing Bell said would haunt me: "You've got Frankenstein's monster." Then, referring to his father and himself, he said, "And you have Carl Clayton Bell's monster."

On the drive back to Houston, I thought about Edward Harold Bell, the grandfatherly-looking man with the twisted frown and ice-cold eyes. The self-described monster. I hadn't been able to convince him to talk in detail about the girls, the eleven he claimed in letters to have sent to heaven. But the man I saw accepted no responsibility. He'd abdicated all free will, claiming he was powerless to do anything but kill. The way he referred to the twelve he'd murdered, the way he tried to hide behind calling the murders "the bad things I've done," that so many small clues linked him to the killings, including a white van matching the description of the one two of the girls were seen getting into?

In my office, I later sat down to test the theory that everything Bell had written in his letters could have been gleaned from newspaper accounts of the murders, the reason those in law enforcement I'd queried had said they couldn't prosecute Bell based on his many confessions. It seemed odd to me that so much would have been reported. Usually, police hold back information like the angles of shots and the type of bindings used.

After I'd searched and found all the available articles on the seventies murders, I put them in chronological order. I didn't consider anything after 1993, when Bell entered his first Texas prison. One investigator had speculated that Bell could be looking up the old cases on the Internet from prison and that was how he knew the facts, but I'd inquired and knew that wasn't possible. Texas inmates don't have Internet access behind bars.

Once I had all the articles before me, I realized that the prosecutors were right: Everything in Bell's written confession was present in one or another of the articles covering the murders, from the angles of the shots into Debbie Ackerman's and Maria Johnson's bodies to the types of bindings used on their hands. "Yeah, but he's been in prison all these years," Fred Paige had told me. If Bell had merely read news articles on the cases decades earlier, the investigator contended that Bell wouldn't have been able to correctly recall so many details. Considering our interview, I thought about Ed Bell's description of the rage that built inside of him and the emotional explosions that he said propelled him to commit murder. When he talked about the killings, he appeared swept back to that time and that place, that moment, standing on the bridge in the oil field, a gun aimed at Debbie and Maria as they cowered below him in Turner's Bayou. Could it all have been the fantasy of an unstable mind?

As much as I believed Ed Bell might be telling the truth, I couldn't know for sure. I had no crystal ball into the past. Unless Bell relayed information only the killer knew, his claim that he was the serial killer would forever be clouded in doubt. Was he toying with all of us? Giving us just enough information to believe he murdered the girls but not enough to prove it? Or was that all he knew, just what had been printed in the newspapers? Were we all listening to the deranged fantasies of a man who had created his own reality?

"Ed, why don't you tell me about one of the killings?" I'd asked. "Pick one, and just tell me everything you remember."

"Not until they let me out of here," he scoffed, his face bitter in rage. "They need to let me out and put the people who did this to me in here. Then I'll talk. I'll tell them everything. But not until I'm on the outside!"

A few months later, I interviewed Ed Bell again. By then, he was housed in the Estelle Unit, a prison hospital. As before, he claimed he was being poisoned and complained that his blood pressure was high. Why was he there? He said that the doctors wanted access to him in order to trick him into "becoming crazy," so they could lock him up in a prison psychiatric hospital "for the fourth time." When he said this, he held up four arthritic fingers and frowned pointedly.

That second visit resembled a chess game, Bell consistently ignoring questions about the girls' murders and redirecting the conversation to his hate for the Program. At times, he looked flustered, angry. But then he smiled and moved on, listing resources he thought would help gain access to FBI files with his picture on them that he was sure existed, ones that spelled out his singular position as the subject of an experiment aimed at "taking a good kid and turning him into a killer."

Was Fred Paige right? Was Ed Bell the Galveston serial killer?

Bell admittedly knew a lot about the killings. He also had possible ties to many of the girls. That was true in one case in particular, the murder of Suzanne Bowers. A former employee of Bell's, a captain on one of the boats Bell owned that ran supplies to the oil rigs, lived with his parents just over a fence line from Suzanne's grandparents.

On May 21, 1977, the twelve-year-old left that same house to walk home to get her bathing suit. She never made it. She was never seen alive again. This was the murder Henry Lee Lucas had once confessed to but later recanted. I asked Ed Bell if he had ever gone to visit his employee at the house behind the Bowers family. "I used to go there off and on . . . he lived there with his parents, so I'd go there sometimes. He worked for me, I guess, about two years."

How often was he at that particular house? "Quite a bit," he answered, with a shrug.

Suzanne Bowers's friend, Sara Groves, had written to Bell in prison, asking him if he'd murdered her friend, and Bell said that he hadn't. "I do not remember hearing about your friend," Bell wrote. "I am sorry for your loss. I can tell you that some people do bad things because of life's experiences. I do not believe that humans are born good or bad."

Even beyond the fact that Bell frequented the home behind Bowers's grandparents', there were other factors that suggested Bell might not be telling the truth. In many ways, the Bowers case was markedly similar to those he claimed to have committed. Suzie looked like the other girls, with her shoulder-length brown hair. Like many of the other murdered girls, Bowers frequented Galveston's beaches and surf shops. Debbie Ackerman and Maria Johnson were last seen getting into a van, and the man who leased the land where Bowers's bones were found described seeing a van on the property around the time of her disappearance.

The final connection: Bowers's skeleton was found in an area linked to some of the other cases, murders Bell claimed to have committed.

"You know, Ed," I said. "A young girl disappeared right there, from the house behind the one your captain lived in with his parents."

Ed Bell said nothing, but his eyes turned frigid, and he glared at me.

I asked, "Her name was Suzanne Bowers. Did you murder that girl?"

Bell clenched his jaw and tied his lips into a taut sneer.

He'd been friendly when I'd arrived, but no longer. Although I asked yet again, Bell never answered my question. He neither admitted nor denied murdering Bowers but glowered at me, furious. I had the sense that my knowing about the case had caught him off guard.

Why wouldn't he talk about that particular case? Perhaps because someone else was involved? According to Groves, an informant told Bowers's grandmother that he'd seen another man kill Bowers, that he was with the killer when she died. And along with the van that was spotted in the field where her bones were found, there was a pickup truck.

From that point on in our second interview, Butch Bell talked about the Program, complaining about the medications he was on and that his head felt swollen. "Maybe it's some kind of mind-expanding drug they're giving me," he said. "They don't want to kill me, just make me suicidal. They're hoping I'll blow my brains out."

At that juncture, Bell excused himself. "I have to go back to my room," he said. "I can't talk anymore. I'm having some pain. But don't tell anyone. No one here. They're causing it."

I knew that I would get no more from Ed Bell that day, and I gathered my things. As I left the visitors' area, Bell stood behind the wire-mesh partition watching, staring, frowning. He looked old and troubled and angry. The last thing he said to me was that he wouldn't see me anymore. My sense was that I'd asked one too many questions about the girls' murders, questions he wouldn't then and might never answer.

That was in 2013, the same year Ed Bell became eligible for parole. The board rejected his application, perhaps because he told them about the Program, or they might have heard his claim that four decades earlier, he'd left a bloody swath across Galveston.

In the months that followed, I continued to write, and Bell responded. While I never got definitive proof that he was the killer, over the course of time he included curt facts about the cases, things like "Maria Johnson had a twenty-dollar bill in her purse." The problem was that if it were true, that fact wasn't recorded in the case file. I couldn't confirm it.

In one letter, Bell described driving the white van that day in front of the Baskin-Robbins, the one seen picking up Maria Johnson and Debbie Ackerman, and I came to believe that he probably did just that. At times, I pictured a younger Ed Bell, his brown hair combed to the side, hanging out of the van window, smiling and urging the girls to climb inside. It was either that or he had a truly amazing memory, one that remembered minutiae he'd read decades earlier in newspaper articles.

Forty-two years after her daughter disappeared, Claire Wilson couldn't tell me what Colette wore the last time she saw her, on the day of the band competition, as she stood on the side of the road holding her clarinet case and waiting for her mother. Ed Bell, however, remembered right down to the color of Colette's purple shorts and that the Mickey Mouse on her shirt was on the front. Yet there were no eyewitnesses, none who came forward to say they saw any of the doomed girls drive off with Bell, and no known forensic evidence tying him to the killings.

Such were the frustrations of decades-old cold cases. As logical as it seemed that Fred Paige must be right, that Bell truly was the Galveston serial killer, in the end, nothing was certain.

THE 1980s

- Heide Villareal Fye: 25, waitress and bartender, left her parents' house to hitchhike to see her boyfriend on October 7, 1983.

- Laura Lynn Miller: 16, the daughter of Tim Miller, last seen on September 10, 1984, using a convenience-store pay phone.

- Jane Doe: third victim found in the Texas Killing Field, unidentified. Her body was found on February 3, 1986.

- Shelley Sikes: 19, a waitress at a seafood restaurant, forced off I-45 on May 25, 1986.

- Janet Doe: fourth victim found in the Killing Field, unidentified, discovered on September 8, 1991.

Chapter 7

The Texas Killing Field
One Father's Crusade

League City, Texas

Dedicated to his daughter,
Tim Miller's Cross.
(Courtesy of Kathryn Casey)

For decades, this clearing in the woods has been notorious, a seeming contradiction for such a quiet site tucked a short saunter off a side road, concealed behind a stand of trees. Little was heard here but the calls of birds, the rush of a breeze through dry winter leaves, and the occasional car on nearby Calder Drive. Yet the spot lay just blocks off I-45, little more than half an hour's drive to the impressive skyscrapers that comprise Houston's high-rise downtown. All around, people were consumed by the pull of daily life. But in this deserted field, time stood still. It was both hallowed and haunted ground, sacred cemetery and blasphemous atrocity, a place that had witnessed all the good and all the malevolence of which man was capable.

In the center of it all, a primitive cross, crudely constructed and weathered, marked its heart, standing as testimony to a father's grief.

This lonely patch of brush-covered, flat, coastal plain scattered with slender pines and the occasional oak was the true Texas Killing Field, a site where, between 1983 and 1991, evil walked. Here the remains of four women lay hidden from the world. Murdered by killer or killers, their bodies withered away waiting for discovery, while those who loved them searched and prayed, hoping they'd be found alive. Anything but dead. Anywhere but here.

"There were nights, I stood here, looked up at the moon and nearly tore my lungs out screaming," Tim Miller said, his tired eyes scanning the desolate terrain. The day—moody and gray with a thick-tented sky—mirrored the mood of the conversation, as Miller stared up into the heavens, appearing to plead for answers. The most important: Who was responsible for the carnage?

Our day's journey began hours earlier in Tim Miller's office in nearby Dickinson, inconspicuously tucked behind a dollar store in an unassuming strip center. A painting of his murdered daughter, Laura—one of the four women whose bodies were abandoned in the field—hung over his head, behind his desk, in the headquarters of the grassroots organization he began in her memory.

Miller is the founder of Texas Equusearch. Since 2000, he and his band of volunteers have traveled the U.S. and the world searching for the missing, on horseback and ATVs, in helicopters, boats, using sonar and drones, wearing scuba gear and spurs. Called in by police agencies and distraught families, Equusearch has investigated more than thirteen hundred cases, bringing hundreds of people home alive to grateful families. They've also recovered more than 170 bodies, giving those who loved the missing answers and permission to grieve. In the process, Tim Miller has been a witness to history, investigating some of the world's most infamous cases, including the disappearances of Caylee Anthony in Florida and Natalee Holloway in Aruba.

Why? A decade ago he stood in the Killing Field, a broken man cursing the demon who had murdered his daughter. Miller had neither name nor face for the predator who devastated his world. The anguish felt crushing. Needing to find a way to reclaim his life, he heard his daughter's voice, pleading with him not to let other families suffer the horror her family endured, the trauma of seventeen months during which they didn't know where she was, what happened to her, or if she was alive. "That day out in the field I made a promise," he said, his raspy voice breaking with emotion. "I promised Laura and I promised God that I wouldn't turn my back on other families who were going through what we went through. I would do all I could to help."

Drawing a deep breath, for a moment Miller was silent. His hands were folded on his lap, and the agony of the decades visible in his deep wrinkles and within his heavily lidded eyes. "People think the worst thing is to have a murdered child," he said. Miller then shook his head as if at the impossibility that there could be anything more painful. But there is. "Waiting for the news, not knowing is worse."

"I think sometimes that if it wasn't for all the rough times growing up, I never could have survived all of this," Miller said. "It infuriates me when I'm at a

Miller in his Equusearch office under a portrait of his murdered daughter. *(Courtesy of Kathryn Casey)*

trial and a defense attorney talks about his client's child-hood, this person who has done something terrible. I feel like, don't play that game with me. I've been there. Adults make choices."

If Tim Miller's shoulders sag, they have reason. The troubles that plagued him began as a small child when his mother suffered a breakdown. As a result, many of Tim's younger years passed circulating between foster homes until a family stepped forward to take him in. Finally, he had a strong father figure, a happy home life.

Still, damage was done. "By twelve, I was smoking and drinking," he said. He married young, and he and his wife, Jan, lived in Ohio, where Tim worked at Ford Motor Company, when their first daughter, Wendy, was born. Laura Lynn Miller was number two, and then they had a son who tragically died of crib death when he was only seven weeks old.

Tim and Jan struggled through, but more adversity waited.

As a child, Laura ran a high fever, one that put her in a coma and landed her in a hospital, yet she recovered and thrived, growing into a good student with many friends. Tim thought their second child had "turned the corner." Laura worked hard in school, getting good grades. Around the house, she was a happy presence, singing into brushes, spoons, whatever was handy as stand-ins for microphones. Laura was a compassionate young girl who ran track in school. One day in the heat of a race, well ahead and in first place, she stopped just before the finish line. Another young girl had fallen and cried out. Instead of forging on to collect the trophy, Laura turned back to help.

Then when Laura was eleven, she suffered a bad bout of the flu. Not long after, she tumbled off a playground slide, and Tim and Jan ended up in a hospital emergency room listening to a doctor explain that their daughter hadn't suffered a simple fall. Instead, a brain scan revealed that the flu's high fever had left behind scar tissue. Laura had a seizure disorder.

"The seizures changed Laura," said Tim. "She didn't feel as if she fit in anymore. She felt different. It was hard on all of us, but especially Laura. She had so many things to struggle against."

Not long after, the family moved to Texas, lured by the flourishing economy. The Gulf Coast was booming, and they settled in Dickinson, not far from the Johnson Space Center. What had been small towns in the seventies were growing. Tim went into construction and dreamed of building a successful company. Yet he worried. As she entered her teenage years, Laura became sullen. "Because of the seizures, she was put in special-education classes at school, and she was embarrassed. She started skipping school," said Tim. "She started hanging around with kids who smoked pot."

Hoping for a fresh start, Tim and Jan decided to move Laura out of Dickinson. In late summer 1984, they found a small, one-story ranch house on Cardinal Drive, a quiet, suburban street, in the nearby town of League City, by car just ten minutes from their current home. Laura would still be able to see her friends, but she'd attend a new school. Shades of brown and beige brick in the front, the house had a garage and a picket fence, an oak tree in the front yard. It was a new beginning for all of them, and Tim was hopeful.

As school approached, Laura registered as a sophomore at Clear Creek High School, and in early September, the family moved into the Cardinal Drive house. Days later, on the tenth, boxes still waited to be unpacked, and the Millers' new home phone wasn't connected yet when Tim rushed off to work. After he left, Laura announced that she wanted to call her boyfriend from a convenience store on the busy corner of Hobbs Road and West Main Street. Jan had to get to work but offered to drive Laura to the store. It all seemed like such a normal morning, but it would turn out to be one they would play and replay in their minds.

At the convenience store, the traffic whizzing past on its way to and from I-45 just a block away, Jan waited as Laura talked to Vernon, her first serious boyfriend. Time passed, and Jan had to get to work, but her daughter didn't want to hang up the phone. "Laura told Jan that she should go on to work," said Tim. "Laura said, 'Mom, it's only a mile. I know my way. I can walk.'"

Laura was sixteen, old enough to drive and get a job. What could happen to her on such a short walk home?

When Tim and Jan returned home that afternoon, Laura wasn't in the house. At first, he assumed she was with Vernon, that they'd gone somewhere together. But then Vernon rang the doorbell looking for Laura. He hadn't seen her. Tim worried but not too much, assuming that his daughter had wandered off with friends. When she didn't come home, Tim and Jan began driving the streets and searching.

When they hadn't found Laura by the second day, Tim became frantic. "I figured then that maybe she'd had a seizure," he said. They called nearby hospitals, and Tim contacted the League City Police Department. The officer who took the missing person report didn't seem concerned; he told Tim that sixteen was an age where teenagers were known to run away from home. The officer insisted that this wasn't unusual, and that Laura would undoubtedly return soon.

Despite the officer's assurances, by the third day anxiety had taken over Tim's life. No longer did he make excuses for Laura's disappearance. He now felt certain that something was very wrong. "I went to see the police again," he said. "I told them that Laura needed her seizure medicine. She didn't have it with her. And she was religious about taking it. She wouldn't not come home."

In response, the officer again told Tim not to worry, that Laura had probably just run off, and she'd be back. "I didn't believe that," said Tim. "I hoped it was true, but I didn't believe it."

That day, Tim's alarm grew when he learned that another young woman had disappeared in League City eleven months earlier, a twenty-five-year-old cocktail waitress and bartender named Heide Villareal Fye.

Pretty with a Farrah Fawcett cut of shaggy blond/brown hair, the mother of a six-year-old daughter, at the time Heide (pronounced Hee-dee) had been staying with her parents, less than a quarter mile from the Millers' new home. Years later, her parents described their daughter as a trusting woman, one who made friends easily. "Heide never met an enemy; everyone was her friend," said her sister, Josie Poarch-Mauro. "She was a carefree sort of girl, and she loved to laugh."

The evening she disappeared, October 7, 1983, Heide told her father, who was watching a baseball game on television with a neighbor, that she'd decided to hitch a ride into Houston to meet her boyfriend.

When Heide failed to arrive at her destination, her family began searching. One of her father's stops was at a

Heide Villareal Fye saw the good, not the bad, in people. *(Courtesy of her family)*

place Heide frequented, the same gas station/convenience store Laura Miller would disappear from the following year, the one on the corner of Hobbs Road and West Main Street, just off I-45. The clerk behind the counter remembered seeing Heide that October evening. In this era before cell phones, like Laura, Heide had used the pay phone on the corner of the building, under a jaunty blue awning and separated from the parking lot by blue concrete barriers.

Certain his daughter wouldn't leave her family, Heide's father searched for her every day.

"My dad was partially paralyzed from a stroke and

walked with a cane, but he went out and searched fields in the area, looking for her," said Josie, her voice heavy with emotion remembering the grief that overwhelmed the family. "It devastated our mother, but our father took it even harder. Heide was the youngest of six, his baby girl. He was heartbroken."

Then came that terrible afternoon the following April, six months after Heide vanished, when a dog carrying something in its mouth emerged from the woods bordering nearby Calder Drive, a quiet country road that angled off I-45. A toddler played on the front porch of a nearby house while his parents stared at the animal, wondering what their dog found in the woods, until they suddenly realized that the object wasn't a ball but a human skull.

When police arrived, they fanned out into the thick brush and straggly trees, searching for clues. Ultimately, attention centered on a patch of land three hundred yards from the house, a Humble Oil field with a narrow road cut through the brush to service a single working well. As if posed, a nearly skeletonized body lay on its back under a tree. Heide's clothes and a necklace were found nearby. When dental records were compared, her family was told that they were a match. While the coroner determined no firm cause, broken ribs suggested that Heide may have been beaten to death.

How was it possible that the body lay so close to civilization without being discovered for so long? The site was less than five miles from the convenience store, and once a week for six months, a worker had driven through the field to service the well, failing to see the woman's corpse concealed in the high grass.

That was April 1984. Five months later, Laura Miller vanished.

Tim Miller considered Heide Fye's murder and worried that there could have been a connection with his daughter's disappearance. He didn't yet know that both girls disappeared after being at the same convenience store, talking on the same pay phone. If he had, he would have been certain there was a link, but instead it sounded believable when the officer he talked to insisted that no relationship existed between Fye's murder and Laura's disappearance. One of the differences, the officer said, was that Fye was a cocktail waitress. "He insinuated that somehow Heide was responsible for what had happened to her because she worked in a bar," Miller said. "He made it sound like she'd asked for it."

Still, Tim wondered. He pushed, wanting to know where the field was, planning to search it himself. "I begged him to tell me where it was," said Miller.

The officer was adamant, however, that the cases weren't connected and that a search of the field wasn't possible. "He said the field was private property and all fenced in," said Miller. "And he told me not to bother Heide's family. He kept insisting that Laura was a runaway, and she'd be back home."

The convenience store phone where Fye and Miller were last seen.
(Courtesy of Kathryn Casey)

Long weeks followed, then months that turned into more than a year, while Tim Miller waited for what he feared would be bad news. Despite all the reassurance from police, Tim didn't believe that his daughter had run away. His heart sprinted in his chest every time the phone rang or a car stopped in front of their house. He waited and worried. He lost his job, and a deep depression took over.

Seventeen months after Laura's disappearance, Tim checked himself into a hospital. It was there on the morning of February 4, 1986, that his wife read a *Galveston County Daily News* article aloud to him. The day before, the decomposing body of an unidentified woman had been discovered in the Calder Drive oil field, the same clearing in the woods where Heide Fye's skeleton had been found. This time four boys on dirt bikes smelled something rotting, tracked down the source, and notified police. When investigators combed the area for evidence, they happened upon a second set of human remains, bones protruding from the ground.

The badly decomposed body and newly found skeleton both lay within two hundred yards of the tree where Fye's bones were recovered two years earlier. The positioning of all three was similar: under trees, on their backs, facing up.

As much as Tim didn't want his daughter to be one of the two unidentified dead women, he took no comfort in a quote from a League City detective: "no local . . . missing person cases seem to be related."

That day, Jan Miller rushed to the League City Police Station. When police asked, she supplied Laura's dental records and samples of their daughter's clothes, in hopes that

One of the last photos of
Laura Miller.
(Courtesy of Tim Miller)

hair could be retrieved for comparison. "I think I knew it was Laura before they told us," Tim said. "I didn't want to believe it, but I already knew."

That Laura's remains had been found brought some relief. That she'd been murdered was horrific, but they now knew she wasn't being held captive, wasn't hurt or sick, and no longer suffered.

Yet that gave Tim little comfort. As he assessed the situation, Tim blamed the police for the agonizing months of waiting without answers. "The way

I saw it, the police were partly responsible. It wasn't long after Laura disappeared that I asked them to look in that field. They wouldn't do it. Wouldn't let me do it. If they'd gone then, Laura would probably still have been dead, but they might have found evidence to stop the guy. At least we wouldn't have had all those months of jumping every time the phone rang. Instead, the cops did nothing, and now they had a third victim, a Jane Doe. Maybe, if they'd done their jobs, she didn't have to die."

There were other similarities between the three women besides the circumstances of their deaths. Jane Doe, like Laura and Heide, was white with shoulder-length brown hair. At approximately five-foot-six to -eight and weighing about 140 pounds, the unidentified woman was judged to be between twenty-two and thirty years old. Her most prominent identifying characteristic: a gap between her front teeth.

When it came to how the women died, there were differences. Indications were that Heide had been beaten. Laura's cause of death was unknown. The Jane Doe—whom the medical examiner estimated died two to four weeks before the discovery—had a bullet hole in her spine.

When police finished processing the scene and took down the barriers, Tim and Jan Miller went to the field, just two miles from their home, to see for themselves where their daughter had been found. It wasn't as Tim had been told. There weren't any fences. If the police had given him the location, he would have found Laura days after she disappeared. The frustration and anxiety that had eaten away at him for so long didn't subside but was joined by anger and an overwhelming guilt. "I was her father. I was supposed to protect Laura," he said. "I failed."

From that day forward, the field became sacred to Miller. Ten months later, just before Christmas, Tim, Jan, and their only surviving child, Wendy, returned to the scene. Tim carried a cross he'd made, roughly hewn out of wood. He drove it into the ground near the spot where Laura's bones were found, and beside it planted a fir sapling. On white rock he laid at the foot of the cross, the family placed objects representing things Laura loved, small statues of a cat, a horse, a turtle, and seashells. "It was a way to mark the place," said Tim, his eyes red and moist, his voice hushed, recalling that day. "It was something we could do for Laura."

Tim Miller and the cross he erected in the Killing Field, where Laura's skeleton was found. *(Courtesy of Kathryn Casey)*

Faced with the inconceivable reality of his younger daughter's murder, Tim tried to let the police do their work while he attempted to put his life back in order but with little success. "I don't think anyone can understand what something like this does to a parent unless they've lived it."

By then his life was already spinning out of control. His drinking had escalated, and the grief was crushing. At home, Laura's room remained as she'd left it. But Tim took to spending nights in the field, lying in wait, hoping to cross paths with the killer. He brought beer and sometimes a gun. "I'd scream, 'You chicken shit, I'm here. Come and get me . . . Motherfucker, I'm here. Come and take me!"

One night, he heard something in the darkness. Tim both hoped and feared that the man who'd murdered his daughter walked toward him, yet that moonless night he'd forgotten his gun. To his relief, what ambled out of the woods was instead a horse.

Not long after midnight during yet another stakeout, Tim stood in the center of this bleak, solitary site and fired six shots from his .357 into the sky. Then he waited for the police, wondering if they were nearby, like he was waiting for the killer to return. No one came.

In daylight, the field called to him as well. Many afternoons were spent inspecting every square foot, certain he'd find some trace of his daughter, her clothes, the cross necklace she'd worn on the day she disappeared, or evidence that would point to the killer. Every day he thought about Laura and how she'd died, wondering if in her final moments she'd called out for him or for her mother.

News of the bodies found off Calder Drive spread. Months earlier, a new movie made headlines and won a fistful of awards. *The Killing Fields* documented the experiences of Cambodian journalist Dith Pran after he escaped the Khmer Rouge and the finding of hundreds of thousands of his countrymen in mass graves. As many on the Gulf Coast pondered the deaths of the three women, the press began referring to the League City clearing as the Texas Killing Field.

In hindsight, Tim Miller would contend that police expended little effort to investigate the three Killing Field murders, and he wondered if some of the reason was political. At the time, the nearby Johnson Space Center flourished with large, expensive homes springing up around it, including in League City. The population in the area swelled, and prosperity brought jobs, stores, and new schools. The small mainland towns around I-45 were spreading, growing so fast with new houses and schools that they grew together to form a contiguous patchwork. "I think politicians and such didn't want people to know what was going on here," he said.

Six months after Laura's remains were found, Tim and Jan divorced. "I can't say that we were a happy family," he said. "There were issues. A lot of guilt. We blamed ourselves."

The years came and went, and Tim tried to pull his life back together. Three years after her body was found, police finally released Laura's remains, and a funeral was held. On a gray granite gravestone, the Millers chose a heart etched with three words inside: DAUGHTER. SISTER. FRIEND. Below Laura's name and dates, her parents included a phrase from an iconic Led Zeppelin rock song, ". . . and she's buying a stairway to heaven."

Walking away from the services that day in the cemetery, Tim looked at nearby graves. One hundred and fifty feet from where he'd buried his daughter, he noticed a gravestone bearing the name Heide Villareal Fye. "It gave me the chills," he said. "They were both out in that field, and they were buried so close."

After the divorce, Tim lived in a house in Dickinson. He worked construction and tried to overcome the pain of Laura's murder. One evening, he walked in and saw her framed photo. Anger overwhelmed him, and he shouted, "Damn you, Laura," picking up the photo and hurling it to the floor, where the glass shattered. Immediately regretful, he fell to his knees and sobbed, begging, "Laura, I'm sorry. Please forgive me. It wasn't your fault."

Then the unthinkable happened, on September 8, 1991, seven years after Laura Miller's disappearance, a couple cantered on horseback on a path cut through the Calder Drive oil field and stumbled upon yet another victim. The badly decomposed body was in the same clearing, again under a tree, three hundred feet from the first three. This time the unidentified woman was dubbed Janet Doe. Fitting the profile, she was white. The ME surmised she was twenty-four to thirty-four years old. Janet Doe was five-foot-three and 130 pounds, and, again recalling the other cases, she had long, light brown hair.

Animals had been tearing away at the corpse, and Janet Doe's skull wasn't with the body but was found three days later a short distance away. At the morgue, the medical examiner found evidence that the woman had been struck on the right side of the face with a flat object. Her cheekbone and jaw were both broken, and the blow had damaged a cheaply made partial upper denture. Yet there were dif-

ferences with this fourth killing, including that this victim,
unlike the others, was placed facedown in the field. For a
cause of death, the medical examiner settled on strangulation.

As quiet as the investigation into the Killing Field murders had been for five years, suddenly it was all over the
newspapers. "Police officials not giving up on murders,"
Galveston's *Daily News* reported. In a quote, police talked
about the problems with the cases, that the women had apparently been killed elsewhere and dumped in the field.
"This is the hardest type of homicide to work and clear,"
a League City lieutenant said. "We have a murder, but we
don't have a crime scene."

America's Most Wanted aired a program on the newly
discovered body, and leads poured in from across the nation,
many from families with missing loved ones hoping to claim
Janet Doe. To try to identify the woman, the medical examiner attempted to rehydrate her decomposing finger tissue to
get prints, then used cameras and lights to expose the ridges.
The effort failed, and like Jane Doe, whose body had been
found with Laura Miller's skeleton in 1986, Janet Doe had
no family or her real name.

Many tried to give the Jane and Janet Doe their faces,
including these by forensic artist Lois Gibson.

Over the following years Lois Gibson, a well-known Houston forensic artist, and others, used their talents to try to give back to the women some of what the killer and death had taken, their faces and their identities. Despite the hard work and good intentions, no one stepped forward to claim them.

Obsessed with his daughter's death, Tim continually contemplated who could have killed her. At times, he had theories, including one in particular, a former neighbor with a shady past. But it was only after Janet Doe's discovery in 1991 that a serious suspect emerged in the eyes of law enforcement. Robert Abel was a retired NASA engineer, one with a top-security clearance who'd been with the space program since the early sixties, a brilliant man who helped engineer the Saturn rocket that carried astronauts to the moon.

Bearded, paunchy, and slight in stature, Abel leased acreage on one side of the Calder Drive oil field beginning in 1983, the year Heide Fye disappeared. Early on, he'd shown a keen interest in the cases, at times lending horses to the investigating officers and giving unsolicited advice. In 1990, the year before Janet Doe's murder, Abel purchased the eleven acres directly adjacent to the Killing Field and opened the Stardust Trail Rides, clearing away brush for paths through the woods and installing picnic tables.

To police, Abel appeared inordinately interested in the murders. Did that mean he was involved, or rather was it simply geography, the proximity of having the bodies found so close to his home?

One reason authorities focused on Abel was that he fit a profile drawn up by the FBI Academy in Quantico, Virginia. Based on a review of the evidence, the feds surmised that the man using the Killing Field as his private dumping ground was a methodical, organized sexual serial killer, one with high intelligence who probably had a history of abusing animals.

Married three times, fiftysomething Abel had a past filled with rocky relationships, and two of his ex-wives told police that their former husband had just such tendencies, that he beat horses with pipes until the animals kowtowed to him. The women described Abel's temper as violent, contending that he flew into rages. One grisly comparison to the way the women's corpses were left to rot in the field came from one of Abel's ex-wives; she said that Abel didn't bury horse carcasses but left the remains on the land, where they'd be picked clean by vultures, coyotes, and other scavengers.

Based on the similarities between the FBI profile and Abel's alleged history, the League City police gained a search warrant for his property in November 1993. For twelve hours, they combed through Robert Abel's land and house. When they left, they took with them .22 caliber guns and bullets, the same caliber used to murder Jane Doe, a gold cap from a tooth, human teeth, newspaper clippings about the murders, and boxes of photos. The teeth and gold cap, they reasoned, could have been souvenirs taken from victims. They vacuumed the rugs, looking for hairs or fibers linked to the killings.

One of the final lines of the search warrant read: "Robert William Abel . . . committed these offenses . . ."

In the end, the search produced no evidence tying Abel to the Killing Field murders. One disappointment was that the bullet removed from Jane Doe, either due to being exposed to acid while the body was being defleshed at the ME's office or from weathering in the field, no longer bore identifying marks that could have indicated whether or not it had been fired by one of Abel's guns.

Yet Abel remained law enforcement's primary suspect, and based on the assertions in the search warrant, Tim Miller discarded his theories about other suspects and instead focused full attention on the brilliant-yet-odd former NASA engineer who walked with a stiff gait. "After I saw how Robert Abel fit the profile, I didn't have a doubt," said Tim. "And from that point on, I made his life miserable."

Spurred on by the belief that Abel was the killer, Miller left angry messages on the man's telephone and confronted him when their paths crossed. Before long, Miller began driving to Abel's house in the evenings and parking on the street, waiting for the man to walk out to pick up his mail. In response, Abel complained to League City police, writing in January 1994: "It has occurred to me that the possibility exists that Mr. Miller has decided to personally vindicate the death of his daughter."

While his sights were set on Abel, Tim Miller continued to search for evidence, hoping to succeed where police failed. In 1998, he leased the property that comprised the Killing Field. At the suggestion of the Galveston County Sheriff's Office, he then brought in heavy equipment, backhoes and pumps, to drain a pond on the land. Keys and change had been found near the water, and there was a theory that perhaps the killer had thrown Janet Doe's purse into the water. The work went on for two days, but all that was ultimately found were scraps of fabric from what appeared to be a woman's blouse, edged in lace.

Could the stains on the Killing Field shirt be blood?
(Courtesy of Tim Miller)

Frustrated, wanting to know what evidence police had that they weren't sharing with him, Miller filed a lawsuit for records from his daughter's case and received pictures of evidence from the investigation. One was of a blue-checked, Western man's shirt that bore Laura's case number on a tag. Tim wondered if stains visible in the photo could have been blood. In 1986, when the shirt was found, DNA testing had yet to be put into use in criminal cases, but by the late nineties, that had changed. Tim would later say that he went to the League City police station, asking to have the shirt tested, only to be told that it had disappeared.

Disappointed in the way the case was being handled, grieving for his daughter and carrying the guilt of failing her, Tim's life continued to unravel. He married again, but Laura's murder preoccupied him. One night in the Killing Field, he pleaded, "Laura, please do not hate your daddy, but it's time for me to put my life back together. I need to say good-bye."

Walking toward his truck, he heard his dead daughter's voice yet again, "Dad, don't quit. Please, don't quit."

"Damn you, Laura," Tim answered. "Just damn you!"

In 1999, Robert Abel told a *Texas Monthly* reporter that the damage done to him by the cloud of suspicion was all-encompassing. "My life has been destroyed. My reputation ruined. I didn't kill any of those girls. I wouldn't know how to kill."

Meanwhile, Tim Miller didn't stop his quest for justice. He consulted a Native American spiritualist and hired a private investigator in attempts to find the man responsible for his personal hell. Consistently, nearly every lead appeared to point to Robert Abel.

Over the years, Miller again took to parking on Abel's street, waiting for him. At times, Abel walked toward him shaking, angry. One night, he shouted at Tim, "All those girls were whores anyway."

Miller jumped from his truck with his gun and came at the man he despised, throwing him on the ground and holding the barrel to Abel's head. "I could murder you now, and I probably should. But if you're dead, they'll probably never find out who Jane and Janet Doe are," Miller said, holding back his rage. "They say you're a serial killer, and you don't have a conscience, Robert. But I'm going to remind you every day for the rest of your life."

Trembling with anger, Tim Miller walked away.

As he drove off in his truck, he judged that he'd crossed

an important line. "I felt like I'd lost my mind," he said. From that confrontation, Miller drove directly to a hospital, where he stayed for ten days. Before long, his preacher began visiting and talking to Tim about forgiveness. "That was one of the healthiest things that I've ever done for myself," said Tim. "The anger was killing me."

After that pivotal day when he'd pointed a gun at Abel, Tim Miller turned his life around.

Over the years, Tim had begun helping in the searches for the missing in southern Houston, including the victims who disappeared on or near I-45 in the years after Laura's death. It was one night in the Killing Field when he made a promise. "I told God and Laura that I wouldn't turn my back on a family looking for a loved one," he said. "I'd always do my best to be there for other families suffering the way we did."

In 2000, Tim Miller began Equusearch, its reputation as a persistent and determined resource to find the missing spreading first across Texas, then the nation. In 2002, he was invited to Washington, D.C., to be in the room when then-president George W. Bush signed a bill setting aside $10 million to expand the Amber Alert program. Miller sat next to Elizabeth Smart's parents at the ceremony, after he and other Equusearch volunteers helped hunt for their daughter. At the time, Elizabeth, who'd been abducted from her Salt Lake City bedroom the previous June, remained missing. "I saw them like I was looking in a mirror," he said. "They were suffering like I had, all those months Laura was missing." The Smart family's story would have a happier ending, when nine months after her disappearance, authorities rescued Elizabeth and arrested her captors.

In 2008, when Caylee Anthony was reported missing, and media across the nation and the world focused on the toddler's case, Tim and Equusearch volunteers traveled to Florida. Looking back, it appeared to Miller that from the beginning Casey Anthony's father suspected that his daughter was involved in the toddler's disappearance. In one exchange, when Miller explained that they'd begun looking for a body instead of a living little girl, Tim Miller remembers George Anthony called his daughter out of her bedroom, and ordered, "Casey, tell Tim where to look."

Instead of helping, as Tim recalled, Casey stalked off.

By then, Tim had transformed, putting aside his anger and the way he saw his old nemesis, Robert Abel. No evidence beyond speculation ever emerged to tie Abel to the killings, and Tim came to believe perhaps police had been wrong and his old enemy wasn't the man who'd murdered Laura. Regretting all he'd put Abel through, one day Tim saw the man on the road and honked. The two men pulled over, and Tim approached Abel and apologized. Admitting that the other man had ample reason to hate him, Tim said he was disappointed in himself for being swept up in the suspicion and tormenting Abel as he had. "Robert, I am very sorry for all the grief I caused you," Miller said.

At that, both men cried.

"I was glad we had that conversation," said Tim. "We finally put it all to rest."

That reconciliation turned out to be especially important in 2005. Tim was in Aruba helping to search for Natalee Holloway, when he heard that Robert Abel was dead. The retired engineer drove an ATV-type vehicle onto railroad tracks and was hit by an oncoming train. Tim heard that Abel was in bad health and rumors circulated that it could have been suicide. In the end, Abel hadn't left a note, and his death was ruled an accident. Miller wasn't certain that was the case. In the small towns around I-45, many continued to believe that the man who ran the stables was the serial killer, and once Abel had that reputation, he'd remained an outcast. "I still wonder if all the suspicion was part of it," said Tim.

Although Abel was gone, the mystery surrounding the Killing Field persisted. That year, yet another billboard went up with sketches of Jane and Janet Doe along a Houston highway. And when Tim returned home after months in Aruba, he discovered a bizarre letter waiting for him at Equusearch headquarters. The words cut out of magazines and newspapers and glued onto a sheet of paper—decorated with demonic symbols including upside-down crosses and the numbers 666—spelled a chilling message: "Abel is not the devil sought by the League City blue fuzz . . . The key to the nightmare field of death . . . Tim Miller it's me you're looking for . . . I was the last man your Laura saw and many more . . . the police won't get me for I am too smart . . . this monster in me . . . more bodies and bones to be found . . ."

That evening, Tim went to the Killing Field and found the cross he'd erected knocked down and broken. He repaired it and stood it upright.

On one hand, Tim Miller's life had turned an important corner, and while he would never forget, he perhaps began reconciling all that had happened. "I know now that Laura's death wasn't in vain. I miss her, and I think about her every day. The holiday seasons are the worst. But because of her death—through Equusearch—we've made a tremendous change in methods used when searching for the missing."

At the same time, he hasn't given up on his quest to give the murdered girls justice. "I've got nearly three decades into this," he said. "We need to get this guy put away."

The Killing Fields murders unfolded over a seven-year period, from 1984 to 1991. Later I would interview a man who said he murdered one of the women, the fourth one, Janet Doe. And he would insist that Tim Miller shouldn't have apologized to Robert Abel, that there was sufficient reason to believe that he was capable of murder. Yet did Abel kill the first three women whose bodies were found in the field? Perhaps not. For as the years unfolded, other evidence came to light, evidence that Tim Miller's instincts might have been right from the beginning and that perhaps he'd known all along who murdered his daughter.

That realization, however, waited in the future. In the meantime, the blood shed during the eighties wasn't confined to that quiet field off Calder Drive.

As the decade counted down, three months after Laura Miller and Jane Doe were discovered, a perky young woman simply drove on the interstate on her way to her boyfriend's house after a hard night's work. Like so many others, Shelley Sikes vanished.

Chapter 8

They Couldn't Prove Murder
The Abduction of Shelley Sikes

Memorial Day Weekend, 1986

Eddie Sikes holding one of the "Search for Shelley" posters.
(Courtesy of Kathryn Casey)

"Lives can change in the blink of an eye," said Eddie Sikes, a sixty-nine-year-old wearing a tropical shirt, jeans, and sporting a trim white beard. We'd been talking for nearly three hours, and it had been a painful voyage back in time, to Memorial Day weekend 1986 and the day his nineteen-year-old daughter Shelley vanished on her drive home from work. "People just don't realize how quickly things can happen," he said, his eyes misting. "Sometimes they forget that stuff like cars and houses don't matter. That what counts are the people they love."

For a moment, Sikes was visibly troubled as he considered what to say next. He was seated in the office of his steel-fabricating plant in Texas City, on the mainland just north of Galveston and not far from League City and the Killing Field. Beside him were thick scrapbooks of yellowing press clippings documenting the tragedy that had shadowed his life for nearly three decades, and in his hands he held a poster produced in the days following Shelley's disappearance. Unlike Tim Miller, Eddie has found some justice—if justice is ever truly possible—but painful questions regarding his daughter's death remain unanswered. And despite the years, closure has never come. "Not a day goes by that I don't think about what happened. It never leaves me. Looking back, it was a crash course in good and evil."

The year Shelley disappeared, 1986, Galveston was in the midst of a building boom, pricey beach communities and condominiums rising on the upscale west end. One of the island's favorite sons, oil magnet George Mitchell, who'd become famous as the developer of The Woodlands, a massive, sprawling, master-planned community north of Houston, had dedicated his expertise and money to helping his birthplace reclaim its past glory. The Strand, the historic district once rotting into disrepair, was renovated, including repurposing an abandoned warehouse into the latest incarnation of the historic and posh Tremont House hotel.

Shelley Sikes in her graduation photo.
(Courtesy of Edward Sikes)

Despite the face-lift, relatively little had truly changed

on the island in the decade since the eleven girls died in the 1970s. As always, the beaches dominated, and it was in summers that the population swelled. Ranked high on a list of local landmarks were the aged Victorians that survived the great storm of 1900 and Gaido's seafood restaurant, founded in 1911. For many, any stay on the island required at least one dinner at Gaido's to be complete. Tourists and locals alike used the restaurant as a meeting place.

In August 1971, Glenda Willis had picked up her friends from Webster, fourteen-year-olds Sharon Shaw and Renee Johnson, in front of Gaido's. Farther down Seawall Boulevard, Willis said good-bye, as Shaw and Johnson walked off promising to return later that afternoon. It would be the last time Willis saw her friends. Months later, she identified Shaw's and Johnson's jewelry to help police ID their skeletons.

Shelley loved working at Gaido's, a Galveston landmark.
(Courtesy of Kathryn Casey)

Fifteen years later on the Saturday of Memorial Day weekend 1986, at 11:34 P.M., Shelley Sikes stood at the time clock inside Gaido's punching out, after a busy shift serving fresh oysters, broiled and golden fried seafood, steaks and drinks.

At just five feet and weighing only ninety pounds, Sikes was petite with a wide smile and big brown eyes. After graduating from Texas City High School, where she'd been pretty much Miss Everything, including most congenial and an assistant drum major, Sikes had gone on to attend the University of Texas in Austin the previous fall. "She'd taken three classes," said Eddie, smiling at the memory. "Music and two dance courses, and I asked, 'What about English and history?' But Shelley really wasn't interested. Her plan was to open a dance studio."

It was a logical strategy for Shelley. She'd been a fixture in ballet, jazz, and tap classes since grade school, and she'd choreographed routines for her high school's drum majors. Loving dance and being center stage, Shelley had a spark about her, a playful nature and a spunky attitude.

Remembering Shelley, Eddie would say that he didn't believe she had an enemy in the world. Instead, she laughed and made friends easily, and she had a penchant for adopting animals, such as the pink Easter chick he gave her and an armadillo he caught that Shelley named Lone Star. She nurtured it for more than a year before it died, then she insisted Eddie dig a hole in the backyard to bury it.

Before Christmas 1985, Shelley called her dad from Austin asking if he'd be

An early photo of Shelley Sikes with her dad. *(Courtesy of Edward Sikes)*

angry if she took time off from college to rethink her future. She was homesick, and he'd later surmise that she missed her boyfriend, Mark Spurgeon, whom she'd been dating since high school. A year behind her, he wouldn't enter college until the coming fall. "I was driving to Austin every weekend to see Shelley," said Mark.

"Not mad but disappointed," Eddie remarked to Shelley about her change of plans.

Shelley in Austin, where she attended the University of Texas. *(Courtesy of Edward Sikes)*

That month, Shelley moved into the Texas City house Eddie shared with his second wife, Denise. Days later, Shelley was hired as a waitress at Gaido's. Eddie wasn't particularly happy about his daughter's new job because it was on the island. "I've always thought of Galveston as kind of a Sin City," he said. "Especially in the summers. There's the beaches, people drink, and there are always guys looking to pick up girls."

Yet Shelley did well at Gaido's and particularly liked working the dinner shifts, when tips were the most plentiful. After work, she routinely arrived home just before midnight. Eddie waited up, and they watched *M*A*S*H* reruns before bed. But on what would become the fateful evening of May 24, 1986, Eddie had taken a holiday-weekend fishing trip to the family lake cottage outside Austin.

That Saturday night, Shelley walked alone through Gaido's door into the parking lot, and climbed into her 1980 dark blue Ford Pinto, intending to drive north onto the mainland to her boyfriend's house, to watch movies. Mark had called about nine thirty, inviting her. "She said she was tired and really didn't want to go out," he remembered. "She said it had been busy at work, and her feet hurt."

Later, the irony of the situation troubled Eddie. On most nights, Shelley would have had a pistol in her car. He had taught both his daughters, Shelley and her older sister, Dana, how to shoot when they were teenagers. But the gun he bought for Shelley was too big for her small hand, and just a week earlier he'd taken it back, intending to replace it. That, however, hadn't happened yet. So on that night, as Shelley drove through Galveston, the Pinto's glove box was empty. It had rained earlier in the evening, leaving the roads slick.

At first, nothing seemed out of the ordinary. On her way to Mark's house, Shelley made a brief stop, driving through a fast-food restaurant and grabbing a burger, then pulled out onto Broadway Street, heading toward the causeway and the mainland. Yet as she traversed the darkened streets, something went terribly wrong.

When Shelley didn't arrive at her boyfriend's house, Mark called Gaido's, and a waiter answered the phone. "Shelley left a long time ago," he said. His next remark would later haunt Spurgeon; with the holiday weekend upon them, the waiter added, "There are a lot of crazies out there tonight."

Not understanding why Shelley hadn't arrived at his house, worried that she could have had car trouble, Mark drove on I-45 toward Galveston, back and forth between his house and the island restaurant, but didn't see Shelley or her car. Increasingly worried, he returned home. At the house, Mark explained the situation to his father and enlisted his help with the search.

This time, when the two men retraced what would have been Shelley's route, Mark searched out the window while his father drove. On the first loop as they left the island and drove north off the causeway, Mark spotted a car parked on the feeder with its dome light shining. Shelley's light sometimes stuck on. "Pull off here," he told his dad.

The car mired in the shoulder's sandy loam was the blue Pinto, and it was empty. Shelley was gone.

Mark's pulse quickened as he looked over the scene. The Pinto's driver's-side window was smashed, glass shards covering the front seat. Inspecting the damage, Mark and his father noted what looked like blood running down the outside of the driver's-side door. The inside, too, was stained with a spray of red on the seat and the front window. Examining the area around the car, Mark noticed the imprint of a bare foot in the dirt beside the roadway. At first, he thought perhaps Shelley had been in an accident, but the blood pattern perplexed him; the way the spatter was scattered about didn't seem right. "Shelley, where are you?" Mark cried out into the darkness, as the occasional car streamed past on I-45. No one answered.

When police arrived, they talked with Mark and his dad. Quickly, it became apparent that the responding officers assumed they'd been called to an accident scene and that Shelley had probably wandered off, perhaps hurt and looking for help. Not appearing overly concerned, the officer wrote up a report. When he finished, he asked if Mark wanted to take Shelley's car and get it off the side of the road. Mark agreed, but his father stepped forward.

"We're not taking that car anywhere," the older man said. "Something's happened here. You need to get someone to pick that car up." Worried that what they were looking at wasn't an accident but a crime, when the tow truck arrived to remove Shelley's Pinto, Mark's father asked the driver to secure the vehicle, locking it to protect any evidence inside.

By then, Eddie was speeding through the night on his way toward Galveston, knowing only that his daughter was missing, her car found, the window broken with blood on the door and inside. A five-and-a-half-hour drive, he stopped halfway and called his wife, Denise, only to be told she had no new information. She'd contacted area hospitals, but none reported treating a girl matching Shelley's description. When Eddie arrived at the scene, fifteen to twenty deputies and police officers milled about. "What happened to your daughter?" one asked.

"I don't know," Eddie answered. "I hoped you'd know that."

Hours passed, without any information coming Eddie's way. When it appeared there was nothing to do at the scene, he drove home to be near the phone. No news surfaced, and by sunrise, Eddie and Denise were at the steel-fabricating plant he owned in Texas City manning the copy machine, running off reams of flyers with Shelley's photo on the top. Word spread, and volunteers arrived and grabbed stacks to post throughout the area. Shelley's mom, Erin, secured a promise through her employer, Amoco Oil, for a five-thousand-dollar reward for her daughter's safe return, and that was added to the posters and flyers. But by then, police had disturbing information that suggested Shelley's situation could be dire.

In the sheriff's office the afternoon following their daughter's disappearance, Eddie, his wife, and ex-wife filled out paperwork to file a missing person's report. In another room, two people who'd driven on I-45 the night before, described to detectives how they saw Shelley's car being pursued by a pickup truck. The first witness, a man, was in his station wagon a little after midnight when Shelley's Pinto pulled up on his right. A pickup hovered behind her, driving recklessly, as if the driver were trying to force her off the road. The Pinto and the pickup barreled past the witness's vehicle. He saw Shelley slam on her brakes and swerve off at an exit, apparently attempting to get away. The maneuver didn't work. While the pickup driver missed the exit, he responded quickly, jumping the grass-covered earth between the freeway and the service road, in pursuit. A short distance down the road, the Pinto spun and slid off onto the shoulder, its wheels mired in the wet earth. That first witness on the scene saw the pickup driver jump from the cab, pull his shirt off and wrap it around his hand, then pound on the car's window.

By the time the man stopped to investigate, the pickup driver had broken the window and was dragging Shelley from her car. To the man witnessing the action, Shelley looked barely conscious. Appearing in a near frenzy, the pickup driver shouted at the passerby that it was a domestic spat and ordered him to get lost. He reluctantly complied when the man put his hand to his back as if he had a gun.

The second statement backed up much of what the first witness had said, but that woman believed that as Shelley was dragged from the car, she was conscious and grasping the car door frame, fighting to prevent the pickup driver from taking her.

When the deputy assigned to update the family explained the situation to Eddie, the reality of what had taken place struck him. There was no longer any possibility that what had happened was an accident, that Shelley wandered off and waited in a hospital bed. Eddie's daughter had been taken by someone who obviously meant her great harm.

At the police station, a forensic artist worked with the witnesses to draw a composite of the pickup driver. The face that emerged was that of an unshaven man with long-ish brown hair, dark eyebrows, and an angry pout. Based on the blood found in the Pinto, they assumed that he'd cut his arm and could be wearing a bandage. Yet while investigators now had an idea of what the man who'd taken Shelley looked like, they didn't have a name or a license number for his pickup truck.

That day and the next, Eddie and the rest of Shelley's family waited impatiently for news, but none came. Not knowing what to do or how to find help, Eddie approached someone he thought would understand what the family faced. He picked up the phone and called John Walsh, whose six-year-old son, Adam, had been abducted from a Sears store in Hollywood, Florida, five years earlier in 1981, his decapitated body found days later. At the time Eddie called him, Walsh was gaining a reputation as a staunch victims' advocate with a special interest in abducted and exploited children. Later he'd go on to become the host of the television show *America's Most Wanted*. "I didn't know if I'd get through, but I did," said Eddie.

Sympathetic, Walsh listened. What he then advised Eddie Sikes to do became an outline for the painful months to come. Walsh told Eddie to do whatever he could to get publicity and pressure the investigators. He said to "keep the case in the headlines to keep the cops out of the coffee shops and out on the street looking for Shelley."

Heeding the advice, Eddie Sikes hired a publicist to promote Shelley's case, and Eddie kept churning out those posters, in English, and later in Spanish, giving them to neighbors, family, friends, total strangers, anyone willing to spread the word. "I think we printed somewhere around three hundred thousand flyers, and we had them in forty-six states," said Eddie. "One friend got them on the backs of eighteen-wheelers that traveled all over the country."

Meanwhile, Mark Spurgeon not only grappled with the uncertainty and fear of what had happened to his girlfriend but also felt as if he were under a magnifying glass. Called in repeatedly to talk to police, he gave statement after statement. Unmarked cars trailed him each time he drove out of his driveway. "I understood why they were doing it," he said. "But at the same time, I wanted them to stop watching me and go find Shelley."

If at first Eddie and the rest of Shelley's family assumed she'd be found quickly, that didn't happen. Instead, days, weeks, then months passed without news. Leads came in and were followed, polygraph tests given, but nothing led to Shelley or her abductor. On his own, Eddie drove every route he could think of off I-45, hoping to find something to shed light on the mystery of what had happened to his daughter.

At times, his thoughts drifted to the Killing Field off Calder Drive. It had been only months since the remains of the second and third victims, Laura Miller and Jane Doe, were found. Was it possible that the man who'd abducted Shelley was the Killing Field's serial killer? Had the evil that stalked that desolate oil field claimed Shelley, too?

The suspicion tormented Eddie, and for days, alone, he walked the field off I-45, searching, hoping yet fearing he'd find Shelley's remains. "I memorized every square foot of that field," he said. "I never found anything."

Desperate to uncover his younger daughter's whereabouts or, if the worst had happened, her remains, Eddie went so far as to hire a plane to fly him close to the ground, crisscrossing the area, looking for a body or an area where the ground appeared to have been recently disturbed. But with no positive results, his mission ultimately appeared hopeless. Shelley had vanished without a whisper.

Months passed, and Eddie's relationship with police soured. Before long, he began following investigators when he heard they were interviewing suspects, sitting outside on the street, watching. "I wanted to make sure they were doing their jobs," he said. And Eddie, his wife, Mark Spurgeon, and Shelley's mom continued to hand out flyers. While Eddie refrained from talking to the press, Shelley's mother and stepmom took on that role, keeping Shelley's name in the news.

At times, the phone rang with tips, sometimes from psychics who claimed to know where Shelley was buried. Although disbelieving, Eddie investigated, not waiting for authorities to follow up. "The police don't always want families to be proactive," he said. "But I was going to do whatever I could to find Shelley. If I had to get crosswise with the police, I was willing to do that."

Time passed until finally, eight months after the abduction, another witness from that horrible night talked to police. Authorities didn't tell Eddie until later what the man said, that there'd been not one but two men in the pickup, and that one of them beat Shelley in a rage before he pulled her from the Pinto.

It was about that time, unable to sleep at night, grieving and frustrated, that Eddie called one of the higher-ups at the FBI and asked him if he had children. The man said he did. "Have you ever been with them in a store and suddenly they disappear? You look for them, and they're gone? You holler for them, but they don't answer?"

"Yeah," the man said.

"I've been doing that for eight months now," Eddie said. "I need help."

The following day, the FBI supervisor called local police, and two agents were assigned to the case, but in hindsight it did little good, because even with the renewed investigation, no answers came. The result was that Eddie Sikes learned a hard truth. "Texas Rangers, FBI agents, detectives, and such, they're all just people," he said. "They're just regular folks, and they can't always solve the cases."

Throughout that year, Eddie and the rest of Shelley's family continued to keep on the pressure with the "Search for Shelley" campaign. Donated billboards on I-45 with Shelley's picture and the composite of the suspect prominently displayed asked for information. And as the one-year anniversary approached, Shelley's family redoubled their efforts, and local newspapers ran updates on the case, more flyers went out, and the reward grew to $12,000. A rally was held in Texas City, and volunteers who attended took home posters to deliver to restaurants, stores, or tape to light posts. Yet there were still no leads.

Then a month later, on June 22, 1987, a remarkable thing happened just over the border in Ciudad Juarez, Mexico; a shaggy-haired man with a beard entered a cantina and saw a poster in Spanish with Shelley's photo. Troubled and drunk, he stumbled back across the bridge over the Rio Grande, to the rundown El Paso motel where he was staying. Hours later, at 4:00 P.M., he called 9–1–1 begging for help, saying that he'd tried to hang himself and slit his wrists. When police arrived, they found the distraught man with two suicide notes, one written on the back of his auto insurance card, in which he claimed to have been involved in the kidnapping of Shelley Sikes.

A still photo taken from the police video of King's first confession.
(Trial exhibit)

The man in the hotel was John Robert King, a twenty-nine-year-old unemployed laborer. Because he was suicidal, King was taken into protective custody and transported to a hospital. The following day, El Paso police returned, read King his rights, and then took an oral statement from him in which he said that he'd been involved in the Galveston abduction of a woman named Shelley Sikes. During that statement, King implicated a friend, a drinking buddy he'd done drugs with, Gerald Pieter Zwarst.

When King checked out of the hospital after a three-day stay, police waited. They brought him to a judge to have his rights read yet again.

Afterward, El Paso officers transported King to the station, where two Galveston detectives, Wayne Kessler, a sandy-haired man, and Tommy Hansen, dark-haired and bearded, waited to interview him. Both had been working the Sikes case for more than a year, and both were eager to hear what King would say. Again, the man who was now the main suspect in the case was read his rights, this time while a video camera recorded every word.

On the video taken that day, King at first rarely looked up at either Kessler or Hansen, instead staring at the wall or the floor, as he recounted in a hoarse voice the events that took place thirteen months earlier. He and Gerry had been fishing in Galveston that day, drinking and smoking pot laced with PCP—phencyclidine—an animal tranquilizer also called Angel Dust known to cause hallucinations, numbness, paranoia, and to contribute to violent outbursts. That night, around midnight, they were in Zwarst's pickup driving off the island, when King saw Shelley in her Pinto.

"I gave her a friendly wave," King told Kessler and Hansen. Was that all he'd done? Whatever transpired between them, Shelley lost patience. "She shot me the finger."

In King's account, Zwarst was behind the wheel. King said he told his friend what the girl had done, and Zwarst "flipped out," forcing Shelley off the road, then breaking the window and pulling her from the car. For the most part, King claimed to be so out of it from drugs and alcohol, that he was barely involved. Yet he admitted helping Zwarst carry Shelley to the pickup truck and putting her on the front floorboard. What were his intentions? King said he did it because Shelley was hurt, and Zwarst said they were taking her to the hospital.

Yet that made little sense. If King only wanted to help Shelley, if Zwarst was the one who pursued Shelley, why did King say he climbed on her in the back of the truck? "I got on top of her. I don't know if I had intercourse with her. Then I heard her whimpering and crying. I backed off."

Later, King said they ended up at his parents' house in

Bacliff, twenty-six miles north of the spot on I-45 where they'd left Shelley's Pinto. At that point, King said Zwarst disappeared with Shelley and a shovel out of the elder Kings' garage.

Only later, King said, did he happen upon a place in the woods behind his parents' house, one where it looked like something had been buried. "I knew there was something bad there, but I didn't want to know what it was." Throughout the entire episode, from abducting Shelley through burying her, King said he was in a drug-and-alcohol-induced haze, in and out of consciousness.

What caused his suicide attempt that brought King to the attention of law enforcement? The constant publicity. "I wanted to deny it. It couldn't have been us. It must have been us. I was going to run from it, get a job somewhere."

Instead, King ended up in that drab hotel room, attempting to hang himself with his shoelaces and slit his wrist with a blade from a disposable razor. When he called his mother, she asked him to call 9-1-1 for help.

"I can't believe I didn't stop Gerry," King said. "He busted the window out . . . or maybe I did? . . . Now that I look back, it seems like a bad dream, a nightmare."

When it came to hitting her, King said he hadn't done that. "I know that for a fact."

"What caused her death?" one of the detectives asked.

"It must have been the shovel," King answered, suggesting that Shelley may have been alive when buried.

There were many contradictions in King's statement, among them that he had no intention to abduct Shelley but that he might have been the one who'd broken out the window. He claimed that he believed they were taking her to a hospital, yet when she moved on the floorboard in front of him, he pushed her down with his foot. In his account, his primary crime was that he didn't prevent his friend from abducting the teenager. "I didn't know what was going on," he said. "It was like I was in a daze or possessed or in a blackout or something."

"You and Gerry were in the truck that night, and he was driving?" Kessler asked.

"Yeah," King answered. He looked up and at the detectives when he said that he worried that Zwarst would try to put the blame on him.

"Do you want to go back to Galveston?" Kessler asked.

"Yeah," King answered.

Four days after his suicide attempt, King was in Galveston being outfitted with a concealed recorder. That afternoon, he met with Zwarst, a thirty-two-year-old unemployed pipefitter. A lanky man, Zwarst had brown hair with sideburns and a mustache. King tried to bait his friend with questions about the abduction, but Zwarst denied knowing what he was talking about. Later that night, Zwarst was arrested and brought in for questioning by Kessler and Hansen. At first Zwarst denied any involvement, but the two detectives kept challenging him, saying, "You're lying."

Finally, Gerald Zwarst admitted he remembered that night. His story paralleled King's in some ways but varied in key facts, including who was driving the car and who forced Shelley Sikes off the road and abducted her.

In his statement, Gerald Zwarst agreed that they were in his truck that night. When it came to who was behind the wheel, however, he disagreed, insisting that King was the driver who forced Shelley's Pinto off the road. After the abduction, they took her to a

Mug shot of Gerald Pieter Zwarst. *(Courtesy of the Harris County Sheriff's Office)*

park, where King put her in the pickup's bed and climbed in on top of her. But Zwarst wasn't sure if his friend had raped her. "The last time I heard any sound out of her was when she was on the floorboard," Zwarst said. "She tried to get up one time, and he kicked her back down."

Neither admitted responsibility for Sikes's murder or confirmed if she was dead or alive when buried.

At two that morning, the four men were in an interview room in the Galveston County Sheriff's Office—Zwarst, King, Hansen, and Kessler—with questions and allegations flying.

"What was obvious from talking to them," Lieutenant Tommy Hansen would later say, "was that it went from flirtatious to bullshit to murder because anger set in. They were flirting with her, and finally she'd had enough. She flashed them the universal signal at that point, and it went from play to, 'Okay, bitch!' It escalated until it was, 'Oh, shit. What have we done?'"

During the interrogation, from left, Hansen, King pointing at Zwarst, and Kessler. *(Trial exhibit)*

"Discuss this so we can find this girl's body and know exactly what you did and how she happened to be dead," one of the detectives ordered at the double interrogation. But that didn't occur. Instead, the two men blamed each other.

"Neither one wanted to take responsibility, which isn't unusual when there are two involved," said Hansen. "And what was really obvious was that Shelley was just in the wrong place at the wrong time."

The interview continued, and King claimed that Zwarst had taken a shovel and the body to the woods. In response, Zwarst countered by saying he didn't even know there was a body, that he was "out of it" most of the time.

"Bullshit!" King charged.

"I don't know anything," Zwarst insisted.

"One of you or both of you know where she's buried," Kessler charged.

In response, King kept pointing at and accusing Zwarst, who did the same in kind until Hansen ordered, "Somebody's lying . . . we want to know where she's at . . . Her family has the right to bury her!"

Yet by that interview, five days after King's suicide attempt, the detectives weren't simply at the mercy of what King and Zwarst wanted to tell them. They had lab results that pegged the blood inside the Pinto as King's, not Zwarst's. Kessler pointed out to King that he was the one who had scars on his arm from breaking the window and the one identified by witnesses as both the driver of the pickup and the one who'd pulled Sikes from the car.

"No, man," King shouted, again pointing at Zwarst. "He knows, man. I swear to God, he was driving."

The bickering continued until Hansen removed Zwarst from the room.

Once they were alone, Kessler talked calmly to King, telling him that the likelihood was that he wasn't remembering everything because he'd been so high that night. "I know you didn't go out that night intending to kill this girl. But what happened happened, and it got out of hand," Kessler said. "Tell me where she is."

Gradually, it appeared that King started to understand that it was likely he'd been the force behind the abduction, and he began wailing like an injured animal, "Oh, man, I couldn't have," he sobbed. "I couldn't have."

"Tell me what happened," Kessler said. "Tell me where she is."

"I can't remember, man," King cried.

"You can't hold it in. Will you tell me?"

Over and again, King insisted he didn't remember anything from that night other than what he'd told them, that Zwarst was behind it all, but the detective wasn't buying the explanation, instead saying that wasn't how it happened, but rather what King wanted to believe. "Clear your conscience, John," Kessler said. "Is she back there [on your parents' property]?"

"She must be," King finally said. "I don't remember burying her . . . Gerry helped me . . . I can't remember."

"Do you remember digging? You say he helped you?"

"I think he did . . ."

"Where did you bury her?"

"Right there out in the back of my mom's house," King said.

"What finally killed her?"

"The shovel, maybe," King said. ". . . Seems like I remember, unless she was already dead, jabbing her with the shovel . . . She was in a grave and the dirt was on top . . . I can't remember doing it, but I can just picture myself doing it."

When he was later read his rights again, a judge would say he heard King mumble something on the order of: "I have to get this off my mind. I done it. I done it. I can still see her body moving when I hit her with the shovel."

The day after the interview ended, Eddie and the rest of Shelley's immediate family met at the sheriff's office to hear what investigators had learned. "I lost it," said Eddie. "I just broke down and cried."

When Eddie first saw the two alleged killers, it was in a courtroom where they were being read their rights. His thoughts were "dark," he said. "I wanted fifteen minutes alone with them."

Believing the case was finally coming to an end, Shelley's mom, Erin, wanted to buy a casket, but Eddie reminded her that they didn't yet have their daughter's body. By then, King had agreed to take Hansen and Kessler to Shelley's grave, to allow them to recover her remains.

Why didn't they ever take that trip? Tommy Hansen would say that he remembered getting ready to take King to his parents' house to look for the burial site when King suddenly asked to talk to a lawyer. "At that point, everything stopped," he said. "Once he said 'lawyer,' we couldn't take him. And after he talked to the lawyer, he was no longer cooperating."

"We were that close to finding Shelley's body," Tommy Hansen said, holding up his thumb and index finger an inch apart. "If King just hadn't asked for a lawyer, he would have taken us to the site, and we would have been able to dig her up. But once he did ask, it was over. It was all over."

In the weeks that followed, Kessler and Hansen obtained a search warrant and six hundred officers, deputies, and volunteers searched in chest-high brush in the woods behind the King house. Cadaver dogs were brought in based on King's claims that he and Zwarst had buried the body there. Helicopters circled overhead, and a forensic team manned gas-emission equipment that was designed to detect vapors released from decomposition. Eddie, his then-wife, Denise, and his ex-wife, Erin, waited and watched, but nothing was ever found.

Speculation built. John King's parents had a new driveway, and rumors circulated that Shelley was buried beneath it. But Hansen and Kessler found records that indicated it was poured a short time before, not after the kidnapping.

Meanwhile, the Galveston County District Attorney at

the time, Mike Guarino, prepared for trial. The main discussion revolved around the charges. Eddie hoped that King and Zwarst would be tried for his daughter's murder. Yet Guarino worried that could be difficult to prove without a body. Instead, he favored aggravated kidnapping. The police had eyewitnesses and multiple confessions from King and Zwarst detailing how they'd driven Shelley off the road and taken her hostage. "We had a good kidnapping charge and an iffy murder charge," said Guarino. "And the truth is that they're comparable charges, both first-degree felonies carrying maximum penalties of life."

One more consideration: There was no statute of limitations in Texas law for murder. If Guarino held back until authorities found Shelley's body, he could go for capital murder and perhaps get death penalties. Without a body, he worried that the odds of a jury's voting for death weren't in his favor.

"But I thought we had a really good case," said Guarino. "I felt good about it."

That didn't change when King's and Zwarst's defense lawyers fought the admissibility of the confessions. The attempt failed, and Guarino pulled together the evidence for the trials. Both were shifted to courthouses outside the Houston-Galveston area, to seat impartial juries. The Sikes case had made headlines for so long, Guarino didn't even fight defense motions to move the trials. "It ensured that it wouldn't be an issue they could raise on appeal," he said. "We just went along with it."

As he prepared, Guarino assessed the men's confessions. In his eyes, he didn't fully believe either King's or Zwarst's accounts. "It seemed more likely to me that they were both in on it," he said. "If it wasn't Shelley, it could have been anyone that night. They were both out of control. All drugged up and drunk. When I looked at what we had, I thought the evidence was overwhelming."

Not long before the first trial, other witnesses came forward, this time men who'd been jailed with Gerald Zwarst the year after the abduction, when he was arrested for public intoxication. They said that during jailhouse conversations Zwarst described helping to pull Sikes into the truck and said that he watched as Sikes was buried. At one point, Zwarst said Shelley Sikes regained consciousness and moved, and that King, as he'd said in the presence of the judge, hit her with the shovel.

Meanwhile, Kessler and Hansen had tracked down Zwarst's truck, the one they were in the night of the abduction. In it, a crime-scene unit found hairs compatible with those taken off of Sikes's brush. In the days before DNA testing, it couldn't be identified as her hair, but it was classified as a possible match.

When Guarino looked at the case, he marveled at the way King had come forward and confessed. The district attorney had never seen a case like it in his twenty-eight years as a prosecutor, and he credited Shelley's family for making it happen by keeping the case in the headlines. "Shelley's family really solved this case. If King hadn't felt the constant pressure, if he hadn't broken down, I don't know that we ever would have figured out that he and Zwarst were the ones."

In the end, John King was tried first, then Gerald Zwarst. In his opening statements, Guarino told jurors that on that night Shelley Sikes could have been anyone's daughter, a good kid who had bright plans for her future. She was simply driving to her boyfriend's house after work when she became an unwitting victim of violence. "There was nothing to tarnish her image, just minding her own business," said Guarino. "There were a lot of things about Shelley that the jury could identify with. It was evil that exists that caused the series of events that took her life."

Witnesses, one after the other, identified King as the one who pulled Shelley from her Pinto, beating her before he even got her out of the car. On the stand, King said that he wasn't a kidnapper and that it was Zwarst who'd abducted

Sikes. Guarino pushed to try to recover Shelley's remains, asking, "Where's the body? Where's the body?"

"I don't know!" King insisted, burying his head in his hands.

"Did you and Zwarst dig up her bones and dispose of those bones?" Guarino asked. "Dispose of them as garbage?"

"No, that's a nightmare!" King said. When Guarino pressed, contending that King abducted, raped, and killed Sikes, he became infuriated. "No! No! That wasn't me, man. I swear. It wasn't me."

"Where's Shelley?" Guarino asked again.

"I don't know!" King answered.

During the breaks, Shelley's boyfriend, Mark, and her family cried together.

Zwarst's trial was similar in many ways, except that by then Zwarst was no longer saying that he remembered King abducting Sikes or much of anything that had happened that night. Instead, he said he'd made that up under pressure from police and that he was so drugged up and drunk that he'd spent most of the night passed out. Guarino described Zwarst's memory as "selective."

"No, I'm telling the truth," he said.

When he took the stand to describe finding Shelley's car along the side of the road at both trials, Mark Spurgeon would remember feeling as if "my blood was boiling," when he looked at the two men. King never looked up at him, while Zwarst impressed him as cocky.

At the conclusion of their trials, King and Zwarst were both convicted and given life sentences on the kidnapping charges. When the jurors gave interviews, they all agreed that they believed that the men had not only abducted but also murdered Shelley Sikes.

Once both men were in prison, Guarino attempted to make a deal with Zwarst, offering him immunity on a murder charge if he would take them to Shelley Sikes's remains.

"We'd consulted Shelley's family, and they wanted to give her a proper, Christian burial," said Guarino.

Zwarst and his attorney agreed, and in September 1990, the convicted kidnapper was hypnotized. Afterward, a massive three-day search was mounted in a park near a power company where King's father worked, one where the family often fished and camped. It was an area John King knew well, so it made sense that he might have taken Shelley there. A white blouse was found, but no bones. Some members of the family looked at it and surmised from its small size and the fact that it had been hand altered—something Shelley did often—that it was hers. Eddie wasn't sure although he did remember that the uniform she wore to Gaido's, the one she would have been wearing on the night she disappeared, had a black skirt and a white blouse. Cadaver dogs also hit on the area, as if there had once been remains buried there.

"I think she was probably moved," said Hansen. "We don't know. They had plenty of time between the abduction and the arrests."

King and Zwarst have both been eligible for parole since 2007. Each time it comes up, the Sikes family protests, wanting them to serve out their sentences. Under Texas law at the time of the offense, a life sentence was a maximum of forty years.

Would Shelley's family stop objecting to parole for the two men in exchange for learning where she's buried? "I think Shelley's mom would," said Guarino. "Families will do things for closure, and it's part of our culture that we bury our dead."

Eddie Sikes disagreed. While he wanted to bury Shelley, he also held firm that Zwarst and King needed to serve the full forty years. And Sikes hadn't given up on the prospect of finding his daughter himself. Thirty years after Shelley's death, her father kept a shovel in the back of his car, and off and on still occasionally stopped and searched deserted fields. "I just have these feelings sometimes," he explained, with a shrug. "I pull over, and if it's someplace I haven't looked before, someplace where it looks like it could be, I start digging."

In the years since the trial, the family has held a service for Shelley at the Baptist church were Eddie was baptized, and on the ten-year anniversary of her daughter's disappearance, Erin placed a marker carved with Shelley's name in a cemetery. "This is the first time I've ever been able to bring flowers anywhere," she said at the time.

At his Hill Country lake house, Eddie built a memorial of his own, fencing in a section with wrought iron and stone and mounting two eagles on posts, dedicated to his lost daughter.

Eddie Sikes holding his scrapbook of clippings on his daughter's disappearance. *(Courtesy of Kathryn Casey)*

In the years following Shelley's death, Eddie Sikes and his second wife, Denise, divorced, and Eddie married Sally, who worked with him at the fabricating company. On the day

I interviewed Eddie, she was at his side, patiently prompting answers to questions when the memories crowded him so that he couldn't think of a name or an event. At one point, he sat in his chair and paged through his yellowing scrapbooks of clippings on his daughter's case. His eyes grew red, and he appeared near tears. Before long, he put the book to the side, as if to try yet again to push it all into the past.

Eddie Sikes was aging, but as I gathered my things to leave, he confessed that he had unfinished business. "I'm not ready to die yet," he said, stroking his full white beard. "There are still things I want to do with my life. The biggest one is that I want to find Shelley's remains. I want to bury my daughter."

Chapter 9

The Bone Doctors
The Trial of Clyde Edwin Hedrick

Galveston County Courthouse

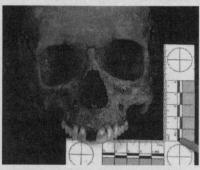

A photo of Ellen Beason's skull taken in 2012. *(Trial exhibit)*

Trials rarely bring true closure, because there is no way to erase the agony when a loved one is lost to violence. Yet the legal system is all we have, the only mechanism available to even attempt to administer justice. Parents of murdered children long for answers and that the persons responsible will be identified, exposed to the world for their atrocities, and convicted of their crimes. They want the killers to pay the price the law deems for such heinous acts.

As I worked on this book, I met mothers and fathers deprived of even basic knowledge of what transpired during the most life-altering events of their lives, the murders of their daughters. For most, there were no arrests, no judges' gavels pounding in courtrooms to signal that it was permissible to attempt to put the nightmares behind them and pick up their lives. The system failed them. Destined to live wondering and regretting, they could only pray that someday the answers would come.

For many, the unknown shadowed them. Eddie Sikes trusted that his daughter's killers lived behind bars but searched for Shelley's remains. Tim Miller buried his daughter but never stopped pondering the identity of Laura's killer.

Only on rare occasions, when it seemed the very stars aligned to light the way, did hope of a resolution emerge undiminished by bitter memories of past disappointments.

Those were the circumstances in late 2012, when Tim Miller voiced a renewed optimism, believing his long journey of uncertainty might have an end. "I think you've come to see me at a good time," he said, a twinkle in his eye. "Can you keep a secret until it becomes public?"

When I agreed, he explained, "We may finally be putting this thing together."

The conversation transpired on the first day I met Tim in his Equusearch office. That afternoon, he sat at his desk and talked, bringing me back to the first years after his daughter's death, when his sights were set on one man, his initial suspect in the killings, a neighbor.

They no longer lived in the same houses. Tim resided on a rural spread, and the man in question had also moved on, eventually landing in the nearby coastal community of San Leon. On his front lawn that Halloween, this man built a macabre cemetery display, one populated by four graves with make-believe stones etched with the names of horror-movie killers. "Four, like the four girls whose bodies were found in the Killing Field," Tim told me, with a disgusted shake of the head. "Like he was saying, there it is. I did it. And no one got me."

Actually, Tim didn't speculate that the man in question murdered all four girls whose bodies were found in the Killing Field, but the first three: the waitress and young mother Heide Fye; Tim's daughter Laura; and the first of the two unidentified women, Jane Doe. The last victim found in

1991, known as Janet Doe, had so many differences, including body positioning, those investigating theorized that she was most likely the victim of a separate killer. "The first three, including Laura, I always thought that maybe this neighbor of mine did them," said Tim. "When the police said it was Robert Abel, for a while I thought it was him. I lost my focus. I now believe that I may have known the man responsible for Laura's killing from the start."

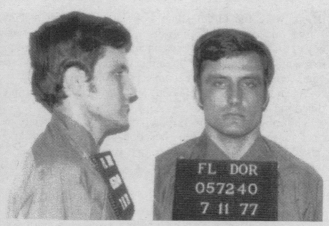

1977 Florida mug shots of Clyde Edwin Hedrick. *(Trial exhibit)*

The man Tim Miller referred to was the first suspect he mentioned to police, an ex-convict named Clyde Edwin Hedrick. In 1977, Hedrick was convicted of attempted arson and sentenced to five years in Florida. In 1984 when Laura disappeared, the construction worker with the prominent forehead and cold, deep-set eyes lived just down the block from the house the Millers had recently moved out of in Dickinson.

What made the man stand out was that Hedrick was the

last person seen with a woman named Ellen Rae Beason. They left a bar together one night in July 1984, and Beason vanished. A year later, her body was found, but based on the evaluation of the evidence at the time, Hedrick wasn't charged with her killing.

After Tim Miller discarded his belief that Robert Abel was Laura's killer, his attention repeatedly centered on Hedrick. Although he had never met him face-to-face, Miller speculated about the man's possible connection to the Killing Field from the moment he heard about Hedrick's link to Beason's death. In Tim Miller's eyes, he saw too many coincidences to be ignored.

First there was the timing: Heide Fye disappeared in October 1983, Ellen Beason in July 1984, and Laura in September 1984. Then Jane Doe died sometime in late 1985 or early 1986. Secondly, the Texas Moon Club, the joint Beason left with Hedrick that night, was the same bar Heide Fye patronized. The place booked local bands, and Hedrick was a regular, spending his nights on the dance floor. Since they both hung out at the Texas Moon, it seemed logical that Hedrick and Fye knew each other. Third: Hedrick's proximity to the Millers' prior home. Finally, on his recurring searches of the Calder Drive field, Tim Miller discovered piles of discarded tiles stripped off roofs. Clyde Hedrick worked for a roofing contractor. "I thought maybe Hedrick used the field to dump garbage from his jobs and visit where he'd left the girls," said Miller.

Yet he had nothing conclusive. In fact, Miller didn't have any direct evidence branding Hedrick the killer, and when Miller relayed his theory to League City police, he said they scoffed. "They told me it wasn't so, that it was crazy," said Tim. "They wouldn't listen."

Despite the disinterest of League City police, Miller continued investigating. He had the club connecting Hedrick with Heide Fye, and before long he had something linking the man to Laura. Not only had Hedrick lived near the Millers, but also Laura's friends said she'd been inside the man's house. They'd gone there to buy pot, and Laura had gone with them. With that information, Tim Miller proved that Clyde Hedrick, who admitted he'd been with Ellen Beason when she mysteriously died, also knew two of the three victims whose bodies were found in the Killing Field: Heide and Laura.

Eager to share what he'd learned, Miller returned to the League City Police Department. Again, he said, the officers brushed him off. "They didn't want to hear it," said Miller. "I knew there was something there, but they weren't interested. I was irate. The police wouldn't listen to me about Laura's being in the same field as Heide, and I'd been right. Laura was out in that field the whole time. I knew Clyde Hedrick was somehow responsible for Ellen Beason's death."

Miller didn't give up. Off and on he stopped at the League City Police Department, looking for reassurance that Laura's case was progressing. "Why is eight years old middle-aged?" he asked a detective one day. When the man asked what Tim meant, he said, "Laura died at sixteen. For her, eight was middle-aged."

Another day when he pushed for an investigation into Clyde Hedrick, Miller said the officer he talked to appeared irritated. Rather than a promise that he would investigate every lead, the man eyed him, and asked: "Why did you kill your daughter and those girls and put their bodies out there in that field?"

"I nearly jumped over the desk to get my hands on that man," Tim recalled. "I had to hold myself back."

The decades passed, and no answers came. Then something happened in 2010. Something that gave Tim Miller his opportunity. Galveston County Sheriff's Lieutenant Tommy Hansen, who more than two decades earlier was one of the investigators on the Shelley Sikes case, made plans to retire. Yet Hansen, by then an affable, white-haired man who wore wide, wire-rimmed glasses, didn't plan to completely leave law enforcement. He had unfinished business to attend to, investigating the area's abundant cold cases. For the first time in the history of the Killing Field murders, an investigator had the opportunity to concentrate on the embarrassment of unsolved cases, and Hansen had help. He would function on a part-time basis as part of a task force that included FBI Special Agent Richard Rennison, working out of the agency's local satellite office. A tall, muscular man with short dark hair and a goatee sprinkled with gray, Rennison had a knack for working cold cases. "I enjoy them," he said. "I like the challenge."

A dogged investigator, Special Agent Richard Rennison sought out cold cases. *(Courtesy of Kathryn Casey)*

Even before Hansen made his change, his attention never completely left the Killing Fields. For decades, he'd kept a blowup of the I-45 Mysteries chart behind his desk. He knew the girls' faces and names by heart. Hansen could recount all their stories. The murders troubled him, as they had so many others. Rennison felt the same way. He'd come up through the ranks, beginning his career as a League City policeman. And of all the cases, the Calder Drive slayings were among the area's most notorious.

Lieutenant Tommy Hansen kept a blowup of one of the I-45 charts behind his desk for more than a decade.
(Courtesy of Kathryn Casey)

So in 2010, as Hansen prepared to retire from his full-time job and start working part-time on the cold cases, Tim coincidentally asked Rennison to stop in at the Equusearch offices. Once the FBI agent arrived, Tim brought up the Beason case. Patiently, Rennison listened, appearing interested. When he left that day, he told Miller that he would talk with Tommy Hansen and get back in touch.

The following day, Rennison and Hansen spent the entire day at Miller's office going through his files and talking to Tim about Ellen Beason and the Killing Field murders. "It was an emotional meeting," said Miller. "I was crying, talking about Laura, and they teared up, too. I told Tommy and

Richard that I always suspected Clyde. I suggested they look into Ellen Beason's death. I said, 'Start there.'"

Sunday, July 29, 1984 was the last day of Ellen Rae Beason's life. A receptionist for a real-estate company, the pretty twenty-nine-year-old, once married, lived at home with her parents and a brother. Friends described Beason as dependable, hardworking, a good cook, yet a free spirit who loved to party and dance and sometimes drank a bit too much. On that night, she walked into the Texas Moon at about 6:00 P.M. The event was a fundraiser to help pay funeral expenses for a local family who'd lost a child in a car accident.

Was Ellen Beason's death an accident or a murder?
(Trial exhibit)

The evening proved a difficult one. After Ellen arrived, her good friend Candy Gifford introduced her to Hedrick. At first, all went well. A disc jockey played rock and roll, and Gifford danced, sometimes with Hedrick. But by nine, a disagreement had erupted between Gifford and her husband. The issue was Hedrick, who Gifford would later describe as hovering around their table. "My husband left, and I followed," Gifford would recall years later.

Not long after, Clyde Hedrick and Ellen Beason walked out the door of the Texas Moon together.

The following morning, Candy Gifford drove past the bar and noticed her friend's car in the parking lot. Ellen should have been at work, and Gifford worried enough to call Beason's mother. The family hadn't seen Ellen since the day before. She hadn't returned home from the club. Days passed, and Ellen remained missing.

"I started asking Clyde what happened, where Ellen was," said Gifford. Hedrick's responses were less than helpful. He claimed that after he and Beason left the bar, they drove around looking for Candy. Later, he took Beason back to the Texas Moon, where she walked off toward a truck, got inside with someone, and drove away. Hedrick said he couldn't describe the truck or the person. That didn't satisfy Gifford, who thought Hedrick must have known something that would help solve the mystery of her friend's disappearance.

Time passed, and Gifford continued to prod Hedrick for answers he didn't supply. Finally, one night four months after Ellen's disappearance, Gifford and Hedrick were again at the Texas Moon. Still determined to find her friend, Gifford asked Hedrick more questions about Beason. This time, Hedrick turned to Gifford, and asked, "Do you want to see where she's at?"

In the darkness, Hedrick drove Candy Gifford toward the Galveston Causeway. Before they entered the bridge, he veered off, toward an open field that ran along a railroad track. There, he guided her on foot through tall brush and weeds, down into a ravine strewn with garbage. He stopped at tires piled on a soiled and torn abandoned couch, pulled the tires off, then tipped the couch back. Gifford recoiled as she stared down at a decomposing body. She spotted a small gold necklace Ellen always wore, and Gifford knew it was her friend.

The account Hedrick gave Gifford that night was that after he and Beason left the Texas Moon, Beason wanted to go to a local swimming hole. Once there, he stayed in the truck, drank a beer, and smoked a joint, while Beason shed her clothes and ran into the shallow water. She invited him to join her, but he refused. Time passed, and when he began calling out to her to return to the truck, she didn't answer. He turned his truck lights on the water, and he saw Beason's body floating. Hedrick said Beason had drowned.

After walking out and pulling her body from the water,

Hedrick said he panicked, thinking others might not believe Beason's death was an accident. Instead of taking her to a hospital, he drove around, eventually dumping her body in the ravine and piling the couch and tires on top of her.

Then Gifford said that Hedrick told her not to tell anyone what she'd seen, a statement she interpreted as a warning that if she did, she or her family could be in danger.

For seven months, Gifford kept Clyde Hedrick's secret, she contended out of fear. Then in July 1985, he trashed her apartment, and she went to the police. The next day, she took officers to the ravine near the railroad tracks, where they moved the couch and exposed Ellen Beason's skeleton.

A macabre find: Ellen Beason's remains in the ravine. *(Trial exhibit)*

When interviewed by police, Hedrick repeated the same account of Beason's death he'd given to Candy Gifford. Days later, his fate rested with Galveston County's chief medical examiner, Dr. William Korndorffer, the man conducting the Beason autopsy. What Korndorffer ruled could have either corroborated or contradicted Hedrick's story. But when the report was filed, it did neither. Instead, Dr. Korndorffer concluded that after examining her remains, he was unable to decide how or why Ellen Beason died. On the autopsy form, the physician wrote "not determined" for both cause and manner of death.

In the end, Clyde Hedrick was put on trial and convicted of abuse of a corpse, sentenced to one year in prison and a $2,000 fine. And Ellen Beason's remains were in a plastic bag inside a casket beneath a granite monument that read, WITH THE LORD.

Yet many continued to believe that Clyde Hedrick had gotten away with murder.

In 1993, although they hadn't indicated any interest in the case to Tim Miller and appeared to rebuff his suspicions, the League City Police Department must have been troubled by the Beason case. That year they exhumed her remains to be reexamined. Instead of sending her skeleton back to Dr. Korndorffer at the Galveston County Morgue, however, her bones were transported to Denton, Texas, to the laboratory of Dr. Harrell Gill-King, director of the University of North Texas Institute of Forensic Anthropology. Gill-King, one of the nation's top forensic anthropologists, spent his career searching skeletons for clues.

Soon after the package arrived, Dr. Gill-King opened the clear plastic bag holding the skeleton to begin his assessment. But he was taken aback by the condition of the bones. In morgues across the nation, it was common procedure to clean bones before examination, removing tissue so indications of trauma can be seen. Apparently that hadn't been done at the Galveston ME's office, because according to Gill-King, when he received Beason's bones, they remained coated with debris and thick layers of connective tissue.

Assessing the task, Gill-King knew any conclusions he came to had to be based on cleaned bones. How else could he see any concealed injuries?

To be sure he had access to the entire skeleton, Gill-King had Beason's bones carefully washed and all remaining tissue peeled off. Once that was accomplished, he started his examination. On the newly exposed surface of the skull, it didn't take long to discover a crack so large that it ran downward from one cheekbone all the way to the other. To have resulted in such a major fracture the skull, one of the thickest bones in the body, had to have sustained a tremendous blow.

To judge when the injury occurred, Gill-King examined the edges of the break. Living bone breaks with rough edges, like a branch off of a tree, while dead bone breaks smooth, like a ceramic plate. On Beason's skull, the edges of the fracture were rough. The patina of the break also matched that of the rest of the skull, suggesting it had aged the same period of time. Those considerations led the forensic anthropologist to decide that the massive fissure occurred at or around the time of Beason's death.

Documenting the injury, Gill-King compiled his report, listing the cause of Ellen Beason's death as blunt-force trauma and the manner as homicide.

For a second opinion, Gill-King then sent Beason's skeleton to Dr. Marc Krouse, the deputy chief medical examiner and principal "bone man" at the nearby Tarrant County Medical Examiner's Office. Like Gill-King, Krouse had no difficulty finding the fracture on the newly defleshed skull, and he, too, judged it was perimortem, inflicted near the time of death. That finding, combined with the way Beason's remains had been found hidden beneath the couch, led Krouse to agree with Gill-King that Ellen Beason had been murdered.

Perhaps the League City police assumed that under such circumstances Dr. Korndorffer would reconsider his opinion. Instead, when the remains were returned to Galveston, the county's chief medical examiner grew angry. The fracture, he insisted to the district attorney, wasn't the cause of death. In fact, the physician asserted that the damage hadn't even been present when he examined the bones a decade earlier. Arguing that it was insulting that Gill-King and Krouse would accuse him of not cleaning the skull and missing a fracture so large a fledgling doctor would have seen it, Korndorffer stood by his original findings.

At that juncture, Galveston's district attorney faced a quandary; if he filed murder charges against Clyde Hedrick, Galveston's own chief medical examiner would testify for the defense.

In October 1997, a crew reinterred Ellen Beason's bones beneath the granite marker. There they waited, until that day in Tim Miller's office, when he suggested FBI Special Agent Richard Rennison and Galveston County Sheriff's Lieutenant Tommy Hansen reinvestigate her death.

Both men remembered the case, and they knew that many shared Miller's suspicions that Hedrick was responsible. "It was one of those cases people didn't forget," said Rennison. "There was the sense that there'd been a killing, and someone had gotten away with it."

With busy schedules it took time, but in November 2011, Hansen and Rennison began looking into the Beason case. Once they did, they learned of the 1993 exhumation, and Gill-King's and Houser's findings, that Beason's death was a homicide. At first, the investigators wondered why nothing had been done, but then realized that it all came down to the conflicting autopsies.

By then, Dr. Korndorffer had retired after three decades as Galveston's top medical examiner, and there was a new district attorney in Galveston County. Hanson and Rennison met with the chief prosecutor in the felony division, Kevin Petroff. "We began talking about exhuming the body again," said Petroff.

On March 28, 2012, for the second time, a backhoe dug into the sandy soil in Forest Park East Cemetery, uncovering a small casket, the size of a child's, holding Ellen Beason's bones. The following day, a captain in the sheriff's department drove north to Denton, to again bring the bones to Dr.

Gill-King for analysis. DNA had already been collected from Ellen's brother Ross, and a specimen was taken from the bones for comparison, to confirm that they were in fact Ellen's. And for a second time, Dr. Gill-King wrote a report documenting the skull fracture, labeling it as the cause of death, and listing his opinion for manner of death as homicide.

Soon after, around noon on April 4, 2013, Clyde Hedrick was arrested for the murder of Ellen Rae Beason. When an officer put the handcuffs on him, Hedrick appeared irritated, saying, "I already done my time for that."

As the events unfolded, and news cropped up on the cold case heading toward a courtroom, Tim Miller watched with interest, wondering if Hedrick was connected to his daughter's death. Then, as the investigation continued, something remarkable happened.

Two months after Hedrick's arrest, a lawyer for an inmate in the Galveston County jail contacted Kevin Petroff at the District Attorney's Office. The attorney had something he wanted to discuss. In the jail, while looking at a newspaper article about Equusearch and Tim Miller, three inmates claimed Clyde Hedrick made damning confessions: nonchalantly commenting that he'd had sex with and murdered Tim's daughter, Laura. During that same conversation, Hedrick allegedly also admitted killing Heide Fye and clubbing Ellen Beason to death with a table leg.

At first, the claims were kept secret. But then that fall, while preparing for trial, Petroff filed a list of extraneous offenses and allegations with the presiding district court, notifying the defense of any additional issues that could come up at the trial. Included was a long list of accusations against Hedrick, everything from drug use to the sexual abuse of a minor. At the end of the documents filed with the district clerk, Petroff included the assertions made by the inmates that Hedrick had confessed to not only killing Ellen Beason, but also Heide Fye and Laura Miller.

Once reporters discovered the official document on

the county clerk's Web site, newspapers and TV stations throughout the Houston area ran pieces naming Hedrick as a suspect in the infamous Killing Field murders. In response, reporters made their way to the county jail, requesting interviews. When questioned, Clyde Hedrick insisted that he'd never confessed to killing anyone and that he was being unfairly accused.

When Miller heard that Hedrick had reportedly made self-incriminating statements involving Laura's murder, Tim was furious. Although he'd believed for many years that Hedrick was a possible suspect in Laura's murder, the allegations of a confession shook him. "It feels like it's happening all over again," he said one day. "It feels like it's ripped the bandages off all the wounds."

As Hedrick's trial date approached, with the published claims circulating that he might be the Killing Field serial killer, it seemed that even more rested on the upcoming proceedings.

Yet despite Gill-King's and Krouse's assessments that Ellen Beason was murdered, the case against Hedrick wasn't an easy one, with Kevin Petroff, Rennison and Hansen repeatedly running into complications. Predominantly: the inability to find much of the evidence.

Over time, records had vanished, including the 1985 autopsy file with all Dr. Korndorffer's photos. League City couldn't find its file from the 1993 exhumation and had yet to locate Dr. Gill-King's photos from that examination. While disappointing, this wasn't unexpected in decades-old cases. "It's not unusual to have missing evidence," Rennison would later say. Records could be misfiled, sometimes systems changed, and data was misplaced, and on the Gulf Coast, evidence could be lost to the flooding brought by hurricanes. "In these old cases, it's really the norm."

Yet it would turn out that the Hedrick case was anything but ordinary.

Perhaps the most surprising twist: Petroff had been requesting that 1985 autopsy file for nearly two years. Although Dr. Korndorffer had retired, his daughter, Brenda Williams, still worked for the ME's Office. She'd repeatedly searched, but it hadn't been found. Then in January, just two months before the trial, Williams asked her father, ill and in a wheelchair, if he knew where the Beason file could be. To her surprise, he responded that he'd taken it home. It was in his storage unit.

"We went to his house," Petroff recounted. "Dr. Korndorffer was pleasant enough, but he was still arguing that he hadn't made a mistake." Despite Gill-King's contention that the bones were encased in tissue when Beason's skull arrived at his office in 1993, and it was his staff that cleaned them, Korndorffer insisted that wasn't true. Instead, the former ME claimed that his assistant cleaned the bones before the first autopsy. And Korndorffer remained adamant that the skull fracture hadn't been there when he first examined Beason's skull in 1985.

Back at the district attorney's office, when Petroff combed through the newly retrieved file and the photos, however, what he found appeared to contradict Dr. Korndorffer. The retired medical examiner had handed over pages of neatly labeled thirty-year-old, 35 mm slides, intended to be slipped into a projector and displayed on a screen. The problem was that based on the numbers on the cardboard frames, sixty-five slides were missing. Of the images Petroff did have, only two were of the skull. Seeming to confirm what Dr. Gill-King contended, in both surviving views of the skull included in Dr. Korndorffer's 1985 slides, the bone remained concealed under a thick layer of tissue, dirt, and debris.

As they prepared in the weeks leading up to the trial, Petroff and his second chair on the case, Kayla Allen, understood that they faced the identical situation to the one that had tabled the case in the midnineties; by then, Hedrick's defense attorney had subpoenaed Dr. Korndorffer. In the courtroom, the two Galveston County prosecutors would be forced to confront the county's former chief medical examiner, who would testify against the state.

Prosecutors Kayla Allen and Kevin Petroff with the skull replica used at the trial.
(Courtesy of Kathryn Casey)

Clyde Hedrick's trial began on the morning of Tuesday, March 25, 2014. Throughout the five days of its duration, Tim Miller sat center stage, in the front row, next to the aisle, behind the prosecutors. Surrounding him filling the first two rows were friends, all Equusearch volunteers, who came to support him. From the defense table, Hedrick glared at Miller, who stared back, refusing to avert his gaze from the man he believed murdered his daughter.

Other interested parties—those with a personal stake in the proceedings—filled the third row: Heide Fye's family, her sisters, one of their husbands, and their daughters. They, too, had come to watch the trial of a man they considered a prime suspect in the murder of their loved one. Often their thoughts trailed back to the day in 1983 when Heide disappeared. "Heide was so full of life, so loved," said Josie Poarch-Mauro, one afternoon. "We want to know who did this, to see the man punished. It's been too long."

Of Ellen Beason's family, her brother Ross appeared anxious and overwhelmed by the drama as it unfolded in the courtroom. He hadn't told his aged mother about the trial, not wanting to bring her back to the time when his sister died. "Ellen's death tore our family apart," Ross said, tears in his eyes.

Yet the missing evidence and the conflicting medical opinions made the case far from certain. Another concern was Hedrick's defense attorney, Jeremy DuCote, known as a hard fighter and an able opponent. At the defense table, his partner and wife, the noticeably pregnant Leigh Love, sat between DuCote and his client. No longer resembling the strapping construction worker who'd left the Texas Moon with Beason on that fateful night, at fifty-nine Hedrick was a heavily wrinkled man who'd lost much of his chin to cancer. Yet his eyes, pale, cold, and empty, hadn't changed.

2013 booking photo of Clyde Hedrick.
(Courtesy of the Galveston County Sheriff's Office)

As in most trials, much of the prosecutors' initial efforts painted the picture, depicting the case's journey. "A woman walks into a police station," Petroff said in his opening statement, dramatically recounting how Candy Gifford first told authorities in 1985 that she knew where to find Ellen Beason's body.

For the defense, Jeremy DuCote didn't disagree. Ellen
Beason died, and his client was with her when it happened.
Yet it wasn't murder, he said, but an accident followed by a
mistake, one Clyde Hedrick had already been convicted of
and served time for. "The fracture in 1994 [the one seen by
Dr. Gill-King] did not exist" in 1985, DuCote contended.
"It wasn't there . . . You will find Clyde Hedrick not guilty."

Through Beason's friends' descriptions, Petroff and
Allen introduced the dead woman to the jury, describing
the fun-loving twenty-nine-year-old who never aged another
day because she'd met a terrible fate that July 1984 night.
When Candy Gifford took police to the ravine, they pulled
back the couch. "I saw the skull first," the officer who'd accompanied her reported.

From the day the bones were recovered, prosecutors detailed the convoluted course the case had taken, including the
1986 trial, the 1993 exhumation, and the interest of the FBI's
Rennison and the sheriff department's Hansen that laid the
foundation for finally charging Clyde Hedrick with murder.

Among the first things Petroff did when Rennison took
the stand was read Hedrick's testimony from the 1986 abuse
of a corpse trial into the record. Once completed, Petroff
asked Rennison if anything in Hedrick's description of the
night Beason died concerned him. "Yes," the FBI agent answered.

Just the evening before, Rennison prepared for trial by
reading Hedrick's testimony, when the FBI agent suddenly
had what he considered an aha moment, when a picture
crystallized. What he'd noticed was Hedrick's description
of finding Beason's body in the water. "He said he saw Ellen
Beason floating," Rennison pointed out. "People don't float
when they drown. Their lungs fill with water, and they sink."

A murmur ran through the courtroom, like breath escaping as the audience filling the benches recalled headlines of
drowning victims being pulled from the bottoms of pools,
ponds, and rivers.

The second thing Rennison noted was Hedrick's own description of the area where he claimed Beason swam, so shallow that he said he walked out to retrieve her body. How could Beason have drowned in water she could stand up in? If she had gotten in trouble, she could have walked to the shore.

The final thing Rennison found unbelievable was Hedrick's claim that Beason had gone skinny-dipping, then tried to coax him into joining her. Instead, Hedrick testified that he drank a beer and smoked a joint in his truck. "A beautiful woman takes her clothes off and tries to get him to swim with her. He doesn't go?" Rennison remarked. "As a man, I thought that was strange."

Gray-haired with glasses and a beard, Dr. Harrell Gill-King resembled the professor he was, when he took the stand and recounted his credentials. While medical examiners most often saw newly dead or decomposing bodies, Gill-King's examinations took place farther along in the death process, when little remained but evidence of trauma recorded on bone. Knife marks, gunshot holes, and as in this case, fractures.

On the Elmo, the document projector that displayed images on a TV screen, Kayla Allen loaded the only two photos marked as coming from Dr. Korndorffer's 1985 autopsy that showed the skull. For the jurors, Gill-King pointed out a thick layer of tissue obscuring the bone. "Is this the way you received the skull?" Petroff asked.

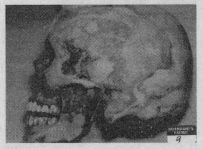

One of the only two known 1985 views of Ellen Beason's skull, still covered in tissue. *(Trial exhibit)*

Gill-King answered that it was. "The skull had not been cleaned . . . there was connective tissue, soft tissue, it covered the bone." After recounting how his assistants soaked the skull in warm water and peeled off the tissue, the anthropologist explained that once the skull was uncovered, the fracture became easily visible. He then used a stereomicroscope to examine the break, noting the rough surface and the fracture's consistent patina that matched the overall discoloration of the skull. Those two findings, he testified, indicated that the injury occurred at or near the time of Ellen Beason's death.

The cleaned skull from beneath, taken in 2012 and showing the fracture.
(Trial exhibit)

"That is some of the hardest bone in the body. It survives fires," Gill-King testified. Such a substantial fracture could only have been caused by "a tremendous blow."

Asked if the damage could have resulted from anything but homicide, Gill-King scoffed, "The possibility that this type of injury occurred without help from someone else is right up there with monkeys typing Shakespeare."

Dr. Krouse agreed when he took the stand, diagnosing that the fracture was the result of substantial blunt-force trauma, and that it couldn't have happened when the couch was put on top of Beason's body, after she was dead. In that scenario, the couch "would have caused damage to the more delicate bones in the face and body, and there is none."

Yet DuCote vigorously challenged both doctors, reminding jurors that Gill-King and Krouse didn't do the original autopsy, and neither had seen the remains when first recovered in 1985. Repeatedly, the defense attorney directed the testimony back to the missing evidence, including autopsy photos and the police report from the first exhumation. Even the fourteen photos Gill-King took of the skull during his first examination had disappeared. "Don't you wish you had your photos . . . those slides, to see if the fracture is there?" the defense attorney asked.

In response, Gill-King maintained he had all he needed to form his opinion.

In his cross-examinations, the defense attorney reminded the jurors of the many things Krouse and Gill-King couldn't tell them, including identifying the alleged murder weapon. Rather than homicide, DuCote suggested that without toxicology reports and a full body to examine, the doctors couldn't rule out the possibility that Beason had drowned or died from an overdose.

While Dr. Korndorffer had been adamant with the lawyers when they met before the trial, neither appeared prepared for the retired ME's stormy demeanor on the stand. Even DuCote, who'd subpoenaed the eighty-four-year-old, handled the feisty old man carefully and struggled to direct his testimony. In the end, he appeared frail in his wheelchair and continually turned to talk directly to the jurors, ignoring the attorneys and the judge who attempted to reel him back in. Yes, he said, his assistant had cleaned the skull, contradicting Dr. Gill-King's testimony. No, Korndorffer said, he didn't know what happened to all the missing autopsy photos including, presumably, many of Beason's skull.

In 1996, the physician had been so insulted by being second-guessed by Gill-King and Krouse that he'd made a video arguing his case. Although the other experts told jurors that signs of hemorrhage weren't useful in this type of a skull fracture, that there often wasn't evidence of bleeding and if there had been any the blood would have deteriorated and disappeared with decomposition, Korndorffer, his voice shaking with anger, insisted that the fact that he'd seen no bloodstains in 1985 was positive proof that at that time no fracture existed.

Cross-examining a fragile octogenarian presented considerable challenge. Kevin Petroff needed to prove his case, yet it wasn't good for the jury to judge that the prosecutor was attacking an old man in a wheelchair. While Petroff proceeded cautiously, Korndorffer sputtered angrily. After the retired ME admitted that the Beason file was the only one he'd removed from the office, Petroff asked why he'd made an exception with that particular case. "Because I was dealing with dirty policemen!" the physician shouted. "They were going to do away with my autopsy report!"

When Petroff asked Korndorffer if he thought Dr. Gill-King was part of a conspiracy, the retired physician speculated that the anthropologist was being used "to convict an innocent man."

Other testimony followed. Another forensic pathologist took the stand, one hired by the defense who initially backed Dr. Korndorffer's views but then retreated when told that Dr. Gill-King's office reportedly cleaned the tissue off the skull and that Dr. Korndorffer had not initially seen the bone defleshed. "If the skull wasn't cleaned, he wouldn't have seen the fracture," she said.

It was late in the trial when the witness Tim Miller waited for finally entered the courtroom, Max Stephenson, one of the inmates in the county jail who claimed to have heard Clyde Hedrick not only confess to killing Ellen Beason but also Heide Fye and Laura Miller. Yet on the stand, Stephenson, handcuffed and wearing his jailhouse uniform, wasn't allowed to talk about anything other than what he said Hedrick told him about Ellen Beason. To do otherwise, to bring up Hedrick's possible involvement in other offenses, could have caused a mistrial or resulted in a conviction, if the jury came back with one, being overturned on appeal.

Clyde Hedrick "told us that he thought [Ellen Beason] drowned," said Stephenson. "He said when he was putting her under the couch, she woke up, and he hit her with a table leg."

On cross-examination, DuCote's second chair, Leigh

Love, implied that perhaps Stephenson lied to get a deal from the state. "You told the FBI guy you wanted your case dropped," she accused.

Stephenson, serving a three-year sentence for evading arrest, admitted that was true but said that Special Agent Rennison had offered him nothing for his testimony.

At the end of the trial, Kayla Allen began closing arguments, reminding jurors of who Ellen Beason was on that final day, a young woman with her life ahead of her. What was important about Stephenson's testimony, she said, was that it matched the scientific opinions, those of Gill-King and Krouse, that Beason's death was caused by being struck with tremendous force by a heavy, blunt object.

"This is a wrongful prosecution of an innocent man," Leigh Love countered. What Clyde Hedrick had done was reprehensible, but he'd been convicted and served his time for abusing Ellen Beason's corpse. Her husband followed, agreeing, arguing that the state wanted it both ways. For decades, prosecutors relied on Dr. Korndorffer's testimony to convict defendants of murder; now they wanted the jurors to ignore his testimony, not to believe him when he said Ellen Beason's skull wasn't fractured in 1985. "It's hard to buy the story of the state that the Galveston ME's Office was so incompetent that it missed a fracture a first-year medical student could find," DuCote said. ". . . Agree with Dr. Korndorffer that the cause of death is undetermined."

The last one to speak was Kevin Petroff, who repeated what the FBI's Rennison had said, that Clyde Hedrick's description of the way Ellen Beason died was illogical. Drowned bodies don't initially float. At first, lungs fill with water, and they sink. Only later will such victims rise to the surface, the result of gases formed by decomposition. Petroff also asked how likely it was that Ellen Beason died in water so shallow she could have stood up and walked to shore. Even more important, Petroff said that the jurors knew that what Dr. Korndorffer said wasn't true, he hadn't cleaned the skull, because Dr. Gill-King had testified that when the remains were exhumed the skull arrived at his office with tissue still covering the fracture. "This is what a government cover-up looks like," Petroff said. "Someone screwed something up and tried to hide it. . . . [Dr. Korndorffer] took the file home . . . put it in his storage area."

After a pause, Petroff reminded jurors, however, that despite all the medical testimony, the case wasn't about the bone doctors or any of the experts. "What we're talking about is the life of a twenty-nine-year-old in 1984 . . ." he said, holding up Beason's photo. "Did she drown in water that just came up to her waist, or did this man who hid her under the couch crush her skull from side to side?"

While murder was the first option on the paperwork, when they returned with their verdict that wasn't the jury's decision. Instead they found Clyde Hedrick guilty of a lesser charge, involuntary manslaughter. While they judged him responsible for Ellen Beason's death, their verdict suggested that they weren't certain that he intended to kill her.

The following Monday, the punishment phase began, and more witnesses testified, mainly family members pleading for mercy for Hedrick. Yet it was one witness in particular who made the greatest impact. A college student who lived with Hedrick as a teenager, the woman initially liked her mother's new boyfriend. That faded, however, as Hedrick exposed himself to her, and she testified she suspected he watched her through a hole drilled into her bedroom wall. She said Hedrick showed her pornography when she was just thirteen, and at fifteen touched her breasts. She cried about a time when she said he gave her something to drink, and she awoke the next morning feeling as if she'd been sexually assaulted. As she voiced her accusations, the jurors stared at Hedrick in disdain, especially the men.

In the end, jurors handed down the maximum allowed, sentencing Clyde Hedrick to twenty years in a Texas prison.

While throughout, the testimony had centered only on Ellen Beason's death, Tim saw the proceedings as his day in court as well, hoping he'd hear Laura and Heide mentioned. When they weren't, he appeared ever more resolute that the matter hadn't ended. One day, he and the rest of Laura's family, along with Josie and all of Heide's relatives, deserved their own trial. But would that ever come?

After listening and viewing the evidence presented at Hedrick's murder trial, Tim talked about two statements he'd heard that took him back to the Killing Field. The source was Hedrick's 1986 testimony at his abuse of a corpse trial, which Petroff read to the jury. First Hedrick mentioned that the field where he'd disposed of Beason's body was one he was familiar with because the company he worked for used it to dump old roofing tiles. In the area around the Killing Field, Miller had also found piles of old, discarded roofing tiles.

Secondly: In his 1985 account of Beason's death, Hedrick had described disposing of her body. On the stand, he said that after he transported her to the ravine, he laid Beason on the ground. Then before he covered her with the couch, he took off the shirt he was wearing, a red Western one, and draped it over her face.

What that brought to mind for Tim Miller was the blue Western shirt he had a picture of in his files, the shirt found near his daughter's remains and tagged with her case number. In the picture, it appeared stained, perhaps with blood. Was it possible that the shirt could be the answer to three decades of questions, that it had the power to finally bring the Killing Field serial killer to justice? Did it belong to Clyde Hedrick? Could it be stained with his DNA?

"Maybe this shirt thing is something Clyde does," Tim mused.

Yet there was a problem. Police had told Tim that the shirt, along with much of the Killing Field evidence, was lost. In the decades since his daughter died, it seemed that like so many cold cases, time and human error had damaged the investigation. What it hadn't diminished was a father's commitment. In no uncertain terms, Tim Miller challenged, "I want them to find that shirt. I want them to keep looking."

In the end, there were indications that authorities could be doing just that. Although unable to comment on ongoing cases, when asked, the FBI's Rennison wouldn't confirm or deny that the investigation continued into whether or not Clyde Hedrick was the Killing Field serial killer. Instead, he smiled, and said, "All I can say is that we haven't closed any of these cases."

While confident that Special Agent Rennison and Lieutenant Hansen continued to look into the murders, in the months following Hedrick's conviction, Tim Miller understandably grew impatient. Five months after Hedrick's trial ended, Miller initiated an action he hoped would push the case forward. On August 25, 2014, he filed a civil action, a wrongful death suit against Hedrick for Laura's murder.

Not expecting to become rich from the suit, Miller had other goals in mind. "I feel like I'm the father to all four of the girls whose bodies were found out in that field. And I want Clyde Hedrick to tell the truth about what happened to them. That's all I want. The truth," Tim said, "and I want him to tell us who Jane Doe is. I want to be able to tell her family what happened to her."

Two weeks after filing the lawsuit, Miller returned to the Calder Drive Killing Field. Surrounded by family and friends, he stood in the center of the clearing during a candlelight vigil. At the ceremony, Tim reinstalled the old weathered cross he'd erected in Laura's memory, repaired and bearing a new plaque with Laura's photo and birth and death dates, to commemorate the thirtieth anniversary of his daughter's death. In addition, Tim and the Equusearch volunteers erected three more crosses in honor of Fye, and Jane and Janet Doe. Then they tied two hundred ribbons to the surrounding trees, each one bearing the name of a missing person.

The very next morning, Tim was in Plano, Texas. A twenty-three-year-old woman was missing, believed to have been abducted, and the family had called asking for help.

Chapter 10

"Fear in Her Eyes"
Mark Roland Stallings
The Murder of Janet Doe

Woodville, Texas

At the end of the Clyde Hedrick trial, so many questions remained. Perhaps he was the serial killer who'd made the Calder Drive field his personal burial ground. Perhaps he wasn't. Perhaps Tim Miller would never know for sure. If it were true, it begged another question: If Clyde Hedrick murdered the first three women whose bodies were found posed under the trees, what about the fourth? Who killed Janet Doe?

Mark Roland Stallings in the interview room. *(Courtesy of Kathryn Casey)*

As I worked through the cases, at first I found no answers. Then one day I read an article out of the *Houston Chronicle* archives about a man named Mark Roland Stall-

ings, who had once been a hired hand on Robert Abel's
League City ranch. According to the 2001 reports, while in
prison on other charges, Stallings confessed to the Killing
Fields murders. Since no charges were ever filed, I assumed
police uncovered evidence that excluded Stallings, but I decided to investigate anyway. In the end, I learned that Mark
Stallings hadn't been cleared. In fact, he remained the prime
suspect in Janet Doe's murder.

"We think Stallings did one of the murders," said Lieutenant Tommy Hansen at the Galveston County Sheriff's
Office, the same Galveston Sheriff's investigator who'd
worked the Shelley Sikes and Clyde Hedrick cases. "We believe he murdered Janet Doe. But he refused to sign a confession, and so far we don't have the evidence we need to
charge him."

Eventually I learned that Stallings not only remained a
suspect in the murder of the final Killing Fields victim but
also in the murders of two women in Fort Bend County, west
of Galveston.

"I was maybe seven or so," Mark Roland Stallings told me,
recounting the first time he put his hands on a girl's neck and
realized that he felt thrilled by her gasp for breath. We were
separated by thick glass and talking via a phone in the maximum security section of a prison just outside the small Texas
town of Woodville. Only sixteen men were housed in the
unit, those considered the most dangerous and the greatest
flight risks. It was an austere place, one where visitors were
meticulously searched coming and going, where access was
carefully monitored.

In these somber surroundings, Stallings reminisced,
describing a time long past when he was still a child, one
whose attention was drawn to forbidden preoccupations. On
that day when he was seven, Stallings played "husband and
wife" with a little girl who might have been eight or so. "For
her age, she knew everything about being sexual. She hit on

me," he said. Aroused, Stallings experimented. "For some reason, I took my thumb and mashed it in her throat."

At that, Stallings held up his thumb and positioned it against his own neck, to illustrate where he'd pressed, at the base, directly over the girl's windpipe. "I saw her face. She had that fear in her eyes. I pulled it back out. She was crying. I apologized, said, 'Don't tell! I won't do it again. I promise.'"

While he never hurt that particular girl again, it would be a promise that Stallings would fail to keep. For according to his own words, there were many women in his future who would be victimized by this man with the cold blue eyes and soft Texas drawl, including one of the murdered women found in the Killing Field.

Talking about his past, Stallings remained emotionless, except during those moments when he recounted the final seconds of a woman's life. Then he grew excited, his voice rising through a thin smile. For Mark Roland Stallings, these apparently weren't tragedies but cherished memories.

In his account of his life, Stallings came of age in the countryside outside Seguin in Guadalupe County, one of the oldest towns in Texas, a center for farming and ranching. In a family of ten children, he described his upbringing as unruly, saying his parents let their brood run with little supervision. As a child, he said he was sexually abused, starting at the age of six, by a woman he never identified.

Violence, too, entered his life early. At seven, he had the encounter with the eight-year-old girl, the one where he thrust his thumb into her throat. At eleven, he claimed to have stabbed a schoolmate on the playground over a dip of snuff, then threatened to slit the boy's throat to convince him to say the stabbing was accidental. At thirteen, Stallings said he raped a young woman at knifepoint. She was eighteen, a relative, and she begged him "not to do anything crazy."

What made him feel justified? He judged her to be a loose

woman, one who gave her sexual favors away. So he felt entitled to do what he would with her.

In the mideighties, Stallings was in his early twenties, married with two children, and working as a laborer. "I got involved with this guy," he said. "We got to know each other, smoked pot and stuff like that. We'd go out on occasion, get blasted. There was this one prostitute I used to mess with."

Her street name was Champagne, and Stallings described her as a white woman with an olive complexion, "real pretty and real nice." All went well until Champagne decided for some reason that she no longer wanted to service Stallings's needs. Perhaps she sensed something about him that worried her. One night when he was out with his friend, Stallings suggested they look Champagne up for a little fun.

"My thing is, it's not up to you when you want to have sex if you're a fucking prostitute," he said, with a sardonic frown. "You sell your body, you disrespect yourself like that, you ain't got no rights."

That evening, Champagne got in the truck with the two men, and they drove off to an abandoned trailer. Once they arrived, Champagne, possibly realizing something was wrong, refused to have sex. They, however, had other plans. Stallings pulled the woman out of the truck, forcing her toward the trailer, while the other man yelled at him to hurry before someone saw them. Inside the trailer, she still refused to do as they wanted, and they fought. "I slammed her upside the head, and I slammed her upside the wall," Stallings said. He beat her and threw her into a back bedroom, where both men forced themselves on her. This time, Stallings said, he wasn't the one who finished the woman off. Instead, after his second go-round with the woman, his friend emerged from the bedroom saying, "I strangled the bitch."

When Stallings investigated, he said that he found Champagne dead with a red scarf tied around her neck. Assessing the situation, he deposited her body in a closet, then rounded up three stray dogs he locked inside the trailer, assuming they'd grow hungry and consume the evidence. Before leaving, Stallings broke the trailer's door handle off on the outside, to keep the curious out. It worked for about two weeks.

"In the paper, it said that they found a female body, twenty-four to twenty-five years old," said Stallings. "I worried for a while that they'd find fingerprints. I was already on parole. I thought about it two or three days, but no one came to talk to me."

Not long after, in early 1988, he met Robert Abel, the man who for a decade would be the prime suspect in the Killing Field murders. The way Stallings characterized it, the two men quickly bonded. "Robert had a dark side like I had a dark side," Stallings told me, his voice grave. "Before too long, we became more than boss and employee."

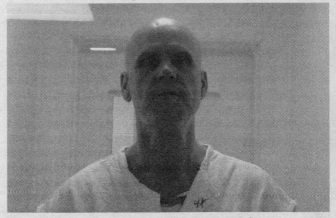

Mark Stallings said he became violent at a young age.
(Courtesy of Kathryn Casey)

In Mark Roland Stallings's account, he and Robert Abel came from very different lives but recognized that they were fellow travelers. The job Stallings accepted was that of foreman on Abel's ranch in Bellville, a small town a little more than an hour northwest of Houston. The land just outside town, two adjoining cattle ranches, had been in the NASA engineer's family since before Texas was a state. A small house anchored the property and the adjacent family cemetery, laid in a grove of trees with headstones dating back to the late 1800s.

On the ranch, Stallings's job became less foreman than laborer, as Abel instructed Stallings on his duties, including tending the stock and doing repairs and upkeep. "Robert didn't want to hire anyone else," said Stallings, who waved his hands expressively, emphasizing his words. "I ended up doing pretty much everything."

Abel fluctuated back and forth, living on his land on the edge of the Killing Field in League City and the family spread in Bellville. When they talked, Stallings learned that Abel shared his view of women. "He'd tell me stuff like women always want to dominate the world . . . make the decisions . . . tell when a man can touch them, when he can't. I said, 'I know. I understand.' I could feel the darkness in Robert. I was relating to that. I was thriving off that myself."

If Stallings told the truth about the events that unfolded in the following year, police weren't wrong when they eyed Abel as someone capable of murder. Before long, Stallings rotated between Abel's two properties, working two to three days a week in Bellville, and the rest of the time staying with his wife in a small cabin in the woods on the League City ranch. It was there one day that Stallings said Abel came to him and asked if he knew where to get a prostitute. In response, Stallings drove to one of Houston's well-known red-light districts, Telephone Road, on the southeast side of downtown. Once there, he pulled over at a small, run-down hotel and picked up a young Hispanic woman who spoke English, then drove her out to the ranch. "We do our thing, and Robert said, 'I want to keep her overnight,'" Stallings said. The next day, Abel seemed on edge, and before long Stallings says Abel told him, "Man, I killed that girl."

That evening, Stallings said he drove to the site where Abel left the woman's body. Once Stallings found it, he tied it with a nylon rope onto the back of a hay baler and pulled it with a tractor into the woods. There he stripped the clothes off and dug a grave, shallow enough to partially conceal the corpse but not so deep it discouraged wildlife. "You can sit out on that property at night and hear the coyotes," he said. "They'll tear a body apart. As far as I know, the coyotes probably strung her from League City to Kalamazoo."

Not long after, Stallings said he returned to Telephone Road, this time alone. On the street, he found another prostitute, one wearing a shirt, brown corduroy pants, and tall brown leather boots. "I tell her, 'Let's go out to this ranch and mess around a bit. I'll show you some cows and shit like that.'"

Once back on Abel's League City ranch, Stallings said he screamed at the woman: "All you bitches. You sell your body, then you make a choice. The way I feel, you ain't got no right to speak about what a person does with your body." By then, Stallings had rigged his truck, removing the lever that opened the driver's side door from the inside, so that the window had to be rolled down to use the outside handle. "The reason was to trap my victim," he said, his voice matter-of-fact.

On this day after he got out, Stallings's prey tried to escape out the driver's-side door. She must have been terrified when she realized that the handle didn't work. Meanwhile, he flung open the passenger-side door and grabbed her. "She kicked me in the chest, and I was outraged," he said, furious at the memory. "Halfway out of the truck, I was like, son of a bitch, and I hauled off and hit her." When he grabbed her leg, her boot slid off, and he began pummeling her with it.

"She's groggy, out of it. By the time I start having sex with her, she's coming to. She tries to bite me, so I punch her a couple of times. I took her sock, wrapped it around her neck, and I choked her out."

As he had with the Hispanic prostitute, Stallings said

he then removed all the clothing from this victim's corpse, dug another shallow grave, buried the woman and left. Not long after, he threw her clothes into a convenience-store Dumpster.

Asked if he could identify either of the two women, Stallings smirked. "I didn't ask no names. These women were whores."

The following day, Stallings bragged to Abel about his exploits and the new corpse buried in the woods. Instead of being impressed, however, Abel quickly grew agitated, not wanting to go to the site to see the body, instead saying over and over that there were too many bodies on his land. Stallings didn't know about the first three victims who'd been found in the Killing Field. He didn't understand Abel's concern, telling his boss that there were only two women buried in the woods. Stallings's appetite for sex and violence whetted by the recent killings, he had plans. With all Abel's acreage, the ranch hand saw no worries about disposal, but Abel insisted he wanted none of it. "I'm sending you back to Bellville," he told Stallings.

"Robert was freaking on me," said Stallings, with a disgusted frown that suggested the older man was weak. In the months that followed, Abel looked tired and stressed, and dark circles framed his eyes. Not long after, he fired Stallings. "It never left me about Robert firing me," said Stallings. "Then I thought I was going to get even."

At one point, Stallings described returning to Abel's property, prepared to murder his ex-boss and anyone else he found there. But when he arrived, Stallings eyed a young boy, maybe eleven or twelve, on a tractor. He didn't know the kid, and he decided he didn't want to kill him. So Stallings simply talked to Abel briefly and quietly left. But it didn't dissuade him from his course of action. He was prepared to do what he had to do to bring Robert Abel down. "I was going to get the son of a bitch."

The county housed trucks in a facility near League City, and one night in 1991, Stallings said he borrowed one, intending to use it to carry out his plan. Again he drove to the same section of Telephone Road, with its run-down hotels and stores. There he found a teenager, pretty, with long blondish brown hair—he gauged between sixteen and twenty—standing alongside the road looking for a John interested in paying for sex. She wore a white shirt with a blue stripe, blue jeans, and tennis shoes. He didn't ask her name. After her body was found in the Killing Field, she'd be called Janet Doe. "I'll do you for ten dollars," Janet told Stallings.

"What do you want it for?" he asked.

"Crack," the girl said, a pipe dangling from her lips. Instead, Stallings bargained with a dealer on the street and bought the girl two rocks. They smoked it. They had sex, then they talked. As Stalling recounts it, the young woman was morose, lamenting the state of her life, and looking for a way out. Estranged from her family, she said her father didn't know what type of life she led. "Why do you disrespect your body like this?" Stallings asked her.

"My dad don't care about me. No one does. I really don't want to be alive." Stallings then listened as, he said, the girl recounted a fantasy, saying: "I want to have sex, and I want to be killed during the sex."

"Well, she's talking to the right motherfucker right here," Stallings said, the memory exciting him. "You know what I'm saying?"

"My intention was to get back at Robert," said Stallings, describing how he suggested they take a ride in the county-owned truck. "So we go back out there." They drove toward League City, then exited the freeway at Calder Drive, coming around the corner and continuing on through the gate and onto Robert Abel's property. Parked in the truck, Stallings asked the girl

The hands of a killer?
(Courtesy of Kathryn Casey)

if she wanted to have sex again. She agreed. She was still in the front seat, when she took her jeans off, and he ordered her to roll over on her stomach. As he moved inside her, he grabbed the seat belt and struck her once, then again in the head, with the metal buckle.

"Pow, I hit her on the back of the head. Bam. She goes, 'Ow!' I hit her again, and her face kind of goes funny. Then I take the seat belt, wrap it around her neck."

Stallings's voice was tight and excited as he described cinching the seat belt tight, strangling the teenager. When he was done, he left her shirt on her, and instead of driving out into the woods, as he had the others, he transported her to the clearing directly behind Abel's property. He said that he didn't know until later that it was called the Killing Field, and that it was there that three bodies had been found years earlier.

"I laid her out, putting her in an empty spot. The others I was hiding. This one, I wanted to be found. She wasn't buried, and she was meant to be found."

"You wanted them to look at Abel? You wanted to get even?" I asked.

"Yeah," he said. "It worked. It sparked a whole lot of shit."

If his story is true, Stallings accomplished what he intended. It was after that fourth body, Janet Doe, was discovered in September 1991, that authorities focused on Abel. Soon the FBI compiled a profile of the Killing Field serial killer, one Abel fit, and Tim Miller started waiting for Abel when the retired engineer walked to the road to collect his mail.

Later in 1991, Stallings was convicted of burglary. Then in 1996, he was in a Texas prison for possession of a firearm and shooting an old man through a window, wounding but not killing him. While incarcerated serving two fifty-year sentences in 1998, Stallings tried to escape, taking a guard hostage with a smuggled-in gun and holding her for four hours. The result: three convictions for aggravated assault and one for aggravated kidnapping. Sentenced to life and not eligible for parole until April 2021, Stallings devised yet another plan to get out of prison. He decided he had a story to tell, and that it could prove his get-out-of-jail-free card.

From prison, Stallings notified authorities that he had murdered women in Fort Bend and Galveston Counties. Before long, the headlines in the state's newspapers read: "Man's confession could solve 'killing field' case."

"Prisoner claims he committed Calder Drive killings," read another on November 3, 2001, in Galveston's *Daily News*.

"I never told them I killed *all* those girls," Stallings said with a wry smile. Instead, he told authorities from Fort Bend about the woman his friend murdered, the one left in the abandoned trailer. And he talked to League City police about the two women murdered and left on Abel's property off Calder Drive. "I did it to get out of here," he said, glancing around the white walls of the narrow cubicle he sat in, a fluorescent light shining overhead, casting the walls and Stallings in an unnatural yellow glow. "I thought while they had me out there, I could figure a way to escape."

For weeks Stallings traveled outside prison walls, shackled and handcuffed, pointing out where he said he'd disposed of bodies, telling parts but, he said, not his entire story. Then, he said, authorities lost interest. "I think they blew it," he said. "I thought they'd want to talk to me more."

It wasn't, however, that they thought Stallings was lying. In the newspapers, Fort Bend and League City authorities agreed that Stallings knew more than he should have about the killings, suggesting he might have been involved. When I called League City and talked to a detective, I was told that Stallings was "a prime suspect" in Janet Doe's murder.

When I pressed further, the man said, "We think he probably did it."

When I reached out to the other jurisdiction where Stallings said he'd been involved in a murder, Fort Bend authorities said the same thing, that they considered Stallings a viable suspect in a murder in their jurisdiction.

The League City detective contended that all the murders of the girls whose bodies were left in the Killing Field remained active investigations. Yet Stallings insisted no one from either jurisdiction had talked to him in more than a decade.

Weeks after I left the prison, trying to determine if Stallings told the truth, I brought Janet Doe's autopsy and the description Stallings gave me of her murder to be reviewed by a friend, a retired assistant medical examiner. After he compared the two, the physician nodded. "It could have happened that way, the way he said he did it. There's not enough here to say for sure that he did it, but it's certainly possible."

Was Stallings telling the truth? He did have a reason to lie. A possible motive: hate for Robert Abel. Although Abel was long dead, perhaps Stallings abhorred the man enough to want to tarnish his memory. But if that was his motivation, Stallings could have added so much more to his tale.

In prison for sixteen years at the time of Hedrick's trial, Stallings didn't know about the allegations against the man. To see what he'd say, if he'd try to implicate Abel in other murders, I asked Stallings if he thought his ex-boss killed the first three victims found in the field behind Abel's house: Heide Fye, Laura Miller, and Jane Doe. Rather than grow his accusations against a man he clearly despised—one who was deceased and couldn't defend himself—Stallings didn't take the bait. Instead, he shrugged and frowned, admitting, "I don't know. Robert never told me he did them. I didn't even know about those girls . . . But I know he did have a dark side. He could have done it."

After Stallings made his claims about the murders in 2001, Abel talked to reporters, describing his ex–ranch hand as "too dumb to string a fence," saying he was relieved that Stallings had come forward, and maintaining that the man's confession cleared him of suspicion in all the Killing Field murders. Others, however, told me that Abel appeared to not believe his own press, and that rather than calm the matter, the former space engineer became increasingly peculiar and obsessed with the cases. "Robert got kind of squirrelly at the end," said one person who knew him. "He started acting oddly. Lots of times, he looked like he was afraid of his own shadow."

Perhaps an explanation lies in something Stallings recounted that happened a few years before Abel died. While in prison, Stallings said he received a letter from a mutual friend. In it, the writer said that Abel was spooked, claiming that the spirits of the dead women, the murder victims, stalked him.

When Stallings got the letter, he was perhaps amused but not surprised. "I believed him," he said. To the ex–ranch hand, the field behind Abel's League City home had always felt haunted. "My wife and I used to go out and sit on the porch of that little cabin in League City. It was so dark out there, no lights, couldn't see two feet in front of you. She starts getting chills and wants to go inside. She said, 'I feel something.' I could feel it, too. It's like you could feel the presence. You can feel the tension staring at you, like the women were trying to say something."

Through the friend, Stallings sent a message back to Abel, telling him that he understood, and that Abel wasn't imagining things; the girls watched him. The theory Stallings proposed was that the girls had moved on to the next world and weren't afraid of Abel any longer since he couldn't hurt them while he remained in this world. The only way to quiet them, Stallings suggested, was for Abel to die and cross over into the next world, where the women would again fear him. Stallings suggested Abel's only recourse was to "join them in the spirit world."

Near the end of our interview, Stallings ruminated that perhaps his suggestion to Abel hit home, since a few years later he drove his ATV onto the railroad tracks and into the path of an oncoming train. "I like to think maybe I had something to do with that," said Stallings, smiling broadly. "Maybe not, but who's to say Robert didn't decide I was right? Maybe that was enough to push him over the edge."

THE 1990s

- Krystal Jean Baker: 13, left her grandmother's house on March 5, 1996, to walk to a friend's house.

- Laura Kate Smither: 12, disappeared on April 3, 1997, while jogging on a rural road near her home.

- Jessica Cain: 17, left a cast party after appearing in a play on August 17, 1997.

Chapter II

Marilyn Monroe's Kin
Krystal Jean Baker

Texas City, Texas
March 5, 1996

Krystal Baker not long before her death. *(Courtesy of her mother)*

Krystal Jean Baker was certainly pretty enough to have been related to Marilyn Monroe. The iconic actress, of course, wasn't always the fabulous MM. As a young girl, she was simply Norma Jean Baker, a child born to a troubled mother. The future actress shuttled between foster homes and relatives, then married while still a teenager. Years after Krystal's death, a paternal uncle would say that he researched the Bakers' heritage and discovered the family, including Krystal, was distantly related to Monroe. Was Krystal a great-niece of Monroe's, as the family legend stated? Krystal hadn't been named for the actress; that they shared a middle name was a coincidence. "I don't know," admitted Krystal's dad, Johnny Baker, a trim man in his fifties. "But my uncle said it was true."

None of that would matter to young Krystal, for she'd die years before Johnny Baker's uncle made his claims. Something else out of the past would prove vastly more important than celebrity ties in the context of Krystal's short life: the stories of the girls who over the years mysteriously met their deaths south of Houston. Johnny, in his soft Texas twang, recounted how even as a boy growing up in Galveston, he'd heard tales of the murders of young women in the area, told in hushed tones as if speaking of the unmentionable. Did he worry about his daughter? "It's not the kind of thing you think could happen to your kid," he said, a painful catch audible in his throat. "By the time you realize it can, well, it's too late."

The heart displayed outside Jeanie Escamilla's home.
(Courtesy of Kathryn Casey)

It wouldn't be difficult to imagine that passersby on the road in front of Jeanie Escamilla's home in Dickinson quickly surmised that the woman who lived inside had a broken heart. From the street, a memorial heart with a young girl's photo was visible, and leaning against a wall stood a cross with Krystal's name and the years of her short life, 1982 to

1996. Jeanie's younger daughter was only thirteen on the day she died, a rambunctious, sometimes headstrong teenager with much to learn and the prospect of a lifetime ahead to do it.

Inside the house, Jeanie and I sat at a table in a corner of a wood-paneled living room. Her long, dark, reddish brown hair fell softly around her shoulders. Dressed in black pants and sweater with a lacy pink top, a heavy cross on a chain around her neck, she initially seemed eager to tell her story. Once the time had come, her hands shook slightly, and she appeared openly apprehensive, whispering that it still hurt to talk about her lost daughter even though it had been more than a decade since Krystal died. The home was decorated in Native American art, paintings, and sculptures, plaques with words of wisdom, and throughout there were statues of angels, including on a lamp table where a figurine of Christ nailed to a cross was positioned beside the Archangel Michael, his sword drawn.

Angels, creatures with the ability to fly away. But for fourteen years, Jeanie couldn't escape the nightmare of her youngest child's disappearance and death. There were no wings strong enough to release her spirit from the despair that filled her heart each time she thought of Krystal's young body, bruised and bloodied. "I've always been tough, all my life," said Escamilla. "When you're a single mom, you have to be. But nothing prepared me for what happened to Krystal. Nothing ever could."

Jeanie Escamilla yearned for her lost daughter. *(Courtesy of Kathryn Casey)*

Spending time with Jeanie, it was evident that her journey had been a long and often painful one. She talked vaguely of a difficult childhood and frequent hard times. Born in Sikeston, Missouri, she came with her mother to Texas. Jeanie married the first time at sixteen, and she had three children, each four years apart. Tonya was eight and Thomas was four when Krystal was born. Pink and blond, Krystal entered the world with a powerful cry and alert brown eyes. When she was three, of all the little girls in her preschool, Krystal was featured in a photo in the local newspaper, dressed as a Thanksgiving pilgrim.

After she and Johnny split, Jeanie and the children lived in a small brick house, while she worked as a hairdresser. Every other weekend, Krystal stayed with her dad in his apartment near the Union Carbide plant where he worked as a chemical operator. In the mornings, Krystal, often reluctant to rise, moaned, begging for more time to sleep, and each year, starting when she was only eight, she took Johnny for breakfast on his birthday. There was something about Krystal that always made him smile. "Just the way she had about her," he said. In the summers, Johnny worked nights, and they lay about the complex pool during the day, Krystal cultivating her tan.

As children so quickly do, Krystal grew up, and for her thirteenth birthday in August 1995, she posed in front of a red car, looking like a Ralph Lauren ad in a hat, blouse, and a skort (half shorts, half skirt), attractive, young and happy.

Although she'd lived near I-45 since childhood, Jeanie hadn't heard of the mysteries in the area involving young girls who'd disappeared and died. As an adult, she'd had little time for gossip or the evening news. "I had bills to pay, and I worked a lot. I was protective of the kids, but the first two were grown-up, and I started not to worry about Krystal as much," she said. "She was a teenager, and I wanted her to be independent. But I watched out for her. She had her first boyfriend, and I talked to him, reminding him that Krystal was only thirteen. He said he understood. It was an exciting time for Krystal. She was giddy in love."

Home in the evenings, the mother and daughter watched TV movies. When they discussed her future, Krystal ruminated about wanting to help people and becoming a nurse. Sometimes Jeanie brought up the pressures teenage girls face. She reminded Krystal that she was there to help, and Krystal promised to come to her before making any decisions that could affect her future. "I was always open with my kids. I wanted them to be able to talk to me about anything," said Jeanie. "At a certain point, you start being not only Mom but friends with your kids."

Yet in many ways, Krystal was still a child, one who needed her mother. One day she wrote Jeanie a letter in which she talked of falling asleep in her mother's arms: "It makes my dreams seem sweeter; knowing the time I share with you is a gift you give me."

That spring all wasn't well at school. Jeanie attended a conference with the principal, when Krystal complained of being bullied. Like Jeanie, Krystal developed early, gaining curves where some of the other girls weren't as yet endowed. The boys noticed, and a clique of girls in the school took note as well. "They were jealous," said Jeanie. "They started verbally abusing Krystal. One day, they cornered her at a park, and some of the girls ganged up on her, pulling her hair." Worried for her daughter's safety, Jeannie called her own mother, who worked for the railroad as a transporter shuffling staff between locations, asking if Krystal could live with her for the rest of the school year. Krystal's grandmother's house was close by in Texas City, in another school district. Moving meant that Krystal would change schools, and her parents hoped that would distance her from the schoolyard bullies. Krystal was less than happy with the situation, not wanting to leave her friends at her old school.

"Just until summer," Jeanie stressed. Looking back, she said, "We didn't know what else to do."

Those were the circumstances in early 1996, when Krystal Jean Baker moved into her maternal grandmother's cottage-like house on South Pecan Drive, a quaint setting with a front porch surrounded by large trees on a street with no sidewalks. The teenager woke up there on March 5, 1996. Since childhood, Krystal suffered recurring ear infections, and that morning she called Jeanie saying she wasn't feeling well. Judging from the gravelly timbre of Krystal's voice that she was telling the truth, Jeanie suggested her daughter stay in bed and offered to arrange a doctor's appointment.

At the beauty salon that day, Jeanie had a full schedule. She went about her work, not worried but planning to make the appointment and pick up Krystal later. Meanwhile at the house in Texas City that morning, Krystal called her dad. "Would you take me to my friend's house?" Krystal asked, explaining that she'd stayed home because of an ear infection. "I need a ride. I left my shoes there."

The shoes were important to Krystal; they were her first pair of heels, not stilettos but heels just the same. Krystal's friend lived in Bayou Vista, a small community south of Texas City at the top of the Galveston Causeway. Krystal's grandmother was at work and unable to drive her, and the teenager sounded eager to get her shoes and see her friend, who'd also stayed home from school that day. Johnny, however, had put in a full night at the plant and needed sleep. Krystal sounded disappointed.

Exactly what time the argument erupted between Krystal and her grandmother would later seem sketchy. Sometime around two o'clock, however, they stood in the driveway quarreling. Krystal's grandmother, upset when she returned home from work and found that Krystal hadn't gone to school, refused to drive her to her friend's house. Krystal, stubborn as teenagers can be, insisted. She wanted her shoes and to see friends who were congregating at the girl's home after school ended for the day. The conflict escalated, and Krystal indignantly stalked off, heading south on Pecan Drive, toward Texas Avenue, the nearest main thoroughfare. Frustrated, the older woman went inside the house and called the Texas City Police Department, asking for an officer to stop Krystal and bring her home.

A little more than a block later, Krystal stood in front of a tire store on the corner of Pecan Drive and Texas Avenue, a few miles east of I-45, trucks and cars whizzing past. For a moment, she sat on a bench in front of the store and watched the traffic, perhaps wondering *What next?* Then she opened the door and asked to use the store phone. The workers agreed, and Krystal began dialing. The first person she called was Jeanie, asking again for a ride to her friend's house. "I couldn't go get her. I had clients all afternoon," said Jeanie. "I told her to go home to her grandmother's. That I was going to make her that doctor's appointment and pick her up later. Krystal told me she'd go back to the house and make peace with my mother."

After she hung up, Krystal, however, didn't do as she promised. Instead, she made more calls, contacting her brother, her sister, and friends, asking each for a ride. None could help her. She stayed so long in the tire store, phoned so many that a worker finally reminded her that it was a business phone, and she couldn't tie it up.

Disappointed, Krystal walked outside into the bright sunshine where the traffic streamed past on busy Texas Avenue. She might again have considered her dilemma: what to do? Her friend's house was five miles away on a route that consisted of two busy roads without sidewalks. Walking meant picking her way along rough gravel shoulders, while traffic kicked up dust beside her. Perhaps she paused momentarily and assessed her options. Or she might have been so angry that she never considered backtracking to her grandmother's house. Instead, Krystal walked east on foot along Texas Avenue. Trucks and cars flew by, beside the young girl in the short silvery cotton dress dotted with white and gold flowers. Around her neck, Krystal wore a necklace Jeanie had given her for Christmas, one with a teddy bear on a chain.

Meanwhile on Pecan Drive, Jeanie's mom explained to the Texas City police officer who responded that she wanted him to find her granddaughter and bring her home. She told him that Krystal didn't have permission to leave. As the old woman had hoped, the officer agreed. He drove off, only to return, however, a short time later, to report that he'd been unsuccessful. Although he'd circulated through the surrounding streets, he hadn't seen anyone fitting Krystal's description. By then, Krystal had disappeared.

"Krystal wasn't a perfect kid, but she was trying really hard," said Jeanie. "She was loving and kind, just kind of spreading her wings. She got mad at her grandmother and left; and then, she was gone."

At three that afternoon, Jeanie called her mother to tell her that she had a doctor's appointment scheduled for Krystal.

"She's not here," the older woman said. When Jeanie asked where Krystal was, her mother explained, "I think she wanted to go to a friend's house, and I told her that I wouldn't take her. So we had a fight. Krystal left, and she hasn't come back."

The rest of that afternoon as she worked on her clients, washing, curling, and coloring hair, Jeanie trailed over to the shop's phone to call Krystal's friends, looking for her daughter. When that didn't result in Krystal's voice on the phone or anyone reporting having seen her, Jeanie called the Texas City police. It was the station's second call that afternoon about the teenager, but the officer who answered the telephone sounded unconcerned. "He told me not to worry, that Krystal was probably with friends and would be home in a matter of hours," Jeanie said. At that point, she wasn't overly alarmed, assuming they were probaby right.

Late that afternoon when she got off work, Jeanie again called her mother and Johnny; neither one had seen Krystal or knew where she might be. It was then that Jeanie started to worry. She drove to Krystal's friend's house in Bayou Vista, the one Krystal begged her grandmother to take her to that afternoon. There Jeanie found a group of her daughter's friends, but Krystal wasn't among them. "We called Krystal and told her to come. She said she would, but we haven't seen her," said one of the girls.

"I guess Krystal thought it would be more fun with her friends than being at her grandmother's house," said Jeanie, shaking her head.

Not ready to give up her search, Jeanie drove onto Galveston Island. In March, the sun set early, and she wound through the darkened streets but saw no sign of Krystal. That evening, Jeanie reluctantly returned home, hoping her younger daughter would call. Not long after, Krystal's boyfriend, Randall, rang the doorbell, looking for her. "That was when I got really worried. Something was really wrong," said Jeanie. "Krystal wouldn't have gone anywhere without telling Randall where to find her."

Frantic, Jeanie redialed the Texas City police, only to be told once again not to worry, that Krystal would be home soon.

On that same evening, as sunset approached, seventy-four miles northeast of Texas City outside Anahuac, an investigator with the Chambers County Sheriff's Office named Bradley Moon stood under the bridge near where I-10 jumped the Trinity River and gazed down at the body of a young girl awkwardly sprawled out on the gravel shoulder.

The call came in at just after five, approximately three hours after Krystal Baker left her grandmother's house, as Detective Moon, a husky, mustached veteran of the department, was getting ready to call it a day. Although the county seat, Anahuac was a sleepy little place, a no-stoplight town where if everyone didn't know everyone, they knew everyone's family, where they lived, and their reputations. Murders didn't happen often in this bucolic setting.

The couple who stumbled upon the body had been fishing in the Trinity River. Before they called police, they covered the corpse with a thin white blanket edged in a ruffle and a plaid shirt, perhaps more for their own peace of mind than for the girl's sake since there was no question that she was dead and far removed from earthly concerns like modesty. The body lay on its stomach, reddish blond hair fanned out across the pavement, pale legs flung askew. Her short, flowered dress was hiked up to her waist, showing thin white panties. Her feet were bare.

One had only to glance to know that she'd suffered. Scrapes and bruises covered her limbs and face, a particularly nasty one above her left eye. Even her toes were battered. Yet it was hard not to stare at the girl's neck. There a thick, dark band formed an angry red slash.

Rather than heading home to dinner and family, Moon and a group of other officers with flashlights searched the area around the body, which had been sectioned off with orange traffic cones. They looked for evidence, any indication of who the girl was, a purse, something left by the killer, her shoes. They found nothing. All they had was a girl's lifeless body and not one thing that indicated who she was or who'd killed her. About the most they could say was that she was dead and that she'd apparently been murdered.

That evening, with the body still on the scene, the local justice of the peace drove out to take a look. In small Texas towns without a coroner or medical examiner, JPs have the duty of pronouncing death. This elected official inspected the young girl's sad corpse and ordered it sent to Houston, to the Harris County Medical Examiner, the facility Chambers County relied on for autopsies.

As Moon and the others watched, the body was placed in a black body bag, then put on a gurney and slid into a body car, a hearse from a local mortuary. As the wagon with its tragic cargo drove off, the officers resumed their hunt, scouring the surrounding area for evidence.

Around that time in Texas City, Jeanie stood across a

desk from a police officer, filling out a report of a missing person. She brought a photo of Krystal with her, and she answered each question. Acid ate away at her insides, as she described her daughter, aching with each word. Yet the officer seemed indifferent. Jeanie left, assuming that police would begin looking for her daughter; instead, the officer filed the form, listing Krystal as a runaway.

Early the following morning, March 6, Brad Moon drove from his office in Anahuac into Houston, to be at the medical examiner's office in time for the nine o'clock autopsy on the unknown female found under the I-10 overpass. By then, the dead girl had a name, but not her own; she was listed as a Jane Doe.

In the autopsy suite, Moon took photos of the injuries on the body, including the heavy bruising across the girl's throat. When he was done, the physician began his investigation. First, the girl's dress and panties were removed and placed into an evidence bag. Next scrapings were taken from under her fingernails. What was found was transferred onto paper then sealed inside a clear plastic bag and slipped into an evidence bag. Both of the evidence bags were marked with the case number and sealed.

Brad Moon was one of the first investigators on the scene the night Krystal Baker died. *(Courtesy of Kathryn Casey)*

Moon didn't usually mind autopsies. He'd been a cop for years and had witnessed a good share of them. "But this one bothered me," he said. "It was the senselessness of it, that it was a young girl."

As Moon stood by, the forensic pathologist cut into the girl's flesh. The head, hands, limbs, and abdomen were examined individually, then described by the physician in detail as he talked into a recorder. Later, a secretary typed up the official report. On it would be noted a one-inch laceration of the vagina. Although no sperm was found inside her, the wound suggested that this Jane Doe had been sexually assaulted. Tiny blood vessels in the girl's eyes, eyelids, and face had burst, indicating suffocation. Homicide, the doctor determined, and the ultimate cause of death was noted as ligature strangulation.

Late that morning, Moon returned to his office in the Chambers County Sheriff's Office and checked the dress, panties, and fingernail scrapings inside the envelopes into the evidence room. He then went to his computer and typed a report on the case describing the Jane Doe as between fifteen and twenty years old with blond hair and brown eyes. Based on lividity, the pooling of blood after the heart stops pumping that turns skin a purple hue, and a lack of rigor mortis, the medical examiner estimated that the girl died not long before her body was found. Once he finished the paperwork, Moon pushed the send button and submitted it to TCIC (the Texas Crime Information Center) and NCIC (the National Crime Information Center) for distribution to law-enforcement agencies.

The case was less than twenty-four hours old, and Moon had a lot of questions. One thing he felt certain of was that the dead girl wasn't local. If she'd been from Anahuac or a neighboring town, either he or one of the other officers on the scene would have been able to ID her.

The days passed. In Texas City, Jeanie dropped in at the police department often, hoping for news on Krystal's case. Each time she did she heard the same assessment, that there was no need to worry, that she needed to just wait, that

Krystal was a runaway, and she'd eventually return home. But Jeanie didn't believe that. One of Krystal's friends had run away the previous year, and Krystal saw the agony it caused the family. Afterward, she'd told Jeanie, "Mom, I'd never put you through that."

Not knowing what to do, Jeanie and her mother searched. They made up flyers with Krystal's photo and began distributing copies to local stores to display in the windows. And they drove the streets of Texas City, throughout the area, looking, stopping at Krystal's friends' homes, hoping to find her, praying that they'd be able to bring her home alive.

Those same mornings in Anahuac, Brad Moon combed through a pile of inquiries about the unknown white female found under the I-10 bridge. He e-mailed out photos and information, but none of the responding departments identified the girl as the one they searched for. Why no one at the Texas City Police Department noticed reports of a Chambers County Jane Doe that fit Krystal's description would be a mystery, but perhaps the reports didn't match up because in Texas City, Krystal was presumed a runaway not a missing person. "That was the way it was back then, standard," said one of the officers. "She was thirteen and she'd left on her own. We didn't have any indication that there was a reason to worry about her safety."

That, however, gave Jeanie no solace. "I was a mother, doing what I could to find my daughter. No one helped me," she said, her voice rising with anger as she was swept back to those days. "No one else was looking for Krystal, so I had to. Every time I called the police, they said she was a runaway. I knew she hadn't run away. I couldn't work. I couldn't do anything. I just kept thinking about my little girl."

One day, Jeanie went to the tire store where the workers told her about Krystal's visit, how she'd stood at the phone calling family and friends, looking for a ride, without finding one. They saw Krystal walk out the door but had no idea where she'd gone.

For sixteen days, each time the phone rang, Jeanie ran to pick it up, hoping she'd hear Krystal's voice. Day after day, Jeanie talked over and again to all her daughter's friends, but heard nothing that helped determine where her daughter could have gone. And Jeanie prayed, she waited, and she hoped.

Finally on March 21, someone at the Texas City Police Department noticed a Chambers County report on the discovery of a dead teenager found under a highway overpass. Photos of the body were pulled up on the Texas City computers. The girl had died just hours after Krystal disappeared. The description of the girl and her clothing matched the report Jeanie had filed. A call came in, and Bradley Moon made his way to Texas City, a copy of the case file in hand.

That morning, Jeanie dressed for work when the phone rang. She'd been at the police department the day before, and there'd been no news on the case, but the officer on the phone said they now had photos to show her. "He didn't tell me that they were pictures of my daughter on a slab," said Jeanie, crying.

At the police station, Jeanie looked at the first picture but either didn't recognize her daughter or didn't want to acknowledge the truth. "That's not Krystal," she said.

The officer put down another, a close-up of Krystal's face taken during the autopsy with a sheet pulled over the shoulders, covering the body. The slash of purple and red around her neck, however, peered out over the top of the sheet. Her heart pounding, Jeanie realized that she stared at her daughter's face. Her eyes trailed down to the ring of welts that extended from under Krystal's chin to her shoulders. "It was horrible," she said. "They pulled out more photos. They were flopping pictures of my little girl in front of me, dead."

Brad Moon would look back on that day and not minimize the pain he saw, yet he insisted they had no choice. Jeanie had to be shown the photos, so she could identify the body. "It was very emotional," he said. "Your heart just broke. I couldn't say the right things. The girl, she was this woman's child."

After identifying Krystal's body from the photos, Jeanie drove home alone. Sobbing, her body shaking, she got out of the car and fell into a ditch that ran along the road. She cried so hard that she couldn't stand up. Her family helped her, carrying her in. Hours later, it was on the news that Krystal Baker, a thirteen-year-old thought to be a runaway, had been found murdered in Chambers County.

That same day, an officer called Johnny Baker at work and told him that his daughter's body had been found. "I thought she was with friends somewhere," he said, his voice a whisper. "I thought that she'd come home."

At one point, Jeanie picked up the phone and called Bradley Moon to ask a question. "Did Krystal have shoes on when they found her?" She didn't. That brought back a memory for Jeanie. Just weeks before she'd disappeared, Krystal had told her mother what she'd do if anyone ever tried anything untoward with her. The teenager looked serious when she said, "I'd scream really loud, kick my shoes off, and start running."

In the days after they learned of her murder, remorse consumed those who loved Krystal. Jeanie, Johnny, and Krystal's grandmother all wished that they'd dropped what they were doing when the phone rang and agreed to pick her up. Jeanie regretted not leaving work, and Johnny that he'd wanted to sleep after finishing his nightlong shift rather than drive his teenage daughter to pick up her shoes. "But how do you know?" he asked. "How could I have known this would happen."

Perhaps there was second-guessing at the Texas City Police Department, too, where officers were now investigating a murder.

In Texas City, Brian Goetschius became the detective on the case, and he began interviewing Krystal's family and friends, documenting the details of the case and looking for a suspect. The reports he heard pegged Krystal as stubborn, perhaps just a little on the wild side. "But she wasn't a bad kid," he said. "Should we have been looking earlier? We did what we were supposed to do. We didn't have any indication that there was anything other than that she walked away."

Brian Goetschius took over the Baker case in Texas City.
(Courtesy of Kathryn Casey)

Meanwhile, Jeanie prepared for a memorial service for her teenage daughter. She had little money, but she borrowed what she could and bought Krystal a white wedding dress, one with a high neckline that extended up to her chin, to cover the wound encircling her neck, and long sleeves to hide her daughter's bruised arms.

When the service started, friends and family lined up at the door, including Krystal's teenage friends. Jeanie fought to hold in her emotions, but at times they overwhelmed her. Texas City officers mingled with the crowd, watching to see if anyone acted oddly. They left disappointed; if the killer attended, they saw nothing that gave him away.

After the doors closed, Jeanie stayed, for the first time alone with Krystal's body. She leaned over the casket, and her tears fell on her dead daughter's face, washing away streaks of the mortuary's thick makeup. Jeanie saw the bruises underneath and that her daughter's left eye was circled in black. "I kissed her and cried, and I cried and cried," Jeanie said. "I said, you're in God's hands now."

Lacking the money for a plot to bury her daughter, Jeanie had Krystal's remains cremated.

The next day in Chambers County, Brad Moon checked out the envelopes holding Krystal's dress, underwear, and fingernail scrapings from the evidence room and transported them to the Jefferson County Regional Crime Lab, where Chambers County had a service contract. The material was logged into a long queue. Months later, when the evidence finally came up for processing, a technician examined the clothing under an ultraviolet light, inspecting it for any substance that could be bodily fluids. The dress material proved a problem. The polished, shiny surface distorted the light. In the end, the technician cut off four small sections of the dress she thought might be stains and sent the samples on for further processing. When the results came back, the fabric samples had tested negative for blood, semen, and saliva.

The only remaining possibility was the fingernail scrapings. But there, too, there was a problem. DNA was just coming of age, and few labs had the equipment to handle what was then such advanced forensic testing. In Texas, one was the Department of Public Safety lab in Austin. In such a large state with so few facilities, the protocol was not to analyze DNA until authorities had a suspect. At the time, it made sense. Unless law enforcement had a person of interest, officers had no one to compare with the recovered DNA.

Yet science was moving quickly, and there were potentially more accurate tests and other breakthroughs on the horizon. So the Jefferson County lab took the precaution of freezing the envelope with the scrapings to hold for another time, perhaps a day when a suspect appeared. And Brad Moon made a second trip to the lab, this time to reclaim the envelope holding Krystal's dress and panties. At the Chambers County Sheriff's Office, he stopped at the evidence room and checked it in for safekeeping.

With no evidence and no suspects, before long in both

Galveston and Chambers counties, the investigators moved on to other cases, ones they had the possibility of solving. "It wasn't that we ever forgot," said Moon. "It was that at a certain point, there wasn't anything for us to do on the case. We didn't have any leads."

One thing Moon did do before putting it to the side was to send the case to Quantico, Virginia, to the Behavioral Sciences Division of the FBI, to be analyzed. When the profile on the killer came back, it theorized that Krystal Baker's murderer could be a serial killer, and that—based on statistical probabilities—the murderer was probably between twenty-five and forty-five and white. The racial information came from theories prevalent at the time that killers most often chose victims within their own racial profile.

Eventually, Jeanie returned to work, but she couldn't forget what had happened to her daughter. She thought of Krystal every day, remembering the injuries that covered her body, thinking about how hard her little girl fought to live. She went to the police station often but came away without answers.

As the case stagnated, Jeanie, who'd once received a poem from her daughter, wrote to Krystal, saying that she had disappeared "like a summer breeze" and calling her "my sweet angel above." On her refrigerator, Jeanie built a memorial, Krystal's photo surrounded by religious pictures and tokens of her love.

Off and on, Jeanie drove to the I-10 overpass in Chambers County that crossed the Trinity River, and stood where her daughter's body had been found. She brought flowers and a cross, and she prayed and thought of all she'd lost, the daughter who would never go to the senior prom, never get married, never have children, never again be held in her arms. Each time she felt her anger rise, the frustration of so many days when the police weren't looking for Krystal because they assumed she was a runaway. "Even if they do run away, the police should look for the kids," said Jeanie. "They could be in danger. They have parents who love them."

The montage memorializing Krystal on Jeanie's refrigerator.
(Courtesy of Kathryn Casey)

It would be many years before Jeanie would discover that in Anahuac, at the Chamber's County Sheriff's Office, someone else hadn't forgotten Krystal, and that this one woman remembered and cared would make all the difference.

Chapter 12

The DNA of a Murderer
Sherry Willcox Never Gave Up

Anahuac, Texas

Sherry Willcox seated at her desk in the Chambers County Sheriff's Office. *(Courtesy of Kathryn Casey)*

"It was the pictures. I couldn't get the pictures out of my mind," said Sherry Willcox, a woman with shoulder-length medium brown hair, kind eyes, and a direct manner who worked as an evidence officer. "Once I had the file in my hands, I couldn't put it away. Krystal's photos bothered me. If it were my daughter, I'd want to know who did this to her.

And I thought there had to be some way to find out, some evidence left behind."

We were in a conference room at the Chambers County Sheriff's Office, and Willcox sat beside Bradley Moon, the main investigator on the murder investigation. Although Moon worked the case at the outset, it was Willcox who took over the quest to answer the question: Who murdered Krystal Jean Baker? "Krystal fought hard to live," said Willcox. "She deserved justice."

"Jeanie was really the one who kept pushing," said Krystal's dad, Johnny Baker. "I tried not to think about it. I didn't want to. But Jeanie kept talking to the police, making sure they didn't forget about the case."

The years had passed, but Jeanie Escamilla's anger and frustration over her daughter's murder never did. She married and moved into the house in Dickinson, placing the pot with Krystal's ashes under a table topped with photos of her murdered daugh-

The container in Jeanie's living room that holds Krystal Baker's remains. *(Courtesy of Kathryn Casey)*

ter. And Jeanie never stopped considering what she could do to get police to focus on Krystal's murder and search for the man who killed her. "I'd go to the Texas City police station, and they'd just tell me that they couldn't do anything," she said. "To me it looked like they didn't care. I was Krystal's mother. She was my baby. And I couldn't let it go."

In 2002, six years after her daughter's death, Jeanie took action. She hired a private investigator to look into the case. By then, television programs and newspaper headlines routinely recounted the vast difference DNA increasingly made in criminal investigations, including decades-old cold cases. Jeanie had read and seen in news footage and TV documentaries how small bits of genetic material could be used to identify a rapist or a killer. She'd never forgotten the condition of her daughter's body, covered head to toe with bruises and abrasions. "Krystal must have gotten something on her. I couldn't see how there wasn't evidence," said Jeanie. "I thought there had to be something that would help them figure out who murdered my little girl."

As part of his investigation, the PI went into the Texas City Police Department and talked to the investigators who'd worked the case but came away with nothing. Then he sent a request to the Chambers County Sheriff's Office for a copy of the file. Sherry Willcox had just started working as an evidence clerk a few months earlier. She was assigned to copy the file and mail it to the PI. As she paged through, she remembered the case. At the time Krystal died, Willcox was a schoolgirl. She'd never forgotten the body found under the I-10 bridge. She remembered her own mother cautioning her at the time to be careful; someone was murdering young girls.

The copies made and in the mail to Jeanie's investigator, Willcox could have returned the Baker case file to the records department, burying it among other cold cases. Instead, she placed it on the corner of her desk. At times, she felt drawn to it, combing through the notes on the investigation, including descriptions of the night the body was discovered. The crime-scene and autopsy photos hit hard. Krystal had been so young, and her life ended in a vicious attack filled with rage. Something about the girl touched Willcox deeply. And she, like Jeanie, assessed the dozens of visible injuries to Krystal's body and considered what that meant. "Krystal put up such a struggle, this child, just thirteen years old," said Willcox. "What she went through that day, I couldn't get past it. I couldn't forget."

Occasionally when Willcox had a break from her duties, she picked up the file on the Baker case. Assessing the photos, her eyes were drawn to a stain on Krystal's white nylon panties. Had anyone ever tested it? Could it lead to the killer? Willcox perused the lab reports and found that Jefferson County had processed the dress and the panties soon after the murder in 1996 and found nothing. But Willcox knew that in the subsequent years DNA and forensic science had made remarkable strides. What were once bits of DNA too small for testing could be replicated and analyzed. Over time, Willcox repeatedly considered the possibility that the evidence could be retested. Yet there were so many potential pitfalls. Had the items been properly stored? If not, they would be useless. But the biggest question: Did the evidence room still have the dress and panties on file?

It didn't take Willcox long to pull the records and determine that the dress and panties remained in the evidence room. Once she had the envelope that held them in her hands, she filled out the forms to have them resubmitted. The next time she drove to Houston to the Texas Department of Public Safety lab, where Chambers County then had evidence processed, Willcox brought the Baker evidence with her. It appeared the effort would be to no avail when the DPS clerk manning the check-in desk saw Jefferson County's insignia on the evidence envelope and asked if the contents had been previously tested. Willcox admitted that it had.

"We can't test then," the clerk informed her. Protocol ruled that since there was nothing new in the case, no suspects, there was no justification for spending tax dollars to retest. Sherry Willcox felt defeated. There was no option other than to take the envelope back to the office. Once she returned the envelope to the evidence room, Willcox considered refiling Krystal's paperwork. Instead, she again placed the case file on her desk. She wasn't yet ready to give up.

Unaware of Willcox's interest, Jeanie had no idea that a

Chambers County evidence clerk was now her greatest ally. Instead, she shook her head in disbelief when the private investigator went over his results with her, saying that records showed that Krystal's body and clothing had been processed and no forensic evidence found. "I just didn't believe it," she said. "My daughter couldn't have fought that hard for her life and not have evidence on her. A hair. A fiber. Blood. Something."

In the years since Krystal Baker's murder, Brad Moon had left the Chambers County Sheriff's Office. In 2005, he returned. When Willcox saw him in the office hallway, she recognized him as the investigator on the scene the night Krystal's body was discovered. "We started talking about the case," he said. "I'd never forgotten it. I'd always wondered who killed that girl. It was one of those cases that I'd never been able to put out of my mind. I thought about it off and on, wondering what we didn't do that we should have done, wondering what we missed."

"When we had an opportunity, we talked," said Willcox, who by then had had the file on her desk for three years. "We tried to think of something we could do to work the case. But there was nothing."

Again years passed, and the case never warmed up. Sherry Willcox returned to school and became certified, so that instead of a clerk she was licensed as an evidence officer. And off and on, she paged through the Baker file and wondered. DNA retrieval and processing continued to improve. Forensic sciences moved ahead. The time came when Sherry decided to take a chance.

On February 6, 2009, Willcox had evidence from an unrelated case to transport to the Houston lab for analysis. Before she left her office in Anahuac, she took Krystal's dress and panties out of the Jefferson County lab envelope and repackaged both into a brand-new DPS envelope, one that didn't indicate the evidence had been previously tested. On the accompanying form, Willcox asked the lab to test for bodily fluids and the presence of DNA. "I didn't ask if we could. I just did it," said Willcox. At the lab, she dropped it off as if it were a new case. This time the clerk didn't question the submission.

Back in Anahuac, Moon and Willcox talked about the turn of events and waited. Meanwhile, in the DPS lab in Houston, the dress made its way through processing. First it was given a visual examination for bodily fluids. This time around, the technician manning the ultraviolet light found an additional four spots of interest. One twist of luck was that rather than fading, with age semen stains become more fluorescent. The lab tech tested the areas with a chemical to determine if they could have been traces of bodily fluids and got a weak reaction. All were around the dress collar. She collected the samples by cutting them from the dress, finally forwarding the samples to the DNA lab for analysis.

Eight months later in August, the DPS lab called the contact number on the evidence envelope and asked for Willcox. Moments later, she walked into Moon's office, crying. "They found semen on Krystal Baker's dress," she said. "They have a DNA profile."

It had been thirteen years since Krystal's brutalized body was discovered, and for the first time, law enforcement had evidence that could lead to her killer. Days later, Willcox and Moon drove to Dickinson to meet with Jeanie and Krystal's dad, Johnny. The two officers explained that semen had been found on Krystal's dress, and that they had DNA to identify her killer. What they needed from Johnny and Jeanie were specimens of their own DNA to use to exclude Krystal's DNA from the mix.

Krystal's parents agreed and swabbed the insides of their mouths for Moon and Willcox, but Jeanie felt both elation and horror. She hadn't known about the tear in Krystal's vagina. Over the years, Jeanie had wondered who'd murdered her daughter, at times questioning if it could have been the girls who'd bullied her at school. Now that Jeanie knew about the semen, she realized that Krystal had been sexually assaulted. "I was devastated," she said. "It made me mad to realize someone had kidnapped my daughter and killed her for a thrill."

The previous years had been a roller coaster for Jeanie. Now there was hope. But there still wasn't a killer behind bars. That wouldn't happen until law enforcement identified a suspect by comparing DNA with the sample found on Krystal's dress. "Please," she asked Willcox and Moon. "Take this. Do what you need to do. But if you find out, don't tell me who this guy is until you have him in jail. I don't want to know."

Back at the office, Moon and Willcox speculated on what else could be done for the case. They had DNA, but they didn't have a match. They didn't have the name or face of the killer. Yet that potential now existed. There was the real possibility that at some point the case could end up in a courtroom. Moon thought about the I-10 bridge, slated to be torn down and replaced. He decided to return to the scene and draw a more precise chart documenting the exact positions of the columns and the placement of the body, before the bridge was gone and their opportunity vanished.

Beneath the I-10 bridge, looking away from the Trinity River.
(Courtesy of Kathryn Casey)

For years, Willcox had been the keeper of the Baker case file. For the first time, she stood where the girl's body had been found. She helped as Moon measured and charted, and she thought about the photos, what Krystal's body had looked like on that awful day. The emotions were overwhelming. Later, back at the office, she paged once again through the file, speculating that perhaps there was something else useful hidden inside. What she found was a notation that fingernail scrapings had been collected. "Would you look this case up and see if you still have the evidence in your freezer?" Willcox asked the clerk at the Jefferson County lab.

"We do," the woman said.

Days later, Willcox walked into the Jefferson lab with a cooler and ice to pick up the sample. As she had with the dress and panties, she transported the envelope with the scrapings inside to the DPS lab in Houston. It was nearly Christmastime, and what Willcox wanted that holiday season was a break in the Baker case.

The year ended, and a few months into 2010, Willcox received more good news; semen had been found in the fingernail scrapings with DNA matching that found on Krystal's dress. An exact match, they came from the same source, an unknown African-American male. Willcox had another piece to the puzzle. By then she'd entered the initial DNA findings on CODIS, the U.S. government's Combined DNA Index System, a database administered by the FBI that included forensic profiles of convicted felons, missing persons, and unidentified human remains.

Finally, on September 15 of that same year, Willcox's phone rang. The caller explained that she had new information on the Krystal Baker case. Willcox's heart jumped when she heard the words, "We have a match."

Chapter 13

"I Saw a Girl Walking"
Kevin Edison Smith

Chambers County, Texas

Kevin Edison Smith.
(Courtesy of the Texas Department of Criminal Justice)

"There was a lot of excitement in the office the day the call came in," said Brad Moon. "Now we had a name, we knew who the guy was, the one who murdered Krystal. But it wasn't someone we would have expected. This guy, he flew way under the radar."

The hit on CODIS matched both the fingernail scrapings and the semen found on the flowered dress Krystal wore that last day of her life. The reason the suspect's DNA was in the system was that in January 2010, he had been arrested in Pointe Coupee Parish, Louisiana. The charge had been a minor one. Pulled over during a traffic stop because he'd allegedly swerved between lanes, officers found a bag of pills in the car, prescription drugs. He was booked on a felony drug-possession charge. In Texas, DNA was collected only from those convicted of sexual offenses and murder, but

Louisiana law required DNA collection in all felony arrests. This man had only minor skirmishes with law enforcement in the past, including being charged after wrangling with police during a 1994 stop for driving under the influence. There were no sex offenses, no truly violent crimes on his record.

Born in 1965, Kevin Edison Smith was the oldest of four children, raised by his mother and an aunt. Smith grew up in the towns bordering I-45, the family living much of the time around the Texas City area, and he'd earned a degree from Galveston's Ball High School. Over the years, he'd married three times, most recently in 2007 to a woman from Opelousas, Louisiana. A pipe welder, he'd had contract jobs in plants throughout Texas and Louisiana, living a transient life, moving on as one job dried up and another opportunity appeared. "He's a really quiet guy, not the kind who attracts a lot of attention," said someone who knew him. "He wasn't the kind who'd stand out in a crowd."

Once they had a name, Moon called in Texas Ranger Joe Haralson to assist with the arrest. Rangers have jurisdiction across the state, enabling them to cross county lines to move in quickly and apprehend a suspect. Haralson had been working out of Texas City since the mideighties, and he'd been involved in many of the I-45 investigations.

Once on board, Haralson helped write

Texas Ranger Joe Haralson in his office in 2013. *(Courtesy of Kathryn Casey)*

the necessary search warrants to get the information they needed to find Krystal Baker's accused killer, Kevin Smith. The method they used was to determine Smith's cell-phone number. Once they had it, they began surveillance on the phone's activity, watching for it to ping off towers. That should have enabled them to narrow down his whereabouts based on his cell phone's location. The problem was that the phone never appeared to be used. For a week they watched and waited. Nothing. Sensing something wasn't right, they investigated and found they had a wrong number.

On September 22, Haralson and the others received a tip; Smith's latest contract welding job was at the Motiva plant in Port Arthur, Texas. The largest facility of its kind in the United States, the refinery is a massive web of steel pipe and machinery owned by Shell Oil and Saudi Aramco with a six-hundred-thousand-barrel-a-day capacity. At the district attorney's office in Anahuac, Haralson notified the Chambers County DA, Cheryl Swope Lieck, that he was on his way to make the arrest. On the paperwork, Lieck noted something rather ironic. "You know it's Smith's forty-fifth birthday," said Lieck, a sarcastic edge to her voice. "When you put the handcuffs on, tell him happy birthday."

At the Motiva plant, Moon, Sherry Willcox, and Haralson waited for Smith, who'd been called into his supervisor's office. When Smith sauntered in wearing his blue work jumpsuit, unsuspecting of what awaited him, he was immediately read his rights and put under arrest. A muscular man, Smith stared at the group around him but initially said nothing. He appeared stunned.

"You're under arrest for the 1996 murder of Krystal Jean Baker," Moon told him. "Her body was found under the I-10, Trinity River Bridge."

"I didn't kill nobody," Smith said. "You've got the wrong guy."

"Your DNA was found on that girl's clothes," Ranger Haralson said, explaining that the match had been made after his Louisiana arrest.

"How in the world did my DNA get mixed up with that?" Smith countered.

"I knew we had the right guy based on the way he was acting, so cool," said Moon. On the forty-five-minute drive, Smith never spoke another word. Back in Chambers County, he was brought before a judge and again read his rights. His bail was set at one million dollars.

Assessing the bruise pattern around Krystal Baker's neck, thicker on the left than the right, Lieck had theorized that the man who murdered Krystal was left-handed. When she saw Smith signing papers in the courtroom with his left hand, she felt ever more certain.

With Smith tucked safely into a cell in the county jail, another duty waited. That afternoon, Sherry Willcox and Bradley Moon drove to Jeanie's house to tell her that there'd been a break in her daughter's case, and that the man responsible for Krystal's death was under arrest. They brought a photo of Smith, and told her that they had a perfect DNA match. "She cried," said Sherry. "And she said thank you."

Soon, Jeanie's phone began ringing, and reporters dogged her. A press conference was held in which Texas City police explained that there'd been an arrest in one of the cases on the I-45 Mysteries chart. A man was in prison for the murder of Krystal Baker. "It took a while to believe it had happened," said Jeanie. "And then it brought it all flooding back, all the grief and the pain."

At the press conference three days later, Jeanie told reporters she'd given up believing Krystal's murderer would ever be found. Although calling the turn of events a miracle, there was something else she wanted more. "If I had any wishes right now, I wish I could wake up and hold my little girl in my arms."

Weeks passed while Smith waited in jail. Then nearly a month after the arrest, a well-known activist and the leader of the New Black Panther Party, Quanell X, drove from his Houston headquarters to the Chambers County jail to talk to Kevin Edison Smith. A muscular, immaculately dressed man, Quanell X had been commissioned by the family to make sure that Smith wasn't being unfairly prosecuted or mistreated behind bars. Later, Quanell X would say that he told Smith's mother and aunt that if Smith "is innocent I will fight them. But if he's guilty of this crime, I will come back and tell you."

In an interview room in the jail, Smith told Quanell X that he wasn't being abused in the jail, but he was being unjustly accused. At first Smith denied knowing anything about Krystal Baker's murder. Then Quanell X warned him, saying that if Smith cried racism, and it wasn't true, "it could backfire on all of us."

It was then that Quanell X explained to Smith that a second DNA test was being run to verify the results of the first, to confirm that the semen found on Krystal's dress tied directly to him. "Man, my wife is going to leave me," Smith said, hanging his head.

As they talked, Quanell X would later say that he asked Smith something else: "Do you think your DNA is going to be found in other cases?"

What Smith reportedly answered was, "I don't know," indicating that was possible. Then it appeared the reality of his situation hit him, when Smith said, "They're going to give me the death penalty."

The conversation continued, and Smith made it clear that he had a grave concern: being put on trial for his life. With that, Quanell X asked Smith if he wanted him to talk to the district attorney, to see if there was the possibility of tabling the death penalty if Smith was willing to tell the truth about Krystal's murder.

In Texas, for a criminal case to be eligible for the death penalty, a murder had to meet certain criteria: involving a special victim, such as a police officer, or happen during the commission of a second felony. That latter qualifier was met in the case since Krystal was a minor. The semen on her dress and the tear in her vagina indicated she'd been sexually assaulted. There was no evidence to suggest she'd agreed to have sex with Smith—in fact, with so many injuries, it was obvious that she'd tried to fight him off—but even if she had, as a child she couldn't legally agree, and any sexual contact with her was a felony.

Shortly after two that afternoon, District Attorney Cheryl Swope Lieck was in a courtroom waiting for a jury to return with a verdict in another case when she got the message that Quanell X said Kevin Edison Smith was ready to confess to the murder of Krystal Baker, but that he wanted something in return. Reluctant to leave the courtroom, she sent a message back, "Are you sure he's not wasting my time?" When assur-

Chambers County DA Cheryl Swope Lieck outside her office.
(Courtesy of Kathryn Casey)

ances came that the offer was a serious one, Lieck left for the jail.

In Moon's office, Lieck talked to Quanell X. "I've explained to Mr. Smith that this is only for this case, not any others," he said.

Lieck was and wasn't surprised. Quanell X had just suggested there could be more cases linked to Smith. "I believe there are others," she said, indicating she understood.

Quanell X said only, "All we're concerned about here today is this case."

A short time later, Moon, Willcox, Lieck, and Kevin

Smith gathered in an interview room, and Quanell X moderated by explaining what the man in question wanted: "Mr. Smith wants assurances that you won't be going for the death penalty."

Once she understood what was being offered, Lieck considered the situation. Like the others, the case resonated for the prosecutor, who'd grown up in the area. At the time of Krystal's death, Lieck had been an assistant DA, and she'd never forgotten about the girl under the bridge. With the DNA evidence, the prosecutor felt confident that she could get a jury to convict and vote for the death penalty. Considering the age of the case she, however, wasn't convinced it would hold up on appeal. And there was something else, that possibility of other cases. She wasn't the only one who thought that there were other victims. Moon and Willcox were voicing the same theories. Smith had been too cool when arrested, and he had a transient past, one where he'd moved from state to state over the years. Lieck wanted Smith alive to answer questions, to have the opportunity to piece together other cases and give other families what relief a confession or conviction could bring.

After a pause to make her decision, Lieck agreed to forgo the death penalty in exchange for Smith telling the truth about his involvement in Krystal Baker's murder. And she reminded him of something Quanell X had already said he'd explained to Smith, that the deal was only for this one case. If there were others, there were no guarantees. "I don't have any jurisdiction over anything that may have happened in another county," she said.

When they explained the situation to Smith, Quanell X said, "She means if there are other bodies that come up with your DNA." When Smith nodded that he understood, Quanell X said to Lieck, "Brother Kevin . . . is not an evil man. A loving family, a wife . . . he was wrapped up in his own personal demons back then as far as drinking alcohol."

"There aren't any do-overs . . . There was a life that was taken," Lieck countered, saying to Smith, "Your DNA was on her . . . I'm not going to bullshit you. You will never get out of prison."

At that point, everyone but Quanell X and Smith left the room so the two men could discuss Smith's options. The death penalty was off the table if he agreed to talk, but would Smith consent to an arrangement that condemned him to spend his life behind bars? A short time later, the others were called back. Smith took the deal. It was then he began talking about the day Krystal Jean Baker died.

In Smith's account, fourteen years earlier he'd worked at the Amoco plant in Texas City, and on that particular day he'd been drinking with buddies after work at Zackie's, a convenience store on Texas Avenue, where he cashed his paychecks. At that time, he said, he'd often get drunk, then pick up prostitutes.

That afternoon, Smith sat on the bench outside the store with other smokers, enjoying a cigarette with his beer when, "I saw a girl walking down the highway." Not long after, he bought a twenty-four-ounce beer for the road and drove off in his green Chevy extended-cab pickup truck.

Approaching the girl, Smith pulled over and lowered his window. Then he started talking, smiling, and offering her a ride, coaxing her into getting into the truck. Krystal must have been tired, her feet sore. She'd been walking for nearly two miles along the dusty highway. Smith was thirty years old, not a bad-looking man, presumably nothing visibly frightening about him. Perhaps he somehow forced her, threatening her with a weapon. But in the version of events he recounted, Smith charmed her, and Krystal ultimately climbed willingly into the passenger seat. Once he had her beside him inside the truck, he turned the conversation to sex. "She said she was eighteen," he told those gathered. "I thought she was a prostitute . . . I was talking to her about some sex . . . oral sex."

The confession continued, with Smith admitting that what Krystal wanted wasn't sex but what she'd been look-

ing for all afternoon, a ride to her friend's house in Bayou
Vista. Smith, however, had his mind made up. He drove a
short distance, then pulled behind a gas station. He promised Krystal money, but again all she wanted was a ride to
her friend's house. Did she try to open the door, to run? Had
he somehow locked her in? What Smith said happened next
was that Krystal "freaked out . . . just started getting crazy
. . . I was trying to restrain her . . . I was drunk."

The teenager, undoubtedly terrified, must have understood the danger. According to Smith, Krystal fought as he
tried to force himself on her, hitting and kicking. Quickly,
the situation turned lethal. "I grabbed her. I choked her," he
said. "The next thing I knew, she'd stopped breathing."

At first Smith insisted he'd strangled Krystal with his
hands, but that didn't sit well with Lieck, who'd read the
autopsy results. When she said that she knew that he'd used
something, some type of a ligature, Smith said, "I had like a
strap . . . I kept in my truck."

With Krystal's dead body slumped in the passenger seat,
Smith then said he drove nearly sixty miles to the Trinity
River Bridge. When asked why there, Smith said he didn't
know the place, only that he'd happened upon it and it looked
like a lonely location, one where he wouldn't be seen. After
he threw Krystal's body out of the truck, he drove off.

The interview continued. A thirteen-year-old girl whose
path just happened to cross with his that day was dead, brutally murdered, but Smith voiced no regret, instead blaming
Krystal. If she hadn't objected, hadn't fought him, had given
him what he wanted, he implied it would never have happened. "I was just playing, and she went berserk," he said.

As she considered his account, the district attorney found
problems. It didn't match all of the evidence. The most
important discrepancy was that Smith claimed he'd only
fondled and ejaculated on Krystal, but that didn't jibe with
the tear in her vagina. Still, what Lieck most needed was to
know if Smith admitted murdering Krystal, and he had.

The meeting ended for that afternoon. If there'd been

any doubt who they were dealing with, what kind of man, it was settled not much later, when a woman came forward, one who claimed Kevin Smith had been her first boyfriend. She said she'd seen reports about his arrest, and she wanted those in charge of the case to know what Smith had done to her when she was a teenager. Along with another man, she alleged that Kevin Smith raped her at gunpoint. Afterward, he terrorized her, threatening her life, killing her dog to frighten her into keeping quiet.

In the days that followed the Chambers County Sheriff, Joe LaRive, urged law enforcement across the entire Gulf Coast to look into unsolved cases they might have that could fit Smith. By then, the Texas Rangers had used employment records to pin down where Smith lived and when. The result was a web of information, suggesting that if Smith had committed other murders, they could have occurred not just in Texas but Louisiana, Oklahoma, Arkansas, Alabama, Florida, and Arizona.

Not long after his confession, although he'd been repeatedly informed of his rights, Kevin Smith attempted to retract all the statements he'd made, claiming that rather than brokering a deal by getting the death penalty off the table, Quanell X had intimidated him into admitting guilt. Moon attempted to talk to Smith in jail about other victims,

The chart depicting cities where Kevin Edison Smith lived.
(Courtesy of Kathryn Casey)

other cases, some on the I-45 chart. Smith denied there were any more to discuss. "No, never," he insisted.

At the jail, Smith's calls were monitored and recorded, and one day he could be heard talking to a family member who couldn't understand why the murder of a teenage girl should land Kevin Smith in prison for life. Rather, she wondered, if seven years wasn't an appropriate sentence. Perhaps she was basing her assessment on the information Smith had given her, his claim that the killing wasn't a murder but an accident.

In jail awaiting trial, Smith's muscles withered, and he lost weight. At hearings, he became belligerent. Not able to pay for an attorney, he was assigned one, Stephen Christopher Taylor, a longtime defense lawyer who'd handled a good share of the county's death-penalty cases.

Months passed, and Lieck wondered if she should prosecute the case, as she'd planned. She wanted to, but there was the possibility that she'd be required to take the stand since she'd been a witness to Smith's confession. In the end, she appointed a special prosecutor, Randy McDonald, who worked both in Houston and Anahuac. McDonald had been the lead defense attorney on a number of high-profile criminal cases, including that of Bart Whitaker, convicted of orchestrating the December 2003 murders of his family. Whitaker's father survived, but his mother and brother died. Faced with the prospect of losing the only remaining member of his family, after Bart's conviction, his father begged for his only remaining son's life. Jurors, however, sentenced Bart Whitaker to the death penalty.

As the Kevin Edison Smith case moved toward trial, Jeanie attended a hearing. Staring at Smith throughout, she thought about all the things Krystal would never do, all the life she'd been robbed of. "He took everything from her," she said. "Looking at him made me feel sick. But I knew I had to be at the trial. I had to be there for Krystal."

Chapter 14

The Devil's Face

Anahuac, Texas
April 2012

The stately Chambers County Courthouse. *(Courtesy of Kathryn Casey)*

In the summer of 2011, vast expanses of the Lone Star State literally erupted into flames. Texans dubbed it the Summer of Fire, as almost 4 million acres burned, destroying nearly three thousand homes. The culprit was drought. That year, even the usually wet spring was desert dry. Months passed without rain, resulting in a parched, brown landscape. A drive through Central Texas passed miles of dying trees, some thick-trunked oaks hundreds of years old. News reports compared the phenomenon with the Great Dustbowl of the 1930s, which attacked the Great Plains. The 2011 drought targeted Texas like an archer sighting a target, including the usually near-tropical Gulf Coast.

As that year drew to a close, weather predictors fretted about the future, forecasting the likelihood of another full year of drought. The state watched helplessly as thirsty trees with no relief shed their bark, their dry trunks splitting and weighty branches collapsing on parked cars and across streets. It felt as if death stalked the state.

This time, however, the experts were at least partially wrong.

Central and West Texas remained dry. But in the new year, the rains came to the Gulf Coast. By early 2012, much of the area appeared renewed, its forests bright with a budding green spring. Backyard water gauges flooded, especially in and around Houston, where storms came heavy and long, overflowing the dammed-up rivers that form the massive lakes that water the vast city. Traveling east from Houston, the landscape was again lush, as I turned off I-10 and drove toward Anahuac in April 2012 for the trial of Kevin Edison Smith, the welder whose DNA had been discovered on Krystal Jean Baker's dress.

A tiny, no-stop-sign town of around two thousand, Anahuac calls itself the alligator capital of Texas. Each year, neighbors celebrate the thick-skinned lizards during Gatorfest. For those passing through, signs along the road ask motorists to be on the lookout for poachers. There was a time when I would have enjoyed the ride, my attention drifting off into the heavily wooded landscape, thoughts of great birds and the morning's first light filtering through a canopy of trees. I instead wondered if undiscovered bodies lay concealed in the water beneath the dense foliage. Startled by my dark thoughts, I shook them off and attempted to focus not on the woods but the road ahead. I kept driving.

The most impressive building in Anahuac was the 1936 Chambers County Courthouse, a grand structure rising out of the flat earth, erected during the Great Depression by

WPA workers for a cost of $276,000. Three stories high, the exterior of the building was ashlar, squares and rectangles of finely hewn stone, with massive art deco lanterns lighting the wide stairs that anchored the main entrance.

Inside the courtroom, the benches were dotted with spectators. Smith's family filled two rows. Many of the other seats were taken by courthouse and law-enforcement workers, weaving in and out, interested in watching what promised to be an important trial. Noticeably missing were Jeanie, Johnny, and the rest of Krystal's family. Texas had what was called "the rule." When enforced, it barred potential witnesses from sitting in on a trial. Usually, the immediate family of the victim was an exception, but for some reason at this trial that hadn't been done. The result was that Krystal's family congregated instead in a nearby office.

At the left front table, Smith sat beside his attorney, an avuncular man with a receding hairline named Stephen C. Taylor. A courtroom veteran, Taylor had experience with high-profile cases. His status as court-appointed, however, rankled Smith, who complained bitterly to his family on recorded jailhouse phone calls that any attorney paid by the state wouldn't have his interests at heart.

Defense Attorney Stephen C. Taylor was well-known throughout the county. *(Courtesy of Kathryn Casey)*

Seated behind the table on the right, the special prosecutor, Randy McDonald, and his second chair, Assistant District Attorney Kathy Esquivel, had case files lined up behind them. Like Taylor, they were prepared and ready to begin.

Gray-haired, mustached, once a Houston prosecutor, McDonald stood before a jury culled from a panel of three hundred of the county's residents at just after nine and began his opening statement, outlining his case. He promised to show that Kevin Edison Smith indisputably murdered Krystal Baker, based not only on DNA but also the defendant's own words, his confession.

From that point on, McDonald relied on witnesses to establish the sequence of events for the jurors. The first called to the stand, Bradley Moon described the scene under the I-10 bridge the evening Krystal's body was discovered. Since she hadn't disappeared from Anahuac or the surrounding area, McDonald had a bit of housekeeping to do. "You observed her body lying in Chambers County?" he asked, to establish that the court had jurisdiction over the case.

"Yes," Moon answered.

On an overhead projector, McDonald displayed photos taken that night. In them, Krystal's brutalized body lay, her legs akimbo. For two weeks, she remained in the morgue, a Jane Doe.

"Were you there when the family identified this girl as Krystal Jean Baker?" McDonald asked.

"I was," Moon said. McDonald then led the investigator through a list of Krystal's injuries, from the gash to her forehead to the bruising on her toes, but concentrating on the hideous wound encircling her neck. On the autopsy table, the teenager looked pale and cold, but it was easy to imagine that before the attack, she must have been brimming with life.

The picture McDonald drew before the jurors described how Smith most likely disposed of the body, pushing it out of his car onto the gravel, then speeding off. "Where the body was dumped, you could drive a vehicle up to that location?"

"Yes, sir," Moon said.

Much depended on the DNA match, and McDonald studiously labored to establish chain of custody for the evidence, confirming that the way it was transported and kept fulfilled legal requirements. In response, Moon described personally transporting Krystal's dress, panties, and the scrapings taken at autopsy from under her fingernails to the lab in 1996 and later picking them up. With that, McDonald handed Moon the evidence envelopes. Wearing latex gloves, Moon opened the first and held up the silver dress covered in white and gold flowers, displaying it before the jurors. In that instant, Krystal became real, not just a name but a young girl in a pretty dress walking down a busy road on a spring afternoon.

When Taylor took over for the defense, he inquired about evidence Moon hadn't produced. Shouldn't there have been aerial shots of the crime scene? Moon said there weren't. Regarding a video taken of the body on the evening it was discovered, Moon said it had been lost over the more than a decade the case remained cold.

On the stand, white-haired Joe Haralson cut an imposing figure, looking the epitome of a Texas Ranger, down to his boots adorned with the image of the organization's badge embroidered in gold thread. Thirty-one years on the job and Haralson had been involved in more than his share of murder investigations, but he still occasionally faced frustration, as in the week during which he helped Chambers County track down Kevin Smith. When they finally found him and arrested him, had it

Texas Ranger Joe Haralson's boot bearing his agency's badge. *(Courtesy of Kathryn Casey)*

been done correctly? Had Haralson or one of those accompanying him read Smith his rights? Since a confession hung in the balance, one the defense attorney, Taylor, objected to being admitted, adherence to the law loomed large.

"I did," Haralson said, verifying he'd made sure that Smith knew he had the right to remain silent and to a lawyer.

Before he gave his confession, Smith acknowledged that he understood his Miranda rights and signed a waiver.

What about the truck Smith drove in 1996, at the time of the killing? It was possible there'd been evidence still inside, perhaps hair or bloodstains tied to Krystal. If her DNA and fingerprints weren't found, however, that could have helped Smith. Haralson said he'd searched for the truck, "but we couldn't find it."

Haralson left the stand and the prosecution's case continued. With the confession groundwork laid, McDonald turned again to the forensic evidence, the all-important DNA match. A series of witnesses verified chain of custody for the clothing and the scrapings, including the former Jefferson County lab tech who initially examined the dress and panties. When Taylor asked if she found any evidence of blood, saliva, or semen on the dress, the woman said, "To my knowledge, nothing was found."

Always, there were reminders of how far science had come, from a time when small quantities of DNA were indecipherable to the present, when tiny amounts of genetic matter could be duplicated and tested.

As the state's tenth witness to take the stand, Sherry Willcox described the hold that the cold case took on her, as she felt drawn to the tragic images of Krystal's body. "It's touching to look at the photos," she said, admitting that she couldn't put them out of her mind. She was the one who refused to file the case away, the one who ultimately found a way to get the evidence retested. "You didn't ask for permission? You just did it?" Esquivel asked.

"Yes," Willcox answered.

"Did your heart jump a little when the DPS lab found DNA on the dress?" Taylor asked.

"Yes," Willcox admitted that it had. The case, it seemed, had become very personal.

"And here we are today?"

"Yes, sir," she said.

It was after Willcox's testimony that something unusual happened. Calling the attorneys to the bench, Judge Carroll E. Wilburn, Jr, asked, "What do we want to do with the skunk in the jury box?"

Trials are emotional, especially for the two families involved, the victim's and the defendant's. In this case, in the old courthouse with few public restrooms, where jurors, witnesses, and family members used the same facilities, perhaps it wasn't surprising that paths crossed. "The skunk" was a juror who'd found herself in the ladies' room with Krystal's mom, Jeanie.

"I don't think we have our witnesses under control," McDonald admitted.

Jurors wear badges, signals that they aren't to be approached or talked to. Any interaction could be deemed an attempt to sway a verdict and cause a mistrial. What had transpired was that the juror in question and Jeanie happened to be in the bathroom together. The woman told the bailiff that Krystal's mom identified herself and showed the woman a photo of Krystal.

As the judge and lawyers talked, Kathy Esquivel was dispatched to caution Jeanie against any future breeches. But the question remained: What was to be done?

An alternate, the potentially compromised juror could simply be dismissed, the trial continued. Yet had that juror talked to the others? Had the contamination spread? The judge mused about how to handle the situation to prevent a mistrial or having the verdict—should Smith be convicted—overturned on appeal. Eventually, the bailiff escorted the woman juror in to personally tell the judge and attorneys her story. In the end, she was released and the trial continued, but only after the judge questioned the remaining jurors, determining that the woman told none of them about her restroom encounter.

At that, the attention returned to the matter at hand, putting testimony before the jurors who would decide Smith's fate. As Esquivel quizzed the forensic scientists, it quickly became obvious that the statistics were overwhelming. The odds that the DNA matched anyone but Smith: one in 332 sextillion for Caucasians, one in 8.591 sextillion for African-Americans, and one in 1.637 septillion for Hispanics. To give a frame of reference, the witness quantified a sextillion, describing it as a trillion billions.

Was it possible that Kevin Smith's DNA had changed over the years? The expert said it wasn't, absent a tissue transplant.

Through it all, a picture emerged of the terror of the last day of Krystal Baker's life.

On the stand, Dr. Dwayne Arthur Wolfe of the Harris County Medical Examiner's Office reviewed Krystal's autopsy for the jury, accompanied by graphic photos. He pointed out the rash of small petechiae, reddish spots and blotches caused by blood pressure rising and bursting capillaries during strangulation. As he described it, Krystal suffered a slow death. Based on the extent of the hemorrhaging, she struggled for life, and Smith fought her, eased up, then tightened the strap around her neck.

"Could this have been done with a welder's belt?" McDonald asked.

"Any kind of belt," the physician confirmed, saying the large abrasions on Krystal's left side were caused from the attacker coming at her from the left rear. When it came to the blunt-force trauma evident on much of Krystal's body, those injuries could have resulted from being pummeled by a fist. The abrasions? Perhaps from Krystal's body hitting the ground as she was thrown from the truck.

"All the injuries look like they were shortly before death," the physician testified, narrowing the time frame to between a couple of hours and minutes before the teenager died. As to the injuries to the right side of Krystal's face, a lack of flowing blood indicated that those happened shortly after death.

The tear to her vagina? The physician identified the cause as an attack with a blunt object. "Could a penis be a blunt object?" McDonald asked.

"Yes," Wolfe answered.

"Or a finger?"

"Yes."

Consistent with the other wounds, the tear in Krystal's vagina happened within an hour of her death.

Yet on cross-examination, Taylor pointed out that there were questions the physician couldn't answer, including where Krystal was when she suffered the injuries and where the dirt came from on her knees. Smith said he'd strangled Krystal in the truck, but could he have taken her to a remote field, assaulted her, and murdered her on the scene? Multiple scenarios were, of course, possible.

Seated in the front of the courtroom, Quanell X made a compelling witness. McDonald led him through the basics, as he described himself as a minister of the nation of Islam and an activist. "Here you were retained as an activist?" McDonald asked. This was an important point. If Quanell X had been in the jail talking to Smith as his minister, the conversation could have been privileged and he could be barred from testifying about its content. But the imposing man on the stand said that wasn't the case.

"Absolutely," he said, limiting his involvement to that of an emissary sent by the family to make sure Smith wasn't being abused or unjustly accused because of his race. Explaining his involvement, Quanell X said he wanted to determine "if this is a case where they picked the nearest brother they could find and threw everything at him including the kitchen sink . . . If I believed he was innocent, I was about to stand with this brother all the way."

Instead, Quanell X said Smith admitted his guilt and wanted to get it off of his chest. The confession was voluntary, he testified, not coerced. "At the end of the day, it's about right over wrong, about justice."

"Did Mr. Smith implicate himself in this crime?" McDonald asked.

"Yes," he answered.

Taylor asked about money Quanell X had been paid by
Smith's family, twenty-five hundred dollars, to look into the
case. The witness agreed he'd been paid, but he said he'd
made no promises other than to find out the truth.

After Quanell X left the stand, the prosecutor recalled
Bradley Moon. McDonald had one last thing he wanted
jurors to hear, Smith's confession. In a hushed courtroom,
the audio played, and Smith described how he'd strangled
Krystal Baker. Then, the state rested.

It seemed there was little for Taylor to work with defend-
ing his client. Science said Smith was guilty and so did the
man's own words. Later, the defense attorney would insist
that if he'd talked to Smith first, he would have cautioned
him against giving the statement. The forensic evidence
might have left some wiggle room, some way to say Smith
had sex with the teenager but not killed her. But the confession had done Smith in.

In his opening, Taylor repeated the justifications Smith
had given during his confession, that he thought Krystal was
eighteen and that she'd gotten in the truck voluntarily, and
that the killing hadn't been planned but resulted from events
spinning out of control.

The single defense witness was Texas City investigator
Brian Goetschius, as Taylor tried to make the point that if
DNA hadn't come through, the case might never have been
solved. When he asked how Krystal's death had affected the
town, the man who by then was a captain in his department
said, "I think it was a community event, sir, that one of our
children was killed."

The jury cleared from the courtroom, the defense attorney then put before the judge the question of whether
or not his client would testify. While Taylor had advised
Smith against taking the stand and putting himself before
the prosecutor for questioning, the decision was ultimately
the defendant's. Agitated and angry, Smith fluctuated back
and forth as the judge demanded a final decision. Although

he'd indicated both possibilities for months, Smith finally announced that he would not take the witness stand.

The charge was capital murder, and since the death penalty had been bargained away, if Smith was convicted, the sentence was automatically life. In his closing, Taylor never argued that his client was innocent but only that jurors should study all the evidence. "We asked you to come here because we needed somebody to make the decision," he said. "This is Mr. Smith's day in court. You have to determine whether the state has satisfied you regarding those facts beyond a reasonable doubt."

Then he reminded the jurors that the charge read not only that Smith had to be guilty of Krystal's murder but also that he had to have done it while committing the offense of aggravated sexual assault of a child. They had to find both crimes had been committed to come back with a guilty verdict.

"The events of March 1996 were tragic," Taylor said. "All I can ask of you is that you go back, take your time, and do a careful and impartial consideration of the evidence."

"The facts are what they are," McDonald countered, when he stood before the jury. "We are here to ask you for justice . . . It's simple . . . either he didn't do the crime at all, or he's guilty of capital murder."

Reminding the jurors of the forensic evidence and the confession, there seemed little doubt. In Smith's own words, he'd said that he'd put a strap or a belt around Krystal Baker's neck and choked her. "He did it until she died."

The semen proved sexual contact with a child, since Krystal was a minor. And the tear in her vagina suggested that it wasn't consensual. "Justice isn't only for the defendant, it's for the victim," McDonald reminded those gathered. "Convict him by his own words . . . What kind of person . . . blames the victim for her own death?"

When McDonald assessed the injuries, he believed that

Krystal hadn't entered Smith's car voluntarily. The abrasions on her body, he said, were consistent with Smith's having wrapped the strap around her neck while he dragged her to the truck. That was why the medical examiner found dirt on her knees.

Behind the defense table, Smith fumed. "I didn't do it," he could be heard mumbling. "I didn't do it like that . . . I didn't do it like he said I did."

"Can you imagine what Krystal Baker was going through?" McDonald asked the jurors. "What kind of person does this? Someone who has no regard for human life."

The jury came back in only forty minutes. By then Jeanie, Johnny, and most of Krystal's family, Bradley Moon, Sherry Willcox, and Texas Ranger Joe Haralson were all in the courtroom. The verdict: "Guilty."

Once the trial ended, the judge pointed at Willcox, who still had chills from hearing the conviction. "That woman right there solved this. If she hadn't done it, this man would still be on the streets."

A cross left by Jeanie Escamilla at the site where Krystal's body was found. *(Courtesy of Kathryn Casey)*

When Jeanie stood in front of the courtroom to give her victim impact statement, she felt as if "a roaring mother came out of me."

"You aren't sorry for what you did," she said, looking at Smith. "You're evil. You disrespected my daughter, my family, and your own family . . . Krystal was my sunshine.

Now I hope that when you see the sun you think of her. It's no longer your friend. How can anyone be so evil?"

As the courtroom cleared, deputies escorted Kevin Edison Smith through a back door to a jail cell. The following morning, he'd be transported to a Texas prison, where he'd most likely spend the remainder of his life.

On her way home to Dickinson, Jeanie pulled off I-10 and drove under the Trinity River Bridge. Traffic roared overhead as streams of cars and trucks sped by unaware of the drama unfolding below. At this lonely site, where her daughter's battered body once lay, Jeanie said a prayer then placed a Styrofoam cross covered in artificial pink roses and a small bouquet of flowers. "I wish I could have seen what kind of woman Krystal would have been," she said. "That devil may have taken her body, but God took her soul. I feel like I've walked through hell, looked the devil in the face, and told him off. Thank God they found him so he never hurts anyone else's little girl."

Chapter 15

Innocence Betrayed
Laura Kate Smither

Friendswood, Texas

A favorite photo of Laura.
(Courtesy of Bob and Gay Smither)

Some families move after losing a child, unable to live in the house their daughter departed from on the day fate ripped her from their lives. Others hold on to the home to safeguard memories, at times designating the girl's bedroom as a shrine, her belongings left undisturbed as if the emptiness awaits an impossible homecoming. To part with a dead daughter's possessions is too hard, too wounding, too accepting of reality, although nothing could convince them that all they've gone through is anything but dreadfully real. For many, the sadness is an unheard voice that ceaselessly whispers of all they have lost.

I wasn't sure what to expect on the day I pulled into the driveway of Gay and Bob Smither's split-level on the west side of Friendswood, yet another of the small towns south of Houston, halfway to Galveston. The community had an interesting past that included devout roots. Founded by Quakers, the Religious Society of Friends, it was settled in 1895. Over the years, the population diversified, and Catholics, Baptists, Episcopalians, and others settled the area, but recalling its beginnings, Friendswood remained the Quakers' Houston-area headquarters. That the horror would unfold in such a place, one founded on a dedication to peace, seemed particularly disquieting.

Like its neighbors, Friendswood was flat coastal plain, the undeveloped areas predominantly pastures where in summers cattle lazily sheltered beneath the expansive branches of oak trees to avoid the harsh Texas sun. Yet where League City and Webster had chemical plants and refineries, Friendswood was a bedroom community, its nearly forty thousand residents for the most part well educated, and relatively affluent, the majority two-parent families with children.

Bob and Gay Smither in front of a tree they dedicated to Laura.
(Courtesy of Kathryn Casey)

The afternoon I pulled up to the L-shaped house, a large yellow Lab slumped unconcerned on the front porch. Worried that it might not take well to a stranger, I called Bob on my cell. "Am I at the right house?" I asked. "The pink one?"

His response was a soft chuckle. "I want you to tell Gay that," he said. "I keep telling her the house is pink, and she said it's not."

Moments later, Bob walked out to greet me, as the dog lazily sauntered toward the house beside us. Laura's father was a thin man, with a cap of graying hair and glasses. He had a quiet, intellectual manner, but a bit of a sparkle in his eyes when he asked me to describe the color of the house for his wife. "Well, maybe it's not exactly pink," I hedged. "Maybe salmon?"

Bob laughed, and Gay, the lilt in her voice from growing up in Zimbabwe coloring her response, shot him an amused grin, and said, "Well, it's not a pink, pink."

They were opposites in some ways, it was easy to see. Throughout our time together, Bob remained reserved although his eyes often clouded over with deep sadness. Gay, well, Gay and her wide smile filled the room with a bristling energy. Although it had been sixteen years, they understandably remained devastated and angry. Gay hadn't given birth to Laura, but never thought of her as anything other than her daughter, and she was the most vocal about the tragedy's terrible legacy. Perhaps there was a reason. "My life sentence is that I gave Laura permission to jog that morning," she said. "I will live with that forever."

"Laura was a force to be reckoned with," said Bob, with a wistful smile.

A home-based electrical engineer who worked as a consultant, primarily in the oil business, he was forty when his first child was born. Laura entered the world on April 23, 1984, a loved bundle of energy. "She transformed my life," her proud father said. "From day one."

From the beginning, Laura was an easy child. Bob and

his first wife, Carol, found they could pack up their daughter and take her anywhere. They went to Grand Cayman on vacation and out to nightclubs to listen to music, all with Laura in tow. "She just never fussed," he said. "She was like that from the start."

Yet all wasn't idyllic at the Smithers' Houston home. In 1985 when Laura was still a baby, Carol died of breast cancer. "Those were tough times," Bob said. "Suddenly, it was just Laura and me."

At that juncture, Gay, an English teacher, was on a worldwide expedition. She'd left her home in southern Africa to travel with a friend, and had already been to England and Greece. An adventurer at heart, she'd worked on a charter boat in the Mediterranean and crossed the Atlantic on a sailboat before she landed in Houston, where she took a job as a nanny. That position ended not long after Carol Smither's death. Laura's pediatrician mentioned Gay to Bob, suggesting that she could care for the toddler.

"I hear you're looking for a job," Bob said on the phone that day.

"Oh?" Gay responded. In reality, she wasn't, at least not in Houston. Instead, she'd been eyeing San Francisco as her next stop. So immediately she questioned why she'd agreed to meet Bob for an interview. Later, it would all seem predestined. From their first meeting, Gay, then twenty-six, fell in love with Bob's little girl. "I couldn't help but love Laura straightaway," Gay said. She still carried the image of the first time she saw Laura in her Care Bear rocker holding her Miss Piggy.

"Gay fell in love with Laura first, before she fell in love with me," Bob agreed.

The couple married in 1986, just after Laura turned two, and in 1988, Gay gave birth to a son, David. The year before, Gay had officially adopted Laura. "I figured someday when she was a teenager, Laura would throw it up in my face that I wasn't her biological mother. You know, say, 'You're not my real mom.' I wanted her to know that she was my first child," said Gay. "But Laura wasn't like that. She never got angry with us. She wasn't the kind of child who pouted. It never would have happened."

Even as a child, Laura was precocious, asking Gay to spell "Laura mad at Mozart," so she could write it down when only three. "Mozart was the family cat, and she'd nipped at Laura," Gay explained. "Our daughter was brilliant and adorable. You couldn't help but love her. Everyone did."

At six, Laura began studying ballet. It seemed a good fit for her, since the little girl with the brown hair and wide smile never walked but danced across a room. "She glided down the aisles at the grocery store. She pirouetted," said Gay.

Their daughter also had her serious side. As early as preschool, Bob noticed that other children sought Laura out to settle their squabbles, asking her to mediate their arguments. They knew she'd think the situation through and try to come up with a good solution. "Fairness was important to Laura," said Bob.

In 1990, the Smithers sold the Houston house and moved half an hour south to Friendswood. They wanted more land, and they found it in a rural setting, a house on a gravel road surrounded by cow pastures and only the occasional neighbor. There, Laura and David flourished.

Meeting her new neighbors, Laura often seemed reticent at first. "She was sizing people up," said Bob. "Once she got her footing, you couldn't quiet her down."

"That was how she got her nickname," Gay said, with a wide grin. This was a beloved memory. "We called her Jabber Jaws."

At first, David and Laura attended a public school. But over the years, the Smithers grew dissatisfied, and Gay began homeschooling, with Bob helping out with math and science. In addition to giving their children a more personalized education, Gay and Bob thought it could make their lives more relaxed. "None of us are morning people," said

Gay. "This way, we didn't have to rush around to get the children out the door."

There were happy days learning together, including family events fashioned around the children's studies. When Laura read Jane Austen, for instance, her parents brought her to the stage on which the dramas were set, by arranging a family vacation in England. Exceptionally bright, Laura began talking about someday attending Stanford University.

In addition to their classes, both David and Laura enrolled in extracurricular activities with other homeschooling families. Laura tried sports, including scuba diving and tennis and other types of dance, but her first love remained ballet. "Laura would get upset when they played the Ninja Turtle theme for modern dance," remembered Gay. "She wanted classical music. She wanted ballet."

Perhaps her interest was fueled partly because Laura was an exceptionally talented and determined young ballerina. She practiced five days a week in between her studies. During the holidays, she earned parts dancing onstage in the *Nutcracker*. "Laura was just beautiful," said Gay. "And so happy when she danced."

In 1996, Laura was twelve and entering the seventh grade, and David

Laura in a dance costume at age nine. *(Courtesy of Bob and Gay Smither)*

was eight years old. That summer, Laura auditioned for the
Houston Ballet Academy, competing against three hundred
children, and won one of only two coveted slots. "She was
beyond excited," said Bob.

From that point on, three days a week, Laura trained at
the academy. Resolute about improving her performance,
when her instructors suggested working out to increase her
stamina, Laura initiated her own exercise campaign. Before
long, Bob and the children became a common sight on the
country roads, Bob jogging while Laura and David rode
bikes beside him.

At that point, much of the area around their home was
going through a metamorphosis. Subdivisions were quickly
replacing what had once been cattle pastures. Contractors
fenced in large tracts. Inside the enclosures, they constructed
block after block of impressive two-story brick houses on
large lots. Even the open field directly adjacent to the Smithers' house was under development, an upscale subdivision in
the making. Still, the family felt safe and isolated from the
problems of the city. "We didn't even lock our doors," said
Gay with a shrug. "We were living family life in small-town
America."

On the night of Wednesday, April 2, 1997, Laura stayed
up late reading a book called *Fit or Fat* by PBS nutrition
guru Covert Bailey, a manual espousing exercise for weight
control and strength. "She wanted to hold her arabesque
longer," said Gay. "Laura was determined to do well in
ballet, as she did with everything."

April 3, 1997, was a Thursday morning like any other. Laura's thirteenth birthday was approaching, and on a whiteboard in her yellow-trimmed bedroom filled with stuffed
animals and dolls, she counted down the days. "Twenty days
until my birthday," Laura wrote that morning.

"She was so excited about becoming a teenager," Bob
said sadly.

Sometime before nine, Bob showered, preparing to meet with a client who was scheduled to arrive at the house in about an hour. Still in her pajamas, Laura popped into the kitchen, where her mother and brother cooked a favorite breakfast, chocolate chip pancakes with bacon. After reading the fitness book the night before, Laura had something on her mind. She worried about her mother. Gay sometimes went on the rotation diet to lose weight. She liked it, since it had recipes and laid out what to eat each day. "The book said you shouldn't go on fad diets. You should exercise to control your weight," Laura said. "Promise me that you won't go on that diet anymore?"

Realizing Laura was genuinely concerned, Gay agreed. Then the almost-teenager asked something that surprised Gay: "Can I go for a jog?"

Busy cooking, Gay didn't believe Laura would really go running that morning since she'd never before gone alone. What Gay answered was: "We're making breakfast."

"I'll be home in time to eat," Laura countered.

Her daughter was growing up. "Okay," Gay said, remaining doubtful that Laura would follow through. Moments later, however, Laura reappeared at the kitchen doorway wearing running clothes.

"When will the pancakes be ready?" she asked. When David said twenty minutes, she responded, "I'll be home in time." With that, Laura, her long dark hair trailing behind her, turned and rushed out the door.

Inside the cheery kitchen, all went on as planned. The pancakes bubbled on the griddle, and David set the table. Soon the steaming circles were on a plate waiting, the bacon crisp, breakfast ready. Bob walked into the room and noticed their daughter's empty chair, and asked, "Where's Laura?"

"She went for a run," Gay said, visibly worried. "She said she'd be home in time for breakfast. She's late."

The Smithers exchanged troubled glances. They knew their daughter well. Laura was reliable, not the kind of child to be even ten minutes late. Immediately concerned, Bob grabbed his keys. "I'll be right back. I'll drive around and find her."

"We were worried she got hurt, that she'd been hit by a car or something," said Gay. "We knew from the beginning for her to be late, something was wrong."

In his small white car, Bob Smither drove the route he and Laura jogged and biked, thinking that was her most likely course. He assumed that any moment he'd see his daughter. Perhaps she'd turned an ankle and needed help. She could be lying somewhere, unable to walk. There was a light mist in the air, the faint promise of approaching rain as he drove the familiar roads watching for Laura. What began as concern swelled into a burgeoning fear as Bob walked into the house and told Gay that he hadn't found their daughter.

"Well where could she be?" Gay asked.

"I don't know," Bob said. "But I'm calling the police."

"Will they do anything? Doesn't she have to be missing twenty-four hours?" Over the years, Gay had heard of cases where police refused to take a missing person report for a full day, a not-unusual situation throughout parts of the country.

"It doesn't matter. I'm calling," Bob said, dialing 911.

To their relief ten minutes later, at approximately 9:55 that morning, a young officer pulled up in front of their house, responding to Bob's call. The officer took a report and left.

Sixteen years later, the day Laura disappeared would be hazy for both her parents. What they remembered most was how hard the rain fell and how frantically they searched. Bob in his car and Gay and David in the family van, they drove the rural roads hoping to find someone, anyone who might have seen Laura. "Did you see a little girl?" they asked. No one had.

Turning onto the vacant land covered with trees and thick underbrush being cleared for a subdivision on County Road 133, also called Moore Road, the main street that ran not far from the house, the Smithers both stopped and talked to the workers. There were few there. A steady rain fell by then, and the construction supervisor had released most of his crew. Had anyone at the site seen Laura? "No, ma'am," the foreman told Gay. She thanked him and drove away.

Their panic continued to build, and at one point when Bob returned to the house, he grabbed a photo of Laura and quickly pieced together a handwritten flyer. That day, the copier would churn out so many copies, it literally burned out. Before long, neighbors who'd heard the disturbing news of a missing child showed up on horseback, offering help. They took off to search the surrounding fields, while the Smithers and close friends grabbed stacks of flyers Bob had piled on the Ping-Pong table and canvassed the closest sub-divisions, knocking on doors, finding no one home.

"It was like Laura had vanished," said Gay. "Our world turned upside down on a dime that day."

On the phone, Gay alerted friends and family, Laura's Scout troop, and her homeschool group. Soon other parents arrived, snatching up flyers and spreading out to the homes in the area, praying and looking, looking and praying. Even the man who arrived for Bob's business meeting pitched in, helping with the search. The police officers told the Smithers not to worry, that children almost always return home, implying that Laura was most likely a runaway. But Gay and Bob knew that wasn't true, and so did an acquaintance of theirs, one who happened to be the chief for the local community college's campus police force. When he heard Laura Smither was missing, he called a Friendswood P.D. captain and vouched for the family, saying Laura would never run away. She wasn't a troubled adolescent but a happy young girl. Something was very, very wrong.

In response, Friendswood P.D.'s chief, Jared Stout, a studious-looking man with thinning brown hair and round, wire-rimmed glasses, immediately reassigned all thirty-nine of his officers to the search for Laura and requested assistance from the F.B.I. At five that afternoon, the special agent in charge arrived at the Smithers' home. By then, more than one hundred neighbors and friends assisted police in the search for Laura, and the rain had pounded down until the gullies and the low-lying areas overflowed. In their living room, the Smithers answered questions, many over and over again.

One of the first things the FBI did was place a tap on the Smithers' home phone, in case Laura had been abducted by kidnappers looking for money. They waited for the phone to ring with a ransom demand, but it never did.

The afternoon blended into evening, when the police informed Gay and Bob that it was too dangerous to continue, and they were calling off the search for the night. Feeling as if their hearts lodged in their throats, the distraught parents knew that despite what the police might do, they couldn't stop, and they continued combing through the fields until well after dark, then returned home only to strategize. All night they paced and talked, off and on standing on their front porch looking out into the darkness, desperate to see their daughter walking toward the house. Around midnight, a man who claimed to be a psychic called, contending that he'd had a vision of Laura in a field near a road. "Any other time, we would have been highly skeptical," said Gay. "But it wasn't any other time, and we were out of our minds with worry."

After listening, Bob and Gay thought they knew the place, and in total blackness with only flashlights to illuminate their paths through the brush, they walked, rain cascading over their faces, calling out to Laura.

"I remember hearing Bob next to me, his voice steady and controlled, like it always is. He was saying, 'Laura. Laura, where are you?'" said Gay. "And I heard my own voice, screaming."

When they returned home at 4:00 A.M., the house buzzed with volunteers and an FBI agent and a police officer who'd been assigned to spend the night. Gay thought it was kind of the authorities to have someone stationed there to protect them, particularly David, in case whoever had taken Laura returned. "We didn't realize yet that we were suspects," said Bob.

By the next morning, a Friday, word of Laura's disappearance had spread like the rainwater spilling over the bayous. David's Cub Scout leader called offering help, and Gay asked him to watch over their son while they worked with the searchers. The house filled with friends and neighbors, while at a nearby softball field, townsfolk the Smithers had never met congregated, eager to help police look for Laura. From there, groups of volunteers fanned out in the continuing rain to comb through the sodden fields. Still, they were resolute. One woman was bitten in the heel by a venomous snake but, when she discovered its fangs hadn't penetrated her shoe, she walked on, eager to help. "We saw the face of God in our neighbors," said Gay. "People we'd never met, total strangers, put their lives on hold and came to help us find our daughter."

At nine that morning, Gay and a friend stood on Moore Road, the main street on Bob and Laura's jogging/biking route, stopping cars, asking the drivers, "Were you here yesterday about this time? Did you see a little girl?"

Many said they had driven that same street around the time Laura had disappeared, that in fact they commuted down that road every morning, yet none said they'd seen Laura. "I handed each one a flyer," said Gay. The drivers sped off, leaving Gay waiting on the road to flag down the next car.

That evening, the local TV stations aired footage of Gay and a friend walking door to door in the rain, handing out flyers. "Everyone wanted to help," Gay said, reliving that moment in her memory, tears clouding her eyes.

When Gay returned to the house, the focus changed, as police again questioned the family, separating Bob, Gay, and David, taking them to different parts of the house. Over and again they recounted the previous morning when Laura vanished. They never refused to answer a question. "We would have done anything they asked, told them anything to bring Laura home," said Gay. "That was all we cared about."

Later that day, Bob grasped what was truly happening. Standing outside of the house, he scolded David for crawling under the deck. When Bob looked over, he noticed an FBI agent watching him with great interest. "I realized we were being observed," said Bob. "But I thought, of course we should be. I told the agent, 'You should look under the deck. And we have a basement. You could search that, too.'" And the police did, over the course of the day removing four large plastic bags filled with potential evidence from the house, much of it Laura's possessions, including her ballet slippers.

At Friendswood P.D., Chief Stout secured a copy of the sex offender registry for Galveston and the neighboring counties. There were more than twenty-one hundred on the list. At the same time, Friendswood P.D. and the FBI compiled the names of men working in the area, including at the nearby construction sites.

Still, the day proceeded without a break. When asked for a comment by the press, Chief Stout remarked about how thoroughly the child had disappeared. "It was as if Laura had been on *The X-Files* and just beamed up."

Another day passed without a breakthrough in the case. The evening of the second day, Bob asked Stout what the plans were for the following morning. The chief answered politely yet steadfastly that the search was over. The police were no longer investing their efforts into looking for Laura. Instead, they would be concentrating on narrowing down the pool of suspects.

As devastated as he felt to think that the official search was over, Bob understood. And as it turned out, that didn't hamper the quest, for the next morning even more volunteers appeared, all eager to help. The media sent out reporters who circulated through the crowd, asking why they were there. Fathers and mothers, grandparents, teenagers, businesspeople, and blue-collar workers said they wanted to do whatever they could to find Laura Smither. Some searched, while others brought baked goods, water, and food for the volunteers. Local merchants donated money to provide dry socks, something sorely needed in the continuing rains.

While the volunteers searched, and the community prayed, Bob and Gay cooperated with authorities. All that week, the Smithers were asked questions, and they continued to patiently answer. "They were interrogations, but nice interrogations," said Gay. "That was their job. We understood. But they did it with respect, so we didn't feel attacked."

As the days wore on, Bob fought to believe that their daughter would be found alive, but it became increasingly difficult. "After a few days, you kind of run out of stories to tell yourself that are going to have a good ending," he said, his eyes downcast and his words hushed. "But I hoped."

Meanwhile, Gay relied on her deep faith. "I went into denial," she said. "I convinced myself that Laura was being held captive, and if I prayed hard enough, she'd be let go." A friend gave her prayer cards, and Gay read them often, putting her heart into every word, dropping to her knees and begging God to bring Laura home.

That didn't happen, but they continued to see in Friendswood an overwhelming desire to help. At one point, the Texas-New Mexico Power Company donated a vacant building to be used as a volunteer headquarters for the search. When Bob called it, someone picked up the phone and said, "Laura Recovery Center. Can I help you?"

"It was incredible," he said.

"That so many people cared about our child was huge," said Gay. "That was our hope."

In the days that followed, Gay and Bob gravitated to the search center, where every morning, hundreds missed work, set aside their own tasks for the day, to search for Laura. There the Smithers asked what they could do. They were told to talk to the volunteers and make up lists of who was working and what each person was doing. "At the time, we thought it was busy work, that they were giving us something to keep us out of the way," said Bob. "But we did it. And later on, it would turn out to be useful."

Yet, at the same time, it was confusing and troubling. In the evenings, the Smithers sat in their house doing what the FBI and police asked, making other lists, this time of all the people Laura trusted enough to get into their cars. So while Bob and Gay felt a deep gratitude for all their friends and acquaintances and the legions of total strangers who were reaching out to them in their time of need, they also found themselves looking at everyone around them as if he or she could be the person who'd taken their daughter. "It grew the suspicion," said Gay.

"It was like a cancer," said Bob. "We didn't believe anyone we knew would take Laura, but we just didn't know. We were desperate to find her."

"The one thing was, everyone who knew Laura loved her," said Gay. "We couldn't believe that anyone who knew her could hurt her."

One week blended into the next, and Laura was still missing. A neighbor talked to a psychic who recommended that Gay burn a candle shaped as a cross. If she did, the psychic said Laura would be found. "I did it," Gay said. "I would have done anything."

Perhaps the psychic was well-meaning. Perhaps he genuinely believed that the candle would bring Laura home. There were so many others, including more psychics and just ordinary people across not only Texas but the nation who called authorities, many of them most likely also with good intentions, saying they'd seen Laura or someone who resembled her. Law enforcement splintered off and used valuable time that could have gone toward the investigation, only to hit one dead end after another.

Yet no one stopped looking. Over the course of more than two weeks, somewhere around six thousand volun-

teers searched for Laura Smither in the fields surrounding
Friendswood. They covered nearly eight hundred square
miles, most of it rural, through snake-infested swamps, deserted oil fields, and cow pastures, terrain deemed the most
likely for the disposal of a body. But nothing was found.

Finally, it was decided that the searching had to end. Too
many people had put their lives on hold with no success. Gay
and Bob, while not giving up hope, didn't protest when the
head volunteers explained that the people of Friendswood
had to reclaim their lives. Some hadn't been to work since
days after Laura disappeared. They had families to support. It was time. Those leading the efforts and the Smithers
agreed on something else as well, that there needed to be
an official event to mark the end of the search, to give the
volunteers some sense of closure.

That meeting was set for the Friendswood Town Hall
on April 20, the seventeenth day after Laura's disappearance. At four that afternoon, three hundred volunteers were
greeted and thanked by the Smithers, who showed a video
the local NBC affiliate had compiled of Laura and the
search. At the meeting, Chief Stout took the stage to speak.
But then something happened. As he addressed the audience, thanking those gathered for all the work they'd dedicated to finding Laura, Stout pulled out his pager. Abruptly,
he mumbled a hasty thank-you and turned and left, literally
running from the auditorium.

"I knew something big had happened," said Gay. "Chief
Stout actually went rigid when he looked at that message.
I thought they'd found Laura. I thought she was coming
home."

That evening, the Smithers held to their practice of not
watching the news coverage, but then, at seven, someone
called to ask about reports on the local news of a body
found, that of a young girl.

"How dare you!" Gay cried. "How dare you call and tell
us this!"

Gay didn't believe it and slammed down the phone. But at ten that night, Chief Stout rang their doorbell. It was true. A decomposing body, nude except for tan socks, had been spotted by a father and son training their dog on the banks of a retention pond bordering a residential neighborhood. The pond was fourteen miles north of the Smither house, and while volunteers had ventured close, they'd never made it that far. In three feet of water, the body was wedged inside a metal drainage pipe with water running across its upper half. The current had stripped much of the flesh from the waist up. But there were indications that it was Laura, including braces on the teeth.

Despite the evidence, Gay asked a favor. "Don't tell us it's Laura until you're sure."

That night, their priest and a close friend stayed with Gay and Bob, waiting for news, praying the corpse wasn't Laura's. Yet they also felt guilty, as if by wishing that Laura was still alive, they were condemning another family to the terrible news that their daughter was dead. The autopsy was scheduled for early the following morning. On his report, the medical examiner would note indications of trauma of the neck—as if she'd been strangled—along with blunt-impact injuries, hemorrhages on the lower body and the buttocks. The manner of death was listed as homicide. "Time of death is consistent with the time of abduction or disappearance."

That afternoon, the FBI agent in charge and the chief again drove up the Smithers' driveway. Bob and Gay anxiously awaited them. "They came to tell us that it was Laura," Gay said, wiping away a tear. "It was two days before her thirteenth birthday. I thought about how she'd been counting down the days."

"Even after we heard, we were in denial," said Bob. "Parents aren't engineered to do this. It was a long time before we were able to completely accept it. Maybe, in a way, denial is a gift."

That night, volunteers guarded the Smithers' house to keep interlopers away, and the next day Bob and Gay faced the grim task of making plans to bury their daughter.

Meanwhile, at the recovery site, along the banks of the retention pond where Laura's body had been found, a make-shift memorial came to life, a field of candles, notes, teddy bears, and flowers. Friends and strangers gathered, bringing crosses and staying to pray for Laura, the Smithers, and the entire community, many undoubtedly asking God to bring the person responsible to justice.

When the ME's Office decided to keep Laura's body to have a forensic pathologist run further tests, a memorial was planned instead of a funeral. The service was held at Sagemont Baptist, the largest church in the area, to accommodate the expected crowds, and ministers and priests from all the area churches participated. It rained hard that day as it had every day since Laura had disappeared, as if the very heavens were crying. Yet more than a thousand braved the bad weather to pay their respects, a final coming-together of those who'd worked so hard and so long to try to find Laura. Throughout the investigation, the community had poured its heart into the search, getting to know the family and learning about the little girl lost. In so many ways, Laura had become everyone's child.

In the end, on May 10, 1997, little Laura Smither, who dreamed of becoming a ballerina, was buried near her mother and grandfather.

Time passed, and Bob and Gay tried to go on with their lives, all the while waiting, hoping that Laura's murderer would be found. The memorial continued to grow at the recovery site for more than a year. At times, friends brought the distraught parents statues, teddy bears, notes, some of the things the community donated to memorialize their daughter. While they appreciated it all, none of it truly helped.

"We were broken people," said Gay.

Over the months that followed, his parents say David

began having problems. "He said Laura was the perfect one.
I'm the naughty one," said Gay. "Imagine how hard it was
for him when she died. And then we found out later that it's
common for the siblings, that they nearly always initially
kind of self-destruct."

Their house became a shrine to Laura, with photos of
her in the living room. Her room was left untouched, the
whiteboard in it still bearing her handwriting as she counted
down the days to her birthday. Initially, the door was kept
closed. "Here was this room that had always been filled with
joy," said Gay. "Now it was like a tomb. And we gradually
came to see that David was suffering. He'd lost his sister,
and his parents were nearly destroyed."

Years later David would compare notes with others
who'd lost a brother or sister through violence and grow to
understand that what he experienced was truly fairly universal. "What I felt was a profound sense of isolation," he said.
"Siblings are often the ones forgotten in these cases. There's
an orphan experience a lot of us go through. We don't just
lose our sibling, but our parents for a time, because they're
grieving."

Perhaps more than anything else, Bob and Gay prayed that
the person responsible would be found and held accountable.
Early on there was hope. That day at the Smither house, the
one when they learned their daughter was dead, Chief Stout
assured them that he'd find the person responsible. "Now
you'll see me turn into the hunter," he told the Smithers.

There were suspects. Within days of Laura's disappearance, law enforcement singled out one man in particular,
one with a violent past: William Lewis Reece.

In October 1996, five months before Laura's abduction,
Reece paroled out of an Oklahoma prison after serving ten
years of a fifteen-year sentence for kidnapping, forced oral
sodomy, and rape. On that fateful April day Laura disappeared, he was in the Smithers' neighborhood, working as

a bulldozer operator in the subdivision under development adjacent to their home.

Around nine that morning, when Laura walked outside and the light drizzle began, Reece's boss assessed the weather and opted to release his crew. Moments later, Laura jogged away from her home, presumably on the route she often took with her father down Moore Road. About the same time, Reece drove away from the construction site, turning onto that very same road.

At least on the surface, Reece appeared to be cooperating. He'd given permission for the FBI to search his house and trucks. He'd even agreed to multiple polygraphs, yet they'd been inconclusive, perhaps, authorities said, because he'd fidgeted and coughed during the pivotal questions.

While Reece had caught the attention of law enforcement, there were other suspects in Laura's death. One was a man who lived in the area who'd made sexual remarks to another young girl. Then there was the tantalizing confession of a man who claimed to have been on the scene when a friend forced Laura into his truck and murdered her. Yet when the trailer where it was supposed to have happened was searched, not one piece of evidence was found. Finally, there was the Harris County Jail inmate who'd been found with a photograph of a young girl resembling Laura in his wallet. None of the other leads panned out, and before long all except the possible connection to Bill Reece were abandoned.

When he talked to the Smithers, Chief Stout gave them the impression that he believed Reece was Laura's killer, but prosecutors argued that they lacked enough evidence to charge him with the crime. Frustration grew.

What was clear in the aftermath of the search for Laura Smither was that something remarkable had happened in Friendswood, Texas. The death of every victim is unique, yet what stood out about Laura Smither was how she inspired thousands to set aside their own lives to fight for a common goal.

Early on, it became evident to Gay and Bob that their community's response had been extraordinary. Even while the search for Laura continued, a father of a missing daughter came to them begging for help. "He saw what was happening on television, how so many volunteers helped us. He wanted to know how to organize his own volunteers to look for his daughter," said Bob. "We helped him as much as we could." In the end, the man's daughter's body was found by volunteers on the same day as Laura's.

Based on that experience, in the months following their daughter's death, Bob and Gay talked with Chief Stout. Looking at the situation, the chief agreed that what had happened in Friendswood was an anomaly, a rare triangle of trust, a coming-together of the family, the community and law enforcement. Perhaps to make some sense out of the tragedy, not long after Laura's memorial service, Bob began pulling together all the notes he'd made about who did what during the search for Laura. The result was a manual of sorts that described how to look for a missing person.

Then something happened that would focus the Smithers' work, an event that would redirect their lives, giving them a cause for years to come. That August, four months after Laura's death, a truck was found on I-45, one that belonged to the C. H. Cain family, who lived on an appendage off the causeway bridge between the mainland and Galveston called Tiki Island. Seventeen-year-old Jessica Cain had been on her way home from a night out with friends when she simply vanished. Her truck was found abandoned, with her purse inside, on the shoulder of I-45. Within hours of the mysterious disappearance, the Smithers' doorbell rang. "It was one of the Cains' neighbors," said Bob. "They were coming to us for help. They wanted to know how to organize the search."

"Here we were, these damaged human beings, and someone was coming to us for help. Something was very wrong if they needed us," Gay said. Yet she and Bob couldn't turn the Cains or any relative of a missing loved one away. They had unwillingly become part of a painful union.

"The hell of not knowing is every parent's nightmare," said Bob. "Until you've walked that road, you have no idea of the darkness."

Chapter 16

A Daring Escape and Pieces of the Puzzle

Webster, Texas
May 1997

Detective turned private investigator Sue Dietrich, taken in 2012.
(Courtesy of Kathryn Casey)

"Ninety-seven was a tough year," said Sue Dietrich, as we huddled together in a small Italian restaurant, planted flush against the southbound Interstate 45 feeder road. Later, Dietrich, a retired cop turned private investigator, lingered in front where I snapped her photo with cars whizzing behind her. The background, of course, seemed fitting, since I-45 anchored the bloodshed we'd come together to discuss.

Inside the restaurant, Dietrich and I toyed with salads and whispered about the summer of 1997, when young women were repeatedly abducted in Harris and Galveston counties. First twelve-year-old Laura Smither, her slain body found in a retention pond. Then in May, Dietrich consulted on the case of Sandra Sapaugh, a woman kidnapped from a parking lot. In August, the missing girl's name was Jessica Cain, her abandoned pickup found on I-45's shoulder.

As we talked, the sadness from Dietrich's many years in law enforcement hung on her like a weighty shroud. Throughout our time together, the aging investigator brought the conversation back to the man she believed responsible for the carnage and accompanying misery. "He's a monster," she said, lips pursed.

At the tables surrounding us, couples and families gathered over steaming plates of pasta, many laughing and smiling. I nodded, signaling that I understood, and I thought Dietrich looked tired. Years in law enforcement had etched deep lines around her eyes.

We'd met for the first time in the midnineties in Alvin, Texas, the same small town where Colette Wilson, the dentist's daughter, had disappeared decades earlier. Back in the day, I paid my bills writing magazine articles, and Dietrich was a feisty blond detective in high heels and manicured nails, one who'd cracked a big case.

Two-year-old Renee Goode, a sweet child with light brown curls, died during a court-ordered overnight stay with her father, Shane. The police quickly wrote off the cause of the child's demise as some unidentified, unexplained illness. But Renee's mom and grandmother believed Shane Goode murdered his little girl to exact revenge against his ex-wife and avoid child support. Repeatedly rebuffed by the police and the county's medical examiner, the two women found no help until they met Dietrich. Unlike many others, she listened and assessed the evidence, deciding those who loved Renee had ample reason to be suspicious. It was Dietrich who interviewed Goode, obtaining a statement that later, along with a second autopsy, led to his conviction for murder.

If any doubt remained, Shane Goode ultimately wrote a confession letter from inside prison walls.

Three years after little Renee's death, in 1997, it was another talent that brought Dietrich center stage in the investigations into the I-45 killings. Along with her duties as an investigator, Sue Dietrich was a certified forensic hypnotist. The lead she ultimately constructed from the clues made all the difference. "If it hadn't been for Sue Dietrich, we might never have seen the big picture," a grateful prosecutor confided. "She pieced the puzzle together."

That spring, Sandra Sapaugh's life was in turmoil.

The mother of two young girls, the nineteen-year-old had dropped out of school in the ninth grade. A striking beauty with long brown hair and a voluptuous figure, Sapaugh did what she could, dancing in topless clubs, to support her children. Her night wasn't going well in the early hours of Saturday, May 17, when she pulled into the lot of a Webster, Texas, convenience store. On this particular evening, she dropped her kids off with their grandparents and drove her red Dodge Astro minivan back to an apartment that until recently she'd shared with her husband, her mission to collect her clothing and her children's things and move out. She left hours later with the minivan loaded and $200 her soon-to-be-ex spotted her to tide her over until she and the children resettled.

Sometime around one, Sapaugh pulled into a Stop & Go on West Nasa Road I, a major thoroughfare that runs east off I-45 toward the Johnson Space Center. Across the street, a Motel 6 where she planned to stay was booked solid, and Sapaugh decided to call a friend. Still years before cell phones became the norm, she parked in front of the pay phone on the outside of the store. As she exited the truck, she noticed a man dressed in jeans, a white, short-sleeved T-shirt, and a black cowboy hat standing beside an oversized white pickup, a dually with four wheels on the rear axle, parked near the store Dumpster. Something about the guy made her uneasy. Quickly, she shuffled inside for change. When she walked out, the man waited, watching her.

"I don't like the way this guy's looking at me," she told her friend on the pay phone. The call ended, Sapaugh shrugged off her apprehension, ignored the stranger, and left. Her plan was to drive across the street to a Waffle House, a small, boxy establishment open all night, where her friend would meet her. She pulled out of the store's lot, glanced in her rearview mirror and saw that the white dually followed directly behind her. Then, as she steered into the restaurant's lot, Sapaugh realized something was wrong with her minivan.

In a parking space near the road, she came to a stop. Moments later, she lowered her window as the man from the convenience store approached. "I noticed that your tire is flat at the Stop & Go," he said with a slow smile. "Why don't I help you?"

Wary but grateful, Sapaugh climbed out of the van to look at her misshapen front driver's-side tire, flat to the rim. Had she run over something? A bad night had just become worse. "I'll see if I have a jack," he said. Sapaugh thought little of it when the man, instead of going to the large aluminum toolbox anchored to the pickup's bed, walked toward the front of the truck and opened the hood.

The young mother had bigger problems; she wasn't even sure that she had a spare. She popped the van's back open to look inside. The man made her uncomfortable, but she'd never changed a tire and needed the help.

"Would you get the rag out of my truck for me?" he called out to her.

In response, Sapaugh strode over to the truck's open driver's-side door and glanced inside. "I don't see it," she shouted back.

"Look again," he said. "It's on the passenger side."

Following his instructions, Sapaugh leaned into the truck, scanning the floor and seat for the rag. It was then that she felt the man at her back. Her mind registered the touch of a knife blade to her throat. Reacting quickly, Sapaugh grabbed for the knife, but the man overpowered her and hastily pushed her inside.

"Get in, and don't yell!" he ordered, clambering in behind her.

Inside the truck, Sapaugh sprawled out on the passenger seat. She flipped over, but her legs were caught, spreading awkwardly across the man's lap. The entire inside of the truck was in darkness, all the lights turned off, but in his hand, she saw the glint of the knife as he growled, "Stay down, bitch!"

Her pulse quickening, she watched helplessly as he threw the truck into drive and pulled out of the restaurant parking lot. "Where are you taking me?" she asked.

"Dallas," he said.

Instead he drove to the Motel 6, the one where earlier Sapaugh had hoped to book a room. If the hotel had a vacancy, she would have been inside sleeping instead of trembling with fear in the stranger's pickup. But this wasn't the time to think about that. Instead, she tried to talk the man into going into the motel office and getting them a room. "We don't have to drive anywhere," she said, hoping to put him at ease. "We can stay here. I'll stay with you." If he went inside to try to register, she might be able to escape. Her fear grew as he put his hand down her blouse and fondled her breast.

The man wasn't interested in a hotel room. That wasn't what he had in mind. Moments later, he'd moved the truck again, this time into the back parking lot of a U-Haul rental agency a short distance away. She shivered with fear as he put the truck in park, then turned toward her and grabbed her blouse, tearing it open. She felt sickened as he put his mouth on her breast. "Take your pants off," he ordered.

"No," she balked. She thought she saw him put the knife

between his legs, as he continued to suck and fondle her breast.

"Take your pants off!" he insisted. Although terrified, she refused.

It was then that he threw the truck into drive and headed west on Nasa I toward I-45. He appeared anxious, eager to get what he wanted. In the van, the man roared orders at Sapaugh. "I said take your damn pants off!"

Out the window, Sapaugh watched stores whiz by and headlights shining, as inside the dark truck she struggled, not sure what to do. When he shouted at her again, she stalled for time, asking, "Can I take my shoes off first?"

"No!" he shouted, but when she argued that she needed to remove her shoes before slipping out of her blue jeans, he reluctantly gave in. By then the truck was barreling northbound on I-45, Webster's lights and civilization fading behind them. In the darkness, the interstate was nearly deserted.

Employing the excuse of removing her shoes, a pair of sandals, Sapaugh pulled her legs off the man's lap. In the passenger seat, she acted as if she were attempting to follow his directions and slowly took off her shoes. As she fumbled with her jeans, she looked about her, searching for a way to escape. It was then that she noticed that the passenger-side door was unlocked. In a single motion, she grabbed the opportunity, seized the handle and swung the door open. Instantly, the man slammed his foot on the brake and snatched the back of her shirt. Not giving in, Sapaugh struggled. Below her bare feet, the interstate's coarse cement surface dashed by. They battled, the truck slowed but still moving, until her shirt finally gave way and tore. He lost his grip, and she fell.

Tumbling from the moving truck, Sapaugh hit the cement hard then rolled across the harsh pavement, skinning the concrete, hitting stones and debris. Once she stopped, every joint ached and her knee throbbed, but she had no time to give in to her injuries. Instead, to her horror, she heard the truck stop ahead of her. Then she heard him shift into reverse.

He was coming back for her.

On her way home from her sister's bachelorette party, Minerva Torres drove her black Dodge Charger north on I-45 sometime after 1:00 A.M., when a barefoot woman startled her by running out of the darkness, staggering in the middle of the freeway, limping and waving her arms. In the backseat, Torres's young nephew yelled, "That lady is hurt. We have to help her! Stop!"

Torres did, pulling the car to the shoulder and parking it, then running to the woman.

"Help me!" the woman screamed. "Please, help me! I jumped from a truck."

"You jumped?" Torres repeated.

"Yes, I jumped from that truck, there!" Sapaugh shouted.

Torres scanned the highway and spotted a white dually pickup pulled off to the side, its headlights turned off but the backup lights lit, as if it were coming toward them in reverse. Quickly, Torres guided the injured woman to the car. The stranger's clothes were torn, and she was bleeding. As Torres lowered the injured woman into the passenger seat, Torres's frightened nephew cried.

"Is that your boyfriend?" Torres asked the injured woman.

"No. I don't know him," Sapaugh said. "He had a knife."

Torres eyed the truck that lurked ominously just ahead. "We need to get out of here."

Hurriedly, Torres threw her car into gear and sped up. Sapaugh saw the dually pull out onto the freeway and take off down the interstate. The man had given up. He was leaving.

At the next exit, Torres pulled off the interstate onto the service road. Her intention was to take the injured woman directly to the hospital. But once they were in the car, Sapaugh pleaded with Torres to take her instead to the Waffle House, where her friend would be waiting. Complying, Torres looped around and drove south to Webster. Once there, she ran from the car into the restaurant. Inside, she shouted at the woman behind the counter to call an ambulance and the police. Back at the car, Torres searched for something to stem the injured woman's bleeding. She found a shirt she pushed against Sapaugh's chest. When the ambulance pulled up, Sapaugh was in the passenger seat, the door open, her feet on the parking lot's surface, dazed, blood streaming down her face and body from gashes and scrapes. Every movement brought excruciating pain.

To the first officer on the scene, Sapaugh described the horror that night had brought and the man responsible. He was white, approximately five-nine, about two hundred pounds, with dirty blond hair and a mustache. And something she'd noticed was that he had bags under his eyes, which she described as "loose facial skin." Although stunned from all she'd been through, she was as precise with the description of the truck, an older model white Ford or Chevy dually pickup with an extended cab, an aluminum toolbox on the bed, and a black stripe along the side. From the sound of the engine, she thought it might have been a diesel.

Torres, who'd grown up working on her brother's cars, gave a nearly identical description of the truck she'd seen on the highway, speculating it was a Ford.

Brought into St. John Hospital in nearby Clear Lake on a backboard, Sapaugh appeared calm as doctors assessed her wounds. She had a gash on her scalp that needed to be stitched quickly to stop the bleeding, a cut above her eye, and abrasions on her left breast. Her hands too painful to move, she couldn't sign a consent form. In her bloodied and torn clothing, angry red lacerations and swollen painful bruises covered her from her face to her feet. Fearing internal bleeding or a concussion, the attending physician checked her into the hospital, wanting to monitor her condition. Three days after she jumped from the truck, her body black-and-blue and sore to move, Sapaugh, still traumatized, left the hospital and checked into a shelter for abused women.

Soon after, she made her first trip to the Webster Police Department to assist officers investigating her case. Once there, she described the man for an officer at a computer, one using Identi-Kit, a program designed to construct composites of suspects. The result was a sketch of a man with baggy eyes, a mustache, stubble on his chin and cheeks, and slicked-back hair. Later that day, the drawing was released in a bulletin to agencies across Texas along with written descriptions of the man and his truck.

The face of Sandra Sapaugh's kidnapper. *(Courtesy of the Harris County Sheriff's Office)*

Throughout the afternoon at the police station, Sapaugh had been on edge, uncomfortable. As precise as she was about the man and the truck, she'd given the police little to work with, since white dually trucks weren't uncommon work vehicles in southeast Texas. There was one piece of information police had hoped for more than any other, one that Sapaugh had been unable to supply: a license-plate number.

The following day, Sue Dietrich's phone rang in her office. "It was a detective in Webster. He asked me to drive to their office to hypnotize a victim and a witness," said Dietrich. "The hope was that under hypnosis, the women might remember more."

Six days after her abduction, Sandra Sapaugh sat in a darkened office with Dietrich and a Webster detective. As a video camera recorded the session, Dietrich asked Sapaugh to describe what had happened to her and everything she could remember about the man and his truck. Dietrich then attempted to relax the woman and put her under hypnosis. Although she'd only used hypnosis on witnesses a few times before, all initially went well. But as Dietrich asked questions, Sapaugh felt drawn back to the inside of the white truck, to that night when she'd feared for her life. In a matter of moments, the young woman became intensely frightened. Thrust back into the truck barreling down the interstate in the darkness, Sapaugh relived the terror, fearing she either had to jump from the moving truck onto the interstate or die at the hands of a killer. "It was hard on her," said Dietrich. "We tried, but she couldn't come up with any more than she'd told us before the session. No license number. She was so upset, we had to cut the questioning short."

Although disappointed, Webster police had one more possibility. The night of the attack, the police found a second witness, a clerk at the Stop & Go who'd just happened to walk out to the Dumpster with a bag of garbage while Sapaugh was inside getting change. The clerk gave a nearly identical account of the man she'd seen standing next to his truck, except for one point, describing his cowboy hat as tan not black.

As with Sapaugh, Dietrich first had the woman describe what she remembered, then put her under hypnosis. This time an additional detail did emerge, that the man wore a gold-nugget pinkie ring. While interesting, that clue gave little more to go on.

In June, a month after her abduction, the Sapaugh kidnapping case was classified as inactive with no leads.

Two months later on August 17, seventeen-year-old Jessica Cain stood onstage at the Harbor Playhouse in Dickinson, seven miles from the Waffle House restaurant where Sapaugh had been abducted. The recent high-school graduate from Galveston's O'Connell High School had moved to Tiki Island, an affluent community on a thumb-shaped appendage underneath the Galveston Causeway, four years earlier. The family had lived on a farm on acreage in East Texas, but moved because her parents heard of drug running in the area. "We thought it would be safer," said Jessica's dad, C. H. Cain.

Jessica Cain, looking over her shoulder.
(Courtesy of C.H. and Suzy Cain)

A hard worker, Jessica had amassed enough college credits in high school so that in the fall she'd enter Sam Houston State University in Huntsville as a sophomore. It would
seem ironic later that her planned major was criminology.

That night at the theater, with Jessica's parents in the audience, the opening was a resounding success, earning the
cast a standing ovation. In a fifties musical revival, Jessica
played a breathless Marilyn Monroe onstage. Caught up in
the exhilaration of the evening, at one point Jessica urged
her father from the audience to do an unrehearsed jitterbug
in the aisle. "That was the way she was, impromptu," he'd
say proudly. "Jessica was bubbly, and she stood out. She attracted attention." Flushed with excitement, wanting to celebrate with her friends, after the performance Jessica asked
her parents if she could attend a cast party at a nearby Bennigan's restaurant. C. H. and his wife, Suzy, gave permission. Most nights Jessica's curfew was midnight, but this
was a special occasion, and Suzy instructed their daughter

to be home by one thirty. The last thing Jessica said to C. H. was, "I love you, Daddy."

From the restaurant that evening, the cast left for the apartment of one of the members. It was after 1:00 A.M. when Jessica told a friend she was tired, not feeling well, and she wanted to go home. Jessica had left her ride, her father's 1992 Ford pickup, at the Bennigan's. At five-foot-four and 140 pounds, Jessica had a fair complexion, a heart-shaped face, medium brown, chin-length hair, and blue eyes. In the restaurant parking lot, the friends who dropped her off saw her get in her truck and pull out onto the road, then drive toward her home.

At the house, Jessica's dad had gone to bed, while her mother intended to stay up and wait for their daughter. At some point, however, Suzy dozed off. When she awoke about two thirty and Jessica wasn't home, Suzy woke up C. H. It wasn't like Jessica, a good kid who followed directions, to be so late. "I immediately panicked," he said.

The first thing C. H., a program manager for Exxon, did was to drive the area, circling back to the theater, the Bennigan's, the places he thought his daughter might be. When he didn't find her, he kept looking. It was about four that morning when he spotted the pickup truck about four miles from the house, on the shoulder of I-45's southbound feeder lane, where the interstate ran through the small town of La Marque, pointed south as if Jessica had been on her way home. When he pulled over, C. H. Cain found the pickup locked, Jessica's wallet, keys, and driver's license on the seat. There were no signs of a robbery.

An odd coincidence was that the Cain family's truck wasn't far from the spot—across the highway—where eleven years earlier Shelley Sikes's blue Ford Pinto had been found mired in the mud. That was the only connection, however, since Sikes's kidnappers, Gerald Pieter Zwarst and John Robert King, couldn't be suspects. Both remained in Texas prisons serving life sentences for aggravated kidnapping.

On this night, police responded fairly quickly, and C. H. explained that Jessica was a responsible young woman, one who knew that the roads could be dangerous. "She drove with the doors locked," he said. With the police, C. H. stressed that his daughter wouldn't have stopped for just anyone. "She had a mobile phone, but not with her that night."

In the days that followed, Jessica's parents reeled from the knowledge that their daughter was missing. "We were in shock, disbelief," said C. H. "We didn't see how it was possible." Ironically, earlier that summer, the Cains had watched the extensive news coverage of the search for Laura Smither, and when Laura's body was found, C. H. cried, wondering how anyone could abduct a child. "We never thought it could happen to us," he said.

On the news the following days, Jessica Cain's parents pleaded with her captor and begged their daughter not to give up. But there were no signs of Jessica. As they had for so many others, thousands of those who lived in the small towns around I-45 banded together, mounting searches. Among them were familiar names and faces from other area tragedies. Bob and Gay Smither counseled the Cains, shoring up their own pain to give them support, and Shelley Sikes's dad, Eddie, and Laura Miller's dad, Tim, helped with the search. Years later, Tim Miller would recall thinking at the time that the whole world must have gone crazy for so many girls to be taken from their families.

Leads were followed, but to no avail, and after approximately two weeks, the searches thinned out, then eventually stopped.

In the bulletins circulated to media about the case, police mentioned two vehicles seen that night, ones that might be connected with the abduction. One was a red Isuzu Amigo, the other a full-sized, light-colored truck with a toolbox on the back bed and lights across the top.

The nineties were turning into another bloody decade in the far southern reaches of Houston. Perhaps few understood how bloody until an article ran in the *Houston Chronicle* on Sunday, September 21, 1997, the month after Jessica Cain's disappearance. Entitled "Elusive Answers," it said the Smither and Cain cases were reminders that many young girls had disappeared and been murdered in the area in the previous decades, dating all the way back to the eleven girls who'd died in and around Galveston in the 1970s. When asked for a comment, Krystal Baker's mom, Jeanie, said, "This could happen to anyone's child."

Accompanying it, the *Chronicle* published the first "Mysteries along I-45" chart, with photos of the girls and details from their abductions. It wasn't that in other parts of the city and across the nation girls, boys, women, and men didn't disappear. It was that this particular chunk of the Gulf Coast appeared to have more than its share of such tragedies, and too many of the cases remained unsolved.

Why? "Get murdered in Dallas, Chicago, inside Houston, and you're dealing with cops who know how to work murders. In these small towns, they see them so rarely, they're over their heads," a seasoned prosecutor said with a frown one afternoon, shaking his head in regret. "These are small agencies, some of the cops have big egos, and the cases cross jurisdictions. It's not unusual for an investigator to guard his cases and not cooperate with other cops from other agencies. That means the folks investigating don't always talk. And that hurts the effort. It can be fatal to an investigation."

In hindsight, it was a cop who did make the effort, one who got in her car and drove to another small town to compare notes, who made a difference.

As the horror unfolded in 1997, Sue Dietrich left her slot as a detective at Alvin P.D. to sign on as police chief of Jessica Cain's hometown, Tiki Island. It was in that capacity on October 3, that Dietrich drove to Friendswood P.D. to chat with her counterpart there, Jared Stout. It was a friendly call, just checking in with the chief of a nearby jurisdiction. Afterward, something interesting happened. "We were talking, and the Smither case came up. He told me about this guy, his prime suspect. Chief Stout was frustrated that they hadn't made an arrest. We talked for a while, and I left. I honestly didn't think a lot more about it. But then I woke up in the middle of the night. I literally sat up in bed and thought, *I wonder if that's the guy*? I thought about the physical description Stout had given me of his suspect and the guy's pickup, and suddenly I remembered that May, and what Sandra Sapaugh told me about the man who had abducted her. The descriptions were so similar, that I picked up the phone and called Friendswood and told a detective that maybe they should compare notes with Webster P.D."

A 1997 photo taken in Houston of William Lewis Reece. *(Trial exhibit)*

The man Stout described to Sue Dietrich was an ex-con, a paroled sex offender from Oklahoma, William Lewis "Bill" Reece, the prime suspect in the Smither case. On the morning of Laura Smither's disappearance, Reece was on his second day on the job as a bulldozer operator at the subdivision under construction just down the road from the Smithers' home. He'd only paroled out of an Oklahoma jail six months earlier after serving time for forcible oral sodomy, abduction, and rape. At about the time Laura set off on her run that morning, Reece drove down the same road after being released from work because of the impending rain.

Within days of Laura's disappearance, Reece had been

questioned, but no solid evidence emerged to peg him as her killer. What spurred Dietrich's memory and led her to recall the Sapaugh case was Reece's appearance, his height close to the man Sapaugh described, protruding bags under his eyes, a mustache, and a receding hairline. And then there was Reece's truck. It matched Sapaugh's description: a white Ford dually diesel with an aluminum toolbox on the back and a black pinstripe down the side. It also resembled the description of the truck seen on the night Jessica Cain disappeared, including the amber running lights across the top.

As Dietrich thought about the similarities, she wondered, if it was Reece who pulled Cain over that night, could the amber running lights have tricked the teenager into thinking she was being stopped by a police officer? "Her parents were adamant that she wouldn't pull over for just anyone," said Dietrich. "I may never know for sure, but I could picture how it could have happened."

A mug shot of William Reece and an evidence photo of the truck he drove. *(Courtesy of the Harris County Sheriff's Office and a trial exhibit)*

By the time Reece was brought in for questioning in Webster that fall, he had an attorney at his side. His mustache had been shaved off, and rather than an aluminum toolbox on the pickup's bed, he'd installed a cowboy camper. The reason he'd been contacted, the officers explained, was to see if he'd be willing to cooperate by participating in a lineup. Reece and his lawyer declined, but the possibility didn't appear to bother the ex-con, as he laughed and joked with the officers, as if the prospect of standing in a lineup wasn't troubling. Not dissuaded, the next day the officers brought a photo lineup to Sandra Sapaugh that included Bill Reece's picture. "That's him," she said, pointing at Reece's photo. "That's the man."

Rough around the edges with a slow country drawl, Reece had grown up on a farm in Yukon, Oklahoma. He'd dropped out of high school in the ninth grade and made money driving trucks, working construction and on rodeos and ranches as a farrier, shoeing horses. He'd married a decade earlier, but that ended in divorce after he'd spent much of the marriage in an Oklahoma prison. Looking at Reece's record, there were similarities between his prior offenses and Sapaugh's abduction. He'd held one of the Oklahoma victims at knifepoint, and one of the women had been abducted along the side of a highway. Her car had broken down, and Reece, just like the assailant in the Sapaugh case, acted as if he were a Good Samaritan, stopping to render aid.

In the early-morning hours of October 16, 1997, police surrounded William Reece's run-down apartment on Fauna Street not far from Hobby Airport south of downtown Houston. They had a warrant signed by a judge for his arrest and search warrants for his home and truck. Reece came quietly. Inside the apartment, officers photographed a black cowboy hat like the one Sapaugh described on her assailant the first time she saw him, at the convenience store. Later, when the truck was inspected, they entered into evidence two knives, including a switchblade-type knife discovered in the pocket of the driver's-side door.

Once Reece was under arrest, he was transported to Houston P.D.'s Southeast Command Center. Sandra Sapaugh waited. In a small room behind one-way glass, accompanied by Reece's attorney, a representative from the Harris County

District Attorney's Office, and an officer from Webster P.D., Sapaugh watched through a one-way mirror as five men filed into the adjacent viewing room. The officer would later say that Sapaugh's eyes locked onto Reece the moment he entered. All the men were instructed to repeat a phrase the kidnapper had uttered, "Stay down, bitch!"

"Number four," Sapaugh said, identifying Reece as the man she'd risked her life to escape that night. "That's him."

As soon as Reece's name hit the newspapers, tips came into Webster and Friendswood P.D., from women who'd encountered him in Houston. Many talked of the way Reece looked at them, how uncomfortable it made them feel. One call was from the Diamond B. Ranch in Friendswood, not far from the Smither house, where Reece shoed horses. The ranch's owner said he had to watch Reece carefully because young women who boarded their horses there complained the farrier gave them unwanted attention.

Something else came up when the caller relayed Reece's reputation at the ranch; four days after Jessica Cain disappeared, Bill Reece did something very strange. Without being asked to, he used his bulldozer to move a large manure pile on the ranch. That spurred investigators to bring in cadaver dogs and equipment to search the pile. Fighting rain, they worked for two days, finding nothing but not abating suspicions that somehow the manure pile was involved in Jessica's disappearance.

The same day as the search at the ranch, Chief Stout in Friendswood went public with his suspicions, announcing that his main suspect in the Smither case was under arrest in Harris County for aggravated kidnapping. Before long, reporters matched up the information, and the news hit the front page of papers across Texas: Stout had a person of interest in the Smither case, and his name was William Lewis Reece.

Not one to shy away from the publicity, Reece granted his own interviews from jail, telling the press that he wasn't the man. "It's a crock," he said, in his slow Oklahoma drawl. "They need someone. They don't have anyone. I know it's not me. They have nothing. They know they have nothing . . . I'm not the kind of person to kill. I would never hurt kids . . . The real killer is still out there."

Yet there was some fascinating evidence uncovered during the searches of Bill Reece's apartment and truck. The state lab analyzed fibers taken from an afghan throw found on the back of his couch and from the truck's floor mats. In both cases, the samples were consistent with fibers recovered from the only clothing still on her body the day Laura's remains were found, her tan socks.

Longtime prosecutors Ted Wilson and Donna Goode Cameron.
(Courtesy of Kathryn Casey)

"If we'd had the evidence to go after Bill Reece for Laura Smither's murder, we would have done it," retired prosecutor Ted Wilson said. It had been fifteen years since Reece's trial, but Wilson bristled at any suggestion that he could have charged Reece with Smither's murder. He was in the office of his second chair on the case, Donna Goode Cameron, who had also left Harris County but landed in Galveston, where she was the district attorney's second-in-command, the office's first assistant. Both Cameron and Wilson were affable, and they talked candidly about William Reece's 1998 trial for the kidnapping of Sandra Sapaugh. Like two tested warriors who've fought the hard battles, they looked back on those days with pride and a sense of what was accomplished, along with perhaps a sadness about what remained undone. "The Smithers believe that Bill Reece murdered Laura, and they think we should have tried him for that, but that wasn't our best case," said Wilson. "It never seemed to get any better for us than that he was in the area."

"We never got to the point where we thought we could prove it beyond a reasonable doubt," agreed Cameron.

Wilson looked at Cameron and frowned, as if revisiting a painful decision. "We had witnesses in the kidnapping case. We had to live with the evidence we had."

Under the best of circumstances, charging Reece with Laura Smither's murder admittedly wasn't the tightest of cases. After all, no one saw Reece with the girl; not a single witness came forward. Those fibers, the ones from Reece's truck floor mat and afghan that matched strands found on Laura Smither's socks? Well, Ted Wilson said it wasn't enough to be conclusive. "We had somebody run the numbers," said Wilson. "We couldn't prove that those fibers could only have come from William Reece's truck. That wasn't possible."

That didn't mean that Wilson and Cameron didn't try. There were bruises documented on Laura's body, and that resulted in speculation that they could have been bite marks. William Reece had distinctive teeth. The front ones splayed out, gaping in the front. A court order secured a dental impression of his teeth for comparison. The results didn't offer any insight. In fact, the experts later doubted that the bruises were even bite marks.

"Could William Reece have murdered Laura Smither? Yes. He was capable of it," said Wilson. "But the waters got muddied for a lot of reasons."

In the spring of 1998, the public became aware of how muddied the Smither case had become. There'd been an error, the kind that can fatally wound an investigation, permanently relegating it to a cold-case file. The scene was the Harris County Morgue. There, Laura's sad remains were improperly handled. The result: hairs were inadvertently transferred to Laura's corpse from another body autopsied in the morgue, another murder victim. Complicating the matter further, the assistant medical examiner who did the autopsy refused to conclusively attribute the hairs to contamination.

At the time the morgue's mistake hit news outlets, reports of the disappointing turn in the Smither case rocked Houston. After such an effort to find Laura, with so many identifying with the family and all they'd suffered, the criticism of the ME's Office from politicians, law enforcement, even folks on the street was scathing. If Wilson pursued Reece for Laura's murder, the ineptitude of the morgue's staff gifted any good defense attorney assigned to the case with a plateful of reasonable doubt to serve potential jurors.

Yet the Sapaugh case wasn't a slam-dunk either. There were potential complications. The first one, said Cameron, was "would anyone care?"

The problems were multiple. Her profession, a topless dancer, invited scrutiny, and the prosecutors worried about how Sapaugh would hold up on the stand. Cameron wondered if some jurors might secretly hold her job against Sapaugh. Wilson was less worried than Cameron. "I didn't care if she danced topless, and I didn't think a jury would either," he said. "If you're kidnapped at knifepoint and have to roll out of a car on I-45, we're in your corner."

As the trial approached, Wilson and Cameron reached out to Reece's two victims in Oklahoma, the women he'd been convicted of sexually assaulting. The prosecutors believed they should be able to present the cases to the jury, based on the similarities to the Sapaugh kidnapping. "Neither one would come. They refused. They were still deathly afraid of Bill Reece," said Cameron.

Preparing for trial, Reece's defense attorney brought motions before the judge for multiple reasons, one of which was a request to bar Gay and Bob Smither from the courtroom. They, understandably, wanted to be there, to look in the eye the man they suspected murdered their daughter, to hear the evidence, and perhaps to hear him be convicted and sentenced by a jury. Anthony Osso, a highly regarded Houston attorney who'd been assigned to represent Reece, however, insisted that some jurors might recognize Laura's parents, and that by their presence, they could taint the trial with suspicion of Reece's involvement in Laura's murder. The judge ruled that the courtroom was open to the public, and the Smithers wouldn't be kept out.

At the same time, Jessica Cain's parents had no plans to attend. On a Geraldo show that aired while Reece awaited trial, they said they didn't believe he was Jessica's abductor. They believed their daughter had been taken and was still alive and was being held captive. On the program, they pleaded with whoever kidnapped her. "I pray that she'll return home, because her daddy and I still want her . . . we want her back home," Suzy Cain said. When asked what they would tell their daughter, she said, "Never give up."

"An abduction is every woman's worst nightmare," Ted Wilson said in his opening statement on April 29, 1998, day one of the Reece trial. ". . . It's more than a nightmare" to Sandra Sapaugh. "Because it wasn't a dream . . . The nightmare . . . became a reality for her . . . She had to make a decision whether to risk her life to save it."

In the audience, the Smithers watched along with a packed courtroom filled with reporters and curious onlookers. The first witness on the stand was the initial officer on the scene that night at the Waffle House, who testified that

Sapaugh was injured "head to toe" and in shock. From the beginning, the man said, the victim had been consistent in her description of her attacker and his truck, even offering such small details as that the truck had manual cranks for the windows and a mounted cell phone. But some of the details, Osso pointed out, didn't match Reece's dually truck. For instance, it had an automatic transmission not a manual one, as Sapaugh described, and the interior seats were blue, not black. Would the jurors find the discrepancies troublesome?

When Donna Cameron questioned Minerva Torres, the twenty-six-year-old described in detail the night her nephew cried as she rescued a bruised and barefoot woman on I-45. How many passersby would have stopped in the darkness? How many would have instead trounced on the accelerator and driven off? If she had, what would have happened to Sapaugh? Torres had seen the backup lights on the white dually. Was the man intending to pursue and reclaim his victim?

On the witness stand, Sandra Sapaugh appeared vulnerable and ill at ease. She wasn't used to such questioning. When she described her family, she mentioned that she now had three children, including a three-month-old infant. At the time of her abduction, the night she jumped out of the truck, Sapaugh didn't yet know it, but she was pregnant.

The questions Donna Cameron worried about had to be asked. What did Sapaugh do for a living? Then and since, she worked as a topless dancer. "Have you ever been arrested for anything?" Ted Wilson asked.

"No," Sapaugh answered. When asked if she saw the man who kidnapped her in the courtroom, she pointed at Reece, wearing a blue suit in his seat beside Osso. "Yes. That's him."

"May the record reflect that William Reece has been identified by the witness," Wilson said. Turning to Sapaugh, he asked, "Were you scared?"

"Yes," she answered.

As the trial progressed, Osso was vigilant, objecting when Sapaugh pointed out things inside the truck she remembered from her abduction, like a notepad with a cord hanging from it. And he hammered on any inconsistencies, questioning if Reece had a mounted cell phone in his truck at the time of the abduction. The truck didn't have manual window handles in the front, as Sapaugh had said. Couldn't that mean she'd been wrong about the truck and man she'd identified? Wilson pointed out with Sapaugh on the stand that Reece's truck had power windows in the front but cranks in the backseat, suggesting that may have been what Sapaugh saw in the darkness.

Much of the testimony centered on the composite, which became state's exhibit number 66. Did Sapaugh tell the officer who drew it that the man had a beard? She answered that she hadn't, and that the darkness around the cheeks and chin were an indication of stubble. In her testimony, she described her abductor's front teeth as crooked, but was that what she'd said earlier? Osso suggested it wasn't, but Sapaugh disagreed. She insisted she'd had a good look at the man, and he was Bill Reece. Osso proposed that perhaps she'd been maneuvered into her testimony by overzealous officers who'd led her to pick Reece from the lineup. Sapaugh denied that it was true, and swore that it was Reece's face she remembered glaring at her that night in the truck.

Why did she decide to jump? Wilson inquired.

"If he was going to kill me, I would just kill myself," Sapaugh testified. Osso stood up to object.

Sandra Sapaugh remained on the stand for much of the next day. Repeatedly, the questions came back to her first statements and what she remembered, how it all compared with the evidence, especially the photos taken of William Reece's truck. Next to his attorney, Reece sat quietly, often his face a blank but at times appearing to jeer at Sapaugh. Osso wanted to know if Sapaugh's judgment could have been influenced. Had she been drinking that night? She denied that she'd had any alcohol, and a doctor later testified that the reading of .007 on her medical records was low enough that it could have resulted from the use of an alcohol swab when her blood was drawn.

Throughout the trial, as he fought for his client, Anthony Osso's attack was two-pronged: pointing out what he referred to as inconsistencies in Sapaugh's statements and the evidence, and secondly what he labeled as a rush to judgment spurred on by suspicions his client was guilty of another crime, Laura Smither's murder.

While there'd been much attention paid to keeping the Smither case out of the courtroom, Osso brought it in, arguing that it had poisoned the trial. The suspicion surrounding Reece regarding Laura Smither's murder became an explanation for why the ex-con was targeted in the Sapaugh abduction. Police couldn't gather enough evidence to charge Reece for Laura's death, so they set him up on the kidnapping charge. Sandra Sapaugh, Osso suggested, had been manipulated into naming Reece as her attacker.

With three talented attorneys in the courtroom, the battle was fierce. Bench conferences abounded as they fought over what would and wouldn't be allowed into evidence, which witnesses could and could not testify.

"My client doesn't have loose skin, does he?" Osso asked, repeating the description Sapaugh gave to police the night of the attack.

But Reece was in the courtroom, sitting within the jurors' view with his saggy eyes. "Yes, he does," Sapaugh countered.

The Stop & Go clerk pointed to Reece, and she, too, identified him as the man with the white dually in the parking lot that night. She noticed the gold-nugget pinkie ring, one the prosecutors had pictures of on Reece's finger.

Back and forth the attorneys argued. Osso pointing out that Reece had a cowboy camper not a shiny aluminum toolbox on the back of his truck, to which Wilson produced a witness who testified that Reece had repeatedly changed the truck, and that at various times it had just such a toolbox.

Sue Dietrich didn't take the stand until the trial's second week, and after Wilson led her through her testimony, Osso attacked her credentials, suggesting that perhaps she led Sapaugh and used her to entrap his client. Wasn't Dietrich simply trying to help Chief Stout in Friendswood make a case against Reece for Laura Smither's murder? "You and Chief Stout needed to find a way," said Osso. Dietrich denied that was true, contending that Sapaugh's description of the man remained the same before the hypnosis and after.

When Osso took over the courtroom, he presented forensic experts who testified that no hair or fibers from Sapaugh were found in Reece's truck, nor any of her fingerprints. The reverse was also true, that no fibers from Reece's truck had been found on the clothing Sapaugh wore that night. But Wilson recounted all that had happened to the victim, from rolling on the pavement, getting in and out of Torres's car, the ambulance, onto the gurney at the hospital, suggesting evidence could have been lost. When it came to those two knives, the state's expert hadn't been able to prove that either had been used to puncture the tire on Sapaugh's minivan. "That doesn't mean that they weren't used," the man insisted.

Finally, Sapaugh had testified that her attacker came at her from behind with the knife on his left hand, but Bill Reece's sister took the stand and testified that her brother was right-handed. On and on the arguments raged, while in the audience Bob and Gay Smither watched, wondering if the man seated in the courtroom with them had murdered their daughter.

Donna Cameron began closing arguments asking, "Does a topless dancer deserve to be picked up off the street at knifepoint and be automatically disbelieved and her testimony discarded?" Rather, Sapaugh was a nineteen-year-old single mother, one who'd dropped out of school to raise her children and was making her living the only way she knew how. But what about Bill Reece? Cameron pointed out that he fit the description, that he looked like the composite, and that his truck was a nearly identical match to the accounts given by all three eyewitnesses: Sapaugh, Torres, and the convenience-store clerk. Reece carried knives with him, and he had a history of sexual assault.

"Inconsistencies are significant," Anthony Osso countered, maintaining the identification of Reece was flawed. "He's the wrong guy!" There wasn't "one iota" of physical evidence tying Reece to the case, and "misidentification is a major problem." It all boiled down to a lack of evidence, in Osso's argument, and the state hadn't proven its case beyond a reasonable doubt.

Ironically it was Ted Wilson who tried to remove the shadow of Laura Smither from the courtroom, when he pointed out in his closing statement that the Smither case wasn't the one the jury was charged to decide. All they had to consider, he said, was whether the three eyewitnesses were telling the truth. That night in the Waffle House parking lot, William Reece had no way of knowing what Sandra Sapaugh did for a living, Wilson maintained. What Reece saw was a woman with children's clothing in her van, a young mother. And he abducted her at knifepoint. If Sapaugh hadn't gotten everything right, it was amazing how much detail she'd remembered.

"If someone holds a knife to you for six to ten minutes, and you thought he was going to kill you, you would never forget him," Wilson argued. "Somebody has got to stop this guy!"

Six hours later, the jurors returned with a conviction. Bill Reece was guilty of aggravated kidnapping.

Although fear kept them from testifying earlier, now that they knew the man who'd attacked them was going to prison, the two women Reece had been convicted of assaulting in Oklahoma summoned their courage to take the stand during the sentencing phase.

The first was a young wife who in April 1986 had been

a nineteen-year-old college student whose Ford Mustang broke down along a highway in a driving rain. Bill Reece pulled over in his eighteen-wheeler, smiled at her, and offered her a ride. She made the unfortunate decision of accepting and climbed into the truck.

The daughter of a police officer described how the saggy-eyed truck driver pulled a knife on her in the truck's cab while they were parked in a grocery-store lot. "I knew he was going to kill me," she said.

When she asked him why he was "doing this," he answered, "I'm crazy."

Inexplicably, Reece duct taped the girl's hands, then pledged his love, saying that he wanted to marry her. "I had to get out of there somehow," she said. And so she played along, claiming she returned his affection. Yet he wasn't about to give her any freedom. In response, Reece forced her into a sleeping bag, zipping it around her like a cocoon. They ended up in a distribution-center parking lot. He had her in the truck's sleeper compartment, where he first tried to undress her. She fought, and he ended up forcing her to perform oral sex. "I thought he was going to rape me. I thought he was going to kill me. I thought he was sick," the woman said on the stand.

She cajoled him into believing that she would marry him and be with him, and he finally released her. Reece was arrested that same afternoon.

"Had you ever been that scared before in your life?" Donna Cameron asked.

"Never," the woman answered.

The second woman testified that Reece was so out of control in Oklahoma that year that one month later, while under suspicion in the first case, he climbed in through the window and raped her, while her babysitter and child slept in the next room. She insisted that she didn't know Bill Reece and had never seen him before that night. She woke up thinking her husband had come home, but it was Reece straddling her, naked, ripping her clothes off, putting his hand to her throat and pushing her down on the bed, while he kneed her between the legs. When she tried to scream, he started to choke her. "If you wake up anyone, I'll kill you," he threatened.

In his closing, Anthony Osso attempted to distance the Sapaugh case from what the jurors had just heard by arguing that the two Oklahoma women had nothing in common with Sandra Sapaugh. Again, he brought up the inconsistencies in the description of the truck, attempting to plant a seed of doubt regarding his client's guilt. And he reminded the jurors that they weren't to consider the Smither case, in which Reece had never been charged.

Once Osso sat down, Ted Wilson rose to address the jury.

"Life isn't always fair," he said, referring to the two women Reece victimized in Oklahoma. They'd done nothing wrong, yet had suffered and would always bear the scars from the attacks. They didn't deserve what had happened to them. In those cases, Reece served sentences that kept him in prison for a decade, but the women "had gotten life."

After his release, Reece left prison and Oklahoma, moving to Houston. Sandra Sapaugh didn't deserve what had happened to her either. "Back at it again, he gets caught again," said Wilson. "And he stands before you asking for mercy . . . This man has shown what he's made of. This man has shown that he's driven to kidnapping and abusing women . . . He is a predator . . . William Lewis Reece needs to be stopped, and you can stop him."

Ted Wilson asked the jury to put William Reece away for life. Instead, they came back with a sixty-year sentence, one that would make him first eligible for parole in 2027, at the age of sixty-eight. "We were happy with that," said Wilson.

After the trial, Bill Reece was shuttled off to a Texas prison while Gay and Bob Smither struggled to find closure.

The following year, in 1999, the Smithers filed a wrongful death suit against Reece for their daughter's death. They were awarded $110 million in a default judgment, when Reece didn't defend himself. "We knew we'd never see a penny. It wasn't about money," said Gay. "But it was all we could do to make him accountable for Laura's murder."

Finally, five years after Laura died, Gay and Bob decided they had no choice. "We had to go on with our lives, if not for ourselves, for our son." The first step was to clean out Laura's bedroom. The process went on over a period of days, as they donated many of Laura's possessions and gifted others to her friends. But there were things Gay didn't know what to do with, including items from the recovery-site memorial and Laura's more intimate clothing. "We decided we'd have a sacramental fire," said Gay.

The blaze was lit in the backyard, and over a day they slowly deposited Laura's things into it, precious items that they were in a sense offering up to the heavens. Their son, David, helped, and so did friends. One after another, they freed Laura's spirit, releasing it in small clouds of gray smoke. It wasn't that it didn't hurt but that it had to be done. Then, when they were finished, in the living room Bob and Gay took down Laura's picture and hung a framed statuette of a ballerina, placing figurines of angels beneath it. They would never forget their daughter, but they had to find a way to endure. And for David, it would mean that he

The memorial to Laura in the Smithers' home. *(Courtesy of Kathryn Casey)*

wouldn't be confronted with the loss every time he walked through the front door.

In time, they began to heal.

In the year that followed, drawn by all they'd suffered, knowing the pain of other families in their situation, the Smithers officially founded the Laura Recovery Center, a nonprofit dedicated to helping communities search for the missing. They used the notes they made during the search for Laura to draw up a handbook, detailing how to harness a community to help law enforcement. It was something they felt called to do. Since then, the Center has assisted in thousands of searches. "We do this in Laura's memory," said Gay. "We do this because it's something we can do."

Yet that day in their living room as we talked about their lost daughter, Gay and Bob Smither made it clear that there was something more they wanted, the one thing they viewed as perhaps having the power to bring some justice. "We still want to see Bill Reece prosecuted for Laura's murder," said Bob, his jaw stern and his gaze rock hard. "We will never know until there's a trial. We want our day in court."

Chapter 17

"I Am Not a Serial Killer"
William Lewis Reece

**The Ellis Unit
Huntsville, Texas**

William Lewis Reece.
*(Courtesy of the Texas
Department of
Criminal Justice)*

It was a breezy, blue-sky mid-March day, picture-perfect, yet I fought a nagging unease on the drive to Huntsville, Texas, ninety minutes north of Houston. My destination was the Texas Department of Criminal Justice's Ellis Unit, where I had a 1:00 P.M. interview scheduled with William Lewis Reece, a man many suspected was a serial killer.

In the time I'd been working on this book, I frequently heard Reece's name; everyone from Sue Dietrich to an FBI profiler, Bob and Gay Smither, the police officers I interviewed and a seasoned prosecutor told me they considered Reece the primary suspect in Laura Smither's murder. There was also speculation that his white Ford dually could have been the vehicle seen on the night Jessica Cain disappeared, her pickup truck found on the I-45 feeder road after she left a theater-cast party.

Yet some investigators, primarily in the Cain case, while not ruling out Reece, saw other possibilities.

For instance, before his death in 2001, private investigator Willie Payne, hired by Jessica's parents, expressed interest in a League City mechanic named Jonathan David Drew, serving a life sentence in a Texas prison for the November 1998 murder of a Houston waitress. What caught Payne's attention and suggested Drew might be involved in the Cain case was that Drew was known to have been in the area at the time. He also had a red Amigo, matching the description of one of the vehicles on the scene the night Jessica disappeared.

Tiffany Dobry Johnston's mother considered Bill Reece a friend.
(Courtesy of Kathy Dobry)

Still, Reece remained not only a viable suspect in the Laura Smither and Jessica Cain cases, but also in at least one Oklahoma murder: that of Tiffany Dobry Johnston, abducted from the Sunshine Car Wash in Bethany, Oklahoma. At the time, Tiffany was a nineteen-year-old newlywed, one who worked two jobs to help pay the bills and planned to attend Oklahoma State University in the fall. The date of her disappearance was July 26, 1997, a little more than three months after Laura Smither's murder and three weeks before Jessica Cain vanished.

What was particularly interesting in the Johnston case was that Bill Reece had a link to the victim. "I knew Billy," said Kathy Dobry, Tiffany's mother. "I knew his family."

Dobry had her ironing done by Reece's mother, who ran a small laundry service out of her home. While Dobry knew Reece had been in prison, she said that at the time she didn't know why. "His mom never said, but I had the impression it was drugs or something. I didn't know it was sex crimes."

Did Tiffany know Reece?

Kathy wasn't sure. Her older daughter accompanied her to drop off ironing at the Reece house on occasion, and Bill Reece had been home at the time. But Kathy hadn't taken Tiffany, her younger daughter, there. Yet Kathy wondered if Reece could have seen her with Tiffany, maybe in a store or just around town. During the time Kathy knew him, she thought of Bill Reece as a friend. She even introduced him to her grandchildren and asked him to deliver something to her older daughter's house. "If I'd known he was a sex offender, I wouldn't have done that," Kathy insists.

On the day Tiffany vanished, her car sat abandoned at the car wash for hours before it was noticed. Like the Jessica Cain case, Tiffany's car was found with her wallet and money inside. In the Johnston case, the body was found quickly, the next day, discarded along the side of a road. Like Laura Smither, Tiffany was strangled.

Early on, police in Oklahoma focused on Reece as a prime suspect. That suspicion never faded.

Although she heard he was a suspect, Kathy Dobry doubted the accusations against Bill Reece. She couldn't fathom that someone she considered a friend would be cold-hearted enough to murder her daughter. Then there were the assurances Reece's mom gave her. "She told me Billy wasn't even in Oklahoma at the time. He was in Houston."

In fact, just days after Tiffany's murder, Reece's mother called Kathy Dobry offering condolences. During that call, Mrs. Reece claimed that police were unfairly targeting her son. Bill was so upset by the unfair accusations, the old woman said that he'd be calling Dobry to talk to her. Not long after, the phone rang again. This time Bill Reece personally told Kathy that he wasn't in Oklahoma but in

Houston on the day Tiffany was abducted. "I didn't kill your daughter," he insisted.

Despite all the conjecture about what William Lewis Reece might or might not have been guilty of, the man I was scheduled to talk to, TDCJ inmate number 00831080, had never been charged with or convicted of a murder. He was serving time in Texas on two counts. The first was theft. One of the investigators on the Smither case wondered how an ex-con recently out of prison bought a bulldozer, an expensive piece of equipment. It turned out that Reece hadn't. The bulldozer Reece used as a contract construction worker was stolen. The second, of course, was the sixty years a jury handed down for aggravated kidnapping in Sandra Sapaugh's abduction.

Was Reece one of the killers who'd made the I-45 area their hunting ground? That was an unanswered question.

My apprehension subsided by the time I sat across from Reece. He appeared thinner than in the prison photo I'd been given, looking a bit drawn. I didn't know if it was true, but I heard that he'd been ill. Clean-shaven, his once-shaggy mop of dark blond hair had thinned. Cut short, he had it skinned back. His complexion had faded as well, a prison pale that looked vaguely unhealthy. His eyes were a washed-out blue. I doubted that those who'd known him fifteen years earlier, at the time of his arrest, would have recognized him. But then, prison and time tended to do that to inmates. It had been my experience that they rarely aged well. The only features that reminded me of the preprison Reece I'd seen on television interviews were his splayed-out, remarkably crooked front teeth, the prominent bags under his eyes, and his continual smirk. Although I'd said nothing that could be at all considered amusing, Reece appeared entertained by my visit.

"How much, uh . . . do I get anything out of this?" he asked. That wasn't an unusual question, but rarely had I heard it so quickly in an interview.

"I don't pay for interviews. I don't pay sources," I said. "What you get is that you get to tell your side of the story. I'm here to listen to anything you'd like to tell me."

At first, it appeared that wasn't enough. "I can't help then," he said, his lips curling into a jeer. He pointed at a group of large envelopes he had on the desk in front of him. "See, I've got everything right here. I've got the Innocence Project working on this. The FBI done cleared me."

"Did you kill Laura Smither?" I asked.

"No."

"What about Jessica Cain?"

He turned away, shaking his head, looking at me warily out of the corners of his eyes. "Who's that?"

As we talked, he claimed he'd never heard of Jessica although investigators I interviewed said they'd made it known to him that he was a suspect in the case. Pam Mitchell, the lead detective on the Cain case, made repeated requests to interview him.

"If they had what they said they'd had . . ." he said, not finishing his sentence. "You see they lied to the public . . . If they had evidence against me, wouldn't they have charged me?"

"There are people who say you're a serial killer, Bill," I said.

"I am not a serial killer," he maintained. "The people who say that, they'll say anything. And I didn't kill that little girl."

"Why do you think so many people think you murdered Laura Smither?"

"I don't care," he said. "There's not a damn thing that links me to anything." When I asked about the fiber evidence—the floor mat and afghan fibers on Laura's socks that reportedly matched samples from his truck and house—he brushed it off, as if it was impossible and not to be considered.

Although early on he'd made motions as if he were going to leave when I refused to pay him, Reece leaned forward in his chair and opened his envelopes, producing copies of search warrants the Friendswood police issued at the time of

Laura's murder. They were warrants tied to other suspects. "They lied when they said I was the prime suspect," Reece said. "There were others."

What Reece didn't mention, but I had been told was that the warrants he held in his hand had been executed, and no evidence was found suggesting the other suspects were involved. The men he was referring to had all been cleared.

"And it's in here, too," he said, holding up a copy of Laura's autopsy. "It said I didn't do it either."

All the investigators I'd talked with about the Smither case, none of them had suggested anything in the medical examiner's report excluded Reece as a suspect. "Show me what you're talking about," I suggested.

Instead, Reece slipped the autopsy report back in its envelope and changed the subject. I brought it back to Laura Smither. "Do you remember what you did that day?" I asked. "The day Laura was abducted?"

"I sure do," he said. Reece then calmly recounted what he said he'd done on April 3, 1997, arriving at work at the construction site early that morning, only to leave when it began to rain. He then drove down Moore Road sometime around nine, approximately the same time Laura left the Smither house to presumably jog down that same country road.

"Did you see Laura?" I asked.

"Nope," he said.

The way Reece told it, all the evidence against him, from the fibers to a knife that was found in his truck, was all manufactured. "That knife was in my apartment on the entertainment center. Now how'd it get in my truck?" he challenged, implying it had been planted by police. "They all know I didn't do it, that nothing at all links me to that girl's murder."

"So what do you think happened here?" I asked.

"I don't care," he said, chin jutting out, defiant. "I had enough from people out there. They all know that I didn't do it."

Behind the prison partition, Reece shifted in his chair

when I asked about his recollection of the day Bob and Gay Smither confronted him in a jail visiting room, wanting to know if he'd murdered their daughter. "I told them the same thing I told you, that I didn't do it," he said, shaking his head.

He'd been an easy target, Reece said, an ex-con just out of prison on sex-crime convictions, one who'd been nearby at the time Laura disappeared. Why was so much attention focused on him? "You don't know your ass from a hole in the ground, what would you do? You got people hounding you. You got a guy who just got out of prison. Let's pin it on him," he said with a fixed, angry grin, explaining why he'd been fingered. "It's all a crock."

"Those charges in Oklahoma?"

"If you look at those, you'll see they've been reversed," he insisted. "I was acquitted of the charges."

But that, too, wasn't true. The abduction case had been returned to the court for a second trial, but it wasn't because of a lack of evidence. It was on what could be termed a technicality, the way the charge against Reece had been written. Certainly nothing that would have exonerated him. Instead, to avoid a retrial, Reece was released for time served.

"One of the girls I knew really good," he said about the women he'd been convicted of attacking in Oklahoma. In that case, he claimed rather than rape it had been consensual sex. The young mother had testified at Reece's Houston trial, however, and under oath said she and Reece weren't friends and that he'd entered her bedroom through the window while she slept.

The second case? Reece maintained he was just being a good guy, that out of concern for the young woman's welfare, he'd given her a ride when her car broke down. He'd never held her captive and forced her to have oral sex, he said, although that's what she said and what he'd been convicted of. As he talked, he often grinned and shook his head, as if it were all too much to even consider. So many were against him, and he'd been abused by the system.

At each opportunity, I brought our discussion back to Texas. "So you never saw Laura jogging down that road?"

"No," he said again.

Again I asked, "What about Jessica Cain?"

Earlier Reece had denied he even knew who Jessica was, but this time he answered differently. "I remember them asking me about that, but I thought they had someone on that . . . Some boyfriend, I don't know." When I said that there had never been an arrest and that he was the one whose name kept surfacing as a suspect, he again shook his head.

"You had a white pickup truck then, a dually with lights on the top?"

"A dually, yeah. A four-door," he confirmed. There was a light-colored truck seen that night, the one Jessica Cain vanished. When I asked if he was there, he answered, "It wasn't mine."

"You've spent nearly half of your life in prison," I commented. That wasn't an exaggeration. Between the two prison stays, the fifty-three-year-old had served twenty-five years behind bars.

"Yeah," he said. "I don't like to think about that."

While he served his time, Reece complained that the world had gone on without him. His father died in 2001 and his mother in 2005. "That's why I'm so angry. I'm in here, and I didn't do any of it."

The Smither and Cain cases weren't the ones that put Reece behind bars, but that was what I was most interested in, so I kept working the conversation back to that evidence, asking again, "What about the fibers on Laura's socks, the ones that matched your blanket?"

"I don't think they have that. I think they're making it up to say they have something," Reece contended. As for the knife that was found in his truck, he again claimed it was planted.

Why did he move the horse ranch's manure pile not long after Jessica Cain disappeared? The way Reece told it, he was just trying to be helpful. Although the owner of the ranch told police that he'd never asked to have the hill of manure moved, Reece insisted that "it was too far out in the road," blocking cars coming for a wedding at the ranch.

In Oklahoma, Reece was already charged with the forced oral sodomy of the college student he abducted off the side of the highway. It seemed particularly brazen to just six weeks later commit the second crime, where he entered through the window and raped the second woman. "He was really cool about it," the arresting officer in the first case told me. "He didn't look the least bit worried."

In Texas, it seemed to be a similar situation; Reece was already under suspicion on the Smither case when Sandra Sapaugh was abducted and, if he was involved, when Jessica Cain disappeared off the I-45 shoulder.

There was one more thing that echoed what he'd done in Oklahoma, something Reece described doing on the day Laura Smither disappeared. In Oklahoma, after he abducted the university student, Reece drove her in the eighteen-wheeler to public places, ending up at a distribution center where he was scheduled to pick up a load, acting as if he had nothing to hide. In Friendswood, shortly after leaving that morning, Reece circled back and drove past the construction site. Why? Did he want someone to see him and believe that he was alone? Was he attempting to enlist an eyewitness to tell police he didn't have a twelve-year-old girl in his truck? "My boss saw me, and I was alone in the truck," Reece told a reporter.

Of course that begged the question: Would anyone have seen Laura if she'd been bound and gagged and forced onto the backseat floor or enclosed in the toolbox on the truck bed?

Our interview continued, and again I asked Reece to describe everything he'd done that day, after he left the construction site. He responded that at the time the FBI asked if he could prove where he'd been. With a sneer, he said, "I done wrote it down for them."

Patiently, I asked him to repeat it for me.

"There were three girls I was seeing at the same time . . . Two of them's married. I went to see this one that I was seeing. She wasn't home, so I went up to Telephone Road and took a ride, went all the way near Hobby Airport to my apartment. I wasn't feeling good. Something I ate that day? I don't know; I was feeling sick. Anyway, I started washing clothes. The steering was hard to turn on my truck . . . My ex-wife called me, and I talked to her on the phone in the morning. Then I left and went to Telephone Road and 518, and this guy put a belt on my truck . . . I had a little old cow dog, an Australian shepherd with me. I stood there while he worked on my truck. Then I went back to the apartment and laid down."

According to Reece, he knew nothing about the Smither case until the next morning, when one of his three girlfriends told him about the kidnapping. "I wasn't worried about the Smither case. I knew I didn't do it." When police contacted him about the Sapaugh case, Reece said he "figured they were up to no good."

Screwing his mouth into a sarcastic frown, he scoffed at the accusations against him. "If I was their prime suspect, there'd be something," he said. "After all this time? All the tests they done and everything . . . They cut my seats up in my truck, my carpet, everything. There's nothing there."

He then talked about his truck, and that he modified it, taking off the toolbox and installing a cowboy sleeper on the pickup's bed, a compartment the size of a small mattress he could lock, large enough to camp out in on the road, or, some of those who pegged Reece as a killer pointed out, to confine a victim. A boxed-in bed with a door, and a toolbox above it. "I added that," he said defiantly.

In prison, Reece worked indoor in the factory that made pants for the guards. His job was to supervise and keep the workers' lines flowing. "I'm not in a cell. I'm in a dorm. Like a stall. It's mine. It's not bad," he boasted. "The food here is all right."

My time drawing to a close, before I left I asked again

why so many saw him as the chief suspect in the Smither
and Cain cases. "Easy out for them. They don't know who
done it or what happened. They fucked up so much, it's
unreal," he said. Referring to Laura Smither, he contended,
"I don't do little kids. I've never been convicted of anything
to do with a child."

"What kind of guy would do something like that? Kill a
young girl like Laura?" I asked.

At first, he simply leaned back in the chair and stared at
me. "He'd have to be someone who's throwed off," Reece
finally assessed. When I looked perplexed by the term, he
explained. "He'd have to be not all there."

That brought to mind the Sapaugh trial, the punishment
phase, when the first of his Oklahoma victims testified.
When she asked him why he'd abducted her, why he was
tying her up and forcing himself on her, what she said he
replied was, "I'm crazy."

As proof of his great success with women, Reece then
again brought up his ex-wife and the three women he claimed
to be seeing during the summer of 1997. "I had four girls I
was with. I didn't have time," regarding murdering Laura
Smither, abducting Jessica Cain, and kidnapping Sandra Sapaugh. For emphasis, he said it again: "I didn't have *no* time,
man. I was too busy."

"Did you carry a knife?" I asked again.

Earlier Reece had claimed that the knife had been
planted, but now he said that he did carry knives for work,
two, a small one on him and a second knife, one in his
horseshoeing box, that he kept in his truck toolbox. On the
ranches, he used it to cut back cuticles on the horses' hooves.

The guard walked past and shot me a look that said my
time had lapsed. I had to leave. As I collected my belongings, I asked, "Bill, do you feel sorry for the Smithers?"

"Yeah, I do, because the police fucked it up . . ." he told
me, his face a model of concern. "The person could be out
running around. They should have gotten the man who
done it."

In the more than a year that followed, I repeatedly asked for a follow-up interview with Bill Reece. Each time he turned down my requests. While he never agreed to see me again, Reece and I corresponded. His letters, a scrawl of half-printed, half-cursive writing across unlined paper, were often angry. Off and on, he made demands. The biggest one was that he refused to agree to another prison visit until I told him what I'd decided about his case. From the tone, it was evident that he wanted me to tell him that I believed he was an innocent man. Only then would he cooperate.

As much as I wanted to interview him in person at least one more time, to have a second opportunity to talk and see where it might lead us, I couldn't tell him that. It wasn't true.

I had reached a standstill with the Smither case. Although I believed Reece to be the probable killer, I feared that no one could ever be certain. Based on our encounters, our one interview and the letters, I doubted, if he was guilty, that he'd ever admit murdering Laura. Consistently, he'd owned up to nothing, still denying that he'd assaulted the two women in Oklahoma.

One of the final things Bill Reece said to me was, "I never killed no girls." Was he being unjustly accused? Or was Reece lying? Could he be the monster so many believed? As in so many of these cases, it felt as if I stood on quicksand, suspecting yet unsure.

Then a remarkable series of events fell into place. In late summer 2014, as I put the finishing touches on this book, Kathy Dobry, the mother of Tiffany Dobry Johnston, the newlywed Reece was suspected of murdering in Oklahoma in July 1997, called me. She had news. The investigation into her daughter's death had been reopened. When the evidence was reexamined and swabs taken at the time of Tiffany's autopsy were resubmitted to a lab, a partial DNA profile had been developed from genetic material found inside Tiffany's vagina. Although further analysis and review might be done to confirm the findings, the test results thus far indicated that the partial DNA profile was consistent with a sample taken from William Lewis Reece.

Not long after, I talked with a reliable source who confirmed what Kathy had told me. As he described it, although it was a partial not a complete profile and therefore not a conclusive match, the numbers were such that it was unlikely that the source of the DNA was anyone other than Bill Reece. The same investigator also verified that authorities now had witness statements placing Reece not in Houston, as he'd told Dobry, but in Oklahoma on the day Tiffany was murdered.

In addition, records showed that a long-distance calling card tied to Reece was used at a pay phone outside a Denny's restaurant seven miles from the car wash where Tiffany Johnston was last seen on the morning of her abduction.

For so many years, Dobry hadn't considered that Reece could have been responsible. To her, he'd always been a friend. But when she heard what investigators had uncovered, that changed. Based on this new evidence, she told me: "I think that he could have done it. I think Bill Reece murdered my daughter."

Meanwhile, I heard that with the Oklahoma news, the investigations into Laura Smither's and Jessica Cain's cases were both being reopened. Seventeen years after Laura was strangled and Jessica disappeared, there was a renewed push to find answers.

As I put this book to bed, there was the expectation that before the end of 2014 the Johnston case would be taken to a district attorney and, if the DNA evidence held up and prosecutors agreed that the case was strong, William Reece could be charged with murder. In the coming years, it seemed possible that he could again find himself in a courtroom, this time charged with murder.

Would the jury believe him if he told them what he told me? "I never killed no girls."

Epilogue

Why Here?

I began this book in the fall of 2011, and it would take three years to complete. Early on, six months into the research, I realized that it was changing me. I watched more carefully, assessed strangers with a jaundiced eye, wondered what hid below the surface. And I became fearful. Not for myself—I've lived much of my life—but for others, the children and teenagers, young men and women I saw on the street. Especially those walking alone, as Krystal Baker had been in March 1996, but even those in cars late at night, like Shelley Sikes on that tragic Memorial Day weekend in 1986.

The pressure built. In late 2012, I spent a day driving to places police call dump sites, the fields where more than forty years earlier Debbie Ackerman's, Maria Johnson's, Sharon Shaw's and Renee Johnson's bodies had been found. I wrapped up for the day by walking through the grass at the Killing Field on Calder Drive, looking at Tim Miller's sad, weather-beaten wooden cross. Around four that afternoon, I was tired and disheartened, troubled. It was difficult not to imagine what it must have been like for each of the girls, how they suffered.

Before heading home, I stopped to buy a drink at the Wendy's on Main Street in League City, a short drive from the Killing Field, a block west of I-45. I stood at the cash register paying when I noticed a teenage girl enter, perhaps thirteen or fourteen. Her long brown hair was tied in a tight ponytail, and although it was cool outside, she wore a scant T-shirt and short shorts, white tennis shoes.

Seated at a table, I rested and checked e-mail on my phone, but my eyes trailed back to the girl. She wasn't attracting attention, merely buying a hamburger and a Coke, taking the tray to a table and eating. She appeared content, unconcerned. I needed to go. If I waited much later, I'd hit Houston's crushing rush-hour traffic. But I stayed. I stayed and watched. As the girl finished her food, she grabbed her purse and left. I stood up. I felt anxious, ill at ease, as I walked out the restaurant door. She cut through the parking lot to the corner, then crossed Hobbs, the side street, before seizing on a break in the traffic to rush across Main to a gas-station convenience store.

I didn't realize at first that I'd followed her to the intersection. When I did, I stopped.

The gas station looked familiar. It was then that I recognized that it was the same convenience store where in 1983 and 1984, Heide Fye and Laura Miller were last seen alive. Until that moment, I hadn't made the connection.

The sun glared off the cars and pickup trucks. A busy street dotted with fast-food restaurants and businesses. A girl alone. The same gas station. I took a deep breath.

"Calm down," I muttered.

Logically, I understood that every day in League City, in Texas, across the nation and the world, teenage girls walk country roads and city streets. They jog like Laura Smither on the morning she disappeared. Like Jessica Cain, they drive home after a night out with friends. The vast majority arrive home safely. I knew my concern was unwarranted, but I couldn't quiet my mind. "This is crazy."

For moments, I thought about returning to my car, but I couldn't make myself. I needed to be sure that the girl was safe. I fleetingly considered running across the street and confronting her, warning her of the dangers, chastising her for going out without a friend, telling her what occurred twice at that very same location three decades earlier. *Didn't she know the dangers?* The teenager, unaware of my interest or my irrational intentions, leaned nonchalantly against the gas-station wall.

"Maybe she's waiting for someone," I whispered. "She probably is."

Moments later a car drove onto the gas-station parking lot, and the girl waved. It stopped next to her, and she disappeared inside. When the driver cut across Main Street and drove past me, I saw the teenager in the passenger seat and the profile of a middle-aged woman behind the wheel, happily chatting.

While I focused on the cases off the I-45 Mysteries Chart that occurred between 1970 and 2000 for this book, the tragedies haven't stopped. In this new millennium, five more photos and names have been added to the list. The first was Tot Harriman, a fifty-seven-year-old woman who disappeared on July 12, 2001, after leaving her son's League City home. Tot lived in Florida but wanted to buy property in the area, to be closer to family. She drove away and was never seen again. Exactly a year later to the day, twenty-three-year-old Sarah Trusty took a bike ride and didn't return home. Two weeks later, her body was found in a Texas City dike.

Terressa Vanegas was only sixteen on the night in 2006 when she walked home from a Halloween party. A man on a motorcycle discovered her body days later on the edge of a Dickinson High School practice field. That same month, the body of Amanda Nicole Kellum, twenty-seven, was found by fishermen near the beach community of Omega Bay, beaten and stabbed.

Taking a few days off from her job in a Beaumont law firm, Bridgette Gearen, a twenty-eight-year-old mother of a toddler daughter, rented a beach house with friends. Waiting for the others to dress to go out, Bridgette walked out onto the sand at dusk in July 2007. Perhaps she wanted to watch the waves or feel the salt breezes. When her friends looked for her, Bridgette was gone. The next morning, her body was found near the shoreline. She'd been beaten, strangled, and raped.

The logical question: Why here?

Galveston County Lieutenant Tommy Hansen had contemplated that question for decades. As a younger man, he investigated many of the cases in this book, and he was one of the two officers who questioned John Robert King and Gerald Pieter Zwarst regarding their involvements in the abduction of Shelley Sikes. In 2013, he helped pull together the case against Clyde Hedrick for the killing of Ellen Beason.

"We have a very distinct group of factors here," said Hansen, his hands arched before him, in thought. "With the beaches, Galveston County is a playground for the fourth largest city in the country. People flood here during the summers. People pass through, and we have no record of their ever being here. They stay on the beach, rent houses or condos, come and they're gone. These are small towns, but during the summer and on holidays, the population swells."

Geographic characteristics, he speculated, added into the equation, including seventy miles of beachfront, a multitude of bayous, and vast undeveloped tracts of land, many with water running through them, offering possibilities for the disposal of a body and evidence.

In addition along with the tourism, the area was highly industrial, workers migrating in for jobs in processing seafood, chemical plants, oil refineries, or for slots on the cruise ships that circulated in and out of the port. "Galveston is a beautiful place, but we have an extremely transient population," said Hansen. As an example of the problems that brought to a criminal investigation, he mentioned 2007's Bridgette Gearen case, one where leads had been plentiful and he hoped to eventually make an arrest. "Bridgette didn't live in Galveston. She was here for the weekend. Neither did any of the suspects or the witnesses," he explained. "It makes the investigation that much more complicated."

Perhaps more frightening was what retired FBI profiler Mark Young contended over sushi in a Houston restaurant one evening. Young, a tall, dark-haired man with a ruddy complexion, wasn't so sure that what was happening along the Texas coastline wasn't transpiring in other parts of the United States, and the world. While some of the cases on the chart appeared to be single murders, crimes of opportunity like the abduction of Shelley Sikes, when it came to at least Galveston in the seventies and the Killing Field, the assumption remained that the persons responsible were serial killers. "At any one time, there are about six hundred serial killers in the U.S.," Young said. "Of those, maybe half are active. The others have aged and stopped killing, or they've stopped for other reasons, like sickness, or they're in prison for other crimes."

Young's bottom line: "Things like this happen all over the world. This isn't a new phenomenon. These guys have always been with us."

Events that unfolded while I worked on this book backed Young's contention that serial predators aren't headquartered in any particular location. In the fall of 2011, police announced that they believed ten bodies found in beach communities on Long Island, New York, were all victims of the same killer, active over a period of fifteen years. Then on May 6, 2013, Amanda Berry miraculously gathered the courage to escape from Ariel Castro's house of horrors in Cleveland, after a decade in captivity. With her came her daughter fathered by Castro and fellow victims Gina DeJesus and Michelle Knight.

Despite the headlines they make, perhaps it's good to remind ourselves that such crimes are rare. The vast majority of murders are committed by family members and friends, acquaintances. Stranger murder is scarce, and the FBI estimates that those by serial killers account for less than one percent of the killings in the U.S.

Still, they exist. Young helped facilitate the entering of the I-45 cases into VICAP, and he spent his career chronicling such crimes and going into the prisons to interview serial killers. Asked for his best advice, the retired FBI agent didn't hesitate. "Don't get in the car. Never let anyone transport you anywhere unless you're sure you know the person and where you're going . . . All the killers I interviewed told me the same thing: When the victims got in the cars, they knew they had them. From that point on, it was all over."

Retired FBI profiler Mark Young spent his career hunting killers.
(Courtesy of Kathryn Casey)

When asked about the girls on the chart, Young acknowledged that anecdotally it appeared that the I-45 area in question had more than its share of unsolved cases. Why the cases weren't resolved was also something that Young considered. One factor, perhaps, was that eleven different law-enforcement agencies covered the area. "They all think of it as their case, and that keeps information from being shared," he said.

I saw that in person one afternoon while interviewing two of the officers involved in the cases. I'd just brought this same subject up. Back in 1992, I'd circulated through this part of Texas writing a book on a serial rapist named James Bergstrom. In *Evil Beside Her,* I documented how Bergstrom jumped jurisdictions to avoid being identified, and how law enforcement in the various communities failed to know what was going on just across their borders. "Is it still like that?" I asked.

The officers said it wasn't although one admitted that in the past, her agency hadn't "played well with others."

When I brought up whether or not there was movement in any of the cases, the woman officer said that she thought there might be a new effort on one, based on what had recently taken place; someone from the Galveston County Sheriff's Office dropped in their offices requesting copies of records.

"Did you give them what they wanted?" the detective asked.

"Not everything," she said, then laughed.

My impression, then, was that perhaps the same old problems plagued the area with its multiple jurisdictions, and that as Young described territorialism helped condemn the investigations to failure.

In the first years after Jessica Cain's disappearance, her father, C. H., attempted to tackle that issue. He lobbied the Texas state legislature for the formation of a new group of officers employed by the Department of Public Safety, the government branch that in-

Jessica Cain in 1997.
(Courtesy of C. H. and Suzy Cain)

cludes the State Troopers and Texas Rangers. This newly formed force would have been composed of specially trained officers designated to strictly investigate abduction cases. In his plan, the team—equipped with helicopters, tracking dogs, all the latest search devices—would move in immediately when there was a kidnapping, to help local law enforcement. That way, experienced investigators would be in charge from the beginning, not small-town police departments that rarely if ever saw such cases.

Unfortunately, C. H. Cain was unable to convince legislators to back the idea.

After working on this book, I have to agree that C. H.'s approach makes sense. Nearly all the victims' families I interviewed voiced frustration with inexperienced police departments. Precious time was often lost and leads too often ignored or mishandled. It wasn't that local police weren't good people who wanted to solve the crimes, but that they had no or limited experience with such cases. "They were basically learning on the job, on my daughter's case," said one father. "They just didn't know what to do."

As my work on this book draws to a close, I consider how far I've come. The I-45 Mysteries/Texas Killing Field chart remains taped on my wall. The girls' faces look out at me, and I hope that, while I haven't brought any of their killers into a courtroom, I have provided insight.

Did I cover every case? No. One of the girls, I found, didn't belong on the chart. Allison Craven's mother returned to the family apartment after running errands in 1971 and found that her daughter was gone. The teenager's remains turned up in a field the following year. Allison has been on multiple versions of the Unsolved Mysteries chart since its inception. She shouldn't have been. Shortly after her death, a neighbor, Henry Doyle Shuflin, Jr., admitted abducting Allison from the complex's laundry room. He pleaded guilty in 1973 and was sentenced to twenty-five years.

In other cases, although I tried to track down family

members and records, I was unable to uncover enough information to include them in the book.

There were also suspects whom I decided to forgo, for the most part because I discovered no evidence linking them to the murders. That doesn't mean something—perhaps DNA—won't come to light in the future, but at this time there was nothing to report. One was a dead drifter named Bobby Jack Fowler who has been linked to at least one murder in Canada, that of sixteen-year-old hitchhiker Colleen MacMillen. There is, at the time of this writing, speculation that Fowler may be responsible for more killings in the Pacific Northwest and Canada. Fowler lived on Bolivar Peninsula, just north of Galveston, from the mideighties through the midnineties, leading to speculation that he claimed victims in Texas as well.

There are also theories that Anthony Allen Shore, already on Texas's death row for one murder and suspected of three others in the Houston area, might be involved in some of these killings. Shore went to high school in the Clear Lake area and preyed on young girls. Thus far there's nothing beyond speculation suggesting he might be involved in the murders of any of the girls on the I-45 chart.

I also certainly don't mean to suggest that these were the only murders in Houston during this time period or the most important, or that only girls and young women fall victim to such homicides.

In fact, coinciding with the time period during which the Galveston Island killings took place, in the seventies, one of the largest and most brutal serial cases in American history unfolded in the Houston area, and nearly all the victims were teenage boys.

On August 8, 1973, Elmer Wayne Henley, Jr. called police to report that he'd just killed a man named Dean Corll. When questioned by police, Henley told a terrifying account of helping Corll abduct, rape, and torture teenage boys. For months after, bodies were pulled from under Corll's home and his boathouse. The press labeled him the

Pied Piper and the Candyman. In the end, authorities theorized that Corll committed at least twenty-eight brutal murders, making him the most prolific killer up to that time in U.S. history. Five years later, in Chicago, a man named John Wayne Gacy surpassed Corll's record by murdering at least thirty-three boys.

For the most part, I now look at the I-45 chart with new eyes. I'm grateful that the Cain, Smither, and Johnston cases are all being investigated. As for the others, the folks I interviewed insisted that there's no evidence left from most of the murders, but I wonder if some might still exist in dusty evidence boxes on forgotten shelves. I've repeatedly asked authorities to look and, if anything is found, to send it out for testing. I hope that happens at some point. Consider the difference Sherry Willcox, the evidence officer, made in the Krystal Baker case. She cared, persisted, and she solved the crime.

Mark Stallings said he left Janet Doe's clothes on when he dumped her body in the Killing Field in 1991. Perhaps those clothes wait in a box somewhere. Perhaps they could be sent to the lab. If DNA was found, that could either confirm or rule out Stallings as the killer. It matters on more than one level. Yes, it could help answer painful questions. But based on what Stallings might be able to tell authorities, it could also identify a victim, give Janet back her name. It's possible that her family still grieves for her, wondering if she's alive or dead.

Through my interview with Stallings, if he's telling the truth, we now know that the description of Janet law enforcement has worked with since her discovery in 1991 may be wrong. For the past twenty-two years, Janet's been labeled as in her mid-twenties or older. If Stallings told the truth, the woman he murdered was a teenager.

Do I have disappointments? Sure. For instance, I requested prison interviews with John Robert King and Gerald Pieter

Zwarst, the two men convicted of abducting Shelley Sikes. I undoubtedly naively hoped to convince them to divulge the location of her remains. It's time. This case needs closure, and Shelley's parents deserve to be able to bury their daughter. King and Zwarst refused to meet with me.

The truth is that despite my best efforts, there are cases in this book that will continue to haunt me, especially that of Laura Kate Smither. I will forever see her face, that endearing smile. Did Bill Reece murder her? Did he abduct Jessica Cain? I hope we know answers to both questions someday soon.

The most frightening thing about these cases? The killers all appeared so ordinary.

If Kevin Edison Smith stood at my door and had a good excuse for being there, I may have let him in. He didn't, after all, look like a killer. But then, what does a killer look like?

What of these men? What shaped them? Why does anyone commit such heinous acts?

A 2005 study published by the FBI listed a set of factors when the perpetrator is a serial killer. One is a genetic tendency, something in a person's psychological makeup that's described as predisposition. The second is an early linkage between sex and violence. Certainly the histories Ed Bell and Mark Stallings recounted during my interviews fit that mold. I don't mean to suggest that their upbringings excuse their crimes, but isn't it important to consider how they were formed? Is there any other way to hope to comprehend why such criminals exist? Perhaps if we understand what fashions them, one day we may find a way to intervene.

It has often been said that evil flourishes within shadow. In the end, if nothing else, I hope this book serves as light into the darkness.

Kathryn Casey
February 2015

Acknowledgments

This has been a long road, but I haven't walked it alone. Off and on, I've been assisted along the way. Thank you to:

- Jane Farrell and Sandy Sheehy for reading and commenting on the manuscript.

- Carey Smith, who helped me weed through decades of newspaper articles, pasting and clipping and never complaining, and who covered a day in court when I had to be elsewhere.

- The folks in the Texas Department of Criminal Justice media office who processed my many requests and arranged my prison interviews.

- Retired Harris County prosecutor Edward Porter, always a good friend, pulled old records to determine the resolution of a case.

- Suzanne Lowe Birdwell for the great map at the beginning of the book.

- Lysa Nistico for clipping photos out of a PDF. I had no idea how to do it.

- Mary Anderson tracked down obscure newspaper articles.

- Private investigator Gina Frenzel sought out contact information for sources.

- Elizabeth Peacock, M.D. and Vladimir Parungao, M.D., who patiently explained medical evidence. If any confusion or mistakes remain, it is on my part, not theirs.

- Dale Lee, Galveston County court reporter, who helped with the evidence on the Hedrick case.

- My editor, Emily Krump, and all the great folks at HarperCollins.

- All those who let me bend their ears and bounce off theories, and those who gave guidance on how things worked and where to look for answers.

Finally, I am deeply grateful to everyone who agreed to be interviewed, especially the victims' loved ones. I thank you for telling me about your daughters, sisters, and friends. I will never forget them.